Main

The Banks Sisters

Complete

The Banks Sisters Complete

Nikki Turner

www.urbanbooks.net

Urban Books, LLC
300 Farmingdale Road, NY-Route 109
Farmingdale, NY 11735

The Banks Sisters Complete

ISBN 13: 978-1-62286-643-4
ISBN 10: 1-62286-643-6

First Trade Paperback Printing April 2018
Printed in the United States of America

10 9 8 7 6 5 4 3 2 1

Distributed by Kensington Publishing Corp.
Submit Orders to:
Customer Service
400 Hahn Road
Westminster, MD 21157-4627
Phone: 1-800-733-3000
Fax: 1-800-659-2436

The Banks Sisters

Dedication

This book is dedicated to my greatest creation, my everything, my only son, Timmond Turner, I could not imagine my world without you! As I watch you turn into a young man, you continue to make my heart smile as you grown into your own. Our bond, and my undying, unconditional love for you, can never waver! Always know that you have the power to do anything you set your mind to do and that without a shadow of a doubt, Mommy always has your back! I thank God for blessing me with you and I thank you for our bond!

&

Every Nikki Turner die hard reader!

Thank you for picking up book, after book, after book, allowing me to continue to create and share my stories with you! I can't express my appreciation for you and I will never take you for granted. Without you none of this would be possible. I love you soooo much! Thank you! Thank you! Thank you!

Chapter 1

A black van had been squatting on the corner of Jefferson Avenue for the past 20 minutes. It was an older model cargo van with limousine-grade tinted windows. It easily blended in with the other vehicles on the busy street, so no one paid much attention to the van. This mistake would cost everyone dearly.

Inside the van, behind the dark glass, were four guys on a major money mission. Each man wore all black and was skeed up on a mixture of cocaine and heroin. All of the men were in possession of two things: rubber masks that their faces would be concealed by, and an AK-15 assault rifle, which rested inside of gloved palms.

"You think we should bounce?" said the passenger wearing a George Bush mask. "Maybe that shit's an omen." George Bush was referring to the police cruiser that was parked in front of the bank that they'd been casing for the past week.

The driver, wearing a Hillary Clinton mask, said, "Fuck that. Police gotta cash their paychecks too. We sit tight, we wait this shit out," he said firmly.

Freddie Krueger, in the back of the van next to Jason from Friday the 13th, agreed with his longtime friend, Hillary Clinton. "We sit tight and we wait this shit out."

Jason was about to toss his vote into the hat when the cop strolled out of the Metropolitan Savings and Loan National Bank with a big smile, got into his cruiser and peeled off.

Once the cop beat the corner it was a few minutes before Hillary Clinton said, "Let's go get this fuckin' paper." He reminded them: "No one gets hurt unless it's unavoidable. But, understand," he looked in each individual's eyes, "nothing is going to stand in the way of us getting this money."

The clickety-clack of the assault rifles being cocked echoed off the van's bare interior. That was the unspoken communication that everybody was on the same page and was ready.

Freddie Krueger opened the sliding door, "Now let's go get this motherfuckin' money!"

On that note, everybody got out and they sprinted across the street, toward the bank.

Meanwhile Inside the Bank:

Fate would have it that it was Simone Banks' first official day on the job, and she was just getting the hang of things.

Jackie, the bank's assistant manager, and the person responsible for training Simone said, "You doing real well to be a newbie. You are such a natural at this," patting her on her back. "What do you do to make this seem so easy?"

Simone was in training to be a manager. Her first lesson was learning to operate one of the bank's seven windows.

"I stay positive and I pray to God," Simone said, holding her breath, hoping that this new endeavor would work out for her. More than anything, she really needed the job to support herself.

"Prayer always goes a long ways," Jackie said in an angelic harmony.

"You're right about that." Simone gave a smile with a nod, warming up to Jackie as she balanced and refilled her drawer.

"Are you sure that you never worked in a banking institution?" Jackie asked with a compliment.

Jackie seemed to be in her mid-fifties. She wore her hair in a tight bun and had an overall good spirit. Simone and she had clicked almost immediately.

"No, just many years of business school combined with a lot of other courses," Simone responded. In fact, Simone was 29 years old and had never had a job in her life. When she was ten Simone and her father made a deal. As long as she went to college, he'd take care of her. She took full advantage of the opportunity her father afforded her, getting degree after degree.

But over the past six months a lot had changed in Simone's life, mostly for the worse. And things wouldn't be getting better any time soon.

At 12:13 p.m. four masked men stormed through the bank's doors.

Hillary Clinton was the first one through the door of the bank, immediately raising his weapon and firing on the security guard. "Get the fuck on the floor."

Before the security guard, a father of two, could reach for his weapon, he ate three slugs to the chest and died immediately.

"Blah . . . blah . . . blah." Fear gripped the entire bank. Customers screamed and the employees were mortified, filling the bank with screams, squeals and madness.

"Keep fuckin' calm, and nobody will get hurt," he said, waving the gun. "Don't fuck with me," he ordered. The patrons did exactly what they were told. After all, he'd just murdered a father in cold blood, it didn't seem like he was taking any prisoners.

Hillary Clinton ordered everyone, "Keep your hands in the air. No fuckin' heroes!"

Simultaneously, the rest of the gun wielding crew followed suit. They came into the bank, guns blazing on some straight gung-ho style, firing shots into the air. The customers dove on the floor or hid for cover.

"Rad-da-ta-ta," roaring bullets blazed through the air like fireworks. Next came the high pitch screams from the patrons. Some automatically hit the floor and ran for cover while the others were stunned. A few just stood still in freeze mode, and waited for instructions from the guys in charge.

The man wearing a George Bush mask was smacking anybody in his way. "Shut the fuck up!" he said, wanting the patrons to fear him more and insight the screams of terror.

The shooting ceased and the robber in the Hillary Clinton mask shouted. "Everybody put ya hands on ya fuckin' heads! If you move em', I'ma put a bullet in your fuckin' head!

Simone prayed to God over and over. Even while praying and being scared shitless, her brain continued to process the horrific scene taking place in front of her very own eyes. Four bank robbers, ten customers and eight employees, alive. One, may he rest in peace, already dead. God, she silently prayed, don't let there be any more.

"Awwww," an ear piercing scream.

The outburst spewed from a woman with bleach-blond hair and red lipstick. The butt of an assault rifle slammed into her face, knocking one of her front teeth out. The tooth caromed off the marble floor and up against a wall.

"Last warning," Jason yelled at the lady as she silently wept.

The oldest of the four men robbing the bank and killing innocent bystanders was only 24 years old. This was the first bank any of them had ever tried to knock off. They were nervous, but the drugs did a good job at helping them hide it. The more fear they instilled into their victims, the more emboldened the young killers became.

Hillary Clinton jerked the trigger of the automatic weapon. *"Barratt . . . Barratt . . ."* He let loose a barrage of bullets again. The drugs had him on some renegade, strong-arm power trip. He was feeling untouchable and invincible.

"Let me be clear. Do as we say, when we say it. If you can do that we gon' take this money and leave without anyone else fucked up. Get it?"

Heads slowly nodded.

Jason, Freddy, and George hit the first three tellers while Ski-Mask maintained control of the room.

"Please don't fuckin' push me."

The teller at the second window got too close to the silent alarm, "Bitch, you touch that button, and I swear on my grandma holy drawers you gone die today!" Jason threatened. He backhanded the teller so hard, her legs wobbled before giving out on her. It was still in question which was harder, the actual smack or her hitting the floor.

Simone still couldn't believe this was happening. She wasn't one to pray in the middle of a room, but with what was going on right in front of her, praying seemed like the best thing for her to do right now. Though things were not looking too good for her, her colleagues, or customers, it didn't stop her. She continued to silently call upon God.

Simone also prayed that nobody made any hasty moves, because she knew these guys were dead-ass serious. The slightest move from her or any of her co-workers could, and would, cost somebody their life. As her thoughts continued to run wild, out of the corner of Simone's eyes, she saw Jackie's finger slowly inching toward the silent alarm. On one hand Simone desperately wanted help to come and rescue them all from the bad guys, but she wasn't willing to risk her life trying to be anyone's hero. Jackie was a braver woman than she.

"Clack, clack, clack," More gunfire erupted, startling her. The guy with the George Bush mask was in the face of teller three.

"Don't give me that fuckin' look," Jason-Mask ran over, jumped over the counter and bashed the next teller in the face. She grabbed her face with both hands and screamed. He grabbed her by the back of the head and rammed her face into the counter. The blow was so powerful that she went unconscious instantly.

This sent everybody else in another frenzy.

"Shut the fuck up," Jason said, silencing the hostages who were in an uproar over the heinous act.

While Bush-Mask and Hillary Clinton-Mask waved their huge weapons around looking at everyone inside, Jason-Mask grabbed another teller by the hair and manhandled her. The poor woman was timid and couldn't help herself.

"Bitch put the money in the bag and no fuckin' dye packs! Hurry the fuck up! Bitch!" He shouted as he controlled her movements by her hair. Tears rolled down her face as she tried her best to place money inside a bag. Her hands shook badly. She managed to empty the money out of the first drawer.

The novice crew emptied the first three stations and moved on to four, five, and six.

"Come on man!" Bush shouted out. "Make that bitch hurry the fuck up!" Just as he saw the man move his hands from his head, Simone saw it too. She wanted to scream out and warn him not to move, "No, put your hands, back up," but the words didn't come out.

The bank robber with the Hillary Clinton mask aimed, fired, and blew the back of the man's head off. The powerful slugs ripped through the back of the man's head and exploded his face across the bank. Brain and blood decorated the shiny marble floors. Blood and brain splatter was everywhere. The place was becoming a massacre.

Everyone's face shared the same expression: disbelief. Betty scooped the money from the draw as quick as her nervous hands would allow. Simone prayed that it was fast enough. Tellers operating window five and six had learned from the others mistakes. Scooping money up in her hands and dropping it inside the bag she moved on to the drawer of the teller that was laying on the floor.

They quickly did as they were told and kept their mouth closed.

The innocent bystanders were horrified and only wanted this nightmare to end.

Window seven, which was Simone's window, was the only drawer that hadn't been hit.

"Bitch you know what's up." A small amount of spit came seeping out of his mouth as he spoke. The man standing over her screaming in her face with the gun in his hand was over six feet tall, yet still several inches shorter than his lanky friend with the Hillary Clinton mask.

Simone froze. Her feet became like blocks of concrete and she couldn't move. In her head, she recited her earlier prayer. She kept praying to God but no matter how hard she prayed that God make her invisible, Jason and his friends could still see her. God either didn't see fit for whatever reason to make her invisible or he had better things to do. Either way, Simone thought she would soon be dead.

Calmly, Hillary Clinton said with the gun in her face, "Bitch, if you want to be the world's flyest corpse, keep standing there like a statue and don't you dare think I'm playing."

Though her face and eyes were filled with desperation and tears, you better believe they didn't have to ask her twice.

Point taken, she wasn't about to die for somebody else's insured money. She started stuffing money into the bag, like it was an Olympic event. She wasn't settling for anything less than a gold medal.

He stood over Simone, mean mugging as she put the last of the cash from her drawer into the bag. After Simone was done, he hesitated.

"Don't fuck with me bitch!" he yelled at Simone. "I'll shoot your pretty little brains all over this counter!" He looked at her with a look of disgust, as if she was holding out on him. She had no clue at all what more he wanted. She had given him everything she had in her drawer but he still wasn't satisfied. For a split second, she honestly thought that it was over for her.

All she could think of and hear in her head was a vague voice saying . . . *Here lies Simone Banks, may she rest in peace.* . . . She envisioned herself in an all-white Donatella Versace gown in an all-white gold trimmed casket.

She convinced herself that she would be all right if she just did exactly as she was told. She was not ready to die. She still was praying to God that he let her live through this. She was taught that if she had the faith of a mustard seed, then God would deliver. As soon as that thought crossed Simone's mind, she began to see bits and pieces of her life flash in front of her. Could this really be the end for her?

Simone couldn't understand, why her? She did exactly what he asked for and now he was going to kill her?

She felt a hard hit on the side of her abdomen. It took her a second to realize Jason-Mask had just hit her with his gun.

"Please don't shoot me! I did everything you asked me to do!" Simone pleaded. Indeed she could feel her life on crash course and all she could do was beg for mercy.

"Bitch! Why in the fuck you playing with me?" he screamed at her. She could see his saliva seeping out of his mouth. He then put the gun to her head and cocked it.

Her heart dropped at the realization that she was about to die. Then out of nowhere she got the strength and boldness to calmly speak out, "I gave you everything and I don't have any codes to anything," She wasn't going down without a fight.

He gave a long hard look in her eyes, with the mean mug and gun still to her temple. Then he said to her, "That there is your Chanel bag right? That there, dat boy bag right?"

"Yes!" She nodded.

"Shit's real?"

Indeed it was. Simone nodded again. At this stage, even if it was a bootleg replica, she would've still given the same answer. "Of course!" she proudly said.

"Well, that shit just saved your life, my bitch been asking for that shit," he informed her.

Simone stared at the purse. It was the hottest bag out and an expensive gift from her father. The matching wallet inside was one of the last purchases she made before all the credit cards were cancelled and her once lavish lifestyle was pulled from under her feet. Though she loved that bag a lot, she loved her life more. Without hesitation, she shoved it too in the duffle bag with the money. There was no way in the world that she was getting hurt over a pocketbook, no matter how hot, expensive, or authentic it was.

He grabbed the duffle bag and clutched on to it so tight, one would have thought that he was Usain Bolt fleeing from a stick-up.

"Nigga, you stealing ladies purses now?" Hillary Clinton asked, shaking his head at his homeboy. Not waiting for an answer he just gave the command. "Let's roll," Hillary Clinton shouted. He backed up toward the door and Freddy Krueger followed. Jason flipped over the counter and hurried toward them, taking up the rear. He turned around and saw one of the remaining tellers press the silent alarm button. He aimed in her direction and squeezed the trigger. Bullets flew like a swarm of bats coming out of a cave. The slugs found permanent homes inside of her face, neck, breast and stomach. Her body dropped and the masked men rushed for the door.

More screams of fear erupted from a couple people, scared shitless, and worried that they could be next. But the guys kept heading to the door.

They were home free and Simone was still alive.

Finally, the nightmare is over! She looked up to the ceiling as if she could see God. *Thank you' Jesus!* Simone thought as the last one of the deadly crew had one foot out of the door and one foot still inside. As she was about to exhale—grateful that she hadn't been too physically hurt, but saddened for those who had—the unthinkable happened.

The dude wearing the Jason mask, stopped at the door and turned around. He randomly pointed the AR-15 into the bank for no apparent reason.

Simone's breath froze into a block of ice, trapped in her lungs. She found herself staring down the muzzle of the assault rifle like a deer paralyzed by the headlights of an incoming speeding truck before the fatal collision. There was no time to duck or move out of the way. Even if there had been a beat or two to get out of the line of fire, the suddenness of the act, combined with her reincarnated fear of dying, held her in place like a straightjacket.

God help me! she prayed.

But it was too late. . . . With a diabolical look, Jason pulled the trigger.

Boom!

Chapter 2

Bush shoved the bank's door open, leading the blood-thirsty crew across the street, through the moving traffic, to the waiting van. Once inside, the crew felt they were home free.

"We did that shit, man! We fuckin' did that shit," Hillary Clinton said with a big smile on his face as he pulled his mask off. "Told you motherfuckers we were going to make this shit do what it do."

"Go! Go! Go!" Bush slapped the back of the head of the driver, putting pressure on him. "Get us the fuck from 'round here."

Hillary Clinton, in return, put the van in gear and pressed on the accelerator. He moved into traffic. They'd done it. They'd robbed the fuckin' bank and it was going to be a'ight.

"We up now!" Hillary Clinton said.

Before the celebration could get in full bloom, Bush noticed the two police cars.

"Shit!" He looked again. "Fuck!"

At the same time, to intensify things more, Jason opened the bag and dug his hand inside, a dye pack exploded. He quickly removed his hand and shouted, "Fuckin' bitch! No! No! No! No! No! Not a fuckin' dye pack!" Jason looked hurt as if someone had just taken his manhood.

"This shot was all for nothin' man?" Freddie shouted out of frustration.

The others looked down at the bag, just as two police cruisers turned the corner and blocked off the street. They exited their vehicles and leaned over their hoods with their weapons aimed at the van.

"Fuck, man, what the fuck we gon' do?" Freddie got a bit antsy when he noticed the cop cars were blocking the one-way street. Two more black and whites turned the corner behind the van, hemming them in.

The vibe inside of the van flipped from jubilant to morose in the blink of an eye. Two black and whites parked nose to nose in the middle of the street were blocking their van from continuing forward.

The driver tried to quickly diagnosis the situation to figure out the best way out.

Jakes crouched behind the makeshift barrier, guns in hand and ready to earn their pay. The two cop cars behind them had turned into six and eliminated the option of backing up.

"It's work call, shawty! My turn now to put in mine! Buckle up, my niggas!" the driver shouted out. He seemed to be getting an adrenaline rush off it all as he put the pedal to the metal.

Underneath the George Bush mask Dougie freaked. "What the fuck we gon' do now?" he said with a shaky tone. The youngest of the four, Dougie was eighteen.

Hillary Clinton—a.k.a. Mike—looked his cousin Dougie in the eyes, "We gon' get it on 'em, meaning go to war or die trying," Mike declared.

Mike was nobody's fool. He knew the odds of them winning a shootout with the RPD were against them. But growing up Black and broke, being the underdog was nothing new. It was their day-to-day norm.

Freddy Krueger—A.K.A Bennie—was 22 years old and had already spent two stints upstate. Going back this time was no option. He knew if he was caught with even a piece of stolen bubble gum, this time, they'd fry his ass for sure. "Court is in session," he said, "and it's being held in the street."

"Then let's get it poppin'" said Jason whose real name was Jason Kill. Jason slammed a fresh clip into the assault rifle. His boys did the same. Then Jason swung the door open. Dougie, Bennie, and Jason hopped out of the van with guns blazing.

Jason let loose, firing on anything in sight. The shots rang out loudly. The slugs from the AR's blew huge holes through the police vehicles, shattering windows and knocking the sirens off the roof. It was a shame Jason hadn't joined the army because he had great aim and plenty of heart.

The police returned fire. Both sides put it down hard. The noise from the shootout sounded like a warm night on the battlefields of Iraq.

A police officer stood up and caught three slugs to the face. His partner fired back multiple times at the man who'd shot his friend and coworker.

Meanwhile other shots were aimed for the driver. The front windshield of the van shattered, the driver slumping over dead. His head fell on the horn causing it to beep continuously. The men knew it was do or die and didn't have any time to waste. The team witnessed their homeboy, Mike, go down, but there was no time to mourn. They would have to pay their respects to him with their war game.

The three masked man jumped out of the vehicle and rolled into the street. They were gunning like skilled soldiers, at war with the boys in blue. They were fueled as they opened fire on the police officers non-stop. The volley intensified. Both sides had lost a man. Neither wanted to drop another but knew there was no surrender or retreat. In no time, mixed with the sounds of guns going off, the air was filled with approaching sirens and first response vehicles.

The fella's bullets tore the cruisers apart. Huge holes popped up over the vehicle, sending two of the cars into flames. That gave the robbers that extra push they needed as they reloaded and continued gunning.

The gun exchange went on for a few minutes. Being outnumbered and outgunned neither intimidated nor deterred the crew from firing their weapons. Two more boys in blue kissed the asphalt as blood leaked from their bodies. The AR-15's bite was as vicious as its bark.

Bennie tried to take cover behind a parked BMW and got chopped down like an oak tree. His body hit the pavement like a drunken monk. Pain soared through his body as if he'd been struck by lightning.

Blood poured from his mouth as he choked, trying his damnedest to hold on as life slipped away from him. He died staring at the Bush mask by his side, but not before letting off a rain of gunshots, going out in a blaze of glory.

Dougie snapped. He'd watched his cousin and best friend die. Even a high school dropout such as himself could predict the outcome for him and Jason. But he swore on everything he loved that he would drop a few more pigs before he died. And he meant it with a passion. He raised up and let bullets fly like birds flying south. The volley temporarily pushed the police down for better cover. Though the police had been trained to deal with these kinds of situations, they also cared if they lived to see tomorrow. Dougie knew that this was his last day and acted as such as he let loose round after round.

But Dougie's camaraderie was his weakness. His emotions overrode his intellect and he made the mistake of checking on Bennie. Maybe he was still alive. He blasted his way to where Bennie lay. He gunned with one hand while checking Bennie's pulse with the other. "What the fuck you doing, Dougie?" Jason screamed, knowing that it was a dumb move and could be detrimental to them. "He's dead."

The reality of his man, cousin, and best friend lying dead in front of him literally fucked him up. His bold plan of attack was no longer strategic. It had suddenly become emotional. Dougie was pissed the fuck off. He rose up and opened fire on everything in his line of fire. The different caliber of weapons sounded like a gun range with everyone firing simultaneously. The sound of bullets hitting metal, glass shattering, screeching tires, and police sirens flooded the air.

As Dougie looked up to hear what Jason was saying, a chunk of his scalp got peeled back. The AR-15 fell from his hands and he flew backward. Then a slug ripped through his head, knocking a huge chunk out. He got hit by another one and another one. He hit the ground, sprawled out like a dead bird.

Jason ran to the van. By luck, or the Grace of God, he managed to make it there. He tossed the deceased driver to the ground, climbed inside, and put the vehicle in drive. He smashed the pedal all the way down to the floor. The van accelerated and sped toward the police vehicles. He rammed into them as they opened fired on the van. He ducked down and floored the gas pedal. He turned the corner and the engine died. He sniffed some coke, opened the door and hopped out with his weapon in hand. Four bullets riddled his back but they didn't stop him. He felt invincible like Scarface. He continued on, as two more slugs ripped through the back of his legs. He fell and quickly flipped onto his back as he placed the gun to his head and pulled the trigger. His brains flew through the top of his head. His arms and weapons dropped at his side as he released his bowels and any of the life left in him. The police officers squatted down behind the parked vehicles as they slowly advanced toward the corpse. Once they saw that he was deceased they lowered their weapons.

The question everybody had on their mind was 'What the fuck just happened?'

Chapter 3

"Doing it now, my nig. We ain't do too bad, either," Spoe said with no emotion. He spoke into his phone in what seemed like a quick, one-way conversation. "Yo, I'm going to finish this shit up and take a shower. By the time you do what you need to do, come through and pick up your bread." He disconnected the phone and threw it in the mix of all the paper he was trying to sort out.

The goose down feathered, crisp white comforter on the king size bed had quickly turned money green due to the bills of American dead Presidents that covered the beautiful bed. While kneeling his sexy, muscular body beside the mattress, Spoe seemed to be quite exhausted. He sorted and stacked the Benjamins, Grants, Jacksons, Hamiltons, Lincolns, and Jeffersons into one thousand dollar piles. He had been counting and stacking the bread for more than an hour. The funny thing was that taking it had been an easier job than counting it. So far the count was better than half a million.

"The fruit from a long day of labor, baby?" Spoe's girlfriend Bunny came into the room, walked behind him, kissed his neck and massaged his tensed shoulders. "That's a lot of money, daddy."

Any presence of her lit up the room and his face. "You know it." He spun around and gave her a long, wet, tongue kiss. "All for us, baby." And he meant every dimension of those words.

Spoe was old school in so many ways, especially when it came to his woman. As the man of the house, he felt it was his responsibility to be the sole provider. All Bunny needed to do was to look amazing, take care of his needs, and make his house as comfortable for him as absolutely possible. She was great at all three and that was something that Spoe never took for granted.

That's the reason why he spoiled her the way he did, providing nothing but the best for them. Matching his and hers Porsche Panerama topped with the Cayenne for him and the 911 convertible for her. The cars were parked in the garage of an expensive condo that overlooked the James River. Their condo has three huge bedrooms with high-end furniture and huge walk in closets filled with the hottest trendy clothes and accessories. Spoe and Bunny's elaborate lifestyle was made entirely possible by Spoe's shill thrill of relieving drug dealers of their proceeds . . . by any means necessary.

When it came to taking money, there was no denying Spoe was at the apex of his game. His peers either respected him, feared him, or both. The one thing that was a known fact about Spoe was that nothing stood between him and his dead presidents. This was another thing he never took for granted. He knew if he wasn't careful, he could get caught out just like the next man.

"How does that feel?" Bunny asked, continuing to massage his neck using her knuckles.

The only thing that he might've cared about more than his money was the love of his life, Bunny. They had officially been together for five years not counting the two years that he had chased her. Though he had more of his fair share of women running behind him, the only one he sprinted after was her. Once he got her, he vowed to never let her go. She was his queen, his prize, his trophy, his everything, and a blessing that he thanked God for every day. No woman had ever captivated him like she did, and he cherished her. He loved her more than he loved his own life. She was his fantasy in an extremely loving, borderline smothering, kind of way. There was no denying that Spoe was obsessed with Bunny and Bunny secretly liked it that way.

As handsome, charismatic, and not to mention rich, as he was, he could have anybody he wanted. There wasn't a day that gone by that he didn't turn down women who threw themselves at him. He couldn't seem to see past Bunny. Rumor had it that Bunny had put something in his food, or worked some kind of Haitian Voodoo, to have him infatuated with her, but that was far from the truth.

The two had an agreement that they took seriously. It was simple: she had him and he had her. So she spent the majority of her time focusing on him and making him happy. In return, he gave his all to making her happy, which meant, as the man of the house, he went and got that bread and brought it back home.

The two were inseparable, spending damn near every waking moment together. Their chemistry, not to mention the sex, went together like music. Every move they made incorporated the other. Even when he went out on "jobs," she was always on call. Just in case something went wrong, she'd be the first one to know.

Bunny massaged his neck then leaned in and started blowing in his ear.

"Baby that feels good." She kept going until he said, "I could use your help to count this babe."

"No problem baby." She kissed his neck and leaned in beside him. "How did it go?" she asked.

"It was like taking steak from a vegan. Easy. Shit went smooth." He paused for a minute, with a smile. "Too smooth. Shit was probably one of the easiest heists we ever did."

"That's cause you the best at doing what you do," she said looking into his eyes then blessing him with a long, intense, *Gone With the Wind* kiss.

"With a cheerleader like you, I can't help but win."

Making her heart smile, she said "You got that right." As she looked up at him, his bulging muscles and black wife beater did something to her.

"Your hands feel wonderful," Spoe said. "But I need them fondling something else right now."

"Oh, really," said Bunny, eager to oblige.

"I need your help counting the money."

She cupped his balls. "Is counting money the only thing I can help with."

If anyone could take his mind off of business, it was Bunny. She was Beyonce-fine, except cuter, if that was possible. Instantly, Spoe's dick grew two inches in the palm of her warm hand. He started to move the already counted money off the bed, leaving the rest where it was.

Bunny smiled knowing what was coming next. Spoe picked her up with ease, his muscles barely flexing with her weight.

Her legs wrapped around his waist. They kissed. It went on for a while. His cotton-soft, dark chocolate skin pressed against hers—the color of caramel—meshed together like the perfect piece of candy. Spoe laid on her on the huge king sized bed, then peeled off his wife beater. Bunny caressed his bulging dick, through his shorts, with the toes of her foot.

For her, Spoe was definitely something to write home about. He was six feet two-inches of pure masculine perfection. Perfect skin. Perfect lips. Perfect body. And yes . . . perfect penis. Even his coal-black wavy ponytail, which hung past his shoulder, was perfect. Bunny couldn't decide which was sexier; her man or the fact that she was about to be made love to on a bed covered in money.

Letting no time pass, Spoe pulled her panties off, filled his hands with her 42- inch hips, and put his best face forward.

Bunny's legs were spread apart like a wishbone, above her head. "Oh my God! Damn! Don't stop!" She cried and begged like a baby for more milk, and Spoe didn't disappoint. When the pleasure got to be too much, she tried to squirm away, only to be pulled back in place by Spoe's strong hands.

He continued to go to work on her hot spot. When she was about to come, he looked up at her with those big doe-gray eyes, and asked if she liked it, as if he couldn't tell by the way her ass had been bucking off the bed.

Every nerve in her body was hyper-sensitive to his touch. Even the tones of his voice, deep and sexy, gave her goose bumps. "If you don't know," she chimed, "maybe you need to keep trying."

"Be careful what you ask for," Spoe said with a mischievous grin. And the party was back on.

In the midst of writhing in ecstasy, she managed to get the begging words out, "Please don't stop." She was at that cross road of lovemaking when she couldn't take any more, yet didn't want it to end.

Bunny just couldn't help herself. When it came to their sexcapades, he always managed to take her to new places in the bedroom. He handled her sexually unlike any other in the bedroom, leaving her no choice, other than to concede to his every wish.

An hour later, the high pitch of squeals of distress emerged from the box spring and mattress, and the faux marble headboard rhythmically drummed against their canary yellow accent wall. A half empty box of Magnum condoms lay on a night table next to the bed.

Bunny and Spoe were still on top of the king sized bed engaged in fervent sex. Lovemaking would come later. On her knees—hairdo soaking wet—tapping Morse Code against the faux marble headboard, Bunny felt as if she was going to explode. Spoe kneeling behind her generous caboose, was hard at work from a southern vantage point. Every forward stroke of his thick manhood submerged his balls deep into her plump, apple-shaped ass. His fingertips sank into her pillow soft caramel flesh as he held on to her hips, trying to control the pace.

"That's right," Bunny moaned. "Fuck da shit out dis pussy, Baby!" She pushed her ass back at him, matching his thrusts as if it was an orchestrated dance.

Spoe welcomed the challenge by upping the intensity. The two of them had been together for years, and years of practice had made Spoe the perfect lover. He knew her every erogenous spot, and she knew his. Bunny thought to herself, no one had ever made her body perform the way Spoe made it feel.

Bunny's eyes were rolling in the back of her head, toes spread and curling, when the phone rang. By the sound of the ringtone, Spoe knew it was Tariq. He also knew that as much fun as he and Bunny were having, it was time to shut it down.

"Fuckkkkk! Baby! That's Tariq," he said and started stroking hard and intense. "Sorry, baby."

Business was business and that was it.

Spoe needed to get the remainder of the now wet money counted and divided before his partner arrived.

Bunny understood that, but right now there was no way she was going to let him go until she got hers. "Uah," Spoe tensed up when she stuck her finger in his butt, then relaxed. This wasn't his first rodeo, and Bunny knew the pressure on his rectum would make him cum quicker. She was already there, making the two unload in unison.

The doorbell rang as they were getting out of the shower. "Perfect timing," Spoe said sarcastically, drying off quickly. He put his towel around his neck and wrapped another around his waist, leaving his hairy chest exposed. He threw on a pair of basketball shorts and a T-shirt.

"Babe, I'ma grab this door while you finish cutting the money for me. Cool?"

"I got this," she said in nothing but a sheer robe. The bell rang again. "Go let 'em in babe."

Spoe looked his woman over one quick time. Her nipples pointed out like cones, accenting her small waist, hips, and thighs. He licked his lips then shook his head. "You know we going for round two tonight, right?" he said as he kissed her before walking off to answer the door.

Spoe headed to let Tariq in while Bunny began to count the money with only her robe on.

Tariq was their most frequent visitor as well as the only person, besides immediate family, that had ever come to their place. "What took you so long?" he asked, when Spoe finally sprung the locks on the door.

Spoe still had a few drops of water on him and his hair was wet from the shower. "What you think I was doing man?" he said as he returned the two deadbolt locks into the cylinders.

Tariq shook his head. "That's all right, bro. I don't need to know the details of you and sis' actions. All that y'all be doing, y'all need to have some li'l Bunnies running around here." He shook his head with a smirk, and took a seat on the oversized sectional sofa. "You got that bread straight?"

"Almost. Bunny's finishing up with it now,"

"A'ight, that's what's up." Tariq trusted Bunny like a sister, so he didn't trip over her counting the money.

A few minutes later Bunny walked into the living room wearing leggings and a crop tank top. Her natural sexy strut should've been bottled up and sold. It could've landed her on a high fashion runway. She handed the bag to Spoe with a heart shaped sticky note on it with the total written on it in red ink. He immediately placed it on the table.

Bunny greeted Tariq with a kiss and a sisterly hug. "What's up T? You good?"

"Yeah, I can't complain, sis," he said.

After the small pleasantries Bunny said, "The total on the money came up to $761 thousand; $380,500 apiece. Yours all there, Reek."

"Not bad huh?" Spoe said with a smile.

Tariq stuffed his half into a backpack. "More than I thought it would be. Life is pretty fuckin' awesome."

They went up in the stash house of some heroin dealers, expecting maybe half a mill at best. It was a pleasant surprise that they had exceeded their expectations. And nobody got hurt in the process. "Can't complain," he said.

The boys sat in the living room talking shop while Bunny fixed sandwiches in the kitchen. "You sure don't you want one, Tariq? I got the roast beef y'all like."

"Nah, man, I just ate."

"Huh?" both Bunny and Spoe questioned Tariq. He never turned down any of Bunny's food.

"Had a little lunch date with a chick and shit."

"What chick?" Bunny asked, being nosey.

"You don't know her." Tariq said nonchalantly.

"Oh, okay. When will I get to meet her?" she asked, getting excited at the thought of having a girl she could bond and shop with while their men got more money than they could spend.

"Chill, Bunny. You're probably not gonna meet her." Tariq explained, "You know I don't keep girls around for too long." Tariq was like that. He was a shy, mild mannered kind of guy with a dry personality, but oddly enough, he had a lot of heart and had no problem at all busting a cap in somebody's ass. When Bunny first met him, she thought of him as a weirdo. But after getting to know him, she learned to love him because he was Spoe's partner in crime.

Bunny laughed and ear hustled, as she always did, on the rest of the conversation.

Bunny fixed two sandwiches, one for her and the other for Spoe. She was sitting on the bar stool eating, when Tariq said to Spoe, "You heard 'bout them simple-ass niggas, Mike and dem, from J-Dubb?"

J-Dubb was the hood's nickname for Jackson Ward, a famous area in downtown Richmond where wealthy Blacks once socialized, owned businesses and allowed themselves to be entertained. It is an area where the legendary actor and dancer Bill 'BoJangles' Robinson, who called Richmond his home and Jackson Ward his playground, had been immortalized by a statue on the corner of Clay and Adams—his likeness suited and booted in the middle of an elaborate tap number for eternity. But now, though slowly being revitalized, Jackson Ward is mostly known for its infamous housing project, poverty, crime, murder and most of all . . . drugs.

Spoe paused in thought. He knew a few Mikes, and J-Dubb wasn't known for producing the city's brightest cats. "Which Mike?" he asked, after drawing a blank.

"Crackhead Mike that Rob juked."

Rob was a careless dope boy from the West End who got caught with his pants down in his stash house with a stripper named Peaches. Peaches was Mike's cousin, and the brains behind the hit. Trusting his dick, a mistake on Rob's part, cost him 32 ounces of coke and his life.

"What about him?" Spoe asked.

Tariq looked at Spoe unable to believe he hadn't heard. "It's been on the news all evening." Then it dawned on him, "Oh, but you and sis been in here on y'all baby making shit today."

Spoe shooed him off. "That's right though."

"On some fuckin' renegade shit. . . . Dude tried to knock off the bank on Jefferson Avenue and got smoked by 5-0 in the process. Them niggas was battling with the police, in the middle of the street, in broad day light, straight on some cold-blooded Wild-Wild-West shit."

Spoe, interest peaked but not surprised, asked, "Fuck outta here. Who was with him?"

Tariq shared what he knew from the news and what the streets were saying. "His cousin Benny and two of his little homies. Five oh sparked all of them." Tariq kept going, not showing one bit of sympathy for the lives lost. "I heard them niggas jacked off too much time inside, all high on that coke and shit. Jakes were laying on them soon as they came out and it was on."

Spoe, bred to put in work, summed up Mike's flaws in one word: "Stupid," then asked Bunny to turn on the television. She was already on it, channel surfing, desperate to find the breaking news story.

A cat commercial was on NBC. Bunny tried the other three local networks. None were showing the news at the time.

"Oh, shit!" A nervous Bunny thought out loud. "You said Jefferson Avenue right? It wasn't the Metro Bank was it?" She asked.

"Yes, it was," Tariq said with a nod.

Suddenly it dawned on Bunny that her oldest sister, Simone, was supposed to start working at that very bank today. Silently, she prayed, *Lord, please don't have let anything bad possibly happen to Simone.*

Then she asked Tariq, "Did anyone working at the bank get hurt?" She crossed her fingers, hoping the answer was no.

That hope crashed and burned when Tariq said, "I think it was a security guard, and at least one employee, maybe two. But I'm not sure 'cause they say the details was sketchy, but I heard that shit was a blood bath inside the bank and outside."

Bunny's blood froze as the chills went up her spine. She immediately reached for the phone.

She tried to call Simone. The phone just rang and the voicemail came on. She tried calling a few more times and still no response.

They were still very close and kept in touch, even though, unlike most siblings, they didn't actually grow up their entire lives in the same house. Like all siblings, they had their differences and would bicker and argue, but make no mistake about it, that was still her big sister, whom she loved dearly and she'd go to war for.

Shit wasn't looking or sounding good at all, but what else could she do but try to keep hope alive?

Chapter 4

Two Hours Later

Bunny stormed out of her house and rushed to her grand-mother's house. When she arrived, Bunny and Simone's younger sisters, Tallhya and Ginger were already there.

Tallhya was twenty-five, two years younger than Bunny, and Ginger, at age twenty-four, was the baby of the bunch. As she took a seat on the living room couch, all three looked at each other but none of them spoke. There was an unspoken understanding between the sisters to just sit and wait for one of their phones to ring. After half an hour of sitting in silence, the only thing that could be heard were Bunny's tall thigh high Tom Ford boots' heels clacking back and forth when she stood up and began striding up and down.

"Can you stop pacing the damn floor, please," Ginger, their youngest sister said. "Just sit your ass down. Everything's gonna be Okay."

Bunny heard her youngest sister, but at the same time, she couldn't help but worry about her older sister.

"God won't take her away from us like this." Tallhya the middle sister chimed in. Out of the four sisters, Tallhya was the soft spoken one. The way she was, you would've thought she was the youngest of them all. She had this gullible inno-cence about her and because of it, her sisters were constantly trying to toughen her up.

"Yeah, because God forbid something happens. On every-thing I love, it ain't going to be nothing nice." She shook her head, "This is some bullshit. She don't deserve to be caught up in no shit like this." Bunny fumed.

Bunny decided to change her scenery and go to the kitchen to sit at her grandmother's kitchen table. She thought maybe if she sat at the table, where she shared so many good memories with her sisters, it would help her feel a little better. Her foot was nervously bouncing off the floor. She'd dialed Simone's number for what felt like the fiftieth time. This time, instead of it ringing like all the other times, the call went straight to voicemail. Simone's phone never went to voicemail. She was always dependable and on point. Out of all of the four sisters, Simone was the oldest and the most responsible.

"Look, if Miss Goodie-Two-Shoes was okay, she would've made a way to call us by now. And she would've seen all our missed calls. She usually answers her phone or calls right back." Bunny made a good point, "Some shit must'a gone down with her. Maybe we should call the hospital and see if she's there"

"Yeah, you right Buns. Her ole considerate ass would've called us by now if she was all right." Ginger had to agree.

"Not the best sign," Tallhya added. "But there's probably a perfectly good explanation."

It didn't help that the police and the bank refused to disclose any information about the robbery, let alone about who'd been injured.

Bunny sucked her teeth. "The bank could at least have fuckin' common courtesy for the employee's families. They could call and say 'look we can't give no details but your sister is Okay'."

"Maybe they're working on getting the employee emergency information" Tallhya said, trying to stay positive

The vibe was glum.

The sister's signature gray eyes, that normally sparkled and lit up a room, were at half-mast.

The captivating gray eyes, high-cheek bones and deep dimples were gifts passed down from their mother, Deidra, who was a deadbeat mom, usually nowhere to be found. Except with Deidra, being conspicuously absent was nothing new. All their lives, the only thing that was consistent with their mother was that Deidra only had time for Deidra. She had only given them two things: life and their enchantingly gorgeous looks.

The sisters were drop dead gorgeous, beauty queen beautiful. In fact, Simone had participated in pageants since she was about nine years old. As a young adult she had even won on a state level. She had that Vanessa Williams regal kind of beauty: sophisticated, well spoken, and educated with a lot of book sense as well as common sense. Bunny on the other hand was a ghetto princess—Keisha from Belly kind of fine. She too had participated in church pageants when she was a little girl and had won Ms. Churchill, East End, and was also the Homecoming Queen. But she never competed in national beauty pageants. Growing up and hanging out with the thugs in her school, she was rough around the edges. She had only attended one year of community college but was very book smart and had more street smarts than any one female should have. She should've been the boy of the bunch, because she was bold, and had the heart of a lion. The girl was overall as sharp as the knife she kept on her at all times.

Bunny and her sisters were raised by their Me-Ma, Mildred Banks. Me-Ma was a strong, God fearing woman that had done the best job she could with her granddaughters. Her daughter Deidra had dropped off all four of them when they were just days old. Even though Me-Ma felt too old to raise kids again, she didn't have the heart to turn her back on them.

Bursting the bubble of silence, Ginger said what they all were thinking. "What if Simone got shot?" Bunny and Tallhya kept their heads down, each sulking in her own thoughts. Ginger continued, "What if she's —"

Bunny cut her off.

"Stop it right there, Ginger." She turned and hissed at her. "Just shut the fuck up. Don't even say that kind of shit." She'd had enough of the negative talking and thinking. "We are not fittin' to sit here and talk no crazy shit like that into our reality. That's what we not gon' do," she said. "You hear me?"

Ginger rolled her eyes.

"It ain't like ya'll wasn't thinking the same shit. I'm just the only one with the balls to say it," Ginger said, challenging her sister. Ginger was the baby but she had always been the tough ass of the four. She was outspoken and unapologetic about the things she said. She was also short tempered and quick to get in somebody's face if they said or insinuated something she didn't like. She was a lot like Bunny except she could get a lot more ignorant. Whereas Bunny was the type to ask questions first, Ginger jumped to her own conclusions and acted on them with no hesitation. But the irony of all this was that Ginger was the most girly girl of the sisters. Always in heels, never in sneakers, Ginger was always dressed like she was about to walk the runway.

Bunny shot Ginger an intense look that Ginger knew all too well. Bunny started walking to get in Ginger's face when Tallhya busted out laughing.

Ginger turned her nose up and asked, "What the fuck is so funny? 'Cause it ain't a gotdamn thing funny about my sister dying."

Tallhya cut her eyes at Bunny, laughed some more, then looked back at Ginger.

Ginger, sitting all proper in her tight jeans and studded stilettos was like, "What? What Bitch? What!"

Tallhya was by now in tears of laughter and couldn't even get her words out, she was laughing so hard.

Bunny, not usually late to the draw, was now getting the joke, and cracked up laughing too.

That's when Tallhya, shared the content of the joke. "You're the only one in here with balls—period!"

Ginger didn't like that at all. She huffed and puffed, "You fuckin' bitch! Your ass makes me fuckin' sick."

"It is what it is Gin. Don't get mad. You set yourself up for that one!" Bunny said in between chuckles. "Now act like you got some balls and take it like a man," Bunny exclaimed laughing even harder this time.

What could Ginger do? The truth was always in a joke. "You got me that time, Tale. I set myself up," Ginger admitted as she joined them in laughter.

All three of them cracked up laughing as if it was the funniest joke ever. Truth was, Ginger did have balls—literally. Born one hundred percent boy, his mother named him Gene. But from the day that she started walking and talking, it was obvious that either God or one of His workers had made a mistake when it came to Ginger's gender. Ginger acted like a girl and always wanted to wear dresses. After a few years of fighting Me-Ma every morning when it was time to get dressed, Me-Ma gave in and let Gene wear what he wanted. Even though he was a boy, Gene had inherited the same high cheek bones and good looks from his mother. This made him the epitome of a pretty boy, so it was easy for him to pass himself off as a girl. All he had to do was let his curly hair grow out.

For this reason, Ginger had always been considered as just another one of those Banks girls. Sometimes they were compared to the Braxton sisters, except the Banks girls were prettier and none of them could hold a note to save their collective lives.

"Fo' real though, that shit was funny," Ginger exclaimed. She knew how to roll with punches and she loved to laugh at a joke, even though it was at her expense this time.

"Hell yea, that shit was funny," Bunny said still tearing and laughing.

Ginger rolled her eyes. The mesmerizing gray eyes, along with a tight body, had seduced many a so-called straight man into her world of cross dressing. She loved that empowering feeling she got when she conquered a straight man and dicked him down. Gene really wanted to get her boobs done but she never wanted to cut her penis off. She actually enjoyed using her 'fun stick' as she called it.

"Will somebody share the joke with me? I could damn sure use a laugh," a visibly shaken Simone said as she stood in the front door way. The sisters were so caught up in their conversation they didn't hear when she unlocked and opened the door to let herself in.

Simone always made sure she looked presentable from head to toe and she always took the extra step to make sure she looked her best. Her appearance right now was a definite indication that she had had a rough day. Her cocoa brown smooth face had smudged eyeliner under her eyes, her make-up was smeared, and she had a small cut on her bottom lip. Her normally long Pocahontas straight black hair needed a brush to it bad. Her black pencil skirt had dirt all over it, and her once crisp white Anne Fontaine shirt was wrinkled and possessed bloodstains. Normally she would have never had a hair out of place, but at this very moment she was just happy to be alive. Simone stood there like a statue.

"Simone!" Tallhya was a thick girl. Not in a fat kind of way though. Even though she could fit some plus size clothes, she was thick in all the right places. She took more after her thick boned grandmother, but either way she was always light on her feet. She quickly jumped up and wrapped her arms so tight around her sister that she almost cut off her circulation.

"Oh my God! I'm so happy you are Okay!" she said. "We've been worried sick about you."

Simone shrugged. Okay? What did that really mean? OK? How could she really ever be OK, the way her life had taken the wrong turn down a dark dead end alley, with one brick wall after another.

Her father, her biggest support system and benefactor, had died six months ago. She was now living back in the hood with Me-Ma because her father's wife, Marjorie, had thrown her out of her daddy's house before his body could even get cold. And today, she had had a gun pointed to her head, felt the feeling of somebody else's warm blood splatter on her, and not to mention, she had almost literally died. Hell no, she wasn't OK.

Not to mention, the police were holding her favorite purse hostage. "I am living, so if that's what we are talking about, I guess I'm OK," she said. "It couldn't get much worse. So, it could only get much better . . . I hope . . . and pray!" she said, trying not to let her tears out, then flashed a fake smile.

Ginger, quick to say the first thing on her mind said, "Girl, we thought yo ass was dead." Bunny and Tallhya stared poisonous darts at Ginger: shut the fuck up sometime, the looks said. "Whatever," said Ginger, "Y'all bitches thought it too."

"How come you didn't answer your phone?" asked Bunny, ignoring Ginger's silly ass. "Bitch, I was worried fuckin' sick about your ass. I drove over here like a bat out of hell trying to hurry up and get here because I just went to pieces when I heard." Bunny started going on a dramatic rant, back to her usual narcissistic self. "And the police probably be here at any time now to take my gotdamn driver's license from speeding."

"My apologies sister." Simone said as sympathetically as she knew how. "I didn't mean to make you do that."

"It's OK, Mona." Bunny said to her sister after making her feel even worse than she already did.

"My phone was high jacked during the robbery." Simone kicked off her heels and plopped down in one of the chairs at the table. "Not to mention my purse. The robbers took it, which is where my phone was. And the police were intensely interviewing us. And the worse part was I had the worst headache the entire time. It was all as if I was living in the Matrix or something."

"Sister, oh my God, that's the worst." Tallhya looked into her sister's eyes wishing that she could fix it.

"Not your Chanel Boy bag?" Bunny asked with a raised eyebrow trying to change the subject. The talk of the violence, and the fact that there was really nothing she could do to get back, was making her mad.

Simone nodded, feeling sick to her stomach as she thought about everything that happened to her today.

"That's why you should've let me borrow it when I asked you for it." Ginger had to get her dig in.

Bunny scooped an unopened bottle of Cognac from her Celine purse. "You look like you could use a drink," she said.

Tallhya's eyes bucked like Bunny had pulled out a snake instead of a bottle. "You know damn well Me-Ma doesn't allow any alcohol in her house," she said as a reminder. "Why are you carrying liquor around in your pocketbook anyway?" She shook her head.

It was Bunny's turn to eye roll.

"Because I'm grown, bitch. Besides," she added. "I knew one way or another a bottle of liquor was gonna be needed, and we all know you don't have none stashed in your room. Either to celebrate, or . . ." Her voice trailed off. What the alternative could've been was best unsaid.

"I told you," Ginger blurted out. "She thought you were dead."

"Shut up, Ginger," Bunny snapped, then told Tallhya, "Get some glasses, please. No back talk and thank you very much."

Tallhya got four glasses from the cabinet. Simone, who never drank anything stronger than a wine cooler, said, "Make mine a double.

Ginger squealed: "Dayum." Then said, "You sure you're a'ight?" As Bunny, splashed a shot in each of the glasses.

The first sip went down as smooth as a ball of fire for Simone, she coughed. But after that, the brown liquor was a soothing as a John Legend song.

"Have you ever seen anyone get shot in the face before?" Simone asked no one in particular. Tallhya and Ginger turned to Bunny.

Bunny downed a finger of the yak. "Fuck y'all look at me for?" she said.

Ginger answered, "You the one always talkin' about how you 'bout that life'. Bust a cap in a nigga's ass. Don't give a fuck . . . and all that ra-ra shit. So have you?"

Before Bunny could reply, Simone said, "I never want to see anything like that again in my life. It was like . . ." She couldn't think of any words that could adequately describe it. "Ghoulish . . . like horrific."

According to the evening news, 13 people in all had died—a customer at the bank, two employees, 6 officers, and the 4 accomplices. It had been the most gruesome day in the new millennium of the history of Richmond City, a city that in the 90's was once called Murder Capitol.

Ginger felt like she was going to throw up. "Ugh. Can we watch something more exciting or can we talk about something else?" she said with a twisted face. "Dayum."

"No you didn't," Tallhya retorted, looking at Ginger skeptically. "You can be so inconsiderate sometimes."

"I just wish my dad was here," Simone dropped her head, "That's all."

"I know," Tallhya said walking over to embrace her sister with a hug.

"But shytttt . . . don't we all. Don't we all wish our dads were here? Ginger said.

"Ginger, you a shady bitch," Bunny shook her head and scolded Ginger with a punch in her shoulder, even though she knew the truth of the matter was that they all at some point or another wished they had a father like Simon, Simone's dad.

Bunny's dad was, and still is, serving a life sentence somewhere in Colorado.

Tallhya's dad, according to Diedra, was a well-known
singer who was married when he knocked Diedra up, and two
years after she was born died of a drug overdose. His manager
found him dead inside a hotel room in St. Louis. And Ginger's
dad, they were all still scratching their head trying to figure
out who that was. The funny thing about that was that Deidra
never offered any kind of story as to who or where he was.

When it came to dads, Simone had been the lucky one.
Simone had a great relationship with him. She was the apple
of his eye and she meant the world to him. In his eyes,
nothing was too good for his princess.

Ginger said to Simone, "So . . . Ms. Touched by an Angel,"
breaking Simone's brief moment of nostalgia, "you gotta go to
work tomorrow or are they giving y'all time off?"

Some things can never be forgotten, Simone thought to
herself.

"I'm never going back to that bank," Simone proclaimed for
the first time, even to herself. "I may never step foot inside
anybody's bank again. I'll do my banking online from now
own. No thank you at all."

"Shit, I wouldn't either." Bunny agreed.

"And I don't blame you." Tallhya got up from the table, put
up the ironing board, and started to iron.

"Awww, hell naw, you know the party is over now, this bitch
about to start her wifely duties." Ginger said.

"And you know she don't play about that." Bunny chimed
in. "And I thought I be on point with my man and his shit, but
this chick right here," Bunny pointed to Tallhya, "she don't be
playing."

Everybody knew all too well how Tallhya rolled when it
came to her men. If Tallhya liked a guy, she not only gave
them the world and everything in it, but she catered to them
in every way. Though she was a little too needy sometimes, a
man couldn't help but love her.

That's exactly how precise she was about them. And
Walter got the best part of the deal when he had married
her. The only way Me-Ma would let him move in and stay

at the house, so they could save money for the big wedding that Tallhya had always dreamed about, was to make it official. So they went to the Justice of the Peace. Walter had been working extra-long hours to make sure that Tallhya's big day was everything that her heart desired. Simone and Bunny didn't understand why they hadn't had a big wedding yet, because they—well not exactly *"they,"* but Tallhya—had won the Virginia state lottery, for one million dollars. And after taxes and fees, she opted for the yearly payout, so that she could get a check every month. After working her ass to the bone, she never wanted to work for anybody another day in her life. Walter had convinced her that they couldn't use their winnings toward their wedding, that that would have to be their nest egg. And she fully agreed, because that was her security. They both agreed that they'd invest their money in addition to him working to pay for the lavish wedding she'd always dreamed about.

"I wish I had a boo like you, Sis," Ginger said sarcastically.

"You make my Home and Gardens ass look bad," Bunny had to admit to Tallhya.

"Look, don't hate me because I'm wife material. All I want is for Walter to be happy."

"Leave her alone. Y'all stop messing with her! I respect that she's submissive," Simone said, wishing she had someone to be submissive to.

Just then Walter, Tallhya's husband, walked into the door, "Honey I'm home." Tallhya ran to greet her man.

"Hey, baby! How was your day?"

"It was great," he said, placing a peck of a kiss on her lips. "Just hungry as fuck. What's for dinner?"

"Good question," Simone said. "I was wondering the same thing, brother-in-law."

"Hey y'all." Walter, a tall, dark and handsome man wearing gym clothes, acknowledged his sister-in-laws. "What did Me-Ma cook? A nigga hungry as shit."

"Nothing . . ."

"Nothing?" Both Simone and Walter sang in unison.

"She's been gone all day. As soon as she heard about the bank, she ran out here so fast she didn't do nothing. In fact, she barely had her wig on."

"Now that's a first." Ginger said. "She was on the move for sure."

Walter looked crazy, like he was about to snap. There was no denying that Me-Ma was the best cook in all of the southeastern part of the Unites States. If for nothing else, he came home every day just so that he could eat her home cooking and always took leftovers to work every day. A man never had to indulge in a restaurant when the kitchen where he resided served food and catered to him better than any restaurant he knew of. "Damn, so ain't shit cooked in here?"

Tallhya could see his frustrations on his face and she ran to his side to resolve the situation. "Don't worry baby. I will get you something to eat," she calmly said, aiming to please her man as her sisters sat and watched. "I'm about to run your shower water, and by the time you get done, I will have your food on the table. OK, baby?"

"OK. I'll settle for that," he nodded, not really happy, but he accepted it.

"You know this shit gets crazier by the day. Somebody better call Me-Ma before this man divorce her." Bunny joked.

"Shit is a crying fuckin' shame if you ask me," Ginger said. "That motherfucker need to cook his own gotdamn food or cook her some. On some real G' shit, he need to take you out at least one night a week on a date night."

"We saving for the wedding, you know that," Tallhya interrupted.

"That nigga makes me sick. He complains about every gotdamn thing. And I don't trust him." Ginger said.

"Yeah, for Christ's sake, somebody please call Me-Ma before we have to fuck him up," Bunny agreed.

Simone reached for the phone and asked, "It's kind of late for Me-Ma to be out isn't it? And you guys said she's been out all day, too?"

Simone called and didn't get an answer and wondered indeed, where in the world was Me-Ma?

Chapter 5

Yield Not to Temptation

"The bible says, if two or more come together, and pray, then their wishes shall be granted, in the name of Jesus," Pastor Cassius Street confidently said to the members of The Faith and Hope Ministry as he led prayer. His straight-legged fitted jeans fit him to the 'T'. The soft material of his designer jeans caressed the top of a pair of his ostrich cowboy boots, as he paced the pulpit. He beseeched in a strong deep voice, dripping with a perfect mixture of confidence and charm.

"I need all my prayer-warriors to get into the spirit. We must," he stressed the word must, "stand in the gap with a Prayer of Protection for the granddaughter of our own, Mother-Mildred Banks."

Sitting in the third row in her usual seat, only using her eyes, Me-Ma thanked the pastor with a nod of encouragement and approval, then bowed her head down for the prayer.

"Lord we honor and praise you in advance for all great things you will bestow upon our life. Lord, we ask you to anoint and protect our sister, Simone. We praise you and we magnify you. We just ask you to have your will done, to keep Sister Simone in your keeping care. We ask Lord, that not a hair be moved out of place, Lord Jesus we know you are a miracle working God."

"Yes, Lord," Me-Ma said aloud and raised her hand.

Me-Ma wasn't one of those so-called Christians who only prayed in times of need. This woman prayed every day, all day. She didn't even have to know the people and she prayed for them. Most of the time when she prayed, it was for other people, rarely for herself.

But Me-Ma's family was an entirely different story. She stayed on her knees for them, especially her daughter, Deidra. She had always been a free spirited person. But when Me-Ma's husband Johnny, Deidra's father, died suddenly of a heart attack on top of his mistress of twenty years, and their fifteen year old love child that lived one street over from them was revealed, Deidra was never the same. Finding out that her loving, idol, role-model of a father was a two-timing woman-izer had damaged her deeply. If she couldn't trust her creator, her father, who could she trust?

From that moment on, Deidra could never connect with people whole-heartedly or truly deeply love. Neither would she commit to anything: a girlfriend, a job, a man, not even her own four beautiful children, who were the spitting mirror image of her. She picked up and disposed of people as if they were trash.

Me-Ma loved her daughter so much and was sure that Deidra's shortcomings were just a test of her faith. Me-Ma's faith was impeccable. She knew that God may not have come when she wanted him to, but he would come in his time. She believed that God was still working on Deidra and would deliver her from her demons one day. Until then she would diligently watch over and pray for Deidra's children; her grandchildren. This was the one reason that she was always on her knees, and in church now with the prayer-warriors, praying for her granddaughter.

Though she was praying for Simone, each of the grand girls had their own issues and could use God's grace and mercy. Tallhya had her battles with obesity and her self-esteem. While Bunny, the ghetto princess, Me-Ma worried to death about. The child was so bold and defiant and, besides God, that girl feared nothing. Gene, a.k.a. Ginger, was an entirely different story. The poor thing had so many demons that all Me-Ma could do was plead the blood of Jesus on that child.

Oddly enough, Simone didn't require a lot of her grand-mother's prayers. Though Me-Ma would never admit it and would deny it to her grave, Simone was definitely her favorite. She loved them all immensely but there was some-thing about Simone's kind and gentle spirit that held a spe-cial place in her heart. The girl walked the straight and narrow and never got in much trouble. Simone was both spiritual and religious. She believed and loved the Lord without a shadow of a doubt. She was raised up in the First Zion Baptist Church and went every single Sunday with her grandmother, even after she went to live with her dad when she was nine. Her dad would drop her off every Sunday so she could attend service with her Me-Ma. Simone sang in the choir and ushered on the usher board. But two years ago, when Pastor Jasper dropped dead of a heart attack on the pulpit, the church, or Simone's feelings toward it, was never the same. Simone hadn't stepped a foot in this church again. It was something about the man dying there that freaked her out.

Me-Ma looked up to God, begging for his mercy on Simone. In the midst, she saw Pastor Cassius' eyes open as he was praying. Then she saw Katrina making googly eyes with the pastor. Me-Ma shot her a look that only a mother could give her child. Cassius looked away quickly, closed his eyes and brought the prayer to a close.

Me-Ma honestly didn't think much of Katrina coming on to the Reverend. It was no secret that damn near every woman at the church had fantasies of being the First Lady. The pastor confessed that he was waiting on God to send her to him. Meanwhile he preached on abstinence, and waited on the one God wanted for him. His most important focus was building his ministry.

"How are you holding up?" Katrina approached and asked Me-Ma. "If I were you, I'd be all to pieces," she said. "But you look so calm. You don't show one ounce of weariness on your face."

Me-Ma was a genuine, kind-hearted woman, but she didn't take mess from a soul. She had seen a lot in foolishness and BS in her day. Me-Ma looked the young lady up and down. Keisha, she thought her name was. Me-Ma had seen napkins with more material than the girl's skirt, leaving nothing to the imagination, except the price to further explore.

"Listen baby, I hear what they saying, but I know I got God on my side and God has the world in His hands, including my granddaughter. And baby, I got faith, and with God who am I afraid of?" she confidently said.

Me-Ma knew the hot little heifer was only being nosey because the bank robbery was all everybody was talking about and the rumors were spreading faster than an STD in a whorehouse.

". . . It was an inside job . . . A million dollars was in the safe . . . The bank robbers were Gangsta Disciples from Chicago . . . One of them got away with the million dollars . . ."

But the one that bothered her the most, ". . . Everyone inside the bank was killed, execution style . . ."

The stories snowballed, one after another, each one wilder than the one preceding it. The church held night services three times a week but today's service had a different kind of energy. As long as it didn't involve them personally, gratuitous violence compelled people to want to talk about it. It didn't matter if it was a bar, on a street corner, or inside a church, human nature was human nature, it didn't change.

Me-Ma took a seat on the pew along with a deep breath, and tried to control her mind from wandering to that place of 'What if?'

"Devil get ye behind me," Me-Ma started to quietly, say to God. "Lord, if it was your will to take her Lord, I just ask you to give me the strength, Lord Jesus."

Then she felt someone put their hands around her from the back. Me-Ma looked up and Simone was standing there embracing her with a hug.

With the sight of Simone, Me-Ma, started screaming, "Thank! You! Jesus!" at the top of her lungs. "Thank you, Jesus! Halllllleeeeluujah!" She said four more times. "My God! My God," she shook her head and tears began to form in her eyes.

This prompted all the prayer-warriors to start shouting all around the church. Me-Ma fell to the ground and begin crying, thanking God.

The Praise and Worship team surrounded her and started singing the gospel hymn, "He Has Done Great Things For Me. . . Greeaaaat Thinggsss . . ."

The rest of the church members started having a big Holy Ghost party while Bunny set in the last pew of the church with eyes hidden behind her big Chloe sunglasses. She was not affected by the way the Holy Ghost filled the place of worship.

The people shouted, and Simone wanted to join them, but she felt weird singing with a church choir she hadn't sang with in so long. The only reason she was even there tonight was because she wanted to personally tell Me-Ma that she was OK. It was just something about the pastor that she couldn't put her finger on.

Pastor Cassius' church was filled with a diverse group of colorful characters of all ages, nationalities, and from all walks of life. The people there were very radical and the fact that they were so dramatic in their acts of praising the Lord, and not to mention, Pastor Cassius, the leader and creator of the whole production with his animated over the top personality, Simone wondered if it could really be legit. Or was it a scam or a show?

Pastor Cassius was a whole other story, he was so flamboyant and in her eyes, everything about him screamed nothing short of a seasoned, homosexual pimp—pimping the pulpit.

He had mastered the Bible. He knew it in and out and could recite it back and forth. His "game" and passion for the Lord was so airtight that one couldn't help but to respect the self-proclaimed "Man of God."

With the most beautiful cocoa skin that looked like it was softer than a baby's butt, he was definitely an attractive man, to the point that all of his primping, the arching of the eyebrows, his big full lips permanently greased with Chap-Stick, along with the pedicures and manicures twice a week, combined with his metrosexual tendencies, turned his handsomeness into pretty.

Me-Ma, who was a wise woman, swore up and down that he was a good man that God himself rescued from the harsh world, and he was nothing short of a walking and living testament of what God can do. But Simone never trusted him. With a name like Cassius Street, who could blame her?

Though all these things were true and correct in Simone's eyes, she couldn't help herself. She had in fact been blessed, and God had spared her from wild bullets that had her name on them. The only explanation was that it was God who had jammed the gun of the robber when she thought she was breathing her last breathe.

Because of God and Jesus Christ, she was able to live on and see another day. That alone was enough reason to praise the Lord. So, she joined in and gave thanks to the Lord.

Pastor Cassius, in his fitted straight leg jeans and cowboy boots, stood before Simone. The rest of the churchgoers watched and listened to every word about to proceed from his mouth.

"My brothers and sisters, what we have just witnessed with our own eyes is nothing less than the work of the Most High. It's God's unchanging grace. It was only our prayers that lead God to allow not one strand be removed from our sister Simone's head. In the midst of a war at her workplace, in the midst of the crossfires and gunshots, and coworkers falling to her left," he dramatically shifted his weight to his left, "and to her right," then did the same thing with the right side of his body. "Ain't God good?" The members started to clap and shout.

His words got the prayer service patrons even more riled up. The Holy Ghost took over. Praising and shouting took place for another forty-five minutes, resulting in a love offering of $212 taken up by Pastor Cassius for Simone.

After the big Holy Ghost party was over, she stood at the door to give hugs and thanks to the church folks for praying for her. Then Me-Ma whispered, "Make sure you thank Pastor here, baby."

Simone shot a look at Bunny that said, "Rescue me," but Bunny, with a smirk on her face, dropped her head, but not before giving her a look that said, "I can't help you with this, big sister."

"Thank you, Pastor, for everything," Simone said. "I really appreciate your prayers and everything you did." She shook his hand, and before she knew it, he had taken her into his arms.

"We hug around here."

"Well, thank you so much for your prayers."

"It was most definitely my pleasure." He flashed his pearly whites at her.

"And I think Pastor has something for you," Me-Ma added.

"Oh, yes," Me-Ma's voice prompted his memory, "Yes," he nodded. "Let's head to my study. Sister, we took a love offering for you and your family."

"Thank you." Simone was surprised at the thoughtfulness of the Pastor. She'd always passionately thought he was a money hungry, ex-pimp drug dealer who was only into the ministry because of the lure of a greater hustle. She hated the fact that maybe she'd have to admit that Pastor may actually be all right after all. Or maybe God was just dealing with him in his own way.

She had to admit, *well, I guess if you think and speak something so long, you start to believe it yourself. Maybe God is really working on him,* she thought to herself as she followed him to his study.

"I think it's about $212.00, and of course you'd bless the church with half of that."

That's a new policy, Simone thought to herself. *They took up the love offering for me and my family, and I have to let the church keep half. Well, I guess half of something is better than nothing. But with this man right here, it's always something,* she thought. Instead she just responded, "Yes, of course, Pastor Cassius."

"You have to be strong and just have faith as you go through this. And know that all of the feelings you are having, God brought you through that ordeal today. He will bring you through feelings of any aftermath you may experience from here on out," he told her as he led her to his study.

"That's right, Pastor. Amen." Me-Ma cosigned. Simone just listened as he continued.

"See, you have to remember that the devil doesn't show up in a red cape and horns. He comes in all kinds of disguises to distract you and throw you off course. You must not yield to temptation," he said as he opened the door to his office.

And they all got the surprise of their life.

"Oh, Jesus. No," Pastor put his hand up and turned his back.

Katrina was in the Pastor's study, buck naked, legs spread eagled wide with a pair of red stilettos on her feet.

***

"Katrina!" Pastor Cassius yelled out. Katrina was so startled to suddenly find herself with an audience that she fell off the desk and crawled under it to shield her naked body.

"I am so sorry about that, Me-Ma. I had no idea she was even in there," a startled Pastor Cassius tried to explain as he closed the door behind him.

"You should be ashamed of yourself!" Me-Ma screamed through the closed door and finished with, "Devil, I rebuke you in the name of Jesus."

Simone couldn't contain herself and burst out into laughter. Damn, that was too funny and so wrong for church.

Me-Ma pleaded the blood of Jesus while Simone got her cash from the reverend and headed back home. She still had to prepare for the aftermath of the bank bullshit in the morning. Even though she didn't plan on working there anymore, she still had to return tomorrow to finish the line of questioning and sign paperwork.

Chapter 6

The Stepmonster

Bunny took Simone back to the bank the next morning so she could get her car. There was a big police crime command center on wheels still outside of the bank to try to collect evidence.

As soon as she got there she was whisked away inside. For the next two hours they asked her pretty much the same questions they'd asked her the day before.

By the time the police were done interviewing all of the bank's employees, Simone was exhausted and beyond ready to go. She asked one of the men who seemed to be in charge, "How much longer do I have to be here?"

Detective Chase Dugan scrutinized Simone carefully with his quick hazel eyes. "You're Ms. Banks, Right? The twenty-nine-year old U of R graduate? And it was your first day at the bank?" He couldn't help but notice how beautiful she was, and chastised himself for being momentarily distracted by it.

"Correct. Correct. And Correct," Simone said, a little nervous, but even more impressed. Dugan hadn't been the officer who'd questioned her earlier, yet he ran off her information without the aid of any notes. "I'm a suspect now?" she joked, but was serious.

Detective Dugan shoved his hands into the pockets of his slacks before saying, "It's my job to know who is who and what is what," he said with a quirky smile. Then: "Actually, we have everything we need from you. And to answer your question . . . No. You're not a suspect."

"Well, what about my pocketbook? One of the robbers had taken my purse and I haven't seen it since."

"Your pocketbook isn't a suspect either." The officer said with a smirk on his face.

Handsome and a sense of humor, she thought to herself. "What I meant to say is, may I please have my purse back so I can go on with my life?" Simone said in a serious tone. She refused to let the officer see that he was having an effect on her.

Detective Dugan, who resembled a younger Denzel Washington, was being a comedian, "I'm sorry. I was just trying to make light of the situation."

Simone had a feeling she wasn't going to like what he was going to say next.

"Your purse is evidence. Therefore, we're going to have to hold on to it for a while."

He was right. She wasn't happy. She looked at him, and said as humble as she knew how, "Look I really need my stuff, my wallet, keys and cell phone. I can't drive my car without my keys. "

After a few seconds of thought, Detective Dugan offered a compromise. "I can get your keys and your phone, but that's it."

"That would be greatly appreciated detective."

Simone went to tell Bunny, who had been waiting patiently. "He's going to get my keys and my phone but that's all. Everything else is being held," she sighed, "for God knows how long."

"That's some bullshit." Bunny said exactly what Simone was thinking but wouldn't say out loud.

"I agree, but this is the struggle."

"I know, Sisi. But it's going to be okay," Bunny tried to convince her sister, then asked, "You need money?"

"No, Buns, I'm good. I have that money the church gave me," she said, knowing she should have taken her sister up on the offer, but she didn't want to accept the dirty money.

"Girl, let me help you. After all, that's what sisters are for."

"Bunny, I appreciate you, but I will make a way."

"How? You just said you're not going back to work again." She looked into her sister's eyes and saw how petrified she was at the sight of being back at the scene of yesterday's nightmare. "And I don't think your trust fund has magically reappeared yet. And even if you do get interviews, that whole thing is a process. It's not like you are going to be able to get paid right away. And honestly, I don't know how far your check for one day at the bank will stretch. So let me help you."

Simone took into consideration what her sister was saying, and knew she was speaking the truth. As bad as she did need the help, she would feel like a hypocrite if she took the money knowing where it came from.

"I can't tell you how much I appreciate you offering me money, but really sis, I will be ok."

"I know you don't want to take it because you feel like it's blood money, but look, money is money. Shit," Bunny sucked her teeth, "it all spends."

"You are right," Simone agreed but still had to kindly decline her sister's offer. "If I happen to change my mind, will the offer still stand?"

"And you know this, Sisi."

Simone looked at Bunny, "Thanks Buns. I love you." She leaned inside the car and gave her a hug.

"Miss Banks," the detective called out to her.

Simone turned to look back at him. He had her keys. She turned to Bunny, told her that she would be OK and said goodbye before going around the other side of the bank to get her car.

After finally getting her keys, Simone bailed out of the bank as fast as her Gucci sneakers would carry her. Outside was a circus of news reporters and yellow tape separating the crime scene from a growing number of curious onlookers. She felt like it was still the day before. She couldn't bear to look at the bank's surroundings. She couldn't get the scene from yesterday out of her mind. There were pools of congealed blood and dead bodies underneath white sheets. The air smelled of death and anxiousness. Simone tried to block it all out, damn near running to her car like an immigrant escaping from a third-world country.

"Miss . . . Miss . . ." One reporter noticed her, prompting the rest of the media frenzy to go after her. It was a good thing that she had a great head start in front of them.

Once she made it to her car, a Mercedes C-350 convertible, she sped off. The Mercedes, as if on autopilot, navigated itself to her father's house, the house Simone had grown up in, the house that now, legally, belonged to her stepmother, Marjorie.

Simone would've given anything to have been able to talk to her dad. He always knew exactly what to say to her, regardless of the situation. No problem was too big, or too small, for daddy dearest. On those rare occasions when Simon, her father, couldn't physically fix what was bothering her, he comforted her with the perfect words, hug, or ear, to make her feel better.

But those moments were gone . . . forever.

Simon was dead. He'd passed six months ago, and that had to be the absolute worst day of her life. She took a deep breath as she parked in front of her father's mansion. She hadn't been there since the day of the burial, when his wife basically packed all her stuff and kicked her out of the house. She hated having to humble herself to ask her stepmother for help, but under the circumstances, she didn't have much of a choice.

Standing on the porch in a funk, Simone punched her key into the deadbolt lock and nothing happened. She wiggled it. Still nothing. Odd, she thought. This was the same exact key she'd been using since she was nine when her father and her first moved into the house. She removed the key from the lock, looked at it, then tried it again.

At that moment, when the lock still refused to cooperate, reality plowed into her like a dump truck carrying a load of shit. She didn't want to believe the ugly truth: The place where Simone had grown up in, and had once called home, no longer welcomed her.

Simone had been front and center at her father's funeral, burial, and wake but for some reason, the full reality hadn't hit her until right at this very moment when her key no longer worked in his house. Her dad was dead. Gone for good. And he wasn't coming back. Deep down, at that very moment, she felt a part of herself softly die.

She was on the brink of breaking down like a discarded, broken lawn chair when the front door flung open. Simone, reaching deep within herself, pulled herself together. Even if it killed her, she thought, she wouldn't give Marjorie the satisfaction of seeing her looking like a stray animal on the porch, yearning to be rescued.

Marjorie stepped out onto the porch, the picture of smugness. "Simone darling." Her exaggerated tone reminded Simone of the late Eartha Kitt. "The doorbell works just fine," she said, pushing the button with her pink and white French-manicured index finger to demonstrate, just in case Simone hadn't for some reason understood.

Simone stood in silence.

Filling the gap, Marjorie asked, in mock politeness, "Now to what do I owe the pleasure?" Then the pretense of cordiality vanished as quickly as it had appeared. Marjorie, as if just noticing Simone, balled her face up in disgust. "By the way, you look a fuckin' mess. In fact, you should be ashamed of yourself walking around here looking like who did it and why. You look despicable."

She had no makeup on her face and had on a velour Juicy Couture sweatsuit. That morning she honestly just wanted to stay in her Me-Ma's house under the covers, but she knew she had to go back to the bank to attempt to get her stuff.

Simone wanted to say, "And you always look like the fake two faced woman you've been since I met you," but instead she bit her tongue to avoid any more of a scene. She just said, "I had a rough twenty-four hours."

Reluctantly, Marjorie invited her in. "Make it quick, honey. I have things to do, people to see, and places to be."

Once inside, under the light, she was able to give Marjorie a once over look and it was official. It was rumored by Ms. Godfrey, her neighbor nextdoor, that Marjorie had been under the knife, getting all types of plastic surgery procedures. Once inside the house, under bright light, the rumors were confirmed. Marjorie's face was tight as fish pussy. She'd gotten a new nose, a facelift and enough botox to fill the holes in the foundation of the Titantic. And if that wasn't enough, Simone couldn't help but notice Marjorie had permanent make-up tattoos in place of eyebrows and lip liner. If her goal was to imitate a frozen clown's face, she'd succeeded with flying colors, Simone thought.

Marjorie led Simone into the living room, which is off to the right of the grand foyer. "I see you've redecorated," she said checking out the room.

Marjorie's face wasn't the only thing that had been drastically transformed into something almost unrecognizable. The paint, the flooring, the furniture, the drapes, everything had been changed. Nothing was really wrong with the way it was before.

"The place needed it," Marjorie said with an edge. "It was a long time overdue."

"Stepmonster," the name Simone used for Marjorie behind her back, had gone too far. The woman had done a master makeover on her outer person and the interior of the house, eradicating any and everything that could conjure memories of Simone's dad. Simone had always secretly disliked Marjorie. To be honest, she hated the woman, but even she had no idea how much of a cold-hearted bitch Marjorie truly was.

Her dad had been married to the woman for twelve years: filled with trips around the world, lavish gifts, romantic dinners, and all the quality time Simon's company would allow him to be away. In return, Marjorie repaid her deceased husband by not even bothering to display a picture in which to honor his memory. Simone had heard of a new beginning, and Marjorie wasted no time starting one.

The house felt cold, devoid of love. "So," Marjorie said, "let's not play games. What is that you want? I'm sure you're not here to give me any decoration tips." Marjorie tightened the belt on her white satin, fur-trimmed robe. Her breasts were hanging like two sacks of sand. It was surprising to Simone that Marjorie had not gotten them done. *I guess even the best surgeon couldn't help those saggy things,* she thought.

Simone gave Marjorie the story about the bank getting robbed, leaving out most of the details.

"I saw it on the news. But exactly what does that have to do with me?" Marjorie asked without any kind of sympathy at all. "You are not dead, so clearly that has nothing at all to do with me."

Simone took a deep breath, and let the comment roll off her back, like water. "One of the bank robbers took my Chanel Boy bag, with my money and ID, everything in it. I need my birth certificate that dad kept in his security box so that I'll be able to get a new ID."

Simone detested having to ask or to need anything from Marjorie. This was the same bitch that contested her father's will, and everything that Simon had left for her. Meanwhile, Marjorie was running through a life insurance policy she'd taken out on him. Simone would bet her life that her father was surely rolling over in his grave. His only child of twenty-nine years was broke, not a dollar in the bank, while his wife of twelve years was living the life of luxury in the fast lane with not one regard for her, or a care in the world.

"So, let me get this right," Marjorie said with a chuckle. "The bank robbers took the bank's money, your money, and your Chanel bag."

The old hag wasn't going to make this easy. Trying not to lose her cool, Simone politely said, "Yes, and my wallet. So I need my birth certificate so I can go to the DMV to get a new ID."

Marjorie's eyes turned dark and the horns went up on her head. "And since they took your wallet will you be asking me for some money too? Is that what your real intentions are? You came to beg money from me?" She spat the words out like they left a bad taste in her mouth.

Simone hadn't considered asking her for money but she thought: *Hell, yes! Well, that would be the least you could do for me. You should have given me the money my dad left me. Instead, you manipulated my dad's will, put me out of his own house and changed the locks on the doors.*

If it wasn't for her mother's mother, Me-Ma, Simone would've been homeless.

Make no mistake about it, Simone loved and appreciated herself some Me-Ma. Growing up, Me-Ma, was always generous, caring, and gracious. It was so sad, but true, that Me-Ma was the closest thing to a mother figure Simone ever had. Besides a little more gray hair and a few more wrinkles, Me-Ma hadn't changed a bit. But Simone had. She was a mature, educated, grown woman whose father had worked hard so that she would always be taken care of, even after he was gone. And now her stepmother manipulated everything and left her with nothing.

It took every fiber of restraint and humility for Simone to answer Marjorie's question. She took a deep breath, slowly inhaled and counted to ten before exhaling.

At that point, she decided why not? What did she have to lose? It was simple. It was either yes or no.

Calmly, she said, "I wasn't here to ask for money but I could use some. I do need money right now. For the basics, gas and food. And I'm going to need to buy a new phone." Doing a few calculations in her head, she figured she needed about seven or eight hundred to get by, but settled for the bare minimum. "Do you think you can give me five hundred?"

The room, smelling like fresh paint and money, was pin drop quiet for a few beats. Out of nowhere, Marjorie cackled like a witch with a black cat up her sleeve. The irritating bewitching laughter went on for a while. Finally, she stopped.

"So, you *need* me, huh," she said. "Where's your mother in your time of need?"

Bringing up Deidra was a low blow, even for Marjorie, thought Simone.

"Wait don't answer, she said, "Let me guess. M-I-A as always," Marjorie added. Besides pushing you out of her pussy that woman has never given you anything. It's just mighty funny how she's never around when you need her."

She was right. Deidra, Simone's mother, had never done a thing for Simone, except pass on her beautiful looks to her, which she was grateful for.

Simone bit her tongue, literally, ignoring Marjorie's childish attempt to make her lose her cool. Simone knew what Marjorie was trying to do. If Simone, snapped on her, Marjorie would use it as an excuse not to give her the money. *Nice trick, but that won't work on me bitch,* Simone thought.

Marjorie, after not getting the results she'd hoped she would, scurried off toward the family room, the bottom of her robe, including the fur trim, flapping in the wind. Simone assumed Marjorie was going to get the money she'd asked for. A few seconds later, Simone heard voices coming from the room Marjorie had just gone into. She couldn't make out the words but recognized that the tone of it was Marjorie and Maria, the housekeeper who had worked for her father for years.

Nevertheless, Simone couldn't make out what they were saying. Simone walked into the foyer taking a seat in a newly purchased high back chair, so that she was closer to the door.

Her thoughts drifted to a conversation she'd had with her father, in this very spot, when she was sixteen. They talked about what time she was expected to be back home from her first real date. She'd made it home thirty minutes before curfew.

The trip down memory lane ended as suddenly as it had had begun. "Here!" It was Marjorie, pushing a crumpled up piece of paper into her palm, a twenty-dollar bill.

No, that bitch didn't! The disrespect burned at the lining of Simone's stomach like a shot of cheap liquor. "What am I supposed to do with this?" She held the twenty-dollar bill by two fingers as if it was a solid dagger. Now Marjorie was just toying with her. She had never felt so belittled in her life.

Marjorie, judging by the twisted smile and the spark of delight simmering in her eyes, made no effort to conceal the joy she felt at Simone's expense. "Darling . . ." she said, bubbling with self-assertion, "you need to take that twenty and run along. I have a date," She made an exaggerated gesture of checking her watch, "and I've wasted enough time with the likes of you."

Simone and Marjorie had never really liked each other, they tolerated one another for the sake of Simon. Growing up, Simone had always given the respect she gave to all adults, as she was taught. But Simone quickly learned that respect wasn't something to be given, it had to be earned. And this trick hadn't earned a damn ounce of anything.

Simone decided to take Marjorie's advice: and get the fuck away from her. As she got up from the high back chair, Marjorie, adding insult to injury, said, "No more freebies here." And she didn't stop there. "You've freeloaded your whole life—Ohhh, daddy's little precious girl. Well, that shit is over. She raised her voice, "Done! Finito! Your daddy's gone and that twenty dollars is the last thing you're ever going to get from me." The smile of glee was replaced by one of unadulterated hate. "You will never see another penny of your father's money. I'm gonna see to that, little girl. And what are you gonna do about it. Nothing! That's what," Marjorie went on. "Because I have the best lawyer in the state, and you don't have shit . . . not a gotdamn thing! Good luck with that in probate court. Now if you don't mind, get the fuck outta *my* house and try to figure out how you're going to feed your grown-ass-self."

Simone seriously considered cracking Marjorie upside her poorly done, surgically-enhanced joker face, but she wasn't a vio-

lent person. The last fight she'd been in was in the third grade with
a girl named Charlotte. Charlotte, a white girl, had told another
girl that Simone's dad looked like the monkey Curious George
from the book the class had to read. After Simone was done
wearing Charlotte's butt out on the playground by the sandbox,
Charlotte would never even say the word monkey again.

"How dare you," Simone said with disdain of her own.
"You have the unmitigated gall to tell me that I need to work
while your selfish ass is running around spending me and my
father's hard earned money like its going out of style.

"You mean my hard earned money," said Marjorie, hands
on her wide hips. "You haven't the slightest clue of the shit I
had to put up with."

Simone gave Marjorie a sideways look as if she was crazy.

Unapologetic, Marjorie said, "I not only had to play mother
to your spoiled ass, acting like I actually gave a fuck if you win
this pageant or that, but I had to make sure you had the nicest
dress for the many proms and homecomings. Chile, please. If
that wasn't enough, I also had to deal with your dear daddy's
tiny-ass dick. That alone should be worth all the tea in China,
having to fake orgasms and please myself for twelve, long years.
That man's dick was smaller than a two years old baby's."

Before Simone had realized it, she'd smacked Marjorie
so hard sparks came from her face. The skin—so tight from
surgery—nearly ripped to pieces. Yet, the expression on her
face never changed.

Simone had no idea what had come over her, but she
wasted no time taking advantage of Marjorie's temporary
shock. Simone cocked back as far as she could and blasted
the witch one more time just because. It felt so good. One of
Marjorie's fur slipper heels wobbled. She lost her balance and
busted her ass on the marble floor.

"You bitch." Marjorie threw the broken shoe at her. The
shoe hit Simone on the arm. A nail, where the heel should've
been, broke the skin and drew blood.

The sight of the blood trickling from her forearm, coupled
with everything else built up inside of her, was more than she
could take. Besides, she thought, it was time to teach this hag
a gotdamn lesson.

She had had enough.

Marjorie was trying to stand up on shaky legs when Simone caught her with a well-timed uppercut. The punch tagged Marjorie's chin like an unwanted tattoo. Marjorie fell back to the floor, kicking, and Simone started squeezing. She wanted to choke some manners into Marjorie, and if Marjorie croaked in the process, so be it. Then maybe all her father's things would revert back to her anyway.

Marjorie's eyes looked for an escape. She made a funny noise—"Ooukkk-o-wokkk," that sounded as if she was sucking a dick. In a morbid sort of way, it was music to Simone's ears.

In third grade, when Simone was tearing a mud hole in Charlotte's little racist ass, it had taken two teachers to get Simone off of her. That was one of the reasons Simone had avoided fighting from that point on. She'd nearly killed Charlotte.

It wasn't until Marjorie's face had turned a funny—not ha-ha funny, but oh-my-god funny—shade of purple that Simone realized what she was doing. Marjorie's eyes, where the irises had been, were now white.

Simone stopped squeezing, releasing the grip from Marjorie's neck.

Desperate for air, Marjorie inhaled—as hard as she could—before blowing out the lung-full of oxygen that kept her alive. With her hand stretched out to hold off an attack, she took a few more precious breaths.

The second Marjorie had a breath to spare, she said, "Get out, bitch! Get the fuck out of my house, before I call the police."

Simone knew Marjorie's wasn't bluffing about the police. "I wouldn't expect your no class wanna-be ass to do anything else but call the police." Simone turned her back, opened the front door, and walked out of her father's house feeling better than she'd felt in a few months. Whoever coined the phrase, "violence never solved anything," was wrong. So, so wrong.

Simone was about to get into her car when she realized it was gone. In the driveway, in the exact spot she'd parked, was a Dodge Neon.

Oh, this hag has really lost her mind!

Simone stormed back into the house like Hurricane Katrina, nearly knocking the door off of its hinges doing so.

Marjorie had somehow managed to pull herself off the floor and was sitting in the high back chair leaning most of her upper body on her legs. Her head jerked up when the door opened. Her eyes looked as if she wished that she'd locked the door.

"Where in the hell is my car, bitch?"

Unable to look Simone in the face, Marjorie said, "Your car is outside."

She put her hand on her hip and said, "I drive a fuckin' Mercedes and the only thing in the driveway is a gotdamn Neon."

Marjorie clutched a lamp. Simone figured Marjorie intended to use the lamp for a weapon, if she needed it. "You don't own shit. The title to that car, registration, license tags they were all in Simon's name, which means I own it now," she spoke in a tone a little above a whisper. "It's all mine."

Simone wished she'd choked the bitch out when she had the chance. She probably could've beat the case if she had: self-defense, crime of passion, or temporary insanity. She'd learned about the different defenses in her criminology class.

Marjorie, holding the lamp with one hand and fixing her hair with the other, got bolder by the second. "I'm the spirit of fairness. The title and the keys to the Neon are in the glove box. You have about ten more days to get it registered. Be grateful."

"Grateful?" Simone questioned.

Simone had no clue where the phone in Marjorie's hand came from. She must have pulled it from her ass, thought Simone. Marjorie dialed 9-1-1. She told Simone, "Now get the hell out of my house." Then into the phone: "Hello, police. I have an intruder inside my home."

Simone walked closer, leaned down, got right up in her face, close enough to smell the scotch on Marjorie's breath. "Listen to me," she said. "No more Mrs. Nice Girl. You hear me? You better make sure every I is dotted and every motherfuckin' T is crossed. That you're papered up with every document you can forge, because I promise you on my daddy's grave," she coughed up a mouth full of saliva and spit right in Marjorie's face, just because, and said, "I'm coming for you."

Chapter 7

As soon as Bunny pulled off from dropping Simone at the bank, her phone rang. The sound of the phone made her heart smile. The ring tone alerted her it was Spoe, the love of her life. She answered right away.

"Hey baby," she said.

"Everything OK?" He asked, wanting to genuinely make sure that Simone was good.

"I honestly, don't know." She sighed. "I'm really worried about her. I just dropped her at her car and she went to pieces. "

"Naw, man," he said concerned and in disbelief.

"Yup, I'm leaving from over here by the bank and this place looks like Hurricane Katrina went through here. They got blocks blocked off from the chase. It just doesn't make any sense, the damage that was done."

"That bad, huh?"

"Yup. And I'm not even talking about the damage done to Mone."

"I thought she was good."

"I mean, she good on the outside but fucked up on the inside."

"What could we do to help, babe. Anything?"

"I offered her some bread."

"That's what's up, you know whatever we can do. We got her."

"Yeah, I know we do, but you know she was on that goody-two-shoes, I don't want to take no dirty money type shit."

"Yeah, but shit if she need help. And if she not going back to the bank and her peoples cut her off. Fuck she gone do?" Spoe asked then gave his two cents. "Trust me that shit going to change real quick."

"I don't know," Bunny said, then changed the subject. "So what's up with you?"

"Everything good. I'm just making sure you and the fam okay, that's it."

"Well, I'm about to swing by Me-Ma's and give this money to Tallhya and tell her to give it to Simone. She may take help from Tallhya rather than me."

"Good idea baby."

"Well, when you get done, let's go to that restaurant I told you about and catch a movie or something."

"You know I'm always up for quality time with the love of my life," she said to him. She could feel his blushing through the phone.

"I can't wait."

"Babe, that's right," she snapped her fingers, just remembering what she needed to run by Spoe. "I keep forgetting to ask you, do you think we could hook Gina up with Tariq?"

Spoe sucked his teeth, "Baby, that's a negative. He's out there right now, doing him." He hesitated. Spoe wanted to make sure that he chose his words wisely. "And you know I don't really think that's wise for us to turn Gina onto him no way. Shit, that's a disaster waiting to happen."

"Damn, baby, you act like my girl chopped liver or something."

"Come on now, baby. I'm not saying that, but you already know. He's not ready. He's on a different time than I am. Maybe a couple years from now he might be ready. But right now, he just having fun enjoying the single life."

"Maybe he needs to settle down," she snapped back, almost taking his analysis of Tariq personally. "Because that life he's living ain't really cool, babes."

"By whose standards though?" he asked, not being intimidated by her views, and then added, "Different strokes for different folks."

"You need to talk to your boy, before one of them chicks catch him slipping and next thing you know, he's in love with a stripper," she started harmonizing that song by T-Pain.

Spoe chuckled at Bunny. She was right, but it was still none of their business.

Tariq was his business partner and a hell of one too. They went back a long way. He had principles, heart, and was trained to go at any time. But most importantly, just like Spoe, he was about that money.

"You crazy, babe, but I'm going to run Gina past him when I talk to him and see what he says," he said, just to shut Bunny up. He knew she'd keep going on and on like an Energizer bunny.

"Can you call him now, please? Because I told Gina I was going to see what's up."

"I'm waiting on him to call me back. I've been calling him all morning and he ain't hit me back yet."

"Sure you don't. The way y'all keep tabs on each other, I can't believe you don't know his exact location."

Spoe knew Tariq was probably up to his normal, but at the end of the day, it's his life. He is a grown man, free to do whatever it is he wants. But still, Spoe needed him to call him back.

"It's almost noon, and I don't know where the hell that nigga at."

Tariq walked out of the bathroom in the nude, over to where his clothes lay. He had stayed far past his normal time he thought, as he picked up his Polo boxer shorts and slipped into them.

Damn, time flies, he thought to himself.

Tariq glanced over to the king-sized bed, where the gorgeous Tiffany Rolay laid on top of the white high-thread-count sheets. The sleeping beauty looked too peaceful to be awakened. Tariq took his time and lotioned down his body. Then he slipped into his clothes from the night before. As he bent over to tie his Air Jordan sneakers, the sun shined through the windows, which provided him the light he needed to tie his shoes.

Tariq walked over to the bed, sat down and ran his finger over Tiffany's soft succulent lips. Her eyes popped open immediately, as if she had just dosed off and didn't know where she was. A smile appeared on her lips when she saw

Tariq's face. "Good morning, handsome! How long you have been up? And why didn't you wake me?" she asked.

"You were in here, knocked the fuck out." He rubbed his hands over her exposed nipple.

"A bitch was tired! Dealing wit' ya ass, on your wanna fuck all night shit. You beat this pussy up, Boo-Boo! I'm soooo sore down there," she said in a girlish giggle.

"You know how I get down. You knew what it was when you got up here last night." He smiled and stroked his own ego, "Major dick-slinging shorty. Now get dat ass up and let's figure out some breakfast."

"Waffle House?" she questioned.

He nodded with a smile. "That's cool."

"A'ight then give me a few minutes. I need to get in the shower and get myself together first."

"Well, hurry up, then. I ain't got all day. My stomach growlin' like a motherfucker."

"Damn! Okaaaay. Work with me, baby! Perfecting this beauty don't come in seconds, but I'm going to make it quick, though. Just for you, Reek," she replied then flicked the sheet off her body and rolled out of bed.

Tiffany stood up and looked back at him, making eye contact and placing a seductive smile on her face. She walked away, swinging her hips, making her backside move like water.

He smiled at her.

Tiffany was a getting money kind of chick. Though he met her when she first started working at Treats Gentleman's Club, in his mind she wasn't the average kind of stripper that he was used to. He couldn't put his finger on it, but it was just something different about Tiffany. Normally he didn't even try to rationalize why the dancers he usually hooked up with danced in the first place. But Tiffany. . . he couldn't figure out why a woman of her caliber would even let men play in her pussy for a few dollars.

Not only was she drop dead gorgeous, she was cultured. The beauty spoke fluent Spanish, French, and some Arabic. Taking away the fact that she took her clothes off for a living, Tiffany was definitely a classy chick, owning the best of everything.

Outside of the club, she wore only the best and latest of gear.
Her purses were fierce, high fashion in the first degree: Hermes,
Chanel, Louis Vuitton, just to name a few. But her shoe game
could give even Imelda Marcos a run for her money.

Tiffany drove a Mercedes SL-65, limited edition, and had a
plush condo. Tariq had only stopped by one time just to see
how she was living, but it was against his principals to stay
or visit any chick. He would never get caught slipping at the
hands of a female. It would be irony at its best.

Anytime that Tiffany had Tariq's attention for more than
a few days, her swag and sex appeal had to be on point. And
everything about her was everything that he liked, almost too
good to be true.

Tiffany stopped at the bathroom door. She bent over and
touched the floor, then looked through both of her legs at him
and started dancing as if she was in the club, giving him a
show. That lasted for a couple of minutes, then she continued
into the bathroom.

Tariq laid back and placed his hands behind his head,
staring up at the ceiling.

*Damn! Tiff bad as a motherfucker. She got that good ole
snappa too. I would hit that shit again, but naw, I got shit
to do in an hour. Matter of fact, fuck that breakfast. I'ma
grab something on my way. Damn, this bitch stay soakin'
the fuckin' sheets with that wet-ass pussy she got squirting
everywhere*, he thought to himself as he looked down at the
wet spot in the middle of the bed.

Twenty-five minutes later, Tiffany walked back into the
bedroom wrapped in a huge white towel and smiled at Tariq.
"You want some more of this good, good?" she cooed.

"We gotta get outta here, Tiff. Later on we could go at it. I
got some shit to take care of."

"So, we going to spend some time again later on?" She coyly
asked with a smile and a raised eyebrow. Tiffany was excited
because she liked spending time with him.

He let out a smirk. "You sound surprised," he teased, knowing why but he wanted to hear her take on what was going on.

"Well, you know the word around the club is . . ." she said, wondering if she should tell him or not.

"I'm listening . . ." he shot back interested in hearing what the scoop was on the stripper-mill.

"You know me and you done got real cool, like real, real cool over the past couple of weeks."

"And we have," he had to agree.

"Well, the word is you kind of like variety. You are like a different woman literally every day kind of dude."

"Is that right?"

Tiffany gave him a playful hit, "You already know. The girls in the club like you because you got a big dick and you will give them a couple a dollars, but they know you not fuckin' the same chick two days in a row."

"That sounds about right."

"So the fact that we've been fuckin' and chilling, it seems like I broke the record."

"You have." He couldn't deny it.

"I must be special." She got ahead of herself trying her hand.

"You are cool, mad cool. But I know your life, and your work, so I already know what it is."

"Meaning?" she asked.

"Meaning you got niggas and you do your thing, which I don't knock. After all I know where I met you at."

"I don't have to have them like that. In fact, I like you. I really do." She looked in his face and said, "I really like you and I want us to be cooler than cool."

"Really?" he questioned.

"Seriously." Tiffany looked in his eyes.

"Time will tell. You just gotta prove it."

"And I will."

"OK," he dryly said.

"Look, I know you think I'm a dollar ho, about my money and all that."

"I do and I don't knock you for that."

"But it's definitely more to me than meets the eye.

"I don't doubt that either."

She tried to pour her heart out to him. "It's more to me than just being on a pole, and I hope you take the time to get to know me."

"Maybe I will. But for now, we are going to take it one day at a time. Every day seems like I learn something new about you, but no expectations, OK?"

"Okay, baby. I won't apply any pressure. But just know that I like you a lot and really feel like we could do anything."

"I feel ya," he said rubbing on her, then changing the subject. "Well, I gotta take a rain check on that breakfast," he said as her phone rang. "And seems like you need to get caught up on returning your calls, because they trying to catch up with you. Duty calls."

Tiffany let out a laugh, "Rain check given! Just know I do collect on those." She smiled as she checked her phone.

"Oh, that's how it is, huh?" Tariq smirked.

"That's right boo. But in other news, I got some news that you could use."

"Go ahead, shoot."

"Well, I know how you and ya man Spoe get down."

"What you talking about?" he asked as if he was surprised.

"Come on now, the whole of Richmond knows."

Prying into his business immediately messed up his vibe. "You say that to say what?"

"Well, I know this nigga that's papered up like a mother-fucker. Real flashy dude, not in the dope game but got this other crazy scam going on. I been to his mini mansion before and it's nice as shit. I mean really nice, no corners cut."

"Get to the point Tiff!" Tariq sat up and looked into her eyes.

"Well, one day I was with him and he was talkin' all this big money shit. I'm like, 'whatever nigga'," she said to Tariq. "'Cause you know, working in the club, niggas always trying impress you. So, you know I heard it all before."

"Ummm-ha."

"So, I'm like 'bye, boy!' Then he got up and walked out of the room and came back seconds later with two big duffle bags. He dumped them out onto his bed."

Tariq didn't blink or utter a word. He just listened and she had his attention.

"Reek, my eyes got big as shit. I ain't never seen that much money in my life. Ole boy looked at me and laughed, then he had the nerve to say, 'I bet you ain't never seen two millions in cash before did you?'"

"Had you?"

"I'd seen a lot of money, but I was lost for words, because I wasn't expecting him to have two million. I thought he was all flash."

"Is that right?"

"Yes," she said making complete eye contact with him.

"He put the money back into the bags and took them back out of the room, then came back like a minute later. I'm tellin' you Reek, it's a sweet lick," she said with excitement.

"So he showed you two million in cash, huh? How you know it was two million?"

"Reek, listen to me, boo. It was definitely a couple of million, trust me."

"Damn, a couple of mill, huh?"

"Yeah, it'll be like taking a bottle from a baby. I got everything mapped out too."

"Who is this nigga?"

"His name is Marky. I think he's originally from New York somewhere."

"So, this shit that sweet huh?" he said with a raised eyebrow.

"Hell yea, it's definitely sweet! I wouldn't bullshit, Tariq. He got it like that! He probably has more than that where that comes from. I'ma be with him tonight. We supposed to be going to dinner then go somewhere else."

"So, you got his address and everything?"

"Yes! He lives by himself, too. I'm telling you, it'll be the sweetest lick you ever had!"

"How you know the bread still there if it was in duffle bags? It probably was being bagged up to go somewhere."

"No, he always got a bag of money laying around. Plus he had it in the car and was bringing it into the house. I'm meeting up with him at the house tonight before we go out. I will lurk and see if the bag is still there."

"You say he gonna be wit' you tonight, huh?"

"Yeah! Y'all could go take the money and meet me later with my cut. You know I'm about my money too," she said jokingly but was dead serious.

"So how much is ya cut supposed to be?"

"Two hundred and fifty thousand, that's all I want."

He smiled.

She quickly said, "You could always give me more if you want."

"A'ight, let me holla at my man. I'ma get back wit' you and let you know if we wit' it. Make sure you answer you phone when I call. This shit better be just how you said it was. Don't waste my fuckin' time."

"Cut it out, Reek. It's all good, boo!" she said then straddled his lap. She kissed his neck deeply and moved her center in a circular motion. He pulled back and looked up in her eyes.

"Where is the money?"

She hesitated. "Now, that I don't know for sure. I'm going to try to roam and see if it's in eyesight. If not, y'all are going to have to find it. I do know that it have to be upstairs somewhere judging by how fast he went and got it, then when he took it back."

"A'ight get dressed. I gotta go."

Tiffany climbed off his lap and picked her dress and six inch Chanel heels up off the floor. She slipped into her body-con painted on dress then buckled the heels around her ankles. Tiffany picked up her Chanel bag, and headed for the door, tossing her red lace panties to him.

Tariq caught them and then placed them in her purse. He trailed a little behind her and watched her bottom bounce underneath the dress. Shaking his head, she had one of the sexiest walks he had ever seen. He got up and walked out of the room behind her, gripping two handfuls of her butt in the process.

Outside, the sun greeted them with a warm kiss on the cheek. The smell of the fresh cut grass and clean air was pleasing to their nostrils. Tariq opened and closed the door to Tiffany's red coupe.

Tariq walked over to his four door Masareti and got inside. He pushed the button, started the engine, and watched as Tiffany drove away.

Biggie Smalls, "Ready to Die," blared through the speakers. Tariq bobbed his head and rapped along with the legend, then drove away. The night with Tiffany was definitely memorable, but it was now time for him to get back to his money. He turned the music down, leaned over and checked his phone. There were a few missed calls from Spoe. He and Spoe were supposed to be meeting, which was on point because he had an earful for him anyway.

"What it do my nigga?" Spoe answered. No hello. No hi. Just simply to the point.

"Mannnnn. . . . Got some shit for you."

"Where you at?" Spoe asked.

"We still meeting?"

"For sure. Just meet me at ya place now bro, I got some heavy, heavy news to drop on you my man!"

"Okay, that's cool. Be there in fifteen."

"I'm like a good forty-five minutes away. We need to really vibe on some real get money shit."

"Say no more."

Tariq turned the music up and rolled his windows down, allowing the morning air to rush in. Tariq smiled like a snaggle-tooth child as he thought about the information that Tiff had given him.

Damn, a million dollars. Two major licks in one month? Damn, life good. Shit, I hope that shit's there. I'm glad I started stickin' dick to Tiff. Who knew it would turn into a million dollar lick in the morning? he thought.

The thought alone of the two million dollar lick had him on cloud nine as he pushed the pedal to the metal of his German engineered car to get to his destination to map out the plan. For the next forty minutes, all he could think of was his million-dollar cut and how Tiffany may have turned out to be an asset after all. She brought his two favorite things to the table: pussy and money. There was no doubt she was slowly becoming the woman of his dreams.

Chapter 8

"Oh, Lord Jesus," Me-Ma screamed. "Say it ain't so." Me-Ma sat at the kitchen table stunned. "This can't be right," she said while reading the newspaper, as she did every single morning.

"What is it, Me-Ma?" Tallhya said as she came running into the kitchen.

"Now, baby," she looked up, giving Tallhya one eye and the *Richmond Times Dispatch* her other. "Walter don't have no kids, do he, baby?"

"No," Tallhya said. "But in about two years we are planning on to have one.

"You sure about that?" Me-Ma asked, with a raised eyebrow. "Yes."

"Why you ask Me-Ma? And you got that look on your face, like something smells fishy."

Me-Ma didn't respond, instead she started reading from the newspaper aloud.

Waltima Joy Ways-Walker, graced the Earth for only 90 short days before she died in her parents' arms at the Memorial Regional Hospital, in Richmond, VA on September 16, 2014. After struggling with inoperable congenital heart disease, she passed gently into the arms of Jesus.

Waltima is the daughter of Walter Walker and Pamela Ways of College Place. She was the answer to their prayers, and they waited for her birth with joyful expectation of their first baby girl. During her brief visit on earth, she enjoyed listening to music, cuddling with soft toys, and being held close by her parents and grandparents. She was loved by all who met her, and will be greatly missed. Her presence on Earth will be missed.

A Memorial Service will be held Saturday, September 20, 2014 at 1:00 p.m. at Mimms Funeral Home, with a reception following at the Military Retirees Hall. Memorial contributions may be made at the Metropolitan Savings and Loan Bank on behalf of: Memorial Fund of Waltima Joy Walker-Ways.

Waltima is survived by her loving parents Walter Walker and Pamela Ways of 1742 College Road, Henrico, VA and a host of other family and friends.

Tallhya was silent for a long minute. Then she said, "Read it again, please." and Me-Ma did.

"It has got to be another Walter Walker. This person can't be him. Walter Walker is such a common name," was her only explanation. "I mean surely if he had a child, he would've told me."

"You think so?"

"For sure, Me-Ma! I'm sure we would've been so deeply involved in that child's life. I know this isn't him," she said confidently.

"I would like to believe that, but I don't put nothing past these men folks," Me-Ma said. "They will have a double life and not think nothing of it. They will act like it's no big deal. Trust me, that's what Joe did to me."

"That was Grandpa, but that's not Walter!"

"That's what I thought. But that no-good-butt Joe was a good husband to me and a greater father to your mother but still tipped off with the woman." She shook her head and continued. "With the woman down the street. Them sons of witches don't have no self-control when it come to their peters." Me-Ma rolled her eyes. This whole thing was bringing back flashbacks of what happened with her husband. "Lord up in heaven, Jesus fix this. Just say it ain't so. I swear I don't want this for you. I want it to be a perfect explanation for this."

"Let me just call and get to the bottom of this."

Me-Ma took her reading glasses off.

"What can make my soul whole," she sang, because in the pit of her stomach, she knew that shit was about to hit the fan. "Nothing but the blood of Jesus."

Tallhya reached for her phone and dialed Walter's number.

"Oh, precious is the flow, that can make me white as snow," Me-Ma sung. "No other fount I know, nothing but the blood of Jeeeesus!"

"Hey." He answered in a voice just over a whisper. No *hey, you*. No *hey, baby*. No *hey, boo*. No *hey, beautiful*. Just simply *Hey*. Before she could address him, he quickly shut her down. "I'm in this place handling some important arrangements. I will call you back in a few." Before she could agree to anything, she heard the dial tone.

No *baby, are you all right?* No nothing. Tears came to her eyes.

"What happened, baby?" Me-Ma asked.

"Nothing." She took a deep breath. "He just said he was about to make some arrangements, and he was going to call me back."

"I pray that there is a perfectly good explanation," Me-Ma said, shaking her head.

Tallhya was at a loss for words. She knew that there had to be a logical explanation, but then the *'what ifs'* started to run through her mind. What if it was true?

Just when the tears started to form in her eyes, that's when she heard the door open and a loud voice call out. "Tallhya . . . Tallllhya . . . Tallllhhhh . . ."

It was Bunny. She took in another deep breath as she got herself together before answering her sister. "Yesssss. I'm in the kitchen."

"Chile, do you have to be so loud."

An energetic Bunny walked into the kitchen and gave Me-Ma a kiss on the cheek. "You look pretty as always, Me-Ma."

"Thank you baby, and where you going looking like you about to work on Second Street?" She questioned Bunny's thigh high tall Tom Ford boots.

"Me-Ma, these boots the style." It was the same answer she always gave to her grandmother. Me-Ma never approved of anything that Bunny wore.

"Says who?" Me-Ma asked.

Bunny didn't take her grandmother's comments to heart. It was normal for her to disapprove of the way she dressed. "All the fashion magazines, Me-Ma." she said with an easy smile.

"Well, they going to hell, and you need to stop looking at those books getting ideas how you should dress. Didn't I teach all you girls to be individuals and be yourself? You don't have to follow the trends, baby."

"I know. I know, Me-Ma. I just look at them to give me some ideas."

"Lord have mercy on you and those people," Me-Ma summed it all up.

"Well, I stopped by because we got a family crisis."

"You right about that." Me-Ma had to agree with Bunny and said, "My Lord up in heaven sure be on time."

"Me-Ma, what you talking about?" Bunny put her hand on her hip waiting for the dig her grandmother was about to say.

"Bunny, Lord knows I'm glad to see you, and I know Tallhya is too." She threw her hands up. "You know God navigated that hundred thousand dollar big car over here because he knew that your sister needed you."

"I know," she agreed. "That's why I came over here, because I wanted to give Tallhya this money," she went into her Louis bag, and pulled out a stack of cash wrapped in a rubber band, "to give to Simone. She's going to need it, but you know she's not going to take it from me."

"I'm not talking about that sister. I'm talking about this sister."

Bunny's eyes shifted to Tallhya and asked, "T, what's going on?"

"Nothing."

"Hog-Mogg and bull crap! You a lie." Me-Ma put her two cents in, looked in the refrigerator, got a bottle of water out and handed it to her. "Chile, if I wasn't a saved a woman, I would tell you go ahead and pull that bottle of liquor out of your purse, because your sister need a drink."

"Me-Ma, what you talking about?" Bunny said, trying to conceal her grin.

"Chile, you know I know everything. I don't miss anything. But right now, you need to carry your sister up there to that

Mimms Funeral Home and get to the bottom of this bull crap that's going on."

"Mimms? Who died?"

"I don't need to go up there," Tallhya said.

"And yes the heck you do," Me-Ma said as firm as she knew how.

"Can somebody tell me who died?" Bunny asked again, wanting to know what's going on.

"Your brother-in-law baby died."

"Huh?" Bunny turned up her face, confused.

"Walter got a baby, I saw it in the obituaries and it said devoted father."

"Oh, hell naw!"

"Watch yo' mouth," Me-Ma pointed to Bunny and then filled her in. "This child don't believe do-do stink, even when it's in the middle of the floor."

"Girl, get your shoes, let's go up there and get down to the bottom of it."

"No. I'm going to wait until he get here. I know it's a perfectly good explanation, right?"

"Get your shoes now, and I'm not going to tell you no more," Bunny demanded. "If it's nothing to it, then it's nothing, but we going to see what's up." Bunny walked out of the kitchen.

"Baby, I know sometimes the truth hurts. Now we hope Walter would not have had a baby and didn't share that bundle of joy with us. At the same time, if he did, you need to know."

"You are right Me-Ma. I do need to know. And even so, I need to pay my respects. Because any part of him, is a part of me."

Me-Ma thought how big of Tallhya that was. "You right baby."

Tallhya got up and went and got her shoes and jacket.

Just then Bunny returned with a small Gucci overnight bag from the trunk of her car. She went into the bathroom and returned quickly, transformed. She was wearing a Pink sweat suit and some Air Jordans to match. She put her Indique straight long hair into a tight neat ponytail and went into the front room. "Come on. I'm ready."

"We not going to start no trouble."

"No, we are going to get to the bottom of it."

"Then why you had to change?"

"Because I stay ready so I don't have to get ready. And no, we not going to start nothing, but make no mistake about it. If a ho get out of pocket, I'm going to handle it."

"Come on, Bunny, we not going for that," Tallhya said, knowing how her sister will fight at the drop of a dime.

"Look, Bunny, give him time to explain. Let Tallhya deal with it. Don't you go over there turning up, you hear me?"

"I'm not," Bunny said as innocently as she knew how. "We are good as long as they don't cause no static. It won't be none if they don't start none."

"Chile, Lord have mercy," Me-Ma said as she was reaching for the phone.

"Who are you calling?" Tallhya asked.

"Your brother. You need to carry him over there with y'all too." Even though the sisters had all accepted Ginger's lifestyle, Me-Ma refused to acknowledge it. After all these years, she still referred to Ginger as a boy. She loved him no matter what, but she prayed every day that God would "fix" her grandson.

"Me-Ma, please, don't call Ginger. I don't want her in my business."

"Chile, please." Me-Ma looked Tallhya in the face. "If this man has lied to us, it's all of our business."

"No, we good. I got it handled. Remember we not going over there to start no commotion." As Tallhya walked out the door to head for the car, Bunny doubled backed to the kitchen and handed Me-Ma a stack of money. "In case you gotta bail us out," she said. Then she burst out into laughter, even though she was dead serious, and headed out the door.

Another ring, Ginger answered.

"Hello, Gene. Meet yo' sisters over at the Mimms Funeral Home. It's a little situation that they are going to get to the bottom of. And baby," she paused, "don't wear none of them stilettos over there neither, if you catch my drift."

Me-Ma grabbed her Bible, and started to pray. Lord knows all parties involved were surely going to need it.

Chapter 9

Lately, it's been hard times;
I'm talking about the financial side

Since the Neon that Marjorie had swapped Simone's Benz out for didn't have a MP-3 jack, or even a CD player, Simone was forced to listen to Anthony Hamilton lament about his imaginary money problems on the car's radio.

> *It's Ruff out there, son*
> *And they say when it rains it pours, (rain, rain)*
> *Raining at My Door . . .*

Simone liked Anthony Hamilton and all. God knows the brother could blow the soul back into a corpse, but the song was killing her vibe, which was already on life support as it was. She turned the volume down on the radio then switched lanes, getting off Interstate 64 at the next exit.

She pulled into the parking lot of a place she knew all too well. Beyond the parking lot were three shiny silver stainless steel warehouses. Each 50,000 square foot structure was filled with cow shit. The company, S&S Topsoil, belonged to her father, Simon, and his best friend Tommy.

At the beginning of every summer, when Simone was growing up, Simon used to bring her to work with him every day, for the two weeks at the beginning of the summer before camp started, and at the end of the summer when it had ended.

Simone hated it with a passion, but her father loved their time together. There was nothing Simon loved more than his only daughter and his company. Not even his wife, Marjorie, but he wouldn't ever admit that to her. Although their summers at S&S Topsoil ended years ago, Simone still used to drop by from time to time and bring her father lunch. This was the first time she'd stepped foot on the grounds since he had died six months ago.

It felt strange, really strange.

As she made her way to the main building, she remembered something that her father used to always say to her. "Inhale," he would say to her. When she acted like she did, he would say, "Deeper than that. You have to really inhale." And then he would say, "You smell that? What does it smell like?"

Simone always responded the same way. "It smells like do-do."

Then Simon would always say the same thing, with the biggest smile, "Naw baby, that's what it smells like when you are stinking rich."

It was something about that smile, and the man had the prettiest set of white teeth. When she got to be older and understood politics, she'd joke with her father about how he should've been a politician. Not only did he have a way with words, he could make anybody believe anything.

Back then, she had taken those moments with her father for granted. Now, memories were all she had of him. And she couldn't get enough of them.

Simone made a right off "Memory Lane," and stepped into the main warehouse. The heels of her Giuseppe booties click-clacked on the vinyl flooring as she made her way to a small but efficient office off to the right.

The lady inside the office looked up from her computer and greeted Simone with a queen sized smile, waving her inside of the cramped office. "Girl . . ." Beverly gushed, jumping up to hug Simone, "where have you been?"

The last time they'd seen each other was during Simon's funeral. Beverly stepped back and with a pair of Never-Miss-A-Thing hazel eyes, studied Simone from top to bottom. Then she said, "What is it?"

Most women were born with a sixth sense, but when it came to reading people, Beverly's gift was extraterrestrial. "I'm fine," Simone lied. She spun around so that Beverly could take a 360-degree of her outfit. Some jeans, fitted sweater and her gold Giuseppe ankle boots. "Don't I look it?"

Although she was like family, Simone didn't want to burden Beverly with her personal problems. But Beverly wasn't fooled. "You look like you could model in *Vogue* magazine. You are damn sure prettier than all those make-up wearing skeletons in designer clothes, and ten times smarter," she said, changing the subject. If Simone wanted to confide in her about anything, she would do so when she was ready.

Beverly wasn't just being nice with her compliments. Simone was fine by anybody's standards.

"I just hope my skin looks as good as yours does when I'm your age, girl."

Bev rolled her eyes, like she was offended by the remark. "I know you didn't just call me old to my face." At 49, Beverly could still pass for a young 30 something.

Simone said, "You are only as old you feel."

"Then I feel like your slightly older sister."

A smiling Simone said, "Cool, I've always wanted an older sister."

"Slightly older," corrected Beverly.

"That's what I meant." Simone smiled at Beverly. Talking to her always warmed her heart, and she knew the woman was genuine too.

After breezing through some light chit chatting, Simone asked if Tommy was in the building. "I need to speak to with him if he's not too busy."

The inquiry took Beverly by surprise. She'd worked for the company for a long time. Simone's father had hired her, personally, two weeks after she had graduated from Reynolds Community College, 22 years ago. So she felt qualified when she said, "Tommy's a damn fool." She looked off into space and then lightly shook her head before speaking. "As good of a man as your father was, may he rest in peace, for the life of me, I could not figure out why he went into business with a scoundrel like Tommy. The man's a pompous pig, with the morals of a housefly."

Simone couldn't help but to burst out laughing. Beverly had definitely hit the nail on the head, but it had totally caught her off guard.

Beverly's face twisted into a frown, like she'd just tasted something bitter or spoiled and needed to spit it out right away. "Yeah, he's here," she finally said.

"Tell me how you really feel," Simone teased. Although she knew Beverly as always kind, she spoke the gospel. Simone often wondered about the answer to the million-dollar question herself. What had her father seen in Tommy that no one else did?

Using the wireless intercom system, Beverly informed Tommy that he had a visitor.

Simone walked to the back of the warehouse, toward where the offices were located. Tommy's was next to her father's old office.

Seeing the door, with her father's name, *Simon Gunn,* still stenciled on the outside stirred up more memories for her. She tried to shove them away. It was hard, but she reminded herself that she needed to take care of what she'd come for before imploding to an emotional wreck.

"What can I do for you, princess?" Tommy was standing in the doorway of his office grinning. "Come on in," he said.

Inside, Tommy's office was enormous; large enough to harbor a midsize aircraft. He hugged her, and whispered his condolences before offering her a seat.

The embrace was tighter and lasted longer than Simone thought was appropriate. Respectfully, she pulled away.

"I need to talk to you about my daddy's will."

They took a seat on a coffee-color leather sofa. "Anything I can do for you, princess. You know good and well, all you have to do is ask. You know without a doubt, Uncle Tommy got ya!" He placed his hand on her leg and lightly squeezed her knee, pretending as if it was an act of comfort instead of perverted lust.

Since the day Simone had turned 18, whenever her father wasn't looking, Tommy gazed at her with lust in his eyes. Her skin felt the heat emanating from his touch. Simone could take care of herself then, and, as a grown woman she could take care of herself now. Simone casually brushed Tommy's hand from her knee, replacing it with her Louis tote bag. She took out a small notebook and pen.

"I would like to ask you a few questions," she said, looking him square in the eyes, "about my father's estate."

Tommy straightened up, putting his sleaze-ball tendencies in check, at least temporarily. "Me and Simon were business partners. Your father's estate . . . well, that's more like *personal* business. And your father's personal business was exactly that, as far as I was concerned."

If Tommy had been connected to a bullshit detector the meter would have put someone's eye out, Simone thought, looking in his eyes.

"Give me a break," Simone chided. "You and my father were friends since middle school. Five decades. I'm not asking you who he lost his virginity to, a question I'm somehow willing to bet that you could surely answer without much contemplation, I'm simply asking you about his will. Anything you can tell me would be helpful and appreciated."

Nothing!

Dead Silence.

Tick . . . Tock . . . Tick . . . Tock . . .

The only sound in the room came from an antique Howard Miller Grandfather Clock.

"Tommy?" she urged, bordering on exasperation from his reluctance to help.

Tommy had a straight face and didn't say a word.

Simon once told his daughter that Tommy lost a ton of money playing poker because he scratched the bridge of his nose every time he bluffed. "I don't know what you want me to say," Tommy was fidgeting. "If I knew anything about a will I would let you know. Why wouldn't I?"

Good question, Simone, thought to herself.

"I don't know anything," he rubbed his nose, and she knew he was lying. "But why are you so anxious about this will."

"Listen, I'm sure you've heard. Marjorie has everything, and I have nothing. Not even a job anymore. The bank I started at yesterday was robbed."

"Not what I saw on the news?"

"Yes."

Hearing her problems somehow prompted him to spark up the conversation. "Did they offer y'all any kind of compensation?"

"No! Nothing! And Marjorie took my Benz from me under my nose."

"She did?" he questioned, not really seeming too surprised.

"Yes." Simone said, starting to feel the emotions coming.

"Well, you know that. You know she's going to milk the situation for everything she can get."

"I know."

"Now you know all the papers we had here, everything went to Marjorie by law."

"Yeah I know."

"I wish it was different." he said, then dropped his head, "Imp, imp, imp. It's a crying shame all the bad luck and the hard time you having."

"I will be Okay," she said about to break down. "I know I will. I'm smart and strong. I will figure out something," she was trying to convince herself, but felt so weak. She couldn't stop the tears from coming.

Tommy took her in his arms and allow her to let loose her tears. "It's going to be Okay. Uncle Tommy got you."

"Thank you, I appreciate you," she managed to get out in between tears.

"I appreciate you too. Don't worry I'm going to help you," he said, then before she knew it, he had his hand in between her legs and started tongue kissing her.

She pulled away. "What are you doing?"

"What you mean? Just relax. I got you." He grabbed her and pushed her back on the couch.

"Stop! No! You fuckin' better not. Let me go," she screamed as she pounded on his chest.

He was still on top of her and his penis was as hard as a rock.

Out of the corner of her eye, she saw a heavy thick glass frame on the table in front of the sofa. She reached for it and slugged it on top of his head.

"Oh, shit," he said out loud and let loose of the tight grip he had on her. Simone was up and out, heading for the door as fast as she could. Suddenly he grabbed her arm and looked her in the eyes. "Listen, as tough as things are for you," he said as sincere as he knew how, "you gon' need a sugar daddy.

If so, I will definitely take care of you. I will pick up where your father left off, if you wanna share some of that sweet, juicy pussy with me," he said then stuck out his tongue and made a motion as if he was pleasuring her vagina with his tongue.

Simone snatched her arm from him, "Go to hell, you disgusting pervert."

He palmed her butt with a smack and smiled, "This the real world baby. Real shit like that exists."

"Fuck you, Tommy," she stormed down the hall.

"If you ever need me, Uncle Tommy will be right here for you."

Chapter 10

The loud pungent smell of weed assaulted his nose as soon as Tariq walked across the doorstep. He closed and locked the door behind him.

"Damn, my nigga. I got a contact and you ain't even took it out yet."

"This that shit. . . . Man this that shit."

"What's the heavy news you gotta lay on me man?"

"I just stumbled across a sting for two million dollars, nigga!"

"Foooo . . . real?" Spoe exclaimed.

"Yeah for real! When you known me to play fuckin' games about this paper?"

"Never." Spoe shook his head. "Run that shit down to me. Make that shit like music to my ears." Spoe put his hands up to his ears. "Two mill, huh? Who gave you the line on this hit?" Spoe needed details. He was the one that usually put the plans together, but he was happy that Tariq had come up with a job for them. He'd still have to check everything out though.

"Tiff did." Tariq said with pride. He was proud that he had a chick that could help them get money and not just spend it.

"Tiff? Who the fuck is Tiff?"

"You know the li'l bad bitch, drive the SL, I been fuckin' wit, Tiffany man."

"Oh, one of the ones from the strip club."

Tariq nodded, "A'ight with that shit now." He laughed at himself. "You trying to say something cause all my joints come from the strip club?"

"And the same strip club at that, but I wasn't even going to mention that shit though."

Tariq laughed at himself. "I'm ridiculous, but the stripper hos love me though."

"Naw, nigga, don't get that shit twisted. They like that money. That's what their loyalty is too. Speaking of which, let's get back to it."

"And I don't never forget it . . . where their loyalty lie."

"Don't ever forget, and when you get ready for a nice chick, Bunny got somebody for you."

"I bet sis do, and I'ma let you know the word."

"No doubt," Spoe said and then asked, "Yo, so is shorty official?"

"Yeah, Spoe, I wouldn't be here right now if I felt for a second that she wasn't official. I been fuckin' wit' her for a couple of weeks now."

"That's a long time for you," Spoe had to admit.

Tariq smiled, "Real talk." He agreed and then got back to the topic at hand. "The bitch couldn't make no shit up like that. She knows how we get down Spoe! She got the address and everything. The nigga got a mini mansion too."

"A'ight, if you fuck with Shorty and trust her word then let's move on it. We are going to have to leave that nigga in there stinking too. Ain't much to it, we got to leave him, when it's that much paper on the line, he won't take that shit sitting down, Reek."

"He ain't gon' be in there, and shorty want two-fifty for her cut too."

Without hesitation, Spoe agreed. "She could get that! Shit, she putting us on to two free mill. Good job Reek, that's a nice sting, sho-nuff," Spoe said, commending Tariq on bringing a lick to the table. Spoe was always the one who tended to stumble across their jobs. But all the excitement aside, Spoe had to ask. "But what the fuck you mean he ain't gon' be there?"

"She going out with him, and while she out with him, we gonna shoot to the crib and take care of what we got to do."

"My nigga, you know I'm not on that B&E type shit. Fuck all that sneaking around shit, Reek." Spoe said disappointed. "Man, you know I like to be in control when we do this kind of shit, so it ain't no slip ups."

"Man I know," Tariq agreed. "I just thought it was a good quick come up."

"But I'll go, my nigg," he said hesitantly, "For a million dollar profit, I'll go," he said again. He was trying to convince himself of how he could sit back and chill, travel the world with Bunny. Then he spoke up again, this time more confidently. "A million fuckin' dollars, you gotdamn right I'm in." Then the two dapped and just like that, it was about to go down.

Chapter 11

Bunny bent the corner almost on two wheels when she pulled up at the funeral home. Like a superhero, she jumped out of the car, ready to solve her older sister's dilemma at hand.

"Bunny," Tallhya called out to her sister, who was hightailing it up the sidewalk of the funeral home. "Bunny! Hold on!" Tallhya hurried up and got out of the car to try to catch up with her sister. "Wait," she called out trailing behind Bunny.

Bunny finally got the hint, and decided to stop in her tracks. She huffed and looked at her overweight sister trying to move as fast as she could. "Well, hurry up then."

Tallhya had put a lot of pep in her step and finally caught up, "Look, we not here for you to act simple, okay?" Tallhya had the most serious look on her face. She knew her sister all too well. What folks would never detect about Bunny was that her looks were very deceiving. Behind every pair of mink eyelashes and red bottomed Christian Louboutin, there was more than meets the eye. In every Celine bag, Bunny packed a sharp blade and had no problem slicing someone up like a piece of deli meat, or slapping the cowboy shit out of anybody she felt warranted it, in regard to herself or anybody she loved.

"Well, they better not start none, it won't be none," Bunny said in a serious tone.

Tallhya grabbed her sister's arm and looked in her eyes. "As I said before we left the house, and in the car on the way over here: we are not here to start nothing. I don't want to cause no drama or be disrespectful in no kind of way. I only want to get to the bottom of this. That's it, that's all," she gave a hard, firm stare and made direct eye contact with her sister. "I'm not fuckin' bullshittin', Okay?"

Bunny saw the passion mixed with the hurt in her sister's eyes. She sucked her teeth and then nodded. "Look Sisi, I'm only here to support you nothing else."

"I know you are," Tallhya said, "and I'm glad you are here by my side."

"That's what sisters are for, right?" Bunny reminded Tallhya.

"I know it sounds crazy, but if I see the baby, I will know if it's his or not."

"Yeah, it does." Bunny put her arm around her sister and they walked side by side. "Sounds like some shit that Me-Ma would say." She chuckled a bit, trying to shine a bright light onto the situation, "You know how them old folks are with babies." She transformed her voice into an old lady's. "Bring 'em here so I can see 'em," she tried to make jokes of the situation as they continued their stride to the entrance.

They entered into the quiet, morbid funeral home. "Yes, may I help you," the spooky looking man, dressed in all-black startled them.

"Yes, we are here to see the baby," Bunny said, making eye contact with him.

"Yes, this way."

The funeral director showed them into the viewing room, where the closed small casket rested on a pedestal. The whole ambience of the room was so gloomy. The second they saw the huge portrait on a tall gold easel of the innocent little baby girl in a beautiful white satin dress, the two were immediately sorrowful.

"This is so horrible," Bunny said, dropping her head. Just the sight of seeing the picture of the little baby girl with so much life in her eyes made Bunny forget all about the intended turn-up and why she had come here in the first place. "It's just . . . " she searched for the word, "it's just so, so, so tragic."

Tallhya couldn't help herself. With tears in her eyes, she stared at the little girl. She was astonished at how she was looking at the spitting image of Walter. Walter had a lot of explaining to do. He had stepped out on her and had a baby with another woman, and never uttered a word of the birth of such a little blessing to her. How could he keep such a thing from her? Indeed, it was a deep betrayal, but Tallhya still felt awful that Walter had lost his daughter. And in a strange way, at that very moment all Tallhya wanted to do was be there for Walter. Though she had not met her "stepdaughter," Waltima, she was sure that knowing her was an amazing experience and losing the bundle of joy, a child, had to be a heart wrenching pain.

Tears had also filled her eyes, and Bunny was at a loss for words. "Are you Okay?" Bunny put her arm around Tallhya and nothing had to be spoken. The embrace simply said it all. "I'm here for you."

The two felt a chilling energy in the room. Bunny had enough. "I'm trying to be sympathetic, but this is so depressing. Can we just get the fuck outta here?"

"Yes, I'm ready." Tallhya agreed.

The funeral director held a box of tissues in front of them. As she took a few tissues for herself and handed a couple to her sister, Bunny asked, "Is it possible that I could have a card with the address, please. I'd like to send some flowers."

"No problem," the well-dressed man said. He reached inside his pocket and pulled out a metal card case, handing her what she asked for.

"Thank you. And you guys really did a good job," Bunny complimented.

"Thank you so much," he said with a smile. "This is our calling." Then he directed them to the hall, to the guest book, and instructed them, "Be sure to sign the book. I'm sure the family would like to know that you were here. That you came by and paid your respects."

"No thanks," Tallhya said.

Bunny interjected, "I think I will," and she proceeded to sign the guest book. The second Bunny had crossed her t's and put the pen down, that's when the door popped open and two ladies entered.

"Yes, may I help you?" the one lady asked, as she looked the two sisters up and down.

"We came here to pay our respects. So sorry for your loss," Tallhya said as heartfelt as she could.

"And . . . who are you?" the woman asked, with a raised eyebrow.

A small chuckle came out. "Kimmy, calm down! I know who she is." A tall confident, slim lady with a body to die for, pointed to Tallhya, then came in closer and spoke up.

The beauty had taken on more curves than a racecar driver. She was drop dead gorgeous, in a rich kind of way. The woman was together in every sense of the word. Her long 26-inch weave stopped at the small of her back and was straight like Pocahontas. "No worries, I know who she is," she pointed at Tallhya in a snobbish kind of way.

"Really?" Bunny questioned, returning the snooty look.

Tallhya only stared at the woman. She was stunned at how fabulous and gorgeous she was.

"That's Natalia, the mark," she boldly said, "You know, the fat, pathetic, desperate, no self-esteem having, stupid bitch that Walter be juicing for all the money and shit. Remember, I told you all about her." She laughed as if it was the funniest thing she had ever thought about. "That's her," she managed to get out somehow, as hilarious as it was to her.

Bunny wasn't having it and had to bring the bewitching laughter to a halt. The cheap version of Pocahontas's laughs quickly turned to cries for help. Before anyone knew it, Bunny had hit her like Foreman hit Frazier. She sent her straight to the floor and out cold, immediately turning the lights out in Pocahontas' head.

"Guess that will teach a no-good, two bit ho to laugh at my motherfuckin' sister." Bunny was pissed and could not resist kicking her a few times. The whole time, she was looking at Kimmy wishing to God Almighty that she would attempt to do anything. "Yes, I'm going to kick this bitch while she down," she boldly said.

The funeral director was in shock. All he kept saying was "Oh, my! Oh, my!" as he was reaching for the phone. Bunny saw him going for the cordless phone resting on the charger. That was the only thing that made her stop kicking Pocahontas. She reached for the jack and tossed it across the room. "Oh, nigga, you gon' call the police on me? You bitch-ass nigga you?" She looked into his eyes and he thought he saw Lucifer himself in front of him.

"Just leave then, please just leave," he cried out.

"Please, sis. Please let's leave," Tallhya said, knowing that Bunny would tear that place up. "Let's just go," Tallhya pleaded with tears in her eyes.

"Okay." she said, and followed after Tallhya, but not before focusing her attention on Kimmy. With fury in her eyes, she said, "Tell that motherfucker Walter, and he can get it too. He's a real coward-ass nigga. And as for this bitch, right here," she pointed down at her, "kindly let her know I ain't finished with her. Let that ho know that since she was down for the get down, every time I see her scheming ass I'm going to wear her ass out."

Bunny kicked Pocahontas, who was still lying on the floor, looking like she was a permanent resident of La-La land. Bunny added, "And that's a promise on her dead baby soul." She headed for the door.

The second Bunny's back was to Kimmy, she jumped on her back and started pulling her hair. This sent Bunny in a rage. Like she was a feather, Bunny swung Kimmy around and body slammed her.

Unsure if the funeral director was trying to break up the fight or get a few licks in, nobody gave a damn. When Ginger slipped into the building and all she saw was this man on his sister, she picked up a folding chair that was in the hallway, tucked away and busted him over his backside. "Fuck off my sister, nigga."

At that point, it was about to get popping, and Tallhya knew they needed to leave out of there. "Come on y'all. Let's get the fuck out of here."

The siblings fled the scene like a shern-head jacked up off of embalming fluid.

Chapter 12

As she drove the shitbox car from the company her dad once owned, tears streamed down Simone's face, and not because she was sad. Nah, she had already been sad for way too long as far as she was concerned. The sadness she'd experienced after her father passed had threatened to swallow her whole, but she had gotten to the other side. She realized that instead of the full-on pity party she had been throwing herself, she needed to be grateful for the time she had with him, the one where all her needs were met, and all the life lessons he had taught her. Hell, she knew up close and personal what it looked like not to have the kind of daddy that she had been blessed to have for twenty-nine years. Two of her three sisters both had trifling, deadbeat, good-for-nothing fathers while Ginger didn't have any idea which of too many to count sexual partners had deposited the lucky sperm into their mother that helped create her. Simone had a daddy, dedicated to her and able to express his love every single day. No matter what, she would always have those memories to fall back on. Right now all she could wonder about is, what would my daddy do?

"Dammit," she spat out to no one in particular at all the emotions spilling over inside of her. So, no, these were not tears of pity or sadness, these were the full expression of the rage bubbling up inside of her at the plain ole bullshit that had gone down today. If her father knew the dirty-dog way Marjorie treated her after he was gone he would have thrown her out on her ass a long time ago. So, come hell or high water, Simone planned to make that happen. She didn't know when, but as long as her ass could breathe out a breath that conniving bitch would pay for the way she disrespected her father's wishes to have his only child taken care of. With God as her witness, she swore the shit was going down.

And the way Tommy, that fake-ass buster, had pretended to be her father's best friend all those years. In reality he was a disgusting predator waiting to pounce on her. His no good ass would get his too she thought as she sat there adding up the offenses. Before she could begin to formulate a plan, Simone glanced down at her phone ringing and recognized the same number she'd seen earlier but hadn't wanted to answer. Of course the first thing that came to mind was that it was one of her favorite stores calling to inform her of a sale or an item she had been waiting on. Being a spoiled daddy's girl, Simone had developed an over the top shopping addiction that had been funded by her daddy. Every high-end clothing store within driving distance of Richmond had her number on speed dial just in case any of her favorite designer's new lines came in. She ticked off her favorites; Louis, Céline, Balenciaga, Chloé, and Prada. Damn, she was missing her former life. She sure did her share of damage, but those days were gone, and she wasn't in the mood to explain to the over eager sales woman on the other end why she hadn't seen her black card running through their credit machines lately.

"I need to ignore that damn call," she thought, but since the person was being persistent she'd have to take out her frustration on them. Simone pulled her car over and answered the call. This no Bluetooth having bullshit was already wrecking her goddam nerves on top of everything else.

"Hello," she snapped into the receiver, for once not using the perfect ladylike telephone manners her daddy had taught to her. The person on the other end of the phone took a deep breath before responding, probably trying to figure out how to deal with the big no that they were guaranteed to hear.

"I'm looking for Simone Banks," the woman on the other end spoke. "Is this her?"

"Yes, this is her," Simone answered, desperate to get off the phone and back to her thoughts. She had a lot of things to figure out, the first being how the hell she'd get another job which was only a close second to when would she put her whole entire foot up Marjorie's ass.

"This is Dr. Cohen's office. The doctor would like to see you at your earliest convenience, today if possible. It's about your test results." Upon hearing that, Simone felt all the blood rush out of her body. That particular statement usually led to the person hearing it to begin playing out worse case scenarios in their head, except this wasn't the first time she'd experienced those words. Her father's doctor started with those words and just a short time later his daughter stood over his wet gravesite as his casket was lowered into the hole in the ground, as buckets of rain fell blending with the outpouring of Simone's own grief.

"I'm sorry, what did you just say?" Simone's voice lost all the anger and attitude as she tried to process exactly what this woman was saying. By the time she hung up, and redirected her car in the direction of the doctor's office downtown, Simone had gone through an entirely different barrage of emotions. She had all but forgotten the mandatory physical she had recently taken that had been required for her new job at the bank. They'd done a battery of tests, including taking blood samples. She hadn't given a second thought to it, especially since she was so young and healthy. Her immediate reaction was to reach for the phone to call her father and have him meet her at the doctor's office. It was a knee jerk reaction before reality came flooding back knocking her into the present. She could have called Bunny, but as much as she loved her sister, the thought of her no-patience-ass in the doctor's office did not comfort her. Plus, all she had to do was call one sister to have them tell the other two and her grandmother. The last thing she wanted was to worry her Me-Ma. Her grandmother would immediately remind her to pray and throw this whole medical thing up to God. Then, Me Ma would insist on meeting her at the office with any available prayer-warrior she could bring from church. In the end she decided to go alone figuring, how bad could it be? Just thinking about how her grandmother would handle the situation reminded her to pray. Her grandmother's feet didn't hit the floor in the morning without a prayer on her lips. Of all her grandchildren, Simone was the only one who maintained a close relationship to God. "Trust in the Lord for He knows your every need," Simone whispered to herself as she entered the office.

"The doctor will see you." The pert bottle blonde stood up and led her into one of the three patient waiting rooms. "You can put this on." She smiled as she handed over a paper hospital gown. Simone took it and had just tied the strings in the back when the door opened. Dr. Cohen, the internist, entered in his white lab coat carrying a clipboard, like something out of a medical drama. Simone had been coming for her once a year checkup since she'd turned eighteen. The doctor she usually saw had recently retired, which is why she didn't really know this man about to deliver some hopefully not so bad news.

"Did you come alone?" his brow furrowed as he approached, staring from her to the papers attached to his clipboard.

"Uh, yeah. I was already in the car when I got the call. I figured how bad could it be?" Simone joked as she waited to see if the doctor would join in. He didn't. Now her ass was starting to really worry.

"I'm sorry to have to tell you this, but your blood tests indicate an abnormality that point to ovarian cancer." He couldn't help but look glum giving this kind of diagnosis to someone so young.

Wait, what? Cancer? I have cancer? My father just died from cancer. These thoughts swirled in her head as she began to dry heave, her mouth feeling dry. She stood up pacing the room like a caged rat. Except it wasn't the room, it had more to do with wanting to get out of her own skin.

"Miss Banks, right now we need to administer a scan and some other tests to determine if you have cancer. But just know that with early treatment this form of cancer has an 80 percent chance of full recovery."

She didn't respond because she couldn't hear anything. It all sounded like the Charlie Brown character, 'waaa waaaaa waaaaa waaaa.' His words were incoherent. Everything started to spin around her and she felt as if she were in some kind of tunnel. She could barely make out the nurse who rushed in helping the doctor pick her up and place her on the examining table. When Simone came to, the nurse was fanning her and rubbing ice on her face.

"What . . . what happened?" she sputtered, although to both the doctor and nurse it appeared obvious.

"You fainted." Both the doctor and the nurse answered. "We tried calling the name of next of kin on your contact forms and the number was disconnected." Simone sat there staring into space, trying to connect, when another woman entered with a glass of water and handed it to her. Simone began to drink, but what she really wanted to do was to throw the glass against a wall and smash it. She wanted to scream, but she couldn't. The doctor, nurse, and assistant fawned over her like a newborn baby. They checked her blood pressure, took her temperature and even offered to get her some food. Simone might have been hungry when she got there but the news of her health crisis dissolved any hunger she may have had. All she wanted was to get home and have Me-Ma tell her that God would take care of everything, that she would be all right.

"We need to schedule this surgery as soon as possible." Dr. Cohen spoke in a calm manner.

"Surgery?"

"Yes, it's a standard laparoscopy so that I can take a look and find out what's going on. We will biopsy a small piece and that will tell us everything we need to know." He'd been doing this for a long time, but ever since the practice switched from regular to concierge medicine the care they showed was something out of the 50's. Hell, they even had an advertisement in the waiting room announcing that they now made house calls. Simone wished she were sitting in her Me-Ma's house with her family around her as she heard this news.

"Do you still have the same insurance? Blue Cross PPO?" the receptionist asked in a syrupy sweet way, as Simone scheduled her laparoscopy. It was the same way the cashiers of all her favorite couture shops spoke to her when they knew she was about to sign for some really expensive shit. Simone didn't even have her wallet. The cop hadn't given it back yet, and if it wasn't for the fact that bitch of a stepmonster had cancelled all of her credit cards she might have insisted he release her wallet.

"Yes," she responded, grateful that at least she could count on something in her life still working even if the reason sucked.

"Let me just get approval for the procedure," she smiled up at Simone, dialed a number and waited. The Bach piano concerto playing took Simone back to all the years of piano lessons that helped her to play this piece perfectly. She even played it at her first beauty competition and of course she won. Simon had been so proud. His attention lasered in on his baby girl up on that big stage making the other girls fade like background players next to her.

The receptionist had to call her name three times to get Simone's attention. She had gotten so carried away with the memories of the music that for a moment she had forgotten where she was or why.

"Miss Banks, the insurance company informed us that your policy is no longer current." The woman's thin lips pursed together, her eyes fixed on Simone as she moved her chair back. The receptionist had experienced the mercurial nature of patients and she didn't want to be caught off guard.

"I'm sorry, that's impossible." Simone sputtered and then had to listen as the woman patiently explained that because she was no longer an employee at her father's company they had canceled her coverage. With everything going on, she hadn't bothered to check her medical insurance status. She hadn't held a real job at her father's company in years, but every two weeks he cut her a check that kept her flushed, able to pursue her interests. She had a three-month trial before she became permanent at the bank, which came with full benefits. But she hadn't planned to go back to the bank after the stick up.

By the time they hustled her out of there, she had received a list of free clinics, mostly in neighborhoods that, just a few months ago, she wouldn't have even dared to drive through. She couldn't bear to look directly into the doctor's face when she left. She felt so embarrassed that her insurance was no longer valid that she grabbed her keys, clutched the paperwork she had been given, and walked back to her crappy car. She didn't know what the hell she was going to do, but she knew not to play around with her diagnosis. Her father had refused to go to the doctor for an annual checkup no matter how much she prodded him over the years. Last year he began complaining of aches and pains. By the time Simone was able to convince him to see a doctor because he felt terrible, his prognosis was dire, with doctors giving him less than a month to live.

"Seriously?" She fumed, watching a meter maid affix a ticket on the windshield of her car. Simone picked up the ticket and threw it onto the ground, giving the meter maid a hard stare just begging her to open her mouth. All of her manners were balled up in her fists, ready to take someone down. Then she realized that the car wasn't in her name, so she wouldn't get the ticket, the only silver lining in this shitshow of a day.

Chapter 13

Me-Ma had too much energy to sit around waiting to hear what happened with her girls down at that funeral parlor, so she did what she always did when worry got the best of her. She put on her blue dress with the white buttons that the girls had gotten for Mother's Day, at some store called Anne Klein. As much as she liked to act like she didn't care about creature comforts, the soft silk and linen fabric against her skin made her feel like the Queen Mother. The blue Taryn Rose shoes that Tallhya insisted she allow her to purchase with her "monthly lottery winnings" certainly made walking the six blocks to the church much easier. "Save your money," she had said. Her words fell on deaf ears, as they usually did when one of her girls made up their mind to do anything. It had been the same with their stubborn mother, Deidra. She had to cover her eyes at the register as the saleswoman rang up the purchase. Me-Ma had lived her entire life being frugal, making the little she and her husband earned stretch to feed every mouth. She would have been happy with the orthopedic shoes her doctor prescribed, but the girls took one look at the 'prison warden' shoes and refused to let her wear them with the dress. "Lord, I hope that wasn't Walter," Me-Ma talked to herself thinking about that newspaper lying on the kitchen table, although she already knew in her heart that it was. She had a strong sense about things like this.

"Tell the truth, shame the devil; tell a lie, shame yourself," she thought as she finished getting dressed for an impromptu visit with the Pastor. Congregation enrollment dropped to their pre 1990's numbers. They were down since the former pastor died. Too many of the older members accused Pastor Street of appearing too secular to be a real man of God in his flashy clothes, but Me-Ma had taken the time and gotten to know him. She had been able to convince some of the old members to stay and to trust that the Lord had brought this man to serve them. Me-Ma had a lot of power in that church, and Cassius took full advantage of it by appointing himself as the son she never had. Oh, he certainly played on her need to be close to God; doting on her whenever she was around, making himself available whenever she needed him. But lately she was coming to the church a lot more often just to talk with him, and that was getting in the way of his extracurriculars, but what could he do?

Unbeknownst to her, she helped raise money for all his pet projects, shaming people into opening their pocketbooks and checkbooks for every little thing he swore would improve the church. Cassius even talked Me-Ma into helping to raise money so that they could televise their Sunday services on some second rate cable channel.

"If one person in pain or shame watches my sermon and because of it finds his way to the Lord, then isn't that what God would want?" Me-Ma contributed generously and convinced the elders that Pastor needed to be given a clothing budget since he shouldn't be responsible for his television wardrobe. She cursed the small-minded people who talked about Pastor behind his back. She'd told many of the parishioners that she would pray for them, but coming from Me-Ma, it sounded closer to a curse. She figured out that to stop the tongues from wagging on the fools running their mouths, all Pastor needed to solidify his image was to find himself a wife and settle down. She couldn't understand why her grandbaby Simone didn't return the pastor's interest.

"Hello, Mrs. Banks," two young girls, in those shamelessly tight-fitting spandex pants that exposed all their business, waved at her as she passed. Boy, did she want to stop and tell those fast children to go put some loose clothes on and start acting like they had some good sense. "Lord, give me strength," she said to herself, realizing that they were barely out of diapers and here they were looking like straight up hoochies shaking their butts at grown-ass men as they passed.

"Girl, come on over here with all'a that ass," one of the older boys shouted as the girls passed. And of course they stopped.

It took everything Me-Ma had not to send those children back to their homes to put on something appropriate, but today she had more pressing matters to take care of. Without meaning to she'd become the neighborhood matriarch. As much as she protested, she wound up accepting the position, since very few adults had the good sense to "pick up after their dogs," as was the old school expression. These were lay down with dogs and get up with flees kinds of people and Me-Ma hated it. Any good therapist would say that her incessant need to help others stemmed from her inability to aid her own child, but she didn't come from that self-help generation where therapy was even an option, so for her she was simply being a good neighbor.

Things had gotten so confusing the past few days that Me-Ma needed to make sure she had her house in order, and not just her religious one. First this thing with Simone nearly getting killed at the bank, and now this thing with Walter, reminded her of the need to get her affairs in order. What better person to help her do that than her pastor. She took all her legal paperwork out of the safe box her husband had purchased all those years ago when their daughter was still a little girl, and stuffed them in her purse.

"We've come this far by faith, leaning on the Lord . . ." one of her favorite hymns played over the speaker system in the church as she entered. The calming music immediately put Me-Ma at peace.

"Trusting in his holy word, he never failed me yet . . ." she found herself getting carried by the spirit, singing along at the top of her voice. God didn't care that she couldn't carry a tune a half a block. All he knew was her heart, and her heart was pure. Clapping hands interrupted her singing, and Me-Ma turned to see Pastor Cassius Street coming down the aisle of the sanctuary. He was the kind of man who dressed to impress, so unless his look was a hundred percent together, he didn't leave his house. His flamboyant purple suit shimmered as he moved up the aisle toward her. The off-white collar shirt, pastel yellow, cream and purple lace tie, and ivory snakeskin shoes had taken him hours of careful planning to match so perfectly, but he would have never admit to that.

"Pastor, you look so handsome." Me-Ma gushed at how put together he was, not like these other men his age who still had their asses hanging out under their underwear. He reminded her of the way men got all decked out in the 70's. He threw his arms around her, hugging her tightly. This little lady may have gotten on his nerves with all of her suggestions and demands, but she sure did help to keep the coffers filled. Cassius had never met a compliment that he didn't like, so he made a point to give Mrs. Banks extra attention for hers.

"I love that dress. Designer?" he asked staring at her appreciatively. The whole point of him being a clothes whore had to do with the way people responded to his efforts. The more effusive they were, the higher up on the patron food chain they went. Well, that and the size and frequency of their donations also contributed to the kinds of time he allocated for them on his schedule. She also had that fine as wine granddaughter who would give the right look as First Lady.

"How is my favorite member? And how is your granddaughter recovering after yesterday's ordeal?" He reached for her hand and held onto it as he stared into her eyes, all sincerity. Cassius made sure to come off as a concerned pastor. He knew better than to let her know that he had a more personal interest in her granddaughter. He fashioned himself a religious Kanye West in need of a woman of equal measure to help raise his profile and Simone was fine enough and educated enough to do just that. She also had that big ole hump on her backside which would make the men jealous and the women envious.

"Pastor, I need help with some important legal matters."

"Absolutely, Mrs. Banks. Anything for you."

"I don't have an updated will that includes my granddaughters. Who knows how long the good Lord will see fit to keep me here on earth?" The walk over to the church had worn down her body. The Pastor led her to his office where they could speak in privacy.

"I am here for you. How can I help you?"

"Will you be my witness?" She leaned close to him. "There are so many things I need to address. I figured if I ran them past you maybe you'd help me come to terms with what I need to do." Cassius nodded his head up and down a little too eagerly but Me-Ma had been so busy thinking about the heaviness of her decisions that she hadn't been paying attention.

"Absolutely, but first, let us pray." The Pastor bowed his head and started to preach the gospel. Me-Ma lowered her head, her thoughts traveling to gratitude at having formed such a close bond with this man of God.

". . . Humble yourselves therefore under the mighty hand of God, that he may exalt you in due time." By the time Cassius released Me-Ma's hand, she had gotten real clarity on what to do next.

"Now you know I love all my granddaughters equally, but the one that I trust the most to handle my business is Simone. She's level headed and fair enough to look after the others. She's also the oldest and most educated so I trust she will handle the legal matters and paperwork more appropriately than my other granddaughters.

"What about your daughter?"

"There is no way I could leave anything to her. Those girls would be homeless and hungry if she got her hands on my property or what little insurance money I have. Lord forgive me for saying this, but my daughter is the reason I need to put things in writing. My husband and I drew up these papers so long ago that Deidra is still the sole heir to everything, and that would be a disaster. . ." Just as Me-Ma started to finish, the door burst open, and standing there owning a pissed off expression, wrapped in a fuchsia colored dress a good size too small with all her woman parts bursting out, stood Katrina. The pastor's face clouded over as Katrina strutted in the office door, only to be replaced by a blank smile, giving nothing away.

"Pastor, may I speak to you?" she said through clenched teeth, her anger so strong she didn't use the good sense God had given her to have manners and acknowledge his visitor.

"Why hello Katrina," Me-Ma jumped in thinking that if this hot-n-tot thought she could be rude on her watch she had mistaken kindness for weakness and was about to get herself old schooled. The arch of Katrina's right eyebrow raised up because this wasn't a sister used to dealing with other women in any capacity. In fact she usually dismissed females in the most rude and arrogant way. She had a body and an attitude made for men and men only, so to have to give some ole biddy her attention fueled her annoyance at the reverend.

"Mrs. Banks," she responded, painting on a faux smile. Now Katrina's legendary bad attitude and temper weren't exactly wiped away, but she realized she needed to play her position since her goal was to become Mrs. Street and First Lady of the church. She couldn't have anything getting in the way of that. Her current position as part time church bookkeeper made it so she didn't have much interaction with the members, but in her new role she'd have to at least pretend to like these people. Cassius stood up, always a gentleman and turned to face his visitor.

"Katrina, I am in the middle of something. I can call you later if you need to discuss the books," he offered, trying to maintain professionalism, but she had an agenda and would not be deterred from it. She sure as hell wasn't playing second fiddle to this old biddy.

"Well, Pastor, excuse my interruption but I needed to stop by and make sure that you were OK. When you failed to show up to the elaborate dinner I had prepared in your honor, the one you had confirmed earlier in the day, I got worried." Her words may have been polite, but this bitch was two seconds from blowing. Well, before Cassius could respond, Me-Ma had grown too tired of this hussy's interruption to put up with another moment of her foolishness and responded for him.

"Ms. Katrina, our pastor was simply being too polite to tell you that he's not interested in whatever you are serving up tonight. Now, you need to get on out of here in that dress you done grown too big to wear and stop embarrassing yourself," Me-Ma said to a stunned Katrina. At first, the fullness of what had just happened didn't register fully to her. She glanced from Cassius to Me-Ma before she had recovered enough to refrain from pummeling a senior citizen.

"He can tell me himself," she growled, her right eye twitching. She couldn't believe this old woman had the nerve to be all up in her business. Katrina assumed that it had probably been too long since she remembered what a good dick felt like, but this old lady needed to stop cock blocking and get her ass to stepping. Katrina had no plans to go anywhere until she got exactly what she had come for. Now the pastor cursed himself for mixing business with pleasure, because this hothead knew entirely too much about him.

"Please, I need a moment," he asked Mrs. Banks as he jumped up and hustled ole girl out of the office and into the hallway where they could have some privacy. Even from inside the office where she sat, Me-Ma could hear the litany of curse words streaming out of Katrina's mouth, and rolled her eyes at the foolishness. Lord, she wished these girls could have just a little dignity. This made her think about her daughter, Deidra, who had called the other day to announce she had taken up with some new under achiever and was living not too far away. Pretty is as pretty does, which was damn ugly as far as Me-Ma could see when it came to her only child. If that girl hadn't been so beautiful, she might have had to develop other qualities like humility and kindness, none of which were evident in her. No matter how many times she had prayed up that child, Deidra, being Deidra, consistently proved to be an utter disappointment to both God and to her mother.

"Sorry for that," Cassius announced as he hurried back to rejoin her. After his "conversation" with Katrina in the hallway, Cassius was anxious to wrap up with Me-Ma. Secretly he was hoping Mrs. Bank wouldn't notice his rush to get her out of there. Katrina had been gracious, well maybe that wasn't the right word, desperate enough to offer him a nooner.

"No problem. It gave me time to sit with the Lord."

"I need to say that as much as I appreciate your desire to add a religious component to this I really think that what you need is a good attorney."

"When my husband and I prepared this last paperwork Pastor Jasper helped us. Then we got a notary to sign it, Gale, who used to be a member here."

"And I would be honored to do that, but these days there are so many stipulations and loopholes that unless you have a law degree you can't figure it out. Not to mention you need to make sure that your document is air tight from what you told me about your daughter. Do you know our member, Sister Lauryn Shelton? She's incredible. I have had the good fortune of sending some of our other parishioners to her and they all raved about her." He tried not to focus on his watch, but the blowjob he had been promised made it difficult to think about wills and deeds and whatever else Me-Ma wanted him to look at.

"I know that child. Her grandmother was a good friend of mine before she passed."

"Great. Why don't you call her office and her secretary will be able to make an appointment for you." No sooner had the Reverend finished with Me-Ma then he found himself with his pants down around his ankles, getting properly serviced by Katrina. There were two kinds of women who could be depended on to give the best blowjobs: either big girls or ugly girls. It was almost like they had something to prove, but whatever the case, they made a lot of men happy. Hell, Cassius thought with a smirk, they were the very reason somebody had coined the term *booty-call* in the first place, because a man of his stature couldn't be seen publicly with them.

The pastor couldn't help but be grateful about the perks of the job. He had them coming and going, and they were more concerned about protecting his reputation, so he rarely had to worry about things getting out. Katrina on the other hand was the exception, and she was already starting to be a problem. He was a little sad that he'd have to end things with her after he shot his load into her mouth. Damn. He loved anyone who could swallow like a professional.

Chapter 14

"Thank you for shopping at Nordstrom's," said James, the cashier. He was a third year sophomore at VCU, working part time for a few extra dollars to party and buy weed. But at that very moment, he would have traded a pound of the most exotic marijuana for a taste of this exotic flower with gray eyes, long bone-straight hair stopping at the small of the back, wearing the tightest designer Robin's jeans and six inch Gucci stilettos, standing at his register. Nordstrom's policy on pushing up on customers was clear: Get caught; get fired.

But pussy trumped policy.

The cashier returned the credit card to the hottie along with two white shopping bags and a receipt for the purchase. "If you need any help with aaaaaanyyyything else, Ms. Green, I put my name and number on the back," James said, gesturing toward the receipt.

You bold, Ginger thought of the cashier and then snickered to herself. *. . . and cute.* But he also wasn't in her league and was clueless. Clueless about her name; the cloned credit card she'd used was in the name of Rebecca Green, and clueless about her sex. Or was he?

Ginger put the plastic away, next to the other four in her cross body Louis bag, and returned the cashier a beautiful smile. "I doubt if you'd be able to handle me," she said, with a raised eyebrow before stepping away toward the store's exit.

Ginger handed both of the bags to Deidra, who was waiting outside.

"Is everything in there?" she asked Ginger, who was the youngest of her children. She'd always been the one who'd tried the hardest to please their mother, even when Deidra didn't deserve a damn thing, which was most of the time. The woman was possibly one of the most selfish women on the planet. All she cared about was herself, and what was best for her; no one else, not her children, not her mother, just herself, Deidra.

Up until this afternoon, as usual, Ginger's plan had been to do her thing solo, especially when she tightened plastic. When doing dirt, she always preferred to do it alone. This was her preference and her motto. Just in case something went wrong, there was no one else to blame beside herself. And she didn't have to break bread with anyone, unless she chose to. But the main reason Ginger preferred to work solo instead of with an accomplice: it eliminated the stress of worrying about that person, down the line, ratting her out in order to get themselves out of a jam.

A crease wrinkled her plans after she got a call from her mother right before leaving the house. For ten minutes Deidra prattled away about a two-week vacation to the Caribbean she and her "friend" were taking. Ginger hadn't bothered asking if her "friend" was a man or not, because Deidra only had male friends.

Before she knew it, Ginger had been persuaded into agreeing to not only get her some things but to let Deidra accompany her to the mall.

Of all the siblings, Ginger was the one who yearned Deidra's approval and jumped through hoops to get it. Deidra took advantage of it every chance she got.

Ginger racked up more than 12 grand in charges on designer clothes, shoes and accessories for Deidra to take on her trip—not including the two shopping bags from Nordstrom's—to five separate, bogus credit cards. "You going to be the best dressed bitch your age on the cruise," she said to her mother.

Just as Deidra was fixing to say something, a tall Black man with a chocolate complexion, walked by. Ginger thought he resembled Morris Chestnut. Chocolate Drop's eyes thoroughly inspected Ginger and Deidra's assets. Before keeping it moving, a smile creased his face, like a dog trespassing on a truck with racks of prime cut filet mignon.

"Amen." Deidra cleared her throat. "Thanks for the compliment," she said to Ginger, referring to being the flyest bitch her age on the trip. "But make no mistake about it," Deidra added, "Deidra Banks look good for *any* age."

Good genes ran in the Banks family, and Deidra was blessed with a closet full of them, enough to pass down to her four children, and plenty left over for herself. Something she proudly announced to each of her children.

As they were leaving the outdoor style mall, Ginger put a little extra in the sway of her hips, matching Deidra's high-heeled strut bounce for bounce. Strangers mistook the two for sisters, clueless to just how clueless they were.

"Where do you want to do lunch?" Ginger asked, enjoying their time together, something that rarely, if ever, happened when she was a child. "It's on me."

"Oh! My! God!" Deidra's heels anchored into the linoleum stopping her strut. Ginger followed the path of Deidra's eyes, which were locked on the bag in the window of the Louis Vuitton store. "Damn," said Deidra obsessing over the design of the purse. "That thing right there would look so good on my arm," she said.

Ginger looked at the small rectangle card, connected to a string, from the inside pocket of the purse: $3200.

This was a problem. Five thousand was the limit on each of her cloned credit cards and she had already run through half of her limit on all of them. It was only one way to cop the bag that her mother wanted. She would have to use two cards, and even then, she would be well over the amount that she usually charged on any piece of stolen plastic.

It was no need in pushing her luck anymore today, "How about if I get it for you next week, Ma?"

"That's cool," Deidra said, sucking her teeth, before pouring a cold glass of guilt. "Too bad the trip isn't next week, huh? I guess I could carry it when I get back from the trip, huh?"

Ginger had to fight to keep from laughing at her mother's shameless attempt to con her. When Ginger was young, the rare times Deidra was around, Ginger would do anything to make her happy and proud of her in order to make her want to spend more time with her. Back then, nothing Ginger did ever worked. To this day, she never quit trying.

"Let me go in and check the temperature." Meaning she wanted to get a feeling for the vibe inside the store. "If it looks right, I will swing it for you. No promises."

"Are you sure that's what you want to do?" Deidra asked as if it was all Ginger's idea. "Because I have no problem waiting."

"Is that right?" Ginger began walking away. "Then we can fall back and go get lunch then. I'm starving," she put her hand on her stomach.

"But since we are already here . . ." Deidra said reaching out, grabbing Ginger's arm before she could take another step. "You might as well . . . aah . . . go ahead and check the temperature."

"Wait here." Ginger flipped her weave and went inside the store.

In her mind, she swore that Deidra was the only person that Ginger ever cared about getting approval from. But it wasn't true. Ginger aspired to be rich, to look rich, and be respected as a rich woman, everywhere she went. This was the reason why she hustled and played with the credit cards the way she did. Not because she needed to, but because she liked the feeling of compliments and the attention she got when she put on the clothes. Unlike Tallhya, she didn't need a man to validate herself. Her beautiful, extravagant "things" never failed her.

The scent of the new Louis' was intoxicating upon entering the store. The smell of richness was the aroma of the place. It reminded her of that new car smell; not that fake shit, the "car-scent", they try to peddle in the auto stores. This smell triggered something in Ginger's head that made her remember how bad she wanted that new convertible Lexus in her life.

One day soon.

"May I help you with something?" The saleslady was an anorexic-looking chick with shockingly bright blond hair. The roots let on that it was so not her real color.

Besides Ginger, there were two other customers in the store, a couple who were being stalked by the only other salesperson looking for a sure commission.

Ginger's instincts told her to fall back, and she'd planned to listen. So that she wouldn't look too crazy, before leaving, she asked to see one of the purses from behind the counter.

It was the same model as the one displayed in the store window. The one her mother almost broke a heel and her neck trying to stop to get a better look at.

Olive Oil flipped her neon hair over her shoulder as if she had better things to do than her job.

This bitch is tripping, Ginger thought. Reluctantly, Olive Oil fetched the bag but not before bluntly informing Ginger of a small detail, "It's forty-one hundred, and we don't have layaway and we never have sales or markdowns."

Ginger exhaled and thought to herself. *Girl, don't even let this definitely in need of a French-fry heifer fade you. Thank the bitch for her help and keep it moving.* But emotions got the better of her. "I'll take the matching wallet also," she firmly said, then plucked two credit cards from her own Louis wallet. "I'm trying to earn frequent flyer miles so divide the total."

Ginger's eyes were glued on Olive Oil as Olive Oil's eyes were fixed on the two credit cards in her hand as she was trying hard not to shit a brick. I'm going to have to see some identification, "Mrs . . ." another quick glance at the plastic then back to Ginger, "Rebecca Paige."

She smirked then added, "Not my but the store's policy."

I'm sure it is, Ginger thought. Since the surge of online shopping, stores rarely asked for ID anymore to confirm credit card purchases. All that was needed was the card number, which Ginger had memorized.

Olive Oil was being a smart aleck, and hating. Either that, or she was hipped to game. *All in all, she better be happy that she's getting this damn commission.*

Negative thoughts were a cancer. Ginger shook the negativity out of her head and into space. She dug into her wallet and found the ID that matched the fake card. The same dude that had hooked her up with the plastic—one of her friends with benefits, had supplied her with a complimentary ID. Doug told her better to have it and not need it then to need it and not have it.

She smiled, thinking of Doug's words in her ears. That's why she fucked with Doug; he was smart and great in bed. Ginger passed Olive Oil the fake driver's license that Doug insisted she take with her. Olive Oil checked the creds. After seeing the headshot of Ginger smiling for the camera above the name Rebecca Paige, she reluctantly swiped the Visa and

American Express, splitting the price of the purchase on the two the cards just as Ginger had asked.

"Thank you, darling." Bag in hand, Ginger showed the raggedy bitch her back and sashayed out of the store.

Without breaking stride, she nodded a "let's go," to Deidra. It wasn't until she was inside of her six year-old Honda, with engine running, that Ginger started to relax. Even then, she still felt a little uneasy, which was odd for her. Usually it was an adrenaline rush, but not today.

"Let's go to Ruth Chris," Deidra said, oblivious to Ginger's anxiety. "I got a taste for one of their juicy, tender steaks."

The mall was behind them. The Honda headed east on 64. On the radio August Alsina's, *"If I Make it Home,"* played.

Ginger turned up the volume. As if they were at the club, three strobes of light bounced off the dashboard. "What the fuck?"

Woop! Woop!

Police. . . .

9:00 p.m.

RINGGGGGG. Spoe and Bunny's house phone rang, which was a surprise because it almost never did.

The two old friends sat on the couch looking at each other, knowing damn well that it couldn't possibly be the call that they were waiting for. Nevertheless, Spoe got up to answer it. He looked at the caller ID and it read: UNKNOWN.

"Hello," he said into the receiver.

The automated recording immediately starting talking, "You have a collect call from . . ." there was a brief pause and then Ginger spoke her name, prompting Spoe to call out Bunny's name, "Ayo Bunny! Babe!"

Then the recording sprung back into action, "From the Henrico County Jail. Please hang up to decline, or press zero to accept."

Spoe couldn't press the zero quick enough to accept the call.

"Hello," Ginger, said.

"Yo," Spoe said, "the fuck?"

"They knocked me off coming out of the Louis store." Ginger was about to give Spoe the details, when Spoe cut her off.

"How much the bail?" Spoe asked as Bunny walked up. He said, "It's Ginger, she down Henrico."

"The magistrate ain't give me no bail," Ginger informed Spoe.

"Don't worry, the judge gone give you one in the morning. Hold your head and Bunny gon' be there to get you," Spoe promised, then handed Bunny the phone.

Bunny took the phone out of Spoe's hand, "Bitch, what the hell happened?"

Spoe corrected Bunny quick. "Don't ask 'em that on them phones. You know them people listening right?"

Bunny nodded to Spoe, agreeing, and then he spoke into the phone to Ginger. "I'm going to be there in the a.m. to get you, OK? So hang in there" and in Me-Ma's voice "Joy going to come in the morning."

Bunny could tell that her last comment mocking their grandmother managed to put a slight smile on Ginger's face.

The rest of evening went by at a snail's pace for Bunny, thinking about Ginger, as well as Spoe and Tariq waiting for Tiffany to finally call.

"Man, this shit is whack. You know we not use to this. Waiting around for a call to move." Spoe was right. He was one of those people that like ritual. He was organic and believed that's how things should be—not forced, but should come when he felt it in his gut. With his balls and heart out of the equation, that was a lot of the reason he was so successful at what he did. He always trusted his instinct.

"Man, she going to call soon," Tariq tried to assure his friend since third grade, as he was a little concerned about the awkward silence between the two of them.

Spoe began to think to himself how he hated breaking his routine of doing things, but then he thought about his cut of the million dollars that could be in his safe tomorrow.

Just then, the phone rang. A smile covered a relieved Tariq's face. He answered quickly the second he saw the caller ID revealing Tiffany's number.

"Yeah, beautiful," he said as he winked and smiled at Spoe. There was no doubt that he was trying to convince his childhood friend that he really wasn't as sprung out on Tiffany as he was. Tariq put the call on speakerphone so Spoe could be privy to the info she had. She let out the address and that was the green light to proceed with their plan.

Spoe went into the bedroom for a quick change into his work clothes. He went over to the bed where Bunny was stretched out watching television, and laid on top of her.

He blessed her with a long passionate kiss. "We just got the call."

"You sure this Tiffany bitch is OK?" she questioned.

"Yes, I guess. Tariq said he bet his life on it," Spoe said.

"He better, and hers too. Hope that bitch value hers, 'cause if she ain't on the up and up, I'm going to deal with her myself," Bunny promised.

Spoe knew that Bunny meant business. His wifey was extremely territorial. He knew that she didn't like the fact that he had to depend on any other woman besides her, for anything. Spoe wasn't going to even entertain the treacherous thoughts of what Bunny would do to Tiffany if the information she gave wasn't on the up and up.

"Well, that girl is all about her money, and she want her cut."

"Seems like it," Bunny agreed.

"Why you say that?" Spoe questioned Bunny as if she knew something that he didn't.

"I looked at her Facebook page and I saw her."

Spoe kissed his wifey-boo again, "You something else," he said, not even surprised that Bunny knew everything, including the girl's last eye exam, there was to know about Tiffany.

"Hand me that phone on the night table," she said to him. He did and she started showing Spoe Tiffany's pictures she had posted on her page.

"You don't be playing, do you?"

"Nope, not when it comes to my man, I don't. Nope, not about mines."

He kissed her again, "I love you woman. You know that?"

"Yes! And know that I love you more." She kissed him back and embraced him tight, then said, "I just wish you could stay here in my arms all night."

"Me too, baby, but duty calls. Gotta go get the bacon."

Bunny sighed, and for a couple beats there was silence between the two. Then she jumped into character. "What you need me to do to help you get ready."

"Nothing. I'm good babe. I got it covered."

"You sure?" she questioned as Spoe got up and slipped into his all black gear. She tried to do any little thing to help him as if he was her son. He didn't mind. He gave her a long hug.

"Go and get that money, baby, and bring it back to Momma," she kissed him and smiled at him.

"You better believe it baby," he said as he headed for the door. "Come lock the door, babe."

Bunny walked behind him. He turned back around and spoke to her.

"And if Ginger call back, let 'em know not to panic. We got 'em as soon as they give a bail."

Once she shut door and watched them get into their work van and pull off, she wondered exactly how Ginger was holding up.

Chapter 15

"Bail denied!"

The decision not to grant Ginger a bond came from behind a bulletproof glass by an overworked magistrate. A deputy grabbed her arm and began to usher her away before a stunned Ginger could respond.

Ginger jerked her arm away. "Hold the fuck up! I didn't even get a chance to speak. Y'all acting like I done killed somebody or something. Damn, even the Briley Brothers got a damn bond."

Deputy Foster allowed Ginger to vent. As long as she didn't get too out of pocket, she was cool. He'd been doing this job, escorting detainees through Henrico Jail, for better than 15 years. Some of them were innocent, but most were guilty as charged. Their crimes were none of his business; he just did his job.

"Are we in America or North-Fuckin' Korea?" Ginger huffed. "Credit card fraud and grand larceny, that's all I'm charged with and I can't get no gotdamn bond. Fuck."

Actually, Ginger had 12 counts of fraud and eight counts of grand larceny, as well as a list of other white-collar charges.

Tightening his grip this time, Deputy Foster directed her back toward post processing, a room where they changed the detainees out of their street clothes and into prison-beige stock jail uniforms.

"I'm willing to bet the reason the magistrate refused to give you bond," he informed Ginger, "is because you don't have a valid ID. You could be a serial killer for all we know. For all he knows, you could be a terrorist. You got four IDs and none of them are you. The Boston Bombers didn't have IDs as intricate as yours. So you can't really blame them for taking those precautions."

Deputy Foster got to a door and handed Ginger off to a female officer to get changed.

"Jane Doe: No Bond," he told his colleague and looked to Ginger. "Behave."

The female's badge read Duncan. Deputy Duncan was short, with chocolate skin, and a military fit body. She sized Ginger up with a pair of hazel eyes. "Small." She was referring to Ginger's size, and it came off more like a statement then a question.

What size smock she took was the least of Ginger's concerns. She had much bigger fish to fry, which was a lot harder to do being that she was the one in the hot pan of grease. It turned out that Olive Oil, the anorexic white chick from the Louis store, had called 5-0. With the omnipresence of surveillance cameras, it had been easy to go back and pick up Ginger's movements. The spotted her leaving Louis Vuitton, putting the bags in the car, she and Deidra leaving the mall, and the license plates of her Honda as they rode off.

"Take all your clothes off and put them in this." Deputy Duncan handed her a small metal basket, "And hurry up. We don't have all day honey."

Chile please. Bitch you much be crazy. Like you really think I'm going to hurry up to get locked down? Think again, Ginger thought as she unbuttoned her blouse slowly.

Two buttons. Deputy Duncan rolled her eyes like, "Get a move on it." She tried to rush Ginger, but Ginger wasn't having it.

She rolled them right back like, *whatever.* The blouse finally unbuttoned, Ginger took off the blouse, folded it up neatly, and placed it into the metal basket. Thanks to all the hormone pills she had taken since age 18, a killer pair of C-cup breasts filled the cup of the Victoria Secret royal blue lace bra.

Deputy Duncan walked her eyes down to Ginger's ironing board flat stomach, then slowly back up to her breasts, with the healthy appetite and appreciation of an admiring lesbian.

"Good," said Deputy Duncan with no shame in her tone. "Jeans and shoes."

Ginger saw the lust written all across Duncan's face, and she milked it, taking her time. Deputy Duncan deaded her fake hurry, enjoying the striptease that Ginger was putting on, while it lasted. Ginger wished she'd worn more clothes.

Finally in nothing but matching lace panties and bra, she struck a pose. Then she gestured for the prison rags to replace the garments she'd disrobed.

Ginger's heart skipped when Deputy Duncan said, "Everything."

With a lot to conceal and nowhere to conceal it, Ginger sighed at the perplexity of her situation.

"You sure about that?" Ginger said in her sexiest voice. "This may be too much for you," she licked her lips and batted her long mink eyelash extensions in a seductive way.

"Trust me, I can handle whatever you got," Duncan shot back. "Now strip."

"Okay, have it all your way," she moaned in a way that she knew turned on Duncan, as she unsnapped her bra, freeing a set of perfectly round mounds of soft flesh, sitting at attention like two puppies awaiting a treat. Deputy Duncan gave a nod at the panties, trying to conceal a smile, but Ginger had other things that needed to be concealed.

They were at ground zero when Deputy Duncan unleashed a wild scream. "Package!"

Thinking that Deputy Duncan had discovered drugs on the Jane Doe's person, and by the sound of her shriek, was engaged in a physical confrontation, Deputy Foster rushed to assist his colleague.

Confused, Deputy Duncan stammered, "S-she'sss a dude," pointing at the seven inches of proof, strapped between Gingers legs and ass cheeks.

"What the fu-ckkkk?" Foster was shocked too.

Chapter 16

Under the pale light of a full moon, Spoe and Tariq stepped from the cover of a thick patch of wood, about half a football field from a white plantation style mansion.

In what little time they did have to prepare, they'd done their homework. It was a Thursday. Every Thursday around 11 p.m., the Bloody Lions Posse left the house together, usually for a couple of hours, but never more than three or less than one. So Spoe and Tariq figured they had at least an hour to find the bread and get ghost, but had decided to only allot themselves thirty minutes to make it happen.

The crib—7200 square feet, on three acres of rural property—belonged to a dread called Dino. Dino was the head of a crew from New York, who were heavily into distribution of cocaine and ecstasy. Even after doing their due diligence, Spoe still couldn't help his feeling of uneasiness, combined with a bad vibe.

"That bitch Tiffany is sure she seen a mill-ticket?" Spoe had to make sure.

Tariq, with his eyes still on the empty house, "She's never steered me wrong before and I'm sure she's not going to start now." Tariq looked his man in his eyes. "She said it was *at least* a million dollars."

"In a suitcase with a gold lion head?" Spoe questioned, then added, "It sounds like some shit you'd see in a movie."

Tariq hunched his shoulders. He had to agree, "True dat. But you know like I know, real life can be crazier than fiction. Take this house for example. You wouldn't think a Black person would be living in it, unless they were the help. The shit looks exactly like Candy Land, the house Jamie Foxx blew up in the movie *Django*."

The sound of barking dogs rang out.

Woof! Woof! Woof! Woof!

The barking originated from two silver back pit bulls. Together the dogs weighed more than 200 lbs, and had heads the size of watermelons.

Spoe gripped the handle of the sub-machine gun hanging from the strap around his neck. Busting a cap in the dog to keep from becoming a Scooby snack wouldn't be a problem. Fortunately for all parties involved, the pits were chained and caged in a 12X12 pen.

"Nah, man, let them live." Tariq suggested. "Let's focus on this bread."

"Tonight is their lucky night," Spoe said, as he looked at the trained attack dogs.

Focused back on the house, Tariq said, "We keep to the script." According to Tiffany, she was upstairs when she'd seen the suitcase. So, she had no idea where Dino kept it. "We toss the house for no more than twenty minutes, and then we out, with or without."

Spoe didn't like scavenger hunts. His preferred method was to snatch somebody up. It never mattered if it was the actual victim, victim's ole girl, or ole lady. He'd torture them until he got what he needed.

Tariq could see his friend's apprehensiveness, but he said, "Spoe, yours is normally riskier than this."

"Yeah, but it's always produced results for us. Big results."

The problem: these dreads originated in New York and had no family in Virginia. To top things off, their entire crew was treacherous to the core. These were the kind of gangstas that would rather die a violent death then bow down to torture.

"A'ight man. It's your play," Spoe said as they crept through the darkness wearing all black. "We'll do it your way." He had no reason not to trust Tariq's judgment, after all the two had been in business together in some sort of way for over fifteen years.

The house was wired with an alarm system from one of the companies that put their sign in the yard as a warning to casual trespassers and kids. For anyone with even average knowledge on how the system worked, the alarm was as usual as the caged guard dog.

Tariq was far from average when it came to disengaging alarm systems. He was a pro. A good alarm took him three minutes to disarm. In 60 seconds give or take they had bypassed the crap system and were standing inside the kitchen. The fridge, stove, and dishwasher were all high-end stainless steel appliances. The island's black marble top matched the onyx-colored floor. The kitchen opened up into an extravagant styled living room: a 70-inch TV mounted over an enormous granite style fireplace, gold tables, white Italian leather sofas and Arabian silk high back chairs. Everything was spotless, not to mention the place looked like a museum.

"Are these cats really drug dealers, or does Martha Stewart live here?" Spoe half joked with a raised eyebrow.

"Shit is unbelievable right?" Tariq was impressed by the one and only lick that he had ever brought to the table.

"It is, but we don't have no time for a tour. We need to get to this money."

"Let's start upstairs," Tariq said, for the first time taking the lead. "Come on."

Spoe followed as Tariq lead the way. They turned left, bypassing the grandiose living room, through an archway and up an oversized spiral staircase, which was also marble and wider than two driving lanes of I-95.

At the top was a loft with more rooms going in either direction, "Man, I know this is yo' show, but in all this house and the time we on, there's no time for roaming. I think it's best for us to split up. You take the rooms to left and I will hit the right, then look for the master bedroom."

Tariq agreed with the plan, adding, "Good idea. We start at the furthest point and work our way back to the loft. Either of us find the loot we holla and we out."

Spoe took responsibility for tossing all the rooms east of the loft; Tariq all the rooms west of the loft.

"Sounds Gucci to me."

They parted like two determined prizefighters, after bumping gloves in the middle of the ring, to their respective corners, except they were retreating to their separate corners of the house, not a ring. Before a purse would be divided, they would have to find it first!

Tariq opened the door of what seemed to be a mini theatre. He didn't think it was a likely place to hide the bread, but one would never know if they didn't look. The walls were textured and red. Thick leather reclining chairs with cup holders, the same ox blood red as the walls, faced the 12 foot wide screen. It was improbable that a suitcase would be able to fit inside or under the recliners but he lifted the seat cushions and felt under each one anyway. The only money he found was $3.17 worth of loose change. He ripped the screen off the wall, checking behind it. Nothing there.

Something caught his attention on the wall near the front to the left of the screen. It was a barely noticeable vertical seam. It was a door, a door with no discernable latch.

The only purpose for having a hidden door would be to conceal something. The question was, what was being concealed? One thing for sure, two things for certain, he'd find out soon enough.

Tariq tried pushing the door, first in the center, then on each corner, hoping it was one of those pressure-spring latches.

Negative.

The seam was too narrow to slip anything between it, so prying it open wasn't an option.

He was wasting time, *Get the fuckin' door open Tariq. Come, on man, this is yo' shit. This the shit you do,* his sub-conscience was talking to him.

Touching the wall, to the right of the seam, he ran his fingers from top to bottom. Nothing. He went out a little wider with his hands, repeating the process.

Bingo!

Camoflauged in the textured sound proofing material was a small button. He pressed the button and the door slid open on a recessed, mechanical track. Inside the space were racks of electronic material. A subwoofer, DVD player, tuner, hard drive, amp, etc.

No money.

Who the fuck goes to this length of secrecy to conceal a stereo? Tariq thought. The answer was no one.

The longer Tariq looked at the audio and video equipment the more he sensed something was definitely offbeat.

What was it? He was wrecking his brain trying to figure it out, but knew he didn't have but so much time to jerk off in there.

The minute he was about to give up, it hit him. He hit himself with the heel of his hand for not pinning it off top. It was the subwoofer. Toshiba made all of the equipment inside of the closet, except for the subwoofer. It was also at least a couple years older than the other stuff.

After closer scrutiny, Tariq was on to the charade. The subwoofer was one of those "in your face" stash boxes. Like the fake rock people hid the spare door key in and left in the front yard. Inside the sham subwoofer were eight neatly wrapped bricks of coke.

It wasn't the million dollars that they were looking for, but it was a heck of a bonus to a great start. Tariq stacked the bricks inside of the duffle bag before moving on to the next room. One room down, four to go.

Meanwhile, Spoe was ready to toss the third room on his end. The first two, besides a couple pieces of jewelry, were a bust. Before he went back to work, he took a deep breath to clear his head.

When Spoe was thirteen and was running wild, an OG name Butter took him under his wing and blessed him with some food for thought.

"Productivity," Butter said, "comes to the brotha that most persistent *and* patient. Remember that, Young Blood." Spoe swallowed the gem whole and kept down. He'd been shining ever since.

Though the master bedroom was bigger than the entire apartment of some projects he'd been in, he didn't get discouraged. If the money was truly there, he'd find it. He flipped the mattress on the king-sized bed, and found a 22-shot Glock. He put the pistol in his waist, got on his knees and looked underneath the box spring.

Nothing at all, but a few specks of dust, was all that he found.

He pulled the bed from the wall and checked behind the headboard. Nothing. He didn't stop there, he continued to look, underneath and behind the oak dresser, chest and the two night tables. Still he came up with nothing. One by one he removed a collection of paintings from the wall, looking for hidden safes. The room had a fireplace almost as big as the one they had passed downstairs. He searched inside the fireplace and around the hearth for loose bricks concealing stash spots. He continued to the floor to ceiling book shelves, bathroom, and a sitting area framed by a bay window. In an antique armoire he found nothing besides a collection of high-end watches in a wooden box.

As he made his way toward a closet, he hoped Tariq was having better luck. He quickly let the random thought go. If Tariq had found the money, they wouldn't still be inside the house searching. They'd be in the truck celebrating, but that wasn't the case at all.

Spoe opened the door to the walk-in closet, which was the size of a two-car garage. Just like the rest of the crib, the design and organization could have been overseen by Martha Stewart herself. Clothes were coordinated by colors and seasons. To Spoe, except for the guns, it seemed like something more suitable for a cat like Nick Cannon than a drug-dealing cat like Dino.

Dudes were seriously strapped. Hanging from a customized pegboard were two AKs, a M-14, a Heckler & Koch UMP, and an array of semi-automatic pistols. Spoe took notice that a few spots on the wall were currently unoccupied, letting him know that Dino and crew were strapped.

Then he noticed something else. On the floor, beneath the guns, was a suitcase. Brown. And embossed in its leather was a lion's head.

Bingo!

God was good! They'd finally found what they'd come for and more than they'd expected.

Motivated by the ease of the score, Tariq wanted to keep searching. "This spot is a fuckin' gold mine." He said to Spoe, adjusting the strap on the duffle bag, weighted down with coke, over his shoulder. "No telling what else we might find."

"Yeah. Like a hot ball and a cold casket." Spoe nodded toward the suitcase in his hand. "I'm Gucci with this."

On their way down the steps, Tariq asked his friend since third grade, "So, when did you start letting the possibility of death hold sway over how you live life?"

Good question, Spoe thought. He was contemplating an answer when the gunshots rang out.

Bbbrrat! Bbbrrat! The barrage of 9mm hollow point from the MP5 hit home, boring through the flesh of its targets. Blood poured through their fingers as they clutched at the fatal holes.

From the elevated position on the stairs, Spoe had a better fight line. He'd spotted the dreads creeping before they spotted him and squeezed off the first shot, dropping two of Dino's men.

Dino watched his two soldier's chests open up right in front of him. With the severity of the wounds, they'd bleed out in a matter of minutes. It was nothing he could do for them but see to it that their killer would die, and hard. The remainder of Dino's crew sparked back, sending the sound of gunfire echoing through the house.

Boom-boom-boom-boom. Spoe shoved Tariq down. "Back upstairs." The odds weren't in their favor going down. "We've got to find another way out.

Bullets slammed into the steps, all around them, kicking up chunks of marble as Spoe and Tariq army-crawled on their stomachs back to the top of the stairs. Attempting to slow down the pursuit, even if only for a second, Tariq fired blindly over his shoulder.

Bbbrrat! Bbbratt! A lucky shot winged one of the dreads in the arm. Tariq caught one in the shoulder and two slugs would've split Spoe's dome if he hadn't moved his head just in time.

When they made it to the loft, Spoe saw that Tariq was bleeding. "You OK?" he asked, and then fired off a few more shots. *Bbbrrat! Bbbratt!*

Boom-boom-boom-boom!

Spoe ducked his head. Tariq fired back. *Bbbrat! Bbbratt!* "Yeah"—*Bbratt-Bbratt*—"It's only a scratch."

Suddenly the shooting stopped. Dino announced, "No way you make it out alive, Sty." His accent was so strong that his words were hard to make out. But their meaning was crystal clear.

Spoe retorted by bucking back, squeezing the trigger. *Bbbratt!*

"You need to worry about your own mortality."

Bbrratt! Bbratt!

"Besides, I've decided not to let the possibility of death get in the way of living," Spoe said confidently.

"Then have it your way, Sty."

Boom! Boom! Boom! Boom!

A downpour of hot lead stung the loft like a swarm of killer bees. They took cover behind the leather sofa, which ate the brunt of the damage. The longer they stayed still, the more their chances of getting away lessened. Tariq looked to Spoe. "What's the plan?"

Boom! Boom! Boom!

Bbbratt!

"Down the hall," Spoe said. "It's a bedroom facing the way we came in. We hit the window and run for it."

"Tariq did the quick math, that's a 30 foot drop minimum." The house had vaulted ceilings.

"Got a better idea?"

Boom! Boom!

Bbbratt! Bbbratt!

"Any plan beats no plan when facing a life or death situation."

"Lead the way."

They eased from behind the sofa, racing down the hall toward the bedroom Spoe, had peeped earlier. Dino and his crew didn't see them dip. Tariq and Spoe hoped to get a 60 second head start before Dino and assassins realized that no one was shooting back. Spoe kicked the window out. The sound of the breaking glass was drowned out by the echo of gunshots. Using the suitcase, he knocked away shards of glass that were sticking out from the frame. Then he threw the suitcase out of the window. Fifteen seconds after abandoning the sofa in the loft, the suitcase landed calmly, with a *thump*, in the backyard. Lucky for it, it didn't have bones to break, but it was a whole other story for a person.

The impact alone from a bad landing could jam their thigh-bones past their pelvis and into their stomach. No walking away from that. Spoe took a quick glance at the door. Then turned to Tariq and said, "See you at the bottom."

Spoe hit the ground hard, but the tuck-and-roll maneuver he used absorbed most of the impact. Besides the tweak in his ankle, he was Gucci. The duffle bag tumbled from the window next, with Tariq right behind it. He nailed the tuck and roll, landing like he'd been on a mission with Field Team 6, and was on his feet.

Boom-boom! boom-boom! The shots came from the window Spoe and Tariq had just jumped from. Bullets kicked up dirt near where they lay.

"Oh, shit!" They didn't expect it to come so soon. They took off running.

"They in d' back yard headin' for d' woods." It was Dino, he ordered his crew to get down there. "And let Brutus and Cleopatra out of their cages."

After hearing their master's voice, the two silver back pit bulls bit the chain on the cage, trying to eat the lock off, to get in on the action.

Slugs followed Tariq and Spoe into the woods. The car they had driven was on the other side, half a mile away.

Spoe's ankle was worse off than he thought. He was having trouble walking, let alone running. And the suitcase, which weighed more than thirty pounds with the money, was wearing him down.

"Let's split up." It was a decision that would later haunt Spoe. "Take the suitcase, I can move faster without it."

Tariq didn't like the idea of splitting up, but with gun-toting Jamaicans and two bloodthirsty pit bulls in hot pursuit, there was no time to debate it.

Reluctantly, he said, "I'll meet you at the car."

Spoe's ankle was throbbing, and he didn't want to slow his partner down. If I'm not there five minutes after you, I'll see you at the crib."

They split up for the second time tonight. The first time was when they searched for the money. Spoe hoped that that bitch Lady Luck was in a good mood and would continue to ride with him. He'd get his answer soon enough.

Spoe's calf felt like it was on fire. Blood poured down his leg. He tried to keep it moving, but his leg called it quits. He'd been shot.

"What I told ya, Sty?" It was Dino, with dogs barking in the background.

"Dead-mon walkin', Sty."

Spoe aimed his gun into the direction of the voice and pulled the trigger but the MP5 didn't bark; its clip was empty.

Fuck!

Dino's turn . . . he pointed the gun at Spoe's head.

Dead-mon walkin'.

Spoe's last thought was of Bunny. Her birthday was next Friday and he was going to surprise her with a trip to St. Thomas. Even the thoughts of the love of his life wouldn't allow him to go out like a sucker. He would never beg for his life from a mother-fucker. Instead he looked that nigga in his eyes and waited. Dino pulled the trigger, making good on his promise.

Dead-mon walkin'.

The bullet penetrated the skull of Spoe's right ear and sliced through his brain as if it was kosher deli meat.

"No mo' walkin'," Dino said, after spitting on Spoe's body. "Just Dead-mon."

He made sure that his crew dumped the body so that if it was ever found, it could never be traced back to him.

Chapter 17

'This is just bullshit!" she screamed pounding the steering wheel of the car, taking out all of her frustration and anger on this piece of shit she was now forced to drive. How could she pray to a God that had taken away everything she had been given, including the only man she had truly ever loved. Everything had been taken away; her father, her sense of safety, her car, credit cards, medical insurance and now her health. What the fuck? Was this some cosmic joke played out for God knows what reason? Life just wasn't making sense to Simone anymore. Just as luck would have it, at a time when she just wanted to be alone to collect her thoughts, her phone wouldn't stop ringing. Her phone was blowing the hell up, but after that last phone call from the doctor she wasn't in any rush to answer an unfamiliar telephone number again. She couldn't bear to get any more bad news today. Then it dawned on her that maybe it was one of her sisters calling because something had happened to Me-Ma.

"Hello?" Simone's soft voice gave no indication that this could be the same person who moments earlier had been screaming at the top of her lungs in a rage.

"This is Detective Chase Dugan, do you have a moment Miss Banks? I need to ask you some questions." Of course the detective sounded polite enough, but after the day Simone had been having, she couldn't bring herself to respond like a normal human being.

"What do you want?" she snapped at him, her voice came out sharper than she expected, but she didn't care enough to apologize.

"I just need you to come in and take a second look at your original testimony. There is a possibility that you may have left something out yesterday. You've gone through a very traumatic experience and often victims subconsciously block out some things that resurface when they go over their statement.

"Detective, I told you everything that I saw happen. There is no way I would, or could, ever forget any of what I saw yesterday."

"I understand, but you would be doing us a great service if you could come down to the station. Oh, and we're ready for you to reclaim your belongings. They have been photographed and logged in, and we won't be needing them. Because the suspects are dead there won't be a trial."

"Fine. I'm on my way." When Simone hung up all her thoughts went to her Chanel bag and the possibility of having order restored in at least in one small area. It was a small yes in the victory column but she'd take it. Luckily she wasn't that far from the station, so she took the back roads and made it there within ten minutes. When she entered the station, she immediately started to feel nervous. Something about being around all those uniforms and guns made her feel very uneasy. Even though she had never committed a crime in her life, Simone could not shake her feeling of discomfort.

You would have thought a purple spotted giraffe or some other creature had entered the room from the amount of interest Simone's appearance had generated. Officer Johnson, a tall, good looking man in his thirties who had never met a woman he didn't find fuckable, motioned to his partner, Darby Cole, a seasoned veteran in his forties with a wife and three kids he magically forgot about on Tuesdays when he visited his mistress. The officers were just about to make a wager on the hottest woman they'd seen in ages without the distance of a television or movie screen between them. This was their thing, betting to see who could date the attractive women, usually damsels in distress who came into the station alone. Their coworkers were busying themselves suddenly finding things to do in Simone's general area so they could at least get a good look at her ass.

"May I help you?" A young white officer, Peterson, jumped the line and rushed over to help Simone.

"Dammit." Johnson and Cole couldn't believe they had been beaten to the punch by one of the rookies, who had as much chance of hitting that as Manson did at being granted his freedom.

Officer Peterson didn't bother to disguise his interest in helping Simone in other ways too.

"I'm Simone Banks, here to see Detective Dugan," she answered glancing around for him.

"Damn, he always gets the fine honeys," another dejected officer across the room joked with his buddy, as if Simone would have been interested in either of them. Like all the other grey-eyed Banks girls, Simone had grown so used to men making fools of themselves for her benefit that it almost didn't phase her. At an early age Simone's father realized that his daughter would have men after her strictly based on her appearance, so he'd made her work so hard on her academics, wanting her to have something other than beauty as currency.

"It's right this way," the officer led her through the station, hoping to use the opportunity to work up his nerve to ask her out on a date. Black women intimidated the hell out of him with their brazen confidence, but he had always been attracted to their beauty. Even though he came from a very old fashioned Italian background where his parents expected him to date "his own kind", all his girlfriends had always been black. "So are you friends with Detective Dugan?" he asked, hoping like hell that this was some business call and he could have his shot at her. Simone pierced him with her eyes, this sister was not in the mood to be his first foray into the dark and lovely club and that was putting it nicely.

"No, I'm a suspect in a crime," she informed him, certain he would lose interest. But if the officer was deterred he certainly didn't show it. Actually, he took that whole innocent until proven guilty thing seriously. It would be another two years before he flipped that script and began to see all suspects as guilty.

"What did you do? Steal a man's heart?" officer Peterson tried, desperate to see more of this gorgeous creature. Her look cut him down and quickly neutered all thoughts of them together just as they arrived at the doorway of the detective's office. Spotting Simone and the young officer, he had to stop himself from chuckling as the cop stared lustfully after her. Detective Dugan had to admit that her beauty put most women to shame, but for him this was strictly business.

"Miss Banks," he greeted her only to be met with the coldest stare he'd encountered in recent memory. This version was decidedly different than the one he'd experienced the first two times he saw her.

"So, can I have my purse and get out of here?" she said.

"Police stations make you nervous, huh?" he asked. His job had taught him to read people quickly and her aversion to the precinct was only one of the things he had assessed in that moment.

"Don't they make everybody nervous?"

"Mostly the guilty ones," he laughed attempting to put her at ease. In his experience, if he could get a person to let their guard down by some friendly bantering, it usually helped him to learn what he needed to know about a person.

"I'm here for my bag," she told him standing there stiffly. Without meaning to, he found himself staring at her. The detective couldn't help but wonder what happened since the last time he had seen her. She had been upset, but under the circumstances, that made sense. But this version of Simone he couldn't quite reconcile with the other one. She acted kind of nasty, which surprised him.

"Yes, and I will give it to you, but first I have a few questions I need to ask you." As soon as she heard that, Simone's arms folded across her chest as an icy-cold frost set in. The detective told Simone, "I didn't realize a woman's purse could cost that much money."

"Then you haven't shopped at Hermés before," she quipped, not giving a shit if she sounded rude. What was really rude was him dragging her in here to pick up belongings the police should have never taken. She really missed her purse. Foolish as that might sound, Simone always cherished her purses and treated them as if they were their own entities. This particular purse was dear to her because it was the last purse she had purchased with her father.

"Excuse me for saying it, but isn't it a bit excessive for a person with your revenue stream?"

"You mean how the hell does a lowly bank teller afford a purse that costs more than my yearly salary? Is that what you want to know?"

"Well, frankly, yes. And it's not like the rest of your wardrobe is off the racks from Kmart or nothing. You have very expensive taste." What he didn't say was it was very tasteful too. Most of the women tromping through here made damn sure you knew that they were flossing expensive shit. They strolled through the doors with their labels on full display to prove they could afford some classy shit, but unless you knew quality, Simone's high end designer clothing slipped under the radar. That quality alone interested the detective, because he wasn't used to people like Miss Banks.

"You think that if I can afford to shop in high end shops then I must be doing something illegal? Is that what it is? I'm a kept woman or a booster? That I lie, cheat and steal for a living? If I were a white woman I doubt you would be so quick to quantify my belongings." She sat back, shooting poisonous looks at him.

"Did I say that?" the detective hated that she had busted him for putting her in a pile with the rest of the people he met in his line of work. If only she knew that he didn't think of her like that. That it was just one of the pitfalls of the job, to categorize the people that you met, good, bad, pimp, hooker, thief, victim. He did not want to admit his prejudices out loud.

"You didn't have to say it. I saw it all over you."

"Fine. You're probably right, but your situation does not add up. You don't have a work history so it's more than a little suspicious that it's your first official day working at the bank, and that very same morning, the bank gets robbed. You wouldn't find that the least bit suspicious yourself? Come on. You seem like a very intelligent woman, be honest with me."

Now Simone had just gone from riches to rags, but she also wasn't going to admit that the detective had a valid point.

"Whatever! But let me tell you that if I were dumb enough to rob a bank, I'd be smart enough not to waste six whole minutes threatening a teller and taking her purse to give to my ghetto fabulous wanna-be girlfriend. Do you feel me? Any girl in the hood with that person would have to flash it and then that would'a led you right to her boyfriend, so the whole thing is just plain stupid if you ask me." She rolled her eyes at him.

"OK. So you don't know any of the perps?"

"I cannot answer that question truthfully because they were wearing masks so I did not get to see their faces. Therefore, I cannot wholeheartedly say that I did not know them. I lived in this neighborhood with my grandmother in my childhood years and then I went to live with my father. Now, I've been living with my grandmother for a few months so it could be that I've seen them around the way if I knew what they looked like. But like I said, I did not get to see their faces, so again, I cannot answer your question." Simone smugly sat in her seat. She was not going to be tricked into answering certain questions in order for the prosecutor to try to turn her words around later and try to implicate her. She was too smart and educated to fall for that. "But I will say this," Simone concluded, "It is highly unlikely that I would have known the robbers."

"Can you at least look at their crime scene photos? Maybe they will jar your memory?" he said before he pushed a set of mug shots at her. He watched her closely to see what her reaction to them would be. The slightest reaction and he would know that she was in on the heist. Simone didn't bother to hide her surprise from the detective. She shoved the photos back toward him. "So, do you recognize any of them?"

"Yes. I recognize all of them. They were just kids from the neighborhood. Jason Kill? He dated my sister Tallhya about five years ago. She fell hard for his swagged-out bad boy behavior. He put her through it, having so many baby mama's, and boy was he mad that she wouldn't give up her birth control to become the next one. He told her that if she loved him then she would have his baby. Me and my other sister, Bunny, told her that if she ever became pregnant by that thug she better keep it moving. We were not going to be related to anybody that stupid. I think it scared her enough not to give up her pills. But she wouldn't give him up because he was her first love. One night she was supposed to go out with him, but our grandmother said she wasn't feeling well. She's actually kind of psychic and something told her to keep Tallhya at home, so she didn't go. He wound up getting shot trying to stick somebody up at a convenience store. Thank God Tallhya listened to our grandmother that night, because he made his side chick go with him to drive the getaway car, and she was arrested and charged along with him. My sister told me he and the girl were sentenced for a few years. I thought he had a longer bid and was still locked up, but when I moved in with my grandmother I saw him around the neighborhood. The rest of the guys, I can't tell you much of. I've seen them around with Jason but I didn't know any of their names." Detective Dugan kept watching Simone. He hadn't expected her to admit that she knew the guys, even after it showed up on her face that she did.

"So you're admitting you knew the ringleader. The one who set up the robbery and got the others to go along. That's interesting." Detective Dugan stared.

"The only thing me and those thugs have in common is the color of our skin and the neighborhood I happen to reside in at the moment. We are nothing alike, and if you try to connect us you will be sorely disappointed. Our social circles couldn't be more different."

"So is there anything about that day that struck you as odd?"

"You mean other than winding up with a gun to my head because a group of thugs decided to rob the bank that morning? Oh, or having these young kids kill the person standing next to me while I feared for my life? Or having a gun pressed against my head? Or watching a man get his head blown off for moving his hands? You mean aside from those events did I find anything odd about what happened yesterday? No, nothing else out of the ordinary officer. "

"Okay, Miss Banks. Look, I'm going to get your belongings." He stood up and left the room, pretending not to pay close attention to her every movement. In his line of work, he didn't come across many sisters like this one. Fine. Educated. And classy. He didn't know her entire story, but based on what he had learned so far, things weren't adding up. She still hadn't explained her high-end tastes or where she got the money to satisfy them, and he guessed that he wouldn't.

When he returned and handed her the bag enclosed in a plastic evidence bag, numbered and logged out, she took it and stood up to leave.

"Don't you want to check the contents, make sure all your stuff is still there?" he asked, used to people wanting to blame cops for any and every thing.

"The bag is worth more than anything in it," she said, removing the plastic bag and leaving it on the desk.

"And if I need to get in touch with you?" he questioned. For some reason he was in no rush to see her leave.

"Oh, is this an indirect 'don't leave town because I plan to catch you lying' threat?"

"Somebody has watched their fair share of cop shows on television." He smiled enjoying the chance to end their meeting on a more civil note. "I know you're not leaving so I'm not worried."

"Really? Because I might sell this bag and skip town," she joked, but what Simone failed to tell him was that as soon as the words were out of her mouth she wished that her words were a real possibility. She knew better than to try to sell her bag though. The bag had cost her father a grip, and the re-sale price wouldn't even be close to half of the original cost. The re-sale would probably only get her a weekend visit to Atlanta, and that wasn't nearly far enough. Not far enough at all from this nightmare.

Chapter 18

"Tiffany!"

"Yes, baby." She said calmly.

"Shit just got crazy! Real fuckin' crazy." Tariq said from the other end of the phone after he'd been waiting for Spoe for the past three hours and he hadn't answered.

"You get the bread?"

"I did, but shit went bad." He sounded worried. "My boy's fucked up," he stuttered. "I think he might even be dead."

"You sure about that?"

"Yeah, I'm sure."

Tiffany took a deep breath. "Come over to my house. You can take a shower and get you some rest. Shit going to be OK. Spoe going to call."

"No! You don't understand. They hunted him down and killed him. I know they did."

"Just calm down, baby. It will be OK. Just come over and let's put our heads together."

"Bet!"

Tariq thought for a second about calling Bunny and filling her in, but he wanted to keep hope alive. He prayed to God, Allah, and everybody else, that his soldier was being a warrior and could endure. Besides he didn't have the heart to break any kind of news to Bunny.

Tariq pulled up to Tiffany's house. Seeing her house from the road gave him solace. Maybe she was right. He did need a shower to clear his head and think.

As he made his way to the front door, he started to think how Tiffany could possibly be "the one." He thought about the years of joking Spoe on being in love and now he himself was falling.

Before he knocked on the door, Tiffany opened the door with a smile on her face which once inside of her house, quickly turned to a frown.

"What the fuc . . .?" He was caught off guard.

"Glad you could make it!" The olive skin Italian dude holding the shotgun waved him into the room, as two other well-armed men kept their pieces trained on a shocked Tariq. "So we meet again. Didn't I tell you that it was a small world?"

Well right there in the mix stood Tiffany. She was wearing the brand new, body hugging Herve Leger dress and Balenciaga leather wedge booties she had, just the other day, suckered Reek into buying after she performed some exceptional deep throat action.

"What the fuck, Tiff?" Tariq made a motion to reach for her but the man who had waved him in turned his gun on him.

"Move and I will blow your motherfuckin' brains out," he promised. Tariq backed off of Tiffany, but the look he gave her promised that he'd kill her with his bare hands.

The treacherous woman didn't bother to look remorseful. She held out her hand, flat palm facing up, to the guy who had to be the one Tiffany called 'Marky', all the while throwing shade at Tariq.

"Told you he'd come," she bragged as the guy laid a thick ass stack of hundred dollar bills on her.

"And you were right. Good job, baby!" He commended her as he laid a juicy deep tongue kiss on her.

"I'ma go into the bedroom, but don't take too long. This gangsta shit gets my juices flowing." He smacked her on her butt as she walked off.

"Bitch, you set me up!" Tariq reached out to grab her before she could leave, but the click of a gun being activated stopped him. He was fucked, and it was all his fault for believing a skanky ass stripper bitch, who made a living fuckin' random niggas for cash, would play fair with a real nigga. He looked at her in disgust.

"Hell, it ain't like you my man or nothing, so there is no need for me to stress myself protecting you. Ain't that what you said?" She laughed as she delivered the gut wrenching blow that had been a direct quote from when he had all the power just a few hours ago. "Well, get back to me when you decide if taking me seriously is an option. Oops! I understand now why that might not be happening." She swung her hips a little extra as she sashayed out of there, shooting him a dirty look over her shoulder. Tariq had always been told that his love of new pussy would one day be his downfall. He hated to think that this might be that day, but it looked that way.

"Look man, no disrespect but I'd been set up. We didn't know nothing 'bout you or your house.

"Yeah," he answered, making Tariq think that he was leaning in his direction. To be fair, it wasn't like he couldn't recognize the validity of his statements if that was all there was to it.

"While you make a very valid point, there is something important that you didn't factor in when you decided to rob me. "

Shit! Tariq thought. *This isn't for the robbery at Dino's, this is from the other night. Damn!*

"You see, I'm incredibly, how shall I say this? I'm protective about my shit. I work real hard at what I do, so when someone or people, like you idiots, believe that you don't have to work because you can just take mine, it pissed me off. You mother-fuckers are under the illusion that it's your right to steal from me? Why? Because you grew up piss poor and no one gave a shit about you? Well boo fuckin' hoo for your non-existent father and your whore of a mother who didn't make sure that the guy she was fuckin' gave a shit."

"No disrespect. It's the nature of the beast. I'm sorry man. I'll give you your money back." Tariq thought about, all the years of his and Spoe's careful hits, and now he was caught out there like an amateur.

"Are you sorry, or sorry you got caught?" He smiled at the man he had at his mercy, sadistically enjoying his fear. "It ain't fun when the rabbit got the gun, huh?"

"Nope."

"Great," he continued, a huge smile of forgiveness plas-tered on his face, as he extended his hand to Tariq, who was filled with a feeling of relief when he saw Marky smile.

The expression on his face turned sour when he felt his arm being twisted straight out of the socket. "Do I look like a fuckin' idiot to you? You motherfuckers stole from me time and time again, and neither of you had the good sense to hide it. No, you two took my money and spent it like it was water and you bitches were Niagara Falls and the shit would never stop flowing." The realization that this was the owner of the majority of stash houses they had robbed rocked him to their core.

"You might know me by my other name." He leaned forward and slowly and methodically unbuttoned his shirt, showing hints of the full body tattoo inscribed with the name Tariq had figured out moments earlier.

"I want my motherfuckin' money!" Ghostman's gravelly voice raised, sounding like a wild beast hungry for revenge. To say that Tariq was shaking in his boots, as Ghostman began to circle him, was an understatement. Considering the crimes he and Spoe had brazenly committed against him, Tariq knew Ghostman wanted payback. The way things were going, he was afraid he'd end up forced to pay with his life.

"I can give you everything we have." He figured that if he offered to pay the guy back, he would have a better chance at leniency. "Yes, everything." Tariq, understanding where this was going, made the promise knowing good and damn well that there was no way his ass was willing to go straight back to ghetto poor, which happened to be a few levels under the poverty line. These were levels so low no one ever talked about them, but they existed in all the lower socio-economic areas.

"And you think what? That it will be repayment for the pain and suffering you caused me?" Ghostman screamed, causing the heathen in front of him to start praying for God's mercy and grace.

"I think you should let me use this." One of the men held up an Uzi and pointed it at Tariq.

"Which one of you geniuses was the mastermind? You or your boy?" Ghostman got right up in Tariq's face as if daring him to lie.

"Me. I'm the one that made all the plans. I found the dope houses, cased them and made all the plans on how it was gonna go down. He just came along to help me. It wasn't his fault, it was all mine." Since Spoe was dead and dead because of him, it was the least he could do. He had not expected Ghostman's reaction.

"So you were the mastermind?"

"I said it because I'm the one that got us into this messing 'round with that bitch ho Tiffany." *Whap! Whap!* The butt of Ghostman's gun whacked Reek across the temple collapsing him to the floor in a heap.

"Where my money at? I mean the rest that you two haven't blown on bitches, cars and dumb shit."

"At our stash house," Tariq admitted, but then he started to hope like hell that Bunny was with her sisters and not laid up waiting for Spoe.

"Look, man, you not going to be able to get it without me. Let me go get it. You can send Tiffany with me. "

"That would mean I trust you to leave this room." His muscle men started to laugh at the idea that Ghostman would do anything that stupid.

"I wouldn't run. I will just go and get your money and bring it back." Reek nodded to Ghostman, a faint smile on his face like he had just figured out the key to saving his ass.

Tiffany came back into the room and made a suggestion. "Have Spoe's bitch bring the money."

Chapter 19

"Bitchesssss, I'm free! The things we take for granted."

"Not quite! You gotta abide by your house arrest rules. Only church outings and that's it."

"You know I'm going to get me some passes to the doctor and some more shit. But bitch I'm free. I will figure out the rest!"

"You gotta stop fuckin' with Deidra, you know that right?"

"I know. I can't believe that bitch left me high and dry!"

"I don't know why you surprised. The bitch been leaving us all for dead since she gave birth to us."

"Damn, I'm hungry as hell." Ginger's words elevated, competing with music, singing and cell phone pinging messages in the car. "Something about almost cutting a nigga's balls off always makes me wanna eat some down South food like barbecue hot links, chicken gizzards, and fried fish with some baked mac and cheese and collard greens."

"Nuh-uh, Gin. That all sounds good except for the chicken gizzards part. That shit sounds nasty. Who the hell eats chicken gizzards?" Bunny exclaimed.

"Bitch, I know you not tryin'a get all uppity on me. Don't act like you ain't had nastier shit in your mouth!" Ginger began making sucking noises while she pretended to be sucking on a lollipop.

"Yea, I suck dick, and what? And I bet you my man's dick taste better than some nasty ass chicken gizzards." Bunny nudged her sister playfully. There was never a dull moment when she and Ginger got together. "I'm driving, and since I'm also the one paying, I say we hit up Mama J's kitchen. All this talk about food got me fienin' fo' some fried catfish, collard greens, and potato salad," Bunny said, starting to salivate thinking about how good that food would be.

"Me-Ma can cook you that shit at home. Besides, why you wanna drive this nice-ass car up into that hood. We don't need to test our luck to see if we can get outta another place alive in one day," Ginger shrieked, ready to make her case until both of them were interrupted by their sister's screams.

"Oh, lord! Oh, lord!" Tallhya cried from the back seat. Her body wracked with sobs as she screamed out in pain like a damn lamb brought to slaughter. Bunny and Ginger jumped in their seats. They had completely forgotten that Tallhya was sitting in the back seat. She hadn't been the same since the other day at the funeral home. This whole time she had been in a zombie-like state. Now it was as if she was coming out of her trance and finally reacting to what had happened.

"No, Lord, no!" she hollered. A look passed between Bunny and Ginger as they drew visual straws to choose which one would be the first to deliver the 'shut the fuck up' sermon to their bereaved sibling.

"Aint like that nigga died or nothing." It was Ginger that started first. "Hell, I never liked his selfish ass no way. None of us did." She sure wasn't lying, but Tallhya was way beyond the point of being able to be reasoned with, especially about the trifling piece of shit she called a husband. All her screaming and hollering had begun to grate on her sisters' nerves and Bunny was a second away from completely losing her shit.

"Tale? Babe, you're gonna be all right." Bunny spoke in the sweetest tone. It was a tone she usually reserved for her man, not one of her siblings, but as bad as Tallhya was right now, she needed to calm her sister down. It was hard for Bunny to sympathize with Tallhya, though. Bunny didn't play that victim role and had no time for crying over no man, especially not one who had the bad taste to cheat with someone else and act like it wasn't his fault. Walter would have been buried alive if it were up to Bunny.

"Hell, no. I'm not gonna be all right," Tallhya finally answered back, flinging her tears and sadness all over the car interior. All this emotional drama had started to affect Ginger's attitude. "How could he do that to me?" Tallhya's voice wailed on.

"That motherfucker ain't thought about nobody 'cept his self. Shit, I bet he ain't never even gone down on you." Ginger snapped her fingers as she rolled her eyes upwards at the very idea that any man would get the chance to leave her unsatisfied. Ginger loved her sister, but saw this whole episode as plain ole stupidity. She had to stop herself from saying as much. "You need to go home and burn all this nigga's shit. Make a great big bonfire in the front yard on some *Waiting to Exhale* type level. I promise you, seeing that shit go up in flames will make you feel better."

"He's my everything. What is my life without him?" Tallhya squealed and kept at it, digging the hole of self-pity a little bit deeper with every sob.

"And that big ole butt girl he had all over him? Did yo' see that heifer?"

"Yes I saw her, and the truth of the matter is, she was pretty and way better looking than me."

"No the hell she wasn't." Ginger said. "That bitch was plastic as these damn titties I bought. That hoe bought all that shit."

"Yes, probably with my money."

"That's why you gotta look out for yourself. Stop giving them niggas yo' money. They don't deserve shit."

"And if a ho stand by and let a man take money from another woman, that ho got a whole other set of issues. I don't care how much of a bad bitch she may appear to be on the outside, but she got low self-esteem to accept that kind of shit."

"You right about that," Tallhya had to agree. "And besides, her breath was stinking, talking about she's Walter's fiancé."

Ginger laughed at Tallhya's weak attempt at badmouthing Walter's mistress. Tallhya had always been the softest out of the four sisters. In school, Bunny had to stick up for her sister, because she was always being taken advantage of by the other kids. She never cursed or talked bad about anyone, so to hear her try to badmouth someone was almost comical.

Ginger busted out laughing again, giving Bunny a high five.

"I'm glad you two find my tragedy so amusing," Tallhya said.

"Oh, Tale," Bunny laughed. "Please don't play the woe-is-me card. This is not a tragedy. You were too good for Walter and you know it. That no-good cheating liar don't deserve you. I know you love him and you're hurting right now, but you are better off without him," Bunny said, reaching in the back to grab her heartbroken sister's hand.

"Amen to that!" Ginger exclaimed, "Now can I get a halle-lujah?" she went on in her best preacher impersonation. She raised her hands as if she was praising in a church. She looked over at Bunny who was giving her the 'time to get serious' look. "Okay, for real though. Walter was selfish and his ass was basically broke, so I don't get it."

"I love him," Tallhya screeched, throwing herself on the mercy of the seat, bucking back and forth, cradling her sides as she droned on.

"Look sis, when you done with all this crying and carrying on, you need to figure out a way to make his ass pay for betray-ing you," Bunny said. She was starting to lose patience for Tallhya's victim bullshit. She couldn't imagine loving a man who treated her the way that she had observed Walter treat-ing her sister. As much as she didn't believe in the whole mod-ern day self-esteem crisis, the girl needed some serious charge by the hour help. She thought about how lucky she had been to find a man like Spoe, who committed himself on the same deep level to Bunny as she did to him. Not to get it twisted, Bunny saw herself as wholly incapable of putting up with any bullshit from anybody, dick or no dick, including Spoe. He didn't expect her to deal with bullshit from him either. "You hear me Tal? This feeling sorry for choosing a loser bullshit has to stop," she admonished her little sister. What Bunny didn't get was how much she sounded like Deidra, who had no patience when it came to tears or neediness. Bunny wished that Simone was with them, because of the four sisters, she was the only one who possessed real compassion and under-standing in emotional situations like this one. Right now, with Tallhya looking and acting so vulnerable, she knew Simone would know how to handle it. It seemed that what her sister needed was to be able to break down and let it all out without being chastised for it, but Ginger and Bunny weren't built for that sentimental stuff. They weren't kumbaya hug-it-out kind of girls. They had tough skin and even tougher hearts. Bunny thought about calling Me-Ma and filling her in on everything that had happened. She decided against it, because as sweet

as her grandmother was, she was very protective of her granddaughters. Bunny was almost positive if she called Me-Ma she
would go Government Grade A Ham on Walter and even the
good Lord couldn't save him.

"You don't understand. I'm not lucky like you are when it
comes to men. I have to take what I can get, and Walter is the
best I ever had," their jilted sister swore through her tears,
sounding like a crazy bitch.

"Don't you ever get tired of accepting so little from the men
in your life? For a big girl, you almost as pretty as my fine ass.
If you thought a little more of yourself you'd bring the men
running." Ginger, like Simone and Bunny didn't understand
why Tallhya allowed a steady stream of losers into her life.
Me-Ma used to say that she had a magnet attraction to Mr.
Wrong. She'd even thought that demanding Walter commit to
her in marriage would guarantee her loser streak would come
to an end, but clearly it didn't.

"Look, honestly, if you feel that way because you are fat,
then lose some weight. Carry your ass to the gym. Watch what
you eat. Go to see a nutritionist and push away from the table."
Ginger knew it hurt, but hell, the truth hurts and some things
need to be said.

Bunny hit Ginger, "Now that wasn't nice, you fuckin' tran-
nie! But for real, Tallya, you are pretty. If you don't like what
you see in the mirror, you can do something about it."

Just at that moment, the phone rang, and Bunny's phone
blew up over the bluetooth. She switched it to her headpiece
when she saw that it was her man Spoe calling from Tariq's
phone. Her sisters were so nosy, but Bunny would not allow
them to live vicariously through tales of her good fortune.
"Ya'll need to shut the hell up so I can hear my bae." Lord why
did she say that? All it did was remind Tallhya of her new
single reality and the boohooing escalated to a whole other
level.

"Bitch, shut up," Bunny snapped at her sister, who was too
far gone to listen.

"Lord why you have to say that to her?" Ginger whispered
at Bunny, then whipped her head around at the hot mess

her sister had collapsed into. Bunny hit the button on her earpiece and tried to make sense of what Tariq was saying. She couldn't really understand what he was saying, because his voice was cutting in and out, but what she could hear was the panic in his voice.

"Shut the fuck up," Bunny screamed, her emotions coming apart at the seams, throwing her sisters off. She had gone from normal to apoplectic, her tone strong enough to quiet Tallhya's wailing.

"Tariq, what did you say?" Bunny said into the phone as she grew intensely focused trying to listen to her man's homeboy. But Tariq's frazzled tone triggered an alarm bell deep inside of her that damn near rocked her to the core. Bunny could tell that something was off. He didn't sound like the man she had watched leave her house to head off to work with her boo. He sounded spooked, giving her an eerie premonition that she tried to shake off as she struggled to hear what he needed from her. She pulled into a parking lot and was finally able to hear him clearly, but what he kept saying wasn't making much sense.

Chapter 20

Me-Ma rode the elevator to the third floor just like it had been explained to her on the telephone. When she got off, she stood facing the glass and marble entryway of the law office of Callahan, Crosby and White. The senior Mrs. Banks didn't normally find herself in places like this and she had to admit, she felt a bit out of place. Me-Ma's first thought was if she had dressed nicely enough for the meeting. Her second, and the most important, was how much would this whole thing cost?

"May I help you ma'am?" a red headed receptionist seated behind the desk looked up to greet her before fielding more phone calls.

"Yes, I'm here to see a Lauryn Shelton," Me-Ma informed the young woman, "I have an appointment"

"Certainly ma'am. Can I have your name please?" the friendly receptionist asked.

"Mrs. Banks" Me-Ma replied.

"Hello, Mrs. Banks. Miss Shelton will be with you in a moment. In the meantime, can I get you some coffee, tea or another beverage while you wait?" the woman asked. Though she was actually thirsty, Mrs. Banks didn't want to waste time sipping on a drink when she came to handle important business. Not to mention that this woman charged by the hour, and how was she to know that hour didn't officially begin until she saw that lawyer.

"No. I would like to see Miss Shelton. I don't have time to waste in here and I am certainly not going to be getting any younger the longer this takes." Me-Ma planted herself at that desk. Her expression told the woman everything she needed to know. As she called Lauryn she also sent her a quick email to let her know that keeping this particular person waiting didn't seem like the best idea. Just as Me-Ma had made up her mind to go off on a tangent, the door flung open and there stood Lauryn Shelton, looking just like her mother and grandmother. *Poor thing*, Me-Ma thought.

"Mrs. Banks, Reverend Street told me to take very good care of you." Lauryn grinned up at Me-Ma who couldn't help wishing that God had been a little kinder to that young lady when it came time to hand out the looks, particularly when it came to that man-size nose fighting for space on her tiny face. Oh, well, at least she was smart enough to have focused on the things she could do something about, like her career.

Miss Shelton wasn't completely unattractive. It's just that her eyes were set too close together and the size and shape appeared better suited to a more masculine profile, but she seemed nice, and that went a long way in life, at least that's how Me-Ma thought. By the time she left that office having handled all her legal issues, Mrs. Banks felt relieved that her daughter and all four of her granddaughters would be provided for exactly as she wanted after she shuffled off the mortal coil.

"Mama," Deidra stood up from her perch on the porch as her mother stepped out of a freshly painted Lincoln town car. Miss Shelton had insisted on having the company driver bring Me-Ma home after they finished with her appointment. Me-Ma had originally planned on taking the bus back, but darkness had fallen by the time they finished with all the paperwork. It had taken a lot longer than she expected to cover all the things she needed to in her will. Normally these things were handled in stages, but Me-Ma let Lauryn Shelton know that she didn't plan on wasting any more time coming back and forth for that hourly wage. She wanted to take care of everything in one day. Considering how dark it was when they finished, Me-Ma agreed to the ride home after Miss Shelton reassured her that she wouldn't be billed for it.

"Where you coming from?" her daughter questioned, as if their roles were reversed and it was Deidra and not Me-Ma who was the mother. Her daughter grew immediately suspicious, especially because everybody knew that Mrs. Banks would never spring for the luxury of a car service.

"Oh, nothing. I was just visiting one of the gals from church and she sent me home in that thing." Her mother waved it off as if it was nothing. Me-Ma didn't feel guilty about her little fib. After all it wasn't exactly a lie. It was closer to the truth than a lot of other things she could have said. Besides, Mrs. Banks didn't see how it would be any of Deidra's business for her to have to explain her whereabouts to her daughter.

"Uh, huh," she muttered, not that great at pretending to feign interest in the affairs of others, even her own mother or children.

"I wish I knew you were coming. I would have cooked a big meal and I would have told the girls. Right now I have no idea where they are for me to tell them you're out here." Me-Ma unlocked the door to let her only daughter inside. "If you're hungry I can fix you something quick to eat. It won't take too long, and from the way you're looking you need to eat something."

"I wish, mama, but I can't stay too long. Lenny is waiting for me," Deidra insisted. This Lenny happened to be the new guy. Me-Ma wasn't sure he'd last with her daughter long enough for them to meet. Her daughter never seemed to have a shortage of suitors, but sometimes the rotation happened so close together that she didn't have much time to get comfortable with the last person.

"This Lenny, is he a good man? Is he nice to you? Treat you good?" her mother hovered and couldn't help but ask twenty questions, still trying to form a stronger bond than the one that broke all those years ago.

"He's great. But he's having a hard time lately. The economy in this climate is hard on Black men." Deidra sounded like she was reading off of a political cheat sheet. She followed her mother into the kitchen and watched as she began to remove pots from the refrigerator and place them on the stove.

"Mama! What are you doing? I told you I can't stay and eat!" Deidra interrupted her mother as she excitedly began to prepare a meal to feed her daughter.

"Yes, baby girl," Me-Ma used the pet name her husband had coined shortly after Deidra had come home from the hospital. "I'ma have this food on the table before you know it." Her mother jumped the gun, fighting to keep her daughter there at least until her grandkids returned. If she had been right about Tallhya's Walter being the same one from the newspaper, Tallhya would surely need her mother, and it would be nice if, for once, it could be the one who brought her into this world.

"I don't have time to eat. I got to go and meet Len," Deidra insisted, becoming anxious as she paced the length of the kitchen floor. "See, we were trying to get enough money together to turn our luck around." Her mother froze in her spot as she realized that this visit mirrored all the others and nothing about it was personal. Deidra only showed up when she needed something, and no matter how much Me-Ma wanted to think otherwise, it always proved to be the case. She needed to borrow money; money that she would never pay back, even though she insisted that it was just a loan. Deidra was always full of empty promises. Once again, money proved to be the only reason her daughter ever bothered to show up.

"The girls are doing good by the way," Me-Ma said, ignoring Deidra's request for money. "Well, not really, actually. They all going through stuff, heavy stuff. They sure could use a bit more of your time De, especially Simone. Don't know if you heard but she had just gotten a job working at the bank when it got robbed the other day. Scared the poor girl half to death. She ain't been back to work since and I'm not so sure she should go back." The whole time Me-Ma talked, Deidra began to pace. If not pacing, she was fidgeting with her hands. She wasn't about the pressure to be nothing to nobody, and her mother trying to make her feel guilty had actually started to annoy the fuck out of her. See, she thought, *that's why I don't come up in here. People always wanting something from me.* Of course the irony of her being there skipped right over her head.

"I don't see how Miss Priss has any choice." Deidra sucked her teeth just thinking about her oldest daughter who ain't never had to do nothing she didn't want to, thanks to that father of hers.

"Please, won't you wait and talk to her." Me-Ma kept trying to get her hard-hearted daughter to spend more time with her own girls. She knew that they were all grown but she knew that they still needed a mother, even one as selfish and narcissistic as Deidra.

"Humh! She better keep that job so she can meet a rich man whose gonna take care of her. That's what's wrong with that girl. Sisi ain't thinking about that. She already hit the lottery with Simon for a father. Hell, if his ass had been as generous to me as he was with her, I would'a stayed with him." Deidra thought about Simon always coming home from his grass fertilizer business with dirt under his nails. She liked her men pretty, decked out in fine clothes and she liked them to take her places. All he could talk about was building his business. Those suckers always talk about getting that money, and she didn't have any reason to believe he'd strike it rich any more than the others who talked a big game to get into her pants.

"He really did love that girl. Shame he's gone." Me-Ma shook her head.

"I would'a thought she'd hit the jackpot when he died. I guess he wasn't as in love with his child as we all thought." Deidra laughed real nasty and petty. You could feel the jealousy shooting out of her. "Didn't leave his only child one damn iron dime. Now she back sucking on your tit, just another mouth to feed." Deidra shook her head at the pure disappointment of her daughter's situation. When she heard that Simon passed she had expected to get in on some of Simone's inheritance, but that proved to be one more damn disappointment. She had always warned these girls that you can't trust none of these men, but they all had rocks between their ears.

"No, he loved that girl. It was that wife who stole that child's money."

"Whatever," Deidra snapped. She had lost all interest in talking about this nonsense. She had to address her own needs and get moving. She went over to her mother and snuggled her head into the crook of her neck the way she'd done since she was little. "Mama, I need you to loan me some money. Just till I can get on my feet." Me-Ma smiled like the thought of giving her child and some anonymous man money one more time didn't break her heart. That smile had to be the only thing standing between her and tears streaming down her face. But just because she always said yes didn't mean she wasn't planning on getting something out of it for herself.

"Baby girl, you wanna go with us to church this Sunday? It would mean so much to me. I can give you some money today and more after the service. That way I'd have time to get to the bank." Me-Ma knew that her daughter's Achilles heel was money. She didn't care what it took, but she was praying that one visit with the Lord would turn her daughter's life around. She'd seen God work plenty of miracles, and as long as she lived she would always pray for the deliverance of her only child.

"Sure mama, I will go with you to church. Maybe I can get Len to come with me. You'd really like him." Deidra's lie swelled up her mother's hope, but in actuality all she wanted was to get that money and get her ass up out of there. Being in that house riled up feelings of discomfort and sadness, emotions Deidra spent her life running from man to man to avoid. Before her father's death, her entire identity had been being her daddy's girl. The moment she discovered her father had another daughter it smashed her world into tiny pieces and left her on a search that would prove elusive. All she wanted was a man she could both love and trust.

"Let me go and get you that." Me-Ma stopped with the pots and went into the living room where she stashed her envelope of cash. Simone was the only one who knew exactly where she kept it, tucked right there in the family bible. Not the one she read every day, that one never left her side. This one had all the names and birthdays of family members written in it. Me-Ma clutched the envelope to her chest as she placed the bible back on the shelf. When she turned, there was Deidra standing in the doorway, watching her.

"Mommy, I really appreciate your help. You know I wouldn't bother you if I didn't need it. Like I said, it's just till we can get on our feet." Whether she realized it or not, Deidra said the same exact thing every time she came begging for money. The last time was less than a month ago, but poor Me-Ma was always just happy to see her daughter. It almost didn't matter to her that the visit was financially motivated.

She opened the envelope stuffed with cash and counted out five hundred dollar bills and handed them to her daughter, who balled them up and stuffed them in her purse. Of course, she kept her eyes on that envelope as her mother returned it to its place in the bible, noticing how stuffed it was with cash. She couldn't believe how cheap her mother was, being she had all that money on her. "I know you got to go but I really wish you could stay and visit to see your girls." Now, a second ago she might have been planning to run out that door once that money hit her hot little hands. Now it seemed her daughter had another plan.

"You know what, that sounds good." Deidra led her mother back into the kitchen. "You want me to help you with anything? Why don't you take those shoes off and go put on your house slippers. Make yourself comfortable mama." The syrupy thickness she put on display for her mother should have made her suspicious, but Me-Ma, like a lot of parents of failure-to-launch children, chose to be blind to most of her daughter's faults. She still blamed all Deidra's problems on her husbands' duplicity. Never ever did she put the fault squarely where it belonged.

"Soon as I get back I'ma cook you those turkey legs you like so much," her mother offered, feeling full of love as she went into her bedroom to change into her housecoat and slippers.

No sooner had she left, Deidra flew into the living room to retrieve the rest of her mother's money. Of course she hadn't expected the door to fling open and for her two youngest daughters to interrupt her plan.

"Mommy!" Tallhya shrieked, dried mascara-streaked tearstains running down her face. At the unexpected sight of her mostly absentee parent, Tallhya went flying toward her. She missed the look of annoyance on Deidra's face. Had she seen it in her current state it wouldn't have stopped her daughter from throwing her arms around her mother's neck and holding on for dear life. The sobs came back in full force.

"Girl, you 'bout to knock me down with all that. Ain't like you skinny like your brother." She rolled her eyes at Ginger, making a mental note to keep him away from Len. *You just never know with these men,* is how she always thought.

"But you don't know what just happened," Tallhya tried to explain. "Walter used me mama. He has another woman." The blubbering and water works caused their mother to take a step backward. She was already upset that their presence had thwarted her plan, and now all this crying and touching her. She wasn't about that at all, 'cause unless she and the other person were fuckin', she didn't see any point in any kind of physical connection.

"And unless you're blind and didn't notice the Dolce skirt and Red Bottom pumps and this fabulous long weave honey, then you on something else, 'cause ain't no kind a man here." Ginger ran her hands up and down her body to punctuate her point, "This is all woman, all the time, 'cause I am strictly dickly." She poked out her lips and swiveled her hips in front of her mother rolling her eyes up toward the sky.

"Look Miss Thang, I didn't give birth to no fourth girl. You have a penis and that's to remind you that you are not female. So if you wanna be a little sissy that's on you and not nothing I did, so don't go blaming me."

"'Course it ain't. You would have had to be here raising me like a mother to know what the hell I am." Ginger's words stung Deidra, but she was too proud and stubborn to let anyone know it, let alone show it.

"You need to respect me. I gave your ass life instead of getting you scraped out of me like I started to do. Don't make me sorry that I didn't." Deidra's harsh words did exactly what she intended. They caused Ginger immediate and irreparable emotional damage. If you caused Deidra the slightest pain, she would maim you permanently if she could. Her scorpion stinger was always ready to strike.

Ginger looked from Deidra to Tallhya, whose reaction to her mother's viciousness was to comfort her little sister. A full two years older than Ginger, Tallhya had more time to grow used to the vicious tornado that was their mother.

"She didn't mean it." Tallhya tried to make an excuse for Deidra, but the damage was already done. Ginger took off for her bedroom with her sister on her heels. Finally, left alone in the living room, Deidra hurriedly grabbed the envelope and ran out of the house. All Deidra cared about as she stepped outside had to do with the loot she had shoved into her purse. Len would be so happy when she showed him what she had gotten.

Me-Ma entered the living room, excited to talk a little more with her daughter. Instead she found herself standing alone. Her eyes immediately went from the space where she kept the bible to the table where it now sat, empty and open.

"I can do all things through Christ, which strengthen me. I can do all things through Christ, which strengthen me. Yes, Jesus, yes. And though I walk through the valley of the shadow of death, I shall fear no evil for thou art with me."

"Me-Ma." Simone entered a short time later, assessed the situation, and helped her grandmother up from her knees where she had been praying. "You all right?"

"Your mother just left." Me-Ma threw her arms around Simone before she could finish, but they both knew exactly what that meant.

Chapter 21

"Everything?" Bunny said wanting to phone Tariq back and confirm the words he had just spoken, because this shit sounded crazy. However, nothing about his tone or words led her to believe he was in the right circumstance to answer her call.

The words kept ringing on and on and on in her head. *They got us, bring all the cash, everything, or they going to kill us.*

The thought of something happening to Spoe would literally kill her. He was everything. Her heart beat because of him.

She ripped through their house, locating the piles of money in all his hiding places. When she was done she had at least a million dollars in cash, money neither of them ever thought they'd have to part with. The memory of the sound of Tariq's voice scared her so shitless she would gladly hand all this cash over and more, just to have Spoe safe at home. In the kitchen, she located the extra set of keys to Tariq's pad, a place she'd actually found for him on the other side of town. Just as she was leaving Tariq's place and wiping out his stash her phone rang.

"Hello." Tariq's number came up on her Bluetooth. She felt relieved to see him calling her back.

"Bunny? Or is it Bunny rabbit? The unfamiliar voice on the other end of the phone snickered to himself, or whoever thought that shit was funny, on the other end. "Tick-fuckin'-tock, you wanna see your man any time soon?" he warned her, full of bravado. Whoever this person was who had her man, she already hated him, but if she possessed anything it was street smarts.

"My friends and family call me Bunny," she snapped, having no interest in pretending to be nice. She figured that she would give this guy the money and then she, Spoe, and Tariq would be on their way.

"Wow! So it's like that? Well I just have one question for you little Bunny rabbit. Where the fuck are you with my goddam money?" he hollered into the phone. The sheer magnitude of his anger came over loud and clear. It threw the normally composed Bunny into a new level of panic.

"I'm on my way. First I had to drop my sisters off and then I had to go to two places on the opposite side of town," she explained.

"You want to see your boyfriend, bae, man, daddy whatever the fuck you people call each other, I suggest you get your ass here right now! You hear me bitch?" He had Bunny all twisted until the moment he called her a bitch. Unlike a lot of women who had been worn down by the overuse of the word in rap songs and popular culture and found it acceptable, she didn't play with any form of being called out of her name.

"I ain't no female dog, so don't call me one," she shot out, getting ready to go ham on him for that shit. Instead of Ghostman coming for her, he actually found her rage funny and burst out into hysterical laughter.

"I'm glad you find me so funny," Bunny stated dryly.

He wasn't laughing at what she said. What he found so hilarious had more to do with how most people treated him. Since his name alone instilled fear everywhere he went, people normally kissed his ass and knew to be afraid when they saw him. To hear her talk to him like that was pretty funny to him.

"Guess I needed a good laugh. I'm giving you twenty minutes to get your ass over here." Bunny glanced down at the *Waze* app on her phone and saw that her estimated arrival time was less than ten minutes.

"See you then," she said, then hung up, noticing her hands were shaking like she had Parkinson's disease or something. She had to slap the steering wheel real hard to stop them from moving like that. Her thoughts drifted back to Spoe. She hoped he wouldn't be upset with her for going against his wishes. He always told her that if he got caught she was supposed to take the money and run as far away as possible. She was supposed to take her passport and leave the country, but she couldn't. She had to try and rescue him, even if it meant walking into a dangerous situation without knowing if either of them would make it out alive.

"I'm Bunny," she told the high class ho who answered the door. Yeah, she had a full head of natural hair that cascaded down her back, and her eyebrows were on fleek, but since she was here it meant they were enemies.

"Umph!" She ran her eyes over Bunny's velour sweat suit and her Louis handbag then snarled at her, but smiled at the duffle bag she was carrying.

"Then you better run your ass upstairs, 'cause Ghostman don't like to be kept waiting." Bunny swore that she saw that girl coming outta Tariq's apartment building a few weeks ago, but maybe she was wrong. She'd have to ask him, she thought as she raced up the stairs. As she stepped inside, three armed men were passing a joint between them.

"Baby!" Bunny dropped the bags loaded down with money onto the floor. She saw Tariq in the corner tied up. He had a look of desperation in his eyes.

"Where is Spoe?"

"Awe, she came for her man. Ain't black love beautiful?" Ghostman joked.

"You got your money. Where's Spoe? Let them go."

He laughed.

"I'm sorry, sis." Tariq said with tears in his eyes. He started to try to fill Bunny in, but Ghostman shut him up by turning his gun on Reek. He shoot Reek in the chest, killing him with one shot, spattering blood all over the room.

Bunny screamed, "Noooooo!" Her heart dropped into her stomach as she stumbled. She was about to pass out from the shock of witnessing the murder of her husband's best friend.

"Why did you have to kill Reek?" she screamed at Ghostman "And where is Spoe?"

"These motherfuckers stole from me, and for all I know you could be the ring leader. Your ass could get the next bullet out of this piece." He waved his gun at her, making the other two men laugh.

"Damn," one of his goons interjected, "That looks like some good pussy she hiding under those baggy-ass pants." Bunny turned and gave him the finger, not caring one fuck that he held a weapon capable of taking her out in one shot. These weren't those normal everyday niggas she was used to dealing with, the ones who talked a good game. These guys didn't care one bit that she looked fuckable. They would just shoot her without hesitating.

Ghostman motioned to one of his men to pick up the bag Bunny had dropped on the floor and bring it to him. He opened it up and checked the stacks. He had to play along.

"And why should I let him live?" Ghostman's sadistic tendencies were fully exposed.

"Please, please don't hurt him," she screamed.

"He's already dead."

Bunny dropped to the floor. Her tears came like a gusher. "You fuckin' monster! You had your money. You had your money." Her words rang out falling onto ears that didn't give two shits. Ghostman was a businessman, and killing the men that stole from him was business.

"Your man stole from me! You think he should have lived to what? Steal from me again? You think I'm fuckin' stupid?"

"Fuck you! Fuck all of you!" she screamed. "How could you?"

"Fuck me? Fuck me?" He reached over and snatched Bunny up off the floor. "If I wanted, I could bend you ass over that table and fuck the shit out of you, then pass you over to these two. They don't get that much pussy, so you can see how that would appeal to them."

"Yeah, I want some of that," the most vocal of the gunmen chimed in. Thoughts of a naked Bunny fighting and struggling while he fucked her was giving him a hard on.

It wasn't fear that kept her from telling him off. Her eyes blazed at him, but Bunny didn't speak. She couldn't. Her grief had taken absolute and total control, rendering her momentarily mute. There was no telling what she would do or say now that he had destroyed her life.

"I may let you off this time, but that would mean you never mutter my name or tell anyone what went down in this room. If you do, you should know that I will find you and let these men do whatever they want to you and that hot little body before they kill you. Do you understand?" A look passed between Ghostman and Bunny.

"Yes."

"I'm not so sure you do." He sneered, moving close to her, raising the gun to meet her temple. "Now here is where shit can get a little sticky. I have to decide whether I should allow you to leave, or if I should let you experience the same ending as this motherfucker here."

Chapter 22

"Somebody get that!" Me-Ma stuck her head out of her bedroom door and hollered over the sounds of the crooning negros in heat playing on one of those speakers Tallhya plugged her iPhone into. That child had been in a bipolar state for a while now; tears one minute, and the next laughing at some funny memory between her and that no good devil of a husband she married. She heard the sound of clopping down the stairs. No doubt it had to be Ginger. She probably had on some ridiculous platform shoes. Ginger loved the way heels accentuated her shapely calves and long legs.

"What?" Ginger gave the messenger the once over. She quickly assessed that he was neither rich nor packing any heat in his pants, which accounted for her wanting him to disappear as quickly as possible.

"Uhm, uhm," the middle aged brother got all tongue twisted staring up at Ginger. Like so many men, he too acted as if he could possibly catch the transgenderitis just from standing too close. If he only knew that he was far from her type. All the begging in six counties couldn't buy him any time with Ginger, so he sure didn't need to worry about her getting too close. That was not going to happen. "I'm looking for a Tall hiy aaa," he blurted out all wrong. Like every other person forced to read his sister's name before they hear it out loud, he mispronounced it.

"She's upstairs. You can give it to me." Ginger reached out for the manila envelope but the messenger snatched it out of her reach, shaking his head.

"She's the only one I can give this to."

"You wait right here, and don't you try and steal nothing," Ginger snapped before darting up the stairs. She slammed open the door to the bedroom that used to belong to Tallhya and Walter, where her sister now lay in a heap crying with some Mariah Carey song playing. Shit had gone from bad to worse.

"Girl you want your delivery you better come and sign for it. Tal, get your ass to the door then you can come right back to this." Ginger hustled her sister out of the room and down the stairs.

"Are you Tall-hiy-aaa?"

"I'm Tallhya," she stuck out her hand. She couldn't be bothered tryin'a explain to someone she would never meet again how to pronounce out her name. All she wanted was for this person to hand over whatever and to go away. She wasn't done crying and feeling sorry for herself so this interruption was just that, another damn interruption. With all the bodies running around that house, her goal of crying herself silly and wallowing in self-pity felt like an impossible task. Ginger came up behind her as the messenger presented her with a clipboard to sign. Once she had finished, he handed over the envelope along with something unexpected.

"You've been served," he blurted out and then ran to his car and took off. The man had experienced one too many irate customers to take any chances, especially since most of the crazies were Black and Latino women. When they got served papers, they reached levels of insanity no man should ever have to deal with. You'd think they'd had no damn idea they were coming.

She tore open the envelope as she closed the door. Ginger stood there trying to figure out the best way to ask for a loan without appearing insensitive.

"Petition for divorce!" She read the top of the legal document in shock. It hadn't occurred to her that this was coming, even after she hadn't heard one word from Walter.

"Girl, you better make sure that motherfucker don't try and take your money. Get your ass to that bank and get your money. I don't trust that motherfucker one bit!"

Now she may have been madly in love and grieving, but Tallhya wasn't stupid. She got herself together and went over to that bank to handle her business. Walter had made a fool of her and she'd be damned if she were going to allow him to continue to do so.

***

"What? What? That is impossible," Tallhya screamed at the bank teller who delivered the bad news. Apparently ole Walter had cleaned out all their bank accounts. A couple of months ago she had added his name onto her accounts in case of an emergency. He'd never so much as touched a dollar and now he had up and taken every single dime she had to her name. Tallhya walked back to her car and just stared at the bank statement the teller printed for her. She kept looking at the zeroes where it said BALANCE. She was overcome with emotions of betrayal. The more she sat there and thought about what Walter had done to her, the more she felt her heart shifting. God knows how long Tallhya sat in her car in that bank parking lot, but when she finally drove home, it was as if a whole new woman was in the driver's seat. A strong woman. A scorned woman. Most importantly, she was a woman with a plan. Before she put her plan into action, she needed to go home and change. She needed a new look to go with her new attitude.

Walter worked at a shipping warehouse over in the industrial part of town. She'd brought him lunch enough times that the guard waved her in as she walked into the building. Tallhya didn't notice that his reason had do with the fact that the security guard was obsessed with watching her scrumptious ass as she walked past him.

"Hi, I'm here to see Walter Walker." The receptionist knew Tallhya by name and picked up the phone.

"Let me tell him that you're here."

"No," Tallhya panicked, then smiled sweetly. "Why don't you let me surprise him?" She winked at the receptionist like they were coconspirators. The woman had grown so bored with the daily monotony that she was excited at the idea of helping out another big girl like herself.

Giving thanks to the Lord for lighting her way, as Me-Ma reminded her earlier, Tallhya went back to Walter's office hell bent on accomplishing what she set out to do. When she didn't find him there she closed the door, sat down in his seat and waited. Sure enough, a few minutes later who should come sauntering in, with not a gotdam care in the world, but her no good husband. The panicked expression on his face shifted to annoyance because this motherfucker was used to ruling over Tallhya.

"What are you doing in my office?" he snarled at her, but unlike the old Tallhya who jumped at his every command, the ugliness of his reaction did nothing to deter her from her focus. She snapped open her extra-large purse and pushed the divorce papers and her bank statements across the table at him.

"This is what the hell I'm doing here. You stole my money? Wasn't it enough that you made a gotdam fool of me? I thought you loved me. I thought you meant your vows when we got married. How could you do this to me?"

"You don't have any money. That's not my problem! Now get the fuck out of my office. Don't you ever show up at my job again, not if you know what is good for you," he threatened. Even after seeing him with that woman, the divorce papers, and him stealing her money, Tallhya still couldn't believe that this person standing in front of her was treating her this way. She couldn't believe this was the same man that she had been so madly in love with just days ago.

"Walter you can't do this. I want my money."

"I done told you that is my money. I have your signature on a document to prove it. Your dumb ass legally signed everything over to me without even realizing it," he smirked. Walter felt real pleased with how well his plan to con Tallhya out of everything had worked. He and Pamela had big plans with that money as soon as he got untangled from this woman.

"You motherfucker." Her arms began to pound into him and she became a madwoman.

"Bitch, you better remember those special little home movies we made, or shall I say that I made when I filmed you sucking my dick, eating out my ass, taking my cum in your face and doing a whole lot of other things. So unless you want everybody in your grandmother's congregation to get a look at your dick sucking skills, you will walk the fuck out of here and never come back. Do you hear me?"

"Yes," her voice squeaked as the realization hit Tallhya that she really had just lost everything. Just like that, her newfound attitude had been torn down to nothing.

Chapter 23

Tallhya's eyes rolled back in her head, not in the praising God kind of way, but in a pissed the hell off to be out of bed this early in the morning when my life is a hot mess and ain't nothing God can do to fix it, kind of way. She had been dragged up into Faith and Hope Ministry one time too many with the promise of grace and salvation. Since nothing she prayed for ever happened, she didn't see any point believing in this mess anymore. But here she sat bright and early in the front row with the unofficial Mayor of this sanctuary, the only person who could convince her to drag her butt up in here, Me-Ma Banks. As much as they tried to be supportive, Me-Ma and Simone were sick to death of Tallhya's crying and carrying on like she had lost something precious. In their estimation, the only thing she lost amounted to unnecessary dead weight.

"Thank you, Jesus! Can you all say, thank you, Jesus!" shouted Pastor Cassius, resplendent in his loud-ass royal blue suit. He danced up and down the stage, shouting and praising like something right out of an old fashioned revival. His loyal flock was jumping up and down, shouting out thank you Jesus like they had just won the Virginia State lottery, and not just another chance to line the Pastor's fattening pockets. Simone sat on the opposite side of their grandmother. She also did not want to be there, but in her defense she had a stronger faith than any of her sisters. She knew that as suspicious as she was of Pastor Cassius, she would glean at least one take-away from the sermon, even if the Reverend made her uncomfortable.

"Good Lord." Ginger's heels click clacked down the aisle as she sashayed her way to the pew where her grandmother sat every single Sunday. Heads turned almost on cue, but like all the Banks girls, she just chalked it up to her exceptional good looks and massive sex appeal. Of course there had been a time, not too long ago, when Ginger used Sunday service to procure her lovers. She had a particular fondness for other people's mates. She preferred married men and men with money, preferably a lot of it. Ginger always joked that she could write the book on the perfect places to meet the down low brothers in the closeted community, and church reigned consistently on the top of her list. Normally though, church and Ginger were not exactly on friendly terms. If it hadn't been for Pastor Street being fine as hell, and straight, at least on the surface, she would have stayed her ass in her bed. Her friends had been whispering about the good Reverend for a while, so it made Ginger curious enough to find out if she could take the man of God for a spin. Plus, she would never admit to it, but her tough act disintegrated when one of her sisters were hurt. If being in church could make them feel better, then so be it. Just don't blame her if she used it as an opportunity to get laid. She slipped in the pew next to her family and paid very close attention to the sermon.

While Cassius led his sermon, Ginger spent that entire time imagining him naked and on his knees servicing her cause. She was a real feminist and preferred to get hers first. The only thing that annoyed Ginger more than being in church was Bunny's absence. Her entire focus revolved around her man Spoe. Now, she appreciated that Spoe was a keeper who treated her sister like gold, but damn, the Negro could share the girl with her own sisters. Ginger hadn't seen or heard from Bunny since the day they went to the funeral place with Tallhya. Spoe called when they were on their way to eat, and whatever it was he wanted Bunny to do must've been important because Bunny canceled all their plans and dropped them at the house like stepchildren. She was acting like she had to go and put out a fire, and had not been seen or heard from since. You would think that with Tallhya in a state of crisis, her older sister would have picked her head up off of her man's penis and shown up, or at least called to check on her.

"Can you see if she's here yet?" Me-Ma craned her neck trying to look clear to the back of the church, many rows back and past a lot of heads, many fitted with fancy hats that could cause a scene at the Kentucky Derby. Simone did a quick look back even though, deep down, she already knew that her mother would be a no show. She hadn't gotten excited about seeing her mom at church because she knew better than to get her hopes up. She did feel bad for Me-Ma though because no matter how many times Deidra disappointed her, she always kept her hopes up. She was destined, once again, to be let down.

"She's not here," she told her grandmother, again.

"This sure is wonderful." Me-Ma smiled, feeling so grateful to have three of her four granddaughters there. It was still early, so she felt hopeful that Deidra was only running late and would arrive shortly. Her daughter had never been on time for anything.

"Me-Ma, she's not coming," Simone wanted to be realistic and tried to soothe her grandmother's disappointment early. Plus, she did not want to spend the entire service checking for her mother, whom she figured was laid up somewhere with her latest loser, because that was her mother's type.

"She said that she would be bringing this new fellow, Lenny."

"There is always a new 'fellow' or two," Tallhya, who had been listening, chimed in, her head and neck going every which way.

"I don't see how you can have anything to do with her Me-Ma. She stole your money and ran out. She's not gonna show up till that money is gone." Now whether she was right or wrong, Simone's tone didn't sit any better with her grandmother. Since she didn't have children yet, she couldn't understand how she felt. For Me-Ma, it was like the saying goes "a mother's love is a mother's love."

"Don't you talk like that about your mother! That is my daughter, my child you're talking bad about." Me-Ma's voice raised, and so be it, because she didn't come from this hiding behind your hand whispering generation. She put her stuff right out there and didn't ever care what anyone had to say. If they weren't paying her bills they did not get a vote, and that included her grandkids. "Just like I love all of you, I love Deidra. You all with your money, money, money ways don't realize that's not how God intended it. You can't put money over people." Even the choir lowered their voices out of respect for Mrs. Banks preaching. It was Sunday, and she sure as hell was giving a sermon. Pastor Cassius must have thought so too, because he waved his hand, commanding the choir to stop singing 'Precious Lord' mid note.

"Mrs. Banks, you are the elder. Me and most of the folks in here want you to have your say. Too often we hush up what the people who have come before us have to say, when they're the ones who can teach us the most lessons. We act as if we have invented loud music, short skirts, and falling in love with the wrong people. Fellow church members and visitors, you need to listen to your elders. Now, Mrs. Banks, would you do us the honor of coming up here to share your message with us?"

Me-Ma looked around silently. Then she stood up, ascended the stage and took the mike like that was her job.

"I was telling my granddaughters that I don't understand this generation one bit. If you don't know, then you will be shocked to learn that when you put anything before God, you will suffer. I'm talking all those fancy Lenny shoes and bags and the stuff you have to spend your money to get." Mrs. Banks was working herself up into quite a frothy lather and she had that Amen corner going. "You need to listen to what I am saying, because God loves you." People stood up and starting shouting back in agreement. The reactions really got Me-Ma shouting and pointing her fingers. She had worked her whole life to build a strong relationship with the Lord, so she knew what she was talking about, and she wanted these people to get it.

"God loves you more than you know. Do you get that?" People kept shouting back agreeing with her. "So you cannot put anything before God and you cannot put anything before your family." Me-Ma took a deep breath, sucking in air to expand her lungs before she continued. "Especially those who have strayed from the Lord, 'cause those are the ones you need to stay on your knees praying the most for, because that is what God would want. When you love someone who has lost their way, you never ever give up on them. You nev . . ." she clutched her hand to her chest. Mrs. Banks' mouth dropped open as her head started to sway back.

"Me-Ma!" Simone's voice raised over the stunned silence as her grandmother collapsed onto the stage. Pastor Cassius Street rushed over to her first. The congregation, many who were present when the last Pastor died, sat there in stunned silence, not believing their bad luck to witness yet another heart attack. Simone, Ginger, and Tallhya raced to the stage as their grandmother took her last breath.

Chapter 24

"Miss Banks, so nice to see you back to work. We all thought you left with the money," Gray McPearson, a 45-year-old workaholic balding manager snidely remarked as she came through the door. His tone couldn't have been more opposite from the desperate married man hoping to get laid when Simone first interviewed with him. He motioned to her to follow him.

The customers in the bank moved about unaffected by the bank robbery that now was classified as yesterday's news.

"Mr. McPearson, I need to talk to you about my job," she started as he flipped through the paperwork on his desk, intentionally ignoring her.

"Yes, Miss Banks," he began.

"It's Simone. Please call me Simone." She took a deep breath, trying to get comfortable being back in this place where she almost lost her life.

"Yes, we do need to talk about your job, Miss Banks," he said coldly. "See, because your first official day on the job coincided with the first robbery this bank has experienced in over six years, I'm feeling a little suspicious of your timing. You understand why I may be a little suspicious of things, right?" Simone actually felt shocked that he cut so quickly to the point. It was one thing to want to fuck the new black girl, because after all she does have multiple degrees from a second tier university, but when she's suspected of being involved in a bank robbery, well, that just takes things to a completely different level.

"I told Detective Dugan everything he needed to know. I could have died in here and you actually think I'm a part of that crime? Are you accusing me of taking part in the bank robbery? Is this because I'm black Mr. McPearson?"

She paused. "Because I am almost positive that if I was a white woman, that thought wouldn't have even crossed your mind." She stared at him, just waiting for this motherfucker to break some law.

"No, that's not what I'm saying." he started to back pedal his ass away from the lawsuit hovering around them.

"Nothing like that has ever happened to me, and I wasn't sure that I would come back to this job. And yes, I knew that it might make me look guilty, but I'm not sure that standing there handing money to the next person holding a gun to my head is the kind of job security that I need." The last thing she wanted was to be classified as a typical ghetto black girl.

"Well, all our feelings aside, are you planning to return to your job at the bank or not?" Mr. McPearson asked, deciding to drop the accusations and just let the authorities handle it.

"Yes, I am, but I can't come back tomorrow as planned. I know that the bank offered me a week off, but there's been a tragedy in my family and I need to take another week."

"Another week? I can give you until Monday," he offered, not so generously.

"Fine." She stood up and walked out of the door. She was fighting to keep it together as she bumped right into Jackie, the assistant manager.

"You all right?" Jackie held Simone by the arm, leading her away from the offices.

"Not sure you want to be seen with the coconspirator to the robbery," Simone warned her as they made their way outside. "But I have been better, a whole lot better," she admitted to Jackie. The admission also came as the first she made out loud to herself. Since Me-Ma passed, she'd been so busy taking care of everybody else and making the funeral arrangements.

"Honey, all you need for them to be suspicious of you is some extra melanin. That's why even though I been here a lot longer than the last three managers I ain't never going to make it past assistant."

"I'm just so tired." Simone's voice matched her emotions, which made Jackie put an arm around her to offer comfort.

"I know sweetheart. But I promise it's gonna be OK. Just trust in God."

"He thinks he can insult me by basically accusing me of being a thief? That's bullshit." Simone lowered her voice. She still heard her father's words in her ear, and did not want to be seen cursing in public.

"Look, those men may have known someone, but it wasn't from the tellers, because we all know that the best day to take this place down is a Friday. That's when we get the money to cash the Government payroll checks, and with the two largest state buildings located a few blocks away, that's a whole lot of money. Hell, if they were smart they would have waited until Thursday night at six after the armored truck drops off the money. Honey, right now I'm just glad we survived. How are you holding up, sugar?" Jackie asked, placing her hand on Simone's shoulder.

Simone stared at Jackie and contemplated whether or not to be honest about how she was really doing. Jackie had been nice to her from the day they met, and she seemed like a good woman. The way Jackie carried herself reminded her of the nice older ladies from church. Right now, Simone really needed someone to be nice to her, and so far Jackie had been the only one to ask of her well-being.

"To be honest Jackie, I'm a . . . shit!" The word had already bounced out of Simone's mouth before she noticed, and too late to stop it, but he was the last person she felt like dealing with today. Detective Dugan stepped out of an unmarked police car and was headed straight toward them. Both women would have had to be blind not to notice him. He had a strong hard body and biceps straining to get out of his shirt that made it hard to look away.

"Damn!" Jackie salivated as the detective joined them. "I'm gonna be late from my break."

"Ladies." The detective nodded his head in greeting as he reached the two, but really he was focused on Simone.

"Officer, I need to clock back in. If you need to talk to me, I'm in my office." Jackie quickly excused herself and hurried back into the bank, trying to beat the clock. Without a legitimate excuse, Simone didn't have any reason to dart away. "Detective Dugan," Simone nodded, taking out her car keys. As fine as he was though, she kept telling herself that she had way too much on her mind to be thinking about a man right now. If her father Simon had still been alive and present he would have been the first one to notice how much alike the two men were, but his baby girl couldn't see it, not yet.

"Miss Banks, I wondered when you would return to work."

"Don't you mean if I was coming back to work?" With everything going on Simone felt particularly prickly and took offense that he would assume anything about her.

"My experience has taught me that most people who experience that kind of trauma in the work place aren't in a position to just quit their jobs. I'm not saying it's easy to go back in there, but you do what you have to do. So, not to be presumptuous, but are you coming back to the job?"

"Yes, but I needed to ask for more time off." She sighed, the full heaviness of losing her Me-Ma finally starting to hit. Out of nowhere tears begin to well up in her eyes. Before she could get a handle on it they began to overflow. Before he knew what was happening, his chivalry took over and he had wrapped his arms around Simone in an attempt to comfort her. Something about this girl made the normally workaholic detective want to push the job aside and get to know her. He'd been on this force a good ten years, and in the thirty two years of his life, he had yet to meet anyone like Miss Simone Banks. That included the girls he came across at Norfolk State University where he graduated majoring in Criminal Justice.

Simone could not get control of her emotions. With everything that had happened the last few days, it was as if she had reached her breaking point and everything was spilling out of her. Detective Dugan stood there, holding her in his arms without saying a word. In this moment, even he felt like he was exactly where he was supposed to be, holding this beautiful, fragile woman in his arms. The familiar way the two of them stood there silently together caused a customer to smile as she exited the bank. She assumed they were in the middle of making up after an argument. She couldn't help but reminisce of how she and her husband would kiss and make up back in their younger days. The chuckling sound the woman made as she passed by embarrassed Simone, who broke away from the detective. Being a private person, this show of emotion was so out of character she didn't quite know how to recover after her breakdown.

"You all right?" He asked, sensing her discomfort. In his line of work he was used to handling woman that were emotionally unstable What he wasn't used to was him feeling so attracted to a woman involved in one of his cases.

"It's my grandmother. She passed away two days ago and I just, I don't know, I think I'm just . . ." Her attempt to blow it off failed miserably as Detective Dugan pulled her close again. This time Simone leaned into him, letting herself go completely, as she closed her eyes, listening to his heartbeat. It felt so good, if only for a moment, to not have to be strong for anyone. The only other man she had ever been able to let herself go like this with was her father. As soon as she started thinking of her dad she completely lost it again as she began to sob while still engulfed in his strong arms.

When she had stopped crying, the detective placed his hands on either side of her cheeks. Even with mascara running down her face and bloodshot eyes, she was still the most beautiful woman he'd ever seen. He found himself taking a step back trying to maintain a professional distance, predicated by the fact that Miss Banks hadn't been officially cleared of the robbery. Years of investigating perps told him that the reasons she appeared suspect had more to do with six degrees of separation, none of it pointing to her guilt. This made him even more anxious to find whoever had helped to set this up because two dead cops meant somebody was going down for this crime. Unless his instincts were way off, he needed to make sure that it wouldn't be her.

"You all right?"

"Yes, I'm fine. I'm sorry I put you in that predicament. Thank you so much, though. I have to go." She darted away. He watched Miss Banks as she got into a car. He made a mental note about the Dodge, because it was a mighty step down from the Mercedes she had been driving the day after the incident when she came asking for her keys. She looked so out of place in that car, which made him wonder what was really going on with this woman. The next thought surprised him. It was that he'd have to find a way to see Simone again, and soon.

Chapter 25

As the church imploded with what seemed like the entire congregation coming to pay their respects to Me-Ma Banks, Simone forced herself to put on a brave face and take charge of everything. She kept herself together and helped her siblings deal with losing their Me-Ma. She stepped up and made all of the immediate funeral and burial arrangements. Luckily, Me-Ma had a life insurance policy that covered all the funeral arrangements. Finally, when she could no longer avoid it, she phoned her mother to inform her about Me-Ma's death. With Deidra's pockets still full of the money she stole from her own mother, Simone knew her mother was too busy spending it to answer or return anyone's calls. After many failed attempts, Simone decided to leave the message she thought that Deidra deserved, "By the way since, you won't call me back, you should know that your mother is dead."

Simone had been so busy making the arrangements and keeping it together that she felt guilty that she hadn't taken care of her sisters. Thank God the elders of the church stepped forward to comfort them. Simone almost burst out laughing when she glanced up to see Ginger being comforted by none other than the speaker for the Lord, Pastor Cassius Street. Simone loved her baby sis to the sky, but the way that child could use any tragedy to slip into a straight man's arms should have been taught in a 'how to get a man' class.

"Honey, you all right?" Pastor Street had somehow managed to detach himself from Ginger, and was standing next to Simone, as she worked her phone trying to handle all the remaining details concerning her grandmother's funeral. In response to the flashy man of God hovering nearby, she nodded, motioned to the phone and took off. *"Ginger, that is all you,"* she thought as she tried once more to reach Bunny, who had been MIA the past few days. *Where are you?* she thought to herself. She was beginning to worry, because it wasn't like Bunny to disappear for so many days without telling anyone at least where she was going. Simone decided as soon as she had a chance she was going to go to Bunny and Spoe's place in hopes of catching her there.

When Ghostman finally freed Bunny and allowed her to leave, she drove around in a fog not sure where she should go or what she should do. She thought about calling Simone but she would probably freak out and call the cops, causing a level of trouble Bunny couldn't escape. She couldn't go back home to Me-Ma and pretend like nothing had happened. That woman had some kind of psychic power or a sixth sense that explained why none of her girls had ever been able to hide anything from her since they were little children. It was as if she could sense when one of them was in trouble. Bunny knew that she could not hide this from Me-Ma, and there was no way she wanted to put her grandmother's life in danger by telling her what happened. Her grandmother had been through so much, but when it came to Me-Ma's family, Bunny knew nothing could keep her from protecting them or helping them, which was why she couldn't go home.

The truth was that there was nothing anyone could do for her. Being alive while Spoe had been killed felt cruel to the point where she started to imagine herself with him in the next life. Bunny had been raised in the church with her sisters and had listened to what happens to the eternal souls of people who commit suicide. As badly as she wanted to end her life, she couldn't do it.

For three days Bunny lay in bed clutching the T-shirt Spoe had worn before he left to pull off the biggest single heist of his career. He had no idea when he walked out of the door that it would finish him for good. She kept drifting in and out of consciousness, only to be reminded when she awoke that the man she loved with every fiber of her being would never come back to her. She hadn't eaten in days. Hell, she could barely think straight. The idea of eating made her feel sick.

She held the dirty T-shirt up to her nose sniffing for Spoe's scent as she imagined him walking through that door. The bleakness she felt startled her. It went deeper than just pain or despair. It felt like it would go on forever.

"Bunny! Bunny!" she heard someone calling out her name, but it felt foggy like it was happening in a dream. "Bunny!" Simone yelled through the door. She knew her sister was home. She'd parked badly in front of her house instead of the garage where she normally left her car. All the noise of banging and the doorbell ringing started hurting Bunny's head until finally she got up and opened the door.

"Shit! What happened to you?" Simone stared at her sister. She had come there to tell her about their grandmother. One look at Bunny, and now she was so worried about her that she didn't know what to do. She closed the door behind her. She led her sister into the living room and sat her on the fancy white couch, the one she picked out of *InStyle* magazine because one of her favorite celebrities owned one just like it. Her hair was matted up, her eyes were swollen and puffy, and she smelled like she hadn't showered in days.

"Bunny, what is going on?" a concerned Simone asked her, "Where have you been?"

"I . . . I . . . he . . ." Bunny who could talk shit in a variety of different attitudes barely strung a comprehensible sentence as she collapsed into her sister's arms sobbing uncontrollably. Simone couldn't remember the last time her sister had broken down in tears, not in years.

"What is it Bunny? You can tell me."

"It's Spoe and Tariq. They're dead. Simone, he killed them." Bunny went mute, her body rising and falling in quiet agony.

"No!" Simone started to cry too and hugged Bunny tightly against her. She couldn't believe all the death surrounding them. For so long they'd been lucky. Lately, it seemed as if they didn't have bad luck they wouldn't have any luck at all. The two sisters lay together for so long the sun set and the house was now covered in darkness. Bunny and Spoe never talked about what Spoe did for a living that provided them with foreign cars, designer clothes, extravagant trips and a place that cost nearly ten grand a month. Simone knew it was illegal, which was the reason she never took any money from them. Bunny assumed that the worst thing that could ever happen would be Spoe getting arrested and going to jail. Then she would wait for him. But she was wrong. Spoe dying was definitely the worst thing that could happen.

"I don't know how I'm going to live without him Sisi," Bunny's voice sounded defeated, fragile even. A few months earlier Simone had said the exact same thing, but about her father. That's how she knew that her sister would learn to survive without the man she loved.

"I need you to come with me." Simone said, pulling Bunny up from the couch. The last thing that Bunny wanted was to leave this house. It was the one place where she felt connected to Spoe. This was their home and she couldn't leave it.

"I can't. I just want to die." Bunny cried.

"Please, Bun-Bun. We need to go. It's about Me-Ma." Just the mention of their grandmother's name brought a hint of a spark back into her. It hadn't crossed Bunny's mind that anything could be wrong, but the concern in Simone's voice did not go unnoticed.

"Me-Ma?"

"Yes, she was at church on Sunday and . . ." A look of horror covered Simone's face jarring her from continuing.

"What?" Now Bunny was sitting up on her own, staring into her sister's eyes waiting for something bad.

"She had a heart attack."

"No, no, no! This can't be. It can't."

"Bunny," Simone hesitated, "She's gone. Our Me-Ma is gone."

Bunny, who had not eaten or even had water in at least three days, simply passed out from the stress and emotional strain.

Chapter 26

Like a bad penny Deidra always managed to turn up at the wrong time in the wrong way. Two days after Me-Ma's death, a friend of a friend managed to track her down in Atlantic City, where she and her dick de jour had gone on a five-day bender, drinking, partying and gambling. As soon as they were broke, Deidra decided to turn on her phone that had not been on in days, and found out her mother had died. To quote the old folks, Deidra got on the first thing smoking and hurried back to Richmond and her mother's house.

"Don't you make any arrangements until I get there, that is my job," She screamed into the phone as that big girl, Tallhya, tried to explain to her everything had already been handled by Simone. She went on to tell her that the final service and burial would happen the next day.

"They just tryin'a get away with something. I don't trust none of them," Deidra complained to her man, Len.

"So you gonna get some inheritance baby?" That was where Len's mind went.

"Hell, yeah, I'm the only child so I get everything; the insurance, the house, all those stocks my father left. Shit, I'm probably going to be paid."

"Baby, that sounds good. Real good." He immediately began counting all the opportunities he would have to help her run through that money before he moved on to his next woman. Len was not what you would call a long term option. Hell, he must have been getting old, because he had been with Deidra a good four months, which had to be about ten times that in dog years, or Len years, as he liked to refer to time. Deidra jumped out of the car before it could be properly parked and rushed inside the house where she had grown up.

"My mother died and none of you could find a way to get in touch with me?" She hollered as soon as she entered and saw her three and a half daughters, that's how she thought of Ginger —a half.

"Well, we couldn't exactly wait until you needed to steal more money from your mother for you to show up now, could we?" Simone who was usually the sweetest of the four got all salty with Deidra, which really pissed her off.

"You did this shit on purpose!" She glared at this disrespectful little bitch. When she got the deed to this property all these freeloading bitches would be sent packing and she didn't give a shit where they wound up.

"Ma, calm down, we did try to find you," Tallhya, always the motherfuckin' peacemaker, tried to insert herself into their conversation.

"Nobody was talking to you. It's little Miss Prissy I was addressing." Deidra pointed her finger at Simone who had the gotdamn nerve to be mugging like she could take her. "Don't get it twisted miss thing. I am still your mother and I can beat your ass just like I did when you were little."

"Wow, well I'm surprised you were around long enough to give me a beating." Simone snapped back , rolling her eyes, the grey eyes that she had the good fortune of inheriting from the mother who had the nerve to come here just to argue at a time like this. Ginger picked up a program off of a stack on the table and handed it to her mother.

"What the hell you handing me this for?" she perused the paper that had all the information about the funeral written on it. Bunny, normally the loudmouth, had been sitting quietly, but now it was her turn to put her mouth into it.

"In case you want to show up to her funeral. Just know that none of us are expecting you to be there. I mean, you didn't have time for Me-Ma when she was alive, so why should we expect you to have time now?" Bunny quipped rolling her eyes at Deidra. Well, that didn't sit well with Deidra, so she got right up in Bunny's personal space.

"I'ma tell all you bitches one thing. When I inherit all this shit you are going to have to find someplace else to live. I want all of you disrespectful hookers to get the hell out of my house.

So if I were you, I would get to packing, and don't you take none of my mother's things, 'cause all this shit you see here, it's mine."

"You can't do that! Me-Ma wouldn't want you to kick us out," Tallhya said from behind her sister Ginger.

"Me-Ma wouldn't want you to kick us out," Deidra mimicked her daughter, adding a whiny tone just to make that shit sound more pitiful.

"It's true. She loved that we all lived together," Tallhya replied in a hurt tone.

"Well, I ain't my mother now, am I?" Deidra snapped as she stormed past them and went up the stairs to root through her mother's things.

"Shit," Tallhya started immediately after she left the room. "It hadn't crossed my mind that mama might end up with Me-Ma's house. What the hell are we going to do? Where are we going to live?"

"This is just so fucked up." Ginger looked at her sisters who had always taken care of her. They were about to be homeless which meant so was she.

"She ain't never been no mother so why would we expect it now?" Bunny said, her voice sounding so far distant, even though she sat right there with them.

Simone, as the eldest, had always felt that it was her job to take care of her sisters, but even she didn't know what to do. They'd all been hit on so many levels this past week culminating in their biggest loss, the rock who had kept them grounded, rooted to this spot together, no matter what.

"I'm broke as a joke," Tallhya added. "Walter done took all my money," She said whining.

"Girl, you gave that man everything. Didn't you learn nothing that Me-Ma taught you about keeping shit for a rainy day? As the youngest y'all should be taking care of my ass. Least Bunny got that money train still rolling fo' sure," Ginger laughed, bumping her sister and tryin'a make her join in. All it did was cause her to burst into tears.

"Maybe we should just rob a bank or something," Simone joked trying to make light of things.

Chapter 27

All Me-Ma's granddaughter's knew that she would have been proud of the way her service turned out, particularly if one didn't include the part where Deidra, no doubt feeling the sting of her perpetual cheerleader now being gone, went nuts. They all knew that as soon as Deidra's dramatic ass got to the church, shit was going to be crazy. And sure enough no sooner had their mother shown up then shit started going sideways. If she had just cried that would have seriously been enough, but she had to go and make sure that everybody in that place knew exactly who she was and that Me-Ma may have acted like the mother to each and every one of them, but she was in fact her only daughter. One of the women in the church stood up and testified to the amazing being that was Me-Ma Banks.

"Me-Ma treated me like family. Like I was her own child," Patricia Hampton, who happened to be a peer of Deidra's, cried after the Pastor asked if anyone wanted to say a few words about the dearly departed. Well, that line snaked all the way down the aisle and out the back door, filled with people wanting to share their experiences of grace delivered by the late Mrs. Banks. Sitting in the front row watching all these shows of heavy emotion for 'her' mother got on Deidra's damn nerves. Before anybody could calm her down and stop her, she was on the stage shoving the latest speaker to the side.

"Y'all think you knew my mother? You think she wanted to mother all of you? Only reason my mother helped so many of you was 'cause she couldn't save me. I am Deidra Renee Banks. I am her only child. Do you hear me? And since this is my mothers' funeral, I shouldn't have to hear your lame-ass stories of how you didn't have your shit together and it was my mother that helped you out. You got that? I'm not interested in hearing about how you all took advantage of my poor bighearted mother. So get the hell off this line and go straight to hell, all of you!" She started mean mugging the people in line to the point where they went running back to their seats. Some of them, more traumatized by Deidra's accusations, darted out of the building.

"Now, now, Ms. Banks. I know that you are grieving for your mother, but this is not the way. Your mother would not have appreciated it." The Pastor hurried over to Deidra hoping to restore order, but if he knew what her granddaughters, all sitting in the front row watching this debacle, knew, he would have stayed minding his business.

"Motherfucker . . ." Deidra started, and her daughters expected, and were not surprised with, what came out of her mouth next. "You need to go back into whatever gay for pay motherfuckin' closet you done crawled your shyster ass up out of . . ."

"Now wait a minute . . ." Pastor Street began, but he had come up against a professional shit talker. No amount of sermonizing for a living would make him a match against the only child of Me-Ma Banks. Well, Deidra lapsed into motherfucker this and motherfuckin' cock sucker that to the point that Ginger felt so sorry for the Pastor. She jumped up and dragged her mother off the stage and out of the building. Just so we're clear, that woman put up a hell of a fight. Most of the people were equally shocked that Ginger was strong enough to take on her mother, in six-inch heels no less.

Of course nobody expected Pastor Street to show up at the repast, especially after the cussing out he got from Deidra. Sure enough, even though he officiated the event, he was ghost at the repast. No one blamed the man for refusing to be anywhere near the person that had publicly delivered the verbal ass kicking. It would take months for him to live it down, no matter how many sermons he continued to deliver on turning the other cheek. By the third such sermon people were snickering and referring to the cheek as his butt cheek. Lord, people can be cruel.

The guest of honor would have been pleased had she seen how many of the ladies of the church went to town on the delicious meals they had donated for the occasion. Me-Ma had reigned supreme as the best cook in Richmond and at least five or six other counties. Her repast served as the first chance for the runners up to compete for her now vacant title. There were roasts, hams, turkey legs, fried chicken, chitterlings, and every single vegetable you could think of. These ladies had put their foot in the preparation, and still everybody remarked on how much they would miss Me-Ma's cooking.

"Everybody all right?" Simone, as the oldest, most organized, and best mannered grandchild, remembered all of her etiquette lessons. She made sure everybody had what they needed. Now I'm not going to paint her as some kind of martyr, that girl liked to keep busy so that she could avoid the sadness lurking underneath all those niceties.

"I wish to hell these people would just carry they asses on home," Deidra, nursing her third drink, sneered to herself. The only reason she didn't act out again was because she didn't want to break anything in this house that would soon be hers now that her mama was dead. But this would be the last damn time any of these stuck-up freeloaders would enter Me-Ma's house, which was another reason she choose not to get out of pocket again. *Let 'em have their good time,* she thought as she strolled around, making a mental catalogue of all the valuables, the picture frames, clock collection, and especially the fine china. Deidra had to make sure none of those things went missing with all these sticky fingered guests.

"Mama, you all right?" Tallhya, the only one of the girls who bothered to check on her, asked, probably trying to make sure she didn't get thrown out with the rest of them.

"Uh, huh, I'm fine." Well, she could be as nice as she wanted, Deidra thought, but soon as the will was read she would be kicked to the curb just like the rest. Do her good to get out there and fend for herself. Hell, Deidra had done it, and so could the rest of them. She wasn't planning on running no charity. She had raised these girls and now they were grown. Now that her mother was no longer around, Deidra chose the opportunity to rewrite history. In her new version, she had been a good mother. Three white men entered the living room. Deidra turned to Tallhya, who had been hovering near her since they got back to the house.

"Who are those men?" she asked Tallhya. Her mother sure did know a lot of different kinds of people.

"I don't know." She wandered over to the men dressed in slacks and leather jackets, not like they were planning this visit. "Can I help you gentlemen?" The one standing in the front of the other two answered.

"We're here to pay our respects."

"Oh, are you friends of my grandmother?" she asked. As they began to make their way into the room, all eyes turned to them. Before he answered, Bunny, who must have seen them enter, came hurrying across the room.

"No, we're friends of hers." The man took Bunny's arm and led her outside.

"What are you doing here?" she snatched her arm away from Ghostman, keeping an eye on his thugs.

"We have a problem," he talked to her like a disobedient child who had disrespected her parent. "That money you gave me was sixty thousand dollars short."

"I gave you everything. What do you expect me to do?"

"I don't care." He leaned in close to her and whispered, "But if you don't want to wind up like your boyfriend, you will get me my money. Seeing how you're experiencing a family issue, I will give you ten days. And don't try and run because it wouldn't help your family."

By the time Ghostman and his thugs pulled away in his Range, Bunny had hit the wall of emotions. She was upset and confused. She had never felt so damn alone. He might as well have told her one million dollars, because she had no idea how she could get her hands on that kind of money. Bunny had long ago left the sanctity of the church, but that was long after Me-Ma drilled into her that when there is nowhere else you can go, that is the perfect time to go to God.

"God, I'ma put this on you."

Chapter 28

One of the most beautiful family of women the receptionist had ever seen approached. "We're the Banks', and we have a meeting with Miss Shelton."

"Can I get you ladies anything to drink?"

"You got cocktails?" the older of the women asked. The receptionist quickly recovered after realizing that the women was dead serious.

"No ma'am, just water, coffee, and soda," she answered, decidedly confused about the cocktail question at ten in the morning.

"Is it free? 'Cause I know how much these big muckety mucks jack everything up," the older woman complained.

"Ma, please let's just have the meeting and then we can get something to eat or drink," Simone interrupted, already embarrassed by her mother's need to prove just how ghetto she was, a source of annoyance to her children.

"Miss Shelton will be right with you," the receptionist said after informing Miss Shelton of her guests. "You're meeting in the conference room. It's right this way." She led them around the corner and down a short hallway to a large glass enclosed room. Imagine their surprise when they found none other than Pastor Cassius Street sitting with a woman about the same age as Simone.

"Hello, I'm Lauren Shelton," she got up, came around the table, and extended her hand in greeting. Everyone but Deidra acknowledged it. She was too busy trying to figure out something else.

"What's he doing here? You did say that this is the reading of my mother's will?"

"Yes, and I need everyone mentioned in the will to be present." She smiled down at Deidra like she was a petulant child.

"Everyone ready?" Lauryn went back to her seat. She seemed a little too chummy with the Pastor, who did everything he could to avoid making eye contact with Deidra.

"We are here today to for the reading of the last will and testament of Marrietta 'Me-Ma' Banks."

"Can we just get to the good part? I'm not planning to be here all day," Deidra snapped, making hand motions for Lauryn to hurry the fuck up.

"Excuse me, ma'am. I will not have you snapping your fingers or disrespecting me in my place of business," Miss Shelton addressed Deidra, "Now please have a seat or I will have security escort you out of the building." This wasn't one of those born with a silver-spoon in her mouth attorneys. Miss Shelton had grown up in one of the worst housing projects in Richmond and had grown up with a lot of Deidras in her day. She was not about to be talked down to.

"That's right, you tell her Miss Shelton! Yes, our mother is not known for her patience." Bunny laughed at the sight of seeing someone shut her mother down.

"Yeah, she has other qualities, like making babies she don't want nothing to do with." Ginger, who had had just about enough of Deidra's nasty comments, decided she had nothing to lose by fighting back. "Is there any way I can legally make my mother divulge which sperm donor is my father?"

"Please, can we just do this one thing for the matriarch of our family without turning it into some high school drama?" Simone had way too much on her mind, like getting back to addressing her health crisis, a possible surgery, going back to work, and probable homelessness, just to name a few.

"I will not be disrespected by none of you little bitches. Mark my words," Diedra snapped. Instead of sending her venom in the direction of one of her children, she glared at the Reverend, still not understanding what the hell business he had with her mother. Although Lauryn knew exactly what had been written on the papers since they were executed not that long ago, she made a show of skimming the document as if looking for the right place to start.

"Mrs. Banks left a very detailed will with everyone present represented." Ginger and Tallhya shared a look of glee, excited for the windfall, when they thought no one was paying attention. Every one of them knew that Me-Ma kept her money tight, so there was bound to be a flow in a few minutes. All four of the grandkids would have gladly exchanged whatever she had left them in the will for another week or month or year with the woman who had raised them, loved them, and taught them to believe in the Lord, even when they didn't want to.

"Go on, what did she leave us?" the biggest mouth in the room pushed.

"To my youngest granddaughter, Ginger, yes, I know I gave you a hard time, but I love you just as much as all the others. If that's what you want your name to be, then so be it. I leave you my family bible and that old Louis whoever his name is purse that you told me is worth so much money. I also leave you whatever you want out of my closet, 'cause your Me-Ma sure had some good taste."

"Wait, she got left some old-ass clothes?" Deidra burst out laughing doubled over in hysteria. "She damn near left you the closet you flew the fuck out of." The rest of the grand-children had to stand in solidarity with Ginger, which was actually hard because Deidra had some serious jokes. Simone and Bunny shot their mother dirty looks, but all she did was roll her eyes and motion for the lawyer to hurry the hell up.

"To my Tall . . . Tall . . . Tallhaaa . . . Tallha . . ." she tripped over her tongue trying to sound out the name.

"She know her damn name, keep going." Deidra had enough of all this hemming and hawing to last a lifetime. Lauryn turned to Tallhya, apologetic before continuing.

"It's not my fault she gave me a name that nobody can pronounce." Her eyes rolled at her mother, who had already made it clear that she was not to be toyed with under any circumstances.

"Your grandmother left you all of her cookware and her recipe books. She also bequeathed you her record collection." Tallhya really just wanted her grandmother back. At the mention of inheriting her recipes, the ones she had taught her to cook by hand, she collapsed into a blubbering mess.

"The rest of you might as well join her, 'cause none of you are getting anything either."

By the time the attorney got to Deidra she was all but celebrating her good fortune. "Read it and weep you suckers!" she sneered before Miss Shelton started reading aloud.

"The house, and all of my money, I leave to the church, the one place that has given me solace in my life. I would like to appoint Pastor Cassius Street as the executor of my entire estate."

"What the fuck is this bullshit?" Simone screamed out, sounding frighteningly like her mother and not at all like herself.

"No! My mother loved me. She would have never left me with nothing. Let me see that paper." Deidra grabbed the paper and tried to decipher what the hell it meant.

"Ladies, God always has a plan. It's our job as human beings to trust that. This is what Me-Ma Banks wanted, so we must respect that." It only took two seconds for Deidra to begin to beat the shit out of him before Lauryn and Bunny were able to pull her off of Cassius, who seemed way too concerned with the state of his appearance than the beat down he just received.

"I can't step out of here in a wrinkled suit."

"Ain't this some shit!" Bunny interjected with her outrage, too.

Chapter 29

Bunny had already lost three days feeling sorry for herself. The clock was already counting down. She knew that Ghostman would not be up to giving her more time. He had that shoot-your-ass-over-nothing vibe, as it was witnessed by the way he killed Tariq over messing with his money. After the complete nightmare of the reading of the will, she decided to drive back to the house, hell bent on getting out from under this mess. There had to be some kind of solution, and she was intent on finding it. Nobody knew that Spoe was dead, so she decided to work that in her favor. As she pulled into the garage, the sight of Spoe's car parked in his space, like he was about to get into it and go about his day, broke her all the way down. She had to sit in her car, dry heaving, tears streaming down her face, until she could compose herself enough to move. That's when this though hit her. She would sell her car.

Thirty minutes later she pulled into the Porsche dealership on the Midlothian Turnpike. She hadn't even parked properly when two hungry salesmen rushed out to greet her, smelling their latest mark.

"I'm looking for Rusty Johnston." Luckily she had found the card of the salesman that sold the car tucked inside a manual in the glove compartment.

"Nice to see you again," the salesmen said. The guy didn't remember that the car had been a surprise and he'd never laid eyes on Bunny in his life. That being said, no one is saying he wasn't happy to see her.

"I'd like to sell my car." An accomplished liar, Bunny spun some story about needing to leave town and that's why she had to sell the car.

"I'm sorry, but you don't own the car," he explained this basic fact to a stunned Bunny, who remembered the day five months ago when Spoe had opened the garage and shown her the matching Porsche's.

"But it was a present. You can't loan somebody a present."

"No, but Mr. Thomas thought you would want a new car next year, so he paid off the three year lease agreement up front. That way you can keep it that long if you wanted, but in case you wanted to upgrade or get a new car, you could."

"So I don't own the car?" Bunny sounded stunned and honestly, didn't get it. The guy was obviously loaded and he paid in cash, which any good salesman knows not to question, even if it appeared really suspicious.

"No, ma'am."

"Did he lease his car too?"

"Yes, ma'am, he did."

"Thank you." Bunny got up, ignoring his suggestions to check out the latest models. For the first time since she got the car, when she got in it all she thought about was what a worthless piece of shit it had turned out to be. She had to find out a way to come up with that money.

When Bunny got back to the house, she started looking around for any and everything that she could sell and make money. There were so many guys that tried to bite Spoe's style. He lived for Gucci, Louis, Giuseppe, and Tom Ford, which made sense, because he and Bunny liked to floss. He has mad style and a wallet to satisfy his appetite. Lots of other men were hating on him, and Bunny realized they would probably pay top dollar for his clothes. Then it hit her that she couldn't run around selling his things. That would look really suspicious. No, she had to be smart about this and not run around halfcocked looking crazy. She had already showed her hand to the car salesman, so the last thing she could do now was to have one of their leased Porsche's go missing.

She remembered that in Spoe's watch box there were half a dozen of the finest time pieces money could buy; a Rolex, two Cartiers, a Franck Muller, Hublot, and a Patek Philippe, his crown jewel that was totally iced out. She crumbled at the idea of parting with them, and emotionally felt herself start to crumble inside. She didn't know why she hesitated to sell these, but she had been with Spoe each time he had purchased one. The look on his face, like a kid buying a new toy, had been priceless. Selling these watches felt like she was giving up a part of Spoe, but as hard as she tried to find a solution, in the end she didn't have a choice. She knew a pretty good fence that could get her top dollar, so she gave him a call and they arranged to meet the next day.

That next morning Bunny was getting herself ready to meet with Billy, the fence, when her phone started blowing up. Ginger called, worried about her because she'd just seen on the news that two bodies had been fished out of the James River.

"One of them is Spoe's friend, Tariq. Where is Spoe?

"I don't know where he is."

"Do you think his body could be in the James River too, and maybe it's washed down to the Bay? I know that happened to one of my lovers' cousins' homeboys."

"I don't know. All I know is that Spoe and Tariq left together, going on a job."

"Are you all right?" Ginger asked her, sounding more upset than Bunny. Of course she already had this information so it didn't come as a surprise.

"Yeah, I guess I am," she answered, sounding weary, as someone started banging on her door. "Ging, let me call you back." She hung up and opened the door, unaware of the shit storm the information about Spoe's death would start.

"All right bitch, get the fuck out of my son's house," Spoe's mother, Wanda, screamed as she stood in the doorway glaring at her. "That is, unless you want me to throw your skinny ass out?" Spoe's family had never much cared for Bunny, especially since Spoe stopped paying all their bills and giving them as much money as they ungrateful asses felt they were entitled too. They felt that since there was a change in his behavior shortly after he and Bunny officially got together, it was because of her. Before she shacked up with him, Spoe spoiled his mama, two sisters and their numerous kids no matter how obnoxious they were. He didn't seem to care that they were using him and always had their hands out demanding he buy them more things, pay their rent, and send them on trips. To be perfectly honest, they treated him like shit and it wasn't until Bunny came along and showed him how he was supposed to be treated that he stopped caving in to his family's demands. She not only took care of him, but worried about his well-being, and showed him a kind of love he never got from his family, even his mother.

While his family didn't care how he got his money, Bunny did. She would remind him that they had enough and that he should think of quitting that life and going straight. She forced him to reevaluate the selfishness of his family, which led to him having a real come to Jesus moment that culminated with him pulling away from his family and cutting them off from the Bank of Spoe. When Spoe stopped coming around and wasn't taking their calls, they all blamed Bunny. To say they were salty or bitter about being cut off was an understatement. As more time passed and they saw Bunny driving around town in her flashy car, they hated her with all their might.

"You heard me bitch. You ain't deaf, are you?" his mother sneered. Now, under normal circumstances, Bunny would have whipped her ass right there, but Bunny wasn't a dumb bitch. Wanda had both of her ghetto-ass daughters with her. Bunny knew she couldn't fight all three of them. They all stood there, frowning, itching to take her down.

"Get the fuck out of my face," Bunny said, wanting to slam the door on them. Before she could stop them, they had already pushed themselves inside. "Get the fuck out of here."

"All this shit in here belonged to my son and we're going to take all of it."

"That's right, you gold-digging bitch!" Shanay, Spoe's oldest sister, placed both hands on her hips, staring down Bunny.

"Let's just kick her ass," Li'l Moni, the baby, balled up her fists and tried to scare Bunny.

"You come near me and that shit will not end well!" Bunny warned them. She had already gone through too much, and wasn't about to let them intimidate her. "This right here, at this moment, is not what you want. I'm trying to compose myself out of respect for Spoe, but right now you need to just leave me the fuck alone!"

"Now, I know that Spoe loved you and would want you to have some of his things, but you are not going to threaten me."

"Bitch probably took all his money too," Li'l Moni snapped trying to rile up her mother and older sister.

"We should call the police," Shanay insisted to the mother. "Throw this greedy-ass ho up out of here."

"Really?" Bunny sneered. "And how exactly are you going to explain your brother's income? I can prove that I live here, so there is nothing you can do to get me out."

"That's the way you want to play this?" Wanda remarked, giving her the stink eye.

"We are taking everything that belongs to Spoe, so you need to move your ass out of the way." Li'l Moni faked like she was about to hit Bunny, whose hands shot up in defense. They all burst out laughing, clowning her. Then they shoved past Bunny and stormed into the bedroom and started grabbing all of Spoe's things.

She couldn't believe these vultures. Less than an hour after hearing about his death they were there stealing all his shit.

"Dammit!" Bunny said to herself freaking out at the realization Spoe's jewelry box was within reach. She had taken it out earlier to get everything ready to meet up with Billy so it wasn't in the safe where it normally would be. She grabbed the box and was about to throw it under the bed when Wanda snatched it out of her hand.

"You tryin'a be sneaky, bitch?" Wanda said as she pushed Bunny to the floor. She sat on the bed and looked in the box. She didn't say a word, but the look on her face was as if she had just won the lottery.

Chapter 30

"OMG! OMG! OMG! What are you going to do?" Simone screeched. Bunny just had explained to Simone everything that happened with Spoe robbing Ghostman. She had just told Simone she had no idea how she was going to meet Ghostman's demands. They were sitting in Me-Ma's kitchen, eating their way through the mountain of food the ladies from the church had brought over earlier. They were grateful that those women now saw it as their job to take care of the four Banks girls in homage to their recently departed sister. "This shit is fuckin' crazy and fucked up!"

"I don't know. I just don't fuckin' have any idea." She shook her head. She knew Simone was upset, because she had only heard her sister curse two times in her life. The first was when her father died, and the second being this one. "There's no way I can get my hands on that kind of money." It all just seemed impossible to her because Ghostman didn't care about her herculean efforts. All he gave a shit about was his money and he was not about to play on that.

"But what about all the clothes and jewelry? Spoe really had serious high end shopping habits. Can't you sell some of his things?"

"That's what I planned on doing. I even had a fence set up to exchange his watch collections for so much money that even after I paid off the debt I'd still be flushed.

"So what happened?" Simone inquired.

"His jealous, money hungry mother and sisters happened. They pushed their way into our spot and took everything I could'a make some cash on. Girl, they even tried to take his Versace drawers. But what the fuck could I do? Wasn't like we were married and I had some legal right to all his illegally gotten goods."

"That is so messed up." Simone sympathized with her sister, feeling incredibly hopeless about the whole thing.

"They were damn lucky I didn't cap one of 'em. The only reason was because I knew even though Spoe had stopped talking to them, he still loved his family. He would have wanted to know they weren't left out there with nothing."

"But what about you? Why didn't he make sure that you were taken care of? That just so fucked up."

"Look, he had my back the same way that your dad had yours. Shit don't always work out the way it's planned. I know Spoe had my motherfuckin' back!" Bunny lashed out at Simone for insinuating that he didn't. Her anger, frustration, and fear were threatening to overflow onto the next person to get out of pocket, even if it was her favorite sister.

"I'm sorry. I shouldn't have said that. I know how much he loved you," Simone offered, backing off. She hadn't meant it the way her sister had taken it. This entire thing was really traumatic, and she was worried about her sister. As the oldest Banks sister, Simone thought it was her job to help her siblings out of their messes. This one was way above her head. The fact that she couldn't help her sister in her time of need pained her.

"Yes, he did love me," Bunny said, her voice sounding fragile and strong at the same time. Unlike Simone's father who had died of cancer, Spoe had been killed. He had been taken from her. If it was the last thing she did, Spoe's killer would pay.

"We have to figure something out."

"No, this isn't on you. It's my problem. I just needed to vent, Simone." Bunny had always prided herself on being able to handle her issues alone, but losing Spoe was too much for her to keep to herself.

"We're sisters, so your problem is my problem. You weren't there when Me-Ma spoke to the entire church, but this is exactly what she meant when she got up on that pulpit and preached. It was about the gift of family and how we don't get to just leave each other flailing in the wind when there is a problem. We have to stick together, and not just when good stuff is happening." Simone reached over and hugged her sister.

"What about the cars?" Simone shouted, excited to have figured out her sister's problem.

"The cars are leased, so I gave his over to his mother, 'cause what good is it going to do me since I can't sell it?"

"What about your stuff? All those expensive bags and clothes?"

"I went into one of those expensive-ass resale stores, but since I didn't have the receipts for none of it the woman didn't want to fuck with me. Everything was paid in cash so they couldn't look it up with my card, and I never saved the receipts. There was nothing she could do. I'm fucked. At another consignment shop, basically after it's sold and they take their cut, it would be like I was selling my stuff for crackhead prices." Bunny shoved her plate of food across the table. There was no way she could have an appetite anymore.

"It's not like I can go to the bank and get a loan. They want collateral, and since they don't mean last season's Chloe bag or Chanel shoes, the only other thing I can put up is my ass." The two of them shared a look, 'cause they were thinking the same thing. "You think if you had a fake ass you could take it to the bank and use it as collateral?" Well that was enough to make them smile.

Lucky for the Banks sisters, God spared no expense when it came to making sure they were fine. They all had bootys that men salivated at, even fully clothed.

"That would be classic." The sisters finally laughed to keep from crying. They high-fived each other, they were clowning so hard.

"Sisi, you work at that bank. You wanna slide your little sister about one hundred grand? You know, to save my life?" Bunny actually started laughing, which proved contagious. Before long both sisters were in hysterics.

"Hell yeah, you and everybody else. Just come to my register and I will personally hand you the money. You need cash to buy a new pair of Louis' for a party? Well, here is three thousand, because you're going to need a new bag to go with it too." Simone mimed handing over the money.

"Well, I really need money to get my nails done . . . in Paris," Bunny spurted out barely able to form the words. Simone played her part to the hilt, sounding like the straight laced bank employee.

"Paris, France or Paris, Texas, because whatever you need, I got your money right here. She laughed before continuing. "The way that damn manager treated me today I should just give you all the money. I told you how he acted toward me when I went today, right?"

Bunny nodded.

"Bwwaaaa!" Simone broke out into gleeful laughter. "Could you imagine his face? I would give anything to see that!" Simone said, her face growing serious.

Bunny noticed Simone's expression change and their eyes met. The two of them grew silent, their thoughts traveling from one to the other.

"Then why don't we just do it?" Bunny spoke first. Instead of arguing or disagreeing, Simone broke into a smile.

"And I know exactly how it would go down." Simone said smirking.

"Why not, right? Let's fuckin' go in there and get that money." Bunny raised her hand to high-five her sister, who just sat there staring at her.

"I was kidding. You do know that, don't you?"

"Well, I'm not. This is the perfect solution," Bunny argued, sounding really adamant. Simone gave her a look to let her know that she thought this was crazy, but she knew her sister. Once Bunny made up her mind it may as well have been set in stone.

"You're crazy if you think you can pull this off. Forget it." The doorbell ringing stopped her from telling her sister in detail how insane she thought her idea actually was. What did she think she could do, burst in and rob the bank all by herself?

"Who the hell is that at this hour?" Bunny got up to answer the door just as Tallhya came flying down the stairs.

"Maybe it's Walter!" she blurted out. Simone and Bunny raced to the door in front of their sister, just as Ginger joined them, stretching from her nap.

"Hello, ladies, may I come in?" Pastor Cassius Street stood on the doorstep in a royal blue suit. Ginger was pissed to be seen in booty shorts and a cropped top without her hair done right.

"Sure, come on in, Reverend," Simone offered, giving her best imitation of Me-Ma, who would always welcome people into her house with a smile, even if that person had been the devil, which this man had already proved to be. The pastor entered, taking a good look around.

"How are you ladies holding up with your grandmother's passing?" he asked in his best caring, concerned, man of God voice.

"We're doing just fine, Pastor," Bunny snapped, refusing to pretend this leper was a welcomed guest. What she really wanted was to give him a beat down for manipulating their grandmother.

"So, I wanted to have a little talk with you ladies to say that what your grandmother did, donating all of her money and property to the church was an amazingly generous thing."

"We're not entirely sure that she did. With all due respect Reverend, we find it a little bit suspicious that she had only had the papers drawn up a week before she passed," Simone told him, trying to keep the rage out of her voice. She had been taught early on that it was better to catch flies with honey, and right now she wanted to catch this snake in his lies.

"Well, anyway," the Reverend continued, ignoring their concerns. "I think your grandmother would have preferred it that one or all of you have the opportunity to buy this house from the church. Wouldn't that be lovely? To keep it in the family?"

"Wait. That's some bullshit!" Ginger's words mirrored what they had all been thinking.

"We need to have our attorney look into this," Simone told him. "The will has to pass through probate before anything can be done with our Me-Ma's things, Reverend."

"Yes, that's right Miss Banks. So that will take thirty days, and by then this property might have already been listed with multiple offers. I just wanted to do the right thing by you ladies and to give you first dibs." He had the nerve to act like he was actually doing them a favor. Simone had to grab

Bunny before she went upside his head. Ginger was already balling up her fist ready to wop him when Tallhya pushed the reverend out the door.

"Thank you, Reverend. We will call you," Simone grabbed him by the arm and hurriedly walked him out of the door, closing it behind him. "That fuckin' crook!" Simone was disappointed in herself that she was cursing as of late, but she was reaching her boiling point. "He is not going to steal Me-Ma's money and get away with it," she stated. The rest of the sisters all nodded, agreeing, but none of them had a solution.

Chapter 31

"How's it going?" Jackie checked in with Simone as she handed over her daily cash, and a receipt she needed checked off and validated that the count was correct.

"I will tell you at the end of the day," Simone said with a smile. "So far things are going well, but the bank hasn't opened yet, so it's going to depend on how many guns I have shoved in my face," she told her, only half kidding.

"We have added extra security measures. There will be another security guard posted outside of the bank between the hours of nine and five. All the studies show that the last hour is the safest. Also, from now on we are going to rotate and distribute marked bills, so that way nobody has them every day. You will know they are the marked ones by the green band holding them together. Last week they had three more cameras installed that are linked to the police station. There is a button near station four that when it's pushed, sends a signal in case of emergency." Jackie pointed at the button on the station next to her.

"That makes me feel a whole lot more secure."

"So the next time somebody thinks they can just rob this bank, they will be on candid camera and the police will have surrounded this place in seven to ten minutes."

"Wow, that's great," Simone answered, thinking how she couldn't wait to tell Bunny this so she can stop with her crazy thinking. Just then, Mr. McPearson stopped in front of her station and added his ten cents.

"We want our employees to feel safe and to know that we're protecting them. What happened at this bank will never happen again. I'm actually looking forward to the next time someone thinks they can just come in here and steal from me," he said with a pompous attitude. Simone didn't know if she was being paranoid, or if this man had actually dared her indirectly to try something.

"That's good to know." She gave him her best fake smile. *What an asshole,* she thought, before turning back to keep counting her money.

"Don't let him bother you. Just be grateful that you don't have to live with his ass." Jackie elbowed Simone to make her laugh.

The rest of the morning went relatively quickly and painlessly with no major issues, before lunch at least. When Simone counted out her bills to make sure all her numbers added up she was actually pleased that it equaled out perfectly. Last thing she needed was for Mr. McPearson to accuse her of stealing ten cents.

"You can take lunch," Jackie told her. "I ordered a pizza and there is still half left in the lounge."

"Thanks, but I need to get some fresh air. Thought I'd head over to Starbucks and grab something." After a quick lunch, she returned to the bank and, as luck would have it, walked in just in time to come across the last person she wanted to see.

"Oh, look who finally got a job." Marjorie quipped under her breath as Simone passed. She decided to ignore her and went to clock in and return to her station. No sooner had she opened her window then Marjorie came over, no doubt to mess with Simone. She waved a handful of hundred dollar bills, money that probably belonged to Simone in the first place.

"What do you want, Marjorie?"

"I just wanted to see what it looked like when a princess actually worked for a living. Your father would be so proud, especially after he paid for three college degrees and the best job you could get only requires a high school diploma. Things must really be tough out there in the real world." She laughed, waving the money in front of Simone's face.

"Look, why don't you do us both a huge favor and walk away." Simone had to do everything she could to keep herself from punching Marjorie in her smug face.

"I see you're not so big and bad now, are you? After all, you don't want to risk the only way that you know how to make

money now, do you? Because I'm not giving you any of mine."
She taunted Simone, loving the fact that by being at work,
her wings were basically clipped so she couldn't fight back or
sucker punch her like last time.

"Walk the hell away from me!" Simone hissed in a low voice,
trying to keep her composure and not alert the other tellers.

"Maybe if you hadn't been such a Class-A brat all those
years, twisting my husband around your little finger, I might
have been more generous to you. But I never liked you. Not
for one single second. Your father may have thought I did, but
that was just great acting on my part honey. See, I knew that if
I were going to manipulate your father into marriage I had to
at least pretend to be the loving stepmother. And I did damn
well for all those years, which is why all this money is mine.
It's the least I should get for putting up with your boring-ass
lousy-fuck father and his second-rate beauty pageant brat. So
as you're slaving away at this little job, just know that I am
somewhere having a great life spending all your dumb-ass
daddy's money and getting the shit fucked out of me on our
bed." Well, Simone had taken all she could.

"Fuck you!" she seethed at Marjorie who now had her
stepdaughter exactly where she wanted her.

"Excuse me? What did you say to me?" she raised her voice
intentionally sounding insulted.

"You heard me," Simone stared, so enraged at her stepmother that she was not paying any attention to amount of
ruckus she was causing. The other tellers and the customers
were starting to stare in her direction but the biggest problem
was walking straight toward her window. "I said fuck you!
You bitch!"

"Miss Banks!" Mr. McPearson arrived at her window in time
to get an earful of the words she had just spit at Marjorie, who
could not have been more pleased with the outcome.

"Is this how you train your employees to speak to your
valued customers? If this is the case, then I may have to take
my seven figure account elsewhere." Marjorie admonished
the bank manager who shot Simone the dirtiest look.

"I'm so sorry about that ma'am. I will have my associate
finish your transaction with us today. I hope this does not

interfere with our business relationship, and as a courtesy we will waive this month's account charge. I assure you this will not happen again," Mr. McPearson said as he turned toward Simone. "Miss Banks, I need to see you in my office right away," he stated before walking away.

"Dammit!" Simone could not believe that she had walked right into the perfectly orchestrated trap that witch had set especially for her. As furious as she was at Marjorie, the person she really wanted to slap was herself for being that gullible. She braced herself as she walked into Mr. McPearson's office.

"You do understand that you are still under a ninety day probation period Miss Banks? That means you are not a permanent employee with the bank and that your behavior during that period is closely monitored. It also means that at any moment we can let you go without a disciplinary hearing. What you said to that woman is more than enough grounds for you to be dismissed, do you understand?" Mr. McPearson barked at Simone as she sat in front of his desk.

"I really need this job," she pleaded not knowing how she would deal if she were fired, and all because of that damn Marjorie.

"When I hired you it was because not only were you educated, but your qualifications made me think one day you could graduate to management. But what I've seen since the robbery makes me think you're not the kind of person who can handle this job. Maybe it's best for you to go back to sitting on your couch or whatever you did before you bothered to get your first real job at almost thirty. I mean, I never really delved into it, but what did you do for a living?" he insisted. As badly as Simone wanted Mr. McPearson to be the second person she told off today, she held her tongue.

"Mr. McPearson, I really need this job."

"I'm just not certain that you're the working type. At least not this kind of work." Simone got that she had just been called a hooker, but she tried to pretend that's not what this asshole manager was suggesting.

"I can handle it. I just . . . I cannot explain in detail my problem with Marjorie, but I really am sorry. And if you give me one more chance, you will not regret it, sir." The look he gave her meant she was out of chances.

Chapter 32

Simone exited the bank to find Detective Dugan leaning against his car parked in front of the bank.

"Can I walk you to your car?" he asked. Instead of answering, she glanced back toward the bank to see if her boss was watching her. The last thing she needed after talking her way into keeping her job was for him to see her talking to Detective Dugan and have McPearson start to think that she's being sneaky or keeping something from him. The detective saw her reaction to him being there and figured out what she had been thinking. "I already talked to the powers that be in the bank and explained that every one of their employees had been cleared of any involvement in the robbery."

"That's nice. A relief," she told him. Though she knew she was innocent, it helped that her boss wasn't still thinking she may have been involved. Something told her that he didn't need another excuse to dislike her. "Is that why you're here?" Dugan, who normally felt self-assured, found himself a little nervous in front of Simone. Maybe it had to do with the reason that he had to see her.

"Uhm, no. Would you like to get a quick coffee?"

"So you're here to invite me to coffee?" she asked, not convinced that was his real intention.

"No," he had to laugh at himself. "You got me. I actually came to ask you to dinner, to ask you on a date," he told her, shuffling from one foot to the other like some adolescent teenager.

"Wait. So I went from being a suspect to being a possible dinner date?" She said this trying to keep a straight face. She was struggling to keep from laughing. She found it a bit comical that Detective Dugan was asking her out after the hard time he had given her.

"Hey look, I was just doing my job," he explained, trying to reason with her.

"And you did your job well," she added.

"All right I get it. This was a bad idea. I'm sorry if I offended you." He took a step back trying to gather himself. It wasn't his habit to mix business with pleasure, and he sure wasn't used to getting turned down, even if it was by the most beautiful woman he'd met in ages.

"You think you offend me?" Simone asked, putting her hand over her chest, acting as if she was surprised.

"I'm sorry Miss Banks. Really. Can we forget I ever stepped over the line and made a real fool of myself asking you out? I get it." He had that look on his face of sheer embarrassment. Simone was really enjoying his discomfort a little too much.

"Get what? That a really cute police officer actually thought I was guilty?" she had to fight to keep herself from laughing.

"No, I didn't say that I thought you were guilty . . . Wait. You just called me cute? Like baby puppy cute or like I should get to know him cute?" He broke out into and infectious smile.

"So where are you taking me on this date?" Simone asked, letting him know exactly what kind of cute she had been talking about. It had been a long time since she'd actually agreed to a date, but she had been thinking about the detective more than she wanted to admit.

"You want to grab a quick coffee and talk about it? I mean, I did drive all this way and waited for you to finish with work." She had been listening, but that was before a Brinks armored truck pulled up in front of the bank. Two armed guards exited and went into the bank. "Hello? Hello?" the detective broke Simone out of her trance, watching the money being loaded into the bank. She glanced down at her watch, 5:30.

"What is your first name Detective Dugan? I cannot go out with someone when I don't even know his first name," she smiled, teasing him a little more. *Damn this girl is gorgeous*, he thought to himself.

"It's Chase, Chase Dugan."

"Yeah, that sounds about right. You look like a Chase. So Chase, you want to go and have a coffee?"

"Sounds good. There's a place around the corner. It's not Starbucks, but I think it's a little more quaint," he told her as Simone allowed him to lead her down the street. So many things were swirling in her head. One of them was definitely how good it felt to have a man this fine want to get to know her better. There was something about the officer that reminded her of someone, but she couldn't put her finger on who that could be.

Chapter 33

By the time Simone and Chase got back to their cars it was way past eight. They'd spent so much time talking about their families and their lives that time had gotten away from them. He had grown up in the area, went away for college and returned, determined to make a difference in his hometown. The whole ride home she kept replaying their conversation and thinking about how comfortable they were together.

When she walked in the door, Bunny was sitting in the kitchen alone, making notes in a book. She didn't even look up when Simone walked into the room.

"What are you doing?" she asked, concerned because her sister had an intense expression on her face when she entered.

"Nothing." She answered without glancing up. Simone came around the table and stood over her shoulder. An immediate feeling of sheer terror shot through her body as she caught a glimpse of what had captured Bunny's attention.

"You can't do it."

"Yes. I'm going to. I don't have a choice." Bunny gave her sister a look of such resignation that she knew there was no way to change her mind.

"This is like when I told you that Marla Thompson was bullying me in third grade and you threatened to beat her up. No matter how much I tried to talk you out of it, you wouldn't listen and you beat the girl up anyway. My little sister came to my rescue," Simone said reminiscing.

"Yup, that's exactly what it's like Simone. You can't stop me," Bunny said without looking at her.

"I couldn't stop you then and I can't stop you now, huh?"

"No, you can't."

"Then I'm going to do it with you."

"No. You must be crazy if you think I'm going to let you do that."

"I'm the insider. I can actually make sure you don't get arrested or killed." Bunny stared at her sister and began considering what Simone had just shared. In the end she fought against it.

"No. And I mean it Sisi. I can take care of myself. I'm the one that was living in the fast lane with a man that ripped people off for a living. Sure, they were drug dealers, but this is my mess to clean up. You never even got a driving violation. You do things the right way and follow all the rules. I couldn't live with myself if I got you caught up in any kind of trouble".

"And look where being a goody-two-shoes has gotten me. Working at a bank for a boss who thinks I'm some ghetto thief anyway. I might as well make sure that he's right."

"I'm not going to let you destroy your life. You're better than this," Bunny said, trying to do whatever she could to talk her sister out of this.

"So who are you going to get to help you? Some of your friends? Bunny, where are all those girls now that your money is running low? You think they won't turn you in if it came to them or you? Family is the only thing you can trust. I will have your back."

"I know why I am willing to risk my life, but Sisi, you can't. I won't let you do this for me." But Bunny knew that Simone was just like her when it came to being stubborn. She knew once Simone made the decision to something, nothing would stop her from it.

"Well, don't flatter yourself. I'm not doing it for you," Simone answered, looking into a confused Bunny's eyes. Now it was time for her to share something. When my father died and that bitch stole all his money, she took something else that I need. She cut me off from my medical insurance and . . ."

"What? Sisi, tell me!" A red flag went off, and Bunny knew that whatever her sister was holding back had to be huge.

"I need to have all these expensive tests and I need them done soon. The doctor thinks I might be very sick, and unless I get these tests I won't know how bad things are and what the best course of action for me to take is."

"Wait. What? Sick? How sick do they think you are Simone?" A now worried Bunny asked her.

"Pretty sick, Bunny," Simone said, trying to keep it as vague as possible, but her sister wasn't having it.

"How sick, Simone? Stop beating around the fuckin' bush!"

"They think I might have cancer," Simone said in a low tone.

"Cancer? No! I can't lose you. Not after Spoe, Tariq, and Me-Ma. Please, God, no." Bunny cried out at the injustice.

"I know, but I'm going to be fine as long as I get the money to handle the medical tests."

"So I guess we're going to do this?" Bunny said, gazing into her sister's eyes.

"Look, I saw that robbery go down and I can tell you everything those men did wrong. They were total amateurs. They didn't even know the bank routines or the best time to rob the place. They just thought that if they busted in like bad asses they would be able to take the place. And those stupid masks were ridiculous"

"We need to hire a driver." Bunny started to flip through her mental rolodex trying to find someone that they could trust.

"And at least one more person. And we need weapons."

"I got guns. Spoe kept all his equipment in a storage place. Nobody knows where he kept them except me and him. I'm sure they're all still there." Bunny's eyes started to water thinking about Spoe. Simone glanced up and saw her sister's damp face.

"Everything will be all right, baby sis." She gave Bunny a squeeze, trying to comfort her.

"I'm all right. Maybe doing this, exactly what Spoe use to do, is going to help me in more ways than one. Because you work there you need to draw the inside of the bank and make a list of all the employees and how many guards."

"And we have to make damn sure that nobody has the chance to put a dye pack inside the bag when they're putting the money in there. That stuff does not come off. And we need the robbery to happen on a Thursday evening."

The two of them were so busy caught up in the details of the robbery that neither noticed Tallhya standing in the doorway, her eyes wide from shock. She cleared her throat dramatically, attempting to get their attention. They both looked up with surprised expressions on their faces.

"So now you bitches think you're Bonnie and fuckin' Clyde?" she asked raising her voice loud enough to wake the neighbors.

"Shhh! Are you fuckin' crazy?" Bunny snapped at her.

"Me! You're asking me? You two are the ones that sound crazy. Y'all bitches think this is the movie *Set it Off* or some shit. If Me-Ma was here she would beat you both with those wooden spoons over there." She pointed to the jar of spoons on the counter that their grandmother used to discipline her unruly charges when they were young.

"We don't have a choice. Or do you have a whole lot of money hidden that we don't know about?" Bunny questioned her, then added a hostile stare for effect.

"No," Tallhya said, looking down at the floor, "In case you two forgot, that no good husband of mine stole all my money, and the bank says I have to sue him to get it back, so I don't have shit," she said looking from one sister to the other with tears in her eyes.

"Look, just don't say anything to anyone please. If we had a choice, we would, but we don't." Simone said with pleading eyes.

"I don't think you two can do this alone. I know that for sure."

"We don't care what you think as long as you keep this shit to yourself," Bunny said with an attitude. They both waited for Tallhya to agree, but she didn't.

"Guess I'm going to have to help, since I don't want to visit you in the state pen." Tallhya's words shocked her sisters.

"What?"

"Y'all are not the only ones sick and tired of being a damn doormat, having everything go wrong. Hell, just less than two weeks ago I had a husband who I thought loved me and a nice size bank account. Now here I am single and broke. Hell yeah I want in. The way I see it, Simone needs to be at work so it doesn't look suspicious. Bunny and I will rob the place, so now all we need is someone to drive the getaway car." All three looked at each other realizing that none of them were the best drivers in the family.

"Ginger!" they all said in unison.

Chapter 34

Bunny drove her sisters to Hopewell, a little town about 30 minutes outside of Richmond, to the spot where Spoe and Tariq kept all their equipment for the robberies. Spoe knew that he had to make sure they weren't ever spotted with the weapons or clothing from the robberies. Luckily, he trusted Bunny, and made her come out with him to learn how to shoot the guns. He didn't ever want her in a situation where she couldn't protect herself. She went from being a novice to an expert marksman.

"Where the hell are we going?" Ginger raised her voice, looking around at the country road with nothing but miles of trees on either side. Occasionally they'd see a small house pushed back from the road, but this was too sparsely populated for the sisters. "This can't take all day, 'cause I got places to go, people to do, and more people to do." Ginger laughed, high-fiving Tallhya.

"You stupid." Bunny shook her head at their youngest sister.

"Not too stupid for you bitches to need me to save your asses. See, y'all can't be talkin' about Ginger and treating her like the pain in the neck little sister when she got skills to pay the bills." She snapped her fingers to solidify her point.

"Whatever," Simone laughed, grateful they could always count on Ginger for some comic relief.

"I'm about to be one bad bitch with a gun in my hands. Then I'll be packing in more ways than one," Ginger joked.

"Ew, stop! Just stop!" Bunny yelled, then proceeded to shoot Ginger a dirty look in the rearview mirror. "Thank God, we're here." Bunny pulled Simone's beat up old Dodge into a hidden driveway. She drove a ways down a road until they came to a shack with a garage.

"I'm not going in there." Tallhya shook her head. Bunny just gave her a look so fierce she jumped out of the car without any more complaining.

"This is serious!" Simone stood there in shock as Bunny unlocked the huge metal cabinet that held a shitload of artillery. Tallhya and Ginger raced against each other, grabbing a gun like they were toys. Tallhya held a semi-automatic pistol, but of course the youngest had to have the biggest and went straight for a machine gun.

"Bam! Bam! Bam! Motherfucker, take that. You're dead," Tallhya shouted to her imaginary victim, who her sisters assumed was Walter. She shot at the cans Bunny had lined up outside on a wall and missed all three of them. Simone, brandishing a Glock, came up next to her and hit all three cans.

"Now Walter is dead for real," she said, winking at Tallhya. Thankfully her father had always made sure that she knew how to defend herself. She had taken shooting once a month since she was thirteen.

"How could I have been so stupid?" Tallhya whined.

"Good dick will make you do some dumb shit." Bunny laughed, thinking about all the things she had done with and for Spoe.

"Ain't that the motherfuckin' truth," Ginger sighed.

"I know," Tallhya started. "But it wasn't even that good," she confessed and they all burst out laughing, because that made it sad.

"All right, we need to get serious," Simone interrupted them, breaking off the fun. "This is a real big deal, so we need to be focused and ready. No thinking about men, or dick, or heartbreak, or any of the people who messed us over. Not now. The slightest mistake can cost us our lives, or our freedom, so the time to joke and have fun is done. You hear me?" She glanced over at her sisters. Even Ginger, who always had a snappy comeback, remained mute and serious. "We are ready to run through what we need to do, because once we —"

"I got this Sisi," Bunny interjected, cutting her off. "I know you're the big sister and you're used to being in charge, but this is my thing."

"No, it's not. You have an immediate need that makes you too invested to take the lead. The other reason I'm going to lead is because I'm the one working at the bank. Do any of you know where the security is stationed? What measures have been put into place recently in order to thwart another bank robbery? Do you even know the best day in order to get the most cash? No. So if you want me involved, you need to let me take charge. I will get you in and out of there safe."

"Fine, but something goes wrong and it's on you!" Bunny announced, throwing up her hands. Simone waited to continue until the wrath of her sister's threat dissipated.

"Every one of us is going to have a job to do. First off, Bunny and I know how to use guns, so Tall and Ginger you both have to learn marksmanship. While I'm at work the next two days you both need to come out here and work on your aim and comfort levels. You can't have any fear. Bunny is going to come up with our disguises and outfits for the hit. Also, Bunny, it's your job to make sure we have the right weapons and burner cell phones. Tallhya, you have a memory like an elephant, so I need you to come to the bank and do a visual walk through. You need to make sure that no one notices you checking out the bank.

"What about me?" Ginger, always wanting to keep up with her sisters, interrupted, her mouth pressed into a pout.

"You need to find a car that no one will notice and we can use for the heist."

"That's easy."

"So everybody has their assignments. My job is to draw a map of the bank and to give you all the details you need to pull this off." Simone surprisingly took to the whole criminal thing. She liked finally being in control.

"You really think we can pull this off?" Bunny whispered to her older sister.

"Yeah, I do. In fact, I know we can do it," she smiled, taking her sister's hand.

Chapter 35

"Girl, what the hell are you wearing?" Ginger asked, then she physically blocked Simone from leaving the bedroom. "Tallhya, Bunny, come quick!" she hollered down the stairs for reinforcements.

"Stop playing. We need to do one more run through before I leave," she insisted, trying to maneuver around her sister. Ginger folded her hands across her chest and gave her the once over before shaking her head at this pitiful display.

"What?" Both Tallhya and Bunny crowded into Simone's bedroom.

"Look at this hot mess!" Ginger pointed at their older sister's outfit, a pencil skirt, button down shirt, a blazer and a pair of pumps.

"What? I like this outfit," she said defending her outfit.

"If you were tryin'a be a librarian or a receptionist you would definitely get the job," Tallhya sassed.

"It's not that bad," Simone insisted, staring at her image in the mirror.

"Unless you are trying to blow someone off, this is not a let's take it to the next level kind of outfit. This is a shut that shit down cause you ain't getting none." Bunny laughed.

"That cooty cat is on some Fort Knox security level." Ginger snapped again.

"But I don't know him enough to sleep with him," Simone insisted, getting uptight about her first date with Detective Dugan.

"How the hell are we related? If he's fine, employed, and interested, then sex is usually on the agenda. How are you even Deidra's child? Our mother likes to fuck, we all like to fuck, except you." Bunny glanced at her oldest sister, who looked embarrassed at this uninvited attention to her sex life.

"It's not that. I like sex just as much as the rest of you, but I want to know that it's not just about the sex. I want a guy to respect me," she told them.

"Girl, they can respect me, but if the sex ain't poppin' then I'm not going to respect them, and the shit will be over. Done. Dead. Finished," Ginger explained, complete with finger snaps.

"Awwwweee, somebody really likes this guy," Bunny teased Simone. "And if that's the case, you don't have to fuck him, but you do have to make sure he wants to fuck you, and that's not going to happen in that outfit." The sisters wore her down and finally convinced her to change her outfit to a fitted black wrap dress that was both classy and sexy. She had an hour to kill before Chase picked her up, so they went over their plans for tomorrow and gave Simone some dating tips too. When the doorbell rang, they all felt ready for the next day, and Simone was ready for her date.

"Hello." Simone blushed as she answered the door. Chase looked damn fine in a pair of dark jeans and a light blue button down shirt open at the neck. She tried to hurry out before the girls embarrassed her, but that didn't happen.

"Don't do nothin' I wouldn't do," Ginger joked, batting her eyelashes and acting a fool. After lots of funny remarks she managed to get them out of there and into his car.

"Have fun you crazy kids," Bunny teased them as they got into the car. As soon as they were gone, the sisters got to talking.

"Damn, he was fine as hell," Ginger exclaimed. "I would have let him arrest me just so he could pat me down."

"You better leave your sister's man alone." Bunny laughed.

"I'm happy for her," Tallhya added. "Lucky bitch!" They all started laughing. Even though Bunny's man had been killed and Tallhya's had left her, they really wanted their sister to find love and to be happy.

"Your sisters really love you," Chase said as he glanced to look at Simone.

"Yeah, they especially love embarrassing me."

"I wish I had siblings. Being an only child I never had moments like that. I wish I had older or younger siblings. You're really lucky to have each other."

"It's definitely never boring," she confessed as he pulled away from the curb. Then, unexpectedly, Chase turned toward Simone, grabbed her hand and kissed it. This was a first for Simone, and she blushed like a little schoolgirl. As he began to drive them to a hip gastropub downtown Simone did not let go of his hand until they reached their destination. After he parked, he insisted she stay in her seat as he came around and opened the car door for her. Simon had always treated his daughter like a princess, opening her door, expecting her to sit before he had been seated, and he had great table manners. He always told Simone that if she ever found a man that treated her the same, to make sure she held on to him because good men are hard to come by.

"Can we grab a booth?" Chase asked the hostess before they took a seat. Simone liked the way he took charge as he sat down beside her. Damn, she wanted to grab him and make out right there, but she didn't. She kept it clean, at least for now.

"So, now I want to hear more about you," she said, staring into his eyes.

"Then you're going to have to stop looking at me like that, because I can't even think. And you have to stop biting your bottom lip like that," he demanded, before leaning in and kissing her. Simone felt herself gasp as his lips touched hers. The electricity between them caused the two to pull back and stare at each other a full minute before they could recover.

"Wow," she exclaimed touching her lips where his had just been.

"Wow, is right. Damn, woman, what are you trying to do to me? I'm trying to be all PG first date, and that kiss took me sailing right past Rated R." She lowered her eyes, afraid he'd see that they were in the same place. Chase placed his hand on her chin and brought her to his eye level. "I like you, Simone Banks. I really, really, like you. Now if I wanted to get laid that's easy. Way too easy. I'm not trying to sound conceited but it's true. I want to get to know you first and foremost. And whether we wind up in bed today, next week or next month it doesn't matter, because I'm still going to want to get to know you. So we can take this as slow as you like or as fast, but I'm on this ride with you." His words rang true to her, but they were also scary. Her whole life Simone had been waiting for a man to be real, honest, and to not try and play her. Basically, she had been looking for a man that reminded her of her father, but those kinds of men didn't come around every day.

"I hear you," she answered, knowing that she couldn't hide the vulnerability in her eyes. She wanted so desperately to believe him and to trust him, but she'd been burned more than once by a brother who came on hard, but when he got what he wanted, he was out.

"I'm not asking you to just hear me. I want you to believe me. Not some surface bullshit, but deep down at the core. Look, I know how this sounds, and I'm the one saying it. What I do for a living requires me to take everything I hear and weigh it, but to never just trust it until I've ruled out all other possibilities. Well, I'm telling you that what I'm saying to you I haven't said to a woman since I was in college and I fell in love freshman year. The relationship lasted three years but it wasn't forever, so we moved on and we're still friends." He leaned in and kissed her again, causing her to get wet between her legs. She felt so exposed that when she glanced up there were tears glistening in her eyes.

"I . . . I just don't know . . ." she stopped herself, getting tongue-tied.

"Yes, you do," he started. They both froze to allow the waiter to deliver their food, although at the moment neither felt any hunger.

"Thank you," they both said to the waiter when he finished.

"If that kiss didn't mean anything to you I need to know now."

"Of course it did, but this is crazy. We just met each other," she began. "You don't just go from going out for coffee to having dinner and talking about serious commitments in just a few days. Yes, I have feelings for you that I cannot explain, considering we barely know each other and the circumstances from which we met, but this is crazy. It's love craziness," Simone told him as she shook her head.

"And what's wrong with crazy love?" he demanded staring into her eyes and making her feel so weak and desperate for him. What the hell had happened to her? Simone had never allowed herself to go there with a guy, not this quick, and probably not ever. God, this man was sexy. Before she could stop herself, her emotions took over and she leaned in and kissed him. She stopped caring if this were real or not and decided that either this would be the biggest heartbreak, or she had finally gotten her love story.

"You think we should eat dinner?" he laughed when they pulled apart.

"Probably," she answered, grinning from ear to ear.

"So what made you become a bank teller?" he asked.

"Desperation. If it were up to me I'd probably be one of those perpetual students always traveling, taking classes and learning new things, but my circumstances had changed and I needed to get a job. I don't think taking that kind of job is fueled by some kind of romantic longing. It was pure necessity on my part, but I've met some interesting people since I started, so it hasn't all been bad." She laughed, flirting with him.

"And she flirts," he teased her. "When I first met you, I thought you were one of those women that needs a man to make at least six figures to get your attention."

"Really? Maybe I am." She couldn't help joking with him. "I need to see your Dunn & Bradstreet rating, your tax returns for the last five years, and I need to go to your house to make sure you're not living with some woman."

"Check!" Chase held up his hand dramatically to flag down the waiter who came running.

"Yes?"

"We need to get the check ASAP." The waiter raced off to handle this request.

"You're kidding right?" Simone asked, curious about this.

"No. I want you to see where I live. Let's go," he said, taking her hand.

"Wait. Wait. I believe you."

"So you don't want to see my house?" he asked challenging her.

"Oh, I'm going to see your house, just not tonight." Simone had a big day tomorrow, and if all went well, then she and the detective would have plenty of opportunity to get to know each other.

"So you're chickening out?" he laughed.

"No, I'm not. As a matter of fact, the next time we see each other I'm going to your house."

"Tomorrow? What are you doing tomorrow?" he asked her, waiting for Simone to wriggle out of it, but she wasn't trying to do that at all.

"Working, and then I'm going to your house," she said matter-of-factly. He leaned in and kissed her, the both of them getting turned on. "Yes. I'm definitely coming to your house."

Chapter 36

All day Simone had to stop herself from watching the clock, remembering that everything that she did was filmed. She knew that she would probably look suspicious if anyone studied the tapes, but that didn't stop her. The bank manager had been particularly pleased with his job at heightening the security as the day wore on without incident. Everything had being going exactly as it should, thanks in part to all the new measures he'd put into place. Yes, this was about to be another great day, he thought as he saw Detective Dugan enter the bank at 5:12 p.m. It certainly helped morale that the Richmond Police Department were making extra rounds into the bank these days.

"How's it going?" Chase surprised Simone when he appeared at her window. She almost had a heart attack, and not because she was excited to see him, which would have been the case at any other time except right now. She was freaking the fuck out about how close this visit was.

"Great," she answered. "To what do I owe this visit, or were you here for another reason?" She tried to fix her face so the smile wouldn't come off as fake. *Don't look at the clock,* she told herself, knowing that it was ticking down to the moment she and her sisters had worked on for the past week.

"No, I came to tell you that I had a great time last night. I didn't want to be rude and text you. I've always felt texts are so impersonal. Plus we said we'd see each other today, and I wasn't sure if you'd remember," he said. Boy did this brother do all kinds of things to her, Simone thought, just watching his juicy lips moving.

"Sure. I remembered. I'm supposed to be going to your place for dinner." She smiled, but inside was trying to figure out how to get him the heck out of there.

"Yes, I can't wait."

"Detective Dugan," she heard Mr. McPearson call out as he was coming toward them. She noticed that he had that look as if he wondered if she were in some kind of trouble.

"Mr. McPearson, I'm just checking on things. Making sure everyone is safe." He winked at Simone as he walked over to greet the manager.

"*Go, go, go, go,*" the mantra kept ringing in her head as she watched the two men having a conversation about nothing. Dammit. She needed him to get out of there or they all would wind up in prison, and that was real.

Meanwhile, ten minutes away

Whose gonna run this town tonight? We're gonna run this town tonight.

Jay-Z and Rihanna's voices filled the old model suburban as the three girls inside prepped themselves.

"This is hot as hell," Tallhya complained about the extra padding she had been forced to wear so that she would look like a dude. They did not want to appear to be three women. Even Ginger had her boy clothes on. This was not the place for five-inch heels and killer nails. Remarkably, she did not complain.

"Can you slow the fuck down, Speed Racer!" Bunny hollered at Ginger, who was having way too much fun in her new role. She had always felt like she wasn't needed in the family, like she didn't have anything to offer. The fact that she was needed by her sisters gave her a rush and made it well worth the risk.

"Ooops, sorry," she commented as she eased her foot off the gas.

"Okay, so you all know the plans. Tallhya, I do all the talking. Don't deviate from what we choreographed. You hear me?" Bunny demanded.

"Yes. Now calm the fuck down," Tallhya ordered her sister as she snatched her Hillary Clinton mask off the floor in front of her and grabbed her beanie. They all shoved their ponytails under the hats.

"Pull over right here," Bunny pointed to a side street.

"Why are we stopping?" Ginger questioned. "That was not in any of the run-throughs that we practiced.

"We need to get rid of all the evidence. Anything in writing has to go." Bunny got out of the car with the papers where Simone had drawn the inside of the bank. She took out a lighter, lit the papers, and waited until they burned before getting back in the car.

Back inside of the bank

Simone breathed a sigh of relief as she checked the clock when Chase started to walk toward the exit. He looked over his shoulder and gave her a little smile that no one else would have picked up on. He held the door for the Brinks guys who entered right on time and handed the bags of money over to the bank manager. He would normally take about twenty minutes to take it down to the safe and lock it up. Once it was in the safe the chance of getting the money was gone.

"Can I have that in all fives?" a sweet old lady who might have been one of Me-Ma's friends requested of Simone. As she began to count out two hundred dollars in fives she felt anxious and really hoped this lady was out of the bank before the robbery took place. The last thing she wanted to do was to be responsible for this old woman having a heart attack. Simone watched the Brinks guys leave the bank as she finished with the old lady.

No sooner had the old lady stepped out of the bank than three people entered the bank wearing Hillary Clinton masks.

"This is a motherfuckin' robbery," Bunny, speaking in a deep, gravelly voice began. *Rat-ta-ta-ta!* Her machine gun made a noise as she pointed it at the ceiling and popped off a couple of rounds. She needed to make her point as Tallhya and Ginger, weapons in hand, hurried over to the registers to keep the tellers from pushing buttons. Simone was glad that they looked like dudes and not women. "Do what I say and no one will get hurt. Now, any of you motherfuckers want to be brave, then that will be your funeral. Everybody down on the floor, now."

All the bodies lowered, fell, or jumped down onto the floor, except the manager, who thought it might be a good idea to reason with them.

"Look, please don't hurt anybody," Mr. McPearson begged as he held up his hands and moved toward Bunny. Luckily there were only four customers in the bank, three tellers, two managers and one security guard. The other guard always went home at five, which is why Simone told them to wait until five fifteen. Bunny took the butt of her gun and slammed it into McPearson, causing him to go down. She wanted to say, *'that's for fuckin' with my sister and for treating her like shit,'* but she knew better. He went down without a complaint. Bunny had to stop herself from glancing toward Simone. In fact, she made a point not to make eye contact with her sister. *Stick to the plan*, she told herself.

"See those bags?" Bunny pointed to the bags Ginger and Tallhya held in their hands. "Fill 'em up," She screamed at the tellers. "Move," she yelled. "And don't touch none of those buttons, because I'm looking for an excuse to use this piece." She waved her gun in their direction.

"Oh my God!" Simone cried just as they had rehearsed.

"Bitch one more sound out of you . . ." Bunny aimed her gun on Simone, ". . . and I will make damn sure those are your last words. You understand?" she barked. Instead of answering, Simone appeared terrified as she shook her head up and down. Then Tallhya slipped into the manager's office where the two huge bags of money were sitting. She grabbed the bags and started walking toward the exit door. Bunny went to the tellers and swooped up the bills they had at their registers. All the while Simone was staring at the clock. This was getting close. Too close. Simone knew she had to take the chance so she coughed. Bunny looked at the clock, grabbed the money and headed for the door.

"Five minutes. Do not move for five minutes, and all of you tellers put your motherfuckin' hands up in the air." And just like that, Bunny, Tallhya, and Ginger were out the door, racing to get into their car. A good two minutes later they could all hear the sound of sirens. Simone knew that it would take five minutes to get to the second car.

"Everybody get up," Mr. McPearson told all the people lying on the floor. Jackie got up and went to check on the tellers.

"You guys all right?" she asked.

"All the employees nodded, a few that had just experienced the last robbery and murders of their co-workers were breaking down. Simone pretended to be affected, shaking as she started crying along with two other tellers. She imagined her father's funeral so that she could make herself cry. She really was worried though. Until she knew for sure that her sisters were safe, she would not be all right. She glanced at the clock. Normally she would be getting ready to leave, but right now the employees were waiting for the detectives to show up so that they could be interviewed.

Chapter 37

"Detective, these robbers were in and out before we arrived. Not at all like the last ones. It's as if they had a playbook that was the exact opposite of the one those four guys used. They even used a similar mask for all three of them, Hillary Clinton, as if they were taunting us. I mean, this may have been the perfect crime." The officer finished as Simone glanced up and saw that he'd been talking to Chase, who must have just walked in.

"There is no perfect crime. We need to look at the tapes," Chase told the detective. Simone froze where she was standing as she worried about what they would find on the tapes.

"We need to set them up in a room. Right this way." Jackie led the men toward the back of the bank.

Simone watched the clock and waited as every single person had been interviewed. Almost an hour passed while she waited, too nervous to call her sisters. The plan was to all meet back at the house. There was no telling if her phone was bugged after that last robbery, so she wasn't taking any chances. It's the little dumb things that get you caught. As she glanced around, she saw one more employee going into the office, which meant that they were almost done. She wondered why they had left her for last.

"Miss Simone Banks." A female officer approached without waiting to confirm if it was the right person. Everybody else had been allowed to go home, so it was obvious who she was.

"Yes, that's me," Simone volunteered and followed the officer down a hallway and into a back office that had been set up with Chase and another detective.

"You all right?" Detective Dugan questioned and smiled as she entered, his attempt at comforting her.

"I'm just really tired," Simone told the detectives.

"This must be hard for you. Especially after that last robbery. And this one right behind it just doesn't make any sense. At least no one was shot this time."

"Yes, thank God. I couldn't have handled that."

"So Simone . . . I mean Miss Banks, this is my partner Detective Franklin," he motioned to the middle age white guy leaning against the wall, watching her with an intensity that made her nervous.

"Hi, nice to meet you Miss Banks," he said, all the while staring at her.

"Nice to meet you too," she answered, trying not to avoid him. She knew that the detectives would look for signs of guilt.

"We need to ask you some questions about the robbery," Chase said, starting to interview her. After last night this seemed so weird.

"Yes, of course. What do you need to know?"

"It doesn't make sense that anyone would hit the bank this soon after the last one. The one thing everyone seems to agree on is that at least one of the suspects was a female, but there is a question about the others. Not everyone agrees on all of the suspects being female." Simone didn't dare mention what had just gone through her head, which was that Ginger would go ballistic if they dared to suggest she wasn't a female, even if she was pretending to be male.

"Yes, I thought it was two girls too," she agreed.

"Our first thought is that these might have been connected to the male bank robbers."

"You think so?" She hadn't thought of that as a possibility.

"We were looking at the surveillance tapes and we couldn't help noticing a couple of things Miss Banks, Detective Franklin commented. She glanced over at Chase and saw him attempt to offer his support with a weak smile.

"Yes, what is that?" she said trying to stop her voice from shaking and revealing that she was scared shitless.

"We noticed that for at least an hour prior to the robbery you kept glancing at the clock," the detective questioned her. Simone had to think quickly on how she would explain herself out of that.

"I had special plans tonight and I guess I couldn't wait. I spend a lot of time being independent, not allowing myself to like anyone, and the truth is I had a date last night with someone I like, and we were going out again tonight." She caught Chase's eyes as he looked up at her, curious about how much she would say.

"Really?" So you were watching the clock because you had a date?" Chase jumped in and asked her.

"Yes, I guess my secret is out. I was anxious about my date tonight," she coughed, and then had to take deep breaths to stop herself from choking. She wasn't entirely lying. She really was looking forward to her date tonight, but she knew that wasn't the real reason she kept looking at the time.

"You all right?" Chase rushed over to the door. "Can you grab us some water?" When he returned he handed Simone a bottle of water.

"I just have this cough that comes and goes."

"Wait. Miss Banks, the reason you were looking up at the clock had to do with your excitement over a date? So you must really like this guy?" Chase questioned her, watching her closely to see if she were embarrassed. Simone scrunched up her face, trying not to die of embarrassment.

"I like him enough to not want to talk about it. I don't know him well enough. I mean he could be a player for all I know."

"But you like him?" he asked again, while Detective Franklin watched the two of them like a tennis match. Suddenly it was as if a light bulb went off.

"Yes. I think so," she admitted.

"Thank you, Miss Banks. That will be all. Partner, why don't you walk Miss Banks to her car. We can get in touch with her if we have any more questions."

"You sure about that? I don't want to step away if you need me," Chase questioned his partner, no doubt feeling self-conscious.

"I'll go and gather my things," Simone explained and left the room with the two detectives watching after her.

"She's a beautiful woman, Chase," his partner teased him.

"Look, I only asked her out after she was cleared from the last robbery. I had no idea that the bank would get hit again and this would become an issue."

"You like her, huh?" he asked, putting Chase, who preferred to keep his work and business life separate, on the spot. The two men worked exceptionally well together over the past four years, but where Franklin was married with children, his partner could, and had, been accused of being wedded to his work. The way he looked at Simone gave his partner some hope. He'd been talking to him about the importance of balancing work and home life, and he hoped this meant that he was actually willing to make a change and to give this woman a chance.

"I do like her, but maybe it's a bad idea trying to mix these two things."

"If I thought that was a problem I would be the first to tell you to proceed with caution. But there is no way that young lady had anything to do with this robbery. I'd bet my badge on it. If you like her, and from what I just witnessed I'd say that you do, then you should go out with her. Hell, I haven't seen you light up at the sight of a woman in years, and the way they throw themselves at you, I would know."

"You're right. But you really think it's going to be all right?"

"What, you don't trust me now?" He gave his partner a stern look to go with his response.

"I'll be right back." Chase agreed.

"Go. And take your time. I want to look at this tape again." He motioned his partner out of the room. It was nice to finally see something other than work on his mind, if only for five minutes, because they had a lot riding on this case.

Chase met Simone at the door.

"I'm around the back, in the employee parking lot this time. I thought it was time I followed the rules. My boss isn't exactly team Banks," Simone told him as they went around the building to her car.

"Look, about tonight." he began. She could tell that his mind was heavy, so she finished his thoughts.

"It's not going to work for a date?" she smiled up at him. "I know you have your hands full." She smiled at him.

"I do. You have no idea. The FBI is threatening to take this case away from us if we don't find the suspects within the next twenty-four hours." He sighed, looking real stressed about the situation, which made her feel torn because she knew that she was the reason for his problems.

"It's all right. I can have dinner with my sisters. I really need to get my mind off today." She lied, because what she needed was to help Bunny give Ghostman his money tonight.

"So now you're cancelling on me?" he looked a little confused, and that actually confused her.

"But I thought that you were cancelling on me," she answered. Even though she wanted nothing more than to spend time with him, she had something much more important on her plate at the moment.

"I might be a little later than I originally planned, but I will let you know. You're not getting rid of me so easily." He leaned in and gave her a kiss that turned passionate, reminding them both of the chemistry they'd had last night.

"Wow."

"Was that okay? I don't know after everything you went through today I thought it might . . ."

"Might what?" Simone asked cutting him off.

"Be nice. A reprieve from the heavy stuff we're both dealing with, not to mention that I've been wanting to kiss you all day."

"Good, because to me that is the best reason." She smiled suddenly wanting to be wrapped up in his arms somewhere far away from this bank. Hell, far away from all of it if that were even possible.

"I got to get back in there. I will call you as soon as I can." He opened her car door and waited until she got in and pulled away before heading back into the bank. The detective couldn't remember the last time he'd spent this much time thinking about anything besides work. Yes, Simone Banks certainly intrigued him, but even more than that she made him feel at home, he thought as he reentered the crime scene.

He kept asking himself how the hell had the same bank been hit in such a short time?

"Nice of you to join us detective," FBI agent Jonathan Marks, Detective Dugan's contemporary and nemesis, quipped, when he saw that Chase appeared annoyed to discover him surveying the crime scene.

"What? You're not honoring the 24-hour threat your superior gave us? Is that how the FBI works these days?" Chase sneered at the man who proved to be a consistent thorn in his side, always taunting the local police that they were inept when it came to doing their jobs.

"Oh, I'm so certain your team will fuck this up that I'm making sure none of the evidence is compromised."

"Your blatant disrespect is getting old, Jonathan." He looked down at the agent, pleased to have a good four inches on him.

"You don't have a problem with it, do you? Because I could call your Sergeant and talk to him," he quipped, watching his team collect whatever they could from the scene. All Detective Dugan could do was watch the smug officer, who had made a habit of stealing his cases to the point that he couldn't help take it personally. Sure he'd been the one to make Detective before Marks, and that made him quit the police force and join the FBI, but you'd think making that leap would have satisfied him.

"I've got work to do." Chase stepped around him and went to find his partner.

"Detective Dugan, tick tock," the agent warned him as he stormed off, as much to get away from him as to try to find the bank robbers.

Chapter 38

Simone left the bank and drove straight home. She knew that if for some reason the cops hadn't bought her story and put a tail on her she needed to go where she said she would be. Her nerves were completely shot as she pulled up in front of the house and parked.

"Dammit!" Simone noticed a new large for sale sign spiked into the grass in front of the house. She hated that damn Cassius Street, and promptly added his name to the list of people she planned to make pay one day for their betrayal.

"We did it!" Ginger raced outside and jumped all over Simone as soon as she stepped out of her car.

"Stop!" she snapped at her sister. "We need to act cool in public." She rushed Ginger inside the house.

"What happened at the bank after we left?" Bunny hurried down the stairs at the sound of Simone's voice.

"Well, Chase and his partner interrogated me for what seemed like forever. But then I could tell that they ruled me out."

"Chase? We like Chase," Tallhya kidded as they entered the living room. Simone blushed at someone else mentioning his name.

"Stop!" she warned her. "So as far as I could tell they didn't think it was three women. They thought that it could possibly be one woman and two guys."

"See, I said you two hoes act like men," Ginger laughed clowning his sisters. "'Cause I'm the only real woman around here."

"Ginger shut up. What else happened?" Bunny demanded. Simone understood why her sister sounded more stressed out than the rest of them, but she needed to fall back. This whole thing had taken its toll on her today.

"They did everything I said that they would; fingerprints, tire prints, they separated all of the employees and interviewed us. It was like they were trying to catch us all in a lie but they didn't know that I was the only one that knew anything."

"So it was that easy?" Tallhya sounded shocked.

"Maybe it was beginners luck?" Ginger suggested.

"We can't ever do it again." Simone preached to them. "This was so scary. My nerves are shot right now. You all have no idea how worried I was sitting in the bank after you three left. I just kept wondering if you were going to get caught and all of us would wind up behind bars. We risked our lives. I still can't believe we did it."

"But we did it for Bunny. Me-Ma was the first one to tell us that we needed to stick together and take care of each other no matter what," Tallhya added.

"Shit. Me-Ma would not be OK with this, but it ain't like we had any other choice. We can't let somebody hurt our sister," Ginger added, getting emotional as she went to hug Bunny.

"Thank you so much, all of y'all. I can't believe we pulled it off. I mean this motherfucker would have no problem taking me out the way that he did with Reek, and you all saved me."

"Shit, after what that asshole Walter did to me I needed to do something badass on some *Set it Off* shit. This new Tallhya ain't about to take no shit from nobody, so jokers like Walter better watch their fuckin' backs."

"Amen, my sister!" Simone, Bunny and Ginger exclaimed as they went in for a group hug with Tallhya. There was just one thing left to do before they could put all of this behind them.

"Guess it's showtime." Bunny got up and went upstairs to get herself dressed. Simone didn't want to let her go alone, but this wasn't about to happen without a fight, because her sister invented stubbornness.

"Either I come with you, or you're not going and he'll have to come here to pick up his money," she insisted as Bunny stopped to weigh what she said before taking a deep breath and answering.

"Fine, you can drive with me, but you can't come inside," Bunny demanded as she strapped on a pair of black patent leather flat Louboutins.

"Damn, I wanna go," Ginger came into the living room whining. The adrenaline of the day had her going nuts. She was ready to race all over town like a bat out of hell and cause all kinds of trouble, which is why her big sisters clipped her wings, at least for the night.

"You need to stay put." Simone warned.

"Damn, Sisi, you are getting in the way of my shit," she complained. "If I hadn't robbed a motherfuckin' bank like a real pro I'd still be going out and getting my swerve on."

"Well, then it's good you're being forced to take a break," Bunny snapped giving her face and attitude. "Give your jaws a break from all that dick sucking."

"And we need to let the heat cool down offa that cash too." Simone piped in.

"So let me get this straight. All the money is too hot to mess with, so that little shopping spree I wanted to go on is not going to happen?" she pouted at the idea that she wasn't going to be as fly as she had been earlier.

"Girl, stay your ass home. We can watch reruns of the news." Tallhya came in from the kitchen eating a slice of peach cobbler pie. She plopped down on the sofa and clicked on the television, flipping the channels for the news stations.

"So we good, Bonnie?" Simone asked, but it came out like more of a warning than a question. All three sisters turned to stare at this new version of their sister who had always been the rule follower with her head on straight.

"I hope you calling her Clyde, 'cause my ass is Bonnie." Ginger just couldn't stop herself from being dramatic, but they lived for her quips, and they all broke out laughing.

"Bunny? You're going to pay off the thug who probably killed your boyfriend, not a date." Simone reminded her rolling her eyes.

"Yeah, well I want to keep him distracted so that he don't know what the fuck hit him until it's too damn late."

"All right. Hurry up! Let's go."

"Somebody is tryin'a get back in time for a late date?" Tallhya kidded her sister. "I can't believe that after everything that went down today you of all people got dick on the brains."

"What's that supposed to mean?" Simone asked getting all huffy and bothered. After all, she was a living, breathing female. Three sets of heads swiveled in her direction and served her some serious side eye. "What?" she asked, still not getting why her sisters were messing with her. "I like him."

"All we know is, for the longest time we thought you were adopted, or Deidra had stolen you or something." Tallhya tried to sugar coat what they had all been thinking.

"Girl, what she trying to say is that your mama Deidra is a ho and her fine ass daughters are not that far behind her. We always wondered why your ass wasn't giving it away too," Ginger told her, snapping her fingers like it was just a given. Bunny jumped in with her piece.

"Well, I might not be as big a ho as some of you," she said shooting looks at Ginger and Tallhya, "but we all got dick sucking skills in the blood and like to fuck, except you, 'cause you be so damn prissy. No biggie. We love you like a sister," Bunny winked, trying to make her laugh, but she was not pleased.

"For all your information I might look like a good girl in public, but I'm a real freak between the sheets. And if we were in a contest I would win on fellatio alone."

"You can't even say sucking dick in public in case somebody hears you being inappropriate, so I know you can't beat me," Ginger teased, loving the look of embarrassment on Simone's face.

"Can we go?" Simone rolled her eyes. "Later for all y'all, and when I go on my date tonight I will remember this."

"Why does she get to go out when I can't?" Ginger complained, but Simone turned to her, all attitude.

"Because I am going to find out exactly where they are with the case tonight and if that happens after the best sex I've ever had, then great." She laughed, shooting a smug look at Ginger as she headed to the door. "That's why."

The two sisters stepped out of the house and got into Bunny's Porsche. She hit the pedal and they were off. They had to stop and get the money from the storage place Ginger had rented earlier in the week. They had Ginger dress in men's clothing to rent the space as Gene in order to cover their tracks. Bunny had to give it to Simone, since her Type-A Virgo personality made sure every single detail of the robbery had been covered.

Bunny left her car in the parking lot of a supermarket. They slipped into the store and came out the back exit where they got into an old Hyundai, a Craigslist purchase that Gene had also gotten for them. They drove the car to the storage locker. Once they were inside Simone cut on the camping light she purchased a few days ago. There, sitting on top of some crates, were the bags of money.

"You need to check inside the bags to make sure there is no dye," Bunny instructed her sister. "I can't get it on my hands, because that would be it." When all the money had been laid out, Simone spotted the marked bills and grabbed them as they counted out the hundred grand.

"I want that motherfucker to pay," Bunny seethed, talking about Ghostman.

"Let's just make sure he doesn't kill you."

They shoved the money in the plastic grocery bags and left. Bunny took out her phone and dialed.

"I'm on my way."

Chapter 39

Bunny felt nauseated as she entered the house where she had last seen Tariq alive and dead. She couldn't believe how terrible it felt in her gut, as if she were reliving the whole thing all over again. Instead of the bodyguards that she had been expecting, Ghostman answered the door himself. Bunny felt her gun rub against her side and wanted desperately to take it out and blow this asshole away.

"So nice of you to come, and right before our little deadline at midnight," he smiled as if they were about to sit down to a lovely dinner.

"Not like you gave me a choice. The way I saw it, either I get you the money or you shoot me and my family dead." She responded in the exact tone he had just used to speak to her.

"There is always a choice," he reminded her.

"Yes, well, I don't exactly see death as a choice. It's more of a sentence imposed onto you or an unlucky kind of fate."

"So, is that my money?" he asked, reaching out for the bag she handed over to him.

"It's not groceries," she snapped back.

"Normally I'm not OK with smart asses, especially women. I prefer my women silent, naked and submissive, at least when I am about to fuck them," he said, leering at her as if he were imaging her in his ideal scenario, naked, ass bent over his coffee table.

"I wasn't trying to be a smart ass. I brought you the money, now can I go?" She asked, knowing that this was not the kind of man who honors his word; at least not unless he wasn't given a choice. He walked into the dining room and spilled the contents of the bags onto the table. A huge grin began to spread across his face.

"So you're happy?" she questioned him.

"Happy? No, but I'm relieved for your sake that you brought my gotdam money that your thieving bitch of a boyfriend stole from me."

"Aren't you going to count it?" she asked him, trying to figure out how to accomplish what she needed to do.

"No, I don't need to count it. Unless you have a death wish, you better have made sure every dollar is there. I know where you live, and you know firsthand that I make good on my threats," he shouted, the saliva from his mouth-spraying Bunny as he moved closer to her.

"I would never ever try and con you. You told me what I owed and gave me a deadline and here I am. That's all."

"Yes, here you are, little bunny rabbit." Ghostman ran up on Bunny and pressed her against the wall. He took his hand and rubbed it over Bunny's breast. She did not even flinch as he moved his hand lower rubbing between her legs. But she did begin to imagine him dead. "You like that?"

"Please, I have to go," she told him, her voice quivering.

"Go? Bitch you owe me for allowing you to live. Yes, you brought the money, but now you have to give me something for being generous by sparing your life. By allowing you to live, I am taking a risk. What guarantee do I have that you will not try to rob me the same way that your 'boyfriend' did?" he said, with a negative emphasis on the word boyfriend. Bunny had to work overtime to keep from freaking out.

"Take off that jacket!" he growled at her. "I want to see what is under that." As she began to remove her jacket, he snatched it off of her. "Now spin around." He motioned for her to twirl, and she knew that if she did he would spot the gun sticking out of the band of her tight skirt. Slowly, she turned, and he was all smiles and bullying until he spotted the gun. He grabbed her by the waist wresting the gun away. "Is this supposed to be some kind of threat? Were you trying to kill me you bitch?" He backhanded her, knocking Bunny to the floor.

"Nooo! I was carrying a lot of fuckin' money and nothing was going to come in the way of me getting this money to you. I had to have protection. What if someone had tried to rob me?" she cried, becoming hysterical as she lay on the floor constricting her body into a tight ball.

"Get up! Come on, get up!" he shouted waving her own gun at her as she slowly stood up to standing.

"I swear I wasn't trying to hurt you," she pleaded with him, knowing it would mean nothing for him to kill her right there.

"You're right. I have a tendency to overreact." He placed the gun on top of the bag of money, basically letting her know that he now claimed it. "It's a personality flaw, my temper, but it's one I hope won't get in the way of us getting to know each other better," he cooed, sounding as if they had just had some lovers spat and not him threatening her life. "Come here!" he crooked his finger in her direction.

"Please. I have to go." She took a step back, pleading with him.

"What? You're not going anywhere." He grabbed her and began groping her again, his hands moving in different directions. Feeling her breasts with one hand, his other palmed her ass. "Damn, you could make some real fans if you got up on the pole, baby." Bunny felt ready to throw up. Instead, she pulled away from him and violently kneed him in the balls, sending him flying backward onto the floor. She knew that if he caught her he would torture and then kill her, so she took off like a bat out of hell flying to the door. She flung it open and raced outside and down the street. By the time he recovered and reached his front door he didn't see any sign of Bunny.

"I'm ready! "Gooooooo! Go! Go!" Bunny told Simone as she got into the car. Simone immediately grabbed the phone that was on the passenger seat and dialed the number she already dialed on the burner phone.

"I need to speak with Detective Dugan." Bunny spoke into the phone using a strong southern accent. A man answered with a deep voice.

"Detective Dugan."

"Hello, I would like to report a man with a gun. He's been bragging that he held up the Metropolitan Savings and Loan. The address is 777 Palm Drive. Hurry. He's armed and dangerous!" she screamed into the phone as she slammed it shut.

"Now we wait." Simone smiled at her sister as they stared into the rearview mirror at Ghostman's house.

Chapter 40

Chase hung up the phone and raced out of his office and into his partner's, where Franklin sat staring at the computer. They'd been checking out all the bank robberies in the area within the last year, trying to find some kind of pattern. With the FBI breathing down their necks they desperately needed this call.

"We got a lead." He informed his partner, who looked up, questions spilling out of his mouth.

"Viable? I mean, do we trust it?" he asked standing up and getting his gun and equipment.

"I don't know, but it's the only lead that we have. The caller said that apparently this guy is armed and dangerous. We should take at least two cars with us to check this out, just in case."

"Let's go!" the two headed into the squad room.

"Captain," Franklin called out as he came into view. "We got a lead says it's our guy and that he's armed. Not sure if the other perps are there or even if this is real, but we need to follow it."

"I agree." the Captain glanced around at his room, "Take Manfred and Douglas, Turner and Reilly, and O'Brien and Anderson. And Palley and Hopper," he called out, igniting the officers who all hurried and grabbed their things.

"I sure hope this is it." Dugan said sharing his concern with Franklin, who nodded letting him know that he was right there with him.

"This thing between you and Marks, it's getting old. That guy, he has such a hard on for you that it's become a real problem."

"Tell me about it," Dugan agreed as they got into their car. The four standard cop cars led by the detectives' Chevy formed a convoy as they sped in the direction of the address. The whole thing had taken seven minutes to organize, and already Simone and Bunny were worrying that Ghostman would somehow get away. The women were parked a block away with a pair of binoculars watching the house.

"There they are," Bunny shouted to her sister, excited when she saw the caravan of cops fanning out in front of the house.

"I want four of you to spread out in case anyone tries to run. Franklin and I will go to the front door, the other four of you follow us," Dugan led them up the steps, where he rang the bell. Usually this is where the threats began in order to convince a perp to open the door, but Ghostman made it so easy for them when he swung the door open thinking that Bunny had come back.

Ghostman was so relaxed because in his mind, women usually begged to be with a man of his influence. He didn't expect her to be any different, so imagine his surprise when he opened the door to the cops.

"Hi, can we come in?" Detective Dugan waved his badge at Ghostman who reacted quickly by trying to slam the front door in their faces. Dugan and Franklin caught the door before he could close it. Ghostman turned and ran to the table grabbing Bunny's gun and aiming it at the cops.

"Come any closer and I will shoot," Ghostman hollered as he stood across the room with his gun pointed at them.

"Let's talk about this," Dugan spoke in that calm voice under pressure that took many years to perfect.

"Fuck you! I don't want to talk to you," Ghostman cocked back his gun.

Blam, blam, blam! From where Simone and Bunny were located, it sounded as if fireworks were going off inside the house.

Blam, blam, blam!

"Nooooo!" Detective Dugan screamed as Ghostman's body was riddled with bullets, sending him falling to the floor. He'd taken the first shot at the detective, who returned the hit, but the four officers running in behind them finished it.

"Dammit," Franklin and Dugan shared a look. This could be bad. Really bad.

"We need to find evidence that this is our guy!" Franklin shouted to the cops. They all fanned out in different directions in the house, desperate to locate whatever could tie this man to the robberies.

"We better hope like hell that this guy had something to do with the robbery. Because if this is just some random crazy person, we are so fucked," Dugan said, commiserating with Franklin.

"Detectives?" one of the officers shouted from upstairs. They went running upstairs and into the home office. Right there on the table sat a bag containing neat bundles of money. The bag also had side pockets, and when Dugan unzipped them, he found three Hillary Clinton masks.

"Bingo!" Dugan and Franklin slapped their palms together. They were damn near jumping up and down. And this was just the beginning of the haul.

"Wait." Dugan stopped to stare at a painting. He went over and moved it slightly, placing a hand behind it.

"What?" Franklin questioned. He knew his partner and he didn't miss one thing. That's what made him so good at his job.

"It's a safe."

"We need an entire team."

"We need to get some forensic specialist, also someone who can break into this safe, and should we invite the FBI for shits and giggles?"

"I can't wait to see a certain someone's face when we show him that we've got this case sewn up."

"That is going to be so damn sweet. I can't wait to see it." The two men shared a delighted look that their bad luck when it came to solving cases was finally turning around.

Chapter 41

Simone and Bunny had just pulled off from watching the drama at Ghostman's place when her phone started to ring. Bunny snatched the phone out of the cup holder and showed it to her sister. Simone pulled over and grabbed the phone as a look of complete fear passed between the two as their worst case scenarios swirled in their heads. Did they find something in that house to tie them to the bank robbery?

"Hello," Simone answered trying to keep her voice level and normal when every part of her was quaking with fear. Bunny placed her hand on top of her sister's to calm her from shaking.

"Miss Banks?" Detective Dugan spoke into the phone using a formal greeting instead of the playful one he had used this afternoon. Simone's face registered her worry. Bunny's hand went to her mouth fighting back her own concern.

"Detective?" she responded, trying to keep the worry from overpowering her words.

"You will never guess how things unfolded after you left," he told her, but she was distracted by Bunny's hands moving, questioning her. She shrugged her shoulders turning back to the call.

"Really what?"

"We found him."

"Found who?"

"The guy who hit the bank. Now we haven't yet identified his accomplices but it's definitely him." Simone couldn't help smile, relieved to be in the clear and touched by the excitement in his voice.

"Did you arrest him?" she asked looking directly at Bunny who pressed herself close to the phone to hear the other side of the conversation.

"No. We had an altercation and he shot at us, and my men wound up killing him, which was obviously not what we wanted. If he were alive he could have led us to the others and now we may never find them. But forget all of that for a moment. We had a date tonight."

"Yes, we did," she couldn't stop herself from smiling, and knew that he could see it through the phone. Bunny moved away, watching her sister.

"Can we rain check it for tomorrow?" he asked.

"Really?"

"Yes. I want to come to your door and pick you up and take you out on a date and not have either of us worry about getting up to go to work in the morning."

"Oh," she answered, feeling way more girly than she had in ages, and really turned on.

"Unless I'm being presumptuous," he said.

"No, you're not, and that sounds perfect," she told him, then proceeded to give him her address.

"I can't wait. And Simone? We really deserve this break," he told her before hanging up.

"So you're going on a date tomorrow?" Bunny asked, fluttering her eyelashes at her sister in jest.

"I guess I am." She laughed.

"We better go and get our money then." Bunny cheered.

"I can't believe we did it!" Simone shouted.

"No. I can't believe how badass my sister is," Bunny boasted as the two hugged, relieved to have gotten away with their crime.

Chapter 42

On their way home, Simone and Bunny decided to surprise their sisters. They stopped and got Chinese food, champagne, and of course the money which they had already switched into grocery bags.

"Your ass went grocery shopping," Ginger complained as they came through the door with their packages.

"Shut up!" Bunny snapped back, taking the champagne out of the bag and passing it to her.

"Oh, hell yeah," Tallhya cheered.

"It's done. Ghostman took the fall, and to make it even better, he's dead. Fool tried to have a shootout with the police." Simone told them.

"We saw it on the news, and they found the marked bills," Tallhya told them as they all danced around.

"And the gun that was used in the robbery matches the gun that Ghostman used to shoot at the cops," Ginger added.

"How the hell did you know it would work out like this?" Bunny asked Simone, who was pouring them glasses of champagne.

"I didn't, but it just made sense. I knew the cops would not give up on finding the bank robbers, and Bunny needed this guy to pay for what he did to Spoe and Tariq, so it made sense," she confessed.

"Now if we can only figure out how the hell to make Walter pay, then that's what's up," Tallhya joked.

"Oh. That is going to happen along with my stepmonster getting exactly what she deserves, along with my father's ex-partner," Simone said as she passed the champagne around.

"And don't forget that bitch-ass fake nigga, Cassius Street. He needs to know that we are coming for him," Ginger added.

"Oh, absolutely. And anybody else you want to add to the list, let me know, because I am forming a plan as we speak," Simone said so calm that it actually sounded more scary than a threat.

"Your ass is just a straight up criminal." Bunny raised her glass to their oldest sister. "Here is to the greatest criminal mastermind in our family."

"I know that's right." Ginger toasted before they put down their glasses and dived into the money, throwing it up in the air.

"Woo, we are rich bitches!" Tallhya shouted as they danced around playfully. They were so distracted having a good time that they didn't notice someone had entered the house and was standing in the doorway watching them, a look of shock slowly turning to pleasure.

"Well . . . Well . . . What do we have here?" They all turned to Deidra smirking at them, an expression of pure joy lighting up her face. "Now you know good and well, either you can do that fed time waiting on you, or run me some of that cash. As a matter of fact. All of that cash in those bags."

The sister looked at each other and on three they were about to tackle her, but then Lenny pulled out a big-ass machine gun while Deidra collected the brown paper bags.

"Didn't Me-Ma tell ya! Easy come and easy go?"

The Banks Sisters 2

Chapter 1

Today was better than yesterday. Tomorrow will be better than right here, right now. But as it stood at this precise moment, life was what it was. And it was a damn good day to be on the Richmond Police Force. Things were finally looking up for Detective Dugan and his dedicated team of hardworking men. They'd been praying for clues that might point them in the general direction of any and all assailants that were running amuck in their fair city. Not knowing if they had a bloodthirsty serial bank robber on their hands or just some daredevil copycats, the stakes were high. All the officers' jobs, raises, and promotions were in serious jeopardy as the mayor demanded results. The wall safe of the now-deceased Ghostman, discovered behind a picture, had finally been cracked wide open by an expert on loan from the next county. The safe's contents had been logged in and were ready to be inspected by a forensic team. A huge stack of assorted currency; several quick claim deeds to homes located in known drug zones; a small spiral notebook; a Breitling watch; and an android smartphone were discovered resting inside next to a gang of snapshots of seminude strippers.

Already designating their victim as one of the perpetrators in the bank robbery committed earlier in the day, Detective Chase Dugan beamed with pride. Not only did they have the masks used in the crime, but a bag containing some of the marked bills. Detective Dugan's desire now was to try to link this crime with the blood fest robbery-turned-homicide earlier in the week at the same branch. "Okay, everyone, take your time on this crime scene. We don't need any mistakes or mishaps. We have damn near every news agency within a hundred-mile radius camped right outside this front door lurking, hoping for a minor or major screwup." With that being said, the overly excited officer of the law looked down at his watch. A far cry in cost in comparison to the one found in the dead man's safe, Chase still felt like he was rich in other ways. Placing a call to the female he prayed would one day be his lady, the smitten detective was elated to share his good news.

"Yes, hello," Simone answered trying to keep her voice level and normal when every part of her was quaking with fear. Her sinner soul was terrified about what was seconds away from being said.

"Yes, Ms. Banks?" Detective Dugan spoke into the phone using a formal greeting instead of the playful one he'd used earlier in the day.

Simone's face registered her worry. "Detective?" she responded fighting to keep her emotions from overpowering her words. She prayed he couldn't easily hear the nervous and guilt sentiments she was experiencing.

"Oh my God! You will never guess how things unfolded shortly after you left."

"Really, how?" Simone asked, scared of his response. She hoped for the best, yet prepared herself for the worst.

"Well, we found him," he fought from shouting out in total elation and jumping for joy. "We got his ass, Simone! We got him!"

"You found who?" she braced herself continuing to playing the dumb role as not to incriminate herself or her sisters just in case Ghostman turned out to be a ho-ass buster and ratted out everyone he could think of.

"We located the guy. The one who hit the bank this afternoon; that's who," the detective laughed with satisfaction in his pitch. "Now we have yet to identify his accomplices, but it's definitely him. He's one of the main guys. He's probably the damn mastermind."

"Really? You think so? How can you tell it was him? Are you serious?"

"Yes, Simone, really, I'm serious as two heart attacks. I think this case is about to be a wrap real soon. Hell, we already have recovered some of the money along with the masks. That's how we know it was him."

"Oh, wow. Did you arrest him? Is he in jail?" The questions started coming one after one. Simone glanced over in the passenger's seat at Bunny praying her new beau would say yes.

"Unfortunately, no," the hardworking detective responded with utter regret. "He's not under arrest. Well, not really."

"Huh? Why not, baby? You said you guys had some of the stolen money and them crazy masks they were wearing, right?" Simone shook her head at her sister, then shrugged her shoulders. Knowing the police caught Ghostman red-handed with all the evidence Bunny had cleverly planted and he still wasn't behind bars was a mystery Simone needed for Chase to solve. "Please tell me why that animal isn't locked up. He and those evil men he runs with need to be in cages."

"Because things didn't work out like that. See, Simone, unfortunately, there was an altercation. Things went real bad real quick once we gained entry. The dude wanted to go for bad; all renegade style. The perp got shot after trying his luck with my men."

"Oh my God! Are you okay?" She showed her genuine concern for his overall safety and well-being.

"Yes, Simone, I'm fine. Thanks for your thoughts. I appreciate it. Matter of fact, you don't know how much it means to me."

"Of course, baby. You're always in my prayers as of lately. But I do just wish that madman was alive so he could tell you who the rest of those reckless monsters are that terrorized us down at the bank."

"Me too, Simone. I wish he was alive so we could have interrogated him about other stuff we think he's involved in. But you're right. He could have led us to the others in on the robbery with him. Now, unless we catch another break in the case, the other crooks can consider his death as a gift from the good man above."

"That's great, Chase, any way it went." Simone acted as if he'd single-handedly brought down the Taliban as she quietly giggled to her sister. "That's a huge relief you got that animal off the street, even if he is dead. Him and his friends were horrible. I hope one day you catch them all before they stick a gun in someone else's face. I'm still having nightmares about both robberies."

"I know, but at least you can sleep well, knowing one of them clowns is out of the picture for good." Chase tried not to smile too much as several of the reporters rushed in his direction. "Look, Simone, I have to go right now, and I need to reschedule our date for tonight, if that's okay with you."

Celebrating in her mind over what he'd just said about Ghostman, Simone happily agreed. "No problem at all. I understand. I'm just gonna go grab some Chinese food with my sister and relax for the evening. Call me later if you find the time. I miss you and can't wait to spend some time with you."

"Aww, that's so sweet of you to say. I miss you too. And for you, I'll make time." The detective placed his cell back on his hip, ready to answer the reporters' multitude of questions.

Simone hung up the phone, relieved that their plan worked, and to top it off, Ghostman was dead. He couldn't be interrogated or forced to snitch on anyone. There was nothing but thanks that they were in the clear.

Chapter 2

"Well . . . well . . . What do we have here? Now you know good and well, either y'all can do that fed time waiting on y'all or run me some of that dough. As a matter of fact, y'all can run me *all* that!" Lenny pulled out a gun and stood guard as Deidra went for the cash. "Didn't Me-Ma teach y'all little hoes . . . easy come, easy go? Stupid asses!"

"Oh, hell, naw, this can't be happening," Bunny angrily blurted out shaking her head in denial. "Not your ass of all people! What the fuck are you doing here?"

"Oh, hell, yes, daughter of mine. This must be my lucky day." Deidra did a little praise dance waving her arms and hands around in the air as if she had the Holy Ghost tucked in her back pocket. "I asked the great hustle gods for a blessing, and here the fuck it is! Just like that . . . It was done!"

"What in the hell you talking about?" Bunny fumed, ready to kick some ass and take names later.

"I mean, damn, we came here to chin check that no good shepherd for Satan whenever he shows up for stealing my inheritance, and *bam!* Instead, we hit the jackpot! Hell, yeah!"

Bunny's impromptu champagne and Chinese food celebration came to a screeching halt, as it did for her three siblings. Smashing her glass down onto the rectangular-shaped kitchen table, Bunny was ready for war and anything that came with it. Still very much in mourning over the untimely death of the love of her life, Spoe, any bitch could get the business if they tried crossing her path—her no-good mother included. "Get the fuck on, lady, before I get pissed. If you think me and my sisters just gonna give you the money we risked our lives and freedom for just like that, you're more twisted in the head than I thought! You straight fucking nuts!"

"I'll be all that and more, but me and Lenny gonna get our share—period!"

"You think so, huh?"

"Yeah, I do. So like I said, run it. Don't keep us waiting! We got shit to do!"

"Seriously? You can't be!" Bunny's resentment grew, and her tolerance level plummeted to zero. She was ready to snap and pop any second.

"Yes, seriously! What part of 'run me all this bread' don't you and the rest of these misfits understand? I know all of y'all can understand English!" Deidra, although she called the streets her home, usually kept herself together. But today, she looked different. Maybe the death of Me-Ma had affected her far worse than she'd let on; but that still was no excuse or ghetto pass on strong-arming the next person's shit.

Coldly staring her mother in the eyes, years of bottled up emotions poured out. Without an ounce of fear for the weapon being held on them, contempt filled Bunny's tone after snatching the brown bag from her mother's greedy clutches. "You and this scheming leech you been laying up with got the game all messed up. You might have stolen Me-Ma's money and got over, but trust, this ain't what you want—gun or not. Not today, bitch. Matter of fact, not *no* day!"

"Watch your damn mouth when you speaking to me, Ms. Thang. I'm still your mother, and make no mistake—I'll still kick your uppity ass with the quickness." Deidra tried to boss up, but her threat fell on four sets of deaf ears.

"My mother? Come on now, Deidra, with all that." Bunny called her by her first name, further proving she had no reverence for the belligerent creature that'd given her birth.

"Yeah, little girl; your damn mother, like I said to all four of you no-good bastards. Run me my shit! Now!"

"You know you ain't been our mother since the day we escaped from that polluted womb of yours. You ain't been a mother to any of us! Never-fucking-ever."

Deidra was unmoved by her child's insults. Always ready to defend her selfish lifestyle, she gladly returned the favor two-fold. "I'm sorry, baby girl, but shouldn't you be somewhere mourning that dead stickup boyfriend of yours, or is one of them other hot-tail bitches he probably ran with doing that? You can say what you want about my man being a leech, but at least he's alive!" she laughed coldly.

Simone, usually the voice of reason, interjected, putting her two cents on the floor before her sister became totally untamed. They had gotten away with robbing the bank, saving Bunny from Ghostman's wrath, and getting him blamed for the crime. Plus the idiot got himself killed, to boot. Today had been a day full of wins, and Simone wasn't going to allow Deidra to break that streak. "Look, why are you here anyway, Momma? Who let you in? And why you just gonna let this man point that thing at us like we some strangers off the street and not your own flesh and blood?"

"First of all, Simone, I don't need any one of you ungrateful little hood rats to let me into my damn mother's house. Just because your daddy came up on the dirt he was peddling and raised you with a silver spoon in your mouth don't mean you can run it any way you want to."

"Oh my God!" Simone fell back, sucking her teeth.

"Yeah, maybe Me-Ma let y'all act all crazy and run off at the mouth, but me? I ain't the one. Shidddd, I'll knock all your heads off like it ain't nothing." Deidra couldn't believe her ears and what she was hearing. Taking a few steps backward, the unfit parent laughed. "If y'all didn't get the memo years ago, I'm grown and come and go as I please around here. Secondly, if you three girls and whatever the fuck you is today," she callously motioned to Ginger as if he were a freak of nature, "don't like what I'm saying, gather my money up and me and my man will be on our merry-fucking-way without anyone getting hurt. Or do y'all want me to call the police? Maybe that nosy, fine-ass cop you talking to Simone . . . How about that? So now that I've made myself once again clear, run me my shit!"

"Say *what?*" Simone paused, wondering how Deidra knew she was dating a policeman.

"That's right, you little neighborhood snitch bitch. I know everything. The streets talking loud, and you and all these rats in heels' names are ringing. Now should I call the police or what?" Deidra smirked, winking her eye at Simone.

"The police?" Tallhya interrupted, swallowing a huge lump in her throat.

"Yes, baby, I said it; the damn police. Didn't you hear me?"

"Are you serious?" Tallhya asked.

"Yes, I'm serious as two heart attacks. Either you girls can cut me and my man in or cut it out. Y'all already let that high-steppin' preacher steal this house and all my mother's freaking money."

"Let . . .?" Bunny, fed up, was once again on Deidra's no-good ass. "We ain't let his crooked ass do jack shit. And since he did con Me-Ma, that means you just gonna gank our come up? Where they do that at? You're a real piece of work—rotten to the core. For sure."

Deidra sneered, glancing up at the wall clock. She'd heard just about enough of jaw jacking from her offspring that she was willing to endure. Done taunting her four children-now-turned-bank-robbers, she was ready to collect what she felt was due to her and bounce. "Well, as far as I see, y'all come up is now *my* come up!" Feeling as if she had the heart of a lion, she brazenly brushed past a noticeably quiet Ginger. Under the twitching eye of Lenny, she bent down attempting to swoop up a handful of unmarked hundred-dollar bills scattered throughout the kitchen floor.

"Hold up, now." Simone roughly grabbed her mother by the forearm, snatching her backward. "Like Bunny said, we not just gonna let you take what's ours. That's not what's gonna go down. We ain't little kids no more—remember that."

Deidra was in no mood to be denied. Me-Ma had already slapped her in the face by leaving the church and Pastor Street the inheritance she felt was hers. Now her kids didn't want to share their come uppings. "Okay, bitches, I'm done playing with y'all. Lenny," she hissed with malice, not being able to bully them as usual with her words, "shoot the first one of these wannabe street-tough hood rats that puts their hands on me! Send them on their way to see Me-Ma." Deidra's voice got louder with each passing word. "Maybe they can ask her dumb ass why she fucked us all over! Shiddd . . . I mean, was that sissy preacher giving her old ass that rainbow dick or what!" she laughed.

That over the top announcement brought a momentary hush across the kitchen. With his palms sweating and the strong smell of cheap wine seeping from his pores, Lenny tried to look as ruthless as possible. Trembling from needing a drink, he fought to hold it together. Just as money hungry as his female companion, the low-life parasite hoped to live large off the enormous amount of revenue he was seeing as well.

"Look, you soulless trick! Have you lost your fucking mind altogether? Do those streets you live in got you that confused that you think you can march up in here making demands and threats like we ain't about nothing? And to top it off, disrespect Me-Ma's good name?" Simone fearlessly stepped front and center. Looking at Deidra like the gutter filth she was, she made it perfectly clear what exactly was and was not going to happen. "You and this fool are out of control, that much is clear, but you're going too far thinking shit will be that easy."

"What you say?" Deidra barked, feeling like she had the upper hand *and* the cops on speed dial.

"You heard me. Y'all clowns going too far, especially *you!*" Without warning or caution, Simone ran up on an obviously nervous Lenny. Now, almost nose to nose, she unloaded her fury and disdain for the stunt he was dumbly taking part of. "You coming up in my grandmother's house pointing guns at people like you some sort of hit man or something; like you so damn gangster with it. Riding with my mother gonna get you killed one day, and today might be that day. If we had the balls to get this money, just imagine what the fuck we willing to do to keep it. You don't want this nigga. I swear you don't!"

Once again, the room grew eerily silent as Lenny's eyes bucked twice in size. He, like the others in the room, didn't know what to say. Tallhya buried her face in her hands, while Bunny's jaw dropped wide open. Ginger, who was playing the background up until this point, finally spoke up. Not wanting his sister to get killed trying to protect them or the stolen money, he looked at his mother, who was so desperate to get, wanting her to stop this madness. "Oh my God, Momma! Damn! Is this what you want? Is money so important that you want Simone or one of us dead to get it?"

With tensions running high, they all waited for a response from Deidra, but received none. Ginger had no more words for his conniving mother. She'd used him and his credit card scams constantly, without any remorse if he got arrested; so be it. Not even bothering to put a single penny on his books, Ginger knew what she was doing now there was no coming back from. Me-Ma was dead and gone, and as far as he was concerned, from this point on, Deidra was as well.

"Ginger, I done told you a million times to stop counting on Momma to change. She wasn't about shit when we was growing up and damn straight about shit now. But I got something for that ass . . . something real serious." Simone's feet were firmly planted where she stood. Still up in Lenny's face, she didn't blink or miss a beat. "Bunny, you and Ginger pick up that money off the floor and put it back in the bags!"

"Hold up, Simone." Bunny raised her eyebrow in protest.

"Naw, sis, I got this; just get the money!"

"Now you talking like you got some damn sense." Deidra, shiftless in her intentions, finally spoke. "Run me my bread; every damn penny!"

Allowing the over-the-top garbage her mother was yacking about to roll off her back, Simone continued telling her siblings what to do. "Bunny, y'all just get all the cash together that's on the floor. And, Tallhya, why don't you go make sure the front door is locked and come right back. Me and Mr. Gun-Toting Lenny right here got some unfinished business to handle."

Despite objections from Me-Ma, Deidra lived her life in the streets since she was a young teen. Seasoned to the game, she knew if you were trying to pull a stunt, run a scam, or plot on a scheme, you needed to be in and out as soon as possible. She knew the more time you spent living in the eye of the storm, the more chances your shit could fall apart. Unfortunately, her bank-robbing daughters knew the same thing; especially Simone. Knowing her mother was capable of snitching to the police if she didn't get her way, Simone knew she had to make a move to make that impossible. Although there was a strong possibility she could have cancer, she'd much rather fight that deadly beast disease than face a judge and whatever part of her life that was left on the earth locked up behind bars. Once again, thanks to her father giving her advance knowledge of firearms, Simone could easily see the once-powerful machine gun her mother's boyfriend-wannabe-henchman was holding was inoperable. The old relic may have been intimidating to some; however, Simone had been through too much over the past few weeks to be scared by a "dummy gun." She'd let her once-beloved mother have her say, but it was time to turn the tables.

"I don't know what you trying to say or do, but my man ain't gonna have no dealings with you whatsoever unless you thinking about putting ya hands on me!"

Simone's voice remained the same as she informed her mother what was to come next. "Believe me, for real—for real—not one of us want to touch you; at least not yet. But this motherfucker right here," she pointed her finger in Lenny's nervous face, "he about to see what it feels like to have a *real* Banks sister on his ass! I'm done being nice." Using both hands, she suddenly shoved Lenny's small wiry frame into the side of the refrigerator. Not scared of him pulling the trigger on the faulty weapon he was holding, Simone snatched it out of his sweaty hands before he knew what had taken place.

"Holding this old shit that don't even fire no more! I told you my mother was gonna get you hurt out in these streets! If she don't give a fuck about her own kids, you think she give a shit about you getting thrown under the bus? Stupid-ass motherfucker!"

Seizing the opportunity, Ginger stepped in, transforming into Gene in a matter of seconds. Delivering blow after blow closed-fist punches to the older man's face and chest area, Ginger broke two of her perfectly manicured nails off into Lenny's rib cage. Practically stomping the cheap wine out of Lenny's skin, Tallhya joined in the free-for-all melee as Bunny collared their mother up.

"Let me go, bitch! Let me the fuck go!"

"Naw, Deidra. You wanted to be here at Me-Ma's house so bad like you running thangs . . . well, welcome your black ass home." Bunny wrapped one hand up in Deidra's T-shirt collar and the other around her neck. She'd been waiting a lifetime to show and tell her mother how she truly felt, and today was as perfect a time as any. Unlike her partner in crime Lenny, Deidra tried to buck but was immediately shut down by Bunny's hands tightening around her throat. "You got some random-ass Negro in here pointing a gun at us? Talking like shit is easy, like thangs ain't hard enough on us! You ain't coming up on shit, bitch!"

Deidra struggled to speak as her mouth grew increasingly dry. "I swear to God if you don't let me go, you gonna regret it!"

"What, Momma?" Tallhya growled from across the room after seeing yet another kick into Lenny's bleeding mouth. "What you gonna do to us that you ain't already did? Abandon us? Lie to us? Cheat us out of our birthday gifts from other family members? Berate us and everything we try to do? What's left, Momma? Huh? What's left? You wanna go dig up Me-Ma's body so you can spit in her face? You foul! I hope Bunny chokes the life outta your ass!"

After making sure Lenny was unable to stand on his own, Ginger, using the manly strength he was born with, dragged him over to the basement door as instructed by Simone. Having no remorse for the beating the fool, Ginger let his battered, bruised body fall recklessly down the old wooded stairs. After hearing the distinct sound of him reaching the bottom, they each paused. Snatching a butcher knife out of the drawer, Simone knew her two sisters had Deidra covered. Holding the shiny blade up to her face, she made sure it was razor sharp. Tilting her head to the side, the nice-sister-now-turned-bad signaled for Ginger to follow her into the basement.

Chapter 3

As much as she wanted to, Bunny loosened her grip, not wanting to actually kill her own mother. As Deidra fought off the disorientation of being close to death, Tallhya closed her eyes, trying relentlessly to not have one of her panic attacks. Fanning her hand in front of her face in an attempt to get some added air flow, she started crying out for Walter's cheating self. Bunny grabbed a sales paper off the table and started waving it in Tallhya's face, begging her to calm down and take deep breaths.

"You bitches gonna pay for treating me like this. And them motherfuckers better not hurt my man anymore! Lenny! Lenny!" The mother of four shouted toward the basement door. "Hold on, love, I'm coming!"

"Shut your mouth! For once, shut your motherfucking ratchet-ass mouth. Don't you see your child is going through something right now, and you calling out for some man?" Bunny frowned at Deidra, who was still down on the floor. "I promise it should've been you and not Me-Ma in that casket! A million of you ain't worth half of the woman she was."

Deidra had not an ounce of compassion for her children and their various troubles. Matter of fact, since they were treating her like what she felt was garbage, she decided to add more heart wrenching fuel to the fire. "Wow, Bunny, tell me how you really feel." She rubbed her sore neck as she spit more venom. "And, Tallhya, I don't know why you crying out for that no-good husband of yours while y'all talking about me running behind some man. I had a taste of that young, curved, uncircumcised dick a few months back. Yeah, when I caught him out at the club with that bisexual dead baby momma of his; showboating hard. I figured with the courtesy of you."

"What?" Puzzled, Tallhya's mouth went dry, as if she was hearing wrong.

"Yup, baby girl, we all partied together off your money and freaked until daybreak." Deidra had no shame exposing a few more hurtful truths. "I mean, the dick wasn't all bad, but it sure ain't worth clowning over. Hell, you might wanna look his baby moms up and let her eat your pussy. She sho' got better skills than Walter do!" A smile spread across her face. She knew exactly what she was doing—throwing rocks at a glass house.

Stunned at what she'd just heard, Tallhya's anxiety level increased as did her anger. It was bad enough her supposed loyal husband had an illegitimate baby with some tramp. And even worse, he'd admittedly stolen her lottery winnings. But now the bum allegedly had sex with her own mother, of all people. If what disgusting acts Deidra claimed were indeed true, that thought alone was more than the average strong-minded person could stand. Tallhya was fragile. Since being served divorce papers, the immediate family knew she wasn't in the mental state to endure any further emotional blows and tried to shield her from as much unwarranted bullshit as possible. Strangely, helping her siblings rob the bank earlier was some twisted sort of empowerment for her. Tallhya was actually feeling good about herself. It was hard, but she was willing to accept the reality she and Walter were over. Now, Deidra had the nerve to show up and drop this cruel bombshell. Divorcing the backstabbing creep was hard enough, but this betrayal was adding insult to injury.

"You know you the damn devil, don't you?" Bunny fumed, knowing her sister had to be devastated.

"You just better be lucky I ain't get a hold of that fine-ass Spoe. I would've really given his dead stickup ass a run for his money—guaranteed."

Slowly easing to the other side of the kitchen, Tallhya oozed with resentment. Her legs were numb. Her broken heart raced as she saw red. Pulling the oven door down, she kept her eyes focused on Deidra who was now preoccupied once again taunting Bunny's recent tragic loss of Spoe. Her mother had to pay for her sins. The injured-emotions daughter saw no other way to make things right. Reaching her hand inside the oven, Tallhya removed one of her grandmother's favorite black cast-iron skillets she'd cook freshwater corn bread in. Raising it high over her head, her fingers tightened. The mentally distraught female's taste for revenge increased. Wanting to silence any more spellbinding revelations, Tallhya brought the heavy cookware crashing down onto the side of her mother's evil face. Hearing the certain sound of her jawbone crack, coupled with Deidra's agonizing pleas for mercy, Tallhya felt vindicated after the verbal tirade she'd just suffered at the hands of her wicked-minded mother. Dropping the skillet to the floor, Tallhya didn't say a word. She just stood there; frozen in some sort of a trance.

"Sis," Bunny loudly whispered, attempting to get Tallhya to snap out of it. After a few seconds, she called out to her sister once more, this time shaking her shoulder. Receiving no response, Bunny had no choice but to leave her standing zombied out in the middle of the kitchen floor. She'd have to deal with Tallhya and this episode later.

With blood leaking out Deidra's mouth and nose, and her face expanding twice its normal size, Bunny knew she had to get her down in the basement with her cohort Lenny as soon as possible. As Deidra squirmed around on the floor getting louder, Bunny didn't want any nosy neighbors or members from Me-Ma's congregation to show up unannounced. It'd certainly not be a good look if they discovered what atrocities were taking place in their beloved matriarch's home.

Quickly retrieving a damp dish towel by the sink, Bunny stuffed it into Deidra's mouth, warning her to shut the fuck up or risk far worse pain. Easily telling her mother's jaw was indeed broken, she was able to jam more of the cloth inside than would be normally possible. Leaning over, she grabbed one of Deidra's feet. Bunny wished she could order a now-bewildered Tallhya to lift the other, but knew at this point she was on her own. Dragging their still-feisty mom across the kitchen floor, Bunny opened the basement door. Yelling for Simone and Ginger to get out of the way, Bunny gave Deidra the same fate as Lenny: a trip down the wooden stairs, face-first.

***

Propped up against a cardboard box of Christmas tree decorations, Lenny was motionless. The inch-long gash on his head, courtesy of the fall, continued to spew blood at a rapid pace. Having broken several teeth when his mouth slammed down onto the concrete floor, Lenny's lips were split open as well. Stepping on the small sharp pieces of his yellow, plaque-stained dental, Simone was in total survival mode as she inhaled the stale dampness of the basement. Her mother's flavor of the month had the nerve to not only be in cahoots with her, but hold them at gunpoint as well. For that, justice would be swift. The beat down he got and the free trip down a flight of stairs was only a small bit of punishment. With the aid of a few old extension cords, she tightly tied his arms. Having cut up a few bedsheets that were hanging on the clothesline, Simone instructed Ginger to wrap the cloth around their nemesis's head so he wouldn't leak his germ-infested fluids all over the place.

"What we gonna do with him, girl?" Ginger was eager to follow her sister's lead. She'd masterminded them getting away with robbing the bank, so she'd earned the right to call the shots.

"We gonna do what we have to do; to him and Momma— *that's* what!" Simone showed no weakness glancing toward the top of the stairs as they heard a small bit of commotion. "We risked everything to get that money up there, and this ignorant fool and Momma ain't gonna take it—let alone get us knocked. I ain't trying to go to jail no time soon. Is you?"

"Hell, fuck, naw! Whatever you say, I'm down. I'm rolling with you." Getting incarcerated for armed robbery was not on her to-do list. Ginger had plans of going on a few elaborate shopping sprees and updating her vehicle. Her share of the money was going to enable her to live life to the fullest . . . drama free. Unlike her sisters, Ginger had absolutely no man problems or health issues at hand. Bunny was mourning Spoe's sudden demise. Tallhya was getting divorced from Walter's conniving ass, and Simone was falling in love with Detective Dugan, and unbeknownst to anyone, possibly had cancer. The illegal revenue was a much-needed distraction for them, and Deidra and Lenny would not become glitches in the system. Just as Simone and Ginger ensured Lenny couldn't break free from his makeshift restraints, the top door opened. Seconds later, Deidra, unceremoniously, made her way down the stairs to join her man.

Moving out of the way just in the nick of time, Simone dodged her mother's body that haphazardly flew down the stairs. Seeing it hit the floor, her limbs flung around like an old rag doll Me-Ma had sitting in the corner of the living room for decoration.

"Damn, girl! What in the hell happened to her head and face?" Simone's concern was short-lived when Bunny filled her in on what she'd said to Tallhya pertaining to Walter. Having had enough of her mother's evil spirit and everything that came with it, Simone had Ginger tie a still-dish-rag-gagged Deidra up with the remaining part of the shredded sheet they'd used on Lenny's head wounds.

"Okay, y'all," she announced seeing both of their problems were temporarily put on hold, "these assholes ain't calling the damn police on anybody no time soon, let alone spending any of our money. Now, let's go back upstairs and check on Tallhya."

Chapter 4

It was the crack of dawn. Detective Dugan had been up all night pressing the forensics team on any reports of additional evidence that could link others to the high-profile bank robbery. After making a positive identification of Ghostman aka Marky Amadeo, he knew this case was about to take him in several different directions all at one time. The deceased was not only involved in robbing banks but was implicated in over a dozen drug-related homicides, to boot. Ghostman was a well-known and connected Italian criminal in the underground world of the city of Richmond. When word spread of his sudden demise, Detective Dugan got call after call from his paid informants, giving him an update on what the streets were saying. While most believed a rival bloodthirsty drug gang originating from New York, the Bloody Lions Posse run by the infamous dread named Dino, had set him up, others rumored it was one of the many strippers he ran with. Maybe even the one whose name the condo was listed in. Wherever the complicated case might take him, a connection with Simone and her family never once crossed his mind.

"Thanks for putting a rush on the items. You know the FBI and the ATF are waiting for us to drop the ball." He stretched and yawned, trying his best to fight sleep.

"No problem, Chase. I got your back." One of the guys from the forensics department handed him several huge manila-colored envelopes. "And just so you know, we got some partial prints of someone other than our deceased gunman. We're trying to see if we can get a hit through the computers."

"Oh, yeah?" He felt more optimistic about not needing the FBI or the ATF's assistance to solve the multiple cases. . . . If he'd only known the key factors to closing all the cases were just a phone call away to Simone.

"Yeah, man. I'll keep you posted. I'm on it. The chief is on my back too."

Having received the discovered android cell phone back from the forensics team, Detective Dugan studied each picture in the gallery, realizing none of the photos belonged to Ghostman. Without hesitation, he knew he'd seen the face in most of the pictures recently on the evening news. It became quickly apparent the cell phone seized from the wall safe belonged to the young man whose body was washed up along the bank of the James River, a well-known dumping ground drug dealers used to dispose of bodies. The detective remembered the man shot in the chest before he was tossed in the murky water's name was Tariq something or another. He, along with a few more bodies, was fished out the latter part of the previous week. After getting in touch with the homicide detective handling that particular case, the weary Chase started the long, grueling task of going through the extensive list of names and numbers in the contact list. Logging in the amount, dates, and times the owner called the most frequent numbers, he tried to find a pattern. After then carefully studying the iPhone Ghostman had on his hip when he was killed, and comparing the two, he felt like he might have been making some sort of headway.

Whoever the heck this Tiffany female is was damn sure getting a lot of play from not only Tariq, but Ghostman as well. Detective Dugan made a mental note as he jotted down her name. *I need to not only find out who she is and where she is, but have a long talk with her. And whoever this last number called from Tariq's cell to "B" might be the link that can shed some light on his connection to Ghostman other than this Tiffany person.*

Having had his people perform reverse number searches on "Tiffany's" and "B's" phones, unfortunately, the exhausted detective came up empty-handed. Of course, he could simply dial the two different numbers on a dry mission, fish around for answers . . . and run the risk of scaring the people off. Or he could do a little background hustle on the owners and see how they'd react when he dropped the information he'd gained on them. Kinda like a surprise attack, throwing them off guard.

Using the social media apps Tariq had on his cell, Detective Dugan was now surfing through the deceased young man's Facebook and Instagram pages. Although he hadn't updated either site in months, it still shed some light on him and the people he ran with. Going through all the photo albums, he finally hit the one marked "FAMILY AND FRIENDS." While Richmond was a big city, some of the faces seemed somewhat familiar, but a few in particular stood out. *I know this damn girl and guy from someplace, but where?* The detective racked his overworked brain as pictures of Bunny and Spoe popped up on the deceased man's phone screen. For the time being, it had yet to dawn on him it was the face of the other dead body that'd washed up on the river and his girl's sister Bunny. Lying down on one of the cots in the rear of the police station, Detective Dugan decided to rest his mind and body. He'd put fresh eyes on the entire case when he woke up. Still behaving like a lovesick teenager, he texted Simone. Good morning, before he drifted off to sleep.

Ginger, Bunny, and Simone all slept under Me-Ma's roof so they could keep a watchful eye on not only their mentally drained sister Tallhya but on Deidra and Lenny as well. Tallhya had yet to mutter one single solitary word since trying to silence their mother once and for all. Out of the four of the siblings, it was no great secret; she was the weakest. Anxiety and panic attacks were part of her extreme depression that stemmed from her being overweight and often teased as a child. Having been the first of the four of them to marry brought Tallhya a small bit of pride, but Walter's bastard love child and betrayal robbed her of that aspect of her life, along with the lump sum of her savings. Thank God she'd taken the monthly payout from the lottery and would not be completely destitute. But for now, in this unpredictable state, Tallhya was no good to her family or herself.

The joint decision was made between her two sisters and brother that she should be committed for observation at the mental hospital. Having tried to end her own life twice before, she was no stranger to the facility. Although Bunny suggested she might make mention of the bank robbery and the fact they were holding Deidra and Lenny hostage in the basement, Simone reassured the pair the physicians would have Tallhya so doped up she would be claiming Mickey Mouse was the president of the United States and Snow White was his first lady.

Leaving Ginger and Bunny to hold the house down, Simone placed Tallhya in her Neon and drove off. Only a block away from Me-Ma's house Simone received a text from Chase saying, Good morning, indicating he'd been up all night. Instead of smiling that the man she was dating was thinking about her, she exhaled, knowing the detective he was still hadn't discovered her secret.

"Sis, you know what's really good, don't you?"

"No, what?" Bunny glanced up from staring at pictures of her and Spoe on her cell.

"We should go down there and just kill the rotten bitch and get it over with. Both her and him," Ginger motioned toward the closed basement door. "I don't know why we wasting time keeping them alive. Y'all know we can't trust Momma or her slimeball man."

Bunny agreed, but just as she was attempting to choke Deidra out the evening before, she couldn't bring herself to actually complete the horrid act. "I swear I know you right. And I wish I could, but the dirty broad still is our mother."

"Yeah, so . . ."

"I mean, dang, maybe we could find another way."

"Another way to do what? Let her wild ass go run and tell the police on us or what? Give her all our money and just say fuck what we had to go through to get it? I don't know how you living, but with me, the struggle is real."

"Naw, Ginger, I mean maybe we could make some sort of deal with her."

"A deal?"

"Yeah, a deal. Like maybe we can offer her some of the money if she keeps her mouth shut. I mean, she already hurt, and it ain't like she could run off at the mouth anytime soon."

"Bunny, are you fucking serious right now? You can't be!"

"Yes, she might take some money and go. Leave us alone for good."

"Yeah, okay, then go broke and keep coming back for more bread, draining our black asses dry until it ain't none left. Stop bugging!"

"But, Ginger—"

"But Ginger my perfect silicone-injected ass! Girl, you know good and damn well Momma and that nothing-ass nigga she running with ain't going for that bullshit. And if you really believe that for one second, you crazier than Tallhya's nutcake ass! They gonna need a room for two! Or did you forget her jaw was knocked the hell off and her no-good shit of a man is also a bloody mess?"

They both giggled at what Ginger said; then Bunny got somber going on to explain that in between Spoe and Tariq getting set up by some random tramp and murdered and Me-Ma collapsing on the church stage, she'd experienced enough death for the time being. If there was a way to avoid Deidra and Lenny getting killed to keep all four of them safe and sound, not to mention free from prison, then great. Bunny was all for it. However, if there was a slight chance that couldn't happen, then her mother and Lenny were both as good as dead.

After their lopsided debate on Deidra's fate, the pair decided to go down into the basement to check on the two conniving crooks. With each creak of the old wooden stairs, Bunny heard muffled sounds coming from the corner where Deidra and Lenny were tied up at. Getting closer, she noticed Lenny had somehow wiggled his hands free from the extension cord and was working on freeing his feet. Terrified of what was going to happen when Deidra's children found out he was trying to escape, Lenny didn't say a word as he stared up into Bunny's face. Hoping for some sort of compassion from the girl, he finally muttered the words he was sorry. Before Bunny could respond, Ginger cut him off, going straight ham.

"Listen up, motherfucker! I know your ass sorry now, but it's too late for all that. You wanna be so damn gangster with our momma like y'all some old played out Bonnie and Clyde, then okay then. That's on you. So deal with the consequences of the bullshit!" Balling up his fist, Ginger socked Lenny in the side of his temple, causing him to black out.

"Okay, Bunny. Help me tie this nickel-slick Negro back up. This time, I'm using this duct tape that was on the shelf. Let me see him get loose from this!" Wrapping the grey tape around his wrist five or six times, Ginger then used the remainder on Lenny's mouth, not wanting to hear his begging voice. "Beg for mercy now, you old fart!" Slowly, he grinded the heel of his shoe deeply into Lenny's backside, undoubtedly breaking the skin. "You'll know the next time to not roll out with our momma!"

"Ginger, come over here," Bunny spoke out using her cell phone as a light. "Look at her; at her face. It got bigger."

Ginger left Lenny alone for the time being and focused on Deidra. Doing as Bunny asked, he leaned over to get a good look. "Damn! You ain't never lied, but hey. God don't like ugly, so there you have it."

"Hold up, Ginger," Bunny reached for his arm as he started to head for the stairs. "We just can't leave her down here like this. It looks like her jaw is infected or some shit like that. And look at her lips. They starting to look almost bluish."

"Good, let them lying lips of hers turn all the way blue. Shiddd, let them turn black. Like I told you in the kitchen, I'm tired of giving a fuck about people who don't give a fuck about me, and that includes her! Now on that note, I'm outta here."

Bunny watched Ginger storm up the stairs. Considering her options, she decided to just try to say fuck it like him and do the same. They'd come too far to head back; besides, she had other things she had to take care of. With thoughts of Spoe heavy on her mind, Bunny double-checked her mother's restraints before saying what she believed were her final good-byes. She might've not been able to speak her final peace with Spoe or Me-Ma, but she'd have satisfaction when it came to her mother.

"You were never a mother to any of us. All we ever wanted was for you to love us. You just never took time to do it like any normal mother would. I guess we weren't good enough, huh?" Bunny lowered herself down to her mother's swollen face and continued, "Don't worry, Deidra, your lying, scheming, no-good ass going to get what's coming to you. I bet you trying to scheme up some plan right now, but guess what? It ain't gonna work. See ya, wouldn't want to be ya!" With those last words to her so-called mother, she climbed up the stairs to be with Ginger.

"Bunny, what took your ass so long? You better not be feeling sorry for that rotten piece of shit down there." Ginger rolled his eyes, hoping he didn't have to tie her ass up as well until Simone got back. He made a mental note to let Simone know how Bunny was acting.

"Ain't nothing—damn! I don't no way feel sorry for her. She deserves everything that happens to her. I'm going upstairs."

Chapter 5

Like Tallhya, Bunny was also mentally drained. Maybe not to the point she required medical attention, but enough to pop a few sleeping pills to get her through the night. Praying for inner peace and strength since the night the love of her life left to meet up with Tariq, she grew sick to her stomach. Even though she was a mourning female, she was a soldier putting on a good front. She was devastated living with the agonizing fact she'd never see Spoe alive again. Denied even the common courtesy or opportunity to view her live-in man's body before his vindictive estranged mother had him cremated, Bunny was dizzy with grief needing closure.

Always ready to get on a ra-ra tip with folk if they got out of pocket, she wanted nothing more than to get revenge on everyone involved in his murder. The fact that Ghostman had gotten killed after she planted the evidence of the bank robbery was of no comfort. Bunny still wanted to come face-to-face with the grimy bitch Tiffany she knew set her man and his best friend up. That stripper ho was the only trick Tariq had been banging recently and had gone as far as even allowing the sack-chasing chick to spend more than two nights in a row at his crib; something he never did.

Tariq used to tell Spoe everything, and in return, Spoe would fill her in. So she knew about the plan to rob some dude that Tiffany claimed was an easy come up. The only thing that bothered Bunny was Tiffany had told Tariq the guy who they were stealing from was some dreadlock cat from New York named Dino that live right outside the county; not some Italian kingpin. Bunny had to know what happened and why. And since Spoe, Tariq, and Ghostman were all dead, the only one that could answer those questions was the forever-scheming Tiffany. Bunny knew that was the bum bitch the night she dropped the cash off to Ghostman; the one that was looking her up and down before Tariq got shot. One minute she wanted to keep it calm and let the cops do their job, while the other part wanted to run up to Treats Gentleman's Club where she knew the ill-intentioned female worked. Trying to get her mind right and deal with the loss of two of the most important people in her life, Spoe and Me-Ma, Bunny wasn't thinking clearly as her emotions were on a roller coaster.

"That's it. I'm through being a victim. That shit is for the birds." Bunny was done crying, feeling sorry for herself. Her man wouldn't want her to be weak. Spoe would want her to make each motherfucker involved in his demise to pay. She knew she couldn't rest until she found out what exactly happened to him that night. And since Spoe, Tariq, and Ghostman weren't alive to tell the awful tale, the only other person who knew what truly jumped was the dirty tramp that orchestrated the entire deadly night: Tiffany.

After making sure the clip was full in one of Spoe's guns she'd begun carrying since his death, Bunny was ready to resume being the beautiful grey-eyed beast she was born to be. "Tonight, I'm going to pay that sneaky whore a little visit down at that club she works at. I know that was her at Ghostman's house looking me up and down like she had an attitude. And if not, one of them bitches down there gonna point her sneaky ass out!" Bunny had to calm her nerves. She had a long day ahead of her and an even longer night. Placing her pistol underneath her pillow, she decided to take a short nap until Simone returned with an update on Tallhya.

The house was finally quiet. Simone was gone, still dealing with the Tallhya situation, and Bunny was upstairs taking a much-needed nap. As Ginger kicked off his shoes, he reached for the television remote. Enjoying a moment to gather his thoughts, he surfed through the channels, finally deciding to watch an episode of *The Price Is Right* in honor of Me-Ma. Just before Ginger was ready to make his guess on the final showcase, he was interrupted by three or four knocks at the front door.

"Who in the hell?" Peeking out the white sheer curtains, Ginger saw it was none other than the infamous Pastor Street. "Oh, no! Not this fake-ass Negro!" Going over to check that the basement door was securely shut, Ginger finally came back into the living room asking, "Who is it?"

"Hello, there. It's Pastor Cassius Street."

"Yes?" Ginger said through the still closed door.

"I wanted to discuss something with you girls if that's okay."

"Like what?" Ginger glanced back over his shoulder to see who had won their showcase.

"Well, can I come in, please? It won't take long."

Finally cracking the door, Ginger stepped front and center. Just as beautiful as his sisters and oozing triple the amount of sex appeal, he licked his lips, informing the man of the cloth that he was the only one home. "I mean, I don't know what you wanna say that hasn't already been said, but if you wanna come in and give me a little one-on-one Bible Study, I'm down. I'm here by myself and open to your word."

Pastor Street had a lump in his throat as he took in a full-length look at Ginger. His long, perfectly shaped legs. His full, pouty lips. The inviting curve of his hips. And the enticing way Ginger stuck his finger in the side of his mouth as he spoke. Pastor Street was definitely intrigued by what he saw. He wasn't fooled one second by who Ginger truly was underneath those female clothes that hugged his body so tightly. Me-Ma had made Gene's sexual preference no huge secret. But that didn't turn the good pastor off; in truth, it turned him on. It was common, unspoken knowledge Cassius Street was a tad bit promiscuous when it came to the single women in his congregation . . . and rumored, a few of the married ones as well. But even though his flamboyant style of dress made some whisper that he was possibly a homosexual on the down low, no one had actual facts, just juicy idle gossip. However, Ginger was different from the rest. His gaydar went off immediately the first time he walked in the church and saw the good pastor prancing and dancing around the pulpit.

"Ummm . . . one-on-one?" He fought his most time-hidden demonlike desires the best he could, but felt himself growing weaker. If there was an opportunity to surface his true desire, he wasn't going to let it walk on by.

"Yes, that's right, Pastor." Ginger licked his lips while tugging down on his tight-fitting T-shirt. "You don't wanna come inside and bless me? Lay hands on me?"

Forgetting the true reason for his impromptu visit, Pastor Street threw caution to the wind. Stepping through the threshold of the door, his manhood twitched in anticipation of what Ginger had in store for him. Although this wasn't his first time at the rodeo, so to speak, this was the first time he was willing to walk on the dark side so close to home. But there was something about Ginger that was calling his name.

"Sooooooo, you're here alone, huh? Where is everyone this fine morning?" His demons were itching to see the light, and he was all for it.

"Yup, I'm here all by my lonesome. All of my sisters are gone doing what they do," he lied, knowing Bunny was upstairs sleeping.

"Oh, yeah?" Cassius grinned as his palms started to sweat and his manhood twitched even more.

"Yup, just me, myself, and I," Ginger flirted, getting closer in his personal space. "And, of course, now you."

Cassius felt his manhood jump once more. As it started to slightly bulge out his trousers, Ginger, with one thing on his mind, got even closer. Pushing the envelope, he then reached his hand down, slowly stroking the pastor's rock-hard stick through his clothes. Receiving absolutely no resistance whatsoever, Ginger seductively unzipped his pants. Using one hand, he pulled his dick out and smiled with satisfaction.

"Hmmmm . . ." Cassius moaned as Ginger's hands made contact with his skin. He wanted nothing else but to feel Ginger's warm lips wrapped around his throbbing dick.

"Yesssss, baby, that's right. Hmmmm . . ." Ginger was pleasantly surprised the pastor's dick was as thick and long as it was. At that point, he could easily see why all the women in the church were going crazy over this man. Before you knew it, Ginger had dropped down to his knees and was giving Pastor Cassius Street the blow job of a lifetime, right in Me-Ma's living room. He wasn't too worried about Bunny interrupting his scene. He just hoped she would be in la-la land till they were all done.

Chapter 6

Simone pulled her rust-bucket struggle-buggy Neon in front of the house just as Pastor Street was walking off the porch. Not sure of what he wanted in the first place, or worse, what he might've discovered in her grandmother's basement, she hesitatingly jumped out of her vehicle. Ready to beg him not to go to the authorities and expose their family secrets, Simone braced herself. "Pastor Street, what are you doing here?"

"Oh, hello, Simone. I really can't talk right now. I must go. I have an important meeting to attend." Stuttering and in panic because of Simone pulling up when she did, he was hella nervous and just wanted to get out of there.

"Huh, excuse me?" she said, confused by the pastor's words and actions.

"Umm, yeah. I can't talk at the present. I have some other business to handle on my agenda today." He looked at his wristwatch as a frantic expression graced his face. His steps couldn't be any faster than a person chasing after a hundred-dollar bill flying down the street.

Simone was totally taken aback. Here this man who spent his life, so it seemed, conning people and always attempting to get in her pants, was busting his ass to leave just as she pulled up. She couldn't understand why he wouldn't slow down enough to explain why he was even here so early in the day in the first place. Was he on his way to the police station? Would she and her sisters all be locked up and on the front page of tomorrow's newspaper? What would Chase say? Question after question raced through her brain as Pastor Street promised to get back in touch with her and her sisters as soon as he possibly could. After that brief verbal exchange, God's servant jumped in his expensive congregation-paid-for vehicle. With the dumbest expression ever known to man, he peeled off as if he was some wild teenager showing out on the block.

Simone sprinted up the walkway. Taking two steps at a time, she ran onto the porch. Busting through the front door as if she was the police conducting a raid, she shouted out for Ginger and Bunny. "Hey, y'all. Where y'all at? Hey!" Simone made sure the basement door was still locked.

"Damn, sis. Why you so loud? What you yelling for?" Ginger smirked, coming out of the bathroom with a bottle of mouthwash in his hands.

"What am I yelling for? Excuse the hell outta me, but did I or did I not just see that damn, no-good, nosy Pastor Street coming out of this house?"

"Pastor Street? Really?" Ginger played dumb, making Simone more agitated.

"Look, fool, stop playing dumb with me. What in the fuck did he want? He didn't go near the basement, did he? Matter of fact, tell me he didn't even come in the kitchen."

"Naw, sis. He ain't come in the kitchen," Ginger teased, waving the green-colored bottle around. "He came in my mouth!" He busted out with laughter.

Simone's facial expression needed no words. She couldn't believe what Ginger was saying or claiming that had taken place. "Okay, so are you telling me that you, Gene, gave Pastor Street some head? Is that what in the hell you standing here saying? You ain't serious, are you?"

Ginger smiled, sucking his teeth. "Yessssss, girl. Right there where you standing. Shiddd, I had his ass catching the Holy Ghost. He asked Jesus to help him as he busted. Sis, I had him promise to take a special love offering for my fine ass."

"Noooooooo," Simone laughed, holding her stomach.

"Yup, and believe it or not, Pastor got some good dick. Hell, I might even start going to church just to get another special offering!"

"Ginger, you lying." Simone couldn't stop smiling.

Bunny came down the stairs wiping her eyes. "Naw, the nasty tramp ain't lying. I thought I heard voices earlier and came down here."

"Say what?" Ginger was not the least bit embarrassed. "Well, I hope your spying ass took notes on how to give fabulous head, because, honey, I'm that real deal! You natural-born females ain't got shit on my jaw game!"

"Oh my God, Ginger, girl, please cut it out," Bunny giggled at his outlandish statements. "Naw, crazy bitch, I ain't take notes, but I did take candid camera video of y'all animal asses going at it." Holding up her cell, Bunny pushed play, showcasing Me-Ma's entrusted pastor and appointed executor of her estate with his pants down past his knees with Ginger, a known transsexual, sucking him off.

Simone fell back on the couch. "See, now, *that's* what I'm talking about. Bunny got his snake butt on video. Now let's see him try to sell this house right from underneath us. I swear if he try that mess, it's gonna be some real scandal-time shit jumping off at Sunday service next week!" Simone had Bunny send the illicit video to her and Ginger's e-mail and as text messages just for backup.

For the first time since her father died, Simone finally felt as if she'd caught a break. Taking a deep breath, then exhaling, she was relieved the pastor hadn't seen Deidra and Lenny, but she knew they had to get both of them out of that basement. After having Tallhya committed, claiming she was hearing and seeing things, Simone had a long time to think on the drive home. As much as she hated the thought of any person dying by her hand, especially her own mother, Simone knew death was the only option pending.

"Look, y'all, I don't know how y'all really feel about that situation down *there*," she nodded toward the basement door, "but we can't risk keeping them tied up much longer. We gonna mess around and get caught up. Remember what I told y'all when we was about to rob the bank . . . in and fucking out as soon as possible."

Ginger was the first to respond, repeating what he'd told Bunny earlier. "Okay, Simone, it's like this. I don't give a flying fish fuck about Momma. As far as I'm concerned, she been dead. So to me, it's nothing. I'll cut the bitch throat myself if y'all need me to step up. Hell, Lenny's too!"

Only needing Bunny to make the decision to murder their mother in cold blood unanimous, Simone and Ginger waited patiently. As Bunny focused on the screen of her cell, the once diva-minded female scrolled by, picture after picture, of her and Spoe. The more pictures she saw of them happy and smiling, the more infuriated she became. With each passing breath, her temper increased. The harsh realization she'd never see her baby, Spoe, again, was more than she could stand. The nap she'd taken earlier had only made her sorrow worse. As her heart raced, Bunny's eyes started to turn beet red. Her life would never be the same without Spoe, and no amount of money from some bank robbery she and her sisters had pulled off would make it better.

Leaping up from Me-Ma's favorite chair, she bolted into the kitchen. As a shocked Simone and Ginger tried to trail behind her, Bunny snatched up the same razor-sharp butcher knife out of the wooden block her sister had used the night before to cut up the old sheet in the basement. Flinging the basement door wide open, the doorknob slammed into the kitchen wall, causing a small piece of plaster to fall from the ceiling. Not even bothering to turn the light switch on, Bunny ran down the stairs. Simone and Ginger looked at each other, not sure if Bunny was true to her actions. No sooner than her bare feet touched the concrete floor, she headed into the corner of the basement. Kicking the box of Christmas decorations out of the way, Bunny's demeanor was unsympathetic. Callously seeing a now-conscious Lenny trying to speak from behind the duct tape, Bunny went to work as if she was a butcher slaughtering a hog.

Huddled in the other far corner of the mildew-smelling basement, Simone and Ginger were silent, never before seeing their sister in this bizarre state of mind. Trying to avoid the massive amounts of blood and mucus that was splattering everywhere, the pair of them wanted to stop Bunny and calm her down but couldn't bring themselves to get in the way of the unpredictable flying blade. Momentarily pausing, Bunny seemed to examine her handiwork on what was once Lenny before turning her attention on Deidra, who was barely clinging to life anyway. Bunny decided to take matters in her own hands and speed her mother on her way.

Clutching the brown knife handle with both hands, Bunny smirked with devilish glee as she raised the butcher knife high, almost touching the low ceiling. "I miss you, Spoe! I miss you, Spoe! I just wanna see you again! I just wanna touch you! I miss you, bae! I love you! You hear me, Spoe? I love you!" With each emotional, tormented word rolling off her quivering lips, Bunny brought the sharp object down rapidly, digging it into the Deidra's upper torso. "I just wanna be with you! I wanna hear you say I love you! Please, Spoe! Please!" Yanking it in and out of the surely dead Deidra's bleeding skin, Bunny then struck the top of her mother's head, and several times ripped open both legs, then ended her gory rampage by lodging the entire shiny blade directly into the heart of the woman who'd given her birth.

Finally out of breath and energy, Bunny became eerily silent. Taking a few steps backward, she causally dropped the butcher knife to the floor. She didn't blink. She didn't move. She didn't show any regret. Not bothering to explain her heinous actions, she then turned to disturbingly acknowledge Simone and Ginger who were still posted in the corner, speechless and in shock. As if on cue, Bunny, covered in two different blood types, crept up the stairs, leaving a trail of bloody footsteps to the bathroom. The murderess got into the shower as if she'd not just bludgeoned to death her mother, Deidra, and Lenny, the man who wanted to be down with their conniving mother.

"Oh my fucking God," Ginger shockingly pressed his hand to his chest.

"You right. Oh my God! I don't know what to say! What the fuck!"

"Girl, what in the hell was that? Better yet—*who* in the hell was that?"

"Who you asking? It was like Bunny was in some sort of strange-ass trance or something. I mean . . . She was acting more zoned out and crazy than Tallhya was last night." Simone shook her head in total disbelief.

"You mean, crazier than you running up on Lenny taking that old-ass gun from him." Ginger gave his sister the side eye and cracked a sarcastic smile, not knowing what else to do or say. "You mean crazier than that shit! Shidddd, I hope that cray cray garbage ain't floating through my DNA! 'Cause if it is, Tallhya gonna have a roommate real soon."

Simone placed her hand on Ginger's shoulder and returned the smile. "Don't worry, Gene, something tells me your DNA is safe."

Standing there a couple of minutes more trying to take in and process what had truly taken place, Simone and Ginger said a little prayer in honor of the very few good moments they'd shared with their now-deceased, selfish, unfit mother. When Deidra Banks wasn't out running the streets chasing dreams that would never come true, she was all right. But those times were limited. Now she was gone and never coming back to cause havoc in their lives ever again.

Wasting no more time going back down memory lane, they had to think quickly and move even quicker. Although they were worried about being disturbed while they were cleaning up the horror-movie-worthy scene, Simone was concerned about Bunny's erratic behavior that made her step off into the deep end like she'd just done. Confused watching her sister go from laughing and joking to heinously butchering two people in a matter of moments was incomprehensible. Zero to a hundred was an understatement in this case.

A lot of things had happened to all the Banks over the course of a month. Each sibling had done a lot of questionable, over-the-top stuff to survive the best way they saw fit. However, this act Bunny had just committed was far most the wildest. Now she was upstairs in the shower humming a love song while she washed their mother's blood splatters off her face. She had just turned causally crazy, just like Tallhya. Simone and Ginger joked they hoped that wasn't a family trait, but getting a closer look at their sister's handiwork, Simone secretly prayed it really wasn't—and if it was, that the bullshit missed her. Before they could get it together and deal with how to get Deidra and Lenny out of the house, they could hear Bunny's footsteps tapping toward the front door.

They both looked at each other, waiting on who would stop her from heading out the door. But before either one made the attempt to do so, they heard the front door slam and a car pulling off, heading to God knows where.

Gathering all the old blankets and sheets they could find in Me-Ma's house, Ginger grabbed two pair of gloves and, ironically, considering the unholy job they were doing, an old "God Is Good" T-shirt to serve as a mask. Simone checked both the deceaseds' pockets for any ID's or personal items. Using a small hand ax, she chopped off their hands with intentions of dumping them separately from the bodies, making it harder to identify them with no fingerprints. After drinking almost a quarter of a bottle of Rémy to get his rattling nerves together, Ginger, along with Simone, started the awful task of not only wrapping the bodies up, but also scrubbing any traces of the murders from the floors and walls. Using all the bleach and other cleaning aids they could find, they disinfected the entire area.

Immediately noticing Deidra's and Lenny's blood seeping through the many sheets and blankets each was surrounded with, Ginger knew transporting the corpses couldn't take place until someone made a trip to their local Home Depot. Otherwise, the trunks of their vehicles would be soiled with evidence to two murders. Switching gears, Ginger instantly went into survival mode by any means necessary—which translated into *"Bitch, stay your black pretty ass out of prison."* As much as Gene loved men and what they had dangling between their legs as he morphed into Ginger, prison was not an option. He ran upstairs after informing Simone he'd be right back.

Thirty minutes later, he returned with three gigantic rolls of double ply industrial painters' plastic. Much to his and Simone's delight, after making sure both bodies were Saran-wrapped totally, the leakage of Deidra's and Lenny's body fluids was contained.

Solemnly, the blank-faced siblings began the grueling task of trying to get their mother and her boyfriend up the basement stairs. After what seemed like a lifetime of pulling, pushing, yanking, and kicking—thank God or the devil—their prayers were answered. Phase one of their disposal plan was complete. Ginger and Simone threw them onto the rear enclosed porch like two bags of garbage waiting for pickup. Unrolling an oil-stained carpet remnant from the corner of the porch, Simone further concealed their unfortunate victims from any prying eyes. Waiting for the right opportunity, they would toss them into the back of an older model van Ginger borrowed from some nine-to-five workingman he often tricked with. Dumping their problems off in a random place was the plan. Then, hopefully, they could find out what was up with Bunny going off like a caged serial murderer possessed with everything bad.

Chapter 7

Detective Chase Dugan was still extremely exhausted. He was drained, not only physically, but mentally as well. He'd pulled an all-nighter working on what he felt was the ultimate case of a lifetime. The brief nap he'd intended on taking in the rear of the squad room almost easily turned into a full-pledged eight hours of sleep. Trying desperately to find a link between the two back-to-back bank robberies was a tedious task, to say the least. With a town full of closed-lipped folk adhering to the "no-snitch" policy, he had to depend on good old plain police work.

There were no major shortcuts this time around. Locking his fingers behind his head, he leaned back ready to do mind battle. Posted at his desk, hoping for a breakthrough, he once again started to examine the seized cell phone. Tapping the blue-colored icon, he was back on Tariq's Facebook page. Not a rookie to the social media game, the detective picked up where he'd left off at. Hell-bent on a mission, he continued navigating through hundreds of pictures in numerous albums. Besides the faces that seemed somewhat familiar to him from earlier, the young victim had an extensive number of pictures and selfies with the same background. Tapping the decent-size cell screen, the pictures became bigger. The bigger they became, the resolution diminished. However, thanks to the detective's 20/20 eyesight, along with being able to zoom in even more on various parts of the pictures, he smiled. He'd finally found a common denominator from Tariq and Ghostman's cellular devices that might link them together in other ways. Apparently, each one of the now-deceased men had strong attractions to strippers that worked at Treat's Gentlemen's Club. One in particular: Tiffany, who just had a huge birthday celebration a few weeks prior.

Hell, yeah! This what I'm talking about! Finally, some sort of break for the kid. I was starting to question my damn self. I knew if I just took my ass to sleep for a little while I'd be good to go. Shiddd . . . It's a good thing I did because it seems like I'ma be taking a trip down to the club later. With a crooked smirk of satisfaction on his face, he tossed the cell on the desk and went to pour himself a cup of strong coffee.

With other officers starting their shift, Detective Dugan filled a few of them in on what he planned on doing later that evening. "Man, I'm telling you, despite all the long crazy hours and bullshit we gotta put up with from the citizens, I love this job. I mean, damn, what other type of gig can have you going to chill at the strip club and get paid to do so? I mean, what can your wife or girl say? You on the clock; city time . . . making money."

One of the married men on the team laughed at his colleague. "You real funny, dude; a real comedian. But why don't you get you a wife—hell, or even a woman, for that matter? Then come talk that bullshit about going to see some seminude female other than your girl and think it's gonna be all good at home. We'll all be bringing you flowers to the hospital!"

Laughing himself at what was said, Detective Dugan realized that hours upon hours had flown by, and he had yet to hear Simone's beautiful voice. He liked her like he'd liked no other woman in an extremely long amount of time. There was something about her from day one that had penetrated the body armor he had built around his heart. Now, just like that, in a matter of days, the educated, poised, bank teller had broken through. Not wanting to lose Simone Banks like he'd done other females in the past from neglect of time due to his dedication to his job, he reached in his pocket, removing his own cell. Going to sit out in his car for a little privacy, he turned on his favorite radio station. With the soulful music playing softly, Chase dialed Simone's number.

It was finally quiet at Me-Ma's house. After all the things that'd taken place since her abrupt death, her grandkids knew she had to be turning over in that fresh grave she was lying in. Yet, some of the factors were put directly into motion by Me-Ma's own hand reaching out from the ground. Leaving not only her money, but the family house as well to Pastor Cassius Street had set off a shitload of events that might not have taken place if her grandkids had other options in place. Playing the unfair hand that was dealt to them, at this point, it was what it was.

Ginger and Simone had both taken showers. The exhausted pair was eager to get their mother's and Lenny's blood mixed with their own sweat washed off of them. It'd been the longest twenty-four-hour time span they'd ever lived through . . . robbing a bank, setting up Ghostman to get knocked, then ultimately murdered, having to subdue their greedy mother and her dim-witted man, watching Bunny slaughter their asses, then damn near breaking their backs dragging their heavy, chopped-up bodies out to the back porch. Simone also had to get Tallhya committed. And lastly, Ginger was extra tired having secured that Pastor Street wouldn't be trying any gank moves on the house the Banks siblings called home.

"No shade, but I still can't believe Bunny bugged out like that!"

"Who in the fuck is you telling?" Ginger replied, rubbing baby lotion on both his swollen feet. "And then got the nerve to play that fraud-ass crazy role."

"Yeah, and then disappear, leaving us to clean her mess up." Simone sat back on the couch chopping it up with Ginger as if they hadn't just witnessed their mother take her last breath. "I keep calling her, and it's going straight to voice mail."

Ginger shook his head while shrugging his shoulders. "Oh well, unless you wanna take another trip out to the crazy house today where Tallhya's at, let that bitch Bunny be. She'll get over it sooner or later. That bullshit business with Spoe, Tariq, and that Ghostman motherfucker got her spooked. It got her in a place in her mind that ain't right."

"Yeah, well . . ." Before Simone could finish her sentence her cell phone rang. Instantly a gigantic smile graced her face.

"Oh my freaking God," Ginger acted as if he was throwing up in his mouth. "Let me fucking guess . . . Detective Good Dick is calling!"

Simone threw up her middle finger at Ginger.

"Hey now, Chase." Simone tried to block all her recent troubles out as she happily answered.

"Hey yourself, Miss Lady. How are you doing this evening? You good?"

"Yes, I'm good. I'm just sitting back handling a few things here at my grandmother's house," she answered, not thinking he could've asked to stop by.

Ginger sat straight up. Ear hustling, he shot Simone the serious side eye, then pointed toward the back porch where the bodies were waiting to be loaded into the borrowed van. Mouthing the words "What the fuck!" Ginger reminded the love struck Simone to not get that carried away with the conversation with this fool that she forgets he's the police. Every single person in the hood they lived in knew, at the end of the day, it was fuck the police. They might've claimed to offer protection, but that was only to some. And Ginger knew that if Chase had the slightest bit of knowledge that Simone was involved in extortion, bank robbery, and the premeditated murder of her own mother, their fledgling love affair flight would be over before it really got off the ground.

"Wow, girl. First things first, I wanna tell you I really dig you. And I really enjoy spending time with you."

"Excuse me, Chase," Simone interrupted, eager for him to get to the point. "But I know you're not breaking up with me, are you? I mean, trying to give me the brush-off?"

"Oh hell, naw, girl. You're not gonna get rid of me that easy. I was just gonna say I'ma be tied up just a few more days trying to close these robbery cases out, and I didn't want you to think that I was ignoring you."

Simone was torn. Part of her was elated her new beau was offering a reasonable explanation of why he would not be as accessible as he would like to be, while the other part of her was worried that the explanation he gave could bite her in the ass, costing her and her siblings their freedom. Not willing to just sit back and wait for the unknown to occur, Simone started to question him on the sly. "Okay, then, Chase, I was about to say . . . I mean, to be honest, I'm really feeling you too."

"Oh, yeah?" He leaned his car seat farther back after turning the radio all the way down. "Simone, I swear I hope you understand. I don't want you to feel some sort of way. It's the job keeping me busy."

"Yeah, of course, I do understand that business comes first. That goes without saying. It's just that I'm so confused about the whole thing in general. I mean, I thought that god-awful man that'd robbed the bank was dead. So it's over with now . . . right? I mean, what else is there to it?"

"Well, kinda sorta. But it's not just that one case I'm working on any more. We think it might be a link to the other one." He offered her an insight on privileged police information. "So until we follow every possible lead, I'm might have to pull a few doubles. Like tonight." He dared not say he was going to a strip club, so he just kept it simple. "It might be a long crazy night for me, but I'll definitely text you later, if that's all right with you."

"Of course, it is, Chase. Keep me posted." Simone's nerves were rattled, to say the least. Hearing what should've been a closed case was now being linked with the first bank robbery had her shook. A damn crime that had absolutely nothing to do with the one they'd committed.

After ending the conversation, he returned to the station and headed to the squad room. Questioning each one of his team members to see who wanted to tag along to Treat's Gentlemen's Club, Detective Dugan had a burning need to tip one stripper in particular: Tiffany. And if luck was on his side, the do-anything-strange-for-some-change dancer would be open to answer a few questions about both the deceased men that seemed so attached to her.

Meanwhile, Simone's mouth grew dry, and she felt dizzy. Sadly, she filled Ginger in on the fact that even though Ghostman was dead and being deemed the mastermind behind the bank robbery they'd pulled off, they definitely weren't out of the woods yet. She informed a now-also-concerned Ginger that Detective Dugan and his men were not gonna leave any stone unturned until they brought every single person that played a hand in both robberies to justice. Nervously, Simone once again called Bunny to give her the update on not just what

Chase had told her but the Deidra situation as well. Just like earlier, she still only got her voice mail. She tried again just for good measure but got the same outcome.

It had gotten dark enough for Simone and Ginger to complete their final task for the evening. Dressed in all-dark clothing, they each put on sneakers, lacing them tight. After Ginger walked around the house making sure the coast was clear, he signaled for his sister to open up the rear door of the porch. On the count of three, Ginger and Simone lifted Lenny's body first. Rigor mortis had set in, and he was as heavy as a sack of bricks and stiff as a board. Even though Ginger was born a man, the struggle was real. It was as if Lenny, even though semichopped up, was repaying them for his murder by being extra difficult to get down the stairs and into the back of the cargo van. Deidra, on the other hand, seemed to be a bit more cooperative. Her frame was much smaller in size, and maybe it was because Simone and Ginger were getting rid of a lifelong headache that made tossing their mother into the van a breeze.

With Ginger behind the wheel, Simone acted as the navigation system, instructing him which way to turn. Finally getting to the murky banks of the James River, Ginger backed the van up. Jumping out of the vehicle, the pair moved as quickly as possible dumping the bodies. Dousing the Home Depot plastic shroud Deidra and Lenny were wearing with lighter fluid, Ginger grabbed a few twigs and lit the ends. Using the twigs as small torches, he dropped them on top of the two. Not waiting to see the certain bonfire-like blaze burn, they rushed back to the van and hit the road. About one mile from the river, Simone set the Ziploc freezer bag containing four hands on fire. Knowing the police would think it was just some random bad-ass kids setting a Dumpster on fire, she tossed the bag in a school garbage can that was full of paper, making the hands burn even faster. In less than ninety minutes after they'd left the house, Simone and Ginger were back at home; no worries; no remorse; no regrets.

Focused on what would be their next move, they both headed upstairs for a much-needed nap to recharge.

Chapter 8

I'm done! I swear I'm so fucking done with the dumb bull-shit! Ain't no bitch or punk-ass nigga gonna take advantage of me any damn more. I let Spoe into my heart, and he left me. He let these fucking streets take him away from me; away from this house; this bed. I don't even know how he took his last breath. What was he saying? What was he thinking? Did he suffer? I know that idiot Ghostman shot Tariq, but where was my baby? Where was Spoe? Oh my God! Shit! Now I'm fucked all the way up! And why? 'Cause some greedy sack-chasing trick-ass pole swinger was trickin' on my man! This some real bullshit!

Bunny used her feet to kick off the thin but expensive com-forter that'd been surrounding her since she stepped foot back inside her condo. The condo that once belonged to her and her man . . . her best friend and confidant. Spoe was supposed to be her hustle partner for life, and now she was forced to be out here flying solo. *That ho Tiffany gonna pay for settin' my man and Tariq up. She thinks it's over? Like Ghostman gonna be dead, and it's all good?* Bunny's mind had been spinning all afternoon. From the point she snapped and sent her mother and Lenny on their way, she'd been harping on the night Spoe left her arms until the moment Ghostman cal-lously announced he was dead. Since that moment, Bunny felt as if she never had a second to slow down and take in what'd truly taken place. Then just like that, when she heard Ginger and Simone talking, she snapped. It was too much yakking and not enough action. She'd killed two people without the smallest bit of remorse. And now, it was the stripper's time to pay. When Bunny got down to Treat's Gentlemen's Club, she was gonna be hell-bent on damn near wrapping that pole Tiffany swung from around her neck—twice.

***

"Hit the strip club, we be letting bands go. Everybody hating, we just call them fans though. In love with the money, I ain't never letting go . . ."

"All right, y'all get your hands out your pants and make it rain on some of these hot-box pretty young things running around this motherfucker tonight. Money in the air makes them legs open wide! Let's see some legs and cash in the air!" The DJ was earning every bit of his salary trying to coax some of the tighter fist pussy-gawkers to cough up some of the dough they were sitting on.

"Girl, I don't know what in the hell is wrong with some of these crab-ass niggas tonight. They acting like the world coming to an end, and they need to hold onto every dollar they can get their hands on," Tiffany remarked, hesitant to even get undressed and hit the stage. "Shiddd, I might as well go back to the crib and chill for the rest of the evening. Watch some damn cable or something. You know what I mean? This may not be worth it."

Sable sat across from the tall top table agreeing with everything her homegirl was saying. Nursing the same glass of cheap wine she'd paid for herself since stepping foot in the club, she wanted to do the same as Tiffany. "I swear, I'm telling you, I was about five minutes away from bouncing outta this dried-up spot my damn self. But you know Cash Dreams having her party tonight."

"Oh, yeah. I freaking forgot. Especially considering it's so whack in here." Tiffany turned up her lip, then rolled her eyes.

"Yeah, I know, right?" Sable giggled out loud snapping her fingers to the music blasting out of the built-in speakers. "But the dumb bitch did support my party and yours, so you know how that bullshit goes. Even if she can't pack the house, we gonna show the skank some love. You already know."

"Yeah, I do. Shit!"

"Well, sis, stop fucking complaining. At least your ass had a few days off relaxing and ain't been posted in this bitch! It's been crazy mad slow, for real, for real."

Tiffany walked away from the dressing area and headed to the bar and ordered a double shot of top-shelf Hennessey from the waitress. Quickly downing the throat-smooth liquor, she tried to get her mind right and get back into the hustle and flow of the club life. Sable was correct. She did indeed have a few days off, but she definitely wasn't relaxing; far from it. Even though Tiffany tried to play the tough role, she was still a female and still had emotions. In between the haunting image of watching Tariq get murked and Ghostman getting his dumb self killed by the damn police, the gorgeous, conniving go-getter was ass out with two of her main sponsors now gone. Trying to be nickel slick and come up, now with both her moneymaking dudes fallen on their backs, Tiffany needed to mess around now and find some new tits to suck off of. Those revenue wells had permanently run dry, and it was only God that she believed help her dodge the bullets of getting caught up behind each one's sudden demise.

True, Tiffany had money saved, but the lavish lifestyle she wanted to live had to be maintained. She had tried repeatedly to get with her other homeboy Dino, who was head of the infamous Bloody Lions Posse. But unfortunately for her, the seasoned criminal moneymaker Dino wasn't returning her calls. She prayed he didn't have a clue she'd low-key sent Spoe and Tariq to break into his mansion and relieve him of all his drugs and cash. Tiffany knew his crew were the ones who really killed Spoe and not Ghostman, but either way it went, she felt it was none of her business. Both the stickup niggas were gonna be dead at the end of that night anyway, so it really didn't matter by whose hand. Their fate just came a little earlier than expected. Now she was back at the strip club seeking her next sponsor. A true hustler is only as good as their next mark; and Tiffany was back on the hunt.

Watching the news, Dino lit a blunt and frowned. It had been well over a week since he'd doubled back home and caught two crooks violating his domain. After having an in-house shoot-out with the guys, Dino's dedicated crew forced both of them to jump from one of the bedroom windows. Suffering bone injuries from the rough landing, the brazen thieves fled into the woods. Swiftly realizing they had not only a huge portion of his money, but some of his drugs as well, Dino let his trained dogs go in pursuit. Luckily for Dino, the two men weren't as quick as they hoped to be. In between the darkness of the night, the many trees, fallen limbs, and holes in the uneven ground, the thieving duo never had a chance. It was like taking candy from a baby. The attack dogs were on their trail immediately and never let up until they earned the fresh porterhouse steaks they were blessed with later that evening. After shooting one of them from afar, Dino ran up, finally getting satisfaction. Firing a fatal shot directly between the eyes, he'd sent one of them home to meet his Maker. Much to his dismay, the other unknown man got away, taking the bag of their ill-gotten gain. Dino's loyal team searched high and low for Spoe's accomplice but sadly, came up empty-handed.

After running the deceased stickup man's pockets, they saw he had not one piece of identification on him, making the task of linking him up with another person or enemy drug-dealing crew practically impossible. There was only one way to positively identify the guy, and that was to let the trained professionals earn their paychecks: the police. Having his men toss Spoe's headshot-wounded body into the James River, Dino swore he'd find not only the person who had his property, but the disloyal motherfucker who'd set him up in the first place. As he focused on news report after news report, he soon saw that his archrival, Marky aka Ghostman had been caught up in a bank robbery and killed by the police. *If I only had that package that was stolen, broken down and circulating in the streets, I'd been on triple-boss status right about now! Now I gotsta make a trip and make this bullshit right. I swear to God if that bum duck that rob me wasn't already floating facedown in the river, I'd shoot him in his head ten more times!*

Interrupted by the sound of his cell phone ringing, Dino looked down at the screen, annoyed when he saw yet another call from Tiffany's good gold-digging ass. *Ain't this about nothing. No wonder this hungry ho keeps calling me back-to-back like she crazy or like I owe her something. That bitch think she's superslick. I see her other meal ticket Ghostman's fag ass is deader than a motherfucker, and now she wanna come back over here and suck on daddy's chocolate pole. Like I'm some sort of fool. These bitches these days be doing the fucking most; like niggas stupid.*

Not thinking she'd have enough nerve to set him up to get robbed, Dino knew anything was possible but chose to not see the writing on the wall. Tiffany, although a do-anything-for-a-dollar type of female, was not on Dino's short list radar of who was guilty. She'd seen him and his Bloody Lions Posse deal with slum-ass dudes that crossed them on more than one occasion and couldn't fathom the thought she'd risk her life going against him, no matter who she was giving her pussy to. Dino swore on everything he loved he had Tiffany pegged. He knew she wanted some good stiff dick every so often when she wasn't into females, a few dollars to put in those overpriced handbags she liked to brag about, and get her car note paid on a monthly basis; nothing more, nothing less. He never thought she would be able to pull off something like that. Besides, she was just another gold-digging hood rat.

Chapter 9

Detective Dugan and Officer Jakes pulled up in front of the semicrowded strip club. Opting not to get valet, they found a parking space on the other side of the block. Even though it was against department policy, Detective Dugan encouraged Jakes to do as he was and leave their pistols and badges hidden in the vehicle. Not wanting to be immediately marked as the police, he felt it'd be better to try to gain more information on the sly. If the bouncers knew they were 5-0, then the DJ would know. If the DJ knew, then the waitress would soon find out; then down the line until every single dancer and even the house mother would know they were cops. Of course, no one wanted to be seen gossiping with the police. Giving a lap dance and getting tipped for it was acceptable. A bitch was being about her paper. But sitting around shooting the breeze about this, that, and the other thing was out of the question. That was . . . unless you wanted to be labeled a snitch. There was already enough dead bodies washing up in the river, so to keep things tight, they were going as regular Joes.

Showing his partner for the night a printed picture of Tiffany, they both exited the car. Making sure the doors were locked, the pair made their way to the club's entrance. After allowing the bouncers to search them and paying the inflated fee to get in, Detective Dugan and Officer Jakes found an empty table. In a matter of minutes, they were seemingly swarmed by countless dancers begging them for a dance or a drink. All sorts of shapes and sizes, the two policemen discussed amongst themselves that no female that'd approached them up until this point was a real showstopper.

"Man, I ain't lying. There's a lot of these chicks that need to give up this bullshit as a career. I mean, they looking tore up from the floor up."

"You ain't lying!" Dugan easily agreed with Jakes. Sipping on his glass of fruit juice, he remarked that the weave most dancers were wearing probably cost more than the car he was driving. After sharing a few more laughs, the reason for their visit was finally called to the center stage. As the house lights lowered, the more the smoke machine kicked in. Before Chase knew it, his mouth dropped slightly open. Licking his drying lips, he stared into the face of one of the most beautiful women he'd seen in a long time. Of course, Simone Banks was a stunna in real life and his girl, so to speak. But this Tiffany girl oozed of the freaky, nasty, sexual "come-fuck-me-rough-and-hard-daddy" demeanor that only wet dreams and fantasies were made of.

Taking out Tariq's cell phone, he dialed Tiffany's number to see if she was the right girl. And as luck would have it, she took her cell out of her bag and looked at it before signaling for the DJ to start her music. Focused on every twist, turn, and spin she made on the brass pole, the man sworn to uphold the law was almost lost as to why he and Officer Jakes were there in the first place. Mesmerized by the multiple flashing lights causing the dancer's bracelet and earrings to sway, sparkle, and stand out on their own, he had to work hard to concentrate.

"They know that's mine. Bust it, baby. Everybody know that's mine. Bust it, baby. Everybody know that's mine." The music played loudly.

Shaking off the erotic trance that had him engulfed, Detective Dugan informed his boy the vivacious female that'd just shown both her breasts and was parting her perfectly plump ass cheeks to the music playing was their girl. She was Tiffany, the possible link to not only two bank robberies, but two homicides as well.

"When she comes offstage I'm going to get her to come and sit with us. Maybe buy her a drink or two and see if we can pick her brain for any info," he anxiously tapped the side of his glass with his fingertips. "Who knows, dude? Maybe with all that beauty she might be brainless. The girl might slip up and make our job that much easier."

"Yeah, you right, Chase," Jakes tried to be informal in case someone was ear hustling and could make out that they were cops.

"If we play this thing right tonight, we might both mess around and get promotions by daybreak. If not," the detective teased still eyeballing the stage and Tiffany's wide ass, "the unemployment office will be calling our names!"

Bunny had taken a long hot bath. After brushing her hair up into a messy bun, she applied her makeup as perfectly as she always did. Coming out of the huge walk-in closet, she was dressed in an outfit that Spoe loved to see her wearing. He always teased that it made her ass sit high and her tits look like they were saluting. Not knowing how the night would turn out, she packed a small overnight bag . . . just in case. Checking the floor-length mirror one last time, she left three sealed envelopes on her dresser, along with her favorite ring given to her by her beloved. Taking the framed photo of her and Spoe out of the bedroom and placing it on the mantle, she smiled. With nothing but her driver's license tucked in her lace bra, five crispy hundred-dollar bills in hand, and her designer overnight bag, Bunny Banks locked up the condo. Leaving the house keys underneath the second flower pot on the left side of the porch, she felt confident. Slowly strolling to her car, she tossed the bag into the trunk.

The revenge-minded female started the engine, then checked her cell phone for the time. *Oh, a bitch gonna pay tonight for fucking over me and my man! It's about to be some real consequences for Miss Ratchet-Ass Tiffany!* Concentrating on one thing and one thing only, she backed out of the driveway, then made her way outside of the gated community. On the way to the strip club Bunny rode in utter silence. There was no need to snap her fingers or bob her head to any music. There was no need to hear upbeat commercials about this party or that or whose upcoming concert was in the weeks to follow. She was deep off into her own zone and wanted to stay that way; at least until the vengeful task she wanted to complete was done. She had to be focused on her task at hand.

With less than five minutes away from pulling up at her destination, a strange sense of pride took over. Bunny began to have more flashbacks of the once-perfect life she and Spoe lived. The life that was now nothing more than a memory. Adding fuel to her already revengeful burning fire, Bunny relived in her mind the last time her lips touched Spoe's and the last time he told her that he'd be forever hers. Seconds later, she was in front of the club handing her car keys to the valet. When the valet asked her how long she would be, she had absolutely no response. Blessing him with one of her five hundred-dollar bills, he automatically kept it up front with her keys close by. As the ecstatic valet and every other man waiting to gain entry into the club watched her walk by, they hoped and prayed Bunny, with all her curves, was going inside to audition for one of the club headliners. After allowing herself to be searched by a dyke female bouncer, Bunny stepped into the dimly lit establishment. Adjusting her eyes, she heard the music bouncing off the walls.

"Best believe she got that good thang. She my little hood thang. Ask around, they know us. They know that's mine. Bust it, baby. Everybody know that's mine. Bust it, baby. Everybody know that's mine."

Like most men who entered the club, Bunny's attention shot to center stage. Taking a few steps toward the seminude performer, Bunny was now sure that was Tiffany. That was the dirty female that she'd seen coming out of Tariq's apartment weeks ago and the one and the same ruthless bitch that was acting all gangster when she delivered the money to Ghostman. Bunny took a deep breath. She felt every beat of the loud-playing music penetrate her entire being. She was starting to feel the exact rage she felt when Deidra left this earth; a cold emptiness. Her head was pounding. A huge lump seemed to be lodged in her throat. No matter how much she tried to swallow, it wouldn't go away. Here, this murderous setting-niggas-up home-wrecking whore was a few feet away, swinging from a pole trying to gank fools out of their money like it was business as usual. Fuck all that! Bunny's world was turned upside down. She had to make shit right for Spoe. Point-blank and period, she had to let Tiffany know what she and her man Ghostman had done to her once-perfect life. She was suffering, so now Tiffany would feel the same type of pain.

Glancing over at one of the empty tables, Bunny noticed that someone's steak dinner had arrived. Guessing the person was either one of the thirsty men at the flashing light-lit stage tipping that cash slut Tiffany or in the bathroom washing his hands, Bunny unwrapped his white cloth napkin and politely borrowed his knife. Standing back in the shadows, trying to be as inconspicuous as possible, Spoe's woman waited for Tiffany to finish her set. *That ho ain't doing no VIP dances tonight unless it's down at the county morgue!*

Detective Dugan and Officer Jakes were too busy enjoying the show Tiffany was displaying that they never noticed Bunny lurking in the shadows at the side of the stage.

"Damn, I didn't even think that was possible to do on a pole!" Detective Dungan took another sip of his fruit juice.

"You ain't lying!" Officer Jakes put his hand up for a high five.

Detective Dungan soon felt a little uneasy when two strippers came by to offer him and his friend a lap dance.

"Can we offer y'all a dance in VIP?" The strippers gave them a little tease with a shake of their asses.

Detective Dungan quickly put his hand up to stop them. "No, thanks, ladies. We already have that covered."

"Let me guess, Tiffany, right?" One of the strippers turned around before shooting them the stink eye.

"That bitch is taking the only money left in this slow-ass shallow-pocket-having club. I'm going the fuck home!" The other stripper followed suit and flipped the detectives off.

"Damn, it's brutal out here, huh?" Officer Jakes chuckled.

"We'll be out of here shortly. It's time to get this show on the road. I'll be right back." Detective Dungan walked toward the stage with a twenty-dollar bill out.

"Damn, Dungan, why do you get to have all the fun?" Officer Jakes laughed.

"It's an unfair world, my friend!" Detective Dungan shouted back.

Chapter 10

Pastor Cassius Street had just finished his evening service with the church's prayer warriors. He was a little bit out of sorts, and they could easily see something was wrong but opted not to speak on it. He knew the Word of the Bible back-to-back, almost word-for-word. That was one of the many attributes he prided himself on. But this evening, he was off. Most of the scriptures he was quoting were off. Whether it was one word or the entire passage, he was off, and he was tongue-tied.

As he stood at the pulpit attempting to preach his motivational sermon, his manhood started to twitch. As much as the flamboyant preacher tried to fight off the evil, illicit thoughts of what had taken place earlier in the midmorning, he couldn't. He couldn't resist the chill bump-raising flashbacks of Ginger touching him. He closed his eyes to block out the sexually charged memory of the man who dressed as a woman caressing his body. Pastor Street didn't want to enjoy Me-Ma's grandson blessing him with the best head he'd ever experienced in life, but so be it. He had definitely enjoyed it. So much so that it was the only thought that occupied his mind and inner being since the moment he'd busted a nut and the second Ginger swallowed his seed. Now he wanted nothing more than to have all the women from the congregation that were known to do his bidding to leave. He wanted them to all say their finally good-byes so he could go into his office and stroke his meat raw while whispering Ginger's name. Having already done so twice in the bathroom, once in his car, and secretly while his parishioners were bowing their head in prayer, he knew he had to have another taste of the girlie man.

"Okay, you ladies make sure to have a blessed night. And please drive home safely. You know the devil stay working overtime out in these dangerous streets."

"Thank you, Pastor. You do the same," they all replied in unison, heading toward their vehicles in the parking lot.

Locking the church doors, without breaking stride, he retreated to the privacy of his office. Dimming the lights, Cassius relaxed, sitting back on his plush black leather couch. Getting comfortable, he repeated Ginger's name as he'd made him do while he was sucking him off. *Ginger, Ginger, oh my God, Ginger! Yes, yes, oh my God, yes, just like that!*

Unzipping his pants, the pastor groped his semihard dick. After squeezing it a few times, then yanking downward, he pulled it all the way out. Exhaling, he marveled how swollen the head was. He'd had plenty of pussy from many a woman and, shamefully, some ass from a few men, but absolutely nothing could compare to the feeling of sheer ecstasy that Ginger had brought about. Now here he was, Cassius Street, a head pastor of a major church in the city, caught up in his emotions feeling some sort of a way about another man. Hitting yet another lick, he shot his thick sperm across the room, landing it on the pages of an open Bible. *Oh my God in heaven! Save me from myself! Please, help me fight this!* The well-respected peddler of the Holy Word hoped his new obsession would not be his downfall.

Trying his very best to keep his mind on the sermon he was writing for the upcoming Sunday, Cassius's thoughts went back to Ginger. Finally giving up on fighting his urges and making love to the palm of his hand, Pastor Street licked his lips. Removing the crumbled piece of paper out of the waste paper basket his new sexual obsession had scribbled his number down on, he briefly stared at it before dialing the digits. Three rings later, the man that'd easily swallowed two loads of his juice back-to-back answered.

"Yeah, this Ginger, so speak on it."

"Hello."

"Yes."

"Hey."

"Hey, who is this?" Ginger asked with a sassy attitude as if the world belonged to him and no one should even consider disputing that fact.

"This is umm . . . umm . . ."

"Look here, who the hell ever this is?" he snapped ready to attack a possible prank caller for wasting his breath. "I ain't got time for the games. Now, final chance; who the hell is this?" After a brief silence from both him and the mystery caller, Ginger went all in for the kill. "Fuck it, I'm about to hang up on your silly self! I ain't about to play no games!"

"Wait, it's umm . . . me."

"And who the fuck is *me?*"

"Pastor Street," he hesitantly replied in a soft tone, as if someone was listening.

Ginger then recognized his voice and somewhat smiled. "Ohhh . . . hey, there, Pastor. You should've said it was you from the jump. I was about to hang up, then add this number to my blocked list of folk that work my nerves."

"Oh, well, umm . . . I'm sorry. It's just that . . ."

Ginger was used to down low dudes who pretended not to like other men being tongue-tied when they spoke to an openly gay man. They had a taste for a little roughhouse backdoor loving but didn't want to admit it to themselves—let alone the world. "Don't worry about it, Pastor. I understand. So tell me what you doing tonight?"

"Tonight?" he answered Ginger's question with a question.

"Yeah, tonight, silly. What you got going on tonight, and can I have the same thing popping as you? I'm bored as hell and ready to have some fun. You up for it?"

Thrown off by Ginger being so forward, Cassius Street's usually boisterous voice was full of confusion as he looked up at a hand carved cross hanging on the far wall of the office. "Well, I guess so. I'm just down here at the church finishing some paperwork." He couldn't help himself to the offering that was urging him all day.

"The church?" Ginger got up, reaching for his shoes, ready to roll out.

"Yes, umm . . . the church."

Ginger had a long day and night. He needed some relaxation after dragging two bodies out of the crib and dumping them. He needed something to get his mind right, and sucking the pastor off again was just what the doctor ordered. "Okay, then, sweetie. I'll be there shortly. Just hold tight and I'll hit you when I'm at the front door."

Saying a few prayers for salvation, asking God to preforgive him for the sins he knew he was about to commit, the good reverend felt like a kid in a candy store. Rubbing his hands together, he didn't know what to do next. Ginger would be here soon, and if he had his way, Me-Ma's grandson's lips would be blessing his manhood with his almighty power.

Throwing the various religious books he had sitting on the arm of the couch into a corner, then tossing a few extra choir robes in the closet, Cassius was ready for whatever. Going into his private bathroom, he brushed his teeth, washed off his dick, and put on a small bit of cologne. Spraying some air freshener around the medium-size room, he anxiously sat back waiting for his cell phone to ring. Twenty minutes later, the pastor's prayers were answered.

"Hey, now, bae. I'm glad you called me." Ginger wasted no time pushing his way through the front double doors into the church's inner sanctuary.

At a loss for words, Cassius nervously smiled in anticipation of the inevitable only seconds from taking place.

"Wow, it's creepy as hell in here at night, by ourself, with all the lights dimmed." Ginger sinfully pranced down the aisleway as Cassius's eyes zoomed in on his perfectly shaped ass.

"It's not that bad," he finally spoke, hoping he hadn't invited the devil inside.

Ginger had not one bit of respect for the church Me-Ma called her second home. Breezing past the area his grandmother dropped dead at, he swooped up one of the blessed prayer candles from the altar. After telling Cassius to lead the way to his office, Ginger grinned, ready to pounce on the man of the cloth.

"Here we go." He motioned for him to step into the office.

"Oh, so this is your private hangout, huh?"

"I guess you can say that."

"Well, I guess this is where you do all your private one-on-one, get-right-with-the-Lawd sessions, huh?" Ginger laughed, kicking off his shoes before plopping down on the black leather couch.

Letting his guard down, the pastor returned the laughter and stopped fighting the feeling. "Yeah, one-on-one." He wanted to jump Ginger's bones and avoid the pleasantries.

Before either man knew what was taking place, they were wrapped in each other's strong arms, sharing a deep, passionate kiss. As their wet tongues darted in and out of their mouths, their poles grew rock-hard. With Cassius being on top, he slow grinded his hips on Ginger's female-like shape. Groping, sucking, licking, biting, tugging, and finally, raw dick fucking until the sun was about to come up, they were both in heaven. Pastor Cassius Street felt he had made some sort of a twisted, yet very secret love connection. While Ginger, on the other hand, was convinced his new lover would gladly sign the lease to Me-Ma's house back over to him and his sisters—where it rightfully belonged. After all, Ginger wasn't about to waste a perfectly good opportunity to be the hero in their die-hard situation.

Chapter 11

"Rhythm is a dancer, I need a companion. Girl, I guess that must be you. Body like the summer, fucking like no other. Don't you tell 'em what we do. Don't tell 'em . . ."

"All right, y'all, show this lovely young lady some love. Bless her with some of that dough you holding onto like you gonna make some cookies tomorrow. Make it rain and show some appreciation for one of the hardest-working females under this roof. The one we call Miss Tiffany." The DJ was still doing what he did trying to coax and encourage the patrons of the strip club to tip. "All right, now, I see two real niggas in the house showing out and showing the way." One man tucked a few twenties in Tiffany's garter belt and returned to his seat where he had a steak dinner waiting. Another man then got up from his table off to the side and whispered something into the dancer's ear. Tiffany smiled, then nodded her head.

"Hey, Chase, what did you tell her?"

"Nothing much. I just told her I was a friend of Ghostman's and wanted to turn her onto something deep. I ain't know how she was gonna react, but I took a chance."

"Damn, guy. And it had her cheesing like that? I mean, damn!"

"Hell, yeah, Jakes. I guess dead or alive, that man's name rings bells."

"Yeah, I guess so."

"Well, she gonna come sit with us as soon as she comes off the stage and goes to the bathroom. Hopefully we can get her to talk."

After returning from pretending he was some sort of Big Willy, the random man brushed by Bunny who was standing a foot or so away from his table. Being the true trick that he was, he, of course asked the fully clothed beauty to join him for a drink while he ate his meal. Getting no response from a silent Bunny who seemed to be in deep thought, he shrugged his shoulder, knowing there were plenty other females up in that spot that were desperate for his attention, and he had more than enough dollars to spread around. "Hey, miss, you forgot to bring me a knife," he caught the apron-wearing waitress before she breezed by to take another order. Putting his attention back on Tiffany, who'd just gathered her tips off the floor of the stage, he saw she was making her way down. Before he could get a chance to signal for the sweaty stripper to come give him a lap dance, the too-uppity-and-arrogant-to-even-speak Bunny had taken a few steps over, unknowingly blocking his view. At that point, he decided to get two other girls to tag team him.

Tiffany was making the best out of an extremely slow night. As she thought, there was no real ballin'-type money circulating. The fact another one of the dancers was having a birthday party at the club meant nothing; it was still whack as fuck on the tip-getting situation. Just as the final song was starting to end on her set, the thirsty headliner was blessed with a few dollars from one man, followed by some uplifting news from the next who approached her. *Dang, I hope this is one of them funny-style guys from out of town that used to be plugged with Ghostman. Maybe he remembers me from being with that dead crazy motherfucker and wants to spend some of that drug money on a sista. I showl in the hell hope so 'cause I could use a come up right about now. Maybe I can set him and his straitlaced homeboy sitting over there stupid asses up too. They dressed like some dorks, so I know they ain't gonna be on that for real for real gangster tip. They probably just gonna give that shit up, no questions asked!* Thinking nothing but positive thoughts, Tiffany took her last swing around the brass pole. Running her fingers through her expensive weave, she then slid down as seductively as possible. Making sure all the men in the club could get a generous view of her G-string-clad ass, she stuck it out, then up in the air as she crawled around the lighted stage. Having collected all her tips, Tiffany grabbed her bikini top that was discarded to the side and pressed it up to her full double-D breasts. No sooner than her seven-inch patent leather skinny heel stiletto touched the carpeted floor, Tiffany signaled to the man she hoped to get some real Ghostman-type money out of later that she'd be right back in a few. She even solidified the deal by blowing him a kiss and letting them know it was on.

Bunny was growing sick to her stomach watching Tiffany. She wanted to throw up. As the minutes dragged by, she wanted to scream and yell. It was taking everything in her inner soul not to run up on that tramp and snatch the female bald. The way she was feeling, Bunny wanted to rip every single strand of weave out of Tiffany's head, then spit directly in her face. Here, this funky-mouth thang was twirling around the stage acting as if shit was all good. She was climbing the pole, hanging upside down, and doing tricks. This belly-rolling bitch was making tips here and there and smiling; grinning all up in niggas' faces. Her no-good ass was living life with no worries or guilt over getting Spoe and Tariq murdered. Bunny trembled. Her heart raced, and her anger increased. Her fingers felt as if they were throbbing, and her legs tensed up. She was only a few yards away from the one person left alive that could tell her how and why Spoe was gone. Tiffany was the reason Bunny slept alone every night, and the reason she had to commit a federal offense and rob a freaking bank. This two-bit stripper had single-handedly made Bunny turn from living the life to possibly doing life if she and her sisters ever got found out. She had to question this wannabe Beyoncé broad. There was no other way around Bunny living any part of a normal life if she didn't get some direct answers from Tiffany . . . and then the gleeful satisfaction of killing her afterward.

What in the fuck! Why is this man trying to speak to me after he just tipped that skank? As if I even look like I'm on the same level as her. Like I'm that damn desperate to want to have a drink with his creepy ass, let alone sit the hell across from him and watch his ugly self eat. Where the fuck they do that at? Certainly not here and definitely not with me. Seething with fury, Bunny was way past homicidal, to say the least. If there was no other person in life she detested, wanting to see dead, it was this diseased twat whore. Bunny coldly eye fucked the rear head of another man that felt compelled by his dick head to tip Tiffany.

Hurry the fuck up, music! Hurry up! Bunny counted down the seconds until the song playing would be over and she and Tiffany could be face-to-face. "Rhythm is a dancer, I need a companion. Girl, I guess that must be you. Body like the summer, fucking like no other. Don't you tell 'em what we do. Don't tell 'em. Don't tell 'em. You don't even. Don't tell 'em. You don't even." Then, just like that, the song ended. Watching her soon-to-be victim like a hawk, she moved over a small bit, making sure she didn't lose sight of her mark in the dimness of the club. Bunny's adrenalin jumped when Tiffany stepped off the stage. She knew it was go time when the sneaky ho headed toward the rear of the club. With ill intentions, Bunny Banks followed.

"Hey, Tiffany, you was throwing down up there," one of the dancers remarked, coming out of the dressing room. "You be making all the money up in this mug."

"Whatever, girl," she nonchalantly replied, waving the female off. "Go on out there and you'll see what's really good."

Bunny fell back a little bit while ear hustling on the sly. Just hearing the annoying sound of Tiffany's arrogant voice made her want to just gut the female right there in the dark hallway—no questions asked. A few feet later, much to Bunny's advantage, Tiffany went into the women's bathroom. Good. I don't have to confront her in front of the rest of these thirsty bitches.

Going into one of the empty stalls, Tiffany unrolled an enormous amount of tissue to wipe the squat-splattered seat dry. Rudely tossing the tissue on the floor, she tore off more, lining the seat before sitting down. After peeing, the seasoned stripper opened her candy-apple red satin pull string bag. Staring down at what couldn't be any more than a few hundred dollars at best, she frowned at her night's take.

"I should just call it a night. Maybe ole boy and his friend got some better shit popping than this slow motherfucker," Tiffany mumbled out loud as she stood to wipe herself. Using the sole of her shiny patent leather boot, she flushed the toilet. Straightening out her tiny bikini top, she then slid the flimsy latch to open the metal door.

Before the arrogant dancer knew what was happening, she had been socked in the face. She saw bright blue and yellow lightning flashes. She wanted to speak but was stunned and couldn't form the words. Dazed from the forceful unexpected blow, her knees grew weak. As she wobbled to stay on her feet, Tiffany leaned against the wall of the small stall. Still dizzy, she could scarcely make out what female had a sharp knife pressed against the upper side of her throat threatening to slice it open.

"If you wanna die sooner than later, then open your big fat mouth and scream." Bunny pressed the blade harder, coming close to puncturing Tiffany's skin. "I'm looking for a reason to just gut the shit out of you anyway! I swear to God, I'm looking for just one damn reason! Open that mouth and you gonna give me one."

Tiffany usually had a lot of mouth. Like a lot of bully bitches like her, she was all talk and not really about that fighting life. She could talk a good game and have other females buffaloed, but at the end of the day, she didn't want no real static. It wasn't in her DNA. Instead of trying to go ham and go for bad, Tiffany just nodded, showing no resistance.

"Do you remember me, ho? Do you?" Tiffany squinted her eyes, finally getting a good look at her infuriated attacker. Her face showed immediate signs of panic realizing who and what this ambush was truly about. "So I guess you *do* remember, huh, bitch? Spoe's girl. His fucking woman!" With the steak knife still lodged under Tiffany's neck, Bunny punched her twice in the side of her lower ribcage. "I need to ask you a few things. And trust, it's in your best interest to answer. You feel me?" Bunny shoved the knife deeper into Tiffany's skin, slicing through the top layer. "And if I even feel you lying, I ain't gonna hesitate to slice your ho-mother-fucking-ass ear to ear."

Tiffany was beyond terrified. Praying for someone to come into the bathroom and save her from Spoe's revenge-seeking wifey, God failed to listen. She was on her own this time and had to either follow instructions or meet the same fate as Spoe, Tariq, and Ghostman. "Okay, okay, sis," she struggled to speak as she bargained for her life to be spared. "What is it? What do you need to know? I'll tell you everything. Please, just don't hurt me!"

Bunny was pissed. Beyond all the harm and turmoil this tramp had brought into her life, she had the nerve to call her "sis," like it was all good. "Listen, you foul bitch! You ain't my sister, and we freaking ain't cool. This is what exactly the fuck it is. Me asking your ho ass what happened to my man Spoe the night he got murdered, and you telling me. So run that fucking mouth, bitch—and nothing else. So where was Spoe when I got to that apartment, and why did you set my people up in the first damn place?"

"Spoe wasn't there. Just Tariq was. I swear to God."

"I know that much, dummy, so don't play with me."

"I'm not! I'm not!"

"All right then. I said, *where* in the fuck was Spoe at then? Please don't make me keep asking you the same damn shit over and over. You making me pissed!"

"Okay, okay, please! Wait! Wait! I'm about to tell you."

"Well, then, tell me and stop all that 'okay, please' crap you blowing out your fucking mouth. Where the fuck was my baby at? Where was Spoe, bitch?"

"Tariq said him and Spoe ran up in Dino's crib, and he came home and caught them."

"Dino?"

"Yeah, Dino."

"Bitch, who in the fuck is Dino?"

"A dude from up in NYC. I was fucking with him."

"What?" Bunny grew puzzled the more Tiffany tried to spin the tale of the deadly night. "Dino from NYC? Look, girl, ain't nobody got no time to be playing word games with you while you stall for time. I ain't trying to hear that dumb shit no more!"

Tiffany took a deep breath attempting to explain what she knew would only make the person holding a sharp blade to her throat angrier. "I told Tariq about this cat I know named Dino. He the head of some dudes named the Bloody Lions Posse."

"The Bloody Lions Posse?"

"Yeah . . . They from NYC."

"And . . .?" Bunny applied more pressure to her victim's neck to further stress the point she was serious.

"And I told Tariq he had a bunch of money at his house."

"Well, how the fuck Ghostman get involved in the bullshit?"

"Tariq and Spoe had hit a few of Ghostman's spots real heavy over the past month."

"So and . . .?"

"I mean, they hit them real, real hard. He wanted to catch up with them and get his money back. He was tired of taking losses."

Bunny thought back to the night she and Spoe made love after one of his and Tariq's biggest robberies ever. *That must've come from Ghostman.* Now some of what Tiffany was saying was starting to make some sense, but Bunny knew there was much more to the deadly story. "Okay, then, why you tell them to hit Dino? Why you set them up to do that shit?"

Tiffany was terrified what Bunny would do if she told her the rest of the story as she knew it. She knew it was ultimately by her hand that all the wheels got set in motion. Both Spoe and Tariq were dead by her decisions—the same decisions that were about to possibly have her pushing up daisies as well. "Ghostman said if they didn't have his money he was going to kill both of them. I knew Tariq wasn't gonna just hand him over all that money, so I turned him on to hit another lick so he wouldn't feel the total loss. Yeah, I did know I was gonna get paid off the top, but you know how it is, sis."

Bunny sucker punched her once more this time, making a kidney the body blow count. "What in the fuck did I tell your ass about calling me that? I ain't your damn sis! And naw, ho, I don't know how it is!"

Tiffany coughed up a small bit of mucus. Tears started to pour out both eyes as her knees grew even weaker. "I'm sorry! I'm sorry!"

"Fuck being sorry. You gonna mess around and be dead. Now like I said from jump, where was Spoe when I got there?" Bunny demanded, tired of the cat-and-mouse game Tiffany was playing. After slowing slicing the side of the girl's face and drawing blood, Tiffany knew she had to reveal the entire truth.

"Tariq said Dino and his crew chased both them down in the woods near his mansion. He said at one point Spoe went down. He said he didn't want to leave him like that, but Spoe told him to take the bags with the money and dope and just get the fuck on." Tiffany was breathing hard as she told the deadly tale. "Tariq said he got a few hundred yards away and heard a gunshot. He said ole boy had some dogs on his ass so he ran to the van he and Spoe left parked on the other side of the woods. That nigga claimed he drove around for about a good hour or so and Spoe never came out of the woods. He called me crying, saying he know Spoe was gone. After that, I told him to at least bring the money over to the apartment. He ain't know Ghostman was there."

"What? So what you telling me is Ghostman ain't kill Spoe?" Bunny was confused. Feeling like someone had let the air out of her emotions, she was almost broken down. The only thing that was keeping her strong was her taste for revenge.

"Naw, he ain't never even laid eyes on Spoe. If what Tariq said was true, Dino and his crew killed Spoe. That was the first time he ever saw Tariq. He'd just heard about both them and knew they was the stickup dudes that was hitting all his spots."

Bunny was infuriated. She couldn't believe what she was hearing. "So why in the fuck did y'all involve me? If Spoe wasn't there, and y'all had the money and drugs they'd stolen from Dino, then why call me? Huh? Why?"

Tiffany knew what she was about to say was gonna get her killed, but she had to roll the dice and take a chance. "Because Ghostman got greedy, and I told him you could get both Tariq's and Spoe's stash and bring it to us!"

"What?" Bunny hissed with undeniable rage. "So that asshole not only had Dino's shit, he made me bring the cash I needed to live off of too? Then had the nerve to come to my grandmother's repast and extort even more money from me?" Bunny was heated. After all, that was the true reason they'd robbed the bank in the first damn place, to repay that bastard.

"Yeah, but, but . . . If you wanna be mad at anybody, be pissed at Tariq's coward ass. I mean, he the one that called you that night, not me. I mean, shit, he and Spoe was stickup boys from off rip, you know that. They luck was gonna run out sooner or later anyway. They was gonna screw up and somebody was gonna end up killing they asses either way. Sis, you know that's part of the game! You know how we do."

That was the last thing Bunny wanted to hear and the last thing Tiffany would say. *Kill this rotten bitch and just get it over with. Make her bleed the way Spoe had to bleed. Make this ho feel the pain my baby probably felt,* the voices in her head kept taunting, urging her to take instant action. Karma had shown up and was about to show out.

Using all her strength, Bunny stabbed the conniving female multiple times in the rear of her skull. In and out with the ease of a butcher slicing meat, she'd tasted her mother and Lenny's blood earlier, so this was nothing. Amused at Tiffany fighting to live to see another sunrise, Bunny sadistically whispered into the dancer's ear to say her final prayers, letting her lifeless body fall to the urine-stained floor as she leaned close, slashing her victim's throat. Tiffany's eyes were eerily wide open, but she was no more.

Reaching over, removing the satin bag that lay by Tiffany's side, Bunny didn't break a sweat. Untying the string, she opened the bag. She removed Tiffany's cell phone along with a crumbled up fifty-dollar bill. Taking the rest of the cash out, she disrespectfully tossed it onto Tiffany's face. Callously, Bunny proceeded to mash some of the filthy currency into the self-proclaimed queen of the strip club's mouth. "Here the hell you go! You money-hungry bitch! Live off this shit in fucking hell!" After that brutal one-sided exchange of rage, Bunny snatched the girl's expensive gold and huge diamond-encrusted monogramed tennis bracelet off her floppy wrist. Not wanting to half step, Bunny then, showing no pity for the deceased, yanked down both of Tiffany's one-carat diamond screw back stud earrings, splitting both lobes. "Thanks, trick. I know Tariq, Ghostman, that dude Dino or some other dim-witted cat whose dick you was sucking sponsored this shit . . . so easy come, easy the fuck go. It's mine now!"

Done doing the deed, Bunny left the small stall. Without an inch of remorse for the slaying or fear of getting caught, she nonchalantly walked over to the sink. Not wanting to have sweaty and bloody palms, she thoroughly washed her hands. Coldly, Bunny smiled as she looked into the mirror admiring herself and who she was. *Perfect as always. Not a hair out of place. Without a doubt, I'm that bitch!*

Going back into the main area of the noisy club, Bunny had no idea whatsoever that her sister's man, Detective Chase Dugan, was sitting only a few yards away. Even if she did know his police ass was in the house, that still wouldn't have halted her plan of the assassination of the cocky stripper. With pride in her stride, she casually walked out the front doors feeling almost whole again. Bunny was now satisfied that Tiffany got what was coming to her for being such a slimeball. The grubby trick had a bad habit of setting paid Negros up, so now she got a little payback. Like Tiffany said when she tried to go momentarily hard, it was all part of the game. Now Bunny would focus on tracking this dude Dino down just like she'd done Tiffany. She now had tunnel vision for making him pay for his sins; him and his boys. They'd taken Spoe from her, now they had to repay that debt in full. Dino and the entire Bloody Lions Posse would wish they were back in NYC when she was done. *In time, baby, I promise I will get them all!*

After the valet pulled Bunny's car up and handed her the keys, she smiled. With pride, she blessed him yet again. This time, with a crumbled up fifty-dollar bill. Working for tips, he would never forget her and her generosity that night.

Chapter 12

Detective Dugan and Officer Jakes finished sipping on their juices while watching a few more females shake their asses and swing from the pole. Looking down at his watch, Jakes finally made mention that it didn't seem as if the girl Tiffany was coming back to sit with them.

"I mean, really, man, how long does it take to go to the bathroom? I done took a full-on dump in less time."

"Maybe she's in the dressing room changing outfits or something. You know how vain these dancers are, especially one as fine as that one is. Maybe she's somewhere giving lap dances or something."

"You think?" Jakes gave Chase the "nigga please" side eye. "It's been a mighty long damn time, and we still out here waiting like some lames."

"Naw, you might just be right, guy. That girl might be slicker than I thought. Maybe I scared her off. I hope not, because she has the potential to be the link we need to close these cases out once and for all."

Just as the two police were exchanging their spate speculations of what was taking Tiffany so long, one of the other dancers ran out the side of the stage as if there was someone or something chasing her. Her arms were flinging from side to side and she called out to Jesus to help her repeatedly. With the piercing sounds of her screaming exceeding the volume of the music blasting through the speakers, all eyes were on her. Through the tears flowing and her painful sobbing, the officers of the law instinctively approached the growing crowd of staff and other patrons to see what all the commotion was about. In a matter of seconds, a tidal wave of gossip swept throughout the club. The distraught dancer tragically had discovered one of her own dead in bathroom stall with her neck sliced wide open.

"I-I-I—" she stuttered as the tears continued to pour out from her red eyes. "I went in there to pee and check my makeup because the dressing room was so crowded, and there was blood on the floor. It was like someone spilled something. It was just running from the stall to the drain. I ain't know what it was at first," she started screaming again as she relived what she'd just seen. "I seen somebody's legs and body when I looked under the door. I tried to push it open, and at first, it was kinda stuck. Then I used my hip and peeked in. It was-it was-it was—" Now damn near hysterical, the stripper was putting on a performance worthy of winning an Academy Award. "It was Tiffany lying on the floor! It was her—Tiffany! Our Tiffany! Oh my God! Her neck was bleeding. It was open—like a big hole open; like something tried to tear her neck from her body! I saw it! I saw it! Her eyes was wide open like she was looking at me or something. There was blood everywhere. Then she had a lot of money stuffed in her mouth. Well, not a lot, but some." The dancer continued with her hysterics, putting on the ultimate performance.

Detective Dugan and Officer Jakes wasted no more time. Immediately, they made the announcement that they were police and for everyone to step back. After practically fighting to clear everyone out of the women's bathroom, they saw firsthand that the wild story the stripper was claiming she'd seen was indeed true. The club headliner Tiffany they were waiting to question about the bank robberies and several murders had been murdered herself . . . only a few yards from where they were sitting nursing two glasses of fruit juice. Without hesitation, the detective called the crime in. Dugan and Officer Jakes then secured the murder scene, trying to preserve any evidence that hadn't already been destroyed or compromised by the stunned dancers, staff, and nosy patrons that all had their cell phones in hand, cruelly recording the unfortunate occurrence.

Finally clearing the scene of all patrons and dancers, Detective Dungan turned to Officer Jakes. "How in the world are we going to explain this shit when we were only feet away? This is not going to be good."

"Well, all we can do now is prepare for our asses being ripped wide open! Shit!"

***

News cameras and reporters were posted outside Treat's Gentlemen's Club. As the early-morning crowds of gawkers gathered, so did the rumors of what exactly had taken place. Throughout the years the adult entertainment establishment was open, there had been more than several shootings outside the perimeter. And more than their fair share of physical altercations inside the dwelling. But this was the first time the rambunctious club had experienced this type of violent crime; a heinous murder in the bathroom.

As the owner and staff were getting questioned, more than close to seventy-five to a hundred patrons had retreated from the club to either avoid contact with the law, having their faces shown on television, or run the risk of their girlfriends, spouses, or significant others finding out where they'd been all evening. This had not been overlooked by the police. Of course, one of them was possibly the killer, but with all the club's security cameras broken, identifying any or all of them would be an almost impossible feat.

"So, you telling me you two knuckleheads were in here when this girl was murdered? What in the hell y'all want me to tell the mayor? Y'all want me to tell him two of my top men I got working on the high-profile bank robberies got their heads stuck so far up in their asses they can't speculate not one person that could've sliced her damn neck wide open like that?" The chief of police was livid. The mayor was up for reelection and was trying his best to get a strong-arm handle on the spike in violent crimes throughout the city. The more disturbed and angrier the mayor got, the more pressure he applied to his handpicked appointed chief of police. Of course, shit rolled downhill, so Detective Dugan and Officer Jakes were facing a full-blown shit storm of it.

"Chief, hold up. Hear me out," the detective bargained, trying to explain. "We were here and did indeed speak to the victim. She said she was going to the bathroom and would return. I mean, we sat right here and waited. There was no way we could have known this was going to happen."

"Like I said, you two sat a few yards away while that girl was being murdered. *My* freaking policemen! On *my* watch!

Damn! Right in there," he disappointedly pointed over toward the roped off bathroom. "First, the string of robberies. Then all these dead bodies washing up on shore. My men just got called out to the scene of two more. These two were stabbed up and set on fire."

Detective Dugan was tired of getting chewed out for trying to do his job and decided to speak out to clear his name, no matter what the outcome. "Okay, Chief, look. She said she was going to the bathroom. I mean, what did you want us to do? Follow her in there and watch her do whatever women do in there? The walls ain't made of glass. How in the hell could we see what was going down? You know like I do, it only takes one second to kill someone if you really want to. Just like everybody else that we done interviewed, we didn't see or hear anything either. There was nothing to indicate something of that nature was going to happen."

The chief wanted to yell and berate his officers further, but unfortunately, he had to step outside and deal with the reporters that were getting small bits and pieces of conflicting information regarding the crime. He knew they were trying to go live with their early news program scheduling, so he felt it best to appease them. "Hey, just do what you need to do to get this bullshit under control! All our damn jobs depend on it! And, Detective, you might as well get ready and get yourself all pretty for these damn cameras outside. If I gotta face this firing squad, you're coming with me!"

Chapter 13

Ginger glanced over at the black leather couch and licked his lips. Pastor Street was just where he'd left him after their last wild go-around; stretched out butt-asshole naked. After all the "special attention" he'd shown the pastor, he finally got the favor returned; more than once or twice. Slowly reaching for his cell, he placed the volume on silent. After making sure the flash was off, Ginger started taking picture after picture of the religious sleeping beauty. Placing the risqué photos in the same file as the scandalous video Bunny had taken at Me-Ma's and sent to him, Ginger smirked with satisfaction. He knew these pictures might come in handy one day, but hoped there would be no need. Placing his cell back in his blue jean pocket, Ginger crawled his perfect female-shaped body over toward the couch. Wanting to get one more taste of Cassius Street's juices before the sun came all the way up, Ginger took all of him in his mouth. As he eagerly sucked and slurped to the tune of the birds starting to chirp outside the church's window, the man of God woke up stiff as a board, and ready to go a few more rounds. With his right hand on the rear of Ginger's head and the left unknowingly on top of a Bible, Pastor Street jerked with pleasure, quickly shooting his early-morning load off into Ginger's warm, moist mouth.

"Hey, you. Good morning," Cassius spoke with none of the shame or bashfulness he had the night before. They'd been pleasuring each other for hours on end, so all the strict formalities were a thing of the past.

Ginger happily swallowed the thick substance before speaking. "Hey, yourself. How did you sleep?"

"Like a baby."

"Yeah, me too."

"Hey, what time is it?" Cassius heard the birds and looked at his watch. He had morning-prayer offerings scheduled. And even though he'd enjoyed the night he and Ginger shared, the money-greedy preacher didn't want to miss out on his extra pocket money. With clothes to get out to the cleaners, he had plans of using this morning's collected funds to pay the tab.

"It's time for me to be getting up, huh?"

"Well . . . it's just that . . ."

Ginger knew what that meant and had no problem with taking the walk of shame. Slipping on his jeans, then his shoes, he bent over pecking the pastor on his bare chest. "Soooo, listen, Cassius. Before I be out, we need to chop it up."

"About?"

"About that deed Me-Ma left to you in her will."

"The deed?"

"Yes, silly Negro, yes, the deed. The deed to the house that belongs to me and my sisters!"

Pastor Street stood to his feet. Grabbing for his clothes that were scattered all about the church office, he looked confused. "I'm sorry, Ginger, but what about the deed?"

"Well, are you going to give us back our damn house or what?" Ginger caught an immediate attitude, shifting all his weight onto one hip. "I know you don't think it's yours to keep. Do you?"

"No, Ginger, I don't think it's mine to keep."

"You damn straight it's not yours!"

"Yes, it belongs to the church. That's the way your grandmother wanted it to be, and shouldn't we honor and respect her wishes?"

"What the fuck you trying to say?"

"Like I told you and your sisters, if you all would like to bid on the house, I definitely don't have a problem with that. I told all four of you this is not personal; it's strictly business."

Ginger was irate. Wanting to destroy everything in the small office, he chilled the best he possibly could. "Oh, so you think it's that easy to gank the Banks sisters? You think we gonna fold just like that, huh? It's going to be that easy, huh?"

Pastor Street sensed the extreme rage in Ginger's mannerisms and took a few steps backward in case he had to retreat. "So was getting the deed back what this was about— me and you? I mean, was that the plan; the big picture? If so, thank you, but no, thank you!"

"It wasn't at first, but if you think you can just take back all that fucking and sucking I done did, you sadly mistaken. But since you feeling like it's whatever, then, let it be. Let it motherfucking ride! I'm about to be all up in my zone!" Ginger placed his hands on his hips and rolled his neck. It was obvious the lustful nature shared last night between the two men had changed drastically. Ginger was not with the games anymore; from anyone. He'd watched Bunny kill his mother and didn't shed a single tear, so as far as he was concerned, wasn't no man, woman, or beast gonna move him. He was unbreakable.

"Wait one minute. First, are you threatening me? Second, didn't you want it too?" Pastor Street then calmly asked like he was some sort of a superhero eyeballing the villain. "Because if you are—"

"Naw, guy, I don't do threats, but man to man, you might wanna tighten that slick tone of yours up. I might dress like a female, but please don't try me! I'm not only good with my mouth but with my hands as well."

"Once again, Ginger, what are you saying? Please just spit it out! I'm not good with all these word and mind games!"

"Nigga, please, fall all the way back. You're the king, or should I say the low-key flaming queen of master fucking manipulation."

"What?" the pastor asked as if what Ginger was saying had no great merit.

"You heard me, chump. I mean, that's how you swindled our grandmother in the first place, ain't it? With that velvet tongue you had buried deep in my asshole last night!"

"Excuse me," he twisted his face not believing how Ginger had flipped in a mere matter of minutes. "I don't take anything from anyone. Now, if these women want to all bless me with gifts of all sorts, who am I to turn down what God has for me? I never asked your grandmother to give the church anything. She did that all on her own."

Ginger headed for the door and evilly giggled before leaving. "Let's just say, Pastor Good-Dick-Sucking-Street, you better stay prayed up fucking with me and mines! You playing like you all rough and tough, but let's be clear . . . Me and my sisters are about that life! By the way, I hope Me-Ma is looking down on you so you better prepare yourself for what's coming your way, Pastor Low-Dick-Loving-Street."

Chapter 14

For the first time in over a week, Simone actually had a good night's sleep. Unlike her siblings, she woke up in her own bed. Tallhya was sedated at the mental hospital. Ginger had gone ho hopping with Pastor Street, and Bunny had checked into a cheap hotel off the interstate to clear her mind. Even though she'd suffered through numerous heartaches, trials, and tribulations recently, she felt as if things might be looking up for her.

The fact that she'd witnessed her mother being killed the day before by her sister in the very house she had slept in meant nothing. Simone was good with it. Fixing herself a strong cup of coffee, she tied the belt on her robe. After yawning, she lazily slid her house shoes across the kitchen floor. Going into the living room, Simone placed her mug on the sofa table. Ready to catch the early-morning newscast, she plopped down on the couch. As she clicked the remote channel surfing, Simone finally came to the *Good Morning, Richmond* program. Waiting anxiously for the cheerful anchors to finish with the first weather and traffic report of the broadcast, Simone watched the breaking news banner flash across the thirty-two inch flat screen. Praying she and Ginger's deadly secret by the James River hadn't been immediately discovered, she bit at the side of her fingernails. God had blessed her to get away with so much shenanigans as of recently, she knew it was only a matter of time before the devil himself stepped in and intercepted her good luck. To Simone's relief, the top story of the morning started with an overnight fatal shooting at a strip club. Taking a small sip of her coffee she turned up the volume.

***

"Accurate reports are hard to come by at this time; however, from what we can gather, it was indeed a homicide that took place in the late hours of the night in the building behind me. The few witnesses that were willing to speak to us off camera say that it was a little after midnight when the victim, now identified as Tiffany K. Ross, age twenty-five, a dancer at Treat's Gentlemen's Club, was last seen exiting the stage. Another employee stated she'd spoken to her briefly before she went inside the bathroom. Our sources also tell us that the bathroom, located a few yards from the main area of the adult entertainment establishment, was the place where she was murdered. Apparently, there was some sort of altercation between her and the assailant. Not yet able to identify the perpetrator, the authorities are looking for some assistance from some of the many patrons that were inside the club at the time when the brutal crime was committed. Earlier, we spoke to the chief of police and Detective Chase Dugan who we are more than familiar with from the dual bank robberies that took place last week."

"Yes, it is true. It was indeed a homicide that took place tonight," the chief confirmed.

"Well, can you maybe tell our viewing audience how the victim was killed? Maybe the circumstances?"

"Well, I, of course, can't give you the particulars of the case as we are just in the beginning stages; however, I can tell you the victim's neck was cut."

"Cut?"

"Yes, our victim's neck was slashed."

"Well, can you give me a description of the suspect you guys are looking for that committed such an awful, horrific act? I mean, is there anything our viewers should be on the lookout for; a license plate number or something?"

The chief had his fill of being in the bright lights of the camera. Without hesitation, he placed his hand on the detective's shoulder. "I'm quite sure you know Detective Chase Dugan. He can answer any other questions you may have, but please make them brief. We all have work to do. Thank you for your cooperation."

Like a small deer caught in the headlights, the detective was slow and cautious with every response he gave the reporters. When he was finished, they had enough to go live, yet not enough pertinent information to ridicule the fact he and his fellow officer were actually on the premises when the murder of Tiffany Ross took place.

"Wow, Chase. You looking so damn good in that Polo shirt and jeans. And those muscles in your arms . . ." Simone was speaking to the television screen as if her detective beau could really hear her impromptu compliments. Without question, Simone was saddened by the reported details concerning the heinous murder. The fact some seemingly innocent female had been brutally killed by having her throat slashed was more disturbing to her than Bunny slicing their mother and Lenny from foot to 'fro. Simone had no worldly idea that the dead dancer had died by the same hands as those two. Nevertheless, she still kept a keen eye on the television just in case they had an additional two discarded body counts to increase the James River's dumping ground count. Enduring what seemed like the longest commercial filled the first eleven minutes of the news, then Simone exhaled. She was sure that if the bodies had been found, it would've made at least the second or third top story. But now, they were covering the weather yet once again. "I might need to call Chase and at least see if he knows or heard anything. I can't be living on pins and needles like this. I can't be caught off guard."

Moments before Simone placed the call, Ginger bolted through the front door hotter than fish grease. Slamming the door with the superstrength of three men, Ginger wasted no time in filling Simone in on the details of his night. "This fool think I'm some sort of a joke; we are some jokes."

"Wait a minute. Hold up." Simone put both hands in the air. "Slow down. I'm confused."

Ginger had to catch his breath. Known to be the flamboyant drama queen of the family, he knew he had tendencies to talk faster than average folk could comprehend. "Look, after that dick-stroker-in-disguise called me last night, I shot right over there."

"Over where?"

"The church."

"Nooo . . . not the church." Simone's eyes bucked as she giggled.

"Yesss . . . bitch, yesss. The motherfucking church. You heard what I said," Ginger replied with no shame or guilt in his voice for violating the house of God.

"Oh, my."

"Yeah, well, when a bitch got there, you know it was all good my way. You know good and damn well I wasn't leaving out of the house any time after ten on a damn Friday night on no dry dick run. If I put my shoes on these pretty, manicured feet and waste my gas, high as that bullshit is, it was gonna be some serious fucking and sucking going on. And I mean *serious!*"

Simone was all in listening to Ginger talk that talk. Never being one to live on the edge, over the years, she'd grown accustomed to live vicariously through her sister's wild-spirited existences. "Please tell me you didn't, Ginger. Please!"

Ginger cracked a smile realizing Simone was being a prude of sorts. "I had that queen bent over begging for more of this bronze pole I was cursed being born with. Then this morning, he had the nerve to get tough toned with me."

"What?"

"Yeah, talking about he wasn't gonna sign over the deed to this house to me."

"Hold up, did he ever say he was?" Simone sat up on the edge of the couch interested in the answer Pastor Street gave.

"Naw, but I don't give a sweet shit about what he actually said or thought."

"Oh, wow!"

"Oh, wow, nothing, Simone. I know his undercover ass ain't think I was giving up all this meat for nothing. There's a price to pay for everything, and I do mean everything."

"I guess so," she giggled.

"Shidd, you guessed right. I mean, sis, he tried to talk all slick, but trust, I got something real deep for that ass. But forget all that right now." Ginger kicked off his shoes and fell back onto Me-Ma's favorite chair to catch his breath. "What in the hell your ass doing up all early on a Saturday morning?"

Simone informed Ginger that she'd wanted to watch the first news report of the day to see if they'd found Deidra and Lenny yet. "I didn't see anything about what we did, but I did see some girl got her throat slashed down at the strip club Spoe's boy Tariq used to hang out at."

"Treat's?"

"Yeah, that's it. And guess who they interviewed?"

"Let me damn guess; your Inspector Gadget boyfriend?" Ginger turned up his lip while rubbing on his feet.

Simone laughed at the comparison. "Yup, Chase's fine ass. He said one of the dancers named Tiffany got her head damn near cut off her body."

"Tiffany!" Ginger leaped to her feet almost kicking over the sofa table. "Did you say a dancer down at that piece-of-shit club? You mean that son of a bitch named Tiffany?"

"Yeah, I think so. Why?"

"Fuck all the whys right about now. Have you spoken to Bunny?"

"Bunny? Naw, not since she left here. I tried calling her again late last night, but I still got the voice mail."

"Shit!"

"Shit, what? What's wrong?"

"Come on, Simone. I know your memory ain't that bad. You know that's the damn female that Bunny said set Spoe and Tariq up, don't you? She said her name was Tiffany, and the ignorant bitch danced at that club. We need to find out where Bunny at. Fast and in a hurry!"

Simone sat motionless. As she replayed the conversation she and Bunny had, it soon came back to her that Ginger was correct. The girl's name was Tiffany, and she was one of the headliners at Treat's Gentlemen's Club. Without hesitation, she ran to the stairs. Sprinting up the stairs and back, she returned with her cell phone in hand. Pulling up Bunny's name, she hit TALK. One short ring and her call was directly sent to voice mail. This time was different than the others because Simone was not able to leave a message since the box was filled to capacity. "I can't even leave a damn message for her ass. We need to go over to her house, like now!"

***

As Ginger drove to Bunny's condo, Simone called Chase in hopes of obtaining information relating to the bodies and Bunny's disappearing ass.

"Good morning."

"Hey, sunshine. Good morning to you also. How did you sleep?"

"I slept well. I just called to tell you that you looked very handsome on the news this morning."

"Wow, you saw that, huh?"

"Yeah, why you say it like that? You looked good to me . . . considering the circumstances."

"Yeah, some dancer messed around and got killed; a real messy scene. But I know you don't wanna hear about all that drama."

He had no idea that was indeed all Simone wanted to hear about. Truth be told, that was the nature of the call in the first place . . . to fish for information not only about the murder at the club and if they had any suspects, but if he'd heard of anymore deceased bodies turning up at the river. "Not really, but I feel so sorry for that girl and her family. I hope you guys find out who did it."

"Yeah," Detective Dugan was distracted by someone coming into his office bringing him some files on yet a few more unsolved cases. "Sorry, Simone. What were you saying, sweetie?"

"Nothing much, Chase. I was just saying I hope you guys have the no-good man behind bars that hurt that girl last night. Doing her like that was a sin and a shame. I hope you locked him up and threw away the key."

"As much as I would love to say yeah, we got the scumbag off the street and get the chief and the damn mayor off my back, no dice. Not only do we have no leads, we don't even know if the killer is a man or a woman."

"A woman?"

"Yeah, Simone. You know, maybe one of the other girls was jealous of the victim's beauty or something." Chase was strangely enchanted by the dead girl Tiffany's perfect angelic face and seductive voice.

"Oh, so you think she was beautiful, huh?" Simone quizzed with envy almost forgetting the reason for the call. "I guess I should be kinda glad you dating me and only me, right?"

Chase smiled, feeling like the female he was so crazy about was also into him the same way as well. "Girl, you know it's no chick in the world I think is more flyer than you."

"Oh, okay, then," Simone laughed getting back on track as Ginger gave her the side eye. "Well, what else is going on? When are we going on another date? You owe me a steak dinner, or did you forget?"

"It's coming, I promise. Just as soon as I think we have one thing under control, though, some other mess pops up. First, the dancer getting killed last night while me and my partner were down at the club, then the two damn burned bodies by the riverbank."

"Down at the club? Two burned bodies? What?" she suspiciously repeated, shocked to hear both admissions. Playing the dumb role, she continued to dry pump him for even more information. "You were at the club last night other than investigating that someone burned up two people? Yeah, Chase, your life is way too busy for me and complicated."

"Naw, sweetie, it's not. I'll tell you what. Can you meet me today for a late lunch? I promise I'll be on time and not let anything stand in our way."

Not wanting to miss out on an opportunity to have a face-to-face with the man who was ultimately holding her and her siblings' freedom, unknowing, in his hands, Simone immediately replied yes before ending their conversation. Turning her attention back to Ginger, she informed him of the details of what Chase had said. "We're gonna have a late lunch. That way, I can really read his face and con the true four-one-one outta his ass!"

Seconds before they pulled into the empty driveway of Bunny's condo, Simone's cell phone rang. Automatically assuming it was Chase forgetting to tell her something, she answered without even looking at the screen. "Don't tell me you're cancelling on me. It only took all of what—two minutes?"

"Yes, hello. Is this Miss Simone Banks?"

"Umm . . . yes, it is," Simone removed her cell from her ear taking a quick look at the screen. Seeing a 1-800 number, she was still at a loss of who it was. "I'm sorry, but who's calling?"

"Yes, this is Capital Health Insurance Company. We're calling on behalf of Tallhya Banks-Walker and the facility she's currently admitted in. You are listed on the admission record as the main contact person."

"Yes, that's right. Is my sister okay?"

"Oh, she's fine as she can be. But we have a problem with billing."

"A problem? What kind of problem?"

"It seems that Walter Walker, listed as her spouse, recently cancelled her health insurance, so we need some other type of payment arrangements to be made by six o'clock this evening or she will be discharged."

"He did *what?*" Simone yelled, causing Ginger to stop from getting out of the parked car. *That low-down son of a bitch! I'm going to personally cut his throat!*

After confirming what her soon-to-be former brother-in-law had done, Simone filled in Ginger. Deciding one day soon Walter would be on their "list" of no-good motherfuckers who went against the grain of the Banks sisters that had to be dealt with, they smiled.

Luckily, Tallhya had taken the monthly payout of her lottery windfall and could easily cover her own medical bills when her next stipend was paid. For the time being, Simone assured the caller she'd be in the office by the end of the day with a check to cover her sister's expenses for the next week or so. Now totally disgusted or confused with most of the men they'd encountered over the past month, with the exception of Detective Dugan, Simone grimaced.

Walking up to Bunny's condo, she then motioned for Ginger to be quiet as they pressed their ears to the door. After hearing no movement or noise inside, Simone retrieved the spare key from the spot Bunny always hid it in. In a matter of seconds, she and Ginger were inside of the expensively decorated condo.

"Okay, now, this bullshit is creepy as a motherfucker. First, the bitch don't answer none of our calls. Then her car ain't here, and now this! What the hell *is* this?" Ginger snatched all three of the letters off of the dresser in Bunny's bedroom. Ripping the envelope open that had his name boldly written across the front, the reason for Bunny's absence became evident.

By the time Simone was finish reading her handwritten preconfession note of sorts, she knew they had to find Bunny as soon as possible. She'd said she was going to make Tiffany pay for what she'd done to Spoe and Tariq. And by all accounts of the tragic events that unfolded the night before at Treat's Gentlemen's Club, Bunny had kept her murderous word. Now they had to find their seemingly disturbed sister and save her from herself. Like the final sentence in the note read, by her own hand she'd be with Spoe, dancing in heaven, before she'd spend one night locked up in the hell that was prison.

Chapter 15

Dino woke up with a new go-getter attitude and lease on life. Knowing he was a true hustler, he never missed a beat. Convinced he could double up and financially rebound from the major lost he suffered at the hands of Spoe and his mystery partner, he lit a blunt, blowing smoke up in the air. Tying his thick, waist-length dreads in a ponytail, he felt the energy of the day in his bones. He'd made things as right as he could with his connect. He had no choice if he and his boys wanted to continue running the narcotic-plagued neighborhoods they were holding down.

Having made several trips up to New York for face-to-face meetings with the main plug, Dino had a lot of explaining to do. Thankfully, the ruthless and rotten leader of the Bloody Lions Posse finally reassured the higher-ups the drug pipeline he'd worked almost a good year and three months on was back secure. He made his foreign investors see that it was only by sheer luck the men that'd infiltrated his home were able to get away with that much product and cash. Showing them plans of not only a new high-tech security system in place, but pictures of one of the culprits, Spoe, being half-eaten by the dogs, they finally were satisfied. Leaving Spanish Harlem with the confidence of the bosses he needed to make money, Dino vowed to never let anyone—man, woman, cat, or dog—get close enough again to know where his stash was.

Now, in less than two hours, the bloodthirsty drug merchant would accept delivery on a new drug package. That blessing from the dope gods would put him not only a little bit back in the game, but all the way back on his feet as well. Considering it was the day of his big prebirthday bash at Club You Know, this come up was right on time. He reached for his phone and dialed the party promoter to ensure that there would be no surprises.

"Yeah, man, you guys got the bottles ready for me or what? I'm not bullshitting around tonight. We trying to turn the hell up in that motherfucker! I need to let this entire city know me and my posse still standing strong and ain't about to fall short no time soon!"

"Of course, Dino. You know we about our business down here at the club. For real, for real. Now, have we ever let you or your people down? I don't think so," the party promoter reassured one of his favorite and loyal customers. "When I say I got you, I got you. Besides VIP, which is practically sold out, we got the flyers posted all around the city; on Facebook and Instagram too."

Having confidence his party would be banging, Dino's mind was at ease. While getting dressed, the seasoned thug grabbed the oversized universal remote. With one click, he turned on not only the television, but the surround system as well. As the thunderous sounds kicked from the various speakers, he abruptly stopped dead in his tracks. He thought he was seeing wrong. He thought he was hearing wrong. It couldn't be, yet seemed as it was. *What in the entire fuck? Oh, hell, naw!* Paying close attention to the suit-and-tie-clad reporter on the midday newscast, Dino's mouth dropped open. The fact that the local strip club he and his boys would hang out at from time to time was the backdrop for a story was nothing. There was always some sort of petty crimes or minor disturbances taking place there. That bullshit was normal at a strip club. However, what was *not* normal was seeing the female's face—who was just calling him the night before like some sort of a stalker—plastered all across the sixty-five inch mounted flat screen.

Tiffany was everything that being a stripper, gold digger, opportunist, slut, ho, and bitch encompassed. She was all that . . . and more. Matter of fact, a master at her craft of hustling men out their cash. Now the always-down-for-whatever female could add another well-deserved title to her extensive ghetto résumé: murder victim. *Damn, I knew that bird was gonna get got one day, but shit . . . Now the sneaky tramp can't suck me off for a couple of dollars no more when a playa get a taste for some of that good head game she got—or rather had.*

Dino didn't know the circumstances behind Tiffany's demise but knew whoever took her out of the game had a good reason to do so. He had no real proof she was behind the deadly robbery at his house, yet, she was one of his suspects, so, fuck her was his mind-set. He was thrown off that she was dead, but that still didn't stop or put a damper on the fact his party was later that night. Dino was feeling himself and wasn't gonna let not no person—dead or alive—bring him down.

After finishing his breakfast blunt appetizer, he went down to the kitchen for the main course he smelled cooking. The infamous drug dealer's personal chef had come in extra early for his birthday and the potent weed had made him as hungry as five men combined.

Bunny spent the night at a cheap motel. Driving a few extra miles outside the city limits, she made sure she parked her vehicle near the rear of the building. Not knowing if someone would be able to shed any light on who committed Tiffany's heinous murder, she felt it best to be as low-key as possible. Not having any remorse for her brutal, but justified actions, Bunny had taken a shower. Feeling a sense of relief, she was totally relaxed. She'd ignored the constant back-to-back calls from Simone and Ginger. Bunny knew they could and would take care of the bloody situation she'd left behind in Me-Ma's basement. And if they couldn't, at this point in the game, she could care less. Bunny felt she had bigger fish to fry. Wrapped in a towel, she lay across the bed gazing up at the ceiling. As she held the pillow and thought of the same thing she'd been thinking about for the past couple of weeks, Bunny prayed Spoe was also thinking of her up in heaven.

Wiping a few tears out of the corner of each eye, Bunny rocked back and forth knowing she had to complete her deliberate task of revenge. Knowing what she now knew about Dino, there was no way in hell his mother wasn't gonna get the same call Spoe's lunatic mother had received. There was no way Dino's woman or jump off was gonna miss out on the feeling of heartache and pain she was enduring. No way in hell was Dino gonna enjoy walking these streets ever again without looking over his shoulder in fear. If Spoe was dead by Dino's hands, then he'd be dead by hers. Lenny's death meant nothing. Tiffany's also meant nothing, and killing her own mother in cold blood meant even less to Bunny. But sending Dino on his way was going to be like hitting the multistate jackpot. Bunny was as anxious to see him bleed out as she was on Christmas morning seeing a tree full of ribbon-wrapped toys.

Climbing out of bed, Bunny turned on the early news report to see if anything would be mentioned about the brazen crime she committed the night before. With wide-eyed anticipation, she sat on the edge of the bed. Not having to wait long, Bunny soon saw Treat's Gentlemen's Club and her sister's beau Detective Chase Dugan taking center stage. Her hands shook and her heart raced as he was being asked question after question pertaining to the case. Attentively listening to every single word reported, Bunny smirked seeing Tiffany's picture then flash on the upper right-hand side of the television. Reading the word "victim" underneath the woman's name who set up Spoe to get murdered brought Bunny even more elation. *No suspects can be identified at this time, and no apparent motive in the slaughter. Hell, yeah!*

As Bunny Banks smiled, she reached over on the nightstand to grab Tiffany's stolen cell phone. Having turned off the GPS tracker before she even hit the corner the night before, Bunny was ready to get down to business. With an inner rage, she started the task of trying to track down Dino. Spoe's devoted wifey had no idea what his grimy Bloody Lions Posse ass looked like or where he lived. However, seeing how Tiffany and he were supposedly so damn close, Bunny knew she could find all the answers she wanted in the smartphone she was holding in her hands. Revenge was at her fingertips.

Like so many other people, Tiffany had all her social media sites easily accessible. She had the app icons on her cell's screen waiting to be tapped. Bunny grinned with total satisfaction as she hit the blue and white Facebook symbol and was directed to Tiffany's personal page. Now having a complete view of her pictures, friends list, and time line, Bunny knew trying to find the infamous Dino would be easier than she thought. In a mere matter of minutes, Bunny was blessed. In the brightest, boldest, and most flamboyant ever flyer she'd ever seen, Bunny saw her man's killer's name big as day, damn near leaping off the screen. Double tapping the picture made it increase in size much to Bunny's delight. As she studied the zoomed-in image, she saw the date of "Dino's Prebirthday Turn Up" was that very same night. Bunny couldn't believe her eyes or luck. Not only did it have a contact number to reserve VIP booths, but it had several of Dino's pictures in the corner of the flyer. *So this ugly-faced mud-duck piece of shit having a damn party tonight at Club You Know! Ain't this about nothing. He out here running the streets getting life in like he some sort of a boss, and my baby gone. But I ain't tripping. It ain't no thang. All that bullshit gonna end real soon for his punk ass. Fucking real, real soon, I promise you that, bitch-ass motherfucker!*

Chapter 16

It was nearing one o'clock in the afternoon as Simone pulled her struggle buggy up into the parking lot of the Mexican restaurant. Checking her makeup in the vehicle's rearview mirror, she was ready to go in and share a meal with her beau, Chase. Hoping the trained detective couldn't see the countless crimes she and her family members had perpetrated since seeing him last, she took a deep breath. Braced with her game face on, Simone confidently walked through the front door. Following behind the hostess, she saw her lunch date had them a table located in the far corner of the room. Seeing Chase's bright smile made her return the favor. Loving the fact that he stood up and pushed her seat in for her made Simone miss her deceased father even more. He always taught her that there were certain things a real man did to prove his true worth to a worthy woman. Chase Dugan had just done one, and she was on cloud nine.

"Hey, now," he kept cheesing, happy to see her.

"Hey, yourself, Chase. How are you?"

"I'm great now that I'm seeing you. You're looking great as usual . . . beautiful smile; gorgeous face . . . the entire package. Everything a man would want or need in his life."

Simone blushed. Automatically, she forgot the real reason she'd taken him up on his out of the blue offer to have lunch. She was here to pump him for information about the criminal cases he was trying to solve, not behave like some immature schoolgirl with a crush on the cute boy next door. Fighting to get back on track and not fall victim to his compliments and endearing gaze, Simone took a small sip from the glass of wine she'd ordered. Seeing how he was still on duty, the police detective wisely decided to let her drink alone and just enjoy the food and her great company. The more she sipped the beverage, the freer she became with touching her lunch partner's arm, then face, then leg. Simone had a lot of stress and guilt she'd been holding onto for the past month, and the wine she was consuming seemed to ease her troubled mind.

Munching on nacho chips and salsa, the jubilant couple exchanged what had been going on in each other's lives. Even though Simone Banks was a little tipsy, she still managed to use her womanly wilds to unearth confidential information. He had no more real solid leads in the bank robbery case. Detective Dugan let it slip that not only did his one lead in that crime run him directly into a brick wall, he also revealed to Simone that the important lead was the stripper that was killed the night before.

"Oh my God, Chase, that's too bad. Did you guys ever catch the man that did that to her? I mean, he must've been a real monster to do something like that. I bet a place like that has to have cameras all over, so it will be easy to at least get that thug soon."

"Yeah, cameras all over that don't freaking work," he remarked feeling like he and his men couldn't catch a break in these random crimes as of late.

"Wow." Simone secretly wanted to shout hooray and do a quick happy dance as she sat still.

"So to answer your question, sweetie, no, Simone." Defeated in spirit, he lowered his head, not wanting to further acknowledge the fact he and his partner were present inside the strip club when the murder took place. It was bad enough having the chief ride his back about not being observant, but not his girl also. "Not yet. The bad part of it is we don't have any strong leads on that damn murder. It's like this entire city has gone nuts over the past month. I don't know if it's something in the water or what. But I mean, it's crazy. The crime rate hasn't been this bad in years. Even the national news is raking the entire department over the coals."

Listening to his Saturday afternoon speech on the state of the city, she was just content he didn't suspect her sister Bunny. Simone took another small sip of her second glass of wine and felt warm all over. The tipsier she became, just like touching on Chase, the bolder her questions also became.

"Listen, honey, don't you think maybe the dancer girl was a bad person that probably was running with the wrong crowd? Maybe drug dealers or whatnot. You know those types of girls are always dealing in something shady. After all, she has lied and schemed to get the fellas to give up their money. Don't you think?" She tried planting the seed of thought in the veteran detective's mind.

"Of course, I do. But it's my job to bring justice to all the families of all victims; even the victims with questionable backgrounds or lifestyles," he explained with a serious tone and demeanor. "It's like these two deceased bodies that were discovered last night out by the James River."

"More bodies?" Simone sobered up quickly. She braced herself for what was to come next. She prayed this wasn't a crazy setup and the police were behind the walls of the restaurant waiting to jump out and arrest her. Maybe Chase had a wire on him and was just making small talk until he gave his surveillance team the signal to reveal themselves. She bravely worked up her nerve and repeated her question. "Did you say more bodies?"

"Yes, sweetie; two of them. We think one is a woman, the other a man. They were badly burned. Our forensics team has noted that both their hands were missing from their bodies. I mean, that's crazy, right? Their hands, of all things. How crazy is that?"

"Missing hands? Oh my goodness, that's terrible."

"Yeah, Simone. We think it might be some sort of wicked serial killer running around the city. I know it seems like a movie plot or something, but at this point, we just don't know."

"A serial killer? Seriously?"

"Yeah, I know, right? Very bizarre but extremely dangerous." He reached across the table holding Simone's wrists, slowly massaging them with his thumbs. "So make sure you and your sisters stay in lighted areas and travel in groups. The chief and the mayor are trying to keep this whole handless body thing under wraps until we have a suspect to parade around the news cameras."

The pair soon finished their short but informative lunch. Having Chase's word that he'd call her later, Simone and he headed toward the front door. Caught up in everything that was Chase, Simone accidentally bumped into a man and woman entering the restaurant.

"Oh, excuse me," Simone politely spoke without bothering to look up.

"Dang, you're bad!" the female rudely replied, causing Simone to give the couple her full attention.

"Oh, hell, naw! Not *you* of all people. You have a lot of nerve walking around the streets coming all out to eat like you just didn't do some old slimeball bullshit! The hospital called me."

"Listen, Simone, don't start with me!"

"Me? Are you serious, fool?"

"Yeah, girl, I don't owe you or that whack job sister of yours nothing! So stay out my face and keep your mouth shut." Walter didn't back down one bit. As his voice got louder, he seemed to be getting closer into his sister-in-law's personal space.

The once meek and mild mannered Simone Banks was no more. Her timid personality was a thing of the past. After all she'd been through, participated in, and seen over the past month, dealing with Tallhya's estranged husband was a piece of cake. "Look, Walter, I'm warning you. I ain't nothing like my sister. If you think you want it with me, you better back the fuck up and think twice. All that bossing her around and having her scared of her own shadow don't work with me. I'm telling you, I ain't the one," she ranted with small beads of perspiration forming in the tiny creases on her brow. "She put up with that foolishness, but trust, I'm not and won't. You don't want to start nothing with me."

"Oh, please, Walter, don't tell me this is another one of them go-for-bad relatives of that crazy whore you fake married to. The one whose money bought me this huge diamond ring on my finger and paid for our trip to Cancun," Walter's lunch date remarked with her hands judgmentally planted on her hips.

"Yeah, baby doll. This is another one of them psychopath dysfunctional Banks sisters," he replied, pointing his finger in Simone's face.

"Oh, yeah, well, you make sure you tell that cross-dressing freak brother of yours the next time he tries to fight two women, my brothers got something for his sissy ass, and that's for real! So whenever you ready, bitch, bring it. I dare you!"

Simone had forgotten about Chase being at her side. Without reservation, she went full throttle on Walter and who she quickly had to assume was his dead baby's momma. The very one that got her ass handed to her at the funeral home. "Listen, Frick-and-fucking-dumb-ass-Frack, neither one of you two want it with any of us. If you think you felt our wrath that day, you best brace yourself. And, Walter, it's bad enough you stole all my sister's money to spend on this trash mouthpiece of shit ho you running with, but then you had the nerve to cancel my sister's medical coverage. You a weak-ass man for that stunt. You know she needed that insurance, and you did her like that after all she done did for your stupid ass."

"Well, forget her and you. The doctors done called me saying your sister up there mumbling about this and that like some lunatic; making all sorts of wild claims about things that couldn't possibly be true."

"What?" Simone twisted her face as if Walter was lying. Yet deep down inside, she knew Tallhya probably was up there in the mental facility telling them who shot King and Kennedy and confessing everything else she'd been a part of the past month or so.

"Hey, if it was up to me, I say let that banner brain broad rot in that motherfucker. I could care less—but not on my dime!"

"Yeah, you better believe that shit!" Walter's companion added her two cents.

Sensing things were seconds from getting even more out of control than they were, Chase stepped in. He had no choice before someone else called the cops. Trying his best to defuse the confusing situation in a calm manner, the police detective stepped in between Simone and her two adversaries. He felt like a ring leader in a bizarre three-ring circus. "Hold up, everyone. Please just be cool and let's try to keep our voices down."

"Man, who in the fuck is you? Don't tell me you another family member of this psycho." Walter flexed, now heading in Chase's direction. "You trying to get some of this rhythm? 'Cause if you is, I'ma gladly bless you with some. Come get it!"

Now in total police mode, Detective Chase Dugan took a few steps backward not only for his own safety, but that of Simone and Walter's shit-talking asses. Showing his badge, he wasted no more time announcing his title, warning the man to maintain his position and relax. "Okay, sir, please step back and lower your tone. You are alarming the restaurant's guests. Not to mention you are threatening an officer of the law with bodily harm. Do you *really* want to go there?"

Walter stopped dead in his tracks. He surely didn't want to be arrested but felt he and his baby momma were verbally attacked first. He complied for the most part but still continued to tell Simone just how crazy her sister Tallhya truly was. "Look, Simone, you and all y'all Banks is straight up nut jobs. Dude, if I was you, I'd watch my back dealing with one of they crazy asses! They all some animals, every last one of them. Their bloodline is tainted."

Chase just stood silent in amazement. He couldn't believe his ears concerning the wild predicament he was abruptly thrust into. If he didn't have such a strange and strong attachment to Simone, he would've arrested all three of them for disturbing the peace and any other criminal charges he could come up with.

"Shut the fuck up, Walter," Simone evilly hissed, ready to snap his neck in two pieces with her bare hands. "You gonna get enough of talking shit to me and about my family. We were the same folks that took your sorry behind in. You ate my grandmother's home cooked meals every single day and night, you ungrateful little nothing of a man! I swear if I saw your ass on fire, I wouldn't even spit on your ass!"

"Naw, Simone, you shut up! The entire neighborhood knows how ruthless y'all family can be when someone crosses y'all; especially that sneaky dead-ass Me-Ma."

"Who in the fuck you think you are? You can't talk about my grandmother like that!" Simone balled up her fist ready to strike, but Chase stepped closer to her.

"Yeah, her cranky hypocrite ass pretending like she so off into the church and the Bible, then sent her grandkid pit bulls down to the funeral home to clown. What old woman does that? That church she was so caught up in, The Faith and Hope Ministry, and that con man preacher is all a joke!" Walter was spewing all the Banks's family secrets out loud for all to hear, especially his sister-in-law's lunch date.

"Yeah, who in the entire fuck does that—sending her people to fight at a funeral home? I hope that old woman burn in triple-hot hellfire for that snake shit she pulled," Walter's girl bravely cosigned, causing Simone to lunge at her.

"Dude, fuck you, her, and y'all dead bastard-ass baby that's pushing up daises. Y'all all can kiss my pretty ass!" Having to be physically restrained by Chase, Simone finally left the restaurant kicking and screaming. As he escorted her to the parking lot, she was still heated and not done clowning. She wanted her fist to connect to Walter's and his bitch's face. "Oh my God, I hate him! I swear I hate that soulless Negro. I fucking swear!"

Chase had never seen this side of Simone. He didn't know what to make out of the blue altercation she was mixed into. She had always been calm, cool, and collected every time they interacted . . . Never showing any craziness or even the hint of it. Even when the bank robbers put guns in her face and had threatened to kill her, Simone was still silent and reserved. Now here she was ejecting threats and having to be dragged out of a public building. "Are you okay now? Relax, Simone. Calm down, please."

The effects of the two glasses of wine had completely worn off. Instead of being in the mood to be loved and felt up by Chase, she was ready to violently lay hands on someone— Walter and his girl in particular. "Wow, I'm so sorry, Chase. I swear I am, but that man knows how to push my buttons. After all he'd done to my sister and our family, he had the nerve to leave Tallhya hanging in the hospital. That's some bold bullshit to do. I never wanted you to see that side of me."

"The hospital? You didn't tell me one of your sisters was sick. How is she doing? Is there anything I can do to help?" he asked, puzzled, not knowing what else to say or do.

Simone tried her best to defuse his barrage of questions. With a straight face, she let Chase know her sister was getting great medical care and would be all right, even though she knew Tallhya was crazier than a bat out of hell. Part of Simone also wanted to confide in him that she had to have some procedures done in the very near future that may prove to be extremely detrimental to her general health and existence, but she opted not to.

Although they were getting closer as the days went by, she still knew she and her siblings were criminals, and he was the law; certainly not a match made in heaven. Instead of being honest, she continued with her mockery of the truth. Further putting on an act, Simone promised to deal with Walter another way when and if she encountered him again. Knowing he had to get back to the office, Detective Dugan made sure Simone got in her car and left the restaurant premises. Watching her taillights turn the corner, he suspiciously rubbed his chin not knowing what to make out of her split personality behavior and all the wild accusations of sadistic behavior her brother-in-law had made. *What the hell was that? That was something I didn't even know she had in her.* Chase's thoughts made him second-guess his lady, but he chalked it up to not knowing the entire situation. Besides, he knew how and what people would say just to be vindictive.

Back at police headquarters, Detective Dugan got settled in his black leather chair. With a strong cup of black coffee sitting on the right side of his desk and a yellow notepad on the left, he was ready for the long haul. Knowing he'd be stuck in the semicool office until the late hours of the night, he took a few minutes to meditate in hopes of getting his mind right. He locked his fingers together after placing them behind his head. Leaning back in the chair, he proceeded to close his eyes. Lost in the darkness, his thoughts started to drift back to the happiness he felt earlier in the day when he had lunch with Simone. He got a warm feeling inside. The detective couldn't help grinning, thinking about how good it felt having her smile at him. His manhood started to jump as he relived the sensation he experienced when she caressed his knee, then upper leg. Thinking about how beautiful she was made him feel like some dumb kid; some crazy teenager in love. He missed that feeling and was giddy that Simone had unearthed those sentiments buried in him.

Unfortunately, as fast as Chase was caught up deeply in his emotions of what he felt could possibly be undeniable love, his keen investigative personality snatched him out of that fantasy and into a feeling that he could only describe as a living nightmare. His perfect princess Simone was a monster in disguise. In a mere matter of seconds, she'd transformed. His possible mate for life made visible her monsterlike tendencies for all the restaurant occupants and him to see. The stunned police detective witnessed her turn from a beauty to a beast firsthand. Simone traded in her diamond tiara for a jagged sword and had no problem doing so.

He knew there was something more to Simone's zero to a hundred drastic behavior change, even if she did despise her brother-in-law. Sure, he'd cancelled the girl's insurance, cheated on her, and had a bastard child behind her back, along with stealing her lottery winnings, so of course, Simone would be heated for her sister's terrible betrayal. That reaction was normal and was to be expected. But Simone wanted blood. She was on the verge of being deranged and homicidal. He'd been on the police force for years and recognized all kinds of sick minded individuals. He'd seen the type of rage Simone had exhibited earlier in ruthless and rotten murderers that were apprehended but coldheartedly showed no remorse. Simone's demeanor when trying to get at Walter and his girl mirrored those traits. It was as if she had no home training. Whatever the true reason was, he knew he'd have to figure that out later on his own time. Right now, Detective Chase Dugan had bigger fish to fry, and the clock was ticking.

Unlocking his fingers, he opened his weary eyes. Sitting upward, he reached for his sports teams' decorated coffee mug. After getting some of the strong brew flowing through his system, the detective in him was alert. With the cracking of his knuckles, he was about ready to connect some dots and solve some of the pending high-profile cases that had been haunting his sleep, the chief's, and the mayor's.

As he looked over the growing stack of papers and reports stuffed into the manila folders labeled after each individual crime, he shrugged his shoulders. *These cases are linked together somehow. If I just set my mind to it, I can see what I've been missing. First things first; where the heck is Tiffany's cell phone? Why isn't it listed in her personal property? I know she had it on her when she left that stage. Now, either the other dancer that discovered her body has it, along with the bracelet and earrings I noticed she was wearing before her death, or the killer does.* Finding the paper he'd jotted the distraught female's number on from the club, he hoped she'd be either honest enough or scared enough to come clean and admit she'd stolen off a dead person.

If that didn't work, Detective Dugan knew he'd have to put a trace on the line through the company provider. Regardless, he was hell-bent on locating not only that phone, but the person or persons that were so brazen to even consider perpetrating a crime that bold in a building full of people. In the meantime, he once again retrieved Tariq's cell phone and pulled up the last number dialed from his line before Tiffany's; someone listed in his extensive list of contacts as just "B."

Chapter 17

Thanks to the news reports and her sister's dim-witted boyfriend, Bunny was satisfied she was not a suspect in Tiffany's murder. Not fearing being arrested, she knew it was safe to go home to the condo. Now somewhat back in her right mind, she decided to return the multiple missed calls and voice mails from her siblings. Knowing Ginger would be the easiest to speak to, Bunny dialed that number first. "Hey, what's going on?"

"Oh, hell, naw, bitch! Don't 'hey, what's going on' me! Where the fuck you been? We been calling you and calling you; blowing your fucking phone up!"

"Dang, I been around. Can't a girl get some alone time? Damn," Bunny smartly responded like she'd done no wrong in not responding to any of their calls.

"Around like where? Girl, me and Simone been by your crib and everything. You know after you ain't call back we was gonna be worried."

"Yeah, I know but—"

"But nothing, trick. You know that slick shit you did going underground was whack as hell, especially considering what went down before you left Me-Ma's."

"Yeah, I know."

"Okay, then, fool, now like I said, where the hell you been, besides, of course, the strip club slicing a bitch's neck?"

"Say what?"

"Bunny, don't play with me," Ginger's voice went from female to male, letting his sister know this wasn't the time to play word games.

"Look, Ginger, I know y'all seen the letters, and I hope y'all understand."

"Of course, we do, but you still just can't disappear like that on us." Ginger's attitude grew sassy with each passing word. "So where you at now because we gotta talk and don't try to avoid us!"

Bunny informed Ginger where she was at. Telling him she had a game plan on deck to settle a few more scores, she told him to get in touch with Simone. "Y'all meet me over here. I got some shit to tell y'all I found out from that slut Tiffany."

"Cool, because we need to put you up on your dead mother's whereabouts amongst other things that done jumped while you was fucking AWOL!"

Bunny sat in the driveway of her condo dreading going inside an empty home. Spoe wasn't there for her to laugh or joke with or to fuss and fight with. It was just her and his calming spirit. A spirit that couldn't touch her; couldn't kiss her; couldn't wrap his arms around her or sadly give her the dick she craved.

Simone made it back home to Me-Ma's in no time flat. Still infuriated from her verbal altercation with Walter and his twisted face jump off, she slammed her car door shut. The amount of force she used caused a small bit of rust to fall from the bottom frame landing on the concrete. Seething with anger, Simone burst through the front door as if she was the police executing a search warrant for two murder suspects in a nursery school massacre. Finding Ginger in the kitchen just ending a conversation, she unloaded the partial 411 on not only what Chase told her at lunch about the cases he was working on, but the battle royal she was about to have with their sister's no-good, soon-to-be ex-husband and his dead baby's momma he's involved with.

Deciding to listen to the rest of Simone's wild escapades in the car, Ginger and she walked out the door and pulled off in Simone's clunker heading toward Bunny's. When the pair finally arrived, they found Bunny's car in the driveway. The door was already unlocked so they let themselves in. Once back inside of the condo, they discovered Bunny's overnight bag thrown on the couch. Walking upstairs, they heard the shower water running and their murderous rampage sister humming. Giving each other the serious side eye, Simone and Ginger shook their heads.

Ginger raised his finger to the side of his head, twirling it around, indicating that he believed Bunny had taken a couple of huge steps off into the deep end of insanity. First, the way she just abruptly jumped to her feet and skin carved their mother and Lenny up like two Thanksgiving turkeys. Then, she washed off their blood and just walked out of Me-Ma's—no words spoken—and disappeared for close to thirty-six hours. Finally, she plotted on, apparently tracked down, then boldly executed a stripper in a nightclub full of potential witnesses like it wasn't shit. Now here, Bunny was taking a shower, humming old love songs like she didn't have a single care in the world. As if she was easy street.

"Hey, girl, we here," Simone yelled out, hoping she wouldn't startle Bunny and become her next bloody victim.

Bunny got out of the shower, dried off, and threw on a track suit. Meeting her siblings down in the living room, she was ready to tell them every detail that had jumped off since she'd last seen them; every gory detail. Starting with the moment she decided to end their mother's useless life.

Simone, Bunny, and Ginger all took a seat at the table. Each not knowing what the other was going to say, Ginger, being a true drama queen, started the ball rolling. Simone knew of his antics and late illicit night of passion with Pastor Street, but Bunny was still in the dark. Pulling out his cell phone, Ginger proceeded to show both his sisters the candid snapshots he'd taken of the good-dick-having-preacher their grandmother admired so before her death. The more each sister scrolled, the more embarrassed they became seeing the supposed man of the cloth exposed. The video Bunny had taken of Ginger giving him the bomb head in Me-Ma's living room on the couch and the floor near the coffee table was bad enough, but these images seemed to be ten times worse. Ginger had somehow managed to get every possible angle captured. He got Cassius Street's good side, bad side, and most shocking of them all, his dark side. Simone and Bunny couldn't believe the nerve Ginger had and found it hilarious. They were amused that the pastor was dumb enough to not notice that

Ginger was snapping away when he claimed to be checking his Facebook page and returning text messages. Ginger was so wild with it he even took selfies with him and the naked sleeping ordained man of the cloth.

"Yeah, you two amateurs see these." Ginger's smile grew wider and brighter each time a new salacious picture was revealed. "Well, these little Kodak moments along with me and my Bible-thumping homeboy's sex tape gonna get us back Me-Ma's house come tomorrow."

"Tomorrow, really?" Simone smirked knowing Ginger was up to no good.

"Yeah, tomorrow." Ginger cleaned underneath his fingernails and rolled his eyes up toward the ceiling. "Let's just say tomorrow at church, right in the middle of service, a fool like me might mess around and catch the Holy Ghost . . . and everything else I could catch in that piece."

Bunny had been strangely quiet but finally chimed in, giving Ginger a high five. "See, now *that's* what I'm talking about! Hit that conniving sack of shit where it hurts. Those church members and them off the chain collection offerings is Pastor Street's bread and butter, so yeah, fuck his hustle all the way up."

"Well, since you in such a fuck-a-nigga's-hustle-up mode, Bunny," Simone eagerly chimed in, "I hope you know you threw some serious salt in me and Ginger's game the other day."

"Huh, what you mean?" Bunny's facial expression changed as she played with a broken clasp tennis bracelet on the table.

"I mean, damn, sis. I know you were deep off into your zone. I could see that. Me and Ginger both could see the bullshit. But, damn, your ass went all Freddy Krueger, Jason, and Michael in that basement."

Bunny innocently bit down on the corner of her lip. "Oh yeah, that."

"Oh, yeah, is right, bitch," Ginger threw his two cents in the conversation. "You just went all Rambo with it and left blood every-damn-where."

"I'm sorry, y'all. I don't know what happened. I just was kinda in my zone. You know."

Ginger wasn't done going in. He had no intentions to let his sister, Bunny, off the hook that easily for going berserk, then dipping like she had a personal cleanup crew on call. "Well, I showl in the hell knows what happened. Your dumb ass cut Momma and that nigga up foot to 'fro, left blood everywhere, and pranced your slap-happy ass upstairs to take a hot shower, then sashayed out the front door leaving me and this crazy-in-love witch to do the cleanup."

"Hey, now. Why I gotta be a crazy-in-love witch? Remember me, heifer? I was the same one that was down in that basement shoulder to shoulder with your crazy ass scrubbing blood and wrapping bodies up," Simone leaped to her feet and announced as if she was seeking an award or politicking for political office. "Have you forgotten *I* was the one that rode with a bag of hands on they lap?"

"Oh, yeah, that," Ginger laughed as if what they did to their mother and Lenny was no big deal.

Bunny was still in the dark, not knowing what to think about what Simone and Ginger were claiming jumped off. "Bag of hands? What in the hell y'all asses talking about?"

Simone was already standing and decided to fill Bunny in. After telling her the trouble they had removing Deidra and Lenny from the basement of Me-Ma's, then dropping them off at the bank of the James River, her sister was finally up to speed. Never getting a total explanation of why Bunny flipped out like she did in the first place, Simone and Ginger decided to just let it go, especially considering Spoe's deceased corpse was discarded at that very river as well. They chalked it up to the small bit of crazy that was rumored to flow through their bloodline.

"Oh, yeah, so while I have y'all attention, let me tell y'all the entire way lunch went down with Chase. Like I was telling Ginger back at the house, things were all good with me and him while we were eating. I mean, real, real good." Simone had a huge smile showing all her perfectly lined teeth. "He told me they did discover Momma and Lenny's bodies."

"What?" Bunny blurted out, still on the verge of panic.

Simone put up her hand for Bunny to calm her nerves. "Naw, sis, don't worry. At this point, like the rest of the bodies they find there, rest in peace, Spoe and Tariq, they don't have any real leads; just speculation."

"Oh, whew, that's good." Bunny placed one hand over her heart and fanned her face with the other. "But what about . . ."

Simone reassured Bunny as well as Ginger that her detective boyfriend had absolutely no idea Bunny Banks was the one that sent Tiffany home the night before. That they were the ones that not only robbed the bank and set Ghostman up, but had killed two people in cold blood. When they were both over that much-needed relief of not going to prison by sunset, Simone hit them with the last part of her lunch. The part that she knew would surely cause them to become just as enraged as she was when it was going down in real time. "Okay, now both of you get ready to hear this bullshit right here."

Bunny and Ginger's full attention was on their sister. After being blessed with the knowledge that they had dodged the bullet of the law, well, at least temporarily, they couldn't imagine what else was more outrageous than that. "Tell us," they both begged, sitting on the edge of their seats.

"Well, when chase and I were leaving, I bumped into a ratchet female by mistake."

"And . . .?" Ginger's eyes bucked, waiting for the story.

"And right off rip, I told the rat 'excuse me,' because it was on me. So you know saying my bad was nothing, you know."

"Okay and . . . Just hurry up and spill the tea, bitch. Who was she? Damn, I'ma grow old waiting for you to get to the good part."

"Real talk, I don't even know her name, but she straight had a message for you. A serious message for that wild ass!"

"For who?" Ginger sucked his teeth as if Simone was lying. "I know you ain't talking about me. Girl, bye. I don't even know who you talking about."

Simone laughed. "Yes, the hell I am; a message for you, that's who."

"What kinda message some random ho got for me?" Ginger got loud and stood up.

"Sit your ass down, Ginger. Well, umm, she said to tell your special brand he/she butt the next time you jump on two women at a funeral home, you gonna get your ass handed to you on a silver platter."

"Oh, hell, naw! Not that lightweight bitch of all bitches! Her and her girl don't want it with me, Bunny, or Tallhya timid ass no more."

Simone told Bunny and Ginger all the things the smart-talking female was blowing out of her mouth. When she had them good and heated about that, Simone hit them with the fact the skank was with Walter. "Yup, y'all. And then *boom* went the dynamite! I was on that trick's head. He started bad-mouthing all of us and Tallhya, and that raggedy good thieving buster even had the balls to drag Me-Ma's name through the mud."

"One day soon, Walter gonna get his for messing over our family," Bunny vowed, meaning every word she was saying. "As soon as I get rid of this other situation I got brewing tonight, his nickel-slick ass is next! I'm sick and tired of motherfuckers thinking they can just do or say any damn thing, and it ain't gonna be any consequences to they actions. That shit is a wrap with me. I ain't buying off into the crap anymore."

Simone immediately peeped game and fell back. She took Bunny's tone and demeanor as an indicator someone or something was gonna feel her sister's unpredictable vicious wrath really soon. "Look, sis, me and Ginger done hogged all the conversation. You did call us over here to talk. So why don't you fill us in on what really jumped off at the strip club last night—your version?"

"I will. First, let me get us a taste of a little something so we can get our minds right. I'm about to put in some more work tonight; some *overtime* in the gangsta department. And I'ma need for y'all to have my back." Bunny got up disappearing into the kitchen to grab the much-needed spirits. Seconds later, she returned with a chilled bottle and three glasses in hand. "Everybody take a few sips because what I'm about to tell y'all about to probably be the realest shit the Banks sisters ever about to do."

Simone took a deep breath as she stared into Bunny's eyes, "Realer than robbing a bank, setting up a drug dealer, and killing our own mother? Damn, sis, pour me *two* glasses!"

Chapter 18

I don't know why I let that mess go down. That entire thing was nothing more than the devil working on me. I should have never given in, Lord. I don't know how I was so weak. I know I've been fornicating with various women, some even married, in my congregation, but like I said, I'm weak. God help me. The devil has been riding my back constantly and won't give up. Please save me from his evil clutches. I'm begging for your divine mercy. That atrocity disguising itself as a woman is no more than a shepherd for Satan. He's a roadblock for your ultimate plan for me. Perched down on bended knees, Pastor Street's fingers locked tightly. In tears, his silent pleas for forgiveness for his homosexual sins his religion condemned bounced off the inside of his brain louder than any noise he'd heard before.

With the wetness of his tears soaking the front of his expensive silk shirt he didn't know what to do or what to say next. Pastor Street had not only disrespectfully violated the inner sanctuary of the church, but also the Word of God. He felt he'd smeared the name of Jesus Christ in his office. He and Ginger were both sinners, yet he could only repent for himself. *I know this thing is gonna come back to bite me in the ass—excuse my language, God—but you know my heart. I know I've been here before in this same type of situation a few years back, but this is much different. I don't know. I just don't know.*

"Hey, baby, I thought I'd find you here. Why didn't you answer my calls?" One of his female parishioners, the church bookkeeper, tapped him on the shoulder with her set of building keys in hand.

"Oh, hey, what are you doing here?" Cassius looked up, shocked someone was inside the locked building with him, yet alone seeing him like he was.

"Oh my God, why are you crying? What's wrong, baby?" Katrina leaned over, attempting to wipe his face but was met with him avoiding her touch.

"Nothing is wrong with me, Katrina. I'm just praying, that's all," he lied, not knowing what else to say. After all, it wasn't like he could be honest with her . . . or anyone else, for that matter. What was he gonna say; I'm asking God to remove craving the taste of a hard dick in my mouth? Hell, naw. That declaration of truth could never work. Pastor Cassius Street announcing that statement would be the scandal of the church, the city, state, and the world.

"Well, I hope you were praying for this hot and wet pussy right here." She raised her skirt, revealing that she had no panties on. Using one finger, she slowly traced the outline of her cat, hoping to arouse the man she'd been sleeping with for the past six months after she persuaded him to stop sneaking around with the elder deacon's granddaughter. Offering him her retirement fund equity for new clothes and the down payment on a summer home near the coast, she felt he was hers.

Trapped by his guilt, he looked away from her. Still wanting forgiveness for his sinful ways, he focused his sights on the hand carved cross that adorned the pulpit. Feeling like he needed strength, he whispered for God to help him be strong enough to say no to this temptation. "Umm, look, I'm not trying to be rude, but not now. I have a gang of things on my plate I'm dealing with."

"Like what?" Katrina fired back with persistence, ready to get her sexual needs satisfied. "I know whatever you're dealing with ain't better than what I got for you!"

"Please, Katrina, not now. Why don't you just go home, and I'll see you at service tomorrow? I need to be alone to think, please."

Not readily wanting to take no for an answer, she asked him if he was sure of his decision, this time exposing her lace bra with her double Ds practically spilling out of her unbuttoned blouse.

Finally convincing her he wasn't interested in any sexual exploits for the evening, he walked the horny female to the door. Being a gentleman, he watched the church's loyal but promiscuous bookkeeper to her car.

Going back into the church, then his office to sit down, his heart and mind were heavy. Knowing he needed to relax, the pastor reached for his Bible for comfort. Before he knew what was happening, he'd lost his religion once more. Wild flashbacks of Ginger and him doing what they did the prior night commandeered his brain. Without reservations of betraying his promise to the Lord, the preacher's right hand was tightly wrapped around his manhood as the left gripped at the tissue-thin pages of God's Word.

Chapter 19

Shocked at the incredible bombshell updates Bunny told them, Simone and Ginger were basically speechless. Her dramatic tales of the last thirty-six hours were that which Academy Award–winning movies were made of. Disclosing the blow-by-blow details of the moments leading up to her going into the women's bathroom at the strip club, until the very second she caused Tiffany to take her last breath, the pair sat motionless.

Simone's jaw dropped wide open while Ginger bit at the sides of her acrylic fingernails. They couldn't believe the nerve Bunny had to pull such a bold feat, knowing there were so many people around. Then have the balls to have the dead girl's bracelet and earrings on the table, saying they were "souvenirs" of the great night she'd had butchering the female. The sheer determination that festered inside Bunny's soul to avenge Spoe's untimely death was to be admired by any gangster that hustled around the entire country. She seemed to be operating on a much different mental brain wave than they were. Bunny was focused. The one-track-mind vixen was set on taking those out she felt was responsible for Spoe's death from the land of the living. As they listened to her new plans to bring Dino to task next, the plot thickened and attitudes heightened.

"That piece of slimy gutter trash thought she was just gonna walk these city streets free and clear? Walk around here carefree like she ain't did jack shit to me and mines? I don't freaking think so. Not on my motherfucking watch. Trust that!" Bunny's rage could be felt with each word that flowed off her angrily poked lips. "She be setting niggas up and think the shit is all good." Bunny saw the expressions on Simone and Ginger's faces and still tried to justify her thought process. "I see how y'all looking at me. I mean, I know Spoe wasn't no damn saint, not by a long shot. I know he and Tariq was going around robbing dudes and getting paid, but they wasn't killing nobody like that nigga, Dino, did. Y'all know they was on some take-and-go type of shit; robbery—not murder."

"Bunny, you know I love you—me and Ginger both," Simone stated as Ginger nodded in total agreement. "But you do know the people Spoe and Tariq robbed probably had to pay someone back that money or get killed. They had bills to pay and financial obligations to their families whether they were drug dealers or not so—"

"That is true, Bunny," Ginger spoke up, also not trying to seem as if she was going against her blood or contradict her statements. "We love Spoe and his homeboy, Tariq, just like you, but—"

"Say *what* now?" Jumping up from the table, knocking over her chair, Bunny was starting to get irate. She could hardly contain herself from screaming at the top of her lungs. "*Seriously,* y'all? For real? That's fucked up. Y'all ain't got my back now?"

"Naw, Bunny, wait," Ginger protested, but sadly, it fell upon deaf ears.

"Naw, girl, *you* wait. Y'all sitting here at the table in the condo my baby paid for with that stolen money talking against him! That's foul as hell!"

"Bunny, whoa, whoa, whoa! Slow down, love. It ain't like that," Simone also tried relentlessly to defuse her sister's anger, but it wasn't working. "We are just saying that—"

"Naw, sis. That's real messed up. Now y'all starting to sound like that pole-swinging-for-dollars tramp, Tiffany . . . blaming Spoe for his own death."

"Bunny, please stop talking like that," Simone begged, not liking this side of her sister she was seeing. "You taking what we saying the wrong damn way. Calm down."

"What other way is it to take? I heard what y'all said!"

"Bunny, stop it! You bugging out for nothing!"

"Naw, y'all straight tripping; acting like he wanted to die or something. I thought y'all had my back. I can't believe y'all two funny-acting bitches right about now! Ain't this some real bullshit!"

Simone loved her sister dearly. She always did and always showed Bunny the utmost respect. The honest fact that she and Spoe lived off ill-gotten gain didn't bother Simone one bit. Although she tried her best to never need to borrow anything from her generous sister because of its origins, she never once judged. Even when she found out she needed the special medical procedures, she didn't want to turn to them. However, she did find a small bit of contempt for Bunny as of late. Even though they'd made a pact since small kids, Bunny was stretching the needle-drawn blood bond to the limits. Me-Ma was a strong supporter of their family charter; if one of the Banks was mad, they were all mad; if one fought, the other fought; and if one was hurt or in trouble, they all were. Bunny had them rob the bank to pay off her and Spoe's debt to Ghostman, which resulted in them having no choice but to eliminate their own mother, Deidra, and her sidekick, Lenny.

Now she wanted them to aid her in making sure this dread-head guy from New York received the same fate as their recently departed mother. "Look, Bunny, you going way too far with this. You need to slow down and think this plan through. We're already living on the edge of the shit we've done recently. It ain't been nothing but God that has stopped us all from being in handcuffs and facing life in prison. Why push our luck? You gotta think! Please!"

Bunny's verbal tirade aimed at her siblings continued. Unable and unwilling to endure any more of the unwarranted attack, Ginger also got in his emotions. Subscribing to the same thought process as Ginger, Simone headed toward the front door, signaling to Ginger she was ready to go. As Ginger reached for the car keys, Bunny ran over, blocking the way.

"Hey, now, I don't give a shit if y'all two weak punks wanna go against the grain. It's all the way good with me. I like rolling solo anyhow. But the other thing I need to know is when we splitting up the bread from the bank robbery? I got shit to do with my share—tonight."

Simone twirled around on her heels ready to put Bunny's hissy fit to rest. "Hey, what did we all agree upon? You wanna get us all knocked or something because you having one of your famous temper tantrums? That shit ain't right, sis, neither is this shit you trying to pull!"

Bunny stood back out of the way of the door. She was a few seconds away wanting to jump on both Simone and Ginger if she didn't get her way. With her arms now folded, daring them to leave without an answer to her question was definitely going to be a gateway to doing just that. "Temper tantrum? Is that what you think I'm doing by asking for my share of the money? Ain't that a fucking trip!"

"Look, you crazy-acting bitch," Ginger interrupted, anxious to go back to Me-Ma's and log onto his laptop. "You keep running around here tonight saying we being fake and we ain't keeping it a hundred with you. And we ain't keeping it real—"

"Yeah? Well, y'all ain't!"

"Wait, hold up, bitch. I ain't done with what I'm saying."

"Well, speed the hell up, then. I told y'all I got shit to handle tonight! I need mines!"

"Okay, girl. Now you trying to strong-arm and act a fool so you can get what you calling your share of the money. Is that right?"

Bunny sucked her teeth, knowing she needed some extra money to floss with later tonight if she hoped to pull off her plan to entrap Dino at his prebirthday party. "Yeah, so what? I need some of my share. What's the fucking big deal? I held my own just like y'all did that day. Now I want to get paid. What's due me!"

"The big fucking deal is I'm about to give you a double dose of reality in your keeping-it-real diet." Ginger's usually feminine-toned voice was three octaves deeper as she began to read Bunny. "You know good and damn well we had a plan. Now me and Simone got stuff we need to do too, but you don't see us breaking the plan or no bullshit like that. And if you wanna keep shit official, bitch, your greedy ass done spent your share when you paid Ghostman ass off. Or did you just conveniently *forget* about that huge chunk of money that went to you? Do you need me to jog your fucking memory?"

"What?" Bunny was dumbfounded. Momentarily silent, she then tried flipping the script like most people did when they are wrong and caught out there. "What are you talking about, Gene? That shit was my idea in the first place, so what? Y'all lucky I cut y'all a piece!"

Ginger immediately got more pissed at his sister and the situation in general. Here, Bunny was wrong as two left shoes and had the nerve to post up and call him by his government name, no less. "Oh, hell, naw! I know you ain't trying to diss me for keeping it real and not being fake like you said we was being. That's real fucked up, but it's all good in the hood, bitch. Do you! Matter of fact, Miss Keeping it Real, do you until the wheels fall off that motherfucker. But don't come crying to me when your ass get handed to you by that New York nigga that don't mind spilling blood, because I'ma prance my pretty ass to the other side of the room like I don't know you! For sure!"

Simone wanted to be peacemaker, however, she saw that might be a losing battle. Bunny had called them out, and that was that in Ginger's eyes. "Look, sis, how much of the money do you need? Maybe you can just spend a little bit."

"Naw, Simone, don't give in to this crybaby-acting bitch!"

"Fuck you, Ginger!"

"Naw, fuck you twice as hard, Bunny! You bugging! Simone, like I said, don't give this rat nothing. She already cashed her share out since she wanna be all technical and shit! Let's keep that shit one hundred!"

Simone stepped in between the two before they came to blows. "Come on, y'all, chill out. We supposed to be family, remember? Us against the world. Maybe we can take a little out of the stash right away."

Bunny reached her hand over placing it on the doorknob. After twisting it, she swung the door open hard, causing the brass decorative knob to knock a hole in the plastered wall. "Naw, you and this greedy whore Ginger can keep that bread. I'm tight on both y'all. Trust me, I'ma make a way to do what I gotsta do; you can believe that much. Unlike you two that sit around and wait for some random faggot nigga or your dead daddy's wife to issue me out money, I make my own!"

"Oh, so it's like that, huh?" Simone tried once more to make peace after Ginger was halfway down the driveway stepping to the car. She wanted to blurt out that she possibly had cancer and wanted to use some of the illegal funds for treatment but just decided to let it go and let Bunny bug out.

"It's just like that, Simone. I'm good. You can be gone like Ginger over there. I guess at the end of the day, all the family I truly had was Spoe and Me-Ma. And considering they both gone, I guess I'm solo out in this world. Now get the fuck on and watch a bitch work!"

Absolutely no words passed between Simone and Ginger on the ride from Bunny's condo. Both concentrating on different issues and concerns, being quiet was a welcome change from the boisterous tirade they'd just endured from their sister. After arriving back at Me-Ma's, Simone went straight up to her room to count and divide up the rest of the money they had left from the bank robbery. If Bunny was to come over and try acting a fool once more and breaking the agreement, Simone would be happy to just give her what she had coming and send her on her slap-happy way.

Ginger was already planning, plotting, and scheming from earlier in the afternoon. No sooner than the mailman had delivered several pieces of mail into the box, Ginger flipped through the various envelopes. Unexpectedly, he was met with one letter in particular that sent him damn near into a rage; a rage that could easily rival his wayward sister Bunny's contempt for seemingly the world. As if things were awkward enough between him and the good Pastor Street, now the fake man of the cloth had the real estate office sending a letter of an upcoming eviction notice and warning if they didn't vacate the property after receiving the notice, the church will be forced to get lawyers involved. From the moment Ginger had torn open the beige-colored document, he knew what had to be done.

Okay, so this down-low son of a bitch think shit gonna be all good. He think he can just send us some punk-ass letter and me and mine gonna fade off into the darkness. Yeah, right, bitch ass. Imagine that! Ginger turned on his laptop and waited for it to boot up. As he waited, he took off his tight-fitting tracksuit and decided to get comfortable. Rescuing his huge dick from being trapped backward between his legs, Ginger exhaled.

The cross-dressing male loved transforming himself each and every morning to the most beautiful female a person would want to see. The male-born diva felt he was being held hostage in the wrong body. In pursuit of being happy, Ginger, formally known as Gene, spent thousands upon thousands of dollars on medicines, vitamins, various treatments, and countless wardrobe items and cosmetics to make right what he knew God got wrong. Me-Ma had always told him that the good Lord didn't make mistakes and one day he was going to have to answer for the way he was behaving. However, Ginger let it be known to his grandmother and everyone else that chose to be all up in his personal business or had an unfavorable opinion, that God did indeed fuck up. And he would deal with the man upstairs when the time came. Standing nude in all his glory, Ginger decided to give his divine lover one more time to get the bullshit right. He picked up his cell and dialed Pastor Low-Down Dick-Loving Ass to give him his only chance to come correct.

"Yeah, hello." Ginger's call was answered in less than two rings to his surprise.

The pastor's tone was cold as he tried to keep it professional. "Yes, Ginger. How can I help you?"

"Okay, you brown-hole secret worshiper, what's the meaning of this crackpot-ass letter you had the real estate office send to our house?"

"You mean the church's house," he swiftly replied with an attitude having been interrupted from beating his meat.

Ginger had about enough. Cassius Street wanted to play hardball, then so be it. "Okay, then, fool, let me cut to the chase. Either you agree to sign back over my grandmother's house or you're going to be sorry. Your undercover ball-licking ass gonna have real problems! Remember . . . What goes on in the dark always comes to light."

"Look here, guy, I don't know what you think you have on me, but trust me when I tell you this. My people love me and believe everything I tell them. So you can claim anything you want happened, but I will just deny it."

"Oh, yeah, Pastor? Is that right? Got them folks wrapped around your short little finger, don't you?"

"Yes, it is that way, Ginger, Gene, or whoever you are going by today. If you and your family want to challenge the legal and binding will your grandmother left, then by all means, do so. I'm not stopping you."

"Oh, don't worry, we will be challenging that bullshit! And don't be disrespectful, you bitch-made nigga." This was the second time today Ginger had been called by his male-born government name and didn't like that or any of the threats being made. Not one bit.

"Okay, then, Ms. Ginger Banks. No problem," he patronized the man whose dick was resting in his mouth not too long ago and who he had just been fantasizing about. "And if there's nothing else I can do to assist you today, then I will see you and your sisters in court or set out on the curb—y'all choice! One."

Ending the heated conversation-turned-argument, Ginger replayed the pastor's smart-talking voice repeatedly in his head. *This guy got it coming real soon. I can't wait until tomorrow morning. I'ma hit everybody in that church with some real amen-type bullshit! By the time I finish with him, he won't be welcome to step through the front or back doors of any church in the United States, Japan, or Russia!*

Stepping into the shower, Ginger allowed the hot water to pound down on his curvaceous body. With the wetness of steam slowly beading up on the smooth walls, he let his head tilt backward. Lost in the warm moisture in the air, his mind drifted to several of the men he'd been blessed to be with. Strangely, Pastor Street kept popping up in his sexually charged fantasies. The more Ginger fought the twisted vision of the man who was causing him and his family so much grief, the harder his manhood became. Leaning over to the metal-framed carousel hanging on the shower wall, he retrieved the bottle of fragrance body wash. Squeezing more than two quarter-size amounts into his already wet palms, Ginger went to work. His right hand clenched, and his body trembled. Up and down; fast then slow; yanking and pulling. Moaning loudly, Ginger's heart raced with anticipation of a feeling. *Oh, yeah, right there. Suck my dick, Pastor Street. Suck this motherfucker until it spit up! Suck it! Suck it! Yeahhhh . . . Oh my*

God . . . yeah . . . Ginger handled his business until he released all his aggression along the side of the white faux marble wall. Out of breath, he fell back from under the steady flow of hot water. Staring at the thick clumpy stream of come slide down and disappear into the drain, he felt he'd enjoyed his fantasy but was ready to put in some real work that would fuck Pastor Cassius Street up in reality. It was time for the good pastor to come clean.

Drying off, Ginger slipped on a pair of shorts. Sitting down behind his laptop, he searched through a small shoe box of black cords. Finding the proper cord, he plugged his cell phone into the computer. Looking for the settings icon on the screen, he transferred his entire photo gallery. Then Ginger proceeded to do the same to the XXX-rated video that Bunny had texted to him. Scanning through the pictures and video, he smiled with satisfaction.

Blessed with the gift to navigate his way through any and all electronics, Ginger started slicing the video, adding music mixed with still frames of the various snapshots of him and Pastor Street. Making what some would soon call a tribute sanctioned by the devil himself, the smut mastermind reminisced as each view of asses in the air, tongues on dicks, and knees getting dirty passed his eyes. *Since that fool wanna play with me, I'm gonna teach him and that entire holier-than-thou judgmental flock of his who is really who tomorrow if I don't get my way. Me-Ma made a big mistake trusting that down-low punk and not her own family. Manipulation be real as a motherfucker in life, but so is revenge!*

Chapter 20

Bunny had taken her time getting dressed for the evening. It was her hope that the rest of her night would go better than the beginning of the day. Having had to argue with Simone and Ginger had given her a major headache and had her blood pressure on bump. She needed some of that money from the bank robbery to make sure she could floss down at the club like she needed to. She wanted to show up and show out. She wanted to make sure she was noticed. Not by just the rest of Dino's sure-to-be-on-deck henchmen, the Bloody Lions Posse, but the main man himself. Luckily, she had the diamond bracelet and earrings she taken from Tiffany to sell at the pawn shop. With more than a few hundred dollars to add with the funds she already was holding, Bunny was ready to play the role.

Carefully, she searched through what seemed like every single expensive clothing item she had hung in both walk-in closets. If this had been a regular night or a regular party at one of the elite Caucasian upscale clubs she liked to hang out at, the choice would be entirely different. However, this was not a regular night and most definitely not a regular party she was going to attend. This was, and would be, a night like none other. This night was like a date with destiny—or the devil—depending on which way one looked at it.

Club You Know was infamous with the younger crowd who liked to dance until the sun came up and get drunk off the watered-down drinks they gulped. Besides, the overpriced bottles of cheap bottom-shelf spirits and the 1980 décor, there was nothing else that stood out about that nightclub other than its known attraction of hood rats trying to come up. Bunny hated to even step foot in such a low-class establishment, but felt she had no other choice. If that's where Dino wanted to play at, then that's where the uppity Bunny needed to be as well. She had no problem swallowing her pride if it meant bringing the man who killed her beloved Spoe to his knees.

Checking herself out thoroughly in the full-length mirror, head to toe, Bunny decided to wear a pair of bright lime-color designer shorts and a cute low-cut Jimmy Choo fitted T-shirt that matched. Slipping on a pair of gladiator-wrapped coiled sandals with nine-inch metallic gold heels, she felt and looked like drug-dealer bait. With her small black crossover purse stuffed with plenty of cash, a tube of her favorite lipstick, her driver's license, and a small but sharp blade hidden in the lining, Bunny was almost ready to head out the door. Fighting the urge to at least call Simone and let her know she was going ahead with the plan even though she had to go solo, the dime-piece diva shook it off and left the condo.

Driving downtown, Bunny pulled up into one of the more expensive upscale hotels. Parking her fancy sports car in the hotel lot, she locked it up and headed toward the lobby. Once inside, she went over to the valet and boldly told him she needed a Metro Car to take her to her destination . . . Club You Know. Originally hesitant to flag for one of their frequently used cars because, first of all, Bunny wasn't a guest at the hotel, and second, the reputation of the hole-in-the-wall spot, the hardworking valet soon changed his mind when she slipped a crisp fifty-dollar bill for his trouble. Not wanting to be seen pulling up in her own vehicle with traceable plates, the car service was the perfect cover.

With phone in hand, a nervous but confident Bunny climbed in the rear leather seats of the full-sized sedan, her adrenalin rushed and her heart raced. Wanting to call Simone once more for an extra boost of encouragement, she opted not to. Before she could tuck her cell back into her purse, it rang. Not accustomed to answering anonymous phone numbers Bunny pushed reject sending the person straight to her voice mail. This was not the time to deal with prank callers, angry girlfriends, solicitors, heavy breathers, or folks who'd just misdialed. Bunny Banks had to stay focused on what she was about to do and who she was about to see. In less than twenty minutes' time, Spoe's Bonnie to his Clyde would be face-to-face with the dreadlocked monster that changed her future forever.

Detective Dugan had his notepad ready. With a pen in his hand he didn't want to mistake anything the person at the other end of the line might say. Whether their impending conversation was long or short, he felt it was best to be prepared. Praying that this could possibly be another person that could shed some light on the reason Tariq was killed and found washed up along the murky banks of the James River, he used his finger to find the recently dialed numbers. Tariq had spoken to Tiffany, and she was now dead and of no help to him and his team. The officer of the law now hoped this mysterious other person listed only as "B" would be able solve the huge mystery. Not knowing if the listed contact was male or female, the trained policeman took a sip of the strong black coffee he was nursing. Part of him wanted to just place the call from the deceased man's cell. Yet, he knew that would alert "B," who could be the murderer, that someone had Tariq's personal property, which was probably the law.

Writing down the number on the yellow legal pad, he pushed *67 before dialing from the phone on his desk. Anxiously he awaited a voice at the other end; feminine or masculine, it didn't matter to Detective Dugan long as he heard answers to his questions. Seconds later, he was met with disappointment receiving the voice mail with a standard provided greeting.

Well, I be damned; it figures. With my luck, five more bodies are liable to wash up on that damn river tonight with connections to these two damn bank robberies. Life ain't fair for a guy like me; it just ain't fair. Frustrated and exhausted, he finally decided to call it an early night. He hadn't got a good night's sleep in his own comfortable bed in what seemed like weeks. Tonight, Chase Dugan decided to say fuck the chief, the mayor, and the citizens that wanted criminals arrested and for them to pay for the multiple crimes taking place across the city. He was going home and didn't care who was against the idea.

I just wanna take a hot shower, kick my feet up on my own couch, and maybe call Simone to check up on her; see if she calmed down from this afternoon. Damn, I hated seeing her act like she did. If I could lock that no-good brother-in-law of hers up and throw away the key for hurting her, I freaking would in an instant! No questions asked.

Pouring the rest of his coffee out into the water fountain, he rinsed the mug and left it sitting on the far corner of his desk. Even though he'd left the police station and was finally en route home, the unsolved cases he was working consumed his thoughts. *Naw, naw, naw! Forget work and dealing with these soulless criminals that run the streets. Tonight is mine. I'm just gonna do what I said; take a good long, hot shower and call Simone.*

The Metro Car pulled up to the front of the club. The driver, not sure if this was indeed the location his seemingly upper-class passenger wanted to be at, glanced over his shoulder. After giving her the eye, he finally spoke, asking her if she wanted him to possibly wait until she got inside the building. He, just like she, noticed the long line of rowdy individuals posted to gain entry. Reassuring him that she'd be fine, Bunny gave him a generous tip and asked for his direct cell phone number, just in case. He happily obliged, then cautiously pulled off into traffic.

Standing directly in front of Club You Know, Bunny's expensive sandals somehow felt they were pressed against concrete that led to a surface they had no business being at. Receiving cold stares from most of the females daring her to jump in the front of the crowd and looks of hungry lust from the men, Bunny ignored them all. She knew by their crude behavior and last-chance-bargain-bin attire, they were certainly not in her league and didn't need to be acknowledged.

Not in the mood for or in the habit of taking part in the traditional waiting in line that some clubs had potential partygoers participate in, she took a deep breath, remembering the true reason why she was here. Opening her purse, Bunny took out a hundred-dollar bill. Folding it over twice, the seasoned veteran tipper made sure the one and two zeros were visible. Confidently, she approached one of the bouncers with money in hand. Wasting none of his time, Bunny quickly slipped the keeper of the peace the folded currency, making sure he saw the denomination. As he was personally ushering her inside the front doors of the jam-packed club, Bunny tapped him on the arm to see if he could further assist her in her plight. When he leaned over, she cupped her hand over his ear so he could hear over the loud reggae music that was blasting off the walls of Club You Know. Informing the six-foot-five muscle beast of a man she also wanted not just a regular booth, but an exclusive VIP booth that was advertised on the event flyer, he took her to one of the party promoters, then made his way back to his post.

"So you need one of our exclusive VIP booths, huh?" The promoter was more than happy to sell Bunny one of the two remaining booths he had available.

"Yes, of course. I need the best booth you have, please."

"No problem, sweetheart." He looked Bunny up and down, realizing she was by far the most gorgeous woman in the entire club. Not wanting to miss his opportunity to possibly get it on, he gave it a shot. "So, hey, beautiful, are you here for Dino tonight?"

Bunny played dumb just as she planned. "Dino? I'm sorry I don't believe I know who that is."

"Well, he's the one that's having the party here tonight; hence, all the reggae music, the smell of weed floating through the air, and jerk chicken on niggas' plates."

"Oh, I'm sorry. I didn't know. I'm not from around these parts. I'm just visiting, so, nope, I don't know this Dino. But if you'd be so kind to take me to my booth, I'd definitely appreciate it. I'm thirsty and want to get away from the heat that's radiating from these people dancing."

Although it was clear she didn't know Dino, the promoter knew just by her brief conversation the grey-eyed model chick was out of his range. Instead, he got her money for the booth and smiled doing so. With only seven of them in total, most partygoers either couldn't afford to be on the top tier of the club or were just content being elbow to elbow with the rest of the sweaty common folk. Whatever the case was, Bunny was escorted up the neon-lit staircase beyond the midpriced range booths, which were full of people popping bottles and enjoying a complimentary Jamaican-themed buffet. Used to all the finer things in life, Bunny immediately took notice that although these people partying in this section were far from being as broke as the fools on the lower level, they definitely weren't on boss status. They were more like junior under-bosses . . . which was not where she desired to be. Bunny always felt like and carried herself like a true boss, so dating another boss was her only option in life.

Feeling like a tropical fish out of water, Bunny was led to her final destination. Pausing as the velvet red rope was unhooked, she nodded at the two bouncers that stood guard on each side of the brass poles. Not more than four feet into the restricted for-true-bosses area, Bunny was met with disapproving side eyes from most of the half-naked-dressed female groupies that surrounded the tables. Smack-dab in the middle of the room was a supersized booth. Clearly, the booth with the most people hanging out, laughing, and having fun had to belong to the guest of honor. The closer Bunny got, she adjusted her eyes to be able to see through the thick cloud of weed smoke that was being blown into the air. Not trying to act as if she really cared who was who at the three-ring circus that was going on near the booth that was obviously going to be hers, she kept her head held high and her fronts up. Standing over to the side, the promoter asked her exactly who she wanted to put on her private list to gain entry to her booth. Announcing the attractive woman could have no more than seven people, including herself, he was shocked to find out she had no one to put on her list; she'd be occupying the huge space by her lonesome.

"Are you sure, sweetheart?" he asked, once more wishing he could join her private celebration. "Because if you need to add anyone at any time tonight to the list, please just let me know. I'm here for you."

Bunny looked over the promoter's shoulder into one of the many flashing lights-framed mirrors that were positioned everywhere. *Oh, hell, yeah, perfect! I can see the man of the hour right over there acting like he own the entire fucking club!* Smiling as she finally saw the crowd move from the main party booth and head toward the fresh food being delivered to the buffet table, Bunny told him she was definitely sure. "I'm sorry, but I'm solo tonight. Is that going to be a problem for me to have the booth?"

"Look, sweetie, you paying, you staying, solo or not," he lowered the clipboard he was going to write the names on and reassured Bunny that with him it's all business when need be, so she was in good hands.

"Okay, great. Then I guess we good then. So it's just gonna be me, myself, and I tonight. I'm having my own private cele-bration, so if you don't mind, I need to get my turn up started." Staring in the mirror at her dread-head target, Dino, making a toast with a bottle of 1738 in hand, she smirked, knowing very soon she was going to have the sweetest revenge ever known to mankind. Feeling herself, Bunny commanded the promoter to bring her the complimentary bottles of cham-pagne she had coming and one glass.

"No problem, sweetie. It's on its way." He excused himself and headed toward the velvet red rope, but not before being stopped by Dino who appeared to whisper something in his ear.

Settling back in her private booth, Bunny checked out the scenery, meaning the other females. It didn't take long for her to swiftly realize she was easily the pageant winner of the bunch. None of the half-dressed-in-cheap-outfitted groupies Dino had surrounding him could hold a candle to Bunny's beauty or body. *This bullshit gonna be a lot easier than I thought. This wannabe shottas fool, Dino, wish the fuck he could ever be on the same level as Spoe was. But that's okay, though. Let him turn up tonight, because his showboat days is definitely numbered.*

Chapter 21

Simone had taken her sweet time. She'd counted every single dollar of stolen bank money they had stashed. After doing so twice to make sure her calculations were 100 percent correct, she divided the cash up into four equal piles. Of course, she'd keep Tallhya's share for her since she was not able to deal with her own affairs. Placing Ginger's portion, and most importantly, Bunny's, in separate plastic bags, she would be ready Sunday morning to just call for another sibling get-together and put an end to all the bickering that had been taking place. Things between them were starting to spiral out of control, and that's the last thing they need if they didn't want to be caught up; division. The original plan to rob the bank where she worked stemmed from sheer necessity. Now, it was turning into an entirely different animal. The money had them all at each other's throats at one point or another since the moment it was in their possession. Simone was starting to feel as if the money was cursed after all the bad luck that'd happened; the house, Tallhya going crazy, their mother being gutted by her very own sister, and not to mention Bunny's newly found desire to get revenge on everyone involved with Spoe's death.

Knowing Ginger was holed up in his room on his computer, Simone knew from past embarrassing situations not to disturb him. Ginger was far from discreet when it came to his sex life, and walking in unannounced was definitely not the thing to do. She wanted to just toss his share on the bed and walk away, but felt maybe if he and Bunny could be back under the same roof sooner than later, they could all find peace as a family again. Going back to her own bedroom, Simone shut the door and started to focus in on her own problems . . . the fear of having to fight the death-seeking devil disguising himself in the form of cancer. *I hate this. Please, God, don't curse me with this. Please. I know I've done wrong in this world. I know I should've not did what I did to my mother, but, God, I swear I didn't know what else to do. I did it for the family to survive. If she told on us, then the family would be separated. Me-Ma wouldn't have wanted that for us. She wanted us to stay together as a unit and stand strong, no matter what. But now it seems like we're falling apart anyhow. God, please help me to be strong!* Lost in her own misery and terrified of possibly having to fight the good fight alone, the normally strong willed and strong-minded Simone started to break down. As she sobbed into her pillow, the distraught female fell asleep. In her dreams, all was good in the world, Me-Ma was still alive, and she and her two sisters and brother were still little kids seeking their mother's approval.

Me-Ma wiped her hands on her apron. She'd been in the kitchen since early morning, slaving away to prepare the perfect turkey-and-dressing meal and baking cakes and pies for dessert, along with her special homemade punch which had everyone feeling thankful to have been invited year after year. Thanksgiving was always a special time in the Banks's household. With plenty of aunts, uncles, cousins, and friends pouring in, the day was more like a huge family reunion other than a day picked to celebrate a handful of Pilgrims breaking bread with some Indians they decided to steal land from.

Moreover, for Tallhya, Simone, Bunny, and Gene, it was one of the few days of the year their wild, free-spirited mother was guaranteed to show her face. Running the streets with this dude and that, Deidra Banks was well known around town for linking up with drug dealers, pimps, and hustlers of all sorts. She was often nowhere her mother and kids could find her if need be. Locating the mother of four if one of the kids hurt themselves, had a parent-teacher meeting, or just plain needed their mother's love and attention was a damn near impossible feat. Deidra cared about one thing in life, possibly two: herself and getting money. However, on this day, Thanksgiving, the poor excuse for a mother and daughter would come around. She'd always put on the perfect-parent face and con all her long-distance living relatives into donating to this and that for the four bastard kids she never provided for in the first place. No sooner than each popped out, Deidra was back searching for the next criminally minded man to be her new potential baby daddy.

"Mommy, please spend the night here with us. Please! Please! Please!" Simone tried wrapping her arms around her mother's long slender leg, attempting to get her way.

Deidra was consumed with fixing her hair just right. She'd been stuck underneath her do-good family all day and was frustrated, to say the least. Used to living life as she saw fit, she'd had just about enough of the entire wholesome environment. It wasn't her scene at all, and it was starting to take a serious toll on her disposition. Annoyed with all the chatter her children were making, Deidra stood back in the mirror. Holding the hot curling iron in her right hand and a half-smoked cigarette in the left, she aggravatingly shook her daughter off of her leg. "Damn, Tallhya, get off my leg. You're gonna make me rip a hole in my freaking stocking!"

On the verge of tears, little Simone fell back onto her right side, correcting her angry mother. "I'm not Tallhya, Mommy. I'm Simone. Tallhya is over there."

Not caring who was who of her offspring, Deidra ignored her tearful child and went on about the business of getting herself together. There was a late-night party that was jumping off at the neighborhood lounge, and come hook or crook, she was going to be in the spot. The tragic fact that she hadn't seen her kids in over five weeks at this point meant absolutely nothing. She'd collected enough money from her family members to party for days on end without a second thought of the gigantic responsibility that Me-Ma had thankfully taken over. Deidra didn't give two rotten shits about that blessed fact. She was out for self and about the business of getting high, drunk, and fucked; all in no particular order.

"Okay, look, Simone, I already done told all of y'all that I wasn't staying in this place longer than I had to. Matter

of fact, y'all should be glad I even came in the first place. But hell, naw, y'all ain't happy for that much. Y'all all sitting over there in the corner, crying like some real little bitches! Especially your sissy-in-training-ass, Gene. You're the worst of them all. You gonna mess around and be straight pussy when you grow up!"

"Deidra! Shut your mouth talking like that to these babies," Me-Ma shouted, coming into the room, Bible clutched in hand. "And I've told you about cursing underneath my roof. I'm not going to tolerate that kind of talk around here or smoking in this house!"

"Whatever, lady, fuck what you talking about," Deidra mumbled, ignoring her mother like she always did. Rolling her eyes to the top of the ceiling, she kept right on curling her hair and smoking her Virginia Slim as if nothing was said. Suddenly she felt the harsh force of Me-Ma's hand slam the Bible across her face. As the cigarette flew out of her mouth, Deidra fell against the dresser.

Me-Ma was heated. She didn't care one bit that she still had guests downstairs. Her only child was out of pocket and needed to be corrected, so she did what had to be done. "Spare the rod, you spoil the child," she huffed, ready to give Deidra some more act right if need be. "I should've laid hands on your no-good self years ago and maybe you wouldn't have turned out to be such a horrible mother to these kids! It just don't make kind of godly sense!"

"Fuck God and you too, Momma," Deidra fired back, enraged from being struck.

Simone, Bunny, Tallhya, and Gene all huddled together in the corner, not knowing what was going to happen next between their mother and grandmother. With their tears flowing in the background, the two elder Banks went head-up, trading insult after insult, followed by blow after blow. Satisfied that she'd put enough of a spiritual, mental, and physical beating on Deidra, Me-Ma ordered her out of the house. As Deidra scrambled to gather her small duffle bag full of belongings, the devout Christian faith mother demanded she only return when she was ready to be a real mother to all four of her children. Hearing the thunderous sounds of the front door slam shut, Deidra Banks's children made the pact that nothing or no one could pull them apart from each other. Of course, Me-Ma agreed. Even when Simone went to go live with her father, she still kept her word; family first above anything else.

Simone was soon awakened by Ginger giggling and knocking at her closed door. Not bothering to wait for her to tell him to come in, he pushed the door wide open. Full of excitement, he jumped on the bed with his still half-asleep sister protesting the entire time. When Simone was finally quiet, Ginger explained he probably would need her help tomorrow at church for a very important presentation for the congregation to view.

"You, Ginger, of all people, going to church without a gun at the back of your head! I must still be asleep and dreaming." Simone wiped out the corners of her eyes.

Ginger had a huge smile plastered on his face as he snapped his painted acrylic fingernails in a circle. "Girl . . . I wouldn't miss Sunday service tomorrow down at the Faith and Hope Ministry under the esteemed leadership of Pastor Cassius Street if Madonna, Cher, and RuPaul begged me to! It's going to be better than any sermon he ever said, and I believe somebody may even catch the Holy Ghost!"

Chapter 22

Excitement filled the club. Taking in the tropical beats of reggae, Bunny bobbed her head to the music while avoiding eye contact with the rest of the people in the club. Thinking back to one of the many fabulous trips she and Spoe had taken, Jamaica in particular, Bunny almost started to have a good time posted at the spacious booth by herself. Nursing her third glass of champagne, she regained focus on the true reason she was slumming VIP style at Club You Know. *Okay, now let me get my shit back together and my mind right. Okay, Bunny, back to the plan.*

Assuming that her mark Dino had yet to notice her, Ms. Banks had to work fast to remedy that situation before he decided to leave and maybe take the party elsewhere. Sliding around the seat, Bunny seductively stretched her long legs outward. Taking another small sip from her tall flute of bubbly, she took a deep breath. It was now time for her to put her plan into full action. *All right, girl, let's get on his thirsty ass! He ain't ready!*

Standing up, she casually checked the mirrors from all angles to see who might be checking for her. Ignoring the cold stares of several females who, nine out of ten times, wished they were her, Bunny tugged down on her T-shirt, making her perfect-size breasts stand more at attention. Already knowing how her ass bounced when she walked in the shorts she had on, she was ready to make a splash. Licking her lips, she moved like a panther toward the long ice-sculpture-decorated table. Getting closer, she happily found the table was filled with every Jamaican delicacy a person could imagine. Removing one of the china plates from the stack, she was greeted by the hired servers dressed in traditional island colors. *Wow, this nigga done tried to do it big up in this low-class dump.*

All right then, I'll eat his little food, but only because a bitch hungry.

Bunny had them give her a small portion of just about everything they had to offer: jerk chicken, beef patties, banana fritters, fried plantain, sausage rolls, curry goat, oxtails, stewed pepper steak, and steamed fish, to name just a few. Without reservations or embarrassment, she reached for another plate but was strangely met with some other hand grabbing the same piece of china. "Oh, excuse me."

"No problem, baby doll. You take the plate. I'll grab another one."

There he was standing there, right in her face. Dino. He had come up to her just as Bunny had hoped. Maybe not while she was ready to feed her face with some of her and Spoe's favorites, but here he was. Now she had to put her plan into overdrive. "Oh, hello, there. Naw, you take it. I probably don't need a second plate anyway."

Dino looked her up and down with admiration and visible fiery lust. "Oh, no, baby girl, you perfect just the way you are. Thick in all the right places, but if you wanna get a li'l thicker in your boom boom, it would always be good with me."

Bunny wanted to be flattered, but this man that stood before her ogling her body was the same hideous piece of filth that had killed Spoe. *How dare he!* she thought to herself. She wanted to spit in his face, and then pull out the sharp blade she had concealed in her purse and stab him right in the heart. *I wish I could just kill this bastard right now. He ain't doing shit but taking up space on earth.* However, Bunny was no dummy. She knew if she really did something like that, his posse would be on her before Dino's body even hit the ground. Sure, he'd be dead, but so would she, or locked up in prison for life. Needless to say, she got ahold of herself and stayed on the path she'd planned. "Well, thank you, I guess. There's just so many great things here to choose from."

"So, baby doll, you like Jamaican cuisine, do you? Let me find out you an island girl at heart."

"Yeah, I do love most of the traditional dishes. And whoever's party this is picked out some of my all-time favorites. It all smells so damn good. I pray it taste as delicious as it looks." Bunny raised her voice to be heard over the earsplitting music.

"Oh, yeah." Dino was now doubly intrigued as he semiyelled as well. The mystery female he'd been checking out on the low since she'd arrived was not only beautiful, but loved all the homeland dishes he craved for constantly. "Well, I have it on good authority that he's a pretty all-right dude. Matter of fact, I heard these were his favorite dishes too. Maybe I can see if he can come and sit with you at your booth; maybe buy you a drink or two."

"My booth?" Bunny played innocent, letting Dino take the lead.

"Yes, girl, your booth. Should I make that happen or not? Maybe he can get his personal chef to share some of his recipes with you. Maybe come and cook for you personally."

Bunny was secretly elated. This night was going better than planned as she agreed to meet the deep-pocket sponsor who had made this entire Jamaican-themed party possible. Of course, she knew she was speaking to the man himself, but she had to play along. If Dino wanted to go through the cat-and-mouse game, then so be it. Bunny was down for anything that would get her closer to Spoe's murderer. With an extra sway in her hips, she turned and headed back to her booth. Less than five minutes later, Dino appeared at her booth with one of the waitresses carrying a bottle of imported European liquor and two glasses. He slid in next to Bunny, and she felt her skin crawl as his forearm touched hers.

"Oh, hey, you," she spoke with a fork in her hand. "I was just sitting back tasting this curry goat and vegetables. It's excellent."

Dino couldn't contain himself any longer. He had to let her know exactly who he was. His ego couldn't stand not letting the most desirable female in the spot know it was because of him that she was enjoying a meal fit for a Jamaican kingpin. "Well, I'm glad you like it. I had my chef prepare it."

"Did you say *your* chef?" She pretended to be surprised and giggled like a silly teenage girl impressed by a guy wearing a new pair of sneakers and driving his parents' car. "Wait a minute. You mean to tell me this whole thing is *you?*" *This stupid motherfucker is working on my damn last nerve; like he some sort of a real boss. I swear if this food wasn't so good I'd throw up in his face.*

"Yup, baby girl, this right here is all me. My name is Dino. This is my party, and yeah, my personal chef did all the cooking. You didn't know?"

Bunny went on with the petty charade she was playing. "I'm sorry, how rude of me. My name is Krissi. And no, I didn't know whose party it was. I'm not from this area at all. I had the driver bring me to a spot that he thought might be jumping. So I got myself a booth; well, the best they had to offer in this place, and here I am."

"Your driver? What do you mean, girl, your driver? And you paid all that money for a booth just for yourself?"

"I had the Metro Car service from the hotel downtown bring me here. And I don't care what the cost is for a good time and good service. It's priceless to make sure you have a good time," she casually remarked, knowing none of the crowd Dino was running with in the club or his Bloody Lions Posse would recognize her. Thank God even though Spoe might have run the streets to get leads on who to hit a lick on, Bunny stayed her uppity self out of the local limelight. Her face and name weren't household and Facebook-rumor ready.

"Hotel? Hey, now, girl. So where you from? Are you here on business or pleasure?"

Bunny acted as if she hadn't heard his question and started to sample more of the food on her plate. "Well, Dino, I must tell you that your choice of menu is off the chain. I haven't eaten food this tasty and authentic since I was last in Kingston."

Dino was now even more intrigued with the woman he believed to be from out of town. Running his fingers through his dreads, he leaned in closer. "Hold tight, baby doll, you've been to Kingston?"

Oh my God, why don't he stop it already? Bunny was sick and tired of him referring to her as baby doll, but she felt that must've been his thing so she went with it, although annoyed. "Of course, I've been to Kingston; several times, matter of fact. Montego Bay twice and Negril, but only once there."

Once again, Dino, the flamboyant shit-talking drug dealer, was almost speechless. In a club filled with hood rats, he'd been bless on the eve of his birthday to link up with a woman of substance and class; someone he thought was on his level. "Okay, then, baby doll, I see you. It seems like you get around."

"If you mean get around as in terms of traveling for business as well as some pleasure when I find time, then, yes, what you say is true. I do get around. Spain, Bangkok, China, Vietnam, South America, Mexico, Peru, and the Bahamas, not to mention your fair Jamaica. Yup, I definitely do." Bunny talked to him as if she was scolding some small child that had butchered the English language. *I don't know who in the fuck this ignorant porch monkey thinks he's talking to! He got me all the way messed up; like I'm one of them ghetto trash-pole-swinging whores like Tiffany he's used to dealing with. He's gonna respect my gangsta one way or another!*

It was very apparent the way he handled most of the women that he came across would not work on this one. She already was shutting him down without any effort, and he was dumbfounded. "Look, baby doll, I didn't mean any disrespect. A rude boy like me just trying to get to know you and all about you." He grabbed Bunny's hand and started rubbing the top side in a circular motion. "You think you can let that go down, baby doll?"

"Okay, then, Dino. Well, we can start by you addressing me as Krissi, my government name my parents blessed me with, okay? And not that baby doll pet name you probably call all these other women up in here that hang on your every word."

"Really?" Dino frowned with a weird smile.

"Yes, really. Do you think that's at all possible? I mean, excuse me, Dino, but I certainly hope you realize I'm not in the same category as these struggling groupies wanting a come up off their backs. I make my own money and lots of it when the opportunity is correct."

Dino was listening with a keen ear, not only the way Krissi spoke, but the roundabout way she was speaking of her travels abroad. He knew she wasn't just a chick from the hood he could treat like a piece of shit, then pass on to one of his posse members. Krissi appeared to possibly be the answer to his prayers; a new lead on a new connect or a female counterpart who was not terrified of being a drug mule. Either one, not excluding just being a fresh hot piece of pussy, he was down for the challenge. "You know what? I don't think that at all. I think you are the hottest female in here, and if you let me, I'm gonna make you mine!"

And here we go. This nigga done fell for the shit, hook, line, and sinker, just as planned. I swear I can't wait to watch this fool bleed out nice and slow for killing Spoe. Bunny sipped on the expensive liquor he'd ordered and grinned in Dino's face, making him believe that what he was saying was all good.

A few minutes of Bunny playing the role turned into a solid hour of Dino ignoring his other party guests. Posted at her private booth trying to plead his case and convince her he was indeed the man around town, Bunny had stomached just about enough. It was a hard task to even lay eyes on the dreadlocked beast who caused her world to turn upside down, but now she had to endure him trying to push up on her. When he started to describe how elaborate of a lifestyle he was living, she wanted to reach across the table and paw his ugly face with her manicured nails. Hearing Dino boast about his imported light fixtures, marble kitchen counter-tops, and solid gold-handle toilet he took a dump on every morning made Bunny tremble with rage, but she continued to play it off as having caught a sudden chill in the air. The icing on the cake was hearing him brag about the tree-lined wooded area that surrounded his estate. Having to contain herself from throwing up in his face again, Bunny slightly gagged knowing what Tiffany had claimed to be true only seconds before she sent her on her way . . . Spoe was chased into those woods . . . hunted down like a wild animal . . . then murdered in cold blood before being tossed into the river. All those heinous, unforgivable acts were committed at the hands of the infamous Dino who was sitting a few inches away.

It was all the normally cool, calm, and collected Bunny could do to stay in character and adhere to the treacherously intentioned game plan. Checking her watch, she informed him she had a prior engagement she couldn't be late for. Dino was visibly disappointed she was about to leave and voiced his regrets. Showing no shame, he begged her to stay a little while longer. Of course, she was not having that. From experience,

Bunny knew men, or people in general, always wanted what they couldn't have. She knew she needed to make sure she was unavailable to Dino on his terms and only on hers. Taking his number while refusing to give him hers, Bunny promised to call him the next day so that they could meet for a late dinner. As she left the VIP area, she looked over into one of the many mirrors seeing Dino still sitting in her booth looking like a lovesick animal in heat.

Oh, hell, yeah! Most definitely I got his ho ass for sure! He thinks he's that deal; I'ma show that nigga how a Banks sister really gets down!

Chapter 23

Sunday mornings were always a big deal in the Banks's household. Me-Ma would prepare a breakfast fit for a king. Everything from pancakes, bacon, ham, scrambled eggs and sausage, to biscuits, waffles, omelets, and oatmeal were liable to be on the menu. Some Sundays when she was really feeling good, she'd prepare all her breakfast treats and invite her church prayer warriors to partake before heading to a long day of two services.

Sadly, since Mildred Banks's death, her granddaughters chose to not carry on that traditional making of breakfast or church a part of their Sunday routine. However, this particular Sunday was different; at least for two out of the four of Me-Ma's grandkids. Ginger was up at the crack of dawn. Having not been able to sleep a wink, the anticipation of coming face-to-face with his Bible-toting fuck buddy was almost too much to bear. He'd taken his shower, brushed his teeth, and shaved his legs. Gorgeous dressed as a woman, Ginger was just as fine when he wore a suit and a tie and went by the name given to him at birth: Gene Jamar Banks. Only bringing Gene back out of the closet on special occasions, this was, no doubt, going to be one of those days.

After spit shining one of the only two pairs of men's shoes he owned, Ginger was beside himself with joy. Getting dressed, he looked in the floor-length mirror and nodded with confidence and satisfaction. By the time Simone had awaken and stumbled still half-asleep to the bathroom, Ginger was downstairs finishing his second bowl of cereal. "Hurry up, girl, and get ready. We need to be holding down the front pew."

"Slow down, fool! I thought your crazy ass wanted to make some sort of big flamboyant entrance," Simone yelled down from the top of the stairs. "I mean, that's what you said last night, or was I mistaken?"

Ginger pumped his brakes nagging Simone to speed up. He knew she would be ready to rock and roll when the time came at church, so that was all that mattered. Still hyped and geeked for the adventure of the day to get started, Ginger went to go stand on the front porch and get some fresh air. Deciding to smoke some weed before Sunday service, he reflected on how he hoped the morning would go and how he would be a hero in all three of his sisters' eyes for getting their family house back in their rightful hands.

The Faith and Hope Ministries choir was in rare form as the doors of the church opened. The choir welcomed in everyone with a spiritual hymn. *"Lord, keep me day by day in a pure and perfect way. I want to live; I want to live on in a building not made by hand. Lord, keep my body strong so that I can do no wrong. Lord, give me grace just to run this Christian race to a building not made by hand. I'm just a stranger here traveling through this barren land. Lord, I know there's a building somewhere, in a building not made by hand."*

Unlike most traditional message bearers of the Lord, Pastor Cassius Street was different. He was known around town for not only being flamboyant and over the top in his choice of expensive clothing he wore around town strutting like a proud peacock, but as a trendsetter in his preaching methods. He didn't wait for the congregation to come inside and get seated to get the Sunday services started; he had the choir greet them in song and celebration no sooner than they crossed the threshold.

"Good morning, little sister. Good morning, brother, and you too, Sister Mabel," Pastor Street happily greeted a family of his parishioners at the door, then another followed by many others. "It's a great day the Lord has blessed us with. The sun is shining bright, and we all awoke to see it! Praise God!" The more openhearted folk that came to worship, the more revenue the conniving preacher saw, not only in the church kitty but his pockets as well. Still somewhat disturbed by his awkward overnight conversation with Ginger—turned argument, then a battle of threats—Cassius searched the crowd of people rushing the door to praise the Lord. Thankfully, he didn't see Ginger, which was a true blessing. *Good. Maybe he and his sisters have decided to give it a rest and just let sleeping dogs lie. I wish they would just give up this silly notion of trying to get back what Mother Banks left to me and this church; well, me, anyways,* he sinisterly pondered.

Just like that, it was as if the devil himself showed up to rain on the parade of glory the preacher was caught up in. Simone Banks had just placed one foot on the stairs of the church and was heading upward. Linked arm in arm with a man wearing a suit and a tie, Pastor Street braced himself for what she possibly might say to him . . . especially if Ginger had divulged their late-night or wild-raw banging or sloppy no-holds-barred oral sex romp in the living room. Now, one of Me-Ma's granddaughters was only feet away, and he knew that could easily spell trouble. Pastor Street hoped Simone would be thinking clearly this morning and would be the normal voice of reason he'd known her to be when dealing with situations in the past.

"Good morning, Ms. Banks."

"Well, hello, there, Pastor Street. How are you this bright sunshiny morning?" Simone returned his pleasantries, still holding onto the arm of the slender-built man. "I trust all is well with you."

Stunned by Simone's nonconfrontational demeanor, the pastor was close to being speechless. Mustering up some words, he finally responded. "Umm . . . Yes, Ms. Banks, all is well this morning. I see you brought a guest to share in worship with us today."

"Whoever do you mean?" Simone looked around still clutching the man's arm.

"Yeah, who is the guest you're talking about, Pastor Street? I was born into this parish and baptized by Pastor Jasper years before you even took over this church." Ginger removed his sunglasses, then smirked. His recent secret fuck-buddy slightly stumbled backward at the sight. Luckily, there was one of the church deacons close by to catch the wide-eyed pastor's forearm.

Having his balance restored, Cassius fought hard to get the lump out of his throat that'd instantly formed, realizing Ginger was not dressed in his usual attire as a female. "Oh my God," he mumbled so that the other churchgoers would not hear him as they strolled by.

"I know, right? Oh my God," Ginger beamed with pride while fixing his multicolor print tie. Feeling smug, he then placed his shades back onto his makeup-removed face and shifted all his weight on one hip. "See, it really doesn't matter what a fly diva like me be rocking; a lace thong up my perfect ass crack or silk boxers so this caramel big-headed python I got dangling between my legs can breathe; I'm still that bitch fools love to hate!"

Simone giggled, watching the nervous Pastor Street start to sweat. "Wow, you better get out of this hot sun and get Sunday service started. I can't wait to hear what your sermon is about today. Me and my special guest, Mister Gene Banks, will be sitting front and center in the pew our grandmother paid for; the one with the Banks family brass plaque attached. I mean, that's not going to be a problem, is it, Pastor?"

Ginger stepped toward Cassius, then leaned inward. "Unless you trying to snatch that motherfucker from underneath us as well!"

With those statements from both Simone and Ginger, they rudely did not wait for a response from Me-Ma's favorite pastor before she collapsed, passing away. Cassius didn't say a word as Ginger let his shoulder deliberately bump into his. The duo then brushed by, marching through the front doors of the church, elated that they'd thrown Pastor Street off his square. Most of the folk in the building didn't recognize Ginger without his makeup and full head of expensive weave, but for the handful of parishioners that did, it automatically set their tongues wagging. Not caring that they were in the confines of the church sanctuary, they still gossiped and backbit.

By the time Simone and Ginger greeted everyone and took their rightful seats front and center, the entire church was either leaning over whispering in each other's ears or was confused about what the true meaning was of Ginger transforming back into Gene after all these years of attending service dressed however he saw fit . . . despite frowns and judgments. The boisterous tones of their supposed Christian voices floating through the packed pews were soon silenced as their always holier-than-thou head of the church walked up toward the pulpit. The choir finished singing the processional hymn and took their seats. Pastor Cassius Street cleared his throat and was ready to start Sunday services.

Chapter 24

Bunny woke up for the first time since Spoe's death feeling whole; like things were finally looking up. She knew her heart and emotions would always bear mental scars from the passing of the love of her life, but she could deal with that if she got satisfaction. Bunny was definitely not back at 100 percent, but she was pretty close to getting there.

Yesterday had been a true test of her patience and how dedicated she was to get what she wanted at the club, yet the beginning of the day wasn't very acceptable. Having a gigantic argument with Simone and Ginger about the stolen money and what they believed to be an unwarranted obsession with her hanging Dino out to dry had taken a serious toll on her mental well-being. As far back as Bunny could remember, she and her three siblings were thick as thieves. And even though they would have small squabbles or disagreements like most kids did with one another, they were raised by Me-Ma to never call the next person out of their name, go to bed mad, or let an outsider come in between them. Disrespectful to her deceased grandmother's memory, Bunny had broken the rules doing all three. Now as she lay in the bed with thoughts of killing Dino the next time she set eyes on him, or the very moment the opportunity presented itself, she knew she had to make things right with Simone and Ginger.

As bad as the brokenhearted diva just wanted to go underground again for a few days until things blew over with her sisters, the truth of the matter was she didn't have time, or the resources, to do so. Thanks to Spoe's greedy mother and good-for-nothing sister taking all the things of value in the condo when they found out he was dead, there was not much of a selection to choose from to maybe pawn or sell to get up on some much-needed cash. She'd already sold the bracelet and earrings she'd stolen off of Tiffany and used that cash for flossing the night before. And now she was down to her last couple of hundred-dollar bills. Bunny did want to make up with Simone and Ginger, that was true. But the fact that she needed for them to agree to come up with her share of the loot from the bank robbery was much more important.

Bunny needed that money, at least a small-size chunk of it, for later on that day and possibly the evening. She was going to call Dino and take him up on his offer for dinner and wanted to make sure she could stunt again, if need be. She'd already got the drug-dealer murderer intrigued and thinking she could maybe be a link to a new connect.

Born with a strange sixth sense, Bunny Banks was beyond excellent at reading people's true facial expressions and mannerisms. Always being told by Me-Ma that she behaved like she'd been here before and knew too much, she quickly realized all she had to do was take a little more time to talk to Dino and get in his head and he'd be practically begging her to be alone with him. Unfortunately for his thirst-trap-pussy-hound ass, it would be to his certain demise. What Spoe's loyal wifey had in store for the dreadlocked leader of the Bloody Lions Posse would be worse than any sexually trans-mitted death sentence disease he could catch from one of the hood rats he was used to banging raw on the regular; that gut-bucket-dead-pole-twirling-for-dollars Tiffany included.

Well, let me get this bullshit over with and call Simone. I need to let her and that damn crazy-ass Ginger know I ain't got time to be messing around. I need some of that damn money; at least a couple of racks. After Simone's cell rang several times, Bunny got the voice mail. Opting to not leave a message, she held the phone in her hand, planning to call back in five minutes. Before she could get a chance to hit redial, a small envelope appeared in the upper left-hand corner and a notification beep. Tapping the envelope-shaped icon, she read the text message sent from her sister.

At church. Ginger bout 2 clown. It's gonna be a show-stopper.

Those brief words were followed by several emojis that had Bunny both laughing and worried. *Oh, well, I'll catch up with*

*them at the house later. I know they can hold it down. I mean,
what kind of craziness can Ginger really do at church of all
places?*

It had been one of the most peaceful nights Chase Dugan
had spent since the crucial spike in crime had started a few
months ago. With what seemed like everyone and their
mother on his back, he was happy to just get some much-
needed rest and relaxation. He'd turned his cell on silent
and plugged it up on the far side of the room the moment
he arrived home. Chase didn't care how many times he saw
the bright light blink in the darkness. The exhausted officer
refused to get out of his bed. He just turned over and pulled
the blanket up over his head.

Feeling refreshed, he wanted to call Simone and invite her
to breakfast but decided to just drive over to her house to
surprise her. After getting dressed, he stopped by the local
Walmart and grabbed a small bouquet of flowers. With the
flowers resting on the passenger seat, he then swung by a
coffee shop and picked her up a large cup of gourmet brew,
hoping she liked his choice. Excited to see Simone, he turned
down her street hoping he was doing the right thing by just
dropping by unannounced. Parking in front of her house, he
noticed Simone's car was parked in the driveway. Smiling, he
got out of the car and headed up the walkway. As he stood
knocking on the door, a longtime neighbor peeked out from
behind her living room curtain. Giving the older woman a
smile and nod, she soon opened her front door asking who he
was looking for.

"Yes, hello, miss. Good morning. I'm here for Simone
Banks."

"Oh, Simone, okay then." She seemed relieved and finally
returned his greeting and smile. "I thought you might've been
lurking around here for Ginger. You know, one of *them*."

Detective Dugan didn't know exactly what the older woman
meant, but assumed whatever it was, it was no near next to
being nice. "Yes, I brought her some flowers and coffee."

"Well, I'm sorry to tell you, but they went to church not too
long ago. I would've went to, but my leg been bothering me."

The neighbor was getting more personal than he wanted to be. Cutting the obviously lonely woman's impromptu pity-party conversation short, the detective asked her the name of the church Simone attended just to make sure. He kinda remembered Walter, the wicked brother-in-law, throwing the name up when he and Simone were arguing. However, keeping the two estranged family members from actually coming to blows was more important at that time than focusing on the name of the church. After verifying the name and location, Chase was on his way with flowers and a now ice-cold coffee in tow. *It will be just wonderful to see her beautiful face before heading in to work. Hope she likes ice coffee.*

Chapter 25

Gazing out into the many faces of his congregation, Pastor Street greeted them once again as he'd done at the entrance. "Good morning, everyone. Praises be to all and welcome to the sacred house of the Lord. It's good to be here, alive and living life the way God intended for us to be." Terrified with each passing word, Pastor Street could not help from allowing his eyes to zoom in on Ginger. Trying his best to submerge his thoughts into the order of service, he kept seeing Ginger nod seemingly in agreement with every statement he was making.

As time ticked on, another song was sung by the choir, a special collection for the senior citizens was taken, and then Sister Katrina took center stage to give the revenue report, as well as the church announcements. In a tight-fitting and scantily clad attire, as always, she made sure to wink at Pastor Street, who was strangely sweating bullets in the cool, air-conditioned sanctuary. One by one, she read off items listed in the programs that were truly of no great importance to most of the bored parishioners. Just before she was about to yield the podium to the pastor to open the doors of the church for any new prospective members, Ginger stood from his seat. Standing in the front row, he smoothly turned to the rest of the congregation. With a taste for pure, uncut ignorance, he stated he had an announcement of praise and a testimony that he was burning to share. Pastor Street jumped to his feet in protest, telling Ginger that what he wanted to do was not listed in the program and highly irregular to do in the middle of the service.

"I'm sorry, Pastor Street, but if I don't say what I want to say, I might just burst. I mean, I'm so thankful for everything that you've done for me over the past few days." Ginger was acting all female as he placed his hand over the center of his chest, blushing. "I've never been so touched by a man at no time. I mean, you really have showed me that there are still good people left in this cruel world we live in."

Shaking in his shoes, Pastor Street wanted to run over and put a gag in Ginger's mouth to stop his chatter. "Please, Mr. Banks," he begged with his eyes locking with Ginger's. "Maybe we can speak about this at a much later date."

"No, Pastor. I would be less than a good Christian if I didn't share my good news with everyone here!"

Katrina, like everyone else, was anxious to know exactly what Pastor Street had done to change Ginger's life so drastically. Maybe one of his condemning-of-homosexual-behavior sermons was the reason longtime member Mildred Banks's cross-dressing grandson was now decked out in men's clothing. And if that was indeed the case, the majority of the parishioners were now wide awake, perched on the edge of the wooden mahogany-stained pews awaiting confirmation of that miracle.

"Let him speak," was one outcry from the crowd, followed by another.

"Yes, testify, Brother; speak your truth!"

Not to be outdone or not seen, Katrina finally spoke out, also asking for Ginger, who, even dressed as a woman, outshined her, to say whatever it was he had to say. "Please tell us what Pastor Street did to change your life for the good. We're all dying to know, Ginger. I'm sorry. I mean Gene," she sarcastically remarked while rolling her eyes to the top of her head.

"Okay, everyone. Well, you all know my grandmother, Mildred Banks. She was here serving the Lord in this very building before Pastor Jasper went on to glory and Pastor Street took over. She was a fixture in this church until God chose fit to call her home, right up there in the very spot our beloved pastor is standing in," Ginger pointed up toward the elevated stage.

"Please don't. Not now," he pleaded with Ginger, once more not knowing what Ginger was going to do or say next. The beads of sweat turned into a shower that couldn't stop dripping off his head. He was in utter desperation for someone to stop this madness. As wrong as it was, he was contemplating faking a heart attack to put a halt to Ginger's declaration.

Ginger grinned, taking great satisfaction in watching the otherwise smart-mouthed preacher squirm. Matter of fact, it was almost the same way he squirmed when Ginger had his tongue buried knee-deep into his Bible-toting ass. "No, no, Pastor Street. Everyone needs to know just how generous and fair-minded you can be. I mean, you blessed me and my sisters, and for that, we will be forever grateful. These fine people should know what you did and follow in your footsteps, to always conduct themselves in a godly manner as a good Christian should do."

Pastor Street's eyebrows rose. He was scared to ask what Ginger was talking about, so he motioned for some of the men from the deacon's board to calmly try to escort Ginger out the side door or into his office so that they could speak in private. "We will speak later, Mr. Banks. You have my word." Hoping the deacon board members could strong-arm him out without another word slipping from his evil mouth was a far cry from a miracle taking place.

"No no no. I need to get this out," Ginger protested. He pulled back from one of the deacon's loose grip. "My grandmother was confused in her last days. She was sick and didn't even know it. Well, during her brief but deadly illness, she signed over our family home to the Faith and Hope Ministry and Pastor Cassius Street. But last night, thank God, the good pastor graciously blessed the Banks family by agreeing to sign that property back to us free and clear. He's truly a vessel for the Lord, isn't he?"

Letting his greed take over his common sense, Pastor Street protested Ginger's claim, praying at the same time that his dirty little secret would not be exposed. "Well . . . That's not exactly true. I did offer to sell them back the property, but we haven't come to terms as of yet. Like I said before, Mr. Banks, we can discuss this later. All this gratitude is truly unnecessary."

Like watching a soap-opera plot slowly unfold, the attentive congregation needed popcorn along with a full glass of communion wine for what was going to come next out of Ginger's mouth. "Oh, I'm sorry, Pastor. I thought when I spent the night with you, the terms were discussed."

"Spent the night? What?" Katrina leaped to her feet, followed by several other women he'd slept with.

Simone hadn't muttered a single solitary word during the whole service. After texting Bunny back that Ginger was about to go ham, she kept her head down focused on her cell. Even when Ginger and Pastor Street started to go back and forth, she stayed with her fingers tapping away on the screen of the phone.

Ginger sucked his teeth and rolled his neck in flaming true diva style. Snapping his fingers, he went on to give his tainted testimony. "Yes, child. Me and him spent the night in his office doing the do." He laughed at Katrina and all the other women seemingly outraged about the announcement. "And y'all already know and can tell from the way he prances around this stage, this brother can put on one hellava show when he wants to. The sex was definitely *all* of that! *Believe me!*"

"Cassius! Say it's not true! Say something!" Katrina shouted, wanting to know if what this cross-dressing freak was saying was indeed true or not.

As the rest of the people shook their heads in stunned disbelief and were totally speechless, some of the preacher's loyal followers tried to put a muzzle on the accusations Ginger was making. Physically having to be restrained from the small but fiery protective group of prayer warriors, Ginger stood by his statements spewing even more words of his brutal truth. "I'm sorry if you all think this dude is anything more than a sheisty con man running game on all you silly-ass women. He's been playing all of you for fools. And all you men who think your wives are safe and he's just giving them a little bit of one-on-one Bible Study sessions when you're at work slaving away to make ends meet—think again. You dummies out punching the clock, and he punching your wives' cat with his manhood."

Pastor Street's pride was damaged, but he still managed to try to stand tall and deny Ginger's awful claims of his vile sins and him breaking every one of the Ten Commandments. "You are nothing more than an abomination against mankind and Almighty God. You think you can come into this sacred sanctuary and defile my name? You are nothing more than a liar and a bearer of false witness. You already have signed a pact with the underworld and sold yourself to the devil! You are nothing more than a freak of nature; an extremely confused, worthless human being. Walking around town, and worse than that, coming through the doors of this church violating his Holy Word!" Pastor Street was sweating up a storm. Putting on a performance of a lifetime, he condemned Ginger, Simone, Bunny, Tallhya, and even the church's beloved lifetime supporter, deceased Mother Mildred Banks, for condoning Ginger/Gene's wicked ways and disgusting lifestyle. "People like you should be thrown in an open dirt pit and burned alive! Amen! Get this abomination out of our church!"

Ginger's skin was extra thick. He'd learned a long time ago to let other people's opinions of him and his lifestyle choice roll off his back. Labeled "different" since birth, Ginger had been picked on as a small child growing up on the block. And maliciously ridiculed by his own mother for behaving too girlie. Called a sissy in grammar school and a fag in junior high, by the time the bullied youth reached puberty and had become a teenager, wearing lip gloss and his sisters' panties were second nature to him. Going against the grain, Gene officially became Ginger at his senior prom when he showed up proudly decked out in an above-the-knee powder-blue lace-and-satin skintight dress with a long chiffon train. Arm in arm with his date, Charles, he had no shame then or now. He felt whoever had a problem with him just had a problem. He wasn't going to change who he was for anyone . . . even for the sake of God.

"Look, Cassius," Ginger said his name like he meant it, "like I told you the other morning when we woke up, don't let this butter-smooth skin and pretty face fool you. I will wear your self-hating ass out! I told you about coming for me."

Pastor Street was not giving up without a fight. He'd built too much of a money-getting venture up to just walk away with his tail tucked between his legs. "Okay, Ginger or Gene or whatever you want to call yourself. You need to stop all these false, slanderous things you're saying before I decide to lose my religion and press charges. You are nothing but the devil right out in the open!"

Ginger had just about enough of being accused of being a liar and the devil, being a fag and an abomination from a first-class hypocrite. It was time for this so-called man of God that specialized in bringing judgment against others to be judged. "Nigga that hides behind the damn Bible and God's so-called Word, you up there talking that yang yang shit about me—like you better than me!" Ginger's voice got louder as all the congregation looked on in shock at what was taking place at their normally uneventful Sunday service. "Well, guess what, you fraudulent asshole? You *ain't* better than me! The truth of the matter is, you *is* me! So hello, my devil brother!"

Ginger had gotten his way and for once he was the hero of the Banks and not just the family freak.

With that being said, complete and total pandemonium ensued throughout the church dwelling. Simone had started sending group text messages to each and every person's phone number listed in the church directory. Thanks to Me-Ma also having the numbers of all the highly revered prayer warriors as well, the entire church was on their feet. Young and old, they couldn't believe what they were watching. It was like some sort of bad dream. Pushing PLAY repeatedly, the women of the church Pastor Street had sexed held their cell phones, worried what disease this biblical monster could've subjected them to, while the men were ready to throw the twisted-thought preacher out on his head. There was nothing the preacher could say or do.

The pornographic smut had been sent to the good pastor's cell as well. Not only were there clips of him and Ginger partaking in oral sex in Me-Ma's living room, but selfies of them hugged up in the church office while he was asleep and audio of his voice saying basically that he takes advantage of women's kindness when need be. The loyal members of the Faith and Hope Ministry were enraged. This was the type of scandal that could bring the church down to its very foundation and have its doors chained, locked, and bolted for good.

Pastor Street didn't know what to say. Here he was standing in front of everyone with all his dirty laundry aired out for all to see. He'd been exposed for the greedy predatory creep he was. Destined to be shunned, he lowered his head, disappearing into his private office before he was literally killed. Shame and embarrassment held him locked in his office until the board of trustees came banging on the door. He paced the floor, trying to come up with a plan to turn everything around. *Everything was photoshopped . . . That wasn't me. I can deny the women of the church I slept with. They wouldn't want their husbands to think they've done wrong.*

"Pastor Street, you must open this door immediately. There are matters we must discuss at once."

With his hands shaking, the pastor unlocked the door. Before he could spin his lies, he was halted by one of the board members.

"Pastor Street, this is outrageous! I thought you were a man of God! That video has been seen by the entire congregation. What do you think our church affiliates will think?"

"That video was the true devil in disguise. That is not me! The devil must've pasted my face to make it look like me. You can't believe that abomination is showing you the real truth." He hoped for a listening ear that could help his fight.

"I can't believe this!" another board member shouted.

"Brothers, you can't truly think I would be shaming the house of God and disrespecting the Word of God in this most outrageous way. Brothers, Sisters, you can't believe this. I'm not that person in those pictures or that video."

"I'm sorry, Pastor, but this kind of scandal can close the church's doors. We must do what's necessary. Please clear your office of your personal items and vacate the premises immediately."

"But . . . But you're not even giving me a chance to speak my truth. I am a man of God and will never bow down to this type of malicious accusations without the right to disclose my truth. This is shameful. What you all are doing to me is unlawful against the church! I can't—and won't—stand for this!"

"Okay, then, let's take a proper vote." The head board member looked around and proceeded. "All those in favor of Pastor Cassius Street to be formally stripped of his robes and connection to Faith and Hope Ministry permanently, please raise your hands."

Former Pastor Cassius Street looked around the room seeing a unanimous vote for his immediate removal, then bowed his head in shame. Forced by the board of trustees and the prayer warriors to immediately sign over the deed to the late Mildred Banks's home and all other dealings attached to her estate, Cassius Street was ultimately disgraced and immediately discredited by the church and all their affiliates from surrounding churches in the area.

"Brothers and Sisters, I believe we have a lot of work ahead of us, and in light of today's events, I think it's best we go home, collect our thoughts, and pray on our impending dilemma. We should meet back here at seven tonight to discuss the future of our beloved church."

All heads nodded yes and quickly dispersed to calm themselves after the storm swooped in earlier, leaving the entire congregation in an uproar. When the board members left the church, they were bombarded with questions by the awaiting members of the church.

"Brothers and Sisters, please, please . . ."

"I want all my donations back! This ain't no church. It's the pit of hell with all this going on," a member shouted.

"Now I understand everyone's concern, and we will address it, but we can say the former Pastor Street is no longer a part of this church or will be of any other after I get through talking to everyone. Now, it's been a trying morning, and well, to tell you the truth, I think we all need to go home and process what has taken place."

There was disappointment heard throughout the crowd gathered, but there was nothing more to be done to correct the damage already displayed.

Although his elusive career was no more, there was more trouble brewing for the former renowned-now-defrocked-and-disgraced pastor. As he snuck his way out of the back of the church and quickly jumped into his car, his phone blared off with text alerts, calls, and even e-mail notifications. He tossed it onto the passenger's seat and pulled off toward his home. The only thought on his mind was how he could recover from this cruel and malicious incident that cost him everything. Tears began to flow, combined with shouts of anger. "You are so stupid! Why didn't you just give them the stupid worthless house? You could have gotten way more in the long run!" He banged on the steering wheel, mad at himself about his greedy actions.

He pulled into his driveway and noticed a familiar car already parked. Cassius's first reaction was to make a U-turn and get the hell outta Dodge as fast as fucking possible. But when he saw the woman strutting toward his car, he knew he would have to eventually face her, and many others that were indulging in his "special" Bible lessons. This was just the first of many.

"Cassius Street, get out of that fucking car now!" Katrina waved her hands as if she was directing a child.

With much hesitation, he slowly parked beside her car, turned the ignition off, and stepped out of the vehicle.

"What in the fuck is you doing? Did you fuck that freak?"

Still in the driveway, Cassius decided on taking this indoors. He sure as hell didn't want the neighbors in his business, and by the tone of Katrina's voice, they soon would come out to see the show. "Let's go inside before you embarrass yourself." He touched her arm to guide her toward the door.

"Fuck you! I ain't going nowhere with your lying ass, you fucking faggot!"

"Please, this is ridiculous that you are even acting this way. Let's go inside, please, Katrina. I can explain everything."

"No, because I have already warned the board that you swindled me out of my retirement money, and they have agreed to pay for all the lawyer fees to press charges on you."

"Oh, is that so!"

"Yes, and by the way, I am pregnant, you stupid piece of shit!"

"What makes you think it's mine? If you fucked me behind your husband's back, who's to say you ain't spreading your legs for another? Now you can leave, or I can call the cops to remove you from my property."

"You piece of fucking shit! As much as I dislike the Banks, I'm going to send them some flowers for the shit show they put on today for outing you."

Cassius watched Katrina stomp to her car still enraged, but he could care less. It came with the territory. Some just play the game better than others. He unlocked his front door and walked inside, struggling with thoughts of what his next move should be. *It's time to blow this joint!*

Chapter 26

Simone and Ginger left through the church doors the same way they had entered . . . arm in arm with smiles on their faces. They felt they were victorious, and it showed in their steps as Ginger held the deed to their grandmother's house in hand. Still hearing the loud panicked voices of folks trying to figure out what had just jumped off and the possible ramifications, the pair was smug. Knowing that their long lineage of family loyalty to that church had come to an abrupt end as of today meant absolutely nothing. Truth be told, when they'd put Me-Ma in the grave burying her, their allure to the church was buried as well. Three feet away from the church stairs Simone was stopped dead in her tracks. She couldn't believe her eyes. She was surprised, to say the least. Chase Dugan, of all people, was leaning against his car. Not knowing what he could've wanted, Simone hesitantly made her way over to his car as Ginger went to his own.

"Well, hello?" she suspiciously spoke with question.

"Hello, yourself, Simone." He raised his eyebrow and smiled.

Relieved he wasn't there to arrest her and Ginger for multiple crimes they'd committed, including murdering their mother, Simone loosened up some and returned his smile. "What are you doing here? Matter of fact, how did you even know I was here? Are you using your police tactics to follow me now?"

"Umm, no, not at all. Your nosy neighbor next door told me," he laughed. "We need her on the damn police force. She sees everything and will let you know, even if you didn't want to know!"

Simone agreed, having grown up next door to her grandmother's porch gossip buddy. "Well, wow, Chase, I am glad to see you. We kinda got out of church earlier than everyone else."

Chase could not contain himself any longer. He had to let her know he'd slipped in church at the end of the first collection for the senior citizens, right before the girl with her boobs hanging out started to read the announcements. "Yeah, Simone, about that . . . I ain't gonna lie. I normally don't go to church; I don't really have the time. But after today, and how your brother blew the spot up . . . It was priceless. I swear on my badge I've never seen or heard anything like it. It was like watching some bad movie that comes on late at night."

Simone's facial expression was that of being confused. She was embarrassed that a guy that she was dating and actually liked saw and heard her family secrets get revealed live and in person. It was bad enough the family was going to probably be shunned from even speaking to most folks Pastor Streets's charities helped, but now she had to contend with this. "Look, Chase, I don't know what to tell you. That slimeball preacher stole, well, manipulated, my grandmother's house away from her shortly before she died. We just wanted it back, that's all."

"Yeah, I see. You and your family play hardball just like your brother-in-law said. Remind me not to get on your bad side!"

The mere mention of Tallhya's husband's name pissed Simone off, making her blood boil. "Yuk, please don't say his name. You know we can't stand him."

Chase agreed not to hint at Walter's name again as he reached in the rear seat of his vehicle, handing Simone the flowers he purchased. "I had some coffee too, but of course, it's no good unless you like cold coffee."

Deciding to ride with Detective Dugan back to Me-Ma's, Simone called Ginger telling him she was good on the ride tip, and she'd see him at home. At that point, he informed her he was going to hang out with a few of his friends in the LGBT community and celebrate his victory over the fake down-low, hate-spewing Pastor Street.

Pulling up in front of the house, Chase quickly observed an expensive sports car parked in the driveway behind Simone's Neon that wasn't there earlier. "Wow, that's a really nice whip. I know that hit someone's pockets hard."

Not wanting him to get the wrong impression and think she and her siblings had money or access to it, Simone played it off. "Oh, that's my sister's boyfriend's car. He's some white guy that plays basketball overseas that's so in love with her, it's crazy. He let her drive his car until the lease runs out next month. So . . ." Having explained her way outta Bunny's dead boyfriend that robbed the stickup man and sponsored the car, Simone was good.

Going inside, Simone offered Chase something to drink and told him to take a seat in the living room. Walking upstairs she found Bunny in Ginger's bedroom plugging in the flat irons. She knew Bunny had been through the wringer and was still suffering from the loss of Spoe, but prayed shit between them could be repaired without further disagreements or fights. "Hey, sis, are you okay? Are *we* okay?"

Bunny knew Simone was making reference to the big disagreement that had taken place over at her condo the night before. Knowing she was wrong as two left feet and had blown the entire thing out of proportion instead of just taking the time out to explain her dire need for a small bit of the ill-gotten gain, Bunny wasted no time taking a cop to her bullshit. "Of course, we are. I mean, we family; sisters. What else can we be but good? That's why I'm in here using this crazy ho's flat irons. She got the best hair-grooming shit in the city, not to mention clothes I may need to borrow if I wanna go hang out in some club with hood rats! Shiddd, a bitch never know which way the wind gonna blow."

Simone was relieved the matter was finally over. She did inform Bunny she'd counted and split the cash up, and her share was wrapped in a bag in the back of the closet in her old bedroom. From this point on, it'd be on each individual to govern their own selves when it came to spending the money. Bunny was overjoyed because this way, she didn't have to further involve her siblings with her plans of Dino's demise.

"Well, Chase, is downstairs if you wanna say hello. He met me at church and brought me some flowers," Simone mentioned, throwing her hand up.

Bunny laughed as she spoke under her breath, "Come on now, dummy. Get your motherfucking life! Why in the hell do I wanna see, say hello, or even give two hot-fire shits about some slow-minded cop that's trying to lock our pretty asses up? If you wanna sleep, bang, or lay up with the enemy, then that's on you. So, girl, bye, miss me on all that! Now, beat it. I need to finish my hair. I got somewhere to be tonight."

Simone could only shake her head and laugh as well. "Okay, then, cool, but when he leave, I gotta put you up on what Ginger did today. Bottom line, Me-Ma's house is back to being ours, point-blank." With that being said, Simone returned downstairs to discover her detective boyfriend looking at the many family pictures her grandmother had showcased on the mantle, sitting on the end tables, framed and hanging on the walls. It was like a small-size shrine to Deidra, Tallhya, Bunny, Ginger, even when he was Gene, and, of course, Simone. "Sorry about that. My sister is upstairs acting silly as normal."

Holding his cell in his hand, Chase informed Simone although he'd love to sit and visit with her, he'd received an urgent call from the chief asking him to come into the office. "Maybe we can eat a late dinner if you're not too busy this evening. How does that sound?"

Cheesing from ear to ear, she quickly agreed. "Yes, it definitely sounds like a plan to me. I'll be home all day, so just call me when you get ready." After walking Chase to his car, Simone returned inside the house and found Bunny looking out the window as the officer of the law drove off. "What you got to say?"

"Nothing to your sprung ass," Bunny teased her sister. "So just tell me what that nut case Ginger did at church before I leave. Knowing him, I know it was straight over the top."

Chapter 27

It was nearing five in the evening and Detective Chase Dugan was back in the office attempting still to bring some closure to a few of his more higher-profile cases. Adhering to the wishes of the chief, he'd been working relentlessly since the very second he'd walked in. Finding out one of the news channels in town was going to do a special segment on the spike in criminal activity in the summer months, the officer's superiors wanted him to be able to give them a little bit more information than what they originally had when the day the crimes were discovered. It was told to him that the murder of Tiffany Ross, along with the more recent floating corpses discovered, would be showcased. That being said, Chase Dugan had to deliver some good news or risk a possible reassignment—fingerprint detail.

Racking his brain for anything that could save his ass, he reached in his desk drawer retrieving Tariq's cell phone. Powering it back on, the detective was once again on the deceased young man's Facebook profile looking at the many RIP posts on his page. Scrolling through them and not seeing anything out of the ordinary, he went back to his photos. Halfway through the second album, he stopped. *Wait one damn minute. Why does this picture look so familiar to me? Am I tripping out because I'm so tired or what? It couldn't be . . . or could it?* Struggling with the same photo he thought might have been someone he'd met before, Chase zoomed in on the face. *Shit! Naw. I must be bugging!* He saved the picture to the device, then cropped out the female standing in the middle with just the initials "B" listed as her name. *Son of a bitch! All this time I've been running in circles chasing my tail like some deranged dog in heat, and here this girl was only a phone call away for real.* Recognizing Simone's sister, Bunny, who was in most of the pictures at their grandmother's house earlier as the same girl Tariq apparently had known was almost mind-blowing. *Okay then, B as in Bunny; Bunny Banks. Now if I can figure out exactly why my victim was calling her before his murder, I'll be one step closer to finding out the who's, what's, and why's to this case.*

Taking his time, he went through picture after picture in album after album, saving any and all photos that had the woman of his dream that he was dating, Simone's sister, in them. *Now what does Bunny Banks have to do with this dude, Tariq, and who is the other guy in the picture she hugged up with? I thought Simone told me her boyfriend was some white guy that plays ball overseas somewhere; that's whose expensive sports car that was in the damn driveway. And what in the hell does Simone's sister have to do with the dead dancer and Ghostman, a drug-dealer kingpin that robbed the bank? Some shit ain't right, and I'm about to find out the real deal on all this twisted mess. This might be the very break I been looking for!*

Bunny called Dino and, as she already expected, he was ready to drop everything he had planned prior to link up with her. She'd fucked his mind so royally the night before, he was practically begging to not only spend time with her, but some money on her as well. Of course, the Jamaican-born idiot was behaving like any other man that had come in contact with a beautiful, classy, refined woman . . . He wanted the pussy. However, he also felt she was a direct plug to the main plug.

Dino had money to burn, and he made sure everyone in town knew it. Yet, the girl, Krissi, was much different than the other trout-mouthed bitches he usually rocked with. She acted like she had so much game, he had to elevate his own to even come close to match hers. She'd traveled all over the world. She'd seen places and eaten cuisine and had experiences that Dino knew was beyond his reach; money or not. The midlevel drug dealer knew some things were out of his reach and jurisdiction, no matter how hood rich you were. Certain people only did business with certain people. He prayed Krissi was one of those people that could introduce him to that underworld and back him on his credibility and gangster, if need be. He was prepared to definitely make it worth her while.

"So you're going to meet me at the hotel for sure, Dino? I have limited time left in town and don't have time to be held up."

"Listen, baby doll, I'm sorry. I mean Krissi. I'd never waste your time. Like I told you last night, I'm really digging you. I wanna just spend some time with you outside that noise box we were in." Dino was not used to bowing down to any female's demands, but she was not just any female, so he took a cop. "Hey, now, I know that spot last night was not top-notch, what you used to and all, but trust, I gotcha next time you're in town."

Bunny held the hotel house phone to her ear and grinned. "Okay, Dino. I believe in you, and I wanna see you as well, away from that environment. So here's the plan. Go to the hotel and grab a suite for us to chill in. I'll call you at about seven on your cell from the lobby, and you can tell me the room number. Is that cool with you?"

Dino was ecstatic. He was going to not only spend time with his opportunity in high heels; he was going to get some of that perfectly shaped ass as well. "Don't worry. I'll be on time and waiting. Is champagne good for you?"

Bunny dug underneath her fingernails scheming as she ended their conversation leaving him to wonder, "Why don't you surprise me? I'll call you at seven." Having already checked into the same hotel she'd used the Metro Car service at the evening before, she kicked up her feet and relaxed, staring out the huge picture window at the downtown sky-lights. In less than two hours, she'd be back in the face of Spoe's killer, and if all went well, Dino wouldn't make it to see daybreak. At least that was the plan.

Police headquarters had been invaded by the news crew cameras ready to shoot footage of the areas in the building that were equip to run different tests on crime-scene evidence. The Forensics Department had received a huge federal grant, and now it was time for them to show and tell. As the reporters filmed one aspect of the crime-fighting efforts segment, Detective Chase Dugan got groomed and prepped for his interview by the chief and the mayor as well. He was told what to say and what not to say. Although he was trained for years on how to deal with nosy reporters, they felt the need to reschool him on the art of avoiding certain questions and making the police force, in general, come off smelling like roses.

After the reporters were finally done grilling him, Chase ducked into the bathroom to wash off the small amounts of commercial powder and makeup their makeup people forced him to wear so as not to appear too shiny faced on the camera. Splashing a few handfuls of cold water on his face, he allowed it to drip down back into the sink. Grabbing a few brown, rough-textured paper towels out of the wall-mounted dispensary, he stared into the mirror. As he double-checked, making sure no signs of the added beauty products were still visible, the wheels in his mind started turning again.

Sitting behind his desk, he used a pencil with an eraser and drew himself a graph. Drawing line after line, he detailed possible ways all the people and potential leads he'd come up with were linked. Still haunted by possible connections Simone's sister, Bunny, had to all of this, he decided to cut straight to the chase and ask Simone. They were supposed to meet for dinner later on, so it would be the perfect opportunity for him to make the needed inquiries without seeming as if he was suspicious of Bunny.

Chapter 28

It was nearing seven o'clock, and Bunny was more than ready to start her date with destiny. Running hot water in the sink, she took one of the winter-white fluffy washcloths and submerged it in the water. After lathering up the soap, she washed her kitty cat, making sure it was fresh and clean. Moving the rag in small circular motions, she imagined it was Spoe's hand touching her the way he used to before his death. A few minutes into her mind being taken over by her fantasy, she was snatched out of the sexually charged trance by her cell ringing. She'd set the alarm to ring at exactly six fifty-five. *Okay, let me get dressed and make this call to this stupid-ass fool.*

Throwing on something supersexy and expensive she'd packed in her overnight bag, Bunny stood in the mirror jocking herself. *Oh, yeah, it's going down tonight. That nigga Dino about to pay for it, Spoe. Don't worry, my baby, I got you!*

Walking over to the desk, she lifted the phone's receiver and pushed the number nine to get an outside line. Dialing Dino's cell phone, the eager, soon-to-be victim answered Bunny's call on the first ring. "Hello, Dino."

His voice sounded like that of a kid about to go on a shopping spree at a toy store. "Hey, now, Krissi. How are you? Did you have a good day? We still on for this evening or what?"

Bunny smiled that she had him going, but at the same time, was slightly annoyed that he came off as so desperate. "Wow, yeah. Slow down with the bombardment of all those questions. One thing you'll learn about me is that if I say I'm going to do something, then you can consider it as good as done."

"Oh, yeah." Dino felt as if he was about to hook up with his soul mate.

"Yeah, dude. I said I'd call at seven, and it's seven. When I'm with you I'm all the way with you. So with that being said, please tell me you got the suite for us to chill in already, 'cause I'm really not in the mood to wait around."

Dino was ecstatic to tell her that not only did he get a suite, he got the best one the hotel claimed to offer. "Yes, baby doll, I mean Krissi. Me and you is good to go. I was going to see if you wanted me to have my personal chef prepare us some late dinner, but I don't have a number to reach you at."

"Oh, yeah, that's right, you don't have my number. Well, I'm quite sure after tonight you'll have my number and a little more than what you was probably bargaining for. Is that okay with you?" Bunny poured the charm on extra thick as she seductively spoke into the phone while tucking two blades in the side compartment of her purse.

Dino hurried up revealing the room number to his dream date and was glad to hear Bunny would be up in ten minutes or so. He checked to make sure the champagne he'd ordered was chilling and the room looked presentable. He'd been watching television and chilling since checking in at five o'clock. Shortly after making sure all his traps were set, he heard two short taps on the door. *Damn . . . Okay, she's here. Shits about to be on and popping. Even if I don't get the hookup on some shit, I'm about to get some of the best-looking pussy I done seen in months!* Rushing over, Dino yanked the handle downward, swinging the door wide open. "Hello, my queen. Please, come on inside."

Listen to this damn fool-ass nigga. He gone! This nigga act like he ain't get some good pussy in who knows how long. Pitiful. Just fucking pitiful. This bullshit gonna be way easier than I thought. "Why, thank you." Bunny stepped into the spacious multiroom suite and smiled. "Wow, okay, I see you up in here doing it big; champagne chilling and even some chocolate-covered strawberries." She picked up the bottle, turning it so she could read the label. "And I see you even got us the good stuff tonight. I'm definitely impressed."

Dino was feeling himself that he'd made Krissi smile, and she was more than satisfied. After opening the bottle and pouring them two glasses, the pair sat down on the plush couch.

Reaching for the huge remote off the coffee table that controlled everything from the climate of the room, the lighting, and the curtains, to the four gigantic flat screens mounted throughout the room, along with the surround sound system, he felt like he was a boss amongst bosses. His house was indeed a showplace, and he could, and would, be proud to bring any female to see where he laid his head at, but it was apparent Krissi was different, and it'd take more than some solid gold fixtures and a marble countertop to impress her. This suite was only the tip of the iceberg for what he had in mind for her. She had potential to be wifey material; the legal-white-dress-standing-at-the-altar type. He knew he'd just met Krissi and didn't even know her last name, but he believed the gods may have sent her to him to make up for all the bad luck he'd been having lately. She was like a gift; a blessing.

After scanning over the hotel menu, they ordered room service. Indecisive over what to get, Dino bossed up getting almost one of everything that they had to offer. Cleverly not to be seen by any of the hotel staff, Bunny conveniently excused herself to the bathroom to freshen up when the small buffet carts arrived with their appetizers, main courses, and desserts. Finally kicking off her shoes, which Dino automatically recognized as being expensive, they sat down, eating, drinking, and enjoying music for hours on end. Bunny wanted her target to be good and relaxed so when the time came for her to send him home to the devil, he wouldn't be expecting it or able to put up much of a fight. The less struggle or opposition to certain death, the better she always believed.

Checking her cell, Bunny noticed it was almost ten o'clock. Having made watching the news a priority due to the recent crimes she'd been unfortunately involved in, and not caught, Bunny had Dino turn the music off and the television on. Glad to have a female that was more interested in current events than who was having a half-off sale on weave was refreshing to him. Together, they listened and watched attentively, as he was just as guilty of heinous crimes as she was and had yet to be brought to justice for them. Five minutes into the broadcast, a special segment was about to air pertaining to crime in Richmond.

"In between all the murders and other crimes, our fair city is turning into a cesspool for criminals to feel as if they can run amuck. Well, the chief, along with the mayor, has revealed to our reporters a plan to not only clean up our city, but other locales within close proximity to ours. We spoke to Detective Chase Dugan earlier, and here's what he had to say about some of the more recent high-profile crimes."

"Yes, we are definitely closing in on more suspects in not only the bank robberies and the cold-blooded murder of exotic dancer Tiffany Ross, but also in the cases of the bodies that have been discovered floating in the James River. We will be bringing certain people to justice by week's end. Some extremely valuable leads have just surfaced, and trust me when I tell you, it's only going to be a matter of time before these animals are apprehended, charged, and locked up behind bars."

Both feeling as if Detective Dugan was speaking to them, their demeanors somewhat changed. Bunny was the first to speak out on the segment. "Wow, so it looks like this city is about to get hotter than July; you think?"

"Maybe, maybe not. I mean, there's always crime in major cities, and they gotta get some scapegoat-ass cop to get on the news and make up shit; lie and say they about to get a handle on the crime. First, it makes for good television, and second, you gotta give the people what they want. And the people wanna believe it ain't gonna never be no more crime, or at the very least, less of it. It makes them sleep good at night just hearing the lies!"

"You think?" Bunny quizzed as she sipped on some more champagne.

"Of course. I don't think, I *know*. And as for that bitch, Tiffany Ross, I knew her. She was a snitch that set dudes up. And between me and you . . ." Dino was trying to prove his dislike for snitches and guys in the game that robbed other cats out in the streets making serious paper and making real bosslike moves just for an easy-ass come up. "As for them bodies that's showing up in that river, niggas can't expect to try to get down on the next moneymaking motherfucker and not suffer the consequences. You hear me?"

"Really." Bunny started to get in her emotions, knowing where this conversation was headed. It was one thing to bad-mouth Tiffany's bitch ass, but now she knew he was referring to Tariq and her beloved Spoe. Motivated by Dino's basic confession, which was his acknowledgment that he had no problem whatsoever throwing a person into the James River that crossed him, Bunny decided to speed up her plan. Suddenly leaning into his personal space, she nudged her head underneath his chin. Using one hand to play with his well-groomed dreadlocks and the other to massage his grow-ing manhood, Bunny wanted to just bang him really good and get it over with.

Dino's head bobbed backward as he closed his eyes. Lifting her chin with his hand he stuck his tongue deep down her throat. Embraced in passion, he slowly worked his other hand down her curvaceous body, resting it in between her legs. Returning the favor, he now was massaging her moist box. Shoving his hand up in her tight-grip pussy, one finger followed by two worked her over until she was practically screaming out his name. Seeing that she was all in, he swooped her off the couch, carrying her to the king-sized bed. Finding no opposition, he raised her dress up devouring her inners. Hearing her moan, Dino dropped his pants, then went in for the kill. Fucking the dog shit out of her like his life depended on it, he was met with Bunny throwing it back on him. She hadn't had sex since Spoe's death, so she was long overdue to get it in.

Almost forty-five minutes later as they both lay exhausted on the bed, Bunny started to feel guilty. Killing Dino was still very much at the top of her to-do list, but the fact that she'd enjoyed the sex so much was starting to eat away at her conscience. Where a part of her wanted to just get down to business and carry on with the rest of the game plan, the freak in her wanted to maybe go another round or two before sending him on his merry way. Fighting the urge to lower herself to suck his huge dick, she grabbed his hand, urging him to go get in the shower to not only wash some of the sweat off his body, but to also get a special blessing from her.

Quick to oblige, Dino jumped up as if he hadn't just put in some serious work and bolted into the bathroom. Turning on the shower, he stepped in underneath the strong flow of hot water, washing his balls as he waited for Bunny to join him.

I can't believe I was all into that nigga sex game like that. I'm so sorry, Spoe; so very sorry. Please forgive me. Don't worry, I'm about to make it right for both me and you. I promise. That ruthless and rotten no-home-training murderer is going to get what he has coming. I love you, Spoe. Talking to herself, Bunny dug into her purse, removing both blades. Holding them tightly, she crept into the steam-filled bathroom. Easily making out Dino's muscular back through the glass door, she felt a strange sense of happiness for what was about to go down. She was seconds away from everything working out the way she planned.

Okay, girl, here we go again! Easing the glass door open, the coldhearted and crazy hood diva stepped her naked body inside. Feeling a slight breeze rush in, Dino knew he was no longer alone in the marble-walled shower. With soap in his eyes and his back still turned, he let Bunny know she was by far one of the most exciting women he'd ever been with, and he hoped to get to know her better in the near future.

Waiting for a verbal response from the female he knew as Krissi, Dino was met with the bitter excruciating pain of not one, but two sharp blades being savagely plunged into his upper torso. Showing no mercy, Bunny brought down one blade overhanded and the other under at a rapid pace, enraged. She repeated the monstrous process until her dreadlocked lover collapsed to his knees. Not saying a word, Dino's lifeless body slumped over underneath the flow of the steaming hot water. Stepping out of the shower to avoid getting his blood even more on her, Bunny allowed him to bleed all the way out until he was well on his way to hell. Bending over his corpse, she cut off one of his dreads as a souvenir. "And, oh, yeah, you ho-ass nigga, Spoe said, 'What up!'"

Leaving Dino facedown in the shower, Bunny washed her face along with her kitty cat in the sink and got dressed. *Fuck him! Let them find him when they do!* Placing a do not disturb sign on the door of the Dino's suite, she casually strolled to the elevator, making sure she was not seen. Returning to her own room, which was located several floors below, Bunny pushed the plastic-issued key into key slot of door 217 and entered. Getting comfortable, she took her cell, which was on silent, out of her purse, along with Dino's dread. Immediately she saw she had several missed calls from the same mysterious number and one voice mail. Lying across the bed, Bunny listened to her lone message and couldn't believe her ears.

"This is Detective Chase Dugan of the Richmond Police Department. I was wondering if you could please give me a call at the number showing on your caller identification. I'd like to speak to you in reference to a few important matters that we are investigating. I need for you to please return this call within a twenty-four-hour time span. Once again, this is Detective Chase Dugan of the Richmond Police Department."

Taking her sister's boyfriend's message as more of a direct confirmation sign from God on what she was intending on doing in the first place, Bunny decided to at least call Simone and let her know that her cop beau was sniffing around for answers. "Hey, sis, this is just a heads-up. Your nosy-ass man just called my damn cell, leaving a fucking message. What the fuck you going to do now, bitch?"

"What? What in the world are you talking about? How did he get your phone number?" Simone panicked, and rightfully so.

"Why don't you tell me?" Bunny wasn't about to sit there and be oblivious that Simone may have slipped up somewhere.

"Well, first, what did he say exactly?"

Bunny was even more determined to go ahead with her original game plan and didn't have time to possibly lose her nerve by a long drawn out emotionally charged conversation. "Look, Simone, I don't know what he knows and certainly don't give a shit at this point. I just wanted you to have a heads-up when dealing with him and to tell you I love you, Ginger, and Tallhya's crazy ass. Oh, yeah, the rest of my share of the money is in the linen closet. Give it to Ginger's greedy ass! Now, bye, sis, I gotta go."

"Bunny, Bunny . . . Bunny . . ."

Bunny had enough of living life without Spoe. Nothing really mattered to her. She'd taken care of everyone she held responsible for his murder, so now she could rest in peace. Now she could go to sleep for good and wake up in heaven dancing on the clouds with her better half, Spoe. Opening a bottle of pills, she swallowed three handfuls to ensure the deed would be done, washing them down with a bottle of wine she'd brought with her. Making sure her hair was perfect, Bunny Banks lay down in the bed, waiting patiently for death to take her to Spoe.

"Bunny, wait, what are you trying to say? Where are you at? What are you about to do?" Simone didn't receive a reply to any of her questions as she was met with the sound of silence. Bunny had hung up. Trying to call back several times, she repeatedly received the voice mail.

Chapter 29

Simone couldn't believe what was happening. She'd been through so much over the past year that she knew she needed some type of therapy if she ever hoped to be right in the head again. She'd lost her father and become almost destitute. Slapped her stepmother and fought off her father's lecherous business partner. Watched her grandmother collapse at church and die, then lose their family home. Been in a bank robbery and planned another. Taken part in setting up a major drug dealer and fought her mother after taking a gun away from her boyfriend. Watched her sister butcher their own mother and that man. Cut off her mom's hands before dumping their bodies and setting them on fire. She committed her sister Tallhya to a psychiatric facility. Tried to fight her sister's husband and his baby momma in front of the man she was hoping to get closer to. And lastly, got shunned from her childhood church because of some stupid dumb shit she had to be a part of in order to set the wrongs right her grandmother left.

Simone had gone too far to turn back and too far to go on. She felt like she was on the verge of having a serious nervous breakdown. Now after all of that, Bunny had just hung up, having her to believe that she was going to kill herself after saying Chase was snooping around. What else could happen she fretted as her head felt as if it was about to explode. While trying to calm her nerves, there was a knock at the door. Praying it was Bunny saying she was playing some sort of cruel, twisted joke, Simone flung the door wide open. Unfortunately, it wasn't Bunny but two policemen.

"Yes, Officers. How can I help you?"

"Ma'am, are you the family of a Mr. Gene Banks?" Their expressions were solemn as they both looked her in the face.

Simone was in a panicked state as she answered, "Yes, yes, I am. I'm his sister. What's wrong with my brother? What's going on?"

The policeman had made these types of house calls before and hated doing so. "Well, it seems he was involved in some kind of what we think was a hate crime. He and several other openly gay men were beaten to death near the park. We need for you to come down to the morgue and possibly identify his body. This is the address listed on his driver's license."

Simone's mouth dropped open. She couldn't speak, and her feet couldn't move. As the room started to spin and she grew increasingly dizzy, the last thing she remembered before blacking out was Chase's voice asking the two officers what they were doing at the house. When she finally came to, she was lying on the couch and Chase was wiping her face with a wet rag he'd gotten out of the linen closet.

"Hey, Chase, did I hear . . ."

Before she could finish asking the question, he answered for her. "Yes, Simone, it was bad news about your brother. He's dead; killed by some idiots."

Simone started sobbing in his arms. "Oh, Chase, not my brother too. It can't be! Why?"

"Simone, I don't know what to say."

"Damn, Chase, I love you so much. My life is so crazy. I wish Ginger was still alive and things were different! I wish I could just turn back the hands of time. If we could just go somewhere and be together . . . just you and me, life would be perfect." Her tears wet his shirt as he grew confused on what to do next. He loved her too and was torn considering he knew there was a direct link with Bunny and the criminal cases he was investigating.

When Simone blurted out that the doctors thought she had cancer and she hoped he wouldn't abandon her, Detective Chase Dugan knew against his better judgment what he had to do . . . forget he'd found the bag of stolen money from the bank robbery he'd discovered in the linen closet and take care of the woman he loved—even if it cost him his badge. At the end of the day, love was all that truly mattered to him. Hopefully, he'd never find out all the Banks sisters' deep dark secrets, because who knows if love for anyone is really that strong!

The Banks Sisters 3

Chapter 1

Everything Exotic

"It's the fuel strainer, and I'd bet my cash on that." Rydah, dressed in an oversized blue Dickies work jumper, threw five one hundred-dollar bills on the hood of the Maserati with confidence. Her hair was done, somewhat, in two messy braids.

Jack, a newbie at Everything Exotic Repair, said, "You're wrong, sweet thing. I'm positive that it's the fuel pump. I know these cars like the back of my hand," he bragged. Jack was a self-proclaimed genius when it came to fixing cars, and he never wasted an opportunity to prove it.

"Just put your cash where your mouth is," Rydah said, calling Jack out on his cockiness. Laughter erupted throughout the shop, and the fellas gathered around.

Jack, pride and ego on the line, dug into the back pocket of his dungarees, fishing out his wallet.

Rydah quickly peeped that the wallet remained closed as tight as fish pussy. "Man, put up or shut up," she said, both chumping and finessing Jack all at the same time. "My money is already on the hood. Alone."

Jack pushed air into his chest. In true male chauvinist form, he said, "I ain't never let no broad talk me down off of nothing." He pried the closed wallet open, peeled out a handful of bills, and tossed it on the hood, matching Rydah's wager. "It's your loss. I was only trying to save you some money, sweet thing."

The other mechanics shook their heads. They had seen it far too many times.

Rydah released an audible chuckle of her own. "Next time, save your breath. You'll live longer." Rydah felt bad for Jack. He had no clue as to what he'd gotten himself into. "You got a lot to learn," she said, "about cars and women."

The line in the sand had been drawn and crossed. There was only one thing left to do—Rydah called for Mickey to settle the bet.

She cupped her hands around her mouth and yelled "Ayeeoo, Michelob!" calling her co-worker Mickey by his moniker.

Mickey was six foot three and thin as a whip, with big hands and feet. And as usual, one of those huge hands of his was strangling the neck of a brown Michelob bottle.

"You're not suppose to have that on the work floor," said Jack out of the side of his mouth.

"No shit!" Mickey gave Jack a quick once over. "You got a lot to learn," said Mickey.

"I keep trying to tell him that," Rydah added. "But he's one of them dudes that knows so much that he don't know shit. Dumb like that."

Jack paid Rydah the same attention that he would've paid to a stain in his drawers—none. After all, she was a woman playing shop in a man's place. What did she know? Instead, Jack stood there, gazing at the beer bottle in Mickey's hand, giving a look that said "unacceptable in the workplace."

Mickey felt the side-stare.

"It's a psychological thing," he said by way of explanation. "It's filled with water. The feel of the bottle manipulates my mind into thinking that I'm having a cold one. It's part of my AA recovery. I haven't had a real drink in more than ten years."

Jack nodded his head. "I didn't know AA allowed you to even be around that type of stuff."

Mickey informed Jack that it was his personal alcohol treatment program. "I invented for myself," he said.

"And it's one that you shouldn't bother to try to figure out," Rydah said, "Just let it go. It works for him, and been working for him for a decade now. And that's all that matters." This time it was Rydah who nodded, but at Jack. "Like I said, you've got a lot to learn around here."

Jack continued to ignore her. Rydah noticed the shade but didn't let it faze her. She knew that the best way to get a man's attention was through his wallet.

"Mickey, we need you to look at this car to settle this bet for us, fair and square."

Mickey caught a glimpse of the pile of cash on the hood of the Maserati. He took the Michelob water bottle to his mouth, took a sip, and shook his head. Then he smiled at Jack. "Man, you let her get you, huh?"

Jack poked his chest out farther than it already was. "She didn't get me. I know these cars like the back of my hand," he huffed.

"Well, your hand must be amputated, because your pockets are about to come up short . . . real short."

"The day a broad beats me at anything, let alone fixing a Maserati, I'll eat shit and die."

"That's a pretty funky way to go, but suit yourself," Mickey said. "If Rydah put her money down, trust me, there's no ifs, ands, or buts. Don't let the estrogen fool you; Rydah knows cars like a gynecologist knows pussy." To Rydah: "No offense intended."

"None taken," said Rydah, knowing that Mickey wasn't throwing shade.

Mickey continued, "If she says the car needs a blood transfusion, the only question you need to ask is where to hook up the damn I.V. Let's get this over with." Mickey scooped up the money, stuffing the bills into his shirt pocket, and motioned for Jack to pop the hood.

Rydah turned her cap to the back and began to remove the plastic wrapper from a cherry Blow Pop. "I'll hold the job of the banker."

Fifteen minutes later, Mickey came up from under the hood, examination complete. "Let me guess: Rydah said it was the fuel strainer and you said it was the fuel pump?"

"That's right." Jack put his hand out to collect.

"Not so quick." Mickey looked at Jack with a small touch of sympathy. "Did you say it was a fuel strainer?"

Jack, who still hadn't got the memo, blurted out, "Fuel pump! I said it was the fuel freaking pump."

"Then you won yourself a losing bet." Mickey gave Rydah her winnings.

Rydah took her money with a smile. "Well, Jack, special thanks to you. Drinks will be on you tonight."

Chapter 2

Ace of Spades

The heels of the nude red-bottom shoes were the first part of her body that he saw after the valet attendant opened the door of the Lamborghini Gallardo. By the time both 6-inch heels kissed the pavement, people were outright gawking. Pockets of bystanders, tourists, and would-be club-goers in line waiting to get into the club were trying to figure out which was more astonishing: the rebuilt custom yellow Lamborghini, or the lady who'd gotten out of it.

God damn she was bad!

She was tall, sophisticated, and overflowing with sex appeal. She carried a red and nude clutch bag under her arm that perfectly matched the form-fitting nude cat suit that clung to every curve of her body. Her gait was as fluid as a fashion model as she strutted past the club's bouncers and velvet ropes, straight to a VIP booth at the hottest party in Miami.

Another stunning woman, wearing a turquoise sequinned dress, reached out and gently grabbed the catsuit-clad woman's arm in a hasty attempt to get her attention.

Rydah stopped to see what she wanted. The girl wasn't a friend, but she'd seen her out often. They had conversed on a few different occasions. "Hey, Sky. What's up?" The music—a Chris Brown song—was so loud that it was hard to hear.

Sky looked Rydah over as if she were a delectable piece of meat, similar to the stares she'd gotten when she got out of her car and entered the club. Sky admired her. "As always, you're looking like a million dollars, girl. Have you decided to date women yet? Because when you do, I'm available." She moistened her lips with the tip of her tongue, which had been pierced with a flawless 1-carat diamond.

Rydah thanked Sky for the compliment. "You're not looking too shabby yourself. I love that dress. However, I'm still strictly dating men right now. But if I ever decide to change lanes, I'll keep you in mind." Rydah had never been with a woman, but several of her friends did. Some went both ways, not sure which team they wanted to suit up for. While others, mostly chicks that had been burned badly by a guy or two, now only strictly dated girls. Either way, Rydah didn't judge.

Sky winked. "You do that. I promise you won't regret it. The grass is fo sho mo' green and mo' wet on the other side."

Flattered, Rydah was unsure how to respond. Sky was cute and all . . . but so was her Bengal cat. But she wasn't interested in dating either of them. Before departing she said, "Keep it sexy, Sky." The music engulfed her as she walked away.

Twenty minutes later, Rydah enjoyed the view and the sounds from one of the ten private VIP balconies which overlooked the main floor from 25 feet above the action. The owner of the club was a friend of a friend, and he comped Rydah the highly sought after spot whenever she wanted it. She was swaying her hips to a Future song when a text notification flashed on the screen of her iPhone 6Plus.

Buffy: Hey girl.

Buffy and Rydah were friends and had met each other about a year ago. The two met in Bal Harbour Mall—both were shopping and had so much in common. Immediately, the two ladies hit it off and had been thick as thieves since.

Rydah: Where R U?

Buffy: On the dance floor w/ a girlfriend f/ church

Is it cool for us to come up & kick it w/ U?

Rydah: Sure. Give the bouncer my name and take the stairs.

Rydah watched Buffy snake her way through the crowd. A gigantic bouncer wearing a tight black T-shirt blocked the door to the stairway. He had to be at least seven feet tall, with a tree trunk for a neck. It would have taken a very determined person—and an M104 Wolverine army tank—to move the bouncer off his square if he didn't want to be moved. Buffy quickly gave him Rydah's name as she was leaning on the rail, looking down. When the bouncer contorted his massive neck to look up in her direction, Rydah nodded her approval, then looked away to make another call.

Upstairs in the posh VIP section of the club, Buffy greeted Rydah with a smile and a hug. "You look great," she said. Rydah returned the compliment. Buffy, staring at Rydah's rear, said, "Girl, your ass looks too perfect to be real," smacking Rydah's backside.

Rydah wasn't wearing any panties, and the playful smack on the rump stung and made her butt jiggle like jelly. Rydah wondered how Buffy would like it if she returned the favor with an open-handed smack to one of her cheeks, and not on the ass. But the thought dissipated as quickly as the sting.

"I don't know how perfect it is," Rydah said modestly, "but it's definitely real." Nothing about Rydah was artificial, including her hair, nails, or demeanor. She had nothing against girls that rocked that way, but she chose not to. Rydah was more than satisfied with the gifts God had blessed her with. Why fuck with God's work?

"I know that's right," said Buffy, stroking her 27-inch copper weave.

Buffy had yet to introduce Rydah to her girlfriends, when some no-manners-having busta-ass dude decided to pour himself a drink from Rydah's freshly-opened bottle of champagne. The drink thief was with a male friend and two females, and the four of them were obviously with Buffy, but Rydah didn't want to assume.

She asked Buffy, who was cheesing ear-to-ear, "Do you know them?" pointing to the drink-stealing busta and his sidekick.

A day and a drink later, as far as Rydah was concerned, Buffy introduced her entourage. "Oh," she said, "that's Lisa from my church and my friend Charlotte who I think I told you about." Lisa and Charlotte were gawking at the lavish suite as if they'd never been off the block. "That's Charlotte's boyfriend, Ken. It's Ken's birthday." Ken was the drink thief. "And that," Buffy continued, "is Ken's boy Jake." Buffy ran it all down extra cavalier-like.

Before Rydah could voice her disapproval of Buffy's arrogance, Buffy tried to clean it up. "I know Wolfe always makes it his business that he hooks you up with this huge VIP suite, and it's always hardly anyone in here with you, so I thought it would be cool. . . ."

"Cool to do what?" Rydah asked, watching Buffy's friends snap selfies and pictures holding her bottles of Ace of Spades. "Take the liberty to invite folks into my space without asking me?"

"It wasn't even like that," said Buffy. When she saw the unyielding look on Rydah's face, she tried to laugh it off. "The more the merrier, right? Live a little. We need to get this party popping! It's not like you don't have enough room, or drink for that matter."

Is she serious? At the moment, Rydah wasn't feeling the excuse or the messenger.

One of Rydah's pet peeves were leeches, especially leeching-ass so-called grown-ass men. She was all for women's liberation and all, but she also felt that a man should be a man and hold his own weight. And the fact that Charlotte's boyfriend had helped himself to a bottle that had been, in fact, gifted to her, was a problem.

"What I got has nothing to do with them," Rydah said. She hated inconsiderate people. She'd seen alley dogs with more manners than Buffy's present company, who had yet to even say hi and were just about finishing the bottle off. She considered calling the bouncer, booting everyone out of her shit. However, she said to Buffy, "Let Ken know that I said happy birthday and all, but he needs to be a gentleman and order himself bottle, and at least offer us ladies some as well."

"Girl." Buffy sucked her teeth. "It's the man's birthday and you got two bottles over there. You very seldom even drink anything. Always having water in your glass, faking like you sipping on something."

"It's principle," she said. "Men need to be men. That's the problem with these new-wave-age dudes."

Ten minutes hadn't gone by and every drop of the champagne was gone. "Ayo, Buffy, can you get more of this where that shit came from?" Ken asked in earshot of Rydah.

Rydah was about to snap, but before she could, Ken's homeboy, Jake, spoke up and said, "Man, don't worry. It's your birthday. I got us! Alllllll of us," he said, putting emphasis on the entire group.

"Very gentlemanly of you." Rydah smiled at Jake.

The server crept into the area almost embarrassed, with two bottles of Absolut vodka, which were the cheapest bottles in the club.

Just then, the sparklers lit up a path heading straight to Rydah's VIP area, and the sexy bottle girls came in toting five more bottles of Aces of Spades. Jaffey, the owner, had comped Rydah since she was low.

Before she knew it, Jake was in the ear of her cocktail waitress, asking for a refund on the cheap bottles of Absolut vodka. Ivy, who was always Rydah's waitress and took great care of her when she came there, didn't want to make a big deal. Besides, Rydah, always tipped her extremely well. Ivy could see the disgust on Rydah's face, and she wanted to defuse the situation before Rydah had the bouncer toss them on their asses.

"Don't worry. I'm going to have Jaffey comp it for you."

"No, don't do such. Make them motherfuckers pay for it," Rydah said.

"It's okay," Ivy said. "I don't want a scene. It's no problem."

Though Rydah never took advantage, she really did have full access to anything she wanted in the club. And Jaffey never spared any expense when it came to showing her a nice time.

"It's the principle," Rydah said to Ivy, and Ivy just looked at her with a coy smile.

"It's nothing. Trust me," Ivy said. "In fact, that slime-ball Jaffey needs to eat something. In my opinion, you never spend enough when you come in here."

"A'ight." Rydah smiled. "Thank you so much. And have the big Wolverine tank bouncer move them motherfuckers outta of here. "

"Gladly!" Ivy smiled.

Her song came on. Rydah used it as a welcome distraction and tried to focus on the lyrics and beat of the tune. She was upset but determined not to let a handful of freeloaders ruin her night.

Rydah began dancing and sipping, intoxicated by the music. Dancing was her second love, after working on cars and bikes.

Ken got the message from down in General Admission. He and his boy ponied up to buy a bottle of Cîroc. They were hugged up with Charlotte and Lisa, acting like big shots.

Buffy, who was tipsy, posted an endless stream of selfies. When she wasn't posting pics, she was banging out texts and what she thought were clever captions for the photos.

Rydah loved to laugh and have fun. She was a closet party animal and free spirit who loved cars, music, and life. A couple of satisfied big spenders approached her about future car projects they wanted her to tackle for them. Others just wanted to show their respect, talk shop, or just flirt. She was a confident man's dream girl: independent, beautiful, and could build a car from the ground.

Buffy, checking for someone to leave with, asked for Rydah's opinion. "What you think about the guy over there?" She nodded. "The one with the big diamond earring and necklace, wearing the red hat."

Rydah looked in the direction where Buffy had nodded. "The Spanish dude?" she asked.

"I don't think he's Spanish," Buffy said. "I think he's light skin. You think I should talk to him?"

Rydah looked more closely. "He look like he's either Spanish or a hip white boy. But he's definitely not black."

"Well, should I go talk to him?"

"Not my style, to go approach. But if you think he's cute, go for it."

Buffy said that she definitely thought that he was cute.

"Then claim him before someone else does."

That's all Buffy needed for encouragement. That . . . and all the champagne she'd drink, courtesy of Rydah.

Rydah watched Buffy half stagger down the stairs through elbow-to-elbow clubbers on a packed dance floor, to the other side of the club to introduce herself. Damn, had Rydah known the girl was feeling the alcohol like that, she wouldn't have even let her go over there.

Meanwhile, Rydah kept sipping and turning up by herself. Before she knew it, Buffy was back, introducing her new friends.

"Rydah, this is Mike and his boy Tiger."

Tiger looked familiar to Rydah, but she couldn't put her finger on where she knew him. Tiger said, "Nice to meet you." And then she remembered. He was one of the dudes eyeing her out front when she arrived. And nothing had changed; he was still staring.

"Sorry. I can't stop admiring you. I saw you the second your feet hit the pavement. You look nice fo' sho. But I bet people tell you that all time, huh?"

"Compliments never get old," she said with a coy smile.

He offered to buy her a drink. "What you sipping on?"

"Water, now."

"In a champagne glass?" he asked as if he didn't believe her.

She seldom drank more than one glass of champagne, and when she did, two was her absolute limit. "I'm a grown woman," she said, "in case you can't tell by looking at me. And I have no reason or inclination to lie, especially to anyone other than the police or a judge, and when I have to, I will do it very carefully."

Tiger stammered. "I–I didn't mean to insinuate that you were lying."

"Yet you did, all the same," Rydah poked, not letting him off the hook.

Tiger recovered well. "Then allow me to make it up to you," he offered. "How about breakfast?"

Naturally, Rydah refused his invitation, but out of courtesy, she allowed the small talk to continue for a while longer. Tiger asked for her number. She gave him a Google number that she used on her business cards.

A drunk Buffy leaned in. "Sooooo fucking out of your reach. Just orbits out of your reach."

He had a stupid look on his face but smiled it off. "I always get whatever I want. Just that simple."

After a few more songs, Rydah danced into the wee hours of the morning and was ready to call it a night. The club was still going strong when she left. Outside, she approached one of the valet guys. "Can I have my keys, please?" She pointed to her car. Since the Lamborghini was parked in front of the club, the only thing the attendant had to do was retrieve her keys from the lock box.

The attendant nodded. "Of course."

Rydah waited, and then she noticed a really familiar face. "Jimbo!"

A five foot tall, flamboyant guy with more gold than Mr. T from the A-Team turned to check out Rydah. He hesitated at first, as if he didn't know who Rydah was, and then he got closer, straining his eyes to make her out, and then said, "Rydah?"

"Ummmm . . . yes?"

"Daaaamn, girl. I ain't even recognize you." He was shocked. "And I ain't even drinking tonight, on antibiotics and shit. And that shit don't even mix."

"How are you?" she asked. "Is everything okay?"

"Yessss, everything cool. Winter cold, and it has been so hot here this winter."

"I know that feeling," she said, towering over him.

"Girl, you look good. Damn good. Your work suit hide a lot," he said, checking her out. "Still loving my Shelby edition you did for me, but wanted to talk to you about making me a bulletproof mobile."

"I can definitely do that, for sure," she said.

"Yeah, I heard you did something similar for them crazy-ass Haitian niggas. I'm like shiiiit . . . let me make sure I don't get caught slipping."

"I got you. Come by the shop tomorrow and let's talk."

"For sure. I'ma get me a suitcase of paper together and be by tomorrow. That's good," Jimbo said with a smile as he walked off.

After a couple minutes, the valet attendant handed Rydah the key to her car and a bottle of water with the club's logo. He shut the door for her once she was in.

Rydah peeled off, going south down Collins, across the Causeway to Biscayne Boulevard. She was about to make the left on Biscayne when the blue lights bounced from her dashboard and rearview mirror.

Whoop-whoop!

"Aw, shit," Rydah said aloud. *The motherfucking police. I wasn't even speeding.*

"License and registration." The officer had blue eyes and red hair.

Rydah had no idea why she'd been stopped. She wasn't speeding. She knew better than that, especially at this time of the morning, after she'd been sipping. "Officer, do you mind telling me why you stopped me?"

If the officer heard her, he showed no indication of it.

"License and registration."

Okay, Rydah thought, *one of those*. This wasn't her first time being pulled over by a racist or overzealous cop. Most police were cool, but certainly not all of them. Rydah put her left hand on the steering wheel, while slowly using her right hand to get her registration from the glove box. Next, she removed her license from her purse, giving both the license and the registration to the officer. She then placed her right hand back on the wheel, next to the left one.

The red-haired officer looked at her picture. "You don't look like your picture, Ms. Banks."

"I guess you could say that I clean up well, Officer. But you still haven't told me why I'm being pulled over, sir."

For the second time, the police officer ignored her right to be told why she was being pulled over. Instead, he zeroed in on the registration of the yellow Lamborghini Gallardo.

"And you are Rydah Banks, the owner of this car?"

The man had her license and registration in his hand, which plainly contained the answer to both his question. Not only did he have selective hearing, Rydah thought, but his eyes must not be all that sharp either. Deaf and blind. She knew she had to be extra careful, or this stop may not end well for her.

She politely said, "Yes, sir. That's correct."

"Are you carrying anything illegal inside the vehicle?"

"Excuse me, sir?"

Now the officer looked at Rydah as if she were the one who was deaf and dumb. "Are you carrying drugs or guns?" he asked.

Here we go, she thought as she blew a long breath of hot air. "No, sir."

When she put her hands in her lap, the officer whipped out his gun as if he'd been waiting for the opportunity to do so all night.

"I didn't say move your hands, did I? Put both hands back on the steering wheel! Now!" Rydah did what she was ordered to do, all while silently praying to God that this stop ended well.

"So," the officer asked, "this engine is rebuilt?"

"Yes, sir. I rebuilt it myself."

"You mean you paid for it?" He said it as if he'd caught her in her first lie. And where there was one lie, there were drugs and guns.

"No, sir. I said what I meant. I rebuilt this engine from start to finish with these two hands." She nodded to her hands, mindful not to move them from the steering wheel until Officer Gung-ho said that it was okay.

"Really?" he said as if he still wasn't completely buying it. "I'd like to see that."

Two more cruisers rolled up on the scene, lights flashing.

Officer Gung-ho said, "Where's the stash box located?" He was cocky.

"There isn't one."

A lot of drug dealers used stash boxes—secret compartments built into the car, usually connected to the electrical system—to transport drugs, guns, and money. Sure, she knew how to do it and was the master at them, but what did that have to do with the cost of gas in Dubai? Absolutely nothing.

"If you're smart enough to rebuild this whole car from top to bottom, how come there's no stash box?"

That's when an officer from one of the other cruisers that had just arrived slammed his door and began walking up to Rydah's car.

The new officer said, "Ma'am, will you please step out of the car." It wasn't a request.

Finishing off the last swallow of water in the bottle, she unbuckled her seat belt and opened the door. Then she slowly stepped outside the car.

"I'm going to ask you to do a few things for me," the new officer said. "I want you to do exactly what I ask, okay?"

Rydah faced the traffic and, as the cars drove by, their headlights beamed into eyes, causing her pupils to retract. People slowed down and stared out their car windows as they passed by the scene, curious but mostly glad it wasn't them being scrutinized by the law.

"Sure." She just wanted to get this shit over in one piece.

"Good," said the officer, as if they were friends. "I want you to hold your arms out like this"—the officer put his arms out like an airplane—"then touch the tip of your nose with the pointer finger of each hand." He demonstrated what he'd just said, and then asked if she could do that.

Rydah quickly and easily completed the task, just as she did the next four tasks after that one.

For the sixth sobriety task, the officer asked her to recite her ABCs, backward. Rydah noticed that the officer didn't bother demonstrating this time. That's because it was called a "sucker's task." That wasn't the official name, but it was called that because the average sober person couldn't do it. An intoxicated person wouldn't stand a snowball's chance in hell. This was the task dirty police asked a person to complete when they wanted to set someone up. Good thing she wasn't drunk. At least she had that going for her.

Rydah began with, "Z . . ." She took a deep breath, thought for a second, then said, "YXW. . . ." She silently replayed the alphabet in her head and said, "VUT . . . S. . ."

Rydah was trying desperately to locate—in her head—the letter that came before *S* when, from a ways up the street, a gold 1978 Cadillac Brougham burled down Biscayne Avenue. The car was almost identical to the one Madea used to elude the police in Tyler Perry's *Madea Goes To Jail*.

Rydah found the letter she was looking for: "R . . ."

The roar of the engine growled louder as the antique car neared the scene where Rydah and the cops were standing.

"Q . . ."

Being that Rydah was facing the oncoming traffic, she could see the imminent collision before the moment of contact. The officer administering the rigged sobriety test to her wasn't as fortunate. The Brougham seemed unsteady, seemingly picking up speed as it got closer. Rydah desperately wanted to get farther off of the side of the road, but she was afraid that if she made any move other than what the officer told her to make, he might shoot.

Because of the light in her eyes, Rydah couldn't see the driver of the old Cadillac, but it was obvious that whoever it was, they were out of control and probably needed to be in her place taking the sobriety test. The car was traveling at 1.5 times the speed limit and swaying. Rydah had a choice: stand there and get hit by this monster on wheels, or move out of the way and maybe get shot. Her heart pounded so hard that if she didn't get hit or shot, she may have a heart attack.

At the last moment, Rydah attempted to jump out of the way to avoid the collision. Officer Gung-ho drew his weapon.

One of the backup officers yelled, "Watch out!" But the warning was too late. The gold hog, being driven by an 88-year-old lady with a bad case of indigestion, ran smack dead into the police cruiser. The impact caused the back end of the cruiser to swing around into the officer, knocking him forty feet into the air. After mowing the police officer down, it spun directly across the spot where Rydah had been standing.

"Oh, shit."

Thank God she wasn't like a deer in headlights. She would've been dead if she had waited one more second before jumping out of the way. Besides the side of her Lamborghini needing a fresh coat of paint, she was good.

The old lady driving the Cadillac was also okay. Not a hair out of place on the gray fox. She straightened up her bifocals, reached in the glove box, and fumbled for a bottle of Tums. She opened it, popped two of the chalky discs into her mouth, and chewed. After swallowing, she said, "That's the last time I'm eating pig's feet. They nearly killed me."

Chapter 3

The Perks

5:37 a.m.

Rydah barely beat the sun home, but not by much. As she stepped through the door of the condo, her phone rang.

"Hey, babe." It was Wolfe, checking to make sure she made it home safe. "How was your night?"

"Great." She didn't bother wasting his time with the stunt Buffy and her so-called friends had pulled. "As always, thanks for the setup."

"It was nothing." Jaffey, the owner of the club, owed him a boatload of money and an even bigger boatload of favors, so copping the VIP whenever he wanted didn't cost Wolfe a dime. But it wasn't like Wolfe was hurting for bread. If he had the inclination to, he had enough money to buy that club and several more of them.

Next month this time, Rydah and Wolfe would have been dating for a year. Once a week, without fail, Wolfe made it his business to take her out on a date. He did everything from a simple movie at his place to a private flight to Vegas for dinner and a show. Rydah wasn't sure how Wolfe stacked so much paper, and she never asked, but whatever he did, he was really good at it. She was sure that it was illegal.

If Rydah was to believe what the streets were whispering, Wolfe had a mean streak. For every dollar of financial stability he possessed, when provoked, he was equally as unstable as a batch of nitroglycerine. It was safer to cross Satan than it was to cross Wolfe. But Rydah had never seen that side of him

She reciprocated by asking how his night was.

"It was uneventful," he said. "So I guess you could say that it was a good night"

"No excitement at all?" she questioned with a raised eyebrow. "Sounds boring."

"Boring is sometimes good," said Wolfe, neglecting to mention using the barrel of his Desert Eagle to play patty cake with a man's tonsils for coming up short with his money. Dude had a temporary lapse of memory that Wolfe's .44 down his throat quickly got rid of.

Wolfe changed the subject, asking, "Do you need anything?"

"Yeah. Two quarts of paint for the Lamborghini."

"Huh?" Wolfe sounded confused. "I thought you were done working on that car."

"Long story," she said. "I'll fill you in over breakfast. I'm cooking. How long before you can get here?"

"I'm going to need a rain check on breakfast, babe. I've been in the same clothes for three days. I smell like a ripe chicken coop. But if you want, on your way to work, you can drop by and pick up this bread that I got for you."

Wolfe was always giving her things. She appreciated it, but she didn't want him to think she dated him for his money. She could take care of herself quite well. She told him, "I don't need any money."

"That's good to know. However, I didn't ask if you needed it. I want to give it to you," he said. "You're not going to deny me the privilege to do that, are you?" Wolfe made it sound as if she were doing him a favor by accepting his money.

"I hope you don't mind me dropping by in my work clothes."

One week later

After hours, Michelob allowed her to have free reign to use anything she needed at the shop. The paint got delivered this morning, a few days early, so she stayed to spray the Lamborghini.

Rydah stopped to admire her progress. She was almost done. Just a few more touches, and when it dried, the car would look as good as new.

She was cleaning the nozzle on the spray gun when her ringing phone broke the silence. She hated being interrupted when she was working. As she was about to pushing the IGNORE button on the screen, Rydah peeped the caller ID.

Damn. She'd been so focus on finishing up the car that she'd almost forgotten that it was Sunday morning.

"Hello, Mom."

"Praise the Lord, doll baby. This is the Lord's day, so let's be happy and rejoice in it."

Every Sunday morning Rydah had breakfast with her parents and faithfully attended her father's church. She said, "God is good."

"I'm making your favorite for breakfast, strawberry pancakes with that special whipped cream you like."

"Thanks, Mom. You're the best," Rydah said as she shut the hood on the car. It went down louder than she would have liked it to.

"Baby, are you still at that shop working on that car?"

"Busted. But I'm just about done with it now. I have a few more little things to do that will take no more than an hour."

"Well, baby, this is the Lord's day, and you need to be praising and thanking Him that it was only the car that was hit and not you. You know God is such a faithful God."

"I know, Mom." She respectfully changed the subject before the sermon began. "I'll be out the door in a second. I'm going to run home to take a shower and grab some clothes, and I'll be there by the time you finish making breakfast. I can do my hair, makeup, and get dressed for church over there."

"Sounds divine," her mother said. "I'll see you shortly then, sweetheart."

Rydah was the only God-begotten child of Evangelist Amanda and Pastor Maestro Banks, and they thanked the Lord every day for blessing them with her. Amanda and Maestro married 48 years ago. For nearly the first two decades, they had tried to give birth to a child, but it just wasn't to be. What a struggle it was for them, as people of such strong faith, to stand before the church and tell the people of God that they can have all the desires of their heart if they just ask God. Well, God knows they had been asking, and yet they kept witnessing the gospel and standing steadfast of God's promises. Then, on their twentieth anniversary, God blessed them with Rydah. Maestro loved the testimony.

"God doesn't always give you what you want when you want it, but he's always on time," her father would say. He'd been preaching the gospel for years, talking to his congregation about trusting God and asking and seeking to receive the desires of the heart. All the while God had yet to bless him and Amanda with a child. Back then, his faith had been tested and was getting weary. But Maestro knew that he and his wife had to be steadfast in God's words and trust him.

Miraculously, on the morning of their twentieth anniversary—which happened to be on Easter Sunday—the phone rang. Maestro's mother was on the other end. His mother, Gladys, explained that her sister's daughter Deidra was en route to the hospital to give birth to a bastard baby that she couldn't take care of. Gladys said that Deidra would allow them to have the baby for $10,000.

Maestro was skeptical. He was desperate to be a father, but he didn't want to do anything that would put his faith in question. He asked, "Will my name be on the birth certificate?"

Gladys said, "If you hurry."

Maestro drove his 1988 Bentley to the Miami International Airport, and three hours after the phone call, he and Amanda were on a flight from the Sunshine State to Richtown, VA. The entire time, Maestro, who was a man's man, secretly asked God for a boy, but as long as the child was healthy, he swore that he would be grateful. He got the latter, a healthy baby girl.

Deidra was not only an unfit mother, but she was also an opportunist. When she saw how well-to-do Maestro and Amanda seemed to be, she had a whole new set of demands: "I want twenty thousand for my baby. Twenty thousand. Not an iron dime less. And I get to name her," she said. "Or no deal."

It was two times the amount they had agreed upon. Maestro had no problem coming up with the extra cash, but he was set on giving the child a biblical name. "We've been thinking about the name Hannah," he said.

Amanda, soft-spoken with warm eyes, said, "It's from the Bible." In case Deidra didn't know.

Deidra nearly exploded. She yelled from the hospital bed, "Hell, no! Fuck, no! No goddamn Bible fucking names for my seed! I suppose you want to turn the child into a fucking nun, too."

Gladys, Maestro's mother, felt badly about the confusion Deidra was causing. As a compromise, she said, "What about Madison?" Madison was a nice wholesome name, and it wasn't from the Bible.

Deidra sucked her teeth. "'Manda, Maestro, and Madison. Oh, what a happy fucking family that will be." There was brief silence, and before anyone else could speak, Deidra said, "I think fuckingggg not!"

Deidra's mother was also in the hospital. Me-Ma was a God-fearing woman herself and never really saw eye to eye with Deidra, but it was her only daughter. Deidra's behavior at the hospital embarrassed Me-Ma. She'd always tried to be understanding and loving of Deidra, but there was no way to understand Deidra's outlandish actions and inexcusable behavior. Deidra continued to show that the only thing the two had in common was their blood. And if Me-Ma hadn't pushed the heifer out herself, she would have questioned that. But for the sake of her sister Gladys and her nephew, Maestro, Me-Ma tried to intervene.

"Deidra, honey, it's bad enough that you are insisting that our own flesh and blood pay you for taking on a child that you spread your legs to have, and now don't want, but now—"

Deidra was like a child spawned from Satan himself. She cut her mother off with a harsh look before she could verbalize the rest of her thoughts. "You have nothing to do with this, Mother. None whatsoever! This is my business and my decision." To Maestro, Deidra said, "It's my way or no way and you can hit the highway."

Amanda and Maestro looked at each other. Maestro's eyes were saying *What should I do?* while Amanda's eyes conveyed the message, *You better not fuck this up. Do whatever she says. Let's just get our baby and get the fuck outta here.*

It took almost everything Maestro had in him to swallow his pride. He told Deidra, "Okay. We'll do this on your terms. What name did you have in mind?"

"That's what I fucking thought," Deidra stated arrogantly. She didn't have an ounce of humility in her selfish body. She didn't even know what the word meant. "Tell me, where did you guys come from?"

Maestro thought: *What does that have to do with anything?* But he answered, "Hollywood. Hollywood, Florida."

No one said anything for at least five minutes.

Then Deidra pierced the bubble. "Her name will be Rydah." No one had a clue as to how she came up with the name Rider, but no one dared question it. "Spell it: R-Y-D-A-H."

Maestro said nothing, though he thought it was a ridiculous name. He quietly prayed that God would let this blessing of their baby go through.

Amanda, not wanting to rock this crazy lady's boat anymore than it was already, said, "Oh my goodness. I love it."

Deidra took a sip of water, piercing her eyes at Amanda, knowing good and well that Amanda couldn't love it.

"What a beautiful Rydah she will be," Amanda said.

"Don't play mind games with me, you fucking homely church lady."

Had it been years ago, Amanda would've mopped the floor with Deidra, but God had her heart and conscience these days. "Honey, I love the name, and I know this little beautiful girl will be a trailblazer and such a blessing to us. We thank you and appreciate you," Amanda said, as nobly and humbly as she could.

"You're welcome," she said. "Now give me my motherfucking cash and take the little bitch with you before I change my mind."

"Oh, my!" Maestro's mother said.

Amanda shot her mother-in-law a look that said, *Please don't piss this girl off.* Nobody wanted a child more than Amanda.

When Maestro wrote the check, Amanda saw demons and dollar signs in Deidra's eyes, and he took full advantage. He signed the check and looked up. "Let us first pray, and then get this birth certificate signed."

Deidra started to spit some disrespectful venom out of her mouth, but she realized that the check wasn't yet in her hand. "Make this prayer bullshit quick," she said under her breath.

Maestro let God lead him in a long prayer.

Not a second after the Amen came, Deidra said, "Okay, enough of all this bullshit. Run me my motherfucking money, because all of this prayer and Saviour bullshit going to seriously make me change my motherfucking mind."

After Maestro and Amanda took the baby, the first second they were alone with their bundle of joy, they prayed the blood of Jesus over her. Regardless of how they'd gotten her, they both knew that Rydah belonged to them.

This morning, church was wonderful, and Rydah enjoyed spending this time with her parents. It was their family ritual; she'd always eat breakfast with them on Sunday morning, attend church, and then have an early dinner. And no matter how old she got—she was 28 now—her parents still felt blessed to have Rydah as their daughter.

Rydah felt the same way about them. Although they weren't her biological parents, she inherited parts of each of them. Rydah learned to appreciate nice things and everything about being a lady from Amanda. Amanda sometimes wished that Rydah was a little more conservative, but she loved the fact that her daughter was more edgy than she ever dared to be, with a twist of class and pizazz.

Growing up, her father took her everywhere with him. Fishing. Ball games. But she especially liked spending time in the garage with her dad, where he tinkered with his cars and built things. That's where she got her passion for rebuilding cars.

Her parents poured every ounce of love they had into her and, in her own way, she made them proud.

Amanda, in her late sixties now, had aged well. If she was the example, the saying was true: "Black don't crack." She was a silver fox.

The lecture that her mother was giving fell on deaf ears, but she pretended like she heard them, and she knew what she had to say to shut her mother up.

"Mommy, I know you disapprove of me going to the club and hanging out, but God protects me. He always has me in His keeping care. And though I wish it were, my work isn't in the church. It's in the streets, and it's in the trenches. I'm looking for the lost, the hurt, the confused, the broken-hearted. And some are, but most of the lost souls are not in the church already. The bewildered in the wilderness."

"Come on now, tell it, baby." Her father egged her on like the members of his congregation did to him. Though her way of doing God's work was unconventional, he was proud that she was there for the young people who didn't know their way to God to point them in the right the direction.

"Those are the ones who need me, and it's up to me to be in these streets and trenches to lead and bring them to church, and then it's up to you all in the church to welcome them with open arms and to save them." Then she looked up at her mother. "Mommy, sorry I'm just not the traditional preacher's kid, that I don't dress like them or pretend to be something I'm not, but one thing's for sure: This heart of mine is pure."

Rydah's speech made her father smile. "That's right, baby."

"God sees all and knows my heart."

Amanda heard her daughter and knew she was preaching the truth. "Well, I just want you to be careful, and Pastor, let's pray over our baby girl for protection and wisdom while she's out in the trenches doing God's work and to save his people."

After praying with her parents, it was time for her to head home to chill out, get some rest, and get ready for work in the morning. Her parents walked her outside to a beautiful purple custom El Camino. Of course, Rydah had done all the work herself.

"Baby girl, this right here is your God-given talent." Her father shook his head in admiration. "What year is it?" he asked, walking around the beautifully crated piece of machinery. "Lord, have mercy. Umph, umph, umph." Maestro and his daughter shared the same deep passion and love for cars.

Rydah, proud of her handiwork, said, "It's an eighty-eight."

Even if he tried, Maestro wouldn't have been able to keep the smile out of his eyes as he nodded his approval. "Is there a particular reason you chose an eighty-eight to restore?" he asked, already knowing the answer.

"Eighty-eight was the best year," Rydah said. Finding one had been a lot of work, almost as difficult as rebuilding it.

"You got that right," Maestro agreed.

"That's the year God delivered you to us," Amanda said, intervening into the subliminal car chat of the two people she loved most in the world. "A blessed year indeed." Amanda gave her only daughter a hug. Rydah squeezed her back.

Like she did every single Sunday, her mother gave her a reusable grocery bag filled with plastic containers—more food than Rydah could consume alone. Thank God she didn't have to. Wolfe always stopped by on Sundays for some of her mother's "gourmet leftovers," as Wolfe called them. Rydah was no stranger in the kitchen, but there was no way she could compete with her mom in that arena. She didn't even attempt to try.

"Amen to that." Rydah tossed the keys to the El Camino to her father to crank it. The engine roared to life. *Vrrrooommm!*

"Music to my ears," he said. "Where's the Lamborghini?"

"I'm not finished touching up the paint," she said. "Couldn't miss our Sunday ritual, so I will finish it up tomorrow after work."

Amanda rolled her eyes. She never cared for the expensive yellow sports car. She thought it was too flashy. Besides, the car had a bad omen about it, she thought. One week, the electrical systems went out on her for no apparent reason. The police stopped her for no reason. And then she was side-swiped by a runaway tank driven by a woman high off of pig's feet.

"I think you should get rid of that car," said Amanda. "It's just not good for you."

"I'm going to get out of here and get ready for work." Rydah knew exactly where this was going, and she wasn't going to in that direction with her mother.

Though Amanda believed in God, she still had always been superstitious about "signs," and Rydah had learned long ago not to argue with her when they disagreed with one of her omens, auspicious or otherwise.

"Get rid of that car, baby girl. I know you could get good money for it."

"Call you once I get home, Mommy! I love you, Daddy!"

Chapter 4

Wheels Up, Guns Down

Miami

Li'l Kim's epic "Not Tonight" blared from the newly installed 1,300-watt stereo that included two shallow 10-inch subwoofers and a complimentary compact class-D amp neatly installed in the bulkhead behind the seats. It was a tight fit, but Rydah fabricated the installation herself. She'd done a total modification of the stock factory system in.

Tell him I'll be back, go fuck with some other cats
Flirtin', gettin' numbers in the summer ho hop
Raw top in my man's drop . . .

Bass hit like a rhythmic explosion as Rydah, along with an army of bikers and hot rods, maneuvered through the holiday-weekend traffic. It was epic.

The Fox Channel 7 news helicopter hovered above the swarm of bikers, broadcasting live. They'd come from all over the country for this: Cali, Baltimore, Richmond, and D.C. were just the tip of the iceberg. The visual could have easily been mistaken for a scene from a summer box-office action movie. For some, the MLK ride was a beautiful sight to behold, while others thought the bikers were a menace to the public roads. Perspective was determined by position. But there was one thing that everyone agreed on: the scene was buck wild.

There was nothing that the police could do about it. The law was clear. Law enforcement weren't allowed to chase the riders through the streets of Miami, and the riders weren't inclined to stop and talk. They came to ride, and that's what they did.

Two of Rydah's cousins, Ronnie and Floyd, flew in from Baltimore to participate in the festivities. They paid a friend to drive their bikes down a day in advance on an enclosed trailer. They would've driven the trailer themselves, but Ronnie, the younger and the flashier of the two, was a self-proclaimed boss and, according to him, "bosses must floss."

The event was billed to promote non-violence and was cleverly coined "Wheels Up, Guns Down." No one was sure exactly who came up with the slogan, but it stuck like cheese grits to a hot skillet.

This was Rydah's type of hype. Her toys were up to par and, if faced with a choice, Rydah preferred breathing the exhaust of a finely tuned engine than smoking a blunt. Any day. The decision wouldn't have been close. Having the opportunity to share the fun with her cousins, who she hadn't seen since they were kids, made it all the more fun. She was down like four flat tires.

Rydah popped the Lamborghini's clutch, dropped the leather gearshift into place, and mashed the gas pedal. Seamlessly, the transmission of the Italian-crafted machinery slipped into third gear, spinning the wheels and snapping her head back as it rocketed forward. She weaved in and out of the traffic like a seasoned pro as bikers among bikers were popping no-hand wheelies, spinning doughnuts, standing on the seats, and at least a dozen other dangerous stunts. She stopped the ongoing traffic so that the three hundred street motorbikes and four-wheelers could have the space to show off.

With the eye in the sky watching down on them, it was open season. Cousin Ronnie threw the front wheel of his Ducati in the air. One foot was on the seat, while the other was on the handlebars. He nailed the trick for two blocks before putting it down.

Damn. Rydah had no idea that her little cousin could ride so well. She was impressed with his skills.

Watching the bikers brazenly display their talents, risking life and limb, got Rydah's juices flowing. Her need for speed and love of motor vehicles ran deep, and the countless crazy colors and engine sizes of the bikes zipping around got her wet between the legs. Rydah was in her element. She was where she loved and wanted to be.

After a few minutes, it was time to move on, not just for the chopper in the sky but for the riders as well. Rydah drove alongside the bikes for a couple of miles, cruising. When she got the signal, she sped a few blocks past all of the illegal bike riders and stopped in the middle of the intersection. Then three more cars, a Mustang (Shelby edition) GTO, '68 Plymouth Roadrunner Hemi, and a 1970 Chevrolet Chevelle SS, followed suit, paralyzing the traffic of any pedestrians or vehicles trying to get by. The only thing the oncoming traffic could do was stop and either be amused or frustrated as the riders showcased more death-defying stunts and tricks.

Rydah's phone rang, but she was too consumed with watching out for the po-po and enjoying the show to answer.

More ringing.

It wouldn't stop.

Fuck!

The annoying phone wouldn't shut up.

Not wanting to take her eyes off the action for even a second, Rydah picked up the jack without giving the caller ID a glance.

She shouted into the phone, "What! This isn't a good time!" She could hardly hear herself speak over the cacophony of screaming engines. She was in ecstasy.

"I've been calling you all weekend, guurrrlll. I want to know when we doing dinner?"

Vrrrrrooooommmm . . . Vrrrrrooooommmm.

"What you say?"

"Dinner!" Buffy was shouting as loud as she could. "When are we going?"

Rydah heard nothing Buffy said. Not a word.

"Let me call you later?"

Vrrrrrooooommmm . . . Vrrrrrooooommmm.

"I'm with my li'l cousins on bike patrol."

Buffy ignored the noise, desperately trying to get an answer to her question. "You promised that we'd sit down and talk," she screamed, "so that I could explain. I even bought you an apology gift! I feel really bad about the other night, and I want to make it up to you! We need to talk! You been putting me off for a minute, and I feel bad and really need to talk to you."

Rydah had heard enough to get the gist of what Buffy was saying. "I know!" Rydah shouted back into the receiver as the bikers continued to do their thing. "I know!"

Vrrrrrooooommmm . . . Vrrrrrooooommmm.

She had been blowing Buffy off ever since the situation they had at the club, but she had promised to meet with Buffy for dinner. She tried to stand firm on her word, even if she didn't feel like it.

Vrrrrrooooommmm . . . Vrrrrrooooommmm.

Buffy wasn't trying to take no for an answer. "You already know you're going to be good and hungry after all that riding. I know you could use some girl time."

Vrrrrrooooommmm . . . Vrrrrrooooommmm.

Buffy added, "All that damn testosterone. Come on now, time to transform."

Buffy had a point. Rydah had been working around the clock at the shop, and when she got off, she stayed at work, fixing her own car. This was the fist day the Lamborghini had been on the street since it was sideswiped.

"Are you still there?" Buffy asked after Rydah didn't respond.

Vrrrrrooooommm . . . Vrrrrrooooommmm.

"Yeah! I'm here!"

Vrrrrrooooommmm . . . Vrrrrrooooommmm.

"So where do you wanna go?" Buffy wasn't going to hang up until Rydah gave her an answer.

"I'm not sure," Rydah told her, "but we will figure it out."

"Okay. Then I'll call you back later?"

"Any time after nine. I'm going to have to go home and clean up."

"Cool! Talk to you later."

Rydah clicked off just in time to see two riders flip a four-wheeler, trying to ride it on its hind wheels. Amazingly, they weren't hurt.

As the day went on, Buffy didn't let an hour go past without calling to keep Rydah on task. Evening came fast. Hours of stunt riding, driving, and holding up traffic quickly turned into nightfall, and it was time for Rydah to say bye to her cousins and head home.

On the way, of course, Buffy called again.

Rydah quickly answered. If she didn't, Buffy would just call back until she did answer. "I'm on the way home," she said before Buffy could ask.

"Great. Did you figure out where you wanted to eat yet?"

All the phone calls were starting to blow her high. Rydah wanted to reschedule, but she knew she'd promised. "No. Not yet. I'll call you back once I get home." Rydah hung up.

Rydah's condo, overlooking the Biscayne Bay, was small but chic. Being home only reinforced the fact that she didn't want to go back out. It was after 10 p.m. and she was tired. Her next thought was to call Buffy and inform her that she'd do dinner with her another day, but she knew that Buffy would not only be disappointed, but she would also keep calling her until that day came. It was probably better to get it over with, Rydah thought. On that note, she married the idea that she was going to hear Buffy out.

Rydah was about to jump in the shower when her phone rang again. *This bitch can't be serious,* she thought. Rydah picked up.

"If you keep calling, I won't have time to get ready," she quickly said.

"What are you talking about, babe?"

"My bad." It was Wolfe. "I thought you were someone else."

"I get it." Wolfe's voice was always low and raspy. If you didn't pay attention, you would miss what he was saying. And he rarely got excited, even when he said he was excited. He was odd like that.

"Are you done riding with your peoples and 'em?"

"I just got in. I'm supposed to be having dinner with Buffy later. I'm trying to get ready now."

"Maybe I could come over and take a shower with you before I head up the road?" He was driving to Jacksonville take care of some business.

"Sounds good to me." Rydah was already hot; might as well put out the fire. "How far away are you?"

"Fifteen minutes."

"I'll make sure the water is hot."

"You do that."

Rydah smiled. She absolutely treasured times like these, when Wolfe dropped by spontaneously to spend real quality time. It was the small things that Rydah enjoyed the most about Wolfe. Based on Buffy's clock, Rydah knew that she didn't have much time, but she couldn't care less. This was about the fifth time today that she strongly felt like postponing the dinner with Buffy.

Rydah lit the fresh cotton–scented candles that she always had around the house and then went into the bathroom, where she ran water into her oversized Roman tub. After getting the temperature just right, she added bubbles, grabbed clean towels, and put them near the tub. As the bubbled water filled the Roman tub, Rydah used the time to run to the kitchen, to her fully stocked bar, and she grabbed a couple bottles of water, a can of Coke, and bottle of Hennessy Black. She put everything on the stand in the bathroom next to a silver ice bucket and two designer champagne flutes. After arranging the items the way she liked, she cut off the piping hot water.

The doorman rang her house phone. He asked if it was okay to let Wolfe up.

In a flash, Wolfe was at her door, carrying an MCM studded backpack on his left shoulder. The smile was the first thing she saw, though. It was a gesture few people got from Wolfe.

When she tried to embrace him with a hug, he quickly pulled away.

"I stink," he said. "I smell like the city. You know how I am about that type of shit. Let me clean up first."

Rydah assured him, "You know I don't care about any of that, baby." Rydah didn't care how Wolfe smelled, But she also understood how he felt. She hated being around people after working on cars all day. The only thing she wanted to ever do was hit the shower and get fresh, so she respected Wolfe for that.

He took his shoes off at the door and then peeled off his jeans and shirt and walked, naked, straight into the kitchen, where he dumped the contents of the backpack on the glass-top table. There were only three things in the bag: a pair of new Versace boxers folded up into a small square, an EBT card, and bundles of cash. The cash covered the table.

When Rydah walked into the kitchen behind him, Wolfe pointed to the food stamp card. "It's like three hundred ninety-four dollars on the card now. Get some groceries. Use it tomorrow for sure. Oh, and if you remember, get me some of that water I like to drink."

"Don't I always?"

"You do." There was that smile again. "And it's supposed to be a fresh four hundred fifty-seven on it on the sixth of each month. The access number on that shit is 2007."

"It'll definitely come in handy," Rydah said. She stole a kiss on his cheek. She didn't cook much, but she still liked to keep the things she liked in the fridge.

Rydah picked up the Versace boxers. "I'm going to put these in the drawer with other ones that I washed, okay?"

"Baby, you're too good to me," he called out.

"Nope. Just good enough," she said back. "The water is hot. Once you're done counting your bread, come on and get in the tub."

"Anything you say."

"Yeah, so you keep telling me," she countered back to him, knowing that that wasn't exactly 100 percent true. Wolfe let her do whatever she wanted to do, within reason, and have whatever she wanted to have, but Rydah had no illusions about who wore the pants in their relationship. That would be Wolfe. And she didn't mind it at all.

While she waited for Wolfe to give her a holler that he was ready, Rydah tried to figure out what she was going to put on for her dinner date with Buffy. While standing in the closet, she yelled back into the kitchen, "Maybe you should help me pick out something to wear."

"Maybe you should model for me? Or maybe you should blow off the dinner date and just lay up with me?"

"You staying in?" she asked with a raised eyebrow. That would've definitely been different, because Wolfe ripped and ran the streets on a consistent basis, chasing money.

"I hadn't planned to. But plans can change. No big deal. Money don't get old," he said, "but people do. If you want, I could stay for a while. Your decision."

It seemed like a good idea: spend the night laid up with her boo. She and Wolfe didn't live together, so sleeping in the same bed together was always a treat. Yet she didn't want to distract him from doing what he loved to do. She was conflicted. On the one hand, something inside of her was saying that it was a good idea. On the other hand, she didn't want to infringe on his plans. If the tables were turned, she wouldn't want him infringing on hers.

Wolfe walked into the bedroom holding a handful of money. "Buy yourself something nice," he said, tossing the stack of money onto the bed.

"I keep telling you that you don't have to keep giving me money. You know I'm an independent bitch, right?"

"That's why I fucks with you," said Wolfe. "But I also don't want you to want for anything. Can you juggle being an independent bitch while acepting an occasional bankroll from her dude? Besides, you do so much for me."

"I do what I do for you because I want to. However, I don't want you to ever think that I'm with you for your money or what you can buy me. It isn't like that," she said.

Wolfe laughed at the irony of her logic. "You make sure I'm good because you fucks with me, but I'm not supposed to do the same thing. Stop playing." Wolfe swatted her on the butt. "Fair exchange is no robbery. That's not just a street maxim. It holds true in relationships also."

Rydah knew there was no need to keep going back and forth with him, because at the end of the day, he was going to do exactly what he wanted to do. She threw her hands up in mock surrender.

"Okay," she said, "you win, Wolfe. Buy me whatever you like whenever you like."

Wolfe compromised. "We're both winners. Another reason why I'm with you."

"Thank you, baby." She smiled. "Give me two seconds to make sure everything's straight in the bathroom."

He walked behind her to the bathroom.

Rydah dimmed the lights and lit the rest of the candles.

Sitting on the top of the commode, Wolfe unstrapped his prosthetic leg and removed it.

Ten years ago, his leg had been removed. The amputation began just above the right knee. What would have been a disability for some people only made Wolfe stronger and so much more ruthless. Losing a leg didn't cause Wolfe to lose any confidence or cockiness. People that didn't know Wolfe before the amputation couldn't tell the leg was missing. He didn't walk with a limp. And for those who had known him over the years, he was so big and so treacherous that they simply forgot or didn't mention it.

Every time he took the prosthetic off, it reminded him of what had happened. As crazy as that night was, Wolfe was grateful it was only his leg. Shit, he'd trade a limb for his life any day.

Wolfe had been in Overtown to drop off some work—two keys of uncut cocaine—to a guy called Panama Jack. Way above the ubiquitous palm trees, the sun shone brightly on blighted stucco and brick houses. It had only been 30 minutes since the sun rose, but the temperature had already reached 82 degrees. This day was going to be a smoker, Wolfe thought. And he only wanted to have his workday over and be home before noon, before the sun was at its peak.

Wolfe preferred to make transactions with weight at this hour because the police were usually worn down from chasing the youngsters around all night. By this time, they just wanted to get off work and go home to their families in one piece.

Panama Jack stayed in a small bungalow-type house in the bad part of the city that, like most of the houses in this neighborhood, was in need of some major repairs. The steps squeaked from Wolfe's weight as he made his way to the porch carrying an army-green knapsack on his right shoulder. No lights were on inside the house, which was odd. Wolfe tapped the door three times then stepped back and waited. The heft of the burner resting on his waist, a 12-shot .40-caliber, pulled at his jean shorts.

Several seconds later, a light flipped on inside the bungalow and the door swung open.

"Aye, boy. I've been waiting on you. How you be, friend?" He spoke English well, but it was laced with a heavy Panamanian accent.

Wolfe had been dealing with the dude for eight months. In that time, Panama Jack was always on time with his bread, and it was never short. Just the way Wolfe liked it.

"I be just great," Wolfe said.

Panama Jack stepped to the side, and Wolfe walked inside the bungalow. The moment the door closed behind him, his instinct told him shit was rotten, and his gut had never deceived him. Wolfe knew he'd been lined up to be robbed.

Wolfe heard a floorboard squeak in the hallway and pulled out his burner just in time to fire down on the two goons bending the corner.

Pop! Pop!

He hit one of them flush in the chest. The other fired back.

Boom!

Wolfe was sandwiched between the remaining goon in the hall and Panama Jack. The living room was tiny, with not much furniture to use for cover—an old sofa, a worn table, and a frayed chair. Wolfe dove behind the sofa and then swung the gun on Panama Jack, letting off two shots. Both shots hit home, slamming through Panama Jack's chest and jaw. He died instantly. Wolf wished the pussy motherfucker had suffered more.

One left.

It only took Wolfe four shots to do it, and he had eight more left in his gun. He slung two more shots down the hallway, just to let the goon know that shit was still hot, and if he wasn't careful, he could revisit his two partners in crime in hell.

Pop! Pop!

The third gunman got bold—or desperate—and advanced forward.

Boom! Boom! Boom!

Pop! Pop! Pop!

The old sofa caught two of the shots. Wolfe's leg caught the third one. It felt like someone had stuck a hot fireplace poker in his leg, but Wolfe ignored the pain for now. He had to get the fuck out of there. Only God knew what other perils were lurking.

Two of the last three slugs Wolfe squeezed off caught the
goon in the chest. Wolfe put two more in his head, just on
general principle, before leaving.

Back in the car, his leg was in excruciating pain, but he
couldn't go to the hospital. Not if he wanted to stay out of
prison, anyway. The hospital had to notify the police of all
gunshot-wound victims, and the police would quickly connect
Wolfe with the three dead bodies he'd left behind. So, he
got drunk and dug the bullet out of his thigh on his own.
Unfortunately, two weeks later, the leg got infected with gan-
grene. He got a friend to drive him to a hospital in Alabama,
where the leg was amputated.

Three dead bodies on the head of an already convicted
felon, even with a shitload of cash, meant he wouldn't be able
to dodge that 5x5 prison cell, so considering he was able to
buy the best prosthetic leg that money could buy, he considered himself blessed.

Chapter 5

The Big Bad Wolfe

Rydah attempted to help Wolfe slip into the tub.

"Please, don't do that," he said. "I'm not helpless." Wolfe hated being treated like he was helpless because he lost a stupid leg. He had his life,and that was more than he could say for the cats that took his leg. A life for a limb; he'd make that trade any day.

"Tell me something that I don't know, Wolfe." She helped him anyway

"I don't need to depend on nobody."

"Except for me," she said, holding his arm as he eased into the hot tub. Once his body was submerged, she gave him a deep kiss that got his dick hard.

That was the thing about Wolfe: he had a major complex about people helping him or seeing him as handicapped. He didn't expect or want folks to treat him any different because he had one leg, and he definitely didn't want to depend on anyone for anything.

His take on folks was: he knew that people came and went into his life, especially chicks, so he made it his business to never depend on anybody. He strived every day to do everything on his own. He put himself through a rigorous physical therapy workout every single day without fail.

There was something about Rydah that allowed him to feel comfortable accepting her help, showing his vulnerability, but he didn't want to slip and make it a habit.

Wolfe said, "You know I appreciate you, right?"

Rydah nodded. "Yeah. I do. But you don't have to keep telling me."

"Fair enough," he said. "But that's the reason why I do so much for you." Though he'd undressed thirty minutes ago, he never shed his confidence. It radiated like the morning sun, along with the 10 carats of flawless diamonds set in the necklace he wore.

Rydah watched as Wolfe adjusted himself in the tub to sit up comfortably. He had perfect posture.

"Make me a promise?" he said to Rydah

"What is it?"

"Promise me that you will never look at me like a crippled, trick-ass nigga who tries to buy affection. The minute I think that, I'm out."

"Wait a second!" Rydah said abruptly and then lowered her voice, letting her eyes meet Wolfe's. "I don't see you as no cripple anything." She was buck naked, standing next to the tub. "And you're far from being a trick-ass nigga, because for one, I don't trick, and I don't fuck with niggas. I date men— not niggas. I care about you because of who you are, not what you have or what you can do. My love for you is genuine. And if you don't get that," she said, turning the tables on him, "then you won't have to leave, because I'll be the one that's out."

Wolfe admired her spunk, her curves, and her confidence as he searched her eyes for deception, larceny, or bullshit. But all he saw in her eyes was love.

"I'll never doubt you again," he said.

She punched him. "You better not." Wolfe could be a bipolar, moody-ass motherfucker sometimes, but she loved him.

Wolfe reached out to her. "Com'ere, baby. When was the last time I told you how beautiful you were? I'm glad you mines." He pulled her closer, coercing her in the tub with him.

Once he had her in the tub, Wolfe leaned into her, licking and sucking on Rydah's perfectly round breasts. She stroked his already rock-hard manhood. Looking in his eyes, she sat down on his dick for a few minutes, gyrating. The tub was big enough to hold the both of them easily, with room to spare. After about and twenty strokes, Wolfe busted inside of her.

"Damn," he said bashfully, "the pussy is so good I'm firing off like Quick Draw McGraw."

"It was mind-blowing while it lasted," she said.

No matter how hard he tried, Wolfe couldn't control himself when he was inside of Rydah. "I'm going to get some of those pills," he said. "I hate getting mine before you get yours."

Rydah rolled her eyes. "Bump that Viagra shit." She had a girlfriend that told her about the effects. "I don't need nobody fucking me for hours on top of hours, stretching my shit all out of proportion. I don't need any highway miles on this." She laughed. "I love the intensity of the sex we have. It's everything."

They kissed.

"Play with my pussy."

He did.

Rydah closed her eyes, enjoying motion of his fingers inside of her. "Besides," she said, "I think I'm getting too old to be getting fucked for hours. It's perfect the way it is."

Wolfe knew that she was stroking his ego, but he smiled anyway. He planned to get the pills first thing in the morning. *I should've been copped them,* he thought.

After Wolfe's fingers accomplished what his dick hadn't, Rydah kissed him. *There's more than one way to skin a cat.* She kissed Wolfe, soaped up the wash cloth, and began washing his chest. She asked if he wanted anything to drink.

"I have water, wine, and cognac."

"Hennessy."

"Coming up." She reached over to the stand beside the tub and poured the drink, and a glass of wine for herself.

Rydah took her time washing him up, and Wolfe was enjoying every second of it. When she was done, she quickly bathed herself, hopped out of the tub, and grabbed two towels—one to dry off her body and the other for her hair. Then she reached for the other towels she'd laid across the chair for Wolfe.

When she tried to dry him off, he said, "I got it. I can do it myself."

"Really, Wolfe? Why do we have to keep going through this?"

"Old habits are hard to break. Work with me," he said.

"I will. Now let me dry your crazy ass off."

"I thought you had to get dressed for a dinner date with what's-her-name?"

"Buffy. Yeah, I do."

"You know you are amazing, don't you?"

"Yes. Among other things." She giggled.

"You got that right. Who other than me has a girl that rebuilt a car for them?"

They made their way to the bedroom, and as soon they were near the bed, Wolfe aggressively took control. He surely wasn't acting like a man with one leg.

Chapter 6

Pimp Or Die

Zzzzzzz . . . zzzzz . . .
Wolfe's phone vibrated.
"Duty calls."
Rydah removed herself from Wolfe's arms.
Wolfe reached for his phone and looked at the screen. "Damn. Forty-seven missed calls," he said.
"You're a busy guy." As soon as the words left her mouth—*riiinnggg*—it was her phone.
Wolfe said, "No more busy than you."
"It's nobody but Buffy."
BUFFY: What's yo status?
RYDAH: Another hour, just out tub.
BUFFY: Cool
Rydah asked Wolfe, "What do you think I should wear? Shorts, jeans, or a dress?"
Wolfe said, "Shorts. And those come-fuck-me boots I just got you."
"The Tom Ford thigh-high ones."
"Those ones."
Rydah pulled out the boots, a pair of cut-off Daisy Duke shorts, and a bedazzled baby T-shirt. "Thanks for the help, babe." She leaned in and kissed him. She got up got dressed and then did her makeup and hair.
Wolfe left the same time as she did, and they both headed out into the world to hold up their ends of the bargain: him business, and her social.

***

Rydah got in her car then realized that she wanted to change her purse. Instead of the crossbody bag that she first decided to wear, she ran back in to get her big Birkin bag. She changed everything out and headed back to the car. Then on the way downstairs in the parking deck, she brushed against some wet paint from the maintenance man who'd painted earlier.

"Shit." She shook her head. Changing clothes would make her run late, but she had to, or not go. She ran back upstairs and changed into some short jean shorts, a black top, and tall thigh-high Tom Ford lace-up-from-the-front-to-the-thigh 6-inch sandals.

Just then, Buffy called, "Girl, where are you?"

"On 95. Where are we meeting?"

"We will decide once we together. Come to The Burger Chef on Sixty-ninth. It's right off the highway."

"Sixty-ninth?"

"Yeah, like I'm right there now."

"Girl, not really feeling that area."

"It's on and off the highway, and I'm right here. Soon as you jump off, I'ma be right there."

Rydah was feeling a bit off beat, and something in her told her not to, but she went ahead and agreed. "A'ight, be there in less than five."

"I'ma be right here waiting."

"Cool." She disconnected the call, and all of a sudden an awful headache came on.

Rydah pulled into the parking lot, which was crowded with a lot of people hanging out. It was Negro Central. Hordes of people were hanging out or soliciting illegal merchandise in the parking lot.

Damnnnn! she thought. *It's a lot of motherfuckers out this bitch. And no fucking Buffy! She said she was here already. I need to get the fuck up out of here!*

Just then, the phone rang. It was Buffy. "Girl, where the hell are you?"

"Right here at the light."

"Girl, I'm leaving."

"Nooooo! Don't! I'm literally right here at the light. And I can't turn on red. Just get you a water or soda from the drive-thru, and as soon as you wheel out, I'm going to be there."

Rydah hesitated. She was thirsty and knew that she should just leave and go back home, but she agreed.

Not even a full 90 seconds had passed before a guy somersaulted into the passenger's seat of her car, Dukes of Hazzard style. All she heard was him hit the leather bucket passenger's seat.

Rydah looked over at the young black guy in her car with his hoodie on. Her first thought was that it was one of the Bike Life guys playing a trick on her. "Who the hell are you?"

Hooded Guy flashed a shiny silver handgun and uttered, "You know what's up. Drive, bitch." He cocked the gun.

Rydah knew by the look in his eye that he meant business. Caught off guard, she couldn't think on her feet. All she did was put the car in gear.

"Bitch, put the top up."

"I can't. It's T-tops," she lied.

"Bitch, stop lying. Don't fucking play with me."

Rydah's hands were tied. She slowly pulled out of the drive-thru. Things seemed to move in slow motion. For a few seconds, she couldn't think straight.

"Turn left and then right. Don't make any crazy moves. And don't try no stupid-ass shit, bitch."

She followed instructions, looked straight ahead, and then took a deep breath. Rydah remembered what the news said about being kidnapped, and those do's and don'ts kept running through her head.

If the kidnapper moves you from one location to another, the odds of you being killed increase.

Yeah, bitch." He smiled and nodded. "I'm going to get a lot of money from you, ho-ass bitch," he spit out with venom.

A lot of money? Hells naw. You's a motherfucking lie, nicka! That was the initial thought that ran through her head. That's when the skid marks went off in her head. She knew she needed to get out of that situation, and quick.

"Turn right at that light, bitch," he demanded.

She looked over at him, and he spit, "Bitch, what the fuck you looking at?"

That was the last *bitch* she was going to be.

It's pimp or die! Kill or be killed! It's survival of the illest!

Indeed, she would make that right turn as instructed.

It was a delayed response, but all of a sudden, she had to take her life back or she was going to die trying. That's when she put the pedal to metal. The CEO of Lamborghini would have been proud how she handled the German engineering and 175 horsepower like a seasoned Lamborghini pro, pulling off a processioned right turn.

SKIRRRRRRRRD!

She slammed on the brakes, bringing the car to a sudden, complete stop. She hit the seat belt and the button that released the door and was making a mad dash like Jackie Joyner Kersey in her Tom Fords, getting down the street, screaming and literally running for her life.

Rydah had about a five-second head start before the kidnapper knew what had just happened and could regroup. He stood on his knees in the car and let off a couple of shots. Then he jumped out like Magic Mike in his Jordans and began to run after her, gunning and unloading the rest of his clip.

Pow! Pow! Pow! Pow!

Chapter 7

When God Got It

Rydah stumbled. She heard the tires on her Lambo speed off. She turned to look and saw her car swerve across the street. He had almost lost control but quickly managed to grab the wheel and took off down the street. The last thing she saw of him were the car's brake lights.

She started creaming at the top of her lungs. "Help! Help! Help!"

"What happened?" a concerned bystander asked.

"I was robbed and my car was stolen," she managed to get out in a panic. "Call 911."

Before she even finished her sentence, it was apparent that someone had called them already. She could hear sirens getting closer and closer, and in the blink of an eye, they were on the scene.

The corner was full of detectives, officers, and bystanders. In the midst of everything, a man brought her phone to her. It had been on her lap and fell out of the car when she jumped out. The screen was shattered, and it wouldn't power on.

Seconds later, Buffy showed up. She seemed distraught. "Oh my goodness. What happened, doll?" Buffy ran up to Rydah and hugged her, sidestepping an officer who tried to keep her away while he asked Rydah a million questions.

"Did you know the person who tried to abduct you? What was he wearing? How old was he? What was his nationality? Have you ever seen the perpetrator before tonight? Would you recognize him if you saw him in a lineup? Do you think that this person was after you, or your automobile? Where did you get an expensive car like that?"

The questions were endless, and the scene quickly turned into a circus.

Someone amongst the growing crowd screamed, "Are you okay, baby?" It was Amanda. Rydah's mother didn't play when it came to her baby. She couldn't give a damn what police had to say. She pushed her way through the thickly congregating group of people.

When she finally reached the front, a police officer stopped her. "I'm sorry, ma'am, but you can't come any closer."

"That's my daughter over there, Officer . . ." She read his tag. "Officer Piper. I have to make sure she's okay."

Officer Piper looked to Rydah for confirmation. Rydah ran over and gave her mother a hug.

"Are you hurt?"

"I'm fine, Mom. Just a little shook up. That's all."

Her father, Maestro, made his way through the crowd after parking the car. After seeing that she was alive, he looked up at the sky and screamed, "God is great! God is great!"

Maestro had the entire set of bystanders coming to Jesus. The makeshift crime scene turned into a praise party.

Amen!

And when it was all said and done, he cursed the person who did this to his daughter.

"May God have mercy on their soul . . . because a wrath is coming!"

Chapter 8

Meet the Parents

"Take me home."

The police were finally done questioning her. Halfway through, the so-called questions began to feel more like an interrogation, and Rydah felt more like a suspect than the victim of a crime.

"The only place you're going is to our house," said Amanda.

Rydah's father seconded his wife's motion.

"We need to spend the rest of the night praising God for sparing your life. It's the least that we can do for our Lord and Savior, Jesus Christ."

Rydah grew up in the church, but unlike her parents, she sometimes questioned *why* or *if* God did all the things people gave Him credit for. For instance, if it was truly God who saved her life, then who was it that tried to take her life away?

Rydah rode in the back seat of her father's Bentley, thinking about what had happened. She reran every detail of the ordeal through head over and over. Maestro was behind the wheel, praying, while Amanda fidgeted with the small gold and diamond cross that she always wore around her neck. The dainty cross hung from a thin chain that she'd had since childhood.

Rydah believed it was her quick thinking and the carjacker's bad shooting that saved her life, but she knew better than to argue with her parents, especially about anything they deemed religious. Instead, she sat in the back seat of the car and thanked God for her life. It must have been her good karma coming back.

Maestro's Bentley pulled into her parents' driveway, and the second they were through the front door, Amanda's phone rang.

"Blessed be the Lord. This is the Banks residence, where we serve an awesome God. Sister Banks speaking."

Rydah smiled. Her mother had always taken great pride in her phone etiquette and salutations.

Rydah watched as her mother carried on a conversation that was obviously about her. "Why, yes, she's alive! A little shook up, but she's so resilient. By the grace of God, my baby had God's favor and was in His keeping care . . . so yes, I'm blessed."

Rydah rolled her eyes.

"Why, yes, he's right here. I'll let you men handle that part. Here, honey." Amanda passed her cell phone to Maestro. "Someone wants to speak to you." Maestro raised an eyebrow. His wife said, "It's William. Rydah's friend."

Maestro put Wolfe on speakerphone and cordially asked, "What can I do for you, Brother William?"

Rydah held her breath as she listened to her father on the phone with her man.

"I know we've never met, Mr. Banks, but I'm a good friend of your daughter's."

"So I hear," said Maestro.

"And I've been looking forward to meeting you."

"Likewise."

"But for now," said Wolfe, "I would like to know if anything was taken from Rydah besides her car." Wolfe had heard about the carjacking from the streets. He tried calling Rydah, but her cell phone kept going to voice mail. He knew she was supposed to be meeting Buffy for dinner, so he retrieved her number from a guy he knew that fucked with her off and on, then gave Buffy a call. A shaky-sounding Buffy was the one who told him that Rydah was okay and had left the scene with her parents.

"Not much," Maestro said to Wolfe. "I think she said she left her pocketbook behind when she jumped out, with her iPad, camera, wallet, gun, and all the other contents." Maestro looked back at his daughter. "Isn't that right, honey?"

Rydah said, "Yes, sir."

The handbag alone was worth ten stacks.

Wolfe said, "If the cat who stole her car has her keys, though security in that building is tight, she still need her locks changed immediately. I can head over and take care of that now."

"That's very nice of you, young man. I'll tell you what—I'll meet you there and give you a hand. I'll also have Rydah alert her security to the situation."

Maestro was a lot like Wolfe in that way. Looking at them, people wouldn't think so, because they seemed so opposite on the surface, but Maestro and Wolfe shared many of the same qualities. For starters, both men were strong, powerful leaders. Maestro led from the pulpit, while Wolfe led from the streets. Each was well respected by his peers, although for Maestro, that respect was manifested by love, whereas Wolfe's was manifested by fear. But respect was respect, and the way it was obtained didn't change the fact that it existed. And both men would do anything for the women in their life. Also, Maestro was much more street savvy than people gave him credit for.

Wolfe insisted he could handle the lock change alone. "No need to bother you with it."

"It's no bother at all," Maestro insisted. "She will need a few items of clothing anyway. Under the circumstances, I think she should stay with us for a couple of days. I'll pick up the clothes."

Rydah felt funny listening to them speak about her as if she weren't there, but she knew that they were only trying to do what they thought was best, so she let it go.

Wolfe agreed. "Not a bad idea. I'll see ya when you get there. Tell Rydah to please give me a call."

"As soon as I get settled in," Rydah said loud enough to be heard over the speaker phone

Wolfe rang the bell.

Since her parents weren't letting her out of their sight, even though Rydah didn't want to, she invited Wolfe over to their house—provided he and her father were still on speaking terms after they met up for the first time at her house.

Amanda answered the door, wearing an apron. "Hello. You must be William?"

Wolfe wore a pair of jeans and a T-shirt with white Gucci sneakers and a matching cap with a blazer. "And you must be Rydah's sister," he said.

What woman didn't like to be complimented? And Amanda was no exception. She ate it up. "Flattery will get you far in this world. Come in. I'll get my daughter. I hope you're hungry."

Wolfe took off his hat. "Actually, I haven't eaten all day. I'm hungry as a wolf," he said, pun intended.

The foyer led down a hall that opened to a large, beautifully furnished family room. Wolfe said, "You have a very nice home.

"Thank you." Amanda asked Wolfe to take a seat while she went to get Rydah and check on dinner.

Rydah walked into the room, barefoot. Wolfe almost didn't hear her approach. Almost. But slipping wasn't something that he could afford to do. Slipping is kin to sleeping, and everyone knows that sleep is the cousin of death. Wolfe wanted no parts of that family tree.

Rydah had on a pair of jeans and a tank top that her father had picked up from her house. They hugged; a long hug. She didn't want to let him go. Wolfe's body felt both hard and warm in her arms. He asked if she was okay.

"I'm fine."

"Dinner's ready." Amanda asked everyone to come to the dining room. She'd made enough food to feed a troop of Boy Scouts, and everything looked delicious. There was grilled salmon, baked chicken, potatoes, seasoned broccoli, shrimp, rice, and some other things that Wolfe didn't recognize right off top, but he was willing and ready to sample everything.

Once they were seated, Maestro said grace.

"Thank you, Father, for providing this food for us to nourish our bodies. Father in Heaven, may you bless those who are about to partake in this meal. Father in Heaven, may you bless the person who prepared the wonderful meal. Father in Heaven, we thank you for sparing my daughter's life as you see fit. In Jesus' name we pray, and let us all say Amen!"

Amen!

The food tasted even better than it looked sitting on the table. And as promised, Wolfe tried it all, including dessert—a flaky-crust apple cobbler that was still warm from the oven.

"Ms. Banks . . ." Wolfe wiped his mouth with a linen napkin. "I can't remember when I've had a better meal."

Maestro wiped his mouth with a linen napkin. "I see the man has good taste. Can't take that from him."

Amanda said, "Thank you. I learned to cook from my mother."

"Well, she taught you well." After a couple of minutes of small talk while their food digested, Wolfe and Rydah excused themselves from the table.

"If anyone wants me," Rydah said to her parents, "I'll be in the den." She then led Wolfe downstairs.

The moment they were alone, Wolfe asked, "Give me some good pictures of that bitch Buffy and that ho's address."

"What for?" Rydah asked.

"Because the bitch set you up, and I don't intend to let it slide, by no stretch of the imagination."

Rydah thought about what Wolfe had just said. She'd thought about the possibility of Buffy being responsible also, but in the end, she had dismissed it.

She said to Wolfe, "I don't think she's smart enough or crafty enough to orchestrate something like that. And it doesn't make sense. Why would she do something like that?"

"Never underestimate what anyone will do at any given time." Wolfe put his hand on Rydah's leg. "And it doesn't matter why," he said. "It only matters that she going to pay for her sins."

"No, Wolfe." She thought about his reputation and some of the things she'd heard about him, and she didn't want that karma to come back on her. "Vengeance isn't mine."

"You right, it isn't yours. . . . It's mine."

Chapter 9

A Vessel of Blessings

Richmond, VA

"Great morning, sunshine."

Gladys Banks was dressed in a long black pleated skirt and flat-heeled leather ankle boots. The fur at the top of the boots complemented the mink mid-length swing jacket. Despite having been on this earth for nearly a century, Gladys was still young at heart and bubbling with energy. Though many of her childhood friends had gone on to see their maker, she remained upbeat and positive about life. A beautiful fall Tuesday morning was as good a reason as any for Gladys to be dressed in her Sunday's best when she strolled into the United Negro Bank of Virginia.

She figured, why deprive the world of getting the very best version of herself, each and every day, regardless of her age or circumstances? She may not be able to always control what happened around her, but there was one thing that she could control. Nobody knew when his or her time on Earth would come to an end, and if that day came sooner rather than later, Gladys wanted to be remembered at her very best. Especially on the first of the month, when it seemed like everybody and their grandmother's mother was at the bank, cashing their social security check.

"Good morning, Ms. Banks." Kim was the head teller at the bank. "I love those boots you're wearing." Kim had been employed at the bank for two decades. She tried to make it her business to get to know all of her customers, and Gladys and her husband, Malcolm, were no exception. In fact, Kim practically knew Gladys's entire family. She considered

Gladys—who was quick-witted and still drove a brand-new Cadillac—to be one of the last of the old-school black Southern belles.

The compliment from Kim brightened Gladys's eyes even more than they already were. She said, "Thank you, darling." Her voice was angelic. "You're always so sweet and considerate. I tell my granddaughter all the time that the prettiest girls are the nicest girls."

Kimberly displayed two rows of even, white teeth before Gladys went on about her health and overall wellness.

"I'm doing splendid for an old lady," Gladys told her. "I've had better days and I've had worse days, but as long as I keep on seeing 'em—good or bad—I can't complain." She added, "Never seen complaining help no one get through tough times, no how." Enough about herself, Gladys took a seat at Kimberly's desk and asked, "How was your vacation?"

"The vacation was wonderful. We went down to our rental house in Hilton Head for a few days."

"Well, I'm sure that it was very lovely. Did your children join you all?"

All of Kim's children were grown. "My oldest boy, Shawn, brought his new wife, and Christina and her husband gave us the news that they are expecting."

"Congratulations!" Gladys's face illuminated with adoration. "I'm so happy for you. It seems like it was not too long ago that you were pregnant with Christina. Now she's giving you your first grandbaby."

Kim agreed. "It seems like yesterday."

"Time flies, sweetie." Gladys locked eyes with Kimberly and spoke from the heart. "So always be good to people and, most importantly, be good to yourself. You make sure you enjoy every precious second God gives you, because there isn't a day that's ever promised to any of us. God can take us home at any given time."

"I'll be sure to remember that," said Kimberly. She loved when Ms. Gladys came in. She was a ray of sunshine. But Kimberly also liked the fact that Ms. Gladys didn't accept any wooden nickels. She was the spunkiest, sassiest, sweetest eighty-nine-year-old she'd ever met. Kimberly prayed that her skin looked like Ms. Gladys's when she got to that age. The maxim "black don't crack" was alive and well.

"How's your son?"

"He's wonderful," she said with even more animation in her voice. She dug into her leather pocketbook and searched for her phone. "He's still in Florida, preaching the gospel and saving souls. Here are some pictures of him." Ms. Gladys retrieved the album folder she wanted and then passed the phone to Kimberly. The album contained fifty-six photos: pictures of her son's church; Maestro on the pulpit; Maestro with his wife, Amanda; the two of them with their daughter, Rydah.

Kimberly had a confession. "I watch your son all the time on television. Every time I watch him it seems as if he's talking directly to me."

"He inherited that from his daddy. Maestro is the spitting image of Malcolm." Malcolm had died in a car crash thirty years ago. Gladys never remarried. "I wish Malcolm could've been around to see the man that his son has become."

"I'm sure Malcolm is looking down on him from heaven, Ms. Gladys."

Gladys looked up at the ceiling and then changed the subject. "I spoke with my son yesterday. He insisted that I spend next winter with him down there in Florida."

"That would be wonderful," Kimberly said. "You get to stay in that beautiful house of his and escape the cold. Sounds like a great time."

"He didn't have to do a whole lot of convincing, I'll tell you that. I love spending time with him and his family, especially my granddaughter."

Kimberly watched Gladys's eyes light up when she mentioned Rydah. "That's one beautiful girl," Kimberly said. "How has she been doing since the carjacking incident?"

Ms. Gladys looked surprised that Kimberly knew about that. She was curious. "How did you hear about that?" The story didn't make national news, thank God.

"Your son talked about it during one of his sermons," she said. "So sad. I also saw some stuff on saw Facebook."

"Facebook? Why would something like that be on the Internet?"

"People were asking her if she was okay, so she addressed it to stop all the rumors, I guess. She said that she gives all praises to God."

Ms. Gladys made the sign of the cross over her heart. "If something would have happened to that gal, I don't even want to think what it would've done to our family. But she's okay now. Rydah is amazing. She's so brave and resilient."

"A lot braver than me," Kimberly said. "I don't know what I would have done in that same situation. But I probably wouldn't have had that kind of quick thinking." And on that note, Kimberly changed the subject. "So . . . how's your sister Mildred? I haven't seen her in quite some time."

Mildred Banks—aka Me-Ma—was Gladys's younger sister, and the two were tight as a fat baby in a leotard. They shared everything, but Mildred drew an angry line in the sand when it came to her daughter, Deidra, and her grandkids. Me-Ma loved those girls to death, and in her eyes they could do no wrong. In that sense, Me-Ma was a lot more gullible than Gladys was.

Like Gladys, Mildred was very religious. The only differences were that Mildred was completely indoctrinated by the church and believed nothing was right if it wasn't in the Bible or quoted by her pastor. Gladys, on the other hand, loved the Lord as much as anyone, but she strongly believed that church was just a building where people came to rejoice in the Lord, and the people inside the building were sinners. She knew there were a handful of saints, but for the most part, people had plenty of shit with them. Being a first lady for over twenty-five years, married to a good man of God, Gladys had witnessed it all: saints, sinners, whores, liars, cheaters, thieves, murderers, gossipers, and plain-old miserable people.

Although Mildred was both a wonderful and great woman, her blind faith in people made her gullible. Mildred only looked for the best in people, even if that person was evil to the core.

Gladys dropped her head and took a deep breath. "God called my sister home about three months ago. She dropped dead while doing what she loved best, praising the Lord. However," Gladys added, "I think it was that goddamn daughter of hers that sent her to yonder. Excuse my language, but that damn niece of mines makes me want to do more than cuss."

Kimberly had her own thoughts about Mildred's daughter, Deidra, and none of them were good. But she kept them to herself.

"Deidra ain't never been worth more than two pennies, but Mildred didn't want to see it. And I believe in every fiber of my body that Deidra and all of her bullshit is what killed Mildred."

Kimberly didn't know what to say.

"I'm so sorry about your sister," she said. "I didn't know." In an attempt to comfort Gladys, Kimberly rubbed Gladys's arm.

Gladys thanked her. "Since Mildred passed away, everything has gone sort of haywire. Some would say it's gone to hell. The pastor at the Baptist church that she was attending convinced Mildred to sign some papers over to him. For the life of me, I don't know why she would think that was a good idea. It goes without saying that the pastor was as crooked as that road in San Francisco." Gladys was referring to Lombard Street, which is notoriously known for its hairpin-winding curves. "Then my nephew, Ginger, you know that was my favorite, outsmarted the preacher at his own game. Did I tell you that the preacher was gay?"

"No, you didn't." Kimberly was thoroughly intrigued with the story, and the bank wasn't too busy this morning, so she listened intently.

"Well, I'm not one to gossip, but you need to take a look at that porn Web site you young kids look at." Gladys leaned in and whispered, "That pastor on there doing all kinds of nasty stuff to both men and women. Almost gave me a heart attack when I seen it. I'll tell you that."

Kimberly whispered, "I think I heard something about Ginger and a preacher." It was impossible to miss. Everyone in the city was talking about the preacher having sex with a known tranny. "But I haven't seen the Web site," she lied.

Ginger was one of Deidra's four kids that were left with Mildred to raise. "Well, it got them their house back. If that child hadn't blackballed that preacher, they would be homeless.

Deidra had four kids—three girls and a boy that wanted to be a girl—whom she abandoned and left Mildred to raise.

Kimberly corrected, "I think you mean blackmailed."

"Whatever. I know he had a set of black balls all up in places where they had no business being. I'll tell you that."

"Well, how are the rest of the girls doing?" Kimberly had attended high school with two of the Banks sisters, Bunny and Tallhya.

"Well, Tallhya went a little crazy for a while, but she's feeling better now, thank God. And poor Simone got breast cancer."

"I'm sorry to hear about their hardships. It sounds like they're really going through tough times."

"God works in mysterious ways. And when it rains, it sometimes come a-pouring. But God don't give us no more than He knows we can handle. Sometimes things have to fall just about to the gates of Hell, and as long as you stand on God's word, He will bring you right on back out that fire."

Kimberly let Ms. Gladys's words marinate as she thought about a few of the things that were going on in her family. "Amen to that," she said. Kimberly punched some keys on her computer. "Hmm. . . ." Something wasn't right.

Seeing the puzzled look on Kimberly's face, Gladys asked, "Is there a problem?"

"Well, there hasn't been any activity on Ms. Mildred's accounts here. No one closed them or anything, and usually—"

Ms. Gladys cut in. "Because that slimy, fake prophet didn't know about that account. That's why. Forgive me for my language, but every time I think about either of them, that no-good pastor or Mildred's trifling daughter, my pressure goes through the roof."

Mildred had opened an account that no one knew about: neither her family, nor her pastor.

"I can imagine. Just take a deep breath and calm down, though. We don't want anything to happen to you."

Gladys followed Kimberly's advice. After taking a breath, she asked, "Who was the beneficiary of this secret account?"

"Well, let me see." Kimberly's eyes bounced from one screen to the other. "There are five beneficiaries. Let me see. . . . Okay, here we go." Kimberly read from the screen. "Simone Banks, Boniqua Bunny Banks, Natallhya Banks, Gene Banks, and Rydah Banks. They will all have to sign, and the money will be divided up and disbursed in equal parts."

Next, Gladys asked the million-dollar question. "Well, how much money is it?"

"Oh." Kimberly said, "I'm not supposed to say."

"Who's going to know? I won't tell. And Mildred is dead, so she certainly can't rat you out." Gladys raised an eyebrow as if to say, *So what's the hold up?*

Kimberly glanced around to see if any of her coworkers were paying attention. After seeing that they were all dealing with customers or minding their own business, Kimberly said, "I can't give you the exact number, but it's north of one hundred thousand."

Gladys wasn't surprised that her sister had so much money squirreled away in a secret account. She confided in Kimberly that, "Mildred was always good with money. She lived like a miser. Me," she said, "I couldn't do it. I'm going to save what I can, but I like to see my money on my fingers, ears, in my house, and in my driveway."

Kimberly said, "You're not too bad at squirreling away money yourself."

"Yeah, but Mildred would rather live like a peasant so that damn grown-ass daughter of hers can live like a queen."

Kimberly said, "Do you mind if I ask you a question, Ms. Gladys?"

Mildred said, "Sure. You're like family. You can ask me anything."

"Why are you smiling? All of a sudden you started smiling when I told you how much money it was."

"I'm just thinking about my sister," she said. "Our momma used to tell us to never let your right hand know what your left hand is doing. I guess Mildred was listening. Everybody thought that she did all of her banking over at Consolidated

Trust and the Credit Union, and all the time she was hiding a fortune right under everybody's noses." *Mildred was smarter than we gave her credit for,* she thought. "That ol' false prophet done spent every dollar that was in the Consolidated Trust account."

"Well, thank God he didn't know about this account. Maybe it can help the girls get back on their feet."

"For sure." Gladys was pleased. "At least something is the way Mildred would have wanted it to be." She was delighted to discover that Pastor Street wouldn't be buying more G-strings and dildos on her sister's dime, but she also had her own business to take care of.

Kimberly handled all of Gladys's regular monthly transactions: she deposited her social security check and her late husband's pension, then wired funds to pay each of her bills. Gladys was never late with paying a bill. It was something she took pride in.

When it was all done, Gladys shook Kimberly's hand and said, "I'll see you next month." Then she adjusted her mink hat, cocking it to the perfect angle.

Before she left the bank, Kimberly asked Gladys to do her one favor.

"Sure," Gladys said. "What is it?"

"I want you to quietly find a way to let the girls know about. . ." Kimberly looked around to make sure no one was listening before continuing. "The new developments."

"Don't worry. I surely will. I will get in touch with them and ask them to call you directly."

"And I can take it from there," Kimberly assured her then turned to go help another customer, her heels click-clacking against the hardwood floor as she strutted away.

Gladys wasn't barely past the door of the house before she called her son down in Florida to let him know what was going on.

Chapter 10

Not A Good Idea

Weston

Rydah loved her parents more than anything in the world, but living under their roof for the past three weeks had been tougher than a microwaved two-dollar steak. She wasn't sure how much more of it she should or could take.

For starters, Rydah was expected to follow the same house rules she had to abide by when she was growing up. According to the church's schedule, dinner was served at 8 p.m. sharp, every single night, unless there was a conflict in her father's calendar. Everyone sat at the table at the same time and held hands as Daddy said the grace. This was non-negotiable. They ate and discussed current affairs and how everybody's day was. There were no phones allowed at the table or television going in the background, only quality time with the family.

Wolfe wasn't even allowed inside of her bedroom. Her parents seemed oblivious to the fact that she was a 28-year-old grown woman with a place of her own. Under their roof, she'd follow their rules and knew better than to even try to request any amendments to their rules.

Rydah felt like she'd forfeited her independence and her privacy at the front door, along with her sex life. When Wolfe ate dinner with them, Rydah could tell that he was tight and uncomfortable, but he'd rolled with the punches. One night after they'd eaten, she told Wolfe that she was horny.

Wolfe replied, "I may be a sinner to the core, but ain't no way I'm fit to get caught with my pants down in Bishop Banks' house."

On top of it all, Rydah was still mildly traumatized. Since the carjacking, she'd yet to drive, and she met with a therapist twice a week. Amanda and Wolfe took turns driving her to the sessions. On Wolfe's days, afterward he would take her out for lunch, sometimes a movie or shopping, just anything he could do to try to make her feel better.

In the evenings, he would come by around 7 p.m. and usually stayed until 11 or 12, chilling with her in the family room, playing backgammon or chess. Tonight they were watching *Family Feud* when the phone rang.

"Hello."

"O-M-G! You finally answered." The high-pitched voice on the other end of the phone belonged to Buffy. "I've been so worried about you," she said, trying her hardest to sound sympathetic. The only thing that transmitted through the phone line was disingenuousness.

"Is that right?"

Nosy-ass Buffy inquired about her whereabouts. "Are you at your parents' house?"

Why the fuck this bitch wants to know where I am? Rydah was about to tell a lie, but didn't. "Yep!"

"Can I come over?"

For a second, Rydah regretted admitting that she was at her parents' house, because she didn't want her bringing any B.S. over there. Then she thought again. She could send the dudes if she wanted to. However, Maestro, a gun collector, had an arsenal of assault rifles and though a churchman, he believed in "Stand Your Ground." Not to mention Wolfe, who'd been itching to murder the culprits. However, she knew that wasn't going down. Buffy had to know better.

Rydah cut her wandering thoughts and came back to the phone call at hand.

"Rydah, you there? I'm going to go ahead and head over that way."

Again, Rydah was honest.

"That probably wouldn't be a good idea," she said.

Buffy asked, "Why not? I want to come and check on my girl."

This bitch can't take a hint.

Rydah looked out the corner of her eye to see if Wolfe was paying her any mind. He was still watching Steve Harvey. "Honestly?" she said. "I just don't think that that would be a really good idea."

"Of course it's a good idea. I wanna come see you. We can have some girl talk. Maybe even drag you out to go to the club tonight."

Like, what the fuck?

"In case you didn't get the memo, Buffy, I just got carjacked three weeks ago. You and me going to a club together is a super long shot."

Turning away from the TV, Wolfe gave Rydah a *who the fuck is that?* look. She acted like she didn't see him.

"Well," Buffy said, "I don't wanna sound insensitive, but do you think you could get me on the guest list?"

Rydah chuckled a little longer than she meant to, because she was honestly at a loss for words.

Buffy was relentless. "No need for you to let your VIP connect fade away," she said, laughing.

Rydah looked at the phone as if it were a serpent, ready to strike. She was speechless, just holding the phone in disbelief.

"So unless you have a damn good reason," Buffy said, "no matter what you say, I'm coming over."

There was a list of things that Rydah wanted to say to Buffy, starting with, *Bitch, you must got bull nuts hanging between your legs.* And *you need to stay as far away from me as you can before Wolfe plants you in someone's flower garden.*

But instead, she said as easily and kindly as she could, "Because my mother thinks you set me up. So it goes without saying that you're not welcome at her house right now."

Buffy was momentarily as quiet as a cat burglar. Finally, she said, "Yeah! You right. Your mother gets real gangsta when it comes to her baby girl. Mad protective." Then Buffy asked the million-dollar question: "So do you think I had something to do with it?"

"I don't want to," Rydah said honestly.

Wolfe attempted to wrestle the phone away from her, but Rydah stood up, moving out of his grasp. They playfully struggled for it again. She mouthed the word *Stop.*

Wolfe was about to put her on his shoulders when the house phone rang. The call was from Virginia.

Rydah said to Buffy, "Hey, girl, I just got a call from my grandma in Virginia. I'll hit you back later." It was a perfect excuse to get off the phone.

Buffy got the last word in. "You know that I would never do anything to hurt you, right?"

Rydah acted as if she didn't hear her.

Click!

Then she answered the house phone, and the call from her Grandma Gladys would change her life forever.

Chapter 11

Out of the Cuckoo's Nest

Chesterfield, VA
aka: Arrest-erfield, VA

Shit! What the fuck am I really doing? Tallhya asked herself. *I know this shit ain't right, but what else am I supposed to do?* She pulled up beside the bank in a car she'd stolen from the valet at a Jehovah's Witness convention. *Bitch, you ain't got shit . . . therefore, you ain't got shit to lose.*

The Last Union Federal Bank. . . .

Tallhya looked at the time of the dashboard clock: 1:38 p.m. This time five days ago, she was in the nut house being fed anxiety pills, tranquilizers, and green Jell-O. When she found out that the hospital couldn't hold her against her will, she checked herself out immediately. Next, she called her sister Simone to get her share of the bank robbery money, only to find out that her cut was severely diminished.

Simone, who had been recently diagnosed with breast cancer, needed money desperately for the doctor and treatments. Simone hated stealing from her sister—especially after using the Baker Act to have her committed into the Westbrook Mental Hospital—but she had no choice. It was literally a life or death decision. She chose to live. Simone used the remainder of the money to do renovations on her late grandmother's house, which Simone and her cop husband were now living in. She would have to make amends with Tallhya later.

Tallhya didn't mind Simone using the money to get treatments and doing the necessary repairs on her childhood home, but she was pissed that Simone hadn't used any common sense and put away any of the hard-earned, ill-gotten money for her. Did Simone think she was never going to get out? However, she tried not to flip out too much, because after all, her sister was doing chemo and fighting for her life. At the end of the day, it was only money, she reasoned. It comes and goes. Simone would be her sister forever.

Besides, Tallhya blamed herself for allowing her sorry-ass, cheating, soon-to-be-ex-husband, Walter, to drive her crazy enough to have to be put in the nut house in the first place. If she hadn't flown over the cuckoo nest, she could've held on to her own cash. *Lesson well fucking learned.*

In the meantime, she had nothing, and in two days, she wouldn't even have anywhere to live. Going back to the house she grew up in to live with Simone and her new husband, Chase, wasn't an option she wanted to entertain. There were too many memories in that old house. Me-Ma was dead. Ginger was dead. Bunny was dead. She would go crazy for real, talking to the ghosts of all of her family members.

Tallhya had met a nice lady who was volunteering at the hospital. Her name was Dorsee Jackson. Tallhya and Dorsee hit it off immediately. She was the one that told Tallhya that the hospital couldn't keep her if she didn't want to be there. Dorsee also told her that, in her opinion, she didn't need all those drugs that they were feeding her. Tallhya stopped taking the pills and a week later checked out. Dorsee offered to give her a place to stay until she could get on her feet. She just failed to mention that room and board would cost $100 a week. Although it was not a lot of money, when there was no money, something as small as $100 seemed to be big. Tallhya had not one iron dime. Besides rent, she needed a phone, transportation, and new clothes. She'd lost a cool twenty pounds in the hospital—the one good thing she got out of being there—and could no longer fit any of her old things.

Tallhya wanted to kick herself for letting Walter swindle her out of her lottery winnings. The moment the money was gone, so was he, and that was the moment she went crazy. It was too much to handle at the time; seeing her husband hugged up with some bitch—a skinny bitch, at that, after he told her that he liked his women with some meat on them. *Just another one of his countless lies,* Tallhya mused. Life sucked, and she had no one to turn to, except doing what she knew how to do.

She pulled the ski mask down over a blond wig and then blew into the plastic gloves she'd swiped from the hospital before snapping one onto each shaky hand. As ready as she would ever be, Tallhya pulled the stolen Toyota in front of the small branch of the Last Union Federal Savings Bank, blocking the doorway. She sucked in on deep breath and hopped out the car.

As soon as she stepped her feet through the double doors of the Last Union Federal Bank, it was on and popping. Feeling invincible, she waltzed into the bank with a BB gun that looked real enough to get the job done—or get her killed. In her fragile and desperate state of mind, Tallhya was cool with either outcome. If she were dead, she would no longer have to worry about money. Heaven didn't charge for things like rent and wings, she hoped.

Inside the bank, there were only three customers. Two of them patiently waited in line while the only teller helped a lady in front. There was another bank employee, dressed in a neat little business suit, sitting in a glass cubicle. Tallhya surmised that she was the bank manager.

"Okay, bitches, get on the fucking floor!" Tallhya waved the BB gun around. "Don't make me say that shit again!" she shouted. "Next time I'm going to pop somebody in the ass to show you that this ain't no fucking joke." Her adrenaline pumped blood through her body like crazy. But no one thought that she was joking. Her eyes, big and wild, weren't the eyes of a person trying to get a laugh. They were the eyes of a person that had nothing to lose.

Once the customers, the teller, and the manager were on the floor, Tallhya leaned over the counter and grabbed a handful of cash out the first drawer. But that wasn't enough. "Get up!" she said to the customer that the teller had been waiting on when she walked in. Tallhya gave her a bag. "Empty both drawers and put the money in here. And don't get stupid over someone else's money. You understand?"

The customer shook her head. She was in the bank simply trying to cash a check; she didn't want to die for anybody's money. Not even her own. "I'll do whatever you say. Just please, please don't hurt me."

"Bitch," she said to the teller, "step away from the damn counter. You ain't setting off no silent alarm today." She saw the teller out of the side of her eye with a stupid look on her face, like she had been busted. That didn't stop Tallhya. She was on a roll.

"You?" She motioned to the lady that had been sitting in the glass cubicle. "Go to the vault and fill this bag up." The bank manager caught the bag that Tallhya had tossed to her. Tallhya walked with her to the vault to keep her honest. Petrified, the bank manager did exactly what Tallhya instructed her to do.

Once both bags were filled, Tallhya took the money and headed for the exit.

Everything went over smoothly. In less than four minutes, she was back in the car. Tallhya tossed the bags on the floor and peeled off.

"Thank you, God!" She didn't find it odd at all to be thanking God for a successful bank robbery.

Driving, trying not to get noticed, she turned up the spiritual music and began to sing a Kirk Franklin song. Until that moment, she hadn't even known that she knew the words, but she sang it like her life depended on it.

"Thank you, Jesus," she said, praising God.

Then, the dye-pack went off. The noise startled her.

"Oh, shit! God damn! What the fuck?" She couldn't help herself, screaming over the gospel music.

In a blink of an eye, the car was inundated with a pink dye. It was everywhere. Smoke took over the interior of the car, even inside Tallhya's mouth and nose, making it difficult for her to see or breathe.

Endless coughing turned into choking, and her eyes were burning. It was unbearable. Tallhya couldn't see where she was going, because the dye had smeared on the windshield like blood. The smoke and the dye did their job overtime.

Boom!

There was a hard bump, and it felt like the entire bottom of the car fell out. Unbeknownst to her, she had driven the car up on the sidewalk and ran head-on into a blue US Post Office mailbox. After she realized that she was okay, she thanked God it wasn't a person she'd hit and that she wasn't dead.

Struggling with all her might, she forced the door open and ran for cover. She was sure the car was going to blow up. She ran into the nearby woods and kept running. She thanked God for Daylight Savings Time and that it was getting dark early.

She disappeared into the sunset and the deep forest, took off her coat and wig. Once she was deep into the trees, she peeled off the gloves and got out of dodge. The blond wig kept the dye out of her real hair, but she still desperately needed a shower.

An hour later, Tallhya checked into a seedy hotel on Jefferson Davis Highway that supplied rooms to crackheads, dope fiends, and prostitutes turning quick tricks. Tallhya took so many showers that the hot water ran out.

Having to leave the bags of money from the bank in the car and only having the cash that she leaned over the counter and took herself, Tallhya had only $210 to her name. She used the money to purchase another week at Dorsee's and get a few groceries.

And the circle was complete. She was back where she started when the day began: broke as joke.

She thought about all that she'd been through, and an overwhelming flood of emotions hit her. She tried to keep the tears from rolling down her face, but the effort was useless.

"God . . . why me?" Tallhya stared upward, toward the cracked ceiling. "I wanna do right," she said to whoever was listening. She dropped to her knees, onto a cheap, worn-out red carpet and said, "Help me, Lord! Help me, Jesus! Jehovah! Father, in the name of Jesus, help me." A steady stream of tears stained her face. "Lord, help me!"

Her prepaid cell phone rang, interrupting her monologue with the All Seeing. When she answered, an automated message said, "You have six minutes remaining."

"Fuck." Could she catch one break? Just one?

"Hello . . . Tallhya?

"Gladys?"

"Don't you recognize your aunt's voice? Lord have mercy," said Gladys, "it hasn't been that long, has it?"

"Of course I recognize your voice, Aunt Gladys. I was just distracted by something."

"Girl, you too young to be distracted by anything but one of them fine young men out there with a good job and love for the Lord. I wish I was your age again."

Tallhya cut her off. "I only have a few minutes, Auntie. I'm on a prepaid."

"A what?" Gladys had no idea what that meant.

"I only have five minutes left on my phone before it cuts off. I have to put some more money on it."

"Well, I have good news."

Chapter 12

Remembrance

Glenn Allen, VA

Established in 1958, Roselawn is a fairly modern cemetery. The lush, manicured grounds, which are aptly named
Memory Gardens, have a spiritual air about them. It's a
certain peacefulness that helps to comfort the mind and soul
of the deceased and their visitors. Those were just a couple of
the reasons why Mildred "Me-Ma" Banks, while she was alive,
chose this particular cemetery for her body to rest once she
was ready to embark on her pilgrimage to heaven.

Chase wheeled the black SRT Grand Cherokee onto the cemetery grounds. Simone sat quietly in the front seat of the SUV,
looking off to her right, staring out the window. The cabin of the
truck was quiet; the couple hadn't spoken for the past 45 minutes, since leaving the house this morning.

After pulling into a parking spot, Chase held Simone's hand.
He could feel the perspiration. He asked, "Are you ready to do
this?"

She wasn't. This was her first time here since Ginger's
funeral. Ginger and Bunny were buried right next to Me-Ma.
Simone had seen to it. After all, she knew that family meant
more to Me-Ma than anything in the world, next to God.

The two got out of the SUV together. Simone exhaled. The
morning was mildly pleasant; the temperature was hovering
around 76 degrees, capped with a beautiful azure, cloudless
sky. Birds sang as they foraged for food and crickets chirped,
trying not to become breakfast for their feathered foe.

She said, "Yes. As ready as I'll ever be."

Chase got out and went around to the passenger's side of the jeep and opened the door for Simone to exit the vehicle. Once she did, he opened the back door, too, and reached into the back seat for the picnic basket Simone had prepared last night. Together, they held hands and walked side by side toward the graves. They'd been married for only a couple of months, but their love was as strong and authentic as a couple that had known each other all of their lives. Love is not measured by time, but how that time is spent together. At least that was the way Simone felt about the subject.

Less than twenty-five yards from where they parked, Simone laid a quilt on the freshly-cut grass, wet with morning dew. It was one of Me-Ma's quilts, hand sewn. From the basket, Simone removed Me-Ma's leather Bible. It was visibly aged, like she was, but strong and dependable, also like she was. Besides the Bible, she removed a single flower from the basket: a purple daisy.

"This is for you," she said, laying the flower onto the head-stone. Daisies were Me-Ma's favorite blossom, and purple was symbolic of royalty. Without question, Me-Ma had been, and always would be, the queen and matriarch of the Banks family.

Simone opened the worn Bible and leafed through the pages until she came upon the passage she wanted: Psalm 91. She read the full Bible passage to her grandmother. When she was done with the reading, both she and Chase, in unison, said "Amen." Simone then kissed her hand and caressed Me-Ma's stone.

Bunny's grave was to Me-Ma's immediate right. When it was time to show her respects to Bunny, Simone put the Bible away, replacing it with an expensive bottle of red wine and three crystal goblets. Simone opened the wine, pouring the fermented grapes into each of the glasses. She set a glass on Bunny's stone, along with a red rose, kept a glass for herself, and handed the last one to her husband.

She toasted: "To family and bad bitches."

Chase touched goblets with his wife. "Amen to that," he said. "Family and bad women. But none finer than my wife," he added, with a consoling kiss on the lips.

Simone sighed. "Bunny loved life so much . . . and so hard," she lamented. "It's hard to believe that she took her own life."

Chase shook his head. "She was so young, also." He was the one who'd found her. He stumbled upon the body in a hotel room while investigating another case. She'd apparently overdosed on a handful of pain pills after finding out that her boyfriend had been murdered and then getting revenge on the person she felt responsible for taking his life.

Chase shared a private thought with Simone, one he'd had on more than one occasion, but never shared, until now. "Sometimes I wonder if somehow I could have saved her. . . ." he said. "If my investigation would have drawn me to the hotel sooner."

Simone thought about what he said. She'd had similar thoughts about ways things may have been different, but deep down, she knew that there was nothing anyone could have done.

She told her husband, "I don't believe that God makes mistakes. He makes things happen exactly the way He wants them to happen. So there was nothing that you, me, or anyone else could have done to change the outcome of what happened."

Slowly, Chase nodded his head. He wasn't a big church guy, but he believed in God. "I guess you're right."

"To my sister Bunny, I don't know why you would do this, in this way. You leave me with so many unanswered questions." Tears formed in her eyes. "But I hope you are at peace finally!" She cried as she poured the rest of the bottle of wine out.

"Baby, don't cry. She's okay. She's with Me-Ma and Ginger."

Not wanting to cry, she tried to suck it up. Simone smiled. "I know that's right. Let us pay our respects to Ginger and get out of here before we guilt ourselves into having a bad day." She was already going into the picnic basket.

Chase said, "Cool. Let's do that."

Simone had brought a rainbow-like Cattleya orchid for Ginger's grave. The flower was indigenous to Costa Rica. It was exotic, over the top, and bold: all the things that made Ginger who she was. Along with the flower, Simone had a copy of *Vogue* magazine with her favorite celebrity donning the cover: The original Don Dada herself, Mrs. Beyoncé Knowles-Carter. Simone read the interview to Ginger before packing up.

As she was putting the things back into the picnic basket, she couldn't help but think if it was symbolic that she was there because she would be joining them soon. After all, she was in the middle of having chemo treatments, and at this point, it could very much go either way. Before she got into feeling sorry for herself, she decided to say a few final words and get out of there.

"To missing my family," Simone said. As she zoned out at her sisters' and grandmother's grave she added, "I have no one but you, Chase."

"And I'm never going to leave you. You are my angel, and I love you more than life itself."

"Thank you, baby." Having him by her side was all she needed, though she really wished she didn't have to be there at all and that she had her sisters there with her. But it truly meant the world to her that he was so supportive and by her side.

The phone rang again, and she looked down at it. "Aunt Gladys?"

"See, I'm not the only one you have." Chase tried to make her feel better.

"Yes." She nodded with a smile. "Aunt Gladys is always right on time."

That she sure was!

Chapter 13

Glamma Gladys

Rydah took an Uber to her grandmother's house. It had been more than two decades since the last time she went there. When she was seven years old and school was out for the summer, Rydah's mother and father had taken her to New York to see the Broadway play *Annie*. On the way back from the Big Apple, they stopped in VA to visit Grandma Gladys. The house was just as she remembered it. White stucco with pink shutters and huge statues of Jesus and Mary standing vigilant in the front yard on either side of the stone steps.

Rydah rang the bell. Lights were on inside the house, but no one came to the door. She punched the button a few more times.

Ding-dong. Ding-dong. Ding-dong.

She thought that she heard noises coming from inside, but still, no one answered. Puzzled, she knocked on the door and rang the doorbell again. Nothing.

Maybe she'd imagined the noise, she thought. She was certain that this was the right address. A car was on the side of the house, covered up. She could tell from the shape that it was her grandfather's Thunderbird. The car was a timeless piece of history in their family. It was one of the reasons she had such a deep passion for cars. She wondered if it still ran. If it didn't, she would fix it.

In the driveway, a brand-new, shiny Cadillac was parked. The vanity plate read *MsG2U*. Rydah had to give it to her. Grandma Gladys never disappointed. The woman was the hippest senior citizen that she knew. This was definitely the right house, but why wasn't she answering the door?

She reflected back to her conversation before leaving Miami:

"*Hey, Glamma.*"

"*Hello, baby.*"

"*I hate to wake you. I know it's super early.*" It was 7:10 a.m.

"*I've been up for a couple of hours now, baby. Just sitting here, having my morning coffee, reading the obituaries. What time do I have to pick you up from the airport?*"

"*My flight leaves in another hour. I should arrive at about eleven o' clock. But I don't need you to come and get me. I'm gonna get a rental.*"

"*I won't hear of it. I'll be there to get you.*"

"*No need, Glamma. I'm gonna need a car to drive around while I'm there anyway.*"

Gladys said, "*You will drive my car wherever you want to go. You can put as many miles on it as you need to.*"

"*And what are you going to drive?*"

"*Chile, don't back talk me. When I pass away, I'm leaving it to you. It's already in my will. So you might as well get used to it.*"

"*Don't talk like that, Glamma. You're not going anywhere anytime soon. Probably outlive us all.*"

"*Thank you, baby, but I'm still not allowing you to drive no rental car while you staying with me. You hear me?*"

"*Okay. Let's compromise then. I'll use my Uber app to schedule a ride from the airport, and I'll use your car once I'm there. But,*" Rydah said, "*that's only if you let me treat you to lunch today.*"

"*I guess I can live with those arrangements. But if you don't get that Uber, make sure you call. If not, you're going to be in big trouble. And trouble with me isn't what you want.*"

Rydah hoped her grandmother hadn't gone to the airport, but if that were the case, her car wouldn't be in the driveway. Rydah put her ear to the door. The TV was on. She knocked again.

When her grandmother finally answered, Gladys smelled like a mixture of White Diamonds perfume and cigarette smoke.

Gladys gave her a big hug. "Girl, you's as pretty as a flower. Let me look at cha."

"Glamma, you been smoking?"

"Nope."

Rydah followed Gladys through the foyer, past the living and dining rooms, and into the family room. The family room smelled like tobacco smoke.

Rydah gave her grandmother side-eye. "You know good and well that you not supposed to be smoking. "

"Now, listen. . . ."

Rydah wasn't trying to hear it. "If you promise to cut back, I won't tell my father that you been smoking like a chimney. And you know he's going to flip, and my mother will lecture you, so . . . oooh, you know how she goes on and on with those lectures. Trust me, you don't want that."

"Wait a minute, missy. I'm your grandmother."

"And I love you to life for being such a great influence on me. And out of respect, I won't give you a lecture on why smoking is like committing a slow but deliberate suicide. Don't you see the warning on the sides of the pack?"

Gladys said, "You a li'l sassy thing, ain't ya?"

"Yup! Just like my glamma," she said, trying to get back on her good side.

"Flattery will get you everywhere. Now, let me get myself dressed so we can start this process to get you your money."

"Thank you, Glamma." Rydah kissed her on the cheek

"Girl, you don't have to thank me. I'm just trying to make sure you get what's yours."

Rydah smiled at her grandmother then blurted out, "What are they like?"

"Who? Your sisters?"

Rydah dropped her head shamefully. "I've never wanted to hurt my parents' feelings by trying to push the fact that I do have siblings."

"Well . . ." Gladys sucked in a deep breath. "Baby, you should live for you. They will understand."

"It's just that I never felt like I was adopted. Ever. Like, never ever! My parents love and accept me for who I am, and the truth is, I've never really inquired about my real family, because I know for a fact that they could never be better than the one I have now."

"Hummmmmph. You got that right." Gladys started to say something, but then she remembered her promise to her son. Maestro made it clear that he wanted Rydah to make her own decisions and develop her own feelings about her sisters. Amanda, on the other hand, felt that Deidra was the scum of the Earth and didn't trust any of them. But Maestro had made his wishes final, and they both agreed that Rydah was a smart girl and that it was best for her to form her own opinion.

"But I do sometimes wonder what my birth mother is like."

"Chile . . ." Gladys chuckled, fanning Rydah off. "Now, my grandmother told me that if you can't say nothing nice, don't say nothing at all. So my lips are sealed tighter than a Ziploc bag."

"And you always told me that the least you could do for a person is to be honest with them."

"You too much, girl. You know that?"

Gladys had always thought her granddaughter was God's gift to the world, and being with her made her remember why she loved this little lady so much.

"Waaaiiiiting . . ." Rydah sang in her sweetest voice, batting mink eyelashes.

Gladys looked her granddaughter over and just admired her. She was beautiful, smart, kind, put-together, and most of all, she was nobody's fool. She knew what Maestro had requested, but at the end of the day, she was *his* mother and the matriarch of the family. And she was more concerned about the wellbeing of her granddaughter that any half-baked promise she may have agreed to.

"Well, Deidra . . ." she said with a disgusted look on her face. "Yuck!" she said in such a nasty tone, out of her normally loving, grandmotherly voice. "The monster that gave birth to you?"

Rydah didn't respond. She just looked at her grandmother and got a kick out of her rolling her eyes at the thought of Deidra, her birth mother.

"Humph . . ." She sucked her teeth. "Chile, please! That thing ain't worth the dirt on a snake's belly. And I'd trust my hemorrhoids more than I'd trust her."

Rydah laughed so hard she almost cried. "Glamma, you know you not right."

"I'm dead serious, girl. And I was being nice because the woman is your blood. Trust me, you don't want to know her. I never saw a wench so low down and dirty. She uses everybody in the most extreme way. Your *brista* was a scammer. Deidra got him to steal all this designer stuff for her and some man, then left him at the mall when he got caught."

"His momma did that?"

"That's not even a small slice of the shitty pie. Deidra never sent the boy one dime. And your no self-esteem-having over-weight sister Tallhya . . ."

"Glamma, don't say that."

"Well, it's true. She pretty. All of them pretty. You look like them, too. Well, your mother slept with the fat sister's husband. That's what drove your sister to the crazy house."

"Are you kidding?"

"No, ma'am. I'm certainly not. I have to go pick her up to take her to the bank as well, so you'll meet her."

"I'm excited."

"She's actually sweet. Kind of gullible, but will give you the shirt off of her back."

Rydah asked, "What about Simone?"

"She has breast cancer and is doing chemo. I spoke to her husband, Chase. He took her to the bank this morning to sign her necessary documents."

"She's married? Does she have children?"

"No children. And I don't know why that girl jumped the broom so damn quick. Maybe she wanted those cop benefits. You know that the state has good insurance and such. I don't know."

"How long she been married?"

"Not long at all. As soon as she got sick, she got married a few days later. She went to the Justice of the Peace, which was very surprising to me, because she's always been a high-class kind of girl. Her daddy—God bless his soul—Simon raised her like her farts never stank. And when he passed, her stepmother took everything she had, including the underwear out her dresser, and sent her packing to Me-Ma's."

"That's sad." Rydah's heart went out to Simone, and she hadn't even met her yet.

"Maybe so, but it made her wise up. And you know how they say so-and-so beat somebody like they stole something. Marjorie did steal something, and I heard that Simone beat the break dust off of that child."

"What about Bunny?"

Gladys dropped her head. "Bunny and Gene both passed away. Gene is your brista—sometimes your brother, some- times your sister. But I will let Simone tell you about that."

"And Bunny?"

"She took her own life."

"Why?"

"Because she was into a lot of deep, dark hell and . . . I think depression over the guy she was dating or something. It never made any sense to me, but I'll let Simone tell you about that when she has enough energy. Just was very sad."

Rydah was temporarily quiet. "She committed suicide?"

"I'm afraid so." Gladys dropped her head. "Umph, umph, umph! She was such a beautiful girl, so full of life."

"Okay. Yes, ma'am." Rydah accepted the info her grand- mother shared with her. She didn't push, but she really wanted to know more.

"Well, I will call and check on Simone and see if she is up for dinner. And if she is, I will make you all your favorite things and you can have some personal, quality time bonding with Simone—and Tallhya, too, if she can come over after. So for now, let's get pretty and get to the bank before it gets too late."

They got dressed, and her grandmother stopped her at the door. "Where is your jacket?" Gladys asked her granddaughter as if she were still seven years old.

"I didn't bring one. Guess I wasn't thinking." With the need to explain herself to her grandmother, she said, "It was ninety degrees in Miami when I left. And it's March. Shouldn't winter be gone?"

Gladys shot her a look. "Girl, that's Miami and this is Virginia, two entirely different worlds. You will not get sick on my watch." Gladys did a beeline to her cedar walk-in closet. "I think I have a mink wrap you can throw over your shoulders so you won't catch a cold."

"Glammmmmm. . . ." Rydah felt like a little girl in the Barbie store. All of the endless furs, in all styles, colors, and shapes. "O-M-G! If I die, just bury me here. Glam, did you will me these, too?"

"Sure did," Gladys proudly said. "A couple to your mother, but most of them to you."

"Put this wrap on and let's get to the bank."

Rydah picked up a beret-style mink hat that matched the wrap her grandmother suggested she wore. "Is it okay for me to take this?"

"That old thing is older than you, sweet pie, but you can help yourself to anything you like."

"Well, here's to vintage." Rydah adjusted the mink beret over her hair, which was styled in Indique tresses that fell down her back. After getting the angle just right, she said, "I've got unfinished business with this closet when we return." The thought of scavenging through her grandmother's closet excited her as much as the perfectly rebuilt engine of a 1970 Mercury Cyclone GT.

Chapter 14

Identical

"Why is Tallhya staying here?"

The parking lot of the hotel was littered with needles and crack vials. Gladys pulled into a parking space near the front. A prostitute, walking with a trick, strolled by the car. The prostitute glanced nervously into the window of Gladys's Cadillac, making sure it wasn't the vice in an unmarked car. Satisfied that Gladys and Rydah weren't po-po, the prostitute—wearing a purple wig and a tight-fitting purple polyester dress, with concave cheeks and dark, lifeless eyes—pulled her trick along by the hand. She was Tallhya's age. Six months ago, before getting hooked on smack, she was a young fly stallion with all the answers. Now she was not only out of answers, but she was also devoid of hope.

Gladys said, "Don't make me into no liar."

Tallhya popped out of room 218 looking tired and disheveled. She waved down below, then took the stone stairs to the parking lot. When she climbed into the back seat of the Caddy, Gladys said, "This is your sister, Rydah. Rydah, this is your sister, Tallhya."

The siblings looked into each other's eyes for the very first time, and both girls instantly felt a familial connection. For a moment, Tallhya thought that she was on the brink of really going crazy again. Not only did Rydah have the Banks sisters' piercing grey eyes, Tallhya observed, but she was also the spitting image of their elder sister, Bunny, who had recently committed suicide after her boyfriend was murdered. Tallhya had to pinch herself to make sure she was awake. But would that work if she were seeing a ghost? She didn't know.

Rydah said, "Nice to meet you, finally."

Tallhya was still trying to discern whether she was smack dead in the middle of a bad dream, or if things were possibly turning around. First, Gladys had called her about some money that Me-Ma supposedly had squirrelled away. God only knew how badly she needed the money. And now she was sitting behind a sister that she never knew she had, that just so happened to look exactly like a sister she'd just lost.

Tallhya was mesmerized by the likeness. Bunny was drop-dead gorgeous in every conceivable way, yet somehow, Rydah was ten times finer . . . more polished. She was stunningly beautiful: skin that looked as if it could star in an Oil of Olay commercial without filters, teeth straight from the Colgate box, hair spun like silk, and the aura of a movie star. Tallhya couldn't pull her eyes away.

Although Rydah and Bunny looked so similar, Rydah seemed to be sweeter, and her confidence was through the roof. She was everything that Tallhya dreamed of being. There was something about Rydah's energy and personality that motivated Tallhya, making her want better for herself. Her feelings weren't motivated by jealousy, envy, or sibling competition. She just wanted what her sister had, but in her own way.

Tallhya was a little nervous when they went into the bank, but Kimberly made her feel comfortable. The formalities of signing the paperwork went over that easily.

Kimberly's eyes were glued on Rydah. "It's unbelievable how you two look alike." Kimberly and Bunny had gone to school together. "Other than your hair being different, the two of you could be twins."

That's when the light bulb went off for Tallhya.

All of the Banks girls had similar characteristics. Even her brother, Ginger, was gorgeous. Tallhya figured that all she had to do was lose weight—a few pounds gone and she would be fine as well.

At that moment, she decided that regardless of what it took, she was gong to get slim.

Chapter 15

Reunited

"This calls for a celebration!" Gladys said. Her skin was glowing. "I got a real nice bottle of wine chilling on ice, and I've set the table with my good China." She admired her spread.

Gladys had cooked everything herself. All the food was placed down the middle of her Mahogany formal dining room table, which sat twelve people. Lobsters, grilled and blackened salmon, shrimp prepared three different ways (fried, steamed, and grilled), scallops, mussels, mixed vegetables, corn on the cob, sweet and baked potatoes . . .

"Looks like Versace china, Glam."

"You already know," Simone said, taking a seat. "Aunt Gladys has always been over-the-top fancy. You can't tell that lady nothing when it comes to some fly shit."

All Tallhya noticed was the food. While her mother often looked hungrily at things with dollar signs in her eyes, there were shrimp in her eyes, telling the story of how she was about to devour that food.

"You got everything!" she said, joining her sister Simone. "Aunt Gladys, you know you shouldn't be doing this to a fat girl."

Rydah said, "Girl, when you go with me back to Miami in a couple of weeks, I got a doctor that's going to fix you right up. He's the same doctor that those celebrity chicks are going to. So you might as well indulge, girl." Rydah admired the food. "Glammmm, this is too fab. You really outdid yourself," she said, giving her grandmother a kiss on the cheek.

Gladys started serving the food. "I ain't outdid nothing," she said. "Glad to do it. Like I said, we're celebrating. You girls only get to meet each other for the first time once. Shoot, it's the least I could do. I'm happy that you girls are united and love each other and all that good stuff. So enough with the thanks, let's just enjoy ourselves."

The girls ate until they felt as if they would pop. Once they were stuffed, Gladys told Rydah to take them to the den. However, Simone insisted that they go out on the screened-in porch so she could smoke her medical marijuana.

"The only perk of cancer," she said after inhaling her first toke of the night.

Gladys came out with a tray of glasses filled with wine and limeade, then doubled back to get chocolate cake, sweet potato pie, and apple pie. "For the munchies," she said.

"Glam, what you know about some munchies?"

"They ain't just start smoking pot this decade, girl. Keep sleeping on your grandma if you want. I've been telling you for the last thirty years that I don't miss much of anything."

Rydah feigned an eye roll. "Excuse me," she said.

Simone got up and gave Gladys a hug. "We appreciate you."

Gladys fanned her off. "That's what family is for, girl."

"And these limeades are the best," Tallhya said. "Always have been." She looked up to the sky. "I know Me-Ma up there smiling at you, Aunt Gladys." Being with Gladys reminded her of how much she missed Me-Ma. Tallhya smiled and looked to Rydah. "Me-Ma knows you would have loved her."

"I know. My grandmother always used to talk about how wonderful she was," Rydah said as Gladys had exited the room.

It felt a little awkward to the girls that Rydah, who was their blood sister, kept referring to their grandaunt, Gladys, as her grandmother. She could see the looks on their faces, but it was her reality.

"Me-Ma was real churchy, but she had a heart of gold," Tallhya said. "She wouldn't hurt nobody, just better not mess with her grand-girls, I know that much! I swear, I miss her so much." Just the thought of Me-Ma made Tallhya's face light up.

"Makes me sad to think about her, she was so wonderful," Simone added. "Since I lived with my dad, I went over there on the weekends and every other Sunday. She made me feel like I was her favorite." She smiled.

"But in fact, she made us all think we were her favorites in her own way. We all accused each other of being her favorite, because she protected us like we were her own cubs." Simone took a pull of her weed. "Now that I think about it, it was probably because she knew Deidra wasn't shit."

"Where is Deidra nowadays?" Tallhya asked, holding her breath.

"Chile, please," she replied, sucking her teeth. "Nobody seen her in a few weeks now." Simone took a long pull of her medical marijuana and reveled in knowing exactly what had happened to Deidra's no-good ass. "Wherever she at, though, trust me, she better off there than here with us."

"It's her normal shit," Tallhya added, shaking her head. "Always have been. Dashing in and out of lives, disappearing—and when she returns, it's empty-handed. Probably somewhere scamming some damn body. Doing some fucking lowlife shit right now as we speak."

"Yup, that's Deidra for ya. Thieving and manipulating," Simone said, blowing the smoke out of her mouth.

"Deidra needs to stop that shit before somebody kills her ass." Tallhya put her two cents in. She hadn't the foggiest idea that her sisters had already whacked Deidra and had no remorse for it.

"Damn . . ." was all Rydah could say. "She sounds pretty bad. She can't possibly, *reallyyyy* be that bad?"

Both Simone and Tallhya said in unison, "Worse!"

"Unlike anything you would ever believe, and because this is supposed to be such a great moment of us being together getting to know each other, we won't waste any more of our time together talking about her. Let's just sum it up: the best thing she did for us was give us life and our good looks, honey," Simone said.

"I concur." Tallhya raised her glass and handed Rydah hers. "To sisterhood."

"Sisterhood!" The ladies toasted.

Rydah was almost scared to tell the girls how great her mother was. She was secretly relieved that Deidra was the worst and she hadn't had the opportunity of meeting her own mother. *Damn shame,* she thought to herself.

"Consider yourself lucky that you never crossed your paths with that sorry-ass bitch," Tallhya said. "I told my therapist that that bitch is dead to me."

"You still salty about Walter's lying, cheating ass?" Simone asked.

"Yes, I am," Tallhya said bluntly. "I sure am!"

"Cheating with Deidra just put the nail in the coffin?"

"Yup. Sure did."

Simone just looked at her sister, and Rydah listened and watched them both. They had the same exact features, eyes and nose, just completely different weights, hairstyles, and personalities.

"I feel better about me, but . . . not him," she said matter-of-factly.

"And aren't you 1033 crazy?"

"Sure is!"

Like a tennis match, Rydah watched her two long lost sisters go back and forth.

"Meaning your crazy ass can probably kill somebody and get away with it?"

"Yup, and not do one day in the pen . . ." Tallhya nodded with a sinister smile. "I could kill your ass with my bare hands for taking me to a goddamn psychiatric facility and telling them people to Baker Act me. . . . Yup, sure could kill your ass dead!" She hit her sister with a playful punch.

"Ummmm . . . you can't beat on a sick woman." Simone tried to be quick on her feet, but she couldn't find the words.

"Oh. any excuse will do. Don't worry, you know-it-all bitch, I won't! I'm not going to kill you, or Walter, for that matter."

With a raised eyebrow, Simone asked, "Really?" She gave a sigh of relief.

"No, you safe. But don't worry, I'm going to get *his* ass. In God you trust, or bet your last dollar that I've got plans for Walter. He's going to pay for exactly what he done to me. . . ." The room was silent. "And he needs to be alive."

"Ummmm . . . do share with us what you're going to do to him."

"I'm going to give him and the world the very best version of myself. Going to be so damn fine, stomach going to be flat and waist going to be *snatched* to the motherfucking gawds, booty popping, boobs sitting up perky. That's what the motherfucker's punishment is going to be." She let out a bewitching laughter. "It gets me high just thinking about how he ain't going to never ever be able to smell the puss ever in this lifetime!"

"That's right, sister," Rydah added. "Sometimes you have to make them sorry, even if they never say sorry."

"Yes, that's why I really need you. I need you to take me to that doctor, you know the one on Instagram that all the celebrities and strippers go to?"

"Dr. Slim Jim or Dr. Snatch or somebody?"

"Yup, him. Sister, I really need you to do this for me. I just need you to give me a ride to the place, let me get my consultation and date, and take me back and let me stay with you until I heal." Tallhya was so passionate in her spiel.

Honestly, when Tallhya referred to Rydah as a sister, that was all Rydah needed to hear. There was something about the word *sister* that just warmed her heart. Growing up as an only child was always hard. Girlfriends who claimed that they were "sisters" came and went and took their sisterhood lightly. Inside, she had always yearned for a real sister, who, no matter what, was bonded to her by blood.

"I got you, sister. Trust me, with Dr. Snatch you going to give not just Walter a heart attack, but all these men and women alike."

"Yesssssss. Check can't clear fast enough!"

Simone gave her sister five. "That's right!"

"Yup, that motherfucker . . . the nerve of him . . . nope, not anymore." For a second, her mind started to venture off into those awful Walter memories, and then Tallhya had a light bulb moment, turned to Rydah, and asked, "As a matter of fact, you think if I ask Auntie Gladys to keep my share of the money, she would?"

"I'm sure she would. Why? What's going on?"

"This motherfucker won't give me my divorce, and he has my money tied up and is trying to come after everything I got.

Being that Simone had me committed, it just didn't make me
look good in the court's eyes, and they gave him control over
my motherfucking money. Makes me so freaking angry every
time I think about it. So, as soon as I get my money from the
Me-Ma situations, what if I gift it to Aunt Gladys?"

"I'm sure it's no problem. But yeah, let's ask her."

Rydah ate, talked, and laughed with her sisters and grandmother. With all the post-traumatic stress and feelings after
the carjacking, it was the first time she had laughed in a long
time. There was something about smelling the Virginia air
that made her happy, or maybe it was just the love of her
grandmother and the feeling of having sisters. She sat and
enjoyed the moment until they heard the doorbell. Honestly,
the sisters didn't care who it was. No one else in the world
mattered but them.

Then, Chase entered into the room, with a strange look on
his face.

"Hey baby! What's wrong?" Simone noticed the stressed
look on his face.

Chase was a really good guy and loved every single thing
about Simone, even the toilet she shitted on. He was a police
officer on the Richmond Police Department and had an idea
about Simone and her sisters' shady past with the bank robberies, as he had been the head investigator. He loved Simone
so much that he told her, "Listen, I'm not sure what your role
was in this whole fiasco of these bank robberies, but I'm going
to let it go. Just make sure it never happens again."

And since then, she had been keeping her hands clean.
She knew that if he dug deeper, he could possibly put her in
prison for the rest of her life, but once he found out that she
had been diagnosed with cancer, he told her he didn't want
lose her, and he had taken care of her ever since. If she survived cancer, and their relationship survived the treatments
and the deadly disease, she would indeed marry him.

Chase insisted that they go to the Justice of the Peace and
get married, and promised her a huge wedding after she beat
cancer.

What did she have to lose? She had no family, really; no
parents, and having lost a sister and a brother only days apart.

The security of knowing she had someone in her corner who loved her to death was enough for her. But knowing everything that she and her sisters had done, and the things that she had manipulated and masterminded, the best thing for her to do was quit while she was ahead. She had a significant other on her side, and the fact that he just happened to be a cop in her pocket was the icing on the cake. Not to mention, the stability on his job and benefits and insurance didn't hurt at all.

"It's bad, babe," he said to Simone with a lump in his throat.

"What is it, honey?" Maintaining a poker face, Simone had all kinds of things running through her mind.

What the fuck is it? What could it be? Is he coming to lock me up? Has he found out about the banks me and my sisters robbed? Then she told herself, *Girl, keep it together. What's worse than cancer?*

"It's your mother." He cleared his throat. "It's Deidra."

"Deidra?" Tallhya asked, shocked. "Well, what the fuck that bitch done did now?"

"She's dead . . ." He paused. "We found a few parts of her body, but enough to identity her with dental records."

"Parts?" Rydah questioned. "Parts?"

"Damn, wouldn't you know it? All of Deidra's bullshit finally came around," Simone said, knowing good and well that she wasn't surprised. She tried hard to think about having cancer and the effects it had taken on her body so she could get some tears, but they wouldn't come right away.

Rydah sat, astonished, then asked, "Are y'all okay?"

Chase's eyes looked at Rydah. She was drop dead gorgeous and resembled the Banks sisters, but she had a certain hotness about her.

Rydah saw Chase looking at her. She had not been formally introduced to him, so she attempted to make light of the situation. "Hi. I'm Rydah, from Miami. I'm their sister. Deidra sold me at birth, so we just met today, and we're bonding. Long story, but that just about sums it up. How are you doing?" She reached to shake his hand.

"Chase," he said, extending his hand. "I'm your brother-in-law. Sorry we had to meet under these circumstances."

"Right?" Rydah said, shaking her head.

"Damn, I knew this day was coming, but didn't think it would be this soon." Tears appeared in Tallhya eyes.

"I'm sorry, Tallhya." Rydah hugged her. "I'm sooooo sorry."

Simone got up and hugged her sister too.

Gladys came in to comfort the girls. On that note, Gladys said, "I know for a fact that Mildred had a life insurance policy on her, too."

Tallhya's tears dried up. "God be working in mysterious ways. He knew I needed this good news."

"Good news?" Rydah questioned. "I know Deidra was a bad excuse for somebody's mother, but her dying isn't good news, is it?"

"No, but if you knew where I was two days ago, how bad Deidra really was, and how bad off and desperate I was, then you would understand."

"She really was a greedy piece of shit," Simone said, "and nobody with a loving mother like what I'm sure yours is would ever understand a rotten woman of such magnitude of shittiness Deidra is or was. And when you look at how she reproduced such beautiful children, you would never understand the pain and let-down she took us through."

"She was really rotten to the core," Gladys co-signed, because it was the truth, but also because she didn't want Simone and Tallhya to look like heartless bitches. "She wasn't no earthly good, and I know she ain't heavenly bound. All that mess she put y'all through, she's going to have to account for that. Judgment Day."

"You right about that. God going to deal with her, then," Rydah said.

"Don't you mean Lucifer?" Simone asked. "Trust me, she ain't getting into the gates of Heaven, not by a longshot."

"Well, at least I know for sure I will be able to get my damn surgery, finally," Tallhya said.

"Damn, are you going to be okay?" Rydah was puzzled.

"Honestly, the best thing that woman could do was die. Trust me, she saved us a lot of pain and suffering. She's never done one motherly thing for us but give us life, because after she brought us into this godforsaken world, we were fair game. All she ever did was lie, steal, and pimp our asses in her own way. Bitch is better off dead," Simone said with malice.

"You got that right," Gladys said under her breath.

Tallhya busted out laughing, and everyone in the room turned their attention to her. "Now irony will have it that the bitch had to die for us to finally get a benefit from her ass."

"The benefit is a financial settlement from all the abuse," Simone added to what Tallhya was saying.

"You're so right, girl." Tallhya slapped hands with her sister. "I bet that bitch running through Hell, hot as fish grease that we get to collect that insurance money."

"I know that's right. Raising hell in Hell. Mad, looking for a reason to trick it out of us if she could." They kept the running sarcasm going.

"Chase, you see what you married into? This family crazy, right?" Tallhya said when she noticed Chase was speechless.

"It is, but it's mines though," Chase said with his chest poked out. He leaned in and kissed Simone.

"Well, I'm here to do anything you need. And I know I speak for me and my grandmother as well," Rydah said, trying hard to console her newfound sisters, even though they didn't seem too much like they needed consoling. "Yes, we are here and will give her a nice memorial. At least put her away nice," Rydah suggested.

Rydah felt as though they were blessed. Richmond had been a blessing. She was collecting money on her grandmother's and her mother's death. Or was it a curse?

"Memorial service? How much is that going to be?" Tallhya asked in a dead-serious tone. "I don't wanna be dipping into my surgery money. Shiiiit, she wouldn't even bury us if the shoe was on the other foot."

Simone spoke, knowing that she needed to cover her own tracks, since it was she, after all, along with Bunny and Ginger, who had killed Deidra, and she had helped them dispose of the body. "Cremate the bitch!"

Chapter 16

MIA

The first few days after returning to Miami went by quickly. There was something about going to Virginia and meeting her family that gave Rydah life and the will to put the memories of the carjacking behind her.

Rydah spent most of her free time preparing for Tallhya's arrival. The two sisters spoke on the phone several times a day.

"Should I get a car? What kind of car do you think I should get?" Tallhya asked.

Rydah tried to convince her sister that transportation would be the least of her problems once she got there. "How many times do I have to promise you that wheels are not a thing? You can borrow one of mines until we get you proper."

"You sure?" Tallhya didn't want to impose on her sister any more than she had to. Rydah had already got her the hookup with a five-star-rated doctor to perform her liposuction procedure. She not only got Tallhya pushed to the front of a 6-month waiting list, but Rydah also managed to negotiate a 30 percent discount. All that, plus, she said Tallhya could stay with her as long as needed.

"Because," Tallhya said, "I have no issues with getting a rental." Tallhya wasn't the freeloading type. She'd been drowning—emotionally and financially—before God answered her plea for help, sending her a much-needed life preserver. Her share of the money Me-Ma left them had literally saved her life. She could now afford the surgery, which would help with her lack of self-esteem, and she'd still have enough money get back on her feet.

"Will you just relax and let your little sister do her thing?" Rydah chuckled.

"What's so funny?"

"I can tell we share the same DNA," she said.

"How so?" asked Tallhya.

"Because I had almost the same reaction to Grandma Gladys when she insisted that I drive her car while I was in Richmond. I didn't want to impose—blah, blah, blah. But really, Tallhya, it's cool. You'll see."

"Okay, but eventually I'm going to have to buy one. I saw this li'l Kia with low mileage that I think I could get a good deal on, but I wouldn't try to drive it to Florida."

Rydah cringed at the image of her sister driving a Kia. She hated that South Korea crap. "Hold off on the Kia, sis. We'll get you whatever you need from down here, even if I have to build it myself," she said. "Hold on to your money, girl. All you need is an airline ticket for right now."

"I need new clothes," Tallhya insisted

"What for?" Rydah reminded her. "You're not going to be able to wear them after the surgery."

That was something Tallhya looked forward to. "But for now I have nothing," she said.

Rydah came up with a compromise. "Then pick up the bare necessities, but nothing more. We'll figure out the rest together after you get here. Just don't go overboard."

Tallhya currently wore a size 16. She had been considered "big boned" for her entire life. That was what the nice people called her. It was hard to envision herself a "normal" size.

"Thank you, sister. You're the best."

Rydah said, "There's only one catch. . . ."

There's always a catch, Tallhya thought. "What is it?" she asked.

"Every Sunday I have to spend the day with my parents. It's sort of like a tradition. We do breakfast, attend my father's church, and then have big dinner. It's non-negotiable. No ifs, ands, or buts. Just on general principle you're going to be expected to roll with the script."

Tallhya thought about her sister's request. Me-Ma was a Bible thumper. When Me-Ma died, they found out that the pastor at her church had scammed her into signing over her house and bank accounts to him, and was then on the down-low getting head and sleeping with her transsexual brother. But in the end, he would have to answer to God for that.

She asked, "Is that it?"

"That's it," Rydah said.

"For a second I thought I may have to sign over my first born or something," she joked.

Two days later, Rydah picked her sister up from Fort Lauderdale-Hollywood International Airport.

"How was your flight?"

Tallhya had taken her advice. She only had two bags: a carry-on and a small suitcase. This was her first time flying.

"The seats are way too small," she said. "Other than that, everything was Gucci."

Rydah put the suitcase in the back of the purple El Camino. The inside was white with purple piped-out seats. The head-rests had her name embroidered into the white leather in pur-ple script. When she turned the key, the engine roared like a cat out of the jungle. The five hundred horses under the hood were so powerful, Tallhya felt the vibrations penetrating her body. Rydah asked her if she was hungry.

"Yup! I could eat. The only thing they gave us on the plane was a tiny bag of peanuts and a half can of soda."

"Shit. You were lucky to get the peanuts for free." Rydah laid down on the gas, burning a little rubber, before peeling out of the airport like the police were hot on her trail. In a matter of seconds, the speedometer reached 60 miles per hour.

Tallhya buckled up. "You better slow your ass down, girl."

"This isn't fast." Rydah turned on the music. "Wicked" by Future blared from the speakers. Then she dropped a few ounces of pressure on the accelerator. The souped up El Camino jetted down the highway like it had wings.

Tallhya was amazed by all the different types of palm trees on the side of the road. They were everywhere.

Cruising at a smooth 85 miles per hour, Rydah navigated the purple rocket in and out of traffic effortlessly. An app on her phone alerted her to road hazards, speed cameras, and squatting cops waiting to make their monthly quotas.

The sisters met Wolfe for lunch at a seafood restaurant in Bayside. Wolfe was on his best behavior. He and Tallhya seemed to hit it right off.

When they were done grubbing out, Wolfe excused himself. "I got business to attend to. I'll have to catch you ladies later," he said. He paid the bill, kissed Rydah on the lips and her sister on the cheek, and bounced.

After lunch, Rydah drove Tallhya to Brickell.

They parked inside the high-rise and took the elevator up to the thirty-third floor.

"Damn, sis!" Tallhya had to pick her mouth up off the floor in order to speak. "Is this where you live?"

"You like it?" Rydah kicked off her shoes. She'd read that besides a lot of unwanted dirt, bad energy clings to the bottom of people's shoes and gets tracked through the house.

What is there not to like? Tallhya thought. The place was fucking amazing. Tallhya imagined herself living this way: three hundred and fifty feet in the air, overlooking the Atlantic Ocean. Right away, Tallhya knew that this was where she wanted to start over.

The two sisters sat on the balcony, talking. Rydah gave Tallhya the 411 on Miami, and Tallhya shared stories about Bunny and Ginger. She kept saying how much Rydah and Bunny looked alike. And the outrageous things she shared about Ginger were straight up made for TV. Before either of them knew it, hours had flown by.

Rydah's phone rang. "I had no idea it was this late," she said before answering it. "It's Wolfe, girl. He's downstairs, on the way up here."

Tallhya said, "I didn't know that he lived here."

"He doesn't," Rydah corrected. "He comes over when he isn't working, though. But he's always working."

Tallhya smiled. "It's good that y'all spend a lot of time together. I like Wolfe. He seems like he really fucks with you hard."

"I do." Wolfe took off his shoes at the door. "That's my baby. For real."

He joined the girls on the balcony with a bottle of gold champagne then went back inside to the kitchen for glasses.

"How romantic." Tallhya examined the bottle of expensive champagne.

"Girl, he trying to impress you," Rydah casually said to her sister.

"Hey, I heard that." Wolfe came up from behind and kissed her on the neck. Rydah took one of the three glasses from his hands. "And it's true," he said. "For you, my dear sister-in-law." He handed Tallhya a long-stem champagne glass. "And yes, I ended my workday early to come and spend time with you. What do you want to do tonight?"

Tallhya's face lit up. "What are our options?" she asked.

"Well, we can do whatever we want. The city is our oyster. You want to party? You want dinner? You name it."

"Hmmmm . . ." Tallhya thought about the choices she was offered. "Decisions, decisions, decisions. A party sounds good, but I would prefer to go out and celebrate *after* my surgery."

"I have an idea," said Wolfe.

Rydah took a sip of the champagne Wolfe had poured. "Do share," she said.

Wolfe told them what he had in mind. "We can have a chef come to us and fix a gourmet dinner here. And when you're healed from your surgery," he said to Tallhya, "I promise you an epic night out on the town to welcome you to MIA!"

Tallhya hadn't yet gotten past the part about the private chef. "Sounds good to me." She smiled, raising her glass for a toast. "To family."

A few glasses of champagne later and a couple of plates from the private chef Wolfe brought in, and the night was coming to a close. Everything was cleaned and put away, and Tallhya was about to wind down when she overheard Wolfe and her sister in a deep discussion.

"So what about that bitch, Buffy?" Wolfe's voice had lost most of its charm.

"What about her?" Rydah said.

"You asked me not to deal with her petty ass until you got back. You're back," Wolfe said. "And my patience is wearing thin."

Wolfe was convinced that Buffy was responsible for Rydah getting snatched, and he was a firm believer in retribution. Rydah was more forgiving.

"Let God take care of her," she said.

"God?" Wolfe laughed. "I'm told that God forgives. I don't," he said. "And neither should you." Wolfe spoke a little too loudly.

Tallhya walked into Rydah's bedroom. She asked, "What are you two lovebirds arguing about?"

Wolfe didn't take too kindly to people interfering in his business. Normally, he would have checked the violator with violence. He didn't discriminate on gender or kin—man, woman, child, mother, brother, or sister-in-law. His motto was that if you were able to commit the violation, you were able to pay the price.

However, he saw the reward in getting Tallhya to see things from his perspective. Wolfe asked Tallhya, "Did Rydah tell you about the girl that set her up to be kidnapped?"

Rydah rolled her eyes.

Tallhya looked from Wolfe to Rydah and then back to Wolfe. For the short time she'd been in Miami, it had been all fun and sunshine, but this sounded serious. "What happened?"

Wolfe gave Tallhya both the facts and his interpretation of the facts. Then he shared how he thought the transgression should be handled. "But Rydah thinks we should leave it in God's hands. I'm just afraid that if God takes too long to act, the bitch might try her hand again. Next time, Rydah may not be as lucky. What do you think?"

One of the main things Me-Ma taught the kids she raised was that if someone fucked with one of them, they fucked with all of them. That's the way the Banks rolled. Me-Ma ain't raise any punks, including Ginger.

Tallhya said, "I think we should beat that bitch's ass!"

Chapter 17

Not My Sister

"And I'm telling you right here and now," Tallhya said to Rydah, "that bitch needs to be dragged. And if you don't do it, I will. That's a promise. I put that shit on Me-Ma, Bunny, and Ginger's grave."

Wolfe got a better reaction out of Tallhya than he expected. She was a natural firecracker waiting to explode. But he played it cool.

"I can't let you do that," he said. They were standing in the entryway of the den, which doubled as Tallhya's bedroom.

Tallhya wasn't trying to hear it. "I'm telling you the God's truth," she said. Her eyes were on the screen of a laptop that Rydah had let her borrow earlier.

Wolfe was curious. "What're you looking for online?"

"Running through that bitch's social media. That's the best way to find out where a bitch at, what she doing, or where she plan to be."

"Word?" Wolfe liked her style.

"Dead ass," Tallhya said, continuing to drum on the keyboard. She was on a mission.

"What you going to do when you locate her whereabouts?" Wolfe asked

"I'm going to do exactly what I promised I'll do—drag the bitch! I ain't never really been much of a talker." Tallhya felt like this was her way of paying Rydah back for being so generous. Also, the way she saw it, in the hood, most big sisters fought at least a dozen battles for their younger sister before the younger sister's eighteenth birthday. Tallhya figured she owed Rydah about a dozen ass-kicking hands, the same way Bunny had kicked ass for her when they were growing up.

God forbid, what if Rydah had got seriously hurt . . . or died? she thought. They never would have met. Thank goodness nothing like that had happened, but at the same time, Tallhya felt that she needed to let these Miami bitches know that there were consequences and repercussions for messing with a Banks girl. Rydah had folks that loved her, folks that weren't going to stand by and let anybody try to fuck her over.

Wolfe loved Tallhya's energy. He wished that Rydah was more like her sister. She was the type of bitch that he needed on his team.

Chapter 18

April Fool's Day

Partygoers filled Club Hoax well beyond its 1,500-patron capacity. Buffy had been scamming, sucking, and saving all year for her mega birthday bash, and the final results were even better than her expectations. Eighty-inch projection screens were positioned throughout the club, and the camera stayed positioned on the birthday girl for the entire night. Buffy hammed up every second of it.

The party was called "The Dirty Thirty," and the theme was the Wild, Wild West. Buffy lived on social media, and she blasted her favorite platforms—Twitter, Facebook, Instagram, and Snap Chat—advertising it as the party of the year.

There were mechanical bulls set up in the middle of the lower level. Anyone that could stay on the mechanical beast for a whole two minutes with the setting on high won a stack. A line of inebriated guys and a few chicks tried their hand at the prize. None of them got close to hitting the two-minute mark.

Half-naked go-go dancers stood on the bar, dropping it like their lives depended on it. You could rent the back of a stagecoach, furnished with a queen-sized bed, for thirty minutes at a time. Mock canons were shot off every half hour. Men walked around in chaps, women in Daisy Dukes, and almost everyone wore a cowboy hat and boots.

Buffy was excited to see her vision come to life. The only thing that excited her more was meeting her new mystery friend. Buffy hoped that the mystery girl she'd met on social media would be as hot as her pictures were. If so, Buffy planned to make love to her like a real cowgirl.

Tallhya walked into Club Hoax rocking black leather Daisy Dukes, ostrich cowboy boots, and a skin-tight, blinged-out T-shirt. Across her chest, she wore two bandoliers, fully loaded with bullets. And she carried two real-looking AK-47s. She gave the security guard her fake name and was escorted straight upstairs to VIP, to be formally introduced to the birthday girl.

Tallhya had successfully catfished Buffy on Facebook. Tallhya had used her real pictures, but said her name was Natalie.

Buffy gave Tallhya a long, thirsty look and nearly fell in love with the color of her eyes. "Thank you for coming." She hoped they were real.

Tallhya blinked, showing off her mink eyelashes. "I wouldn't have missed it for all the pussy in Bangkok," she said. Tallhya once heard the line used in a movie, but she couldn't remember its name.

Amused, Buffy took a harder look. "You remind me of someone I know," she said.

"That's not a very original come-on," Tallhya said. "But I'll give you a pass, because I hear it all the time."

The D.J. played a Trina cut and the girls went nuts.

"You are so pretty," Buffy said. She liked girls with a little meat on their bones, as long as they were cute. "Are you really into girls?" she asked.

"Not at the moment," Tallhya quipped. "But the night is young." She thought to herself that this shit was easier than she expected. She could just take the bitch home, get her drunk, and then slit her throat with a kitchen knife. But if she got knocked, she could kiss her surgery and her life good-bye. The only two states that executed more people than Florida were Texas and VA.

Fuck that!

"True." Buffy was clueless as to Tallhya's real intentions. "The night is young," she said. "And so are we. Young and free to do anything we want. Anything."

Tallhya smiled. This was the type of attention that she craved to get from men. But it no longer concerned her, because after her surgery, she would have to fight the guys off with a stick.

She didn't respond to Buffy's remark.

Breaking the momentary silence, Buffy said, "This shit is going to sound corny, but I was in love with the girl who you remind me of."

"Was?" Tallhya feigned like she gave a fuck. She asked, "What happened?"

Buffy contemplated the question. *After Rydah wouldn't give me the time of day, I got one of my homeboys to carjack her bourgeois ass.* Then she said, "She was straight."

Tallhya joked, "Don't ya hate when that shit happens?"

"In the worst way. But I never thought I'd rebound with one of my social media fans."

Did this bitch just call me a groupie? Getting this bitch drunk, taking her to a hotel, and poking her with a sharp knife is starting to look like a good idea again. Who the fuck does this ho think she is, a broke Nicki Minaj?

"Fan this!" Tallhya reared back and coldcocked Buffy with one of the fake assault rifles. Buffy dropped like a thot's G-string backstage at a rap concert. She screamed, "That's for my sister Rydah, ho!" Then she commenced to ram her ostrich boots upside Buffy's head.

The one-sided melee was like something from an MMA fight, and the entire smackdown was being recorded live on 23 different projection screens.

People were screaming, "Stomp the bitch . . . stomp the bitch . . . stomp the bitch!"

And Tallhya didn't disappoint. She zoned out. She envisioned the faces of her cheating-ass ex, Walter, and his new bitch in place of Buffy's and got to whaling even harder.

"Stomp the bitch . . . Stomp the bitch . . . Stomp the bitch!"

Finally, security showed up. Better late than never, if you were the one getting your face stomped out. But Buffy would have given anything for them to have gotten this crazy bitch off of her a little sooner.

A big black guy wearing a tight yellow T-shirt, who looked like he came straight up off of WrestleMania, snatched Tallhya up like she weighed no more than a ham and cheese sandwich. He had her a good three feet off the ground, carrying her across club's floor, kicking and screaming. The next thing Tallhya knew, she was out the front door on her ass.

A stranger walked up. "Are you okay?"

Tallhya was out of breath. "I'm fine," she said.

The guy handed her a closed bottle of water. "You look thirsty."

She hadn't realized how dry her throat was until the cool water hit the inside of her mouth. *Damn, that shit taste good.* She'd been on an adrenaline rush, and now the rush was quickly turning into an adrenaline crash. She sat on the bench, drinking the cool bottle of water, smiling at how she'd kept her promise. She'd beat the brakes off a bitch at her own Dirty Thirty birthday party.

Thirty definitely had a dirty start for Buffy.

Tallhya was smiling at the ordeal when a massive headache came on. Tallhya took another long drag of water and she was done! She collapsed to the ground, out for the count.

Chapter 19

American Dream

Twelve hours later

Tallhya woke up on a pissy mattress in a small, dark room that—besides the urine—smelled like old clothes and mildew. She had no idea where she was or how she got there. The last thing she remembered was mopping the floor with that bitch Buffy and getting thrown out of the club. And then she recalled someone offering her a bottle of water. After that was a blank canvas.

She tried to wipe the mucus away from the corners of her eyes, but she was unable to carry out the task. Each of her wrists was encircled with a heavy plastic tie. The plastic ties were intertwined with one another, creating a virtual handcuff. The same contraption was used on her feet. Someone had made her a prisoner. When she attempted to yell out for help, her screams were shortstopped by a rag, which was packed inside her mouth. She had to breathe out of her nose

Click.

Someone cut on a flashlight and pointed the beam into her face.

"I see you're finally awake," said a voice from behind the flashlight. His accent was Haitian, and he spoke with the casualness of a friend or lover. "I'm going to remove the gag," he said, "but when I do, you must promise not to scream. Okay, Tallhya? Nod your head if you understand."

The bright LED light caused the decibles from the drum-like noise reverberating inside her head to increase two-fold.

If you get that fucking light out of my eyes I'll agree to whatever you want, she thought. But since, at the moment, she couldn't speak, she nodded.

The guy with the flashlight and the Haitian accent approved. "Good," he said, then: "I told you that she would be cooperative."

Tallhya and Flashlight weren't the only two in the room?

"They all cooperative when they tied up and shit," said his partner.

Flashlight: "Don't be so negative."

The partner said, "Whatever. Let's just move this shit along."

Flashlight removed the rag from her mouth. "Okay, Tallhya, I need for you to answer a few questions for me. Okay?"

Tallhya had few questions of her own, starting with, "How do you know my name?"

Flashlight said, "I'm psychic. I know many things." To prove his point, he said, "Your name is Natallhya Banks. You're thirty-two years old, and you're from Richmond, Virginia." Then he laughed. Tallhya missed the joke. "Besides," said Flashlight, "it's all right here on your Virginia ID."

Her predicament was getting worse minute by minute.

"What do you want with me?" she asked.

"What do I want?" Flashlight echoed. "Well, Tallhya, I want what everybody in America wants—money! It's the American dream, no? Okay," he said, "your turn is over. Now I ask questions. And your answers will determine whether or not you make it back to Virginia alive, or end up in Mexico selling pussy."

Tallhya said, "I don't have any money."

"Well, as you know, I've already been through your wallet, and based on the stuff I found on your person: two grand worth of hundred-dollar bills, a Consolidated Bank platinum card, an iPhone 6Plus with a Swarovski crystal custom case, Christian Louboutin lipstick, Chanel chain purse . . . Tell the broke shit to someone that don't know better," he said. "I'm sure there is more money somewhere."

Tallhya begged him to believe her. "Trust me," she said, "there isn't any money." After the $150,000 life insurance policy Me-Ma left was divided three ways, Tallhya had spent everything but the twenty thousand she had put up at Rydah's house. Most of if was for the surgery, and the other grand was for a good weave.

Flashlight said, "I'll be the judge of that."

"I take it you're out here on vacation," said the partner. "So if you wanna be back with your family and friends, you need to figure out where to get one hundred and fifty thousand dollars."

"I don't know anyone with that kind of money."

Flashlight wasn't buying it. "You better think about it real hard, then."

Tallhya, just a couple of weeks ago, felt like she had nothing to lose. In fact, she hadn't cared if she lived or died. Now, her life had changed. She had met her sister, who was kind and pushed her to win and wanted nothing less than the best for her. Her self-esteem was building, and finally she had the financial resources to change her lifelong battle with obesity. And after she got her lifestyle under control, she would help others as well. Ironic how at this very moment she wanted nothing more than to survive, to live, to be healthy, and to strive.

"So," the partner said, "who are you out here on vacation with? We take travelers checks." He had a mean look plastered on his face.

For some reason, when Tallhya looked at him, all she saw was his mug shot picture in her mind, with that mean and ugly disposition written all over his face.

Tallhya told the truth. "I'm visiting my sister."

The partner nodded his head.

"Now we're getting somewhere," he said. "What your sister do out here?" He took a not-so-wild guess. "She a dancer?" Half the street girls in Florida either danced or ran scams.

"No," Tallhya said, a bit too defiantly. "She works at a car shop."

"Fuck!" Flashlight rolled his eyes. "That shit no good. What about family back home?"

"Two of my sisters are dead, and the other one has cancer. My mother is dead—and when she was alive she never gave me a dime." Tallhya chose not to mention Me-Ma or the money she left behind. It would only complicate things more than they already were, she thought.

Flashlight or Mean-Mug didn't seem to be moved by her losses. "What about your nigga?"

"He left me for a skinny bitch and cleaned out my bank account before he dipped."

"Fuck! It must really suck being you," Mean-Mug surmised. "You may be better off to everyone selling pussy for a living."

Flashlight tried to make her better understand the predicament. "You know what it's like working whore houses in Mexico? Fucked up. Nigga after nigga, wetback after wetback. You'll be servicing about twenty to thirty smelly dicks each night. You seem like a cool person that's caught a few bad breaks. You've come through before, and I believe that you can get through this. Get us the money so that you can go on with your life."

Think, bitch! Think! Think!

Tallhya stared off into the darkness. A few weeks ago, she was in the crazy house being coerced to take meds she didn't need. That seemed like Disney World right now.

Mean-Mug got an idea. "Does your sister have a dude?" He held Tallhya's phone in his hand. "Who can we call?"

Tallhya started to lie and say no, but the fib died on her lips. "Yeah," she said. "She has a boyfriend, but I don't know him like that. He may not care enough to pay the price for me. We just met a few days ago. I just met my sister for the first time not even a month ago."

A phone rang with a "We Are Family" ringtone. It was Talhya's.

The partner killed the call, got the number, and then Face-Timed the caller back. When Rydah answered, he pointed the camera toward Tallhya on the urine-saturated mattress with no sheets. He held it just long enough for Rydah to get a brief visual of Tallhya's predicament. Then, the kidnapper texted Rydah from Tallhya's phone.

Tallhya: 150K to get her back alive!

On the other end of the phone, Rydah was speechless, but she texted back right away.

Rydah: I'll give you whatever you want. Just don't hurt my sister.

Flashlight's partner handed him the phone. "Look at this shit, man." After Flashlight read the message, they both thought the same thing: *Bingo.*

"I thought you said that your sister worked on cars for a living. What does her nigga do?" Mean-Mug was trying to hide that he wasn't pleased and now he wanted to know if there was a way that he could squeeze more.

"I don't know," Tallhya said honestly. "All I know is that his name is Wolfe and that he's from down here somewhere."

Neither guy could hide behind their poker faces how Tallhya's statement had surprised the hell out of them. The name Wolfe represented money and danger. Everybody in the streets knew that Wolfe was caked up. But the name also meant trouble. Wolfe was an egotistic, ruthless, certified sociopath.

Flashlight said, "Well, Tallhya, your sister seems to be more worried about you than you thought. She says that she's willing to pay to get you home safe. For that, I'm not going to put the rag back in your mouth. But if you act stupid, I'm not only going to gag you . . ."

The partner pulled a pistol from his waist and finished Flashlight's sentence. "I'm going to fuck you with this."

"I–I wont try anything," she stammered. "But I need to use the bathroom. Is it possible to untie me?"

"Piss on yourself, bitch. That's what you been doing."

"But since my sister is paying you, please cut me some slack," Tallhya calmly asked. "Honestly, you don't have to worry about feeding me. Just get my diet pills out of my purse and I will be okay," she said.

"She is human," Flashlight said.

"Get that bitch a bucket and give her them leftover bum-ass wings that I got from The Office the other night."

Mean-Mug looked like he was about to change his mind. He stared her in the face, and she looked as innocent and hopeless as she could. In return, Flashlight placed a bucket and styrofoam takeout tray of old chicken wings in front of her. However, Mean-Mug still studied her.

To reassure them that they were making the right decision by untying her, she said, "I promise I won't do anything crazy."

But she couldn't speak for Wolfe.

Chapter 20

The Shake Down

Tallhya was left alone in the room. She used the time away from her abductors to pray. One after the other, she prayed to God, Me-Ma, Ginger, and Bunny. It was the same prayer each time: *Please help me!*

She even asked (via prayer) for help from her no-earthly-good mother. Maybe the woman who gave birth to her would be a better mother from the grave than she was in real life. One thing for sure, Tallhya surmised, was that reaching out to her mother, whether she was in Heaven or Hell, couldn't make her situation any worse than it already was. Like Me-Ma used to say, "Closed mouths don't get fed."

To the best of her knowledge, it had been about two hours since Flashlight and his partner were last in the room. She couldn't be sure, because she didn't have a watch, and of course she didn't have a phone.

After praying, Tallhya used the time trying to utilize meditation techniques she'd learned from a psychologist while in the crazy hospital. It was useless. Each method required her to do two things: (1) Take deep breaths and (2) Clear her mind completely of all thoughts.

The first one was easy enough, but she didn't have a snowball's chance in Hell of clearing her mind. She was way too nervous for that shit, and there was no logical grounds to relax and clear her mind.

The small room was pin-drop quiet. For some reason, Tallhya's mind kept going back to when she was in that seedy hotel after the bank robbery. She was destitute of not only money, but of hope as well. She'd spent the few pennies she'd gotten from the robbery on the hotel room and food. She wasn't sure if the bank's cameras had captured a good image of her and if the police were hot on her trail. She'd only had

six minutes on her prepaid phone, and with nowhere else to
turn, Tallhya had cried out to God. Lo and behold, He had not
only showed up, but He showed out! In what seemed like the
blink of an eye, God had changed her life significantly.

Tallhya kept reminding herself that this was no different. If
He thought that she was worth saving then, why would God
allow her to be thrown to the wolves now?

Deep in thought, Tallhya began hearing voices. Was she
hallucinating? What were audible hallucinations without
images called? *Crazy*. Was God trying to speak to her, or was
her mind playing tricks on her?

Turned out that it was neither. The voices manifested from
the devils outside the room where their captive was tied up.
Prince (aka Flashlight), and his partner Abe (aka Mean-Mug),
weighed their options.

Sitting on a ratty sofa, Prince expressed his concerns. "I
don't think it's the right move, trying to shake that nigga
Wolfe down."

Prince and Abe had been friends since the sandbox and had
always been tighter than fish pussy. They were like peanut
butter and jelly, different but complimenting each other.

Abe wholeheartedly disagreed with his homeboy's rational-
ity. "Fuck Wolfe! He not exempt from the game." Abe, sitting
across from Prince in a mismatched corduroy recliner, was
adamant. "It's 'bout time somebody man up and get at dude.
Shiiiit!" he exclaimed. "Might as well be us."

Prince shook his head. He'd heard wicked stories about
Wolfe—each more treacherous than the next. The man was
not only vicious, but he was also relentless. Prince once
heard that Wolfe waited a whole year to murk a dude who'd
dinged the door of his new Bentley parked in a Wal-Mart
parking lot. Wolfe investigated the indiscretion for months.
He wrote down the plate number of every car parked in his
section of the lot and questioned them all. When Wolfe
finally found out the identity of the perpetrator, dude was
serving a six-month skid bid in Turner Guilford Knight
Correctional Center for driving without a license. When he
got out, Wolfe gave the careless asshole the opportunity to
pay what it had cost to get the ding out. He'd even saved
the receipt. Dude made a fatal mistake of thinking Wolfe's
request was optional.

"Wolfe isn't going to let no shit like that go without serious repercussions and consequences. You know that's right." Prince made sure his buddy understood what they were agreeing on.

"Like I said," Abe spit, "fuck that one-legged, cripple-ass nigga! You scared of a gimp? Just say you scared, bro," Abe teased. "A scared-ass nigga is what I ain't ever known you to be. Guess this some new shit you on."

"It's not about being scared," Prince said. He set the empty beer can down on the floor. "This chick was supposed to be a quick lick until we got all the details down on the armored truck heist. Get us enough cash to hold us over."

"Never count unhatched eggs," Abe sagely said. "That armored truck play is set to go in motion in a few weeks. This shit here . . ." he said, "is here and now. I'm not passing up on nooooo fucking bread, bro. This is how we play it. We call the sister back and tell her to tell Wolfe to cough up the hundred fifty K or we kill Tallhya. And after we kill her, then we gon' find his bitch and make him pay to get her back, too."

"Man, that's real ambitious, and I like your ambition," he told his buddy. "But the last thing we need is to be going to war with Wolfe!" Prince fully understood the dangers of fucking with a nigga like Wolfe, but all Abe saw was money signs. He felt that their team was invincible.

"Once we take the armored truck out, we'll have enough bread to go to war with whoever." Abe was sure about that. "Bet that, my nigga."

"That's not the point," said Prince, speaking with plenty of logic.

"Money is the point, my man. Always has been and always will be. Anything else is pointless. So let's just focus on the grind: one bitch, one truck, one lick at a time."

Prince chuckled. "Speaking of bitches," he said, "here comes yours."

"Heyyyyy, boo. I called your phone. Why you ain't answer?"

"Busy." Abe looked annoyed. "And didn't I tell you not to come over here unannounced?"

"What was I supposed to do?" Buffy said. "I needed to speak with you, and when I called, you didn't answer."

Abe was blunt. "What da fuck you want?"

Buffy shouted, "I want to kill that bitch!"

"So go ahead and tell the entire fucking neighborhood?" a twisted-face Abe said.

"I! Want! That! Bitch! Dead!" Buffy screamed, emphasizing each word to get her point across. "And I want her to die a fucking slow, painful death!"

In the other room, Tallhya could hear everything and recognized Buffy's whiny voice. Her heart dropped.

Fuck! Ain't this a bitch. If it weren't for bad luck, I wouldn't have any luck at all.

She didn't like the way this was going. When she first heard Buffy's voice, her heart dropped. Now it was racing 90 miles per hour.

"I want that bitch dead!" she heard Buffy scream.

Fuck, the feeling is mutual. She tried to be optimistic. *They won't kill me as long as they think they can get paid.* However, optimism was hard to maintain when one's survival hung in the hands of a bitch one just stomped out. After they got the money, what would keep them from killing her then? Her existence would no longer hold any value for them. In fact, it would be the opposite; she would be a liability.

Before she knew it, Tallhya began to hyperventilate. Tears and sweat rolled down her cheeks. Then she heard a voice in her head. This time it really did emanate from inside of her.

You got God!

The three simple words calmed her down.

You got God!

Then she heard Me-Ma's voice. *"And with Him, who can be against you?"*

Then came Bunny's voice. *"Bitch, if you don't drag that motherfucking bitch again and beat the living shit and fucking daylights out of her when you get out of here! Teach her about fucking with us Banks sisters!"*

Next was Ginger's voice. *"Biiiiiitch, you never crack under pressure! If you don't get your game face on! Focus on getting out of here in one piece and getting skinny mother-fucking skinny and fly and stunt on all these motherfuckers."*

Then lastly, she could hear typical Deidra in her head. *"I know good and well you ain't stunting these motherfuckers. Focus on that money—play your role and figure out how to get their plans on that armored truck. Fuck everything! Fuck your feelings! Focus on that money!"*

"Calm the fuck down," Abe said.

"Calm down? Look at my motherfucking face." Buffy turned so that Abe could get a better angle. She turned the volume down on her voice a few notches, but she was clearly still angry. "That bitch fucked my face up completely."

Abe had to agree.

"Yeah, your face is fucked up." Her face was red and blue and swollen.

Prince said, "Day-um!" and turned away. "Bitch got a mean hook. Remind me of my sister!"

Buffy ignored Prince and whined to Abe, "I had to get stitches and everything . . . ." She was laying it on thick.

Tallhya thought, *Good for that bitch! A permanent scar! Bitch is going to always remember me and my sister, even if I'm dead! Mission accomplished.*

"I want y'all to handle that bitch," Buffy said. "I want her dead. She embarrassed me at my own shit. I want her and her sister Rydah to die! Both of them dead! I hate them bitches."

Prince said, "Ain't that the same chick you wanted to lick just a few months ago? Now you want her dead because her sister retaliated on some shit you instigated and lined up?"

Abe left the emotions out of the equation. Once the emotions were gone, all that was left was the money. He said, "Miss me with that shit, Buffy. She's worth way more to me alive than dead, any day of the week. Matter of fact, I'ma hit you up later. Just go on home, lay low, and let your mug heal," he suggested. "Instead of running 'round these streets all destructive and shit."

"Go home and do what?" she questioned.

"For once," Abe said, "just do what I tell you to do. Go home. Stay off the phones and social media. Don't let nobody know shit. Just keep your mouth shut. Do everybody that justice, please."

"A'ight." Buffy acquiesced. Then she said, "Are you going to pick up when I call you?"

"Stop fucking playing with me, Buffy, and do what I say to do, a'ight?"

It seemed like hours, but it was only a few beats of silence. For a second, Tallhya thought that they were going to come into the room. Then she heard a door slam. Hard.

"That bitch is bad news, man . . . bad fucking news!" a disgusted Prince said to Abe. "She gon' get you killed before it's all over with. And me too, if I ain't careful. Shit!"

"At the end of the day, Buffy be 'bout that paper," Abe said. "How many of them fake, flossing-ass niggas has she lined up for us?" Abe asked. "A boat load. That's how many. A fucking boat load. More than you can remember. That's how many. As long as she keeps food on our plates, she's all right with me. So be grateful."

"For sure," Prince said. "She's come through in the past, but everything gets old sooner or later. I'm just saying that the bitch may have run her course. Bit by bit, you sacrificing pieces of your swag and your good sense fucking with this chick. You put too much faith in her. A snake is a friend to no one. It's only a snake. Just because it doesn't bite you right away doesn't mean that it never will."

"I have to admit," Abe said with a nod, "she is a heartless bitch. That's her best quality, though."

That was the first thing the two lifelong friends had agreed on all day

All Tallhya wanted right now was to be released and get out of there, get her surgery, heal, and start living the life that she should have been living a long time ago.

As time turtled by, Tallhya continued to lie on the pissy mattress, exercising patience and faith, and somehow tuning that smell out.

Suddenly, Abe walked in. Before she could sit up, he grabbed her by the hair with one hand and punched her in the face with the other. He hit her so hard she went out.

"That's for giving my bitch a black eye on her birthday." When she woke up, he wrapped his hands around her neck, choking her. That was all she remembered before blacking out again.

"Miss?"

Someone was trying to get her attention.

"Miss?"

When she came to, Tallhya only had vision in one eye. The other was covered with some type of bandage. She could barely see out of the one that wasn't covered. Everything was blurry. People were standing over her, but she couldn't make out much of anything else. A few beats later, she realized that the people standing over her were paramedics.

Everything seemed to move in slow motion.

Tallhya heard a lady with a high-pitched Spanish accent speaking to someone as the medics strapped her onto a stretcher.

Someone said, "They dumped her from a green van. I thought she was dead."

"Thank you, ma'am. Do you mind coming downtown to give a statement and look at a few photos?"

"I'm kind of busy."

"It wont take long"

"Well . . ." the Spanish lady reluctantly said, "okay. But I only have a minute."

"Yes, ma'am."

A paramedic with red hair asked, "Does she have a pulse?"

There were two fingers on her wrist.

"It's weak, but she has one!" He wore his hair in dreads.

Red Head said, "Thank God, ma'am, that you called when you did."

Tallhya could feel the gurney being lifted into the back of the ambulance. She felt sick to her stomach.

Speaking into the radio, one paramedic said, "We have a black woman in her late twenties, early thirties, possible heroin OD."

OD?

Other than the drugs administered to her at the mental hospital, Tallhya had never abused a drug in her life.

"No track marks," said Red Head.

"Probably a recreational user."

Tallhya tried to respond, but her body wouldn't cooperate.

"Vitals low."

"Oh, shit!"

"What?"

"Her heartbeat's dropping rapidly. She may not make it."

Chapter 21

Lunch Money

Rydah had wired the $150,000 to the bank account the abductors had specified. Wolfe came through with the cash like it was lunch money. He didn't want to give in to suckers trying to shake him down, but he felt bad for Rydah that these fools were holding Tallhya, doing who knows what to her.

Rydah felt horrible. God forbid if Tallhya didn't live. She would never forgive herself. She kept running everything through her head from the day of Tallhya's disappearance.

Wolfe took the phone away from his ear and said to Rydah, "Stop beating yourself up, babe!" He'd been on the phone with everybody he trusted, trying to find out how this had happened. Right now he was talking to a guy named Jack Fishy. Jack Fishy was an ex-bail bondsman and ex-bounty hunter turned private investigator. Everyone called him Fishy.

Fishy had a reputation of being able to find anyone, anywhere. People in the street joked that Obama had hired Fishy to find Osama Bin Laden.

"I need your services," Wolfe said. "Someone snatched my sister-in-law and shook me down for a hundred fifty G."

Fishy said, "I'm on it. It shouldn't be hard following a trail of money that large." Within five minutes, Fishy knew that the money had been transferred through a Bahamian bank. "As you know, peoples who transact a lot of shady money or just wants to duck taxes think of Nassau as a baby Swiss banking system. But it isn't as sophisticated as people think. I'm on it, Wolfe."

The street's lips were tight for the moment, or no one knew anything. And someone always knew something.

Vexed, he hung up the phone. "I promise, baby, when I find out who's behind this . . . I don't even want the money back," he said. "But on everything I love,"—which wasn't much—"they going to pay dearly."

Rydah knew better than to say anything to try to stop him. Nor did she want to.

Wolfe saw the anxiety etched in Rydah's face. "Baby, I promise you everything will be okay." He took her into his arms. It hurt Wolfe seeing Rydah broken up the way she was. This was the very reason why he hated being in a relationship, because your enemies targeted the things you loved most.

"Why haven't they called? We paid them what they asked for."

Rydah had to ask her parents to use their account to wire the money. She didn't want to tell them, but she didn't know what else to do.

"They'll call," said Wolfe, but in his heart, he knew that it could go either way. They could kill her just as easily as they could release her. It was 50/50.

Rydah felt helpless and angry, and she secretly wished that Buffy paid for what had happened. Every time she thought of all the tragic ways she wished Buffy would die, Rydah had to ask God for forgiveness.

The text came from a private number

Unknown: Your sister is on the way to the hospital.

Rydah almost threw up. How bad was she hurt?

Chapter 22

The Lady Lagoon

"Someone probably slipped you a roofie," the doctor concluded. "You said the last thing you remembered was drinking the water, then waking up in a strange place?"

It had been a few hours since arriving to the hospital, and Tallhya was laying in the bed, trying to take everything in. She still couldn't believe what had happened, or that she was alive to tell the story.

"Yes."

"Do you remember being given drugs of any kind?" the young Spanish doctor asked with a raised eyebrow.

"Yes! Ummm . . . no . . . ummm, I don't know." Tallhya searched her brain but couldn't be sure. "I don't remember."

"Was there any kind of intercourse?" he asked.

"No!" A pause. "I don't think so."

The doctor patted her on the shoulder. "You are safe now. We will take good care of you."

Once the doctor left, Rydah said to Tallhya, "Miami isn't the place for you to be running the streets alone. What the hell were you thinking about? I work late for one night and everything goes to shit."

Wolfe said, "Let's just focus on the fact that Tallhya is here with us now."

"I guess you are right, but I still don't like what happened to my sister."

"None of us do. And whoever's responsible will pay for it."

Tallhya thanked Wolfe for coming up with the money. "I promise I will pay you back."

"Don't mention it," Wolfe said. "Just keep me out the doghouse with your sister," he half joked.

"I'll do the best I can."

Wolfe then asked, "Did Buffy have something to do with this?"

"She told them to kill me. But they said I was worth more money alive than dead."

"What else do you remember?"

"Not much."

Rydah's parents entered the room, and that was Wolfe's signal to exit, but he didn't want to make it obvious, so he stayed for a few minutes longer.

Maestro came with people from his church, rejoicing that Tallhya was alive and safe. Amanda couldn't stop talking about how the two sisters needed to be more careful and stop being so trusting.

Wolfe held face as long as he could, but it was time for him to leave. He needed to hit the streets and get to the bottom of things. He said his good-byes and left the room.

Wolfe was at The Lady Lagoon on business. The manager told him that the owner would be out to see him shortly. To pass the time, Wolfe copped a seat at one of the strip club's ten bars, nursing a Heineken and a double shot of Remy. On stage to his left, a half-naked dancer gave him the eye. She was mixed: half Chinese and half black, but it was obvious to anyone with eyes that the black genes were the more dominant of the two. The honey was as thick as a bowl of oatmeal and fine as a summer evening on a white-sand beach. Wolfe wasn't the least bit interested and ignored her advances.

The Lady Lagoon was open 24/7, had four stages, and kept at least forty strippers on payroll at all times, even on the slowest nights. On the weekends, there were sometimes as many as two hundred girls making niggas throw money like it was water and they were trying to put out a fire.

The owner of The Lady Lagoon was a man named Jaffey Logan, a serial club owner and legend among anyone in that circle. He had a long history of owning spots throughout South Florida, mainly Miami, and he had his hand in every part of the industry, from clubs to liquor to promotions to prostitution. Jaffey knew as much about running night clubs as Sam Walton knew about retail. In the 80's and 90's when the nightlife scene was at an all-time high, Jaffey sat at the top of the mountain and collected an avalanche of money. Unfortunately, when the bubble burst, the paper evaporated as quickly as it came.

After finishing his phone call with the liquor warehouse, Jaffey exited his office donning a fresh pair green gators and a green linen suit. He was told that someone was waiting to see him, and that someone was no other than Wolfe. Adjusting the angle of his hat, Jaffey wondered what Wolfe wanted with him. Wolfe wasn't the type that frequented clubs of any kind, unless it was an absolute necessity. Never for pleasure.

Jaffey spotted Wolfe sitting at the bar and reluctantly began walking in that direction. He owed Wolfe a little over ten million dollars.

Wolfe was still facing the bar when Jaffey snuck up behind him. The music was blasting. Jaffey was about to tap him on the shoulder.

Wolfe said, "I wouldn't do that if I were you."

How the hell did he see me? Jaffey wondered.

"Have a seat." Wolfe finished off his cognac and placed the empty glass on the bar.

"What brings you to this side of the Intracoastal, my man?" Jaffey wasn't used to Wolfe just popping up. "I thought you said I could have until the end of the month to make that payment. After Memorial Day."

When the recession hit in '08, puncturing the real estate market, Jaffey reached out to Wolfe for help. Wolfe knew that Jaffey was a legend in the business, but he also knew that Jaffey had vices. If Jaffey hadn't been an owner, he would have been an owner's best customer. He loved women, gambling, cocaine, and flossing, a mixture that, more times than not, led to a dead end.

In all actuality, it wasn't a really good idea for Jaffey to have his own strip clubs, because he indulged with the help too much—but no one could deny that he knew how to get the people to come to not just the strip clubs, but the party clubs as well. That was why Wolfe floated Jaffey the first $2 million. He genuinely had love for the dude. Wolfe also believed in Jaffey, although he knew that he would probably never get all of his money back.

Jaffey always did what he could, and everything wasn't about money. Because Jaffey knew people in high places, he was better off to Wolfe alive than dead. So Wolfe continued to bankroll his clubs, but not lately—the buck had stopped, but the tab was still there, and Jaffey always paid something. He never wanted be on Wolfe's bad side. Who in their right mind would?

And this was why Jaffey rolled the red carpet out to Rydah at any club she wanted to go to. Most times she was treated better than a lot of so-called celebrities. Jaffey made sure that all of his staff knew who she was, and if they didn't damn near bend over to kiss her ass, they were fired on the spot. It was the least he could do considering the ballooning tab that he owed her man.

When Wolfe said, "I'm not here about the payments," Jaffey breathed easier. Until then, he'd been holding his breath.

"Then what can I do for you?"

"I need all of the surveillance tapes from Club Hoax."

Jaffey was both relieved and confused. He was relieved that Wolfe hadn't come for an early payment, and he was confused as to why Wolfe would want the surveillance tapes from Club Hoax. "Is there something I should know about? You never struck me as the type that needed to check up on his woman."

Wolfe said, "How and when I check on my lady is none of your business. But that's not the reason I'm asking for the footage. I got a hunch that the footage may clarify for me."

Jaffey knew better than to ask what the hunch was about. Wolfe was relentless and methodical when he had had a hunch. Best to leave well enough alone. "No problem," he said.

Wolfe made it clear what he wanted. "I need all the footage—from both inside and outside the club—for the past three weeks."

"It's going to take me a day or two to get it together, but you got it." He didn't want to make Wolfe upset. "And for the record," he said, "I always treat Rydah like the queen that she is, giving her carte blanche."

"Appreciate it," Wolfe said.

"Don't mention it. She's so beautiful and classy and carries herself as a lady."

"Yeah, she sure does," Wolfe bluntly said.

Jaffey nixed the ass-kissing and small talk and got straight to the request. "I'll make the call immediately. And as for the payment, I'll have it for you right after Memorial Day. It's always real fruitful for me around those times."

"For the entire city," Wolfe said.

Wolfe finished his Heineken, talked to a few people who were vying for his attention, and then kept it pushing. Business as usual.

Chapter 23

The Fonz

Tallhya was discharged from the Memorial Regional Hospital at 9:17. Rydah had been waiting there to pick her up since six in the morning. Outside, the sky was slate gray and gloomy. Tallhya thought it was apropos to the way she felt inside.

Due to the injuries she incurred—two fractured ribs and a bruised eye socket—the doctor informed Tallhya that any cosmetic surgeries she'd planned would have to be postponed for at least six weeks. Six weeks was the "if she was lucky" date.

The news hit her like a cement bag in the gut, knocking what little wind was left in her already nearly depleted sails.

Rydah decided to make a detour before taking Tallhya to her parents' house, stopping by a little trendy diner downtown, where the food was always on point. Rydah ordered two of the specials; two eggs (prepared any way you like), home fries, bacon, sausage (or ham), and buttered toast with jelly. As always, the cook did his thing. The food was delectable.

Rydah chomped off half a sausage link in one bite and chased it with a forkful of cheesy scrambled eggs.

Tallhya's plate went untouched.

"Why aren't you eating?"

"Don't have much of an appetite."

If she couldn't get her surgery, then Tallhya figured she would starve herself to lose the weight. She was tired of being labeled "the cute big one" or "the fat Banks sister."

Rydah took another bite of the sausage. "You should at least try your home fries," she said.

"At least be woman enough to stare," Tallhya said loudly enough for the two women who were stealing glances at her when they thought she wasn't looking. "Bitches!" She said to Rydah, "Can we get out of here?"

Pushing her plate away, Rydah said, "Sure. If you don't want to be here, we out." Rydah dipped into her purse, pulling out a couple of twenty-dollar bills and a ten. She left the money on the table.

Back in the Lamborghini, Tallhya said, "You could've taken a doggie bag."

"Now you say that shit." Rydah jokingly rolled her eyes. "I didn't want to make you stay anywhere you didn't want to be. I just thought you might have wanted something good to eat after chowing down on hospital food for the past three days. And that place makes the best damn home fries in the city."

"My bad."

Rydah hung a left on Biscayne. "Nope. It's my bad for not asking if you were cool with being out so soon. We can hit 'em up some other time."

For weeks afterward, all Tallhya did was eat, sleep, and cry. When she wasn't sleeping, she was crying, and when she wasn't crying, she was sleeping. Once or twice, she managed to do both at the same time, eventually crying herself to sleep.

When she was asleep, she often dreamed about life after she got the surgery done. The image was the same every time she had the dream: a skinny version of herself rocking a tiny bikini on a sandy beach. And then she would awaken and start crying all over again. It seemed as if everyone in the state of Florida was thin, taunting her for being out of shape. Deep down, Tallhya knew that she was being irrational, but it was how she felt.

In her eyes, the only good thing that had happened to her since being released from the hospital was Aunt Amanda. Like the mother Tallhya never had, Amanda nursed and catered to her every need every single day. Tallhya secretly wished that Amanda had been her real mother instead of Deidra. That it was she who had been adopted by her Uncle Maestro, instead of Rydah.

Day by day, with Amanda's help, Tallhya recovered from her injuries. During this time, since Tallhya had seemed to sink deep into depression, Rydah and Tallhya barely spoke.

Rydah hated it. She'd finally been reunited with one of her estranged sisters, and they weren't doing anything together. All Tallhya wanted to do was lay in bed, tuning out the world.

Rydah could no longer take it. She burst into the guest room where Tallhya was staying. "Enough is enough!" Rydah shook her. When Tallhya opened her eyes, Rydah screamed, "Bish, get out the bed and get dressed. And when you're done, put these on." She handed her sister a pair of big-framed Chopard sunglasses. "We're going out today, and I'm not taking no for an answer."

Tallhya looked at Rydah like she'd lost her mind. "Why you gotta be so damn loud—waking me up and shit?" With an exaggerated yawn and stretch, she said, "I was sleeping good."

"It's freaking one o'clock in the freaking afternoon," Rydah told her. "Time to get up."

Just then, Amanda came into the room, carrying a tray. "Time for brunch." Amanda had cooked French toast and bacon, and she'd put fresh strawberries and blueberries in a bowl on the side so that Tallhya would have the option to put the fruit on her French toast or eat it separately. Rydah swiped a piece of bacon as Amanda placed the tray on the night table beside the bed.

"Don't mess with my food."

"Oh," said Rydah, "now all of a sudden you full of energy and stuff."

Tallhya ignored her.

Rydah asked Amanda, "How does she just get to sleep the days away? Didn't you give her the house rules, the ones you implemented on me?" The house rules had always been, *If the banks are open, you should be out of bed.* "It's unfair."

"You treat her better than me," Rydah said in a little girl's voice.

Amanda waved off Rydah's complaints. "The girl is healing from a traumatic event. Wait until she gets her strength back."

The way she's being pampered, Tallhya may never get her strength back, Rydah thought.

Tallhya stuck her tongue out behind Amanda's back, teasing.

"Rules are rules. In this house, nobody is allowed to sleep past nine a.m.," Rydah said, pulling the covers away from

Tallhya, almost forcing the linen to land on the floor. "Now get up!"

"Mother Amanda, she keeps bothering me," Tallhya complained. "Tell her to let me rest. And she's being mean to me, too."

"You a snitch now?" Rydah rolled her eyes.

"Rydah, that's no way to treat your sister."

Rydah sighed. "Mommmm. . . ."

"Especially," Amanda reminded her daughter, "the sister that you claimed to have been waiting your entire life to meet. Did you know that Rydah used to cry herself to sleep at night because she wanted a sister to play with?"

"And once she has one, she's mean to me."

"But she needs to get up," Rydah protested. "She just can't sleep her life away."

Amanda agreed with Rydah. "Some fresh air would do you good, Tallhya. But you girls have to promise to be safe and not overdo it."

Rydah quickly said, "We know. Now get up, my dear sister, so we can get some fresh air as our beautiful mother has requested." Rydah smiled, side-eyeing her sister. "Honor thy mother and thy days will be longer. Those are the Bible's words, not mines."

Tallhya tried one last excuse. "I have nothing to wear. Remember, I didn't bring any clothes because I thought I was going to be doing shopping for my flat stomach and small waist after the surgery."

"Mm-hmm. I knew you were going to try to pull that. That's exactly why I got you this." She went into her backpack and pulled out a Pink sweat suit. "You got thirty minutes to shower and get dressed. Hurry up."

Before leaving the room, Amanda suggested that Tallhya should put something in her stomach. "And drink some juice," she said. "Hydrate, dear, hydrate!"

Forty-five minutes later, outside in the driveway, Rydah had another surprise for her sister.

Tallhya was tongue-tied. Parked in the driveway was a white four-door BMW 645. "Stop playing, Rydah. This is for me?"

"It was a salvage. I redid the entire thing myself." Rydah handed her the keys. "For you, my sister."

Rydah shouted. "Oh! My! God!"

"Now let's go to the mall and get you a few outfits. My treat."

After a couple of hours of shopping and a few stores later, Tallhya said, "I'm hungry."

"Me too."

The sisters decided to have lunch at a place called Gourmet Dărê. It was a new chic restaurant that Rydah had been wanting to try ever since the doors opened to rave reviews six months ago. They were seated by their hostess near a 500-gallon aquarium that was home to a colony of tropical fish of every size and hue.

The two had been giggling and laughing since they sat down.

Rydah drank her lemonade from a crystal champagne glass. "Girl, you so crazy."

"Naw," said Tallhya, "that's you." At the table, they were discussing a multitude of topics like family, relationships, movies, and purchases they'd made earlier that day.

Rydah told Tallhya, "I think you should've gotten the silver Swarovski crystal shoes instead of the black ones."

Having a bit of buyer's remorse, Tallhya agreed.

"Don't get it twisted. You can never go wrong with black, but those silver ones were everything. Like, because you are my long-lost sister," she said, "I would've splurged for them both if you wanted."

Tallhya took another bite of her entrée; it was the best grilled salmon she'd ever eaten. She said, "You know you are more flamboyant than me. You're so much like Bunny it's scary. Y'all two would've stayed fighting over each other's clothes."

"For real?" Rydah couldn't help but get excited when she talked about the siblings she'd never met. "I wish I could've known her."

"I promise you would have loved her and hated her at the same time, because her paws would've stayed using her five-finger discount on your stuff," Tallhya said then changed the subject to something less sad. "Do you think that my feet will drop a size after my surgery? I read that somewhere online."

"Ummmm . . . I never heard that one before."

"Ladies . . ." A guy walked up to their table.

The two sisters eyeballed him.

"Not to intrude or be rude, I'm sure that you hear it all the time, but it's worth saying it again: you two are so beautiful. Are you twins?"

"Thank you for the compliment," Tallhya said. "And no, we're not twins."

"But we're sisters," Rydah chimed in. It felt good to say she had a sister. Plenty of girlfriends had come and gone, claiming to be her sister until they got bitchy and petty, but this was different. No matter what happened, good or bad, nothing could change the fact that their blood bonded them together forever.

"Really?" said the gentleman. "Your father must have strong genes."

"You mean our mother," Tallhya said. "We look like our mother."

"Well,"—he tipped his hat—"let her know that she did the world a real great service by giving birth to such beautiful beings."

Rydah was about to tell the stranger to fuck off, but in a nice way, when the waiter approached with the one-hundred-dollar bill, placing it on the table.

In true gentlemanly fashion, the stranger picked it up. "I would love the honor of taking care of the tab for two beautiful ladies." Before they could say no, he dug into the pocket of his linen trousers and came out with a black American Express card.

For the first time, Rydah checked him out. He was carrying three bags: two from Saks-Fifth Avenue and a Hublot watch boutique bag. His skin was smooth and brown like expensive chocolate. He was at least six feet tall with a short haircut, and he was very dapperly dressed in a linen button-down shirt, Louis loafers (no socks), and a diamond-studded Rolex watch.

Rydah knew that Miami was the hub for credit card scammers, aka swipers, and she was well aware that they came in all shades, colors, and sizes. There was no stereotype to put them in. Miami was home to the most sophisticated scammers in the world.

Rydah studied him, knowing that in Miami there were three classes of people: the haves, the have-nots, and the haves who have not paid for a damn thing, aka the scammers. If she had to bet on it, there was something and everything about this fella that said he was definitely a have.

Tallhya thanked the stranger for his generosity.

He smiled and said, "Mind if I sit for a second?" as he slid into the booth beside Tallhya.

"Looks like you already did."

"Forgive me if you think that I'm being too presumptuous. It's not every day that a man gets to sit next to a gorgeous lady such as yourself. I like to take advantage when life offers me opportunities as such."

Tallhya instantly noticed that his cologne was intoxicating and his swag was definitely on point.

Rydah said, "Thanks for picking up our bill, but um . . . I don't even know what to call you. My name is Rydah; and you are?" She extended her hand.

He cleared his throat. "My name is Alphonso. But my endearing friends call me Fonz."

"I'm Natallhya, and my endearing friends call me Tallhya.'"

"Well, Tallhya, I hope to one day be able to call you Tallhya."

This guy was really pushing it at Tallhya, hardcore, Rydah noticed, but Tallhya was being reserved. She wanted yell to her sister, "Don't let him get away!"

Tallhya was intrigued, but she was also skeptical. She asked, "Do you live around here?"

"On Sunny Isles."

"Fancy," Rydah said, knowing that Sunny Isles was dubbed the French Riveria of Florida, filled with high-rise, high-dollar condos on the ocean.

"I like it," he modestly said.

"And who are you shopping for?" Tallhya nodded toward his bags

Again, he beamed that enticing white smile. "I got myself a suit, a couple of shirts and a little watch."

"A Hublot is no *little watch*," Rydah said. "I think it would be better described as a timepiece," she said as her eyes pierced the bag.

Fonz turned to Tallhya. "May I ask if you're married or not? I mean, I don't see a ring or anything."

"Nope," Rydah answered for her. "She's not married."

"Relationship?"

"My sister is new to town," Rydah said. "She's been divorced for quite some time now."

"Well, this question is for you, Natallhya. Are you open for dinner with me, let's say, any time in the next couple of days?"

"Ummm . . ." Tallhya wasn't sure how to respond. "I don't even know you," she said. "And I'm not in the business of really hanging out with strangers."

"That's why we should go to dinner, to get to know each other."

"Well, ummm . . ." Tallhya hesitated, turning red. The truth of the matter was that she was a little intimidated. Walter was the only man she had ever really dated, and he stole all of her money and tore her self-esteem down to dust in the process. She couldn't believe someone as handsome as Fonz wanted to get to know her. What was his motive?

Sitting down, he must not be able to tell how big I am, she thought. *But what if he doesn't care?*

Tallhya wasn't ready to take the chance of entertaining the idea of someone actually liking her and getting her feelings hurt. It was almost easier not to open up that can of worms than to gamble with her feelings.

As if he could read her mind, before Tallhya could turn him down, he said, "Let's at least exchange numbers. Take it back to the old school. Get to know each other a little over the phone, and then dinner? Can you go along with that?" He was confident in his delivery.

Not nearly as confident as Fonz was, Tallhya said, "I guess."

Pulling out his phone, Fonz wasted no time. "So, what's your number?"

Tallhya gave it to him, and Fonz locked it in.

He asked, "Are you going to answer when I call?" Her phone rang. "That's me. Lock me in."

"I wouldn't have given you the number if I didn't plan to answer," she said.

"And what's your number, sister? Just in case Natallhya doesn't answer, I'm going to call you to get her on the phone for me. Deal?"

Rydah laughed.

Fonz said, "I'm dead serious."

Rydah could see that Tallhya was a little shell shocked, so she took it upon herself to ask the tough questions. "Exactly what is it that you want with my sister?"

Fonz responded by saying, "I'm not sure what your question is."

"What are your intentions with my sister?" she said, rephrasing her query.

"Just to get to know her better."

Tallhya interjected. "That's what they all say."

"Well, I'm not them all by a long shot," countered Fonz. "But if you don't give me a chance, I can't prove you wrong."

"Give the brother a chance, sis. And if he's full of shit, you already know we'll deal with him."

"I'm shaking in my boots."

Rydah said, "You should be."

"All I'm asking is to be given a chance," Fonz said. He stood up. "But I'm not going to intrude on your time or space too much longer."

Both Rydah and Tallhya were pleasantly impressed with him. Tallhya thanked him for paying their restaurant tab again.

"Hopefully it will be the first of many." Before parting, he said, "I'm going to call you tonight, okay? Pick up and hear me out."

Rydah assured him, "She'll listen as long as you're not blowing hot air."

"That's all that I ask of you. The ear of a good girl that's not all caught up in the streets."

When Fonz left, Rydah exclaimed, "Girrrlllll, he was fine! And he threw himself at you. You're sitting there acting all nonchalant and shit, like you a boss playa or something."

Tallhya wasn't as optimistic. "He's only seen me sitting down," she said. "He has no idea how big I really am."

"Girl, please. Dude sat beside you, checking you out like you was the last top model or something. He was so engulfed in you that he hardly even knew I was sitting over here."

"I just don't have the energy for all the bullshit, lies, and let-downs that come with an insincere relationship."

"I'm not asking you to marry the dude. Just go out to dinner and get to know him. See what he's talking about. Have a nice time. You owe it to yourself."

Tallhya nodded. "I'll do it." She giggled. "Dude was hella cute, wasn't he?"

"Like a cold drink of water. Now, let's hit up a couple more stores, sis!"

Chapter 24

Bad Time to Post

Good food, a handsome gentleman, and countless shopping bags filled with fabulous finds later, before they knew it, the time had flown by and the stores were closing. The shopping spree was nearly over as the girls headed to the car, giggling.

Rydah had never seen Tallhya so happy. "Today was definitely a good day," she said as they neatly placed their bags into the trunk of the BMW.

Tallhya couldn't front. "I had a blast. Thanks, sis—for everything. Who knew what some fresh air and a little retail therapy could do for the sick and shut-in?"

"Well, I'm not one to say I told you so, but . . ." Then her phone chimed. "It's a text from Mom. She wants me to remind you to take your meds."

"Damn! I'd forgotten, too."

Rydah said, "And you know it took her forever to compose that text message. She old school."

They laughed.

Rydah closed the trunk while Tallhya headed to the driver's side of the BMW. "You cool with driving still?" Rydah asked. "If you're tired, I can take the wheel."

"I'm good. You going to have to pry that steering wheel from my cold, dead hands."

"I hope not." Rydah was about to get in on the passenger's side before she changed her mind. "Let me go get us some bottled waters so you can take your meds. I don't wanna hear Mother's mouth," she said. "And trust me, you don't either." She laughed as she reached for a few singles out of her billfold. "Hydrate! Hydrate! Hydrate!" Rydah imitated her mother.

"I know that's right. You don't want her to beat your ass for not looking after her new favorite daughter," Tallhya teased.

Rydah said over her shoulder, "You wish," as she walked away from the car.

Tallhya cranked the engine and cut on the A.C. As she waited for Rydah to return with the waters, she checked on social media. It had been a while since she had been on any of the sites.

The moment she began scrolling Facebook, she saw it. Buffy had blasted her timeline with selfies, one after another.

Another one.

Who the fuck posts this many selfies wearing the same outfit, just slightly different poses? Tallhya answered her own question. *This bitch Buffy, that's who.*

For some reason, the pictures of Buffy smiling made her more furious by the second. She didn't think Buffy had a right to be happy, posting all over social media like nothing had happened. Tallhya looked into the rearview mirror. When she took off the sunglasses, though it wasn't as bad and it was healing, the bruise was still visible on her eye. Her blood rose by a couple degrees, instantly.

Tallhya slapped the steering wheel of her car. *This bitch ain't learned about posting yet! That was the way I got at yo' ass the last time.*

Tallhya studied the screen. Then it hit her. *Wait a minute!*

Buffy was at Bal Harbour Mall . . . the same mall she and Rydah were at.

God works in mysterious ways, doesn't He?

She zeroed in closer and studied the pictures. In a few of the photos, Buffy was with two other chicks. If the last couple of photos were an indication, they were on the second level parking deck, one level below where she was parked. It was indeed a small world, with so many big possibilities.

Tallhya looked over her shoulder. Rydah was making her way back to the car. Tallhya geared it into reverse as Rydah got in.

"Here you go."

Tallhya took a sip of the water. "Buckle your seatbelt," she said. "Tight."

Rydah's expression said, "What's up?" as she buckled her safety belt.

Tallhya simply said, "Today may be our lucky day." Then she smiled at her sister and tapped the gas. The engine of the Beamer purred.

On deck 2, Buffy stood in the middle of the lot, still posing and taking selfies, paying attention to nothing but the angle of her camera. Tallhya zeroed in on the little ho and mashed the gas. In her mind, she planned to kill Buffy by running into the bitch at 50 mile per hour, breaking bones as if they were twigs, killing her instantly. A hit and run.

The worst part of the whole thing would be that they would probably have to get rid of the car, at least for a while. But there was no reward without sacrifice.

The Beamer was five feet away. Just before impact, three words ran through Tallhya's head—*Slow. Painful. Death.—* causing her to stomp the brakes. She wanted Buffy to suffer. The car slowed, but the at fifty miles per hour, the anti-lock breaks weren't designed to stop the car instantly. The Beamer clipped Buffy's side, knocking her off her feet. Buffy flew a couple feet into the air in one direction, and her blond wig in another.

A "What the fuck?" expression was plastered on Rydah's face.

With no time to stop, the driver of a Honda Accord ran into the back of the Beamer. Tallhya couldn't care less about the damage to the car or who saw what she did next.

Tallhya jumped out of the car. Rydah reached in her black Celine purse, came out with a .25-caliber pistol, and jumped out of the car, seconds behind her sister.

Tallhya stood over Buffy, who was bruised and bleeding. "Slow and painful, bitch?" Tallhya wasn't thinking straight. All she wanted was retribution. "Be careful what you wish on other people, because it may come back to bite you."

Buffy looked as if she wanted to cry, hoping Rydah would feel some semblance of pity and help her.

Rydah burst her bubble. "I don't give one solitary fuck about your tears, bitch." She pointed the .25 directly at Buffy's dome. "You set me up to die."

Buffy had a broken leg and a laceration on her forehead. "No," she said, still crying. "It wasn't like that."

Tallhya said, "Know this, bitch . . ." She didn't really care what Buffy thought it was like. "Every time I see you, I'm going to whip yo' ass. And I put that on my grandma's grave!" To get her point across, Tallhya punched Buffy in the face.

Two guys approached. At first they thought that it was the mall's security or undercover police, but then Rydah recognized one of them. They were Wolfe's people.

"Did Wolfe tell you to follow us?" she asked.

JoMo, the one she knew, nodded.

The other guy moved swiftly. He opened the trunk of the BMW and took the bags out, placing them in the back seat of the Benz that they were driving. JoMo instructed Rydah to take the Benz home. "Wolfe will call you shortly," he said.

"We don't want her dead," Rydah told JoMo.

"That's no longer your problem," JoMo said coldly.

"I'm serious," she said.

"I hear you," said JoMo.

Rydah searched his expressionless face for an indication as to whether he was lying. JoMo's reputation was as ruthless as Wolfe's, and that was scary for Buffy. Her last minutes amongst the living could very well be spent in the trunk of a car.

If it was true, there was nothing more Rydah could for her. She tapped Tallhya on the shoulder. "We gotta roll."

Buffy started screaming for help. JoMo's friend put a piece of tape over her mouth, silencing her.

Rydah gave her one last parting bit of advice. "You need to learn not to fuck with us Banks sisters," she said.

Chapter 25

Not Stable

Rydah knew better than to go to her parents' house, so she went home. Wolfe showed up a few minutes later.

When he walked in, the two ladies were sitting on the plush white leather sofa, talking. They got quiet when they saw Wolfe. Looking at each other, they both knew that they were in big trouble.

Tallhya took the blame. "It's my fault, brother-in-law."

Rydah was angry with Wolfe. "You had someone following us and you didn't even tell us?"

Wolfe was blunt. "Damn right. And it's a good thing that I did."

Rydah shook her head as Wolf poured himself a drink.

"So your first day out of the house," he said to Tallhya, "you roll over a bitch in broad daylight, damn near killing her?"

"Basically," said Tallhya, cucumber-cool.

"So . . ." Wolfe started.

Tallhya cut him off.

"Like I told Rydah, if the police show up, then I'll take the weight. I just got out the asylum and I got papers that say I'm not stable. They know I'm not working with it all."

"Really?" Wolfe looked at Tallhya with a raised eyebrow.

"I know you're mad, but I couldn't help myself. When I saw that bitch giggling and flossing on social media, fifteen feet below where we were parked, I had to react. I guess I wasn't thinking."

"That was where you went wrong," Wolfe said. "You weren't thinking. If you're going to do something that's against the law, the first rule is to always think it out first, then react."

Wolfe sat on the sofa, enjoying every moment of Tallhya's rant. She was a firecracker and he admired her heart. He secretly wished that Rydah were more like her. But then he thought again. Having two loose wires on his hands, in his home life, may be too much headache. It would grow old. Though he loved Tallhya's unpredictability, there was still something about Rydah's easygoing, peaceful spirit that tended to balance him out. She was definitely the Yin to his Yang.

"I told that bitch I'm going to beat her ass every time I lay eyes on her, and I meant it."

"Calm down," said Wolfe. "I got it from here."

Tallhya was cool with Wolfe taking care of the problem. She just had one request. "Whatever you do to her," she said, "make sure that it's done slow and painfully. The bitch deserves it."

"I said that I got it, didn't I?"

"Yes! I know you have it, but she told those guys that she wanted us to die a slow and painful death."

"Well, I got her. Let me handle her."

Rydah was still stuck on the fact that Wolfe had had them followed. "You could have told us what you were doing."

He sat down between the two ladies. Wolfe shook his head. "You back on that again?"

"Yes. I'm back on that."

"Never the one to throw anything in your face, but it was a good thing I did have you followed."

Rydah didn't want to admit it, but secretly, she was glad that he had. If JoMo hadn't intervened when he did, there was no telling how things may have turned out.

She asked Wolfe, "What did you do with Buffy?"

All he said was, "I got her."

That wasn't enough for Rydah. "Is she dead?"

Wolfe shook his head. "She's safe, just where she needs to be."

Rydah could tell when Wolfe was lying to her, and he wasn't. To ease the tension in the room, she kissed him on the cheek. "Thanks, babe, for having our back. You're always on point. That's one of the reasons why I love you so much. You're the best, and I'm glad you belong to me."

"Yeah," Tallhya said, "them dudes rolled up like the feds, moving all professional and shit."

"Yeah," Rydah joked, "but that didn't stop Tallhya from wanting to beat the life out of Buffy, though."

"I was like . . . what the hell, if the police here, I'm going down anyway."

"And she knew I was right there with her."

"Yup, pistol in her hand, wanting a bitch to move the wrong way," Tallhya said.

"Sure was. I had to have my sister's back."

"Y'all two something else. Double trouble, for real."

"So," Rydah said, ignoring the last comment, "if you didn't kill her, what did you do with her?"

Wolfe sucked in a lungful of air. "She's locked away, babe."

Tallhya said, "I want to see her. Can you take me to her? I'm still not done with her ass."

Here in this house, with Tallhya, was the only time in his life that he ever felt the need to explain himself and exercise his patience.

"Listen . . ." Wolfe addressed them both in a firm voice, letting them know he was now in charge, in case this was ever in doubt. "This girl will be handled. Trust me. I'm more pissed than you will ever know. However, you two have gotta fall back and let me handle it the way I see fit. In a way that won't come back to haunt you later. Is this understood?" He shot a look at them both.

Rydah nodded.

Tallhya was quiet.

"He'll take care of it," Rydah assured her, and there wasn't a doubt in her mind that Wolfe would handle Buffy. "Trust me. She's light work for him, sister."

"I know," Tallhya said. "Just hate making promises I can't keep."

"Sometimes you gotta pass the baton to the next runner. You did your part, and you did one hell of a job. Hell, you held it down better than a lot of the niggas I know." He gave credit where credit was due.

Tallhya appreciated the compliment. "Thank you for that." All her life, people had walked over her and never appreciated her efforts. Even her own sisters sometimes treated her like the reject fat sister. Even after they robbed multiple banks together, Simone repaid her by having her Baker Acted, leaving her in a crazy house. No one even came to visit. It felt good to finally have a sister that loved her for her and had her back. It was all she ever wanted.

Everyone was quiet.

Then Wolfe said to Tallhya, "You still haven't been out to really see the town. Since you've been here, there's only been misfortune. Time to change that. I think you sisters need to bond. Do some tourist stuff, girl stuff. Don't worry about this Buffy broad. Put that in your rearview mirror. It's in my hands now."

"And the guys?" Tallhya asked. "What about them? Mean-Mug and Flashlight?"

"Working on it."

"When you get them, can I at least come and spit in their face? For violating me."

He chuckled. "You got it, li'l sis."

"Promise?"

Wolfe reflected back to the day, when he was twelve years old, that he watched his father smack his mother because she "allowed" the dinner she'd cooked for him to get cold. He remembered the sound it had made, a cracking noise that reverberated like the whip of an angry horse jockey.

Wolfe had told his dad: *If you ever hit her again, I'll kill you.*

He told Tallhya, "I always keep my word."

Chapter 26

Legwork

The sisters agreed to lay low and let Wolfe deal with the situation. Tallhya had absolute and complete confidence that Wolfe could and would handle it, but at the same, she just couldn't leave it alone. She felt like she owed Wolfe for the $150,000 he had used to get her back. Although Wolfe said not to worry about the money, Tallhya was determined to repay him. No one had ever done anything like that for her, and the fact that Wolfe wasn't her man, that he did it because of the love he had for her sister, was real gangsta. Tallhya hoped that when she found a man of her own, he would be half the man Wolfe was. She felt like as long as she was overweight, she'd never get a man.

During her last checkup, the doctor said that at the rate at which she was healing, her body might be able to withstand the surgery she wanted in about three and a half more weeks.

No matter how hard she tried redirecting her attention to other places and things, her mind kept going back to the conversation she'd overheard between the two guys she referred to as Flashlight and Mean-Mug.

" . . . It isn't personal, just a part of the game. The American Dream. . . ." Flashlight had said.

Time to turn the tables. How? She thought. *Think. Think. Think.*

She had an idea.

When Mean-Mug and Flashlight were holding her captive, they had mentioned getting some "bum-ass wings" from The Office. Up until now, she'd forgotten about it.

She'd googled The Office, and it came back as a strip club. Not much of a lead, but it was definitely a good place to start.

If her hunches told her anything, they were coming back for those "bum-ass wings."

Tallhya packed bottled waters and sandwiches in a small cooler and put the cooler in the car—a Maxima, not the BMW Rydah had rebuilt for her. She never saw the Beamer again. Wolfe told her to forget about the car. Easy for him to say. That was the nicest car Tallhya had ever had.

For two days, Tallhya used the Maxima to stake out the parking lot of The Office. On the second day, she broke luck. A burgundy Lincoln with tinted windows pulled into the lot. It was the one she called Mean-Mug.

She picked up the phone to call Wolfe, then changed her mind. Instead, Tallhya watched Mean-Mug's every move, following him for a couple of days. On the second day, Mean-Mug met up with Flashlight.

They seemed to be doing some research of their own. Tallhya surmised that they were working on the armored truck heist that they'd discussed. After she was sure, she made a trip to Best Buy to purchase one of those long-lensed, paparazzi-style cameras. She also copped spyware apps from a tech novelty store.

She used the services of a stripper to get the spyware onto their phones. It was easy. The stripper simply had to offer each of the guys her number. When they clicked on her text, the spyware would infiltrate their system. With the spy apps installed, Tallhya could see everything they saw on their jacks. Everything. Phone calls, texts, e-mails, and pictures—even Internet traffic.

Rydah and Tallhya both shared the responsibility of monitoring the devices. It was a tedious job. The boys used their phones like a couple of high-school girls.

Tallhya's phone rang. It was Simone. She put the phone on speaker.

A hyped Simone said, "Hey, girl. You with Rydah?"

Tallhya responded, "She's right here. She can hear you."

Rydah shouted, "Heyyyy!"

Simone asked, "What are y'all doing?"

Rydah and Tallhya shot a conspiratorial look at each other. "We'll tell you later," Rydah said.

"Trust me," Tallhya added, "you don't even want to know."

Simone said, "Let me be the judge of that."

Rydah hunched her shoulders as if to say to Tallhya, "It's up to you."

Tallhya spoke on their behalf. "We been doing a lot of sight-seeing and eating on the beach," she said, bending the truth. They'd been keeping Mean-Mug and Flashlight in their sights and eating sandwiches while they waited. "You know—white sand and blue water."

"Just showing her the city," Rydah said. "Enjoying each other's company."

A pause.

"Oh," Simone said.

Tallhya knew Simone like a book, and by the sound of that "Oh" Simone blew out her mouth, Tallhya knew that her sister was a wee bit jealous of the way she and Rydah were getting along. She rubbed it in.

"We're having a ball. I've never had anyone in my entire life roll out the red carpet like this. I mean Rydah, her parents, and our brother-in-law . . . I swear, they outdid themselves."

Simone asked, "For real?"

"Enough about me," Tallhya said, knowing that Simone would want to hear more. "More importantly," she said, changing the subject, "how are you?"

Simone, sounding excited, said, "I Just finished my last round of treatments a couple of weeks ago. And everything looks good."

They both screamed, "Yesssss!"

Simone said, "I'm feeling a lot better. The doctor said that I should get some sun. Relax. I'm thinking about coming to Miami for a few days."

Rydah couldn't contain her smile. "You serious?"

"As cancer," she joked.

It was one of those jokes that was only funny because the person was making fun of herself.

"Damn, sis, your timing couldn't be much better. I got something big simmering in a pot that could use your special touch. Still early, but it's definitely coming together," Tallhya said.

Simone asked, "Really?"

"If you're up to it."

Simone said, "Don't worry about me, little sis. I feel as well as I've ever felt in my life."

"I hear you."

"Then spill the tea."

"Still researching . . . but trust me, it's going to turn out something big. I just know it."

"Let us know what day you're going to get here," Rydah said to Simone.

"Whatever day my little sister says that she needs me. I could use the excitement."

"Talk to your husband, see if he will let you steal away," Tallhya suggested. "See how soon you can get here and call us back. Meanwhile, I'm still doing my homework, but it's going to come together soon."

They disconnected the phone call from Simone and when they did, Rydah asked, "Ummmm, are you going to share what you have been all closed-lipped about and where you been spending all this time?"

"I will soon, sister. Just know I'm not getting in any trouble. Just chilling, that's all. Researching some stuff."

"You sure?"

"Positive," Tallhya assured Rydah.

"I know you. . . ."

"Listen, the second I get the info I need, I promise I will share it. A few more pieces to the puzzle have to come together. Don't worry. We going to be on some damn Wonder Twins shit. I promise."

Chapter 27

A Chef Salad?

When the phone rang, Tallhya looked at the screen and thought, *What's the catch?*

It was Fonz.

If nothing else, she thought, *the man is persistent. And a helluva looker.*

Since they'd exchanged numbers three weeks ago, Fonz had made it his business to phone Tallhya at least once a day. Some days he called more than once, and he was always pleasant, polite, and so damn poised. Tallhya hadn't quite figured out what his game was yet, or why he seemed to be so interested in her.

"Hello?"

"Good afternoon, gorgeous." His voice sounded like chocolate for the ears. "How was your day thus far?" he asked. Even his bullshit small talk sounded sincere.

"Who, me?" She was on a stakeout, hunched down in the driver's seat of the Maxima with a pair of binoculars and a cooler packed with a turkey sandwich, fresh fruit, and water, watching Mean-Mug. She'd just followed him to a house in Miami Gardens. "Same ol', same ol'," she said. "Uneventful."

Fonz saw an opening and took it. "Maybe I could do something to break the monotony." Until now, he'd kept his word and only used her number to kick it on the jack. No expectations and no promises. An opportunity to get to know one another. "Let's say I take you out for dinner? To a nice restaurant."

She didn't say anything because she was focused on an older lady who came out of the house. She must have been Mean-Mug's grandmother.

Fonz took the opportunity of her silence, ran with it, and went out on a limb. "Do you like crab cakes? I know a place that makes some of the best crab cakes in the city." As soon as the faux pas came out of his mouth, he mentally kicked himself. What if she didn't like crab cakes? Or worse, if seafood made her sick? He'd given her a built-in excuse to turn down his offer. "They make lots of other great things also," he said, trying to recover from his slip.

When Tallhya opened her mouth, the truth fell out. "I just so happen to love crab cakes. It's a date," she said. Too late to take it back. Damn.

That was the fat bitch that accepted his offer, not me. She needed to get a grip on that.

"Then," with cobra-quick reflexes, Fonz said, "I'll pick you up at eight." He finished before she could change her mind. "That's good for you?"

The only thing she'd eaten all day were two apples. She said, "Eight's fine, but instead of picking me up, I'll meet you there. Just text me the info."

"Deal."

At 7:45 p.m., Fonz handed the keys to his new Rolls Royce Wraith to the valet. The three hundred thousand–dollar automobile rolled off the showroom floor with 624 horses under the hood. It was the most powerful Rolls ever produced.

Fonz cautioned the valet attendant. "Be easy with her. She has a tendency to get feisty with drivers she doesn't know."

"Sir," the attendant proudly said, "I promise to treat her like the queen she is."

"Thank you."

Fonz would've literally had a coronary if he'd witnessed the rubber the attendant left tattooed to the cement while spinning the Rolls' wheels, but his mind was occupied with his date for tonight.

Tallhya pulled up to the restaurant fifteen minutes later. The same valet attendant that had abused the Rolls, parked her car.

Inside, a six-piece jazz band performed a Miles Davis piece. Fonz met her in the lounge area, where patrons waited to be seated.

"You look amazing," Fonz complimented.

"Very nice choice," Tallhya said, admiring the ambiance of the place.

"The lighting was off when I first arrived."

"Really?" Tallhya asked with a raised eyebrow.

"That's until you arrived and lit the entire place up."

Blushing all over, she was glad that one of the hostesses, attired in a black-and-white suit, ushered them to a reserved table for two.

"Right this way." The hostess spoke with a slight accent which Tallhya didn't recognize.

"Nice table choice," Tallhya said once they were seated. They were close enough to the band to be entertained, but not too close where their conversation would be drowned out by the volume of the music. Fonz took the liberty of ordering a robust red wine, along with a light appetizer, bread, and salad.

Fonz did everything he could in order to make Tallhya feel comfortable, but none of it worked. In her mind, she looked and felt overweight. She'd worn all black too, with a waist shaper underneath her clothes to appear slimmer than she was. It was too tight, and she could barely breathe. It sucked everything in, but her fat girl tricks weren't holding up to their end of the bargain.

Fonz was good at small talk. Conversing with strangers seemed to come natural to him, as if it were something that he had to do for a living.

Just like a con artist, Tallhya thought.

The band was jamming out to a George Benson cover when the waitress returned. She asked if they were ready to order. She was looking at Tallhya as if Fonz was a regular and she already knew what he liked. In fact, Fonz seemed familiar with quite a few people in the restaurant, both staff and patrons.

Yet he remained the ultimate gentleman at all times.

"Take your time. But if you're unsure of what to try, order as many different dishes as you like." Coming from some people, the line would've sounded mean-spirited, but not from him. "We can sample them together," he said. "That's good for me, because everything is so delicious here, and my mind tends to want some of it all, but my stomach won't let me have it all."

"I'll have the chef salad."

"And what dressing would you like with that?"

"I would like to have it dressed up in a couple of crab cakes and a juicy fillet mignon." That's what she wanted to tell the skinny-ass heifer. "French dressing is fine," was what she really said.

As if he could read her mind, Fonz ordered the seafood platter with extra crab cakes. "We can share," he said. "Oh, and would you throw in a few extra prawns, please?" Fonz said as he handed the menu to the waitress.

Fonz seemed to be everything she needed and wanted in her life. He smelled good, looked good, could dress his ass off, was classy and articulate, and seemed to have his shit together. He seemed to really like her, made her feel comfortable, and had the potential to romance the hell out of her.

This nigga is just too damn good to be true. That was the exact moment that Tallhya decided that after this date, she would never see or talk to Fonz again.

Her stomached growled.

Shut the fuck up!

Chapter 28

Doggie Style

Three weeks later

Wolfe's dog kennel was 6 feet by 9 feet by 4 feet, fabricated from solid steel. On a table next to the kennel was a box of chicken and a can of dog food. Wolfe opened the can of Alpo, spooned it into a metal dog bowl, and slid it through a feeding slot.

For the first week, Buffy left the dog food untouched, but after a while, when she knew that there would be nothing else to eat, she couldn't wait to chow down on the canine cuisine. Unable to stand up in the 4-foot tall cage, Buffy crawled through her own feces and piss to reach her meal.

"Not so much fun when the rabbit got the gun," said Wolfe.

Buffy's eyes stayed glued on the bowl of dog food.

"I was taught to treat people in accordance to the way they treat me." Wolfe chomped down of a piece of fried chicken. "So," he said, "you thought it was entertaining to see my sister-in-law beat up, raped, and drugged, huh?"

Buffy continued to eat. She knew that she only had five minutes. After that, Wolfe would take the bowl from the cage—whether she was done or not.

"One question," he said. It was the same question he asked every day. "Who were the other two guys?"

Buffy answered the same way she'd answered before. She said nothing.

Wolfe's phone rang and he took the quick call. When he hung up the phone, he smiled.

"I just got two calls back to back. I got info on who your partners are. You got about an hour to decide if you wanna give them up before they throw your ass under the bus."

"They will never throw me under the bus."

Wolfe started laughing as if it were the funniest thing in the world. "We'll see, bitch!"

Chapter 29

Gotcha

Zzzzzzz . . . Zzzzzzz . . . .

Tallhya was sleeping like a baby when the spy app she had
connected to Mean-Mug's phone vibrated, informing her that
the phone was in use. She woke up immediately.

Mean-Mug: IHOP on Biscayne at 11

Flashlight: Cool. Riccardo is with me

Tallhya leapt out of bed, hopped into a pair of jeans, a
T-shirt, and sneakers. Then she drove straight to the IHOP
and waited.

Tallhya waited patiently in her car, smiling on the inside, in
disbelief that her plan was finally coming together.

All of her life, she had been pushed around and given
orders by family members. Now she was the one who had
researched everything, and though it wasn't her plan, she was
masterminding a major robbery.

Everything was falling into place. The guys were meeting
with Riccardo, the driver of the armored truck, and they were
putting the finishing touches on their plan.

She sat in the blue Mercedes AMG and watched as the guys
arrived, ate, and listened in as they were securing their final
plans.

"So Riccardo, man, if you wanna pull out, let us know right
now."

"I'm all in."

"And you sure you are going to be the driver, right?"

Riccardo answered, "Been doing it for the past three years."

"Now, are you sure that the one guy is going to be a rookie?"

"Yes. It's going to be his first day out of training and his first
day riding along without having his trainers with him."

"And they assigned him to your truck?"

"Yes."

"And you sure that this is going to be a day to do it?"

"Yes. We have extra money to deliver to the three major companies in that area. And on top of that, the people at auction we would've picked up. So at the point we discussed, that's where you have to take the truck down."

"Okay. We got it."

"After all is said and done, you will do the interviews with the police. You don't know anything. And once you cleared from them, at midnight that night, we will meet you with your cut."

"A'ight, cool. That's sounds about right," Riccardo said.

"So it's all set in stone, right?"

They gave each other five. "Man, this shit is going to be great. And we going to eat."

"To money, and a lot of it." Flashlight toasted with their glasses of lemonade.

They shook on their plans and Riccardo left. Meanwhile, Flashlight and Mean-Mug sat there, gloating about how things were going to be great.

"Told you it was coming sooner rather than later."

Mean-Mug nodded. "Yeah, you did." He gave his boy a hand slap.

Mean-Mug and Flashlight were as happy as a faggot with a bag of dicks. Life was about to be great for them. They sat in their booth discussing how they were about to come up and how life was about to be great for them.

They strolled out of the IHOP excited that their plan was about to come into motion.

Tallhya sat in the car and was excited that things were finally coming together for her.

Chapter 30

Ice Cream Truck

Rydah was relaxing on the couch with the TV remote, channel surfing, when Tallhya rattled her key into the lock and stormed into the house. Rydah looked up.

"Damn, girl," she beamed at her sister after seeing how happy she was. "Pass that shit over and let me inhale whatever the hell you been on."

Tallhya was smiling like an only child on Christmas morning with a room full of presents. "I got something I have to tell you."

For the past few days, she'd been keeping her movements close to the vest, but now it was time to share her plan with her sister, friend, and confidant.

Rydah perked up, tossed the remote onto the table, and gave her sister her full attention. Taking a shot at what had Tallhya so giddy, she said, "Did you finally meet up with Fonz again?"

"He did call me, but that's not it." Tallhya copped a seat.

"What did he say?"

"I mean, we talked, but right now I just don't have no time for him, though." She didn't bother explaining to her sister her way of thinking, because she didn't feel like hearing Rydah's optimism when it came to Fonz. Plus, she had bigger fish to fry right now, like this plan that she had been babysitting for quite some time now.

"Okay, okay." Rydah was done guessing. "If it's not a guy, then what is it?"

"I found a way to get a freakin' shitload of money, but I'm going to need your help to pull it off."

Joking, Rydah said, "What, bitch, you plan to rob a bank or something?"

Tallhya said, "Nope." She was thinking, *But you're close.* "I plan to rob an armored truck."

"Now I know you've been smoking something." Rydah waited for the punchline to what she thought was a joke. When the punchline took too long to come, Rydah said, "Nobody's robbing anyone's truck, girl. You aren't that hard up, and you ain't broke."

"Just hear me out," said Tallhya. "It's not as crazy as it sounds. I promise."

All types of warnings went off in Rydah's head. Up until that moment, she thought that her sister was joking. "I'll be a monkey's aunt," she said in disbelief. "You serious, aren't you?"

"Yup."

"Well, let me stop you right there, sis. We're not going to be robbing anybody's truck. Not an ice cream truck. Not a candy truck. Not a trash truck. And certainly not an armored truck. Girl, have you lost your mind?"

"If you're done," Tallhya said, "I'd like an opportunity to explain. Give me that."

There was nothing on God's green Earth that could come out of her sister's mouth that would convince her to rob an armored truck, but for shits and giggles, Rydah agreed to listen. "I'm all ears."

Tallhya told Rydah everything. The more she spoke, the better she felt. For the past couple of weeks, keeping what she was doing secret from her sister had been eating her alive.

After hearing everything, Rydah said, "Listen. You already know I got your back like a tight bra strap."

Tallhya could hear the sincerity in her sister's tone.

"But I wouldn't be much of a sister if I wasn't honest. And honestly, I don't think that this is a very good idea."

Tallhya was not perturbed. "Tell me that a million dollars don't motivate you."

"I'm not saying it do or it don't, but—"

Tallhya cut her off. "I understand. I know this type of shit isn't who you are. I still love you all the same. But this won't be my first time doing this type of thing."

Tallhya told her about the bank jobs they'd pulled back in Virginia. "And most of all," she said, "this shit is personal for me." She wanted to make Flashlight and Mean-Mug know that they'd fucked with the wrong bitch.

Rydah looked her sister dead in the eyes. "I get it," she said. "But can we find a better way to achieve that than robbing a truck? We smarter than those niggas, and there's a way that we can outsmart them. I know there's a better way."

"I don't think so."

"I disagree." Rydah shook her head. "There's always more than one way to skin a rat."

Tallhya wasn't trying to hear that. "You're always looking at the things from the righteous perspective. God and the Universe can't handle everything. Sometimes you have to trap the rat yourself. It's more satisfying that way. At least it is for me. Can you respect that, sis?"

"Of course I do, but I also know there has to be a smarter way. If we can just put the emotions aside and utilize our intellect . . . because doing life in the pen is not where we want to end up."

"Well, that's a risk we take. But if we get away with it, then look at the reward."

Rydah was operating with tunnel vision and could only see it her way. "I'ma respect your way, but you're going to have to respect mines."

Chapter 31

What's Going On?

The sound of the front door opening and closing ceased all talk about the plan to rob the armored truck. The room was thick with awkward stiffness when Wolfe entered the house.

"What's going on with y'all? The tension in this bitch is tougher than leather," he said, then planted a kiss on his boo's lips.

Rydah kissed him back. "What you talking about? We good."

"Seems like a sisterly squabble is in progress."

"We ain't got nothing but love for each other," Tallhya said defensively.

"Sometimes we gotta agree to disagree," Rydah added.

"You got that right," Tallhya quipped.

Rydah was so busy trying to hide what they were talking about from Wolfe that she hadn't noticed that he was carrying something. "What's the deal with the briefcase?" she asked, diverting the subject away from her and Tallhya's disagreement.

Wolfe plopped down on the sofa between them and set the leather briefcase on the glass coffee table. He fingered the numbered dials on the front of the case, popping the locks. He removed a large manila envelope that contained pictures.

When Wolfe began to spread the photos out onto the table, the sisters' eyes got as big as eggs.

"That's them motherfuckers right there," Tallhya said, pointing at the flicks. "That's the one I called Flashlight, and this is the one I nicknamed Mean-Mug.

"That's Abe and Prince," Wolfe informed them.

"Wow." Rydah was puzzled. Pointing at a guy in another photo, she said, "That's the dude named Tiger that I told you tried to holla at me that night at the club, the night I went out and all that stuff happened with Buffy and her leeching-ass friends." Then she looked again. "That's the guy Ken and Jake."

Wolfe drew the conclusion. "All them motherfuckers were working together that night, running the scam."

"But the dude Tiger wasn't with them. He didn't come into the picture until later."

"Right," Wolfe surmised, "because they wanted to have multiple opportunities at getting at you."

"Mean-Mug and Flashlight was after us both?" Tallhya asked, a little confused.

"You mean Abe and Prince," corrected Wolfe. "They were after Rydah. They figured that her parents were rich enough to pay any amount of ransom to get their only daughter back, hence the failed carjacking. And after they botched it, Rydah never rolled out by herself again, so they didn't get another shot. However, they somehow found out that the two of you were sisters. Saw an opportunity with you, Tallhya, and took it." Wolfe's voice was as calm as a summer breeze, but his eyes were as deadly as a tornado.

"So . . ." Rydah finally let the truth sink in. "Buffy really did have something to do with me getting carjacked?" In her heart, she already knew this, but seeing the proof was different. "Our entire friendship was bullshit." She tried to shake it off, but the thought was still disheartening for her to believe.

Wolfe was blunt. "You knew what it was off top, baby."

"I did, but to have more concrete proof . . . that shit hurts. I'm human."

Wolfe looked at her. In many ways, Rydah was very naïve and innocent. Those were a couple of the characteristics that drew Wolfe to her. That and the fact the she was the most beautiful girl Wolfe had ever met.

"Most people don't have a heart as genuine as yours, babe. Most people are sheisty and evil and solely motivated by jealousy or money," he said.

"I know, baby. I know!" Rydah said, laying her head on Wolfe's chest. He put his arms around her.

"Never change your heart, baby. In more ways than one, because your heart is so good, and we are profoundly connected. It just makes me better."

"Awwww, that's so sweet and well said."

"Real talk. A good woman is the only thing that can make a rotten nigga sweet."

"Thank you, baby."

"All that sweet shit don't mean I ain't going to deal with these niggas, though," he said.

"What now?" Rydah asked, already knowing the answer. It was written all over Wolfe's face.

"I'ma have them niggas scooped up," he told her.

"Then what? I mean, after you have them scooped up?" she asked.

Wolfe was honest. "You don't want to know," he said.

Tallhya felt no pity for them. She said to Wolfe, "Don't forget what you promised me."

Wolfe glared at her. "I gave you my word, didn't I?" He wasn't used to being questioned, and he didn't care for it. The only reason he didn't make a big deal out of it was because she was Rydah's sister. If she wasn't, he would have taught her to stay in her place.

"I know you haven't had a lot of experience dealing with real brothers, but real niggas do what they say and say what they mean."

"My bad, brother-in-law. You right. But you didn't have to put me in my place like that," she said, trying to bring light to a dark topic.

"Actually, he did," Rydah said. "You needed that."

"I did," Tallhya admitted. "So, now that we know their identities, how do you plan on going about it?"

"I'ma deal with it."

Tallhya asked, "Can I ask for a small favor?"

"I have to know the favor before I can say yes."

"Can you hold off for a couple days before you get at them them?" Rydah asked. "Please, babe, I need you to do it for me."

Tallhya looked at her sister and smiled. "Please, brother. Please?"

Wolfe thought that this was an odd request, especially coming from Tallhya. If he'd read her correctly, she was the type that wanted wrongs righted. Quickly. "Something you need to tell me?" he asked.

Tallhya was quiet, going back and forth with herself mentally, trying to determine if she wanted to share with Wolfe what she knew. On one hand, she wanted to be real with him, but on the other hand, she knew that he wouldn't let them rob the truck. And he definitely wouldn't allow Rydah to participate in her scheme.

Wolfe waited.

Tallhya asked Rydah, "What do you think?" Wolfe was her man. Let her decide whether they should keep him in the dark.

"This is the same man that had us followed. He's like Big Brother. He sees everything."

Tallhya said, "Damn." How could she be so stupid? "You already know, don't you? You're just testing me."

Wolfe said nothing.

"Well, you won't believe what I found out."

"Try me."

Chapter 32

401K

Riccardo, an 8-year employee of the Cashmore Armored Truck Company, exercised an enormous degree of patience and precision wheeling the 10-ton steel behemoth through the constipated byways and highways of South Florida. The truck didn't handle as well when it was weighed down with cash, and today, they were at the truck's limit. The company was short on help, so Riccardo and his two partners were asked to pick up the slack, pulling an additional route on top of their all ready busy regular route.

Riccardo pulled the truck into the loading area of the Hard Rock Casino. "You guys ready for this one?" The Hard Rock was hosting a popular nationally televised poker tournament. Fifteen hundred players signed up to play, each ponying up a $10,000 entry fee.

From the back of the truck, Teddy said, "Yep. Let's do this." He and Mike were the hoppers, the guys that got in and out of the truck. There were two buttons, one located in the front and the other in the back of the cab, that had to be pressed at the same time in order to release the lock on the cab's door. Riccardo and Teddy hit the buttons, disengaging the hydraulic locking system.

Teddy and Mike hopped out of the back of truck to load the money. They wore blue and black security uniforms and carried badges and guns. It took twenty minutes to load thirty bags of legal casino money onto the truck. The rest of the money was designated to be delivered to the Federal Reserve Bank for safekeeping, but before it got there, one more pickup needed to be made. It was a small bank branch on Seventh Avenue.

Riccardo maneuvered the truck into the cramped parking lot, nearly clipping the bumper off of a green Camry. Once he got the truck where it needed to be, he said to Teddy, "This is it, my friend. One last stop. You ready?"

It was Teddy's last day on the job. He'd put in his retirement papers last month after he'd paid his faithful dues to the company with not one mishap. Teddy had given Cashmore thirty years of service. It was still hard to believe that after today, it would be over.

"Yep."

They hit the buttons.

Riccardo said, "Make it epic."

"I will."

Teddy smiled as he and Mike hopped out of the vehicle, clueless how true that innocent remark would be.

Riccardo sat in the driver's sear in front of the bank thinking, *There is no turning back now.* He planned to leave the company in about two more years himself, after everything blew over. That was how long he'd decided he'd have to continue to do this job in order to not draw suspicion. He knew that the company would require him to do PTS counseling. And who knows? If he played his cards right, after the Post Traumatic Stress counseling, if he was lucky, the company may even put him on disability. But if all else failed, he'd just have to do this job for another two years or so and that was it.

He inhaled a lung full of air. *The hardest part,* thought Riccardo, *will be laying low and not spending any of the money.* When he quit, he would move back home to the Dominican Republic and live like a king.

Yup! He had it all figured out.

Life is good, he thought as he sat at the wheel of the truck, smiling, waiting patiently for show time.

Teddy made his way out of the bank. He was feeling himself, knowing that today would be his last day of having to look over his shoulder, carrying someone else's money. His mind was so gone on the plans he'd made for him and his wife once he retired that he wasn't paying attention to details—like the man dressed in black who had just crept up from the sewer Riccardo had intentionally parked next to. Teddy was three feet from the truck.

Mike, who was waiting in the back of the cab, opened the door. That's when Abe shot a heavy stream of commercial-grade pepper spray into his eyes, disarmed him, and then cuffed him with plastic flex-cuffs. As rehearsed, Prince snuck up behind Teddy and cracked him across the skull with the butt of his gun. Once Mike's limp body crumpled to the cement, Prince disarmed him.

For the sake of the cameras, they had Ken from the club, whose birthday it had been that night, put a gun to Riccardo's head. On cue, a white van rolled up with Tiger behind the wheel, and another masked guy walked up and had his gun held on the two guards who were both out cold.

Abe and Prince began to fill the van with bags of cash.

"Holy shit!" Abe said when he caught a glimpse of how full the truck was. Neither man expected there to be so many bags money, or that the bags of cash would be so heavy.

Ken, the accomplice who had the gun on Riccardo, who was also the timekeeper, announced that they only had thirty seconds. Abe and Prince picked up the pace.

Abe said, "We need more time." They were loading the van as quickly as they could.

"We don't have it," said Prince, "if we want to be able to spend any of it."

"Five seconds," said Ken, the timekeeper. "Time to wrap this shit up."

Abe and Prince, with regret, each tossed their last bag into the van. The truck was still one-third full. It almost literally made them sick that they would have to walk away without it all. There was no other choice; they would have to leave it. Ken jumped into the van.

Abe walked over to Riccardo. He had one last piece of unfinished business. He said to Riccardo, "Thanks for nothing!" and then pulled the trigger. Twice. He shot Riccardo twice in the head just for the fuck of it, since he was pissed about having to walk away with only a portion of the money.

Before any of his accomplices knew it, he ran over to Theodore and shot him in the head, and then Mike, too, never even hearing either beg for their lives.

"Fuck you do that for, man?" Prince snapped, "You gon' bring the heat!"

"Because I'm pissed the fuck off!" He spit the words out. "Fuck them dead motherfuckers! And anybody else who stand between me and this paper!"

Chapter 33

Gut Instincts

When the white van pulled off, Tallhya wasn't far behind them. She had the entire thing on video. It was their insurance policy. She texted Rydah as she followed them, already knowing their next move before they even made it.

Tallhya: Everything good on ur end?

Rydah: Mild hiccups but working it out.

Tallhya:We don't have time for no hiccups. Pls don't f' this up! We only have one shot!

HONKKKKKKKKK!

A dump truck heading down Seventh Avenue laid on the horn and smashed the brakes in order to dodge the boy running across the street.

The boy was actually Rydah in boy's clothes. She was carrying a tool box. She'd done a little work on the Suburban that Prince, Abe, and their crew planned to switch into.

The tracking device Rydah had installed on the truck gave her eyes on it. She watched from her smartphone as the fellas transferred the money from the van to the Suburban.

The crew had taken off their masks and black jumpsuits, changing back into street clothes. On the way, they'd transferred the bags of money into colorful storage totes to conceal the bags.

They were home free, or so they thought, when the engine in the Suburban suddenly died

"What the fuck?" said Abe. "Shit!"

What the fuck was right. . . .

Prince got out of the van and looked under the hood, searching for the problem. The truck was only a year old, with not even 10,000 miles on it.

Frustrated, Abe kicked the wheel. "Fuckkkk!" he screamed, frustrated.

Prince said, "It has to be something simple," reassuring his partner, who was already on edge after taking the life of two innocent security guards, having to leave a truck full of cash, and now to have his car break down with what cash they did have in it. It was turning out to a pretty fucked up day, and he knew these kinds of days usually sent Abe off his rocker.

"Our luck can't be this bad," Abe said.

Prince spotted an Advance Auto Parts store down the street. He told Tiger to take the walk. "I think it's the battery."

"Shit." Tiger was reluctant to go. "I don't trust you with the bread," Tiger said.

Prince, still keeping his cool, said, "We go back too far to start not trusting one another now. If I was going to put any shit into the game, I would've laid you down back there with Riccardo." Prince looked his friend in the eye. "Money ain't never came between us, but if we don't act soon, we ain't gon' have shit."

Tiger noticed Abe looking at him with frustration and knew he was a time bomb. He glanced at Ken, who was down for Tiger either way. He then thought about the bags of cash that he so desired, and how they had come too far to start bickering back and forth within the crew.

Tiger glared at his even-tempered friend, Prince. "The deviation of the plan got me thinking crazy. It's all good. We go back too far for this shit."

"Look," Prince said, "we need to get moving before we get made."

"You right," Tiger said. "I've never been around this much paper before. The shit got me thinking crazy."

Just then, a state trooper pulled up alongside the Suburban. "Everything all right, fellas?"

"Yeah, Officer. We just need a jump. We just drew straws for who would take the walk to the store," Prince spoke up.

"Who lost?" the trooper asked.

"Huh?"

"You said that you drew straws," the trooper said.

"Right." Abe pointed to Tiger. "He did."

On that note, Tiger started making his way down the road. The trooper smiled and tilted his hat as he drove off slowly. Everyone in the truck exhaled a sigh of relief.

Prince said, "That shit was close as fuck."

Abe was feeling himself. "Close is only good in horseshoes and grenades. We can't be stopped."

The moment they let their guards down for one second, two vans rolled up, and before they could blink, had them boxed in. Nowhere to run, they were caught slipping.

"Oh, shit!"

They were surrounded.

"Police! Don't move!" The police jumped out of the van quicker than a lightning bolt.

Tallhya watched the entire thing through binoculars from a couple blocks away. *Damn*, she thought. *They swooped in as if they'd been informed.*

Abe looked around for an escape. One of the cops said, "Don't even think about it, motherfucker," as if he could read Abe's mind.

Prince slowly put his hands up, shaking his head in disgust. "Ain't this a bitch."

"Yup! Sure is! A real pretty one!" the redneck officer said.

Prince asked, "What are the charges?"

The Caucasian cop said, "Just shut the fuck up, motherfucker!"

Innocent bystanders were gawking, looking for something to post on social media.

As the police perp-walked them to the van, Abe did a double take at the crowd of onlookers and managed to meet eye-to-eye with Tallhya. She was sitting in front of the Wing Station, eating Buffalo wings and wearing an American flag scarf tied around her head.

He thought his eyes were playing tricks on him. He squinted to make sure it was her. That's when Rydah stuck her middle finger up, flashed a huge grin, and silently made him read her lips when she moved them to say, "Yeah, motherfuckerrrr!"

But out of her peripheral vision, she saw Simone, dressed in a police uniform, jump into the Suburban and pull off.

Chapter 34

For the Love of Money

"Money . . . Money . . . Moneeeeyyyyyyyy. . . .
You wanna do things, do things, do things, good things
with it.
Talk about cash money
Talk about cash money—dollar bills, y'all."

The O'Jays' 1973 hit single "For the Love of Money" played on repeat from Rydah's Beats by Dre Pill.

Rydah, Tallhya, and Simone celebrated their victory of outsmarting the guys who had caused them all types of hurt and pain by singing, dancing, and playing in more than six million dollars in cash. Being around so much money made them euphoric. The sisters were on a rush that had them riding higher than the thirty-story condo that overlooked the city of Miami.

Tallhya lowered the volume slightly on the portable speaker. "God bless mu'fucking America," she said, worn out from doing splits and the Roger Rabbit as she took her seat at the table. Rydah and Simone followed suit. The table was overrun with money; more money than a middle-class family made in a lifetime.

"I still can't believe we really did this shit." Tallhya shook her head in disbelief. "We actually pulled this shit off."

Rydah said, "I told you that there was more than one way to skin a cat, didn't I?"

"We are waaaay smarter than those motherfuckers, and it had to be a better way to do it than us doing it."

"You sure did." Tallhya had to admit it. "That shit was easy."

"We literally made them bozos do all our dirty work for us, and we just collected on the back end."

"Pimps up, hoes down! We pimped the hell out of them," Rydah said.

"We sure did," Tallhya said. "You should've seen that nigga's look on his face. I think he shitted a brick after he made eye contact with me."

The girls laughed.

"And the driver, that was the guy named Tiger, the guy who was trying to holla at me and I shot him down. And the other guy was Ken. The girl Charlotte that Buffy knew from church, Ken was supposed to be her boyfriend, but it was all larceny. All that shit was one big scam."

"And that's why we came up," Tallhya said with a funny face.

"And we deserve every penny of this cash," Simone said, looking at the all the cash on the table. There was still, what seemed to be countless more bags in the corner, waiting to be opened and counted. "This is it, sisters! We are set for life, and we can do what we want. But most importantly, we can live happily ever after."

In the bliss of everything, Rydah happened to look up, and she couldn't help but notice the words *Breaking News* flashing across the 80-inch flat-screen television.

"Hold on, hold on, hold on," Rydah said, grabbing the remote and turning up the volume.

"This is Lisa Sanchez from WYGH-Action News, Miami, reporting live from outside a bank on Seventh Avenue, where a murder and armored truck robbery took place early this afternoon on this hot, Miami day." The reporter was standing in front of the yellow crime scene tape in front of the bank.

"This morning, Theodore 'Teddy' Solomon kissed his wife good-bye and left for work, as he had done for the last thirty years. When he got off, he'd planned to stop and pick up a rental tux for his retirement party. The party would include his loving wife of forty years, his three biological children, and the twenty-seven foster kids he had taken into his home over the years. The retirement party was planned for tomorrow evening, celebrating his thirty years of devoted service to the Cashmore Armored Truck Company. However, those plans, along with his life, were both highjacked at the hands of what authorities believe to be four dangerous, masked men."

Lisa took a dramatic pause, looking at the notes on her phone.

"Now," she continued, "the video you are about to see is very graphic, and should not be viewed by children or anyone with a weak stomach to violence."

Lisa looked into the camera with a sympathetic face as she proceeded with the news.

"Mayhem and madness started this afternoon when Truck 651 was making its final pick up at the First National Republic Bank, when Mr. Solomon took his final walk out of the building. He was only two steps away from the truck and the rest of his life when it went down. When Michael Fuqua opened the door to let Mr. Solomon back inside, a masked man assaulted him with high-grade pepper spray. Then, the assailants shot Mr. Fuqua in the head, which then gave them full control over the truck carrying millions of dollars."

Surveillance footage from the area cameras ran across the screen, showing the masked suspects murder the guards and load a white van with the stolen money.

"If you look to the left of the screen you can see the man driving the van monitoring a stopwatch. When they reached the designated time, they stopped, leaving more than three million dollars behind. Then they shot the driver of the truck, Riccardo Santana, in the head, and drove off."

"Oh, shit!" Tallhya jumped up from the table.

Her sisters paid her no mind.

Simone fanned her quiet, while Rydah turned the volume on the television up a few more notches.

"Don't shush me!" said Tallhya

"Three honorable men are dead. An undisclosed amount of money is missing. Such a sad day for the devoted security officers and the people of Miami." The reporter lowered her eyes, shaking her head as if she herself were in mourning. "Our condolences go out to the families of these three men. Back to you, John."

The screen shot back to a camera inside the studio to the male news anchor.

"So sad, Lisa."

"Yes it is, John"

"Now, Lisa, we know that you devote your life to being the first to deliver the latest and most accurate news stories."

"I truly do, John."

Tallhya said, "You bitches better not shut me down. I think we may be in real fucking trouble."

Rydah hushed her sister. "Let's hear the entire piece before we jump to any conclusions. This is where the story gets good. This chick right here always has some shit for yo' ass. She always gets the low down on everything and takes pride in delivering the tea before anybody else."

The camera shot back to Lisa. "Now there's something," she said, "that I found quite interesting, and so did the authorities." Lisa worked the viewers as she confidently sucked the camera in with her ocean-blue eyes. "What most people don't know is that armored trucks are used to move much more than just money. Although we usually assume the trucks are carrying cash, these vehicles may be transporting anything of significant value, and this was the case here today." She used her hands to express herself, putting up one finger.

Tallhya said, "Y'all listening to this bitch when I'm trying to tell you that we are fucked. Fucked in the ass with no lube. No Vaseline. No nothing!"

Lisa Sanchez went on to say, "I happen to find it mind-boggling that this particular armored vehicle, Truck 651, was carrying highly sensitive and classified electronic files of the FBI's undercover operatives, witness protection lists, and some of the FBI's top informants' relocation addresses and pictures, along with more top secret and very sensitive, highly classified information."

Lisa looked into the camera and put up another finger to try to make her point. "Now, the fact that millions of dollars were left behind makes me think that the money wasn't the motive, but the information was. And the money was just a perk."

Then, Lisa looked into the camera, threw up her hands, and shrugged her shoulders. "This is just my own personal theory and observation, which does not reflect the views or opinions of the powers that be here at WYGH-Action News, Miami."

After the brief disclaimer she said, "I haven't been able to get the authorities or police to confirm or deny that the information was removed from the truck. However, I have a source that is absolutely positive that Truck 651's manifest did indeed indicate that such files had been picked up and were being transporting to the Federal Reserve Bank to be held overnight, and were then to be moved to the Pentagon on Monday. Again," she said, proudly breaking the news story, "it is not confirmed that this information was stolen. This is just my two cents, and as always, it's my duty to keep you abreast of all info as it becomes available.

"This is Lisa Sanchez, and do note that I'm the first and only anchor on scene here, allowed behind the yellow tape. Until next time . . ." She smiled. "Back to you, John."

Rydah was already up from the table, going through the other bags that they hadn't counted yet, looking for the jump drives that Lisa had spoken about.

"You think we have that too?" Simone asked as she got up from the table, standing nearby, anxious to see if they had it.

Tallhya came over, standing between the two sisters. "Why y'all over here searching for damn rats and shit? The same way they got that footage from outside the bank, they can get footage from one of the buildings where we jacked the Suburban."

Rydah looked up from the bags of money she was searching through. "Bitch, that's what your ass been whining and throwing a tantrum for?"

Tallhya looked at Rydah like she wanted to smack her. "For once, when I need you to be fucking serious, you all relaxed. This is the shit that can send our asses to the pen for fucking life, bitch! And usually you are the more mature one, and you are taking this shit lightly."

"That's not going to happen," Rydah said nonchalantly. "I disarmed every camera within half a mile of there."

"What?" Tallhya knew nothing about disarming no cameras. "When? And how you know to do that shit?"

"That's why I was running a few minutes behind schedule, because I was setting up a device that distorts digital cameras for up to a half mile. If a bitch was in the vicinity and wanted to make a Snapchat on her phone, she was shit out of luck. Equipment and towers were down."

Tallhya wasn't sure how something like that worked, but she was glad that it did. She said, "You the best, sis."

"Awww, hell," Simone said. "You two bitches done drove me to smoke." Her phone rang. "I'm going on the balcony to take a smoke and talk to Chase."

"Don't tell that nigga none of our business," Tallhya reminded her. "You hear me?"

Simone stopped short of the glass balcony door and looked Tallhya smack dead in the face. "Don't disrespect me like that, Tallhya. I've never told him any of our family secrets, and I never will. Ever!" She rolled her eyes. "Just have my cut right when I get done smoking." She gave Tallhya the finger before shutting the balcony door behind her.

Tallhya eyed Rydah.

"You know that bitch don't get an equal third, right?"

Rydah laughed. "You crazy."

"Nah. I'm dead-ass fucking serious." Tallhya explained why. "First, she's not the boss of this job. That would be me. She did very little, and she stole all my money last time."

Rydah got serious. "So what are you proposing?" she asked. "And are you taking into account how that is going to make Simone feel?"

"Since she's our sister, by default we going to look out for her. I love Simone. She's my blood, and I would never let her be fucked up." Tallhya thought about a number. "Three hundred thousand. That's enough for her to live off, and she will be happy with that."

Rydah asked, "Are you sure?" This was the first she'd heard about Simone stealing money from Tallhya. Curious, she asked, "What about us? How do we split the rest?"

"Down the middle," Tallhya assured her.

"What about Wolfe? We have to look out for Wolfe," Rydah said, getting straight down to business.

"I'm going to give him his hundred fifty K back, plus a healthy bonus for having our back."

Rydah thought about it. "That sounds fair."

Simone was on the balcony talking to Chase with a face covered in smiles. Rydah crossed her arms, studying Simone's body language.

She asked Tallhya, "How much you trust her?"

"I trust her," Tallhya said, "but not with my money . . . or her judgment when it comes to my mental state. I know for a fact that she would never rat on us, but still, that shit she did to me . . ." Tallhya had yet to fully forgive Simone for putting her in a crazy house and spending her money, leaving her with nothing. And she wasn't sure if she ever would. It didn't matter that Simone had a good reason for spending the money. "I love her, but I'm sorry, I just ain't over it."

Simone stubbed the cigarette out and pulled open the balcony door. "Congrats, baby. I'm so happy for you, and we're going to celebrate big time. My sister and I are going to take you out. We're all super elated for you! Love you much. And I'll see you soon."

Simone disconnected the call and walked over to Rydah's bar, fanning herself. Though she was cool as a cucumber talking to Chase, she was starting to panic.

"Vodka! Bitches, I need vodka!"

Rydah and Tallhya exchanged glances, not knowing what to think.

Tallhya said, "You're not supposed to be drinking."

"Or smoking, for that matter," Rydah added.

"It's not about what I'm 'not supposed' to do, but what I need."

"You don't *need* no drink," Tallhya said.

"Or to smoke, either," Rydah added with her arms crossed, looking at her sister. "Especially not smoking. You just beat cancer."

"Look, if you have a problem, you can talk to us about it. Drinking won't make it go away," Tallhya said.

Simone ignored her sisters nagging, continuing to scan the labels on the countless liquor bottles on and underneath the bar. "Where in the hell is the vodka? And Rydah, I thought you didn't drink like that. So how come you got every fucking top shelf liquor in the store?"

"What's going on, Simone?"

Simone inhaled and then blew out the used air. "I got both good news and bad news all in the same call."

Tallhya tried to keep it positive. "Give us the good first."

"I'm going to be able to spend more time with you. A lot more. Because Chase and I are moving to Miami."

This didn't make sense. Tallhya said, "Chase can't up and leave his job on the police force."

Simone found and poured that drink. She took a shot straight to the head and then poured another. "Chase just got a call from the Attorney General of the United States. He got a promotion. The promotion comes with a huge raise and a relocation to . . . guess where? Miami. They want him to put a task force together to solve city's top unsolved bank robberies. Starting with this armored truck heist."

Rydah poured a drink of her own. "Get the fuck outta here."

"Say that shit one more time." Tallhya couldn't believe what she just heard. "This nigga seems to be drawn to us like bees to sugar."

Simone agreed. "I know. He's boarding his flight now. They are flying him in on a military jet so that he can get started right away before any of the evidence gets cold. I'm going to meet him at the airport."

Rydah went back over to the table, sorting, stacking, and putting the money away.

"Well, we wanted to talk to you about your cut." Tallhya said.

"Whatever y'all decided to give me is cool with me. I don't expect a third of it. Plus, I know I owe you, sis," Simone said to Tallhya.

"You right. But I got you. I ain't going to do you like you did me."

"Whatever you give, I'm going to have you hold on to it for me . . . for now, please. I can't go around him or stay in the hotel with him with a duffel bag of cash," Simone said, looking off into space. "This shit feels too close for comfort. It's like history is repeating itself."

Simone reflected on how she met Chase in the first place. It was her first day working at the bank, which was the first job she'd ever had in her life. That job was at a bank that got robbed on that very day. Although she had nothing to do with the robbery, initially the police looked at her as a suspect.

Chase was the lead detective on the case, and after it was all said and done, she ended up being the leading lady in his life. After Simone, Bunny, Tallhya, and Ginger started robbing banks, he was investigating those too, and he suspected the sisters. However, in the end, he told Simone that he loved her so much that if they did have something to do with it, he would let it go. He told her to just never do it again.

Rydah sat beside her sister, comforting her. "It's not history repeating itself," she said. "Because it's nothing to investigate. And no one in this room is ever going to rob anything again. We are set for life. That's it, that's all."

"I need a Valium," Simone said. "I know one of y'all post traumatic, psychotic bitches gotta have one. Valium or Xanax—something."

"We got you," Tallhya said. "Don't worry. We Banks, right?"

"A'ight. Let me pull myself together. I'll take a shower and do my makeup. I want to look halfway decent when I get to the airport to meet Chase."

"Okay, sis. Everything will be okay," Rydah assured her sister, and Tallhya joined in for a group hug, which was interrupted by Tallhya's phone ringing.

"Hello." She paused. "This is she. How can I help you?"

Tallhya listened. "Why sure . . . yes . . . oh my goodness. Thank you so much!" Tallhya's smile could've lit up the entire North Pole.

When Tallhya got off the phone, Rydah said, "Damn, girl, do share the good news."

"Dr. Snatch's office called and said they had a cancellation. They can fit me in on Tuesday for the surgery. Bitchessssss . . ." She did a pirouette on the floor. "I'm about to be a skinny bitch."

Simone and Rydah laughed as Tallhya pranced around the house, singing.

"Tell Chase to tell them people at his job, right out the gate, that his sister-in-law needs a get-out-of-jail-free card for walking around buck naked on South Beach." Tallhya was hyped up. "I might not ever put on clothes again. My everyday outfit is going to be a skimpy bikini."

They laughed.

Their laughter was interrupted by Tallhya's phone again. "I swear, if these people are calling me to cancel, I'm going to snap and just go ballistic." But when she looked down at the phone, she saw that the call wasn't from the doctor's office.

She answered, "Hey, brother-in-law."

"Just calling to make good on my word," he said. "You still interested in having your way with these nothing-ass motherfuckers or not?"

"You already know how I feel, brother-in-law."

"Then I'm going to send you the address. Ask Rydah for the directions."

"A'ight. I will be there soon." Tallhya hung up the phone. "This day can't get any better than this."

"What now?" Simone asked.

Tallhya didn't want to tell Simone what she was about to go do, so she changed the subject. "Don't you have to get dressed and get ready to get to the airport? And you shouldn't take that Xanax and drive."

"Especially after drinking vodka and smoking. You need no Valium," Rydah added.

"Blah, blah, blah. But whatever, I hear y'all. Rydah, can you drop me off?"

Under her breath, Tallhya asked Rydah, "What's the deal with the address? Wolfe told me to ask you to explain."

"He has a code that he uses. Whenever he texts you the address, switch the first and the last numbers with one another. If the police see the address, it won't match the real one."

"Gotcha." She nodded. "That's smart."

"You know Wolfe got everything covered and will always stay a few steps ahead of the game," Rydah reminded her sister.

"A'ight, sisters. I gotta go handle my business," Tallhya said, lifting up her shirt in front of the mirror, putting on her waist shaper. She tried to rush getting all the hooks latched together.

"That contraption is going to kill you before you can even get on Dr. Snatch's table," Simone said, watching her sister squeeze and snap herself in the girdle.

"I've been telling her, but it falls on deaf ears. You know she treats that thing like it's an American Express card. She isn't going to ever leave home without it," Rydah said.

"I can honestly say that she lost a lot of weight since she been here with you, and Miami is doing her good."

"Between the eating better, diet pills, and the damn waist shaper, she be working it out," Rydah had to agree.

"I hear you bitches talking about me like I ain't here. But I'm about to be out."

Tallhya headed for the door and slipped on her shoes. Before she bounced, she said, "There's one thing that I know. We've all been through the fire. We argue. We fight. But it doesn't change the fact that when everyone is gone—Momma, Daddy, Granny, man, friends, and foes—at the end of the day all we got is each other. No matter what."

"No matter what!"

"No matter what!"

Chapter 35

Hurricane Wilma

Coral Gables

Wolfe had purchased the four-bedroom home during a down cycle of the real estate market eight years ago. It was a corner lot, built on a dead end, tree-lined street. The main thing that attracted Wolfe to the property, besides the foreclosure price, was the soundproof, semi-underground storm bunker. This was something extremely rare for Miami, but the prior owners had the 1,000-square foot, fully functional bunker built after the category 4 hurricane that pimp-smacked the coast in 2005. The natural disaster, which was labeled Hurricane Wilma, racked up $16.4 billion in damages, mostly throughout Broward and Palm Beach Counties.

Wolfe used the house as a fictitious rental property to justify a small portion of his untaxable income. He could give two fucks if anyone ever really rented the property. It was only one of thirty such spots. In fact, this particular location had intentionally never really been occupied.

The storm bunker was the perfect place to take care of business that he wanted to go undetected, such as enhanced interrogations in search of sensitive information.

Wolfe caged both Abe and Prince down alongside Buffy in the soundproof bunker, each in their own fabricated, reinforced dog kennels. He'd already killed the two other partners. Disposing of their bodies was easy. Florida is occupied by an estimated 1.25 million alligators, and Wolfe knew just where to find a family of hungry gators that appreciated good fast food delivery from time to time.

Wolfe sat at his desk, eating a piece of red velvet cake as he watched the surveillance footage, which seemed to have him quite entertained when the gators ate into the two accomplices.

"Damn, another one bites the dust," Wolfe said, making sure the destruction of his prisoners' friends were in surround sound, so that Buffy, Abe, and Prince could hear their partners in crime scream their last cries, begging for their lives.

After witnessing firsthand what Wolfe was capable of, it didn't take long for Abe to sing like a young Frankie Beverly before the rumored throat cancer. But Wolfe was taken aback by the lyrics of the song.

Wolfe took another bite of his cake and got up from the desk. He dug into an old tool bag and came out with a pair of oversized needle-nose pliers. Abe's eyes stretched to double their normal size when Wolfe reached toward his family jewels. His face was already leaking from the brutal beating Wolfe had administered with a bat.

Abe stammered, "I'm t–telling the t–truth."

Wolfe busted the pliers to bite down on Abe's left testicle. The coiled muscle ruptured under the pressure. Abe passed out from the pain.

When he recovered, Wolfe said, "There's one remaining, for now. If I find out that you're lying, you won't have any."

Sweating golf balls at the mere thought of losing another testicle, Abe said, "It was Jaffey! I swear on my son's life. Jaffey set it all up."

Wolfe, silently still holding the bloody pliers, gave Abe a hard stare as if to say, "Keep going."

Abe quickly obliged. "Jaffey paid us twenty thousand to carjack Rydah. We were supposed to hold her for ransom, and then smoke her after you paid the bread. When Rydah got away from the nigga I sent, Jaffey nearly had a heart attack. I swear."

Jaffey? That country, pimp-costume-wearing motherfucker played me for a chump, Wolfe thought. *But why?* All Wolfe had ever done for Jaffey was bankroll him the dough to stay afloat.

Then he reflected on the conversation he'd had with Rydah the other night, when he was trying to convince her that it was Buffy who'd set her up, answering his own question: *People are motivated by jealousy and money.*

The plot never changes, only the people.

Chapter 36

Surprise

Sitting in the waiting room of the doctor's office, Tallhya glanced at the dials of her new Rolex. It was 10:25. The watch was a gift from Rydah; she'd bought one for both sisters. Being that Rydah had spent very little of the money that they'd inherited from Me-Ma, the gifts were a legitimate purchase.

But where the hell was Rydah? Tallhya wondered. She was supposed to have met her there twenty-five minutes ago. It wasn't like Rydah to not be on time. She was the most prompt person Tallhya knew. In order to keep her mind from running wild with speculation, Tallhya focused on the "Before and After" pictures that the receptionist had given her on the iPad.

The doctor was late as well.

Tallhya was getting impatient. Surprisingly, the weekend had flown by. She was at the lab at 9 a.m. sharp, getting her blood work done. Now she was waiting to see the doctor for her pre-op. If everything was okay, God willing, the doctor would schedule the tummy tuck and liposuction procedure for the next day. She prayed that all of the blood work come back correct. Tallhya wanted nothing to get in the way of her new beginning.

"Natallhya Banks." It was the receptionist.

Tallhya jumped up, quickly making her way to the open door that separated the waiting room from the main part of the clinic.

A waiting nurse flashed a smile. "My name is Kendra." Tallhya followed her down the hall to a room. Inside, the nurse took her vitals, blood pressure, and pulse. Then, after asking a few questions, Nurse Kendra informed Tallhya that Dr. Snatch was running late. "But I'm going to let you chat with Dr. McNeil to at least give you an idea of what to expect.

That'll be one thing out of the way. I know firsthand you must have a lot anxiety and questions."

Tallhya thought that she sounded very professional and sympathetic. "Actually," she said, "I just want to get the whole thing over and done with, so that I can heal."

"I was the same way with my first surgery," the nurse said. "I was also filled with a mixture of anxiety and excitement all at the same time."

Tallhya gave Nurse Kendra a hard once over. She was tall and lean, with not an ounce of fat on her toned body. "If you don't mind me asking," Tallhya inquired, "how many surgeries have you had?"

"Oh, honey, let's just say that I'm an old pro at it."

She may be a pro, Tallhya thought, but nothing about Nurse Kendra seemed old. "Would you mind telling me some of the things that you've had done? I'm just curious. You look so fit."

"Let's see . . ." said Nurse Kendra. She started counting the procedures off on her fingers. "I've had the tummy tuck, lipo on my back and thighs, a butt lift, breast implants, breast lift, rhino surgery, cheek sculpture, Botox, and probably a few other things I forgot to name."

"Wow." Tallhya was amazed. "Well, you look damn good," she said. This bitch looked like she had the best body that money could buy, and her face was beautiful as well. Judging by the Florida State class ring she wore, nurse Kendra was probably somewhere in her late forties, and she looked like a retired runway model.

Tallhya asked, "Who was your doctor?"

Tallhya beamed from ear to ear when she heard nurse Kendra say, "Dr. Snatch and Dr. McNeil are the only people in the world that I would ever let do a procedure on me."

"Then I'm glad I made the choice to come here."

"Trust me, sweetie, you are in good hands. And I'm not just saying that because I work here," she assured Tallhya. "These guys are the absolute best."

"That's good to know. But my procedure's still going to be done by Dr. Snatch, right?" Dr. McNeil seemed like a good guy, but Tallhya had paid the big bucks to specifically get her body snatched by Dr. Snatch. He was the one with the long waiting list, the huge following, and did all the work on the celebrities. She hadn't come this far to be baited and switched for the sidekick.

"Yes, Doctor Snatch will be doing your work. But like I said, Doctor McNeil is just as good. Trust me. So this is how it's going to work," she said. "Doctor McNeil will be in in a second to speak with you. And in the morning when you check in, Dr. Snatch will go over the procedures again, do drawings, and show you where he will be cutting."

"All right, I guess." For the first time, Tallhya felt nervous.

Nurse Kendra sensed it. "Everything is going to work out fine. Trust me. You are going to be snatched to the gawds."

Tallhya thought that it sounded kind of tacky coming out of the mouth of a preppie and proper Caucasian chick.

"Can't wait. If my sister comes in, will you make sure they send her back? You'll recognize her. She's a skinny, already snatched version of me."

"Sure thing." Nurse Kendra shut the door behind her when she left.

Three minutes later, the door opened. When Tallhya looked up, she got the shock of her life, and so did Dr. McNeil.

"Fonz. . . ."

Both of their mouths dropped the second they locked eyes.

"Tallhya. . . ."

Not only did her name sound like a melody when it flowed off his tongue, but the smell of his cologne and his starched white coat damn near paralyzed her. She was so embarrassed. All she wanted to do was run away and disappear, but she wasn't leaving that office going anywhere until she got her pre-op and everything finalized to be on that table in the morning.

"OMG! You are a doctor?" She stopped herself from putting her clothes back on and running out of the room. "How come you didn't tell me you're a plastic surgeon?"

"You never asked. And," he said with an accusing stare, "*you* never told *me* that you were getting surgery."

"I just met you. Why would I tell you something that personal?"

"Because I'm your friend, and I would have been concerned that my friend is going into the hospital, under anesthesia, to have a major surgery."

That sounded good, but her getting plastic surgery was still none of his business. She kept her thoughts to herself.

Fonz said, "Would you be offended if I shared a personal observation?"

"It can't get any more personal than this. I don't have a shirt or bra on. And I'm under this gown."

Blushing, Fonz said, "I don't think that you need surgery. I think you are stunningly beautiful the way you are."

"If you believe that, then you must be blind," she said. "I'm like, way overweight."

"And you carry it well. I think you are gorgeous to the naked eye. However, it doesn't mean anything at all."

"What do you mean?" she asked. "You see so many beautiful women. I bet you tell them all how beautiful they are."

"Only if it's true," said Fonz. "I admit, for the past twelve years I've seen some beautiful women, and I sculpt women into nearly flawless creatures. But none of that means anything if the person isn't beautiful inside."

Tallhya wanted to call Fonz on his bullshit, but she also wanted to believe that he was really being sincere.

"Anybody's outer appearance can be transformed into what the world thinks is beautiful," said Fonz. "But what's most important is a person's heart."

When she rolled her eyes, he said, "I'm telling the truth. A person's manners, their vibes, their principles, humility, their will to love, understand, and appreciate other people, places, and things. . . . Those are the things that make a person gorgeous."

The compliments rolled off of his tongue so effortlessly, and if he said it a few more times she would have believed it. Tallhya found herself not wanting to debate with him. Her mind was asking her why had she'd ducked so many of his calls and pretended to be so busy.

Because you were out planning bank robberies and torturing niggas, bitch, she tried to convince herself, but she reminded herself what the reality was. *You are afraid of getting your heart broken again! You've got to let go of that Walter shit.*

"When I met you, I was immediately gravitated to your magnetic beauty. Even though you acted tough and gave me the run around, I would've bet that under all that posturing there was somebody who just wanted to love someone and have someone to love her."

"This is really deep, and I love the content of the conversation," Tallhya said, fronting as if Fonz wasn't saying everything she wanted to hear, "but this is like, really awkward. My friend-slash-phone-buddy turned out to be a surgeon in my doctor's office."

"You forgot to mention you dumped me after our wonderful evening at dinner."

Tallhya skipped over that conversation. "Fonz, I'm in a gown having a conversation that's making me melt. This just need to stop." She honestly didn't want to offend him. "Or continue to another time. Like, seriously."

"My apologies. It just felt so natural."

"Talking to women you barely know while they're wearing a gown is what you call natural?"

Fonz chuckled. "I don't want to ever make you feel uncomfortable. And I have a patient waiting for me. Why don't you get dressed? Afterwards, you and I can go have coffee, chat a little bit, and by the time we return, Dr. Snatch should be back, and he can finish up."

"Sounds good," Tallhya admitted.

"I sense a but. . . ."

"No buts. I'm just still a little shocked to find out that you're a doctor, that's all."

"What did you think I did for a living?"

"Honestly?"

"That's the best way to answer a question."

"I thought you were some type of scammer." They both laughed. "I'm serious," she said.

"Like a credit card scammer?" he asked

"I didn't know."

"What gave you that impression?"

"Ummm . . . ." She was getting tongue tied from all the butterflies floating around in her stomach. "It's Miami," she said, as if that would explain it.

"A credit card scammer?"

"I'm sorry. If it's any consolation, I'm glad you are not."

"Get dressed," he said, smiling.

"I'm still having my surgery," she said. "I won't let you talk me out of that."

"I know better than to even try to, but I'm going to make sure that you are safe doing it." He walked out of the room and Rydah walked in.

"Is that who I think it is?"

"Yep!"

"Well, I guess he's exactly what the doctor ordered," Rydah said.

Chapter 37

Two Things

Jaffey arrived at The Lady Lagoon strip club every morning at the same time, rain or shine. Regardless of the duties Jaffey had to perform throughout the night and into the early morning as the owner of multiple clubs, often involving beautiful women in the wee hours of the morning, his routine never deviated. Today was no different. Jaffey pranced into The Lady Lagoon draped in a one-of-a-kind tailored gold silk suit, a coffee Versace silk shirt, and a pair of two-tone brown Mauri gator tie-ups, at 11 a.m. sharp.

The A-shift manager, Mike McKinney, and his crew had been in the club since eight o'clock working to get everything in order. Girls, food, liquor, cigars, condoms, cleaning supplies, bathroom amenities . . . the list of things that needed to be done to run a successful strip club was endless. Mike was a competent manager, capable of getting the job done, and he was also married to Jaffey's sister.

Mike was restocking the bar when Jaffey walked in. He'd already diluted the top-shelf liquors by 20 percent with spring water. The added water brought in an extra $125 dollars per bottle, minimum, depending on the brand.

When Mike looked up, Jaffey waved him over.

Mike made his way to the end of the center bar where Jaffey was standing. "What up, boss?"

Jaffey hated being called boss, and that was the exact reason why his brother-in-law enjoyed doing it so often. But Jaffey ignored the dig. He had more pressing matters to deal with.

"Have you heard from Prince? He was supposed to contact me a couple of days ago."

Mike wiped his hands on a towel that was hanging from his belt. "Not a peep," he said. Mike sensed that something had Jaffey uptight. "Is there something you need me to do? You want me to reach out?"

It just doesn't make sense, thought Jaffey.

First, Prince had been secretly pulling these kinds of kidnapping and robbery jobs for Jaffey for quite some time, and he'd always brought him his share, if for no other reason than he knew that Jaffey kept the jobs rolling in for Prince. If Prince had gotten knocked, it would've been blasted all over the news. And if he wasn't in somebody's jail, then where was he? Jaffey consciously wanted to dismiss the obvious answer: Prince had run off with the money.

But Jaffey knew that not wanting something to be true doesn't make it so. Fuck. He needed his cut of the armored truck money to pay Wolfe and get him off his back. It would have been massively fucked up on so many different levels, because the whole heist had been his idea. He'd been planning this thing for over a year now, and to not get any proceeds at all from it would be fucked up.

"Just let me know if you hear anything."

Mike chose not to dig at his brother-in-law this time when he said, "Okay, Jaffey. Is there anything else that I can do?"

"Just keep doing what you're doing." Jaffey said, "You're doing a great job." He checked on a few small things before going to his office to hit the phone.

The door to Jaffey's office was solid oak, and the deadbolt lock was engaged and disengaged by a keypad mounted on the wall to the left. His privacy was worth every penny of the 3 Gs he'd doled out for the system.

The code for the lock was his mother's birthday: 06-02-34. He typed it into the keypad. She'd passed away eight years ago. When the deadbolt disengaged, Jaffey flipped on the light switch on the side of the wall. LED track lights lit up the space like an operating room. Jaffey liked it that way. Life was shady enough as it was.

The moment he took a seat behind his desk and powered on the computer, Jaffey heard a noise. It was unmistakable.

Click-clack!

The hard plastic barrel of a Glock pressed against his freshly shaved head.

Wolfe's voice was menacing. "Who told you that Rydah had a sister?"

A shaky Jaffey said, "No one."

Wolfe reared back and cold-cocked Jaffey upside the head.

"An innocent person would have asked what I was talking about. The reason you didn't was because you already knew."

"I–I have no idea what you're talking about, Wolfe. I swear."

"Too late," said Wolfe. He smacked Jaffey with the gun again, this time harder. Blood poured from a gash on the top of Jaffey's head onto his one-of-a-kind silk suit.

"Fuck!"

"You are right! Now, shut the fuck up!"

"But I'm telling the truth."

Wolf said, "Your slimy ass wouldn't know what the truth looked like if it was fucking you in the ass without a condom."

Now Jaffey knew exactly where Prince was at. Wolfe had him. Obviously Prince had run his mouth, or Wolfe wouldn't be there with a gun to his head. Prince was probably dead.

"What do you want me to do?" Jaffey knew better than to keep lying. It would only make matters worse. "I'll do anything. Please, just don't kill me."

"Two things."

Jaffey was shaking. The temperature in his office was set to 69 degrees, but Jaffey was sweating bullets and blood. "Anything," he begged. "Anything."

Wolfe said, "You're going to sign over all three clubs to me. Then you're going to get your ass out of Florida—today—and never come back. Either that or eat a fucking bullet."

Florida was the only place that Jaffey had ever lived, and the only place he ever wanted to live. All he knew how to do was run nightclubs in South Florida. It was what he was good at. But it wasn't worth dying for.

"No problem." He was crying. "I'll do whatever you want me to do. The papers for the clubs are in the safe at my house."

Wolfe already knew where the papers were. He grabbed the laptop on the desk that Jaffey used to survey everything, and slipped Jaffey out the back door of the club in order not to draw attention.

Wolfe had driven a 1986 refurbished Impala to the club. He made Jaffey get in the driver's seat. "You drive."

It was a 20-minute car ride to Jaffey's beach house. They pulled into the built-on garage, which was connected to the kitchen. Wolfe walked Jaffey into the beach house.

"Get the papers." He shoved the gun into Jaffey's back, coaxing him toward the safe behind the oil painting in the bedroom. Jaffey spun the combination lock: 26 left, 32 right, 13 left.

"Stop right there!" Wolfe shouted. "You think I'm stupid?" Jaffey acted as if he had no idea what Wolfe was talking about. "Back away from the safe." Jaffey took two steps to the side. "You would have loved to put your hands on his gun, wouldn't you?" Wolfe removed the baby 9 millimeter from the wall safe, along with the paperwork and some chump change, about 40 grand in cash.

Jaffey said, "I'm going to need a couple of days to leave the state."

"Too bad, because you don't have it. Now sign the papers."

Jaffey did as he was told. He had to bide his time. He would leave, but it wouldn't be forever. Wolfe didn't own the state of Florida, and he didn't own him.

"Now back date them to a year ago." Wolfe stood over his shoulder.

Jaffey did exactly what he was told to do.

"And here, sign this too." Wolfe had had his attorney draw up the papers to make sure that the deal was airtight and couldn't be contested whatsoever by any of Jaffey's family.

Jaffey did so.

After Jaffey was finished signing the paperwork to Wolfe's liking, making Wolfe the sole owner of all three clubs, Wolfe shot him in the head.

Bang! Bang!

Lights out.

Chapter 38

Hoes Over Bros?

"Sister Ivy . . . Sister Ivy . . ." The faint voice seemed to get closer and closer. She was trying to hurry to her car.

Sister Jackie attempted to get her attention once more. "Sister Ivy . . . ."

Sister Ivy was trying to leave. The service had stretched out 40 minutes longer than usual. Ivy didn't have the luxury or the time to listen to Sister Jackie spill the tea on their church "friends." But she liked Sister Jackie, so she stopped.

"Yes?" Sister Ivy was in her late thirties but looked 25. She was drop-dead gorgeous, sophisticated, and had an air of sexiness about her. Dressed in all white, she turned around, flashing two full rows of pearly whites. "What's going on, Sister Jackie?"

Clutching at her heart, Sister Jackie said, "Oh, Lord." She always had to be dramatic. "Chile, you got me sweating like a Hebrew slave running down them there steps trying to catch up with you." She was breathing heavily. "You know how this girdle be, and these hot flashes," she joked. It was funny because it was true. "I just wanted to tell you how happy I am that you decided to join the Usher Board. We desperately needed some new, young blood."

Sister Ivy chuckled a little and ignored the slight that Sister Jackie had thrown at the other members. "I'm happy to be on the team," she said.

"Well, you need to know that the Ladies Auxiliary Board Number Six is going to be meeting on Wednesday at seven p.m. for a quick meeting before prayer service."

"Okay." Sister Ivy's smile exaggerated her naturally high cheekbones. "I wouldn't miss it for the world."

Sister Jackie noticed that she was headed to the car. "You not going to have dinner with us in the Fellowship Hall?"

"I have other plans." She hoped that Sister Jackie would grab hold of the hint and not hold her up too much longer with the small talk.

"Awwww. Sorry to hear that. I was looking forward to chit-chatting with you over dinner. You know Sister Donna cooks a mean piece of chicken. And that ain't the only bird she knows her way around, but you ain't heard it from me. Anyway," she added, "you know every first and third Sunday we serve dinner in the Fellowship Hall."

"I'll keep that in mind," Sister Ivy said. "We can catch up on Wednesday at the meeting." She said good-bye and kept it pushing to her car.

Once she was in her car, she carefully perused her phone for missed calls and texts. Out of twenty-four missed calls, none of the numbers were from Dade County Jail. That was a good thing. They were mostly business calls. No strange numbers, and nothing at all from Prince. Why in the world hadn't he called her?

"Help me, Jesus." Ivy made it her business to make it to church every Sunday to formally ask God to protect not only herself, but Prince, from any harm.

She thought about what the pastor had said: "Seek, and ye shall find. Ask, and the door shall be opened. Ask, and it shall be given.'

Ivy asked God to protect Prince. So she didn't worry. If she was going to worry, then there was no need to pray. And if she prayed, there was no need worry. He would be fine, she told herself. And right now, there was money to be made, ongoing bills to pay, and plenty of fabulous shit to buy.

Get your mind right, Ivy. Prince is good, she had to tell herself several times.

Once she made the thirty-minute drive home to her luxurious condo, she took a deep breath and ran into her house to change out of her church gear. When she came out, she reminded herself of what she always claimed her motto was: *Hoes before bros*.

Ivy looked in the rearview mirror to make sure her lipstick and her game face were painted on properly, and they were.

Game on, bitch.

She then started her Porsche 918 Spyder and let the engine of the best of German engineering run wild as she made the fifteen-minute drive to her other house. Ivy punched the six-digit code into the keypad, and the gate swung open. She drove the Spyder down the long, winding driveway, past about a dozen other late-model exotic automobiles. It was a collection of whips that would make the heart of a certified luxury whip aficionado skip a beat.

Pau, the bodyguard and butler, met her at the door. He was as big as a sumo wrestler—not fat, but solid as a tree trunk. She asked, "Is Molly here?"

Pau nodded. "Yeah, ma'am."

Every time she walked through the oversized French doors, she was reminded of how much she loved the place. She paid for it with cash about ten years ago, one of her proudest investments. It came equipped with all the amenities that any overprivileged girl could ever want: an infinity pool that peek-a-booed over the Atlantic Ocean, three Jacuzzis, two saunas, a game room, eight bedrooms (three of them masters), and ten full bathrooms. The house was home to a lot of history, sex, and her multimillion-dollar empire, and although she refused to call it what it was, the house was also a first-class, high-end brothel.

And Ivy was the madame!

The mansion housed at least twelve girls at all times, women from all over the world. All of her girls lived a life of luxury, courtesy of Ivy. Let Ivy tell it, she provided them with more indulgences than the richest, most privileged kept woman.

Her ladies were above the rest and sported the best of the absolute best clothes, the best shoes, drove the best cars, were seen by the best cosmetic surgeons, and had access to the best parties and the richest customers. But the ladies were constantly reminded that everybody had to pay the piper; there were no free dances. This meant that to pay for their keep, they had to please her clientele, some of the richest and most powerful men in the world.

Ivy kept them so intoxicated on living, dining, and traveling first class that many of them thought that fucking a few

rich men a night, if needed, was the least they could do to pay
her back. Others were happy to be a part of her stable. They
already liked sex and were willing to fuck for free pre-Ivy, so
why not live lavishly while doing it? The richest men were
usually old, and old men didn't keep it up long, so most of the
time, the work wasn't *hard*.

Ivy called out for Molly, her bottom whore to the core.
They'd been together for many years. When they met, Molly
was an illegal alien from Brazil who couldn't pronounce a
syllable of English if she needed it to save her life. Ivy found
her left for dead in the alley of a strip club in the hood. She
had OD'd on pills. Ivy nursed her back to health and then
helped her get her green card. Since then, Molly had not only
been loyal, but helped her make a lot of money. More money
than either girl had ever dreamed of seeing.

Molly was a long-legged brunette with a beautiful golden
complexion and gray eyes. She now spoke three languages.
She also liked to walk around the house in bathing suits that
were barely large enough to cover her private parts.

Ivy asked her, "How did everything go while I was away?"
She hadn't been at the house since Saturday morning.

Molly went to the safe inside her room that was cam-
ouflaged to look like a piece of furniture. "Great. I tallied
everything up for you."

"No problems?" Ivy questioned.

Molly hesitated.

"Spit it out," Ivy said. "You're getting soft on me. Stop trying
to protect those hoes. They don't give a fuck about us. You
know these bitches. They come, they go. Only thing that stays
true is you and me. Now spit it out, Moll—"

"It isn't that," Molly said. "I know they don't breed bitches
like us anymore."

Ivy agreed. "You ain't never lied, Moll. That cloth we cut
from, they just don't make. Now tell me what happened."

"It's Juicy."

You could almost see the anger ooze from Ivy's pores. "That
bitch still fucking up, huh?"

Molly said, "The new girls are bringing in the most money
right now, but they're drawn to Juicy. They can learn nothing
but bad habits from her."

Ivy nodded. "What else?"

"I found out that she hasn't been forthcoming with all of her tip money."

"Is that right?"

"I'm afraid so," Molly said.

"This is good," Ivy said.

"I don't understand," said Molly.

"Don't worry about it. You will. Soon enough."

Molly searched Ivy's face for a sign as to what she had in mind. Ivy's face was a blank canvas. Molly changed the subject. "I was about to have the chef make me a salad. You want one?"

Ebony, the live-in chef, was the ex-wife of Ivy's deceased brother. Ivy looked at Ebony like a sister, but she kept her at a distance all the same. However, Ebony loved Ivy like the sister she never had.

Ebony wore many hats in the house. She was the chef, the dietician, the herbalist, the nutritionist, and the personal trainer for the ladies. Ebony was damn good at what she did. She could have gone into business for herself and made more money than Ivy was paying her . . . a whole hell of a lot more. But like Molly, Ebony was loyal to Ivy, except for a different reason. Ebony was loyal to Ivy because she'd loved Ivy's dead brother more than life itself, and she promised him she'd always have his sister's back.

Ivy took one forkful of the salad and blurted out, "Damn, girl. I can't front. This shit is the bomb. Oh my goodness! And just to think, a lady from my church tried to get me to stay and eat some greasy-ass chicken they were serving."

Ebony took pride in her cooking. "Hell to the naw."

"Girl, I've traveled the entire world, and I ain't never had nobody make a seafood salad as good as this. What's in it?"

"Shrimp, lobster, and crab meat for the most part, and some other treats."

"Lord have mercy!"

There was no greater compliment. Ebony said, "Aw, thanks, Ivy."

Ivy helped herself to another serving. "I'm going to start going extra hard this week with my training," she said.

Ivy worked out harder than any woman Ebony had ever met. She was strong as an ox but still looked like a woman. "Girl, you look great."

Ivy gave credit where it was due. "You got some of these bitches' abs cut up like a bag of raw dope."

If the other girls in the house were cut up like dope, then Ivy must have been chiseled like a flawless diamond. Body was tight, fit, and rigid. It was clear that missing a workout hadn't been on her agenda in a very long time.

Ebony modestly said, "Well, I'm only doing what I signed on to do." She was cheesing, because she knew that she was damn good at what she did.

Molly had to agree. "For someone that's self-taught, you are amazing."

"Thank you, but y'all need to cut it out with the compliments. You know that shit go to a bitch's head." Ebony cleared the dishes from the table.

Ivy asked Molly, "Do we have any guests here?"

"Not yet. The Sunday pool party is set to begin in another hour or so. I scheduled a few girls to go down to Fontainebleau for their pool party also."

That's all Ivy needed to know. She rose up from the table. "Juicccccccyyyyy!" Ivy started toward the pool.

Molly nudged Ebony in the side. "Oh, shit! This is about to get ugly."

Molly followed behind Ivy out to the pool, where Juicy was sitting with a few of the other girls around her, cackling. They were listening to Juicy tell old ho stories.

"Juicccccccyyyyy!"

Juicy got up and was on her feet fast.

"Yes!"

"Come here, bitch!"

"Coming, Madame." Juicy quickly made her way over to Ivy. "Yes?" she said with a refreshing, confident smile.

Ivy cocked back and punched her square in the face, breaking her nose. You could hear the bone crack from fifty feet away. "Get me my money, bitch!"

Juicy starting bawling alligator tears. She stammered. "I–I–I . . . ."

"*I* my ass, bitch!" Ivy smacked the stutter from her mouth. "Bitch, don't play with me."

Juicy fell to the patio like a bad hairdo. The girls that had been eating up Juicy's ho stories were petrified, looking on in shock. And that was exactly what Ivy wanted to happen. She could administer one good ass-whooping and snatch the attention of the entire house to set an example.

Once she knew all eyes were on her, Ivy kicked Juicy in the face with the toe of her high-heeled Jimmy Choos. Ivy hadn't even busted a sweat. That's what the hoes didn't know. Ivy had rumbled with some of the best men, so toe-to-toe with a bitch was featherweight work.

"Bitch, get yo' ass up before I tear into your ass for real."

Juicy pulled herself up. She had a broken nose, two black eyes, and a busted lip. She was afraid to look Ivy in the face.

"Now carry your scary ass upstairs and get my motherfucking money, bitch! Not fucking part of it! Not half of it! All of it."

Juicy took off, but she was moving too slow for Ivy's liking. Ivy couldn't care less that the girl was injured. Ivy grabbed Juicy by the hair and dragged her up the stairs.

"You hoes think these tricks care about y'all? Trust and believe they don't. They are only loyal to me. Hoes come and go, but I'm the one that consistently provides them with services and favors. Remember that shit the next time one of you decides to try and short me in any way."

Juicy handed Ivy the money she'd stolen.

"Bitch, you owe me an extra five hundred for breaking my nail while I was whipping on your larceny ass."

Juicy humbly said, "No problem."

"And mop this blood up off of my marble floors." To the rest of the girls, she looked each of them up and down then calmly said, "Now, doll babies, get back to your Sunday festivities."

Ivy made eye contact with Molly, who had always played the good cop around the house, and headed off to the room to see about Juicy.

A few minutes later, she pulled Ebony to the side.

"Have you heard from Prince?"

"Naw. I called him because he was supposed to train with me, but he ended up being a no-show, which is odd." Ebony looked up from the icepack she was putting together to take to Juicy.

"And he didn't call you back?" Ivy asked.

"As a matter of fact, he didn't." She looked off. "Which is so unlike him. You already know how that dude feel about his sexy."

"Hmmmm." Frown lines somehow managed to appear on Ivy's Botox-filled forehead. "That's odd," she said.

"A'ight," she said to Molly, who had just returned from checking on Juicy. "I gotta go make a run. Hold it down for me until I get back." She kissed her on the cheek. "I'll call you shortly."

"Okay," Molly said.

Where the fuck is Prince? was the only thing on her mind when she left the mansion.

Prince was Ivy's little brother, her only biological living family, and honestly, the only thing besides Benjamins, that Ivy actually gave one solitary fuck about. Their other brother, Lucas, was killed taking up a beef that was meant for Ivy. Actually, it was Ivy that the bullet was meant for, not Lucas. After Lucas's death, Ivy made a vow that she'd always take care of Prince.

However, it wasn't a simple promise to uphold. Prince was his own man and hated walking in the shadow of his older brother. The only thing he hated more was being referred to as Ivy's little brother. And he damn sure wasn't in the business of taking money from a woman, especially not one that shared his same DNA!

Ivy pulled up in front of the valet at The Lady Lagoon. The first person she saw was Mike. "Where in the hell is Jaffey?" she asked

"In his office, as far as I know."

"I've been calling that motherfucker and he ain't answering." Ivy was pissed. "That motherfucker got some nerve to be ignoring me, as good as I am to him."

Mike had learned long ago not to take sides when it came to Ivy and Jaffey. "Y'all two and y'all bullshit." This was normal between those two. They went back and forth all the time, fussing about pussy and money.

Ivy said, "Have you seen my brother over here?"

"I haven't seen or heard a peep from him," Mike said. "As far as I know, Jaffey hasn't either. As of two hours ago, anyway."

Ivy slipped past Mike, heading to Jaffey's office.

She banged on the oak door. "Open the fucking door."

Mike came up with a novel idea. "Maybe he's not in there," he sarcastically said.

Ivy turned to Mike. "Did you see him leave?"

"Nope. But that doesn't mean shit. Nigga be in and out all the time."

Ivy screamed, "Open the door or buzz him!" She wasn't upset with Mike, but he was the only person available right now for her to take her frustration out on.

"He's not answering," Mike said after buzzing the office.

Ivy stood with her arms folded, while Mike kept trying.

"Open up the door, Mike. This silly motherfucker could've had a heart attack or something. You know what happened the last time he took all those Viagara and tried to fuck those three young bitches."

Mike was silent for a minute. "Turn around," he said.

"Nigga, please!"

"Turn around." Mike held his ground.

Ivy turned around slowly.

Mike punched the code into the keypad, hoping that Jaffey wasn't in there with some chick's legs on his shoulders. That's the type of shit that may get Mike fired, regardless of whether he was married to Jaffey's sister.

"Damn . . . "Mike said once he went inside. "He isn't here. His computer is gone too. He must have gone out the back door."

Ivy stood there with a raised eyebrow. "When he gets back, let him know that something is wrong with my brother. And he better not have anything to do with it, or I swear on Lucas's grave . . . and you already know how I roll. I will get to the bottom of this."

Chapter 39

All Work

Since his arrival in Miami, Chase had worked around the clock. He temporary living accommodations with Simone were a sparsely furnished two-bedroom apartment in corporate housing. He transformed the second bedroom into a makeshift workspace. Dozens of boxes, filled with reams of paperwork, lined the walls. The bed was littered with manila folders, brimming with files. Photos of crime scenes, suspects, and witnesses were either taped or thumb-tacked to nearly every square foot of two of the four walls. But every lead either came to a screeching halt before gaining any traction, or took off into a thousand different directions, like the windshield of a car shattered by a BB gun. After a while it became difficult to ascertain where one lead began and another lead ended. Witnesses looked like suspects, and suspects turned out to be witnesses.

In an attempt to break the monotony, Simone slipped into the self-imposed prison that her husband called an office. In a heavy voice, she said, "All work and no play makes Chase a dull boy."

The see-through lingerie number she wore was about an inch or two negligent of covering the area where the undercarriage of her plump caramel ass connected with her toned legs. Simone's perky breasts stood at attention like obedient solders, standing sentry above her pancake-flat stomach. She'd waxed or shaved every hair on her body besides her head.

For as far as Chase noticed, she might as well have been dressed in baggie jeans, covered in dog manure. The room reeked of old coffee and stationery. His clothes were unkempt, and puffy, dark bags loomed heavy underneath his eyes.

"I have to break that Cashmore case," he said.

Of all the cases that have been piled on him . . . she thought. *Wouldn't you know it would be the armored truck that he was obsessed with.*

Simone played it cool. At least this time he was investigating a case in which she and her sisters weren't the actual bandits. This time they'd only taken the money from the people who had really taken the money. Wasn't that different?

"Baby, you have get some rest. You can't continue to run on coffee and fumes."

"I can sleep when I die," he said. "Or once I solve the case. Whichever comes first."

Being awake for eighteen straight hours not only made him fatigued, but also caused him to be frustrated and cranky. Chase just wasn't thinking clearly—and maybe that was a good thing. Simone wasn't sure. On one hand, she loved her husband and wanted to help her man, but not if it ended with her and her sisters going to jail,

"Maybe you should get some rest, regroup, and start fresh in the morning. I promise to make the break worth your while."

Chase ignored her.

Simone pouted. Twirling a strand of hair with her fingers, she asked, "Is there anything I can do to help you? Would like for me to make you a drink, or something to eat?"

He snapped. "No. I don't want a fucking drink." The moment the outburst was out of his mouth, he wished that he could have swallowed his words. But it was too late. The stress from the job was making him crazy. He thought the promotion would enhance their lives. He'd only been in Miami for two weeks, and the job was already driving a wedge between them. The two love birds never used to argue before.

"My apologies." He begged her, "Baby, please forgive me."

"I know you're stressed, but you can't just snap on me or shut me out," she said. "Allow me to help. Can you talk about it?"

Chase didn't want to talk about it, but he didn't want to be in the doghouse with Simone in addition to the headaches at work.

"There were some electronic files that were stolen from the Cashmore heist." He sighed. "You wouldn't be able to fathom the potential shit storm it will create if in the wrong hands. Every law official in this entire country is on edge." He looked at her with complete despair in his eyes. "The name of every confidential informant ever used in the entire country is on those files. It could turn the law enforcement world on its head. So pardon me, please, if I'm being an asshole. Okay?"

"I've never seen you this way."

"I've never had literally no clue as to where to turn on a case before," he said. "It's like the perpetrators have fallen off the face of the earth. No one has a clue as to where the files are. And the fact that I was promoted with such high regards, I have to deliver the goods."

"And you will." Simone hated seeing her husband this way.

"That's easier said than done," he shot back. "You don't understand. This one case could make or break my whole career."

"And you will break it open. I know you will." Simone encouraged him, "Come on, you got this, baby! Let me put on a pot of coffee—mine black and yours with a shot of Cognac. And let's work this thing out one step at a time."

Though Chase knew better than to discuss his case with anyone, he decided to take Simone up on her offer.

Hell, he thought, *right about now, I need all the help that I can get. And at the end of the day, Simone and her sisters have masterminded bank robberies before, so maybe, just maybe, she can bring something to the table.*

Chapter 40

A Sucker-Punch

"Honey, I'm home!" Wolfe entered the house, but no one said anything, which was extremely odd, he thought, after leaving his shoes at the door.

"Babe?" He called out, and nothing. This was definitely not normal. After a long day in the jungle dealing with knuckleheads, debts owed, larceny, and bullshit, he was used to Rydah greeting him at the door, embracing him with hugs, kisses, affection, and nothing but love.

"Rydahhhh . . . baby!"

Still nothing.

Something was definitely wrong. Wolfe pulled his Desert Eagle out of his pants and crept through the house, not knowing what to expect. He was trying to shake his feelings of caring, but he just couldn't. All kinds of things ran through his head, and he hated the thought that if something happened to Rydah, it would truly have a huge effect on him. He hated that he cared for her and had vested interest in not only her, but her family too. He knew a man in his line of work shouldn't be this attached to anything or anyone.

For a split second, he thought about turning to walk out the door and out of Rydah's life forever. However, as much as his mind told him to do so, his heart wouldn't let him go anywhere.

He took the safety off, put one in the chamber, and started to assess the situation. He crept through the house one step and room at a time. He popped into the bedroom, and Rydah seemed to be in another world.

"Hey, beautiful!" Wolfe said as he entered into the bedroom. Rydah was staring off, so deep in her thoughts that she hadn't even heard him come in.

"Hey, babes." He came in closer, startling her.

Rydah snapped out of her trance and was shocked to see him with a gun in his hand. "Hey, you scared the shit out of me. I didn't even hear you come in." She was confused.

"That's not like you," he said, taking the clip out of the gun and placing it on the night table. "Where was your mind? It seemed to be on the other side of town." Wolfe could sense something was wrong.

"Just a lot on my mind."

"Well, I'm here to listen."

"I don't know where to start, and I'm not ready to talk about it yet. Still processing."

"Well, I'm here, and after all that we've been through, you can trust me. And when it comes to you, I'm definitely a good listener."

"So you remembered where I live, huh?" Rydah said nonchalantly, referring to her not seeing Wolfe in a few days.

"Stop that!" He came in and kissed her with a long tongue kiss. "How could I forget? This is where my heart lives." Wolfe hadn't been to Rydah's house in over a week. He'd been busy with tying up the loose ends with Abe and Prince.

She chuckled. "You are so funny. You smelling all good," she said, getting a sniff of his Bond No. 9 cologne. "Fresh shower *before* you come in. That's new."

"Work, baby. Cold, callous, dirty work."

"I bet. Seems like . . . nut-busting work, if it's the kind that calls for a fresh shower."

"Oh, that's what you think? That I've been fucking with some bitch?" He put up his defense.

"You said it, not me. I've never known you to come in here smelling like Neutrogena body wash combined with Bond No. 9 cologne. You usually all funky, dropping your clothes at the front door. But now all of a sudden you come in here all fresh and clean. Change in behavior. I'm watching you."

"Ain't even like that. I've been dealing with them niggas. Once I was done I burned my clothes. For my own safety, I had to take a shower. I couldn't come across town like that. Funky is one thing, but DNA, blood, and bullshit is another."

"I respect that."

But now all I want is a good night's rest, spooning with my baby." He took her in his arms.

"That's fair."

"How did the surgery go?" He changed the subject, trying to lighten the mood.

"It went well. She's happy. But the guy who we met at the mall, Alphonso, he turned out to be a plastic surgeon at Dr. Snatch's office. I thought he would have talked her out of it."

"Shiiiit. You know nobody was talking her out of that. She was determined. But it went good, right?"

"Yeah, it did. Just resting, healing. Mom taking good care of her, so you know she enjoys Mom spoiling her and all that."

"I already know she sucking that in."

"Yup. She has an appointment tomorrow. All her drains will be removed, and I asked Mom to drop her over here after so I can talk to her."

"You know we about to have a beast on our hands for real."

"Yeah, don't I know it. When she's skinny, she's going to be something else."

They both laughed at the thought at how off the chain Tallhya was going to be with her new physique.

"What do you have planned tomorrow?" he asked.

"No real plans. I just have something important to talk to her and Simone about, that's all," Rydah said.

"I respect that." He nodded, not wanting to pry. "Well, we about to be in the club business." He put the manila folders and envelope on his side of the night table.

"Really?" Rydah asked. "How so?"

Wolfe yawned, not wanting to get into it tonight. "I will tell you all about it tomorrow when I wake up, okay?"

"Okay, baby." Rydah was curious, but she had much bigger things on her mind and couldn't really focus anyway, so tomorrow was better for her too.

Wolfe was so tired from being up for days that the peaceful vibe in the comfort of Rydah's home made sleep finally come down on him. He took his clothes off and jumped in the bed. "I'm tired and just want some sleep," he managed to get out. Before she could offer him something to eat, he was out like a light.

Rydah watched as the man, who never seemed to sleep without one eye open, was deep in slumber in her bed, snoring. She felt good to know that he was finally getting the rest he needed.

While Wolfe slept the night and the next morning away, Rydah couldn't get one ounce of sleep. Her mind was so heavy, and it seemed like the time until she would get to talk to her sisters turtled by.

Finally, Simone arrived and hugged her sister.

Luckily, it wasn't as awkward as she thought it would be, just the two of them alone without Tallhya. During the hour they talked, Rydah learned that she and Simone were more alike than she thought.

"So how are things going with Chase being in town now?"

"I have barely even seen him. It's like I'm just here to keep his bed warm. He's working so much that we literally only sleep in the same bed. He's up and out before me, and comes in way after I'm asleep. I try to wait up for him, but most nights I end up falling asleep."

"I'm sorry."

"Don't be. It's not your fault. He keeps telling me to go out and enjoy the city. And I want to," said Simone, "but it hasn't been easy. I don't know anyone. And I don't like bothering you."

"You don't bother me at all, sis. I want us to spend more time together. I'll be glad to help with whatever you need."

"I can't even get Chase's opinion on simple things like that, because he's been so obsessed with this case and all." She shook her head, wishing that things were different.

"Is it the armored truck heist or the cold cases that mainly have him so stressed out?" Rydah asked.

"It's both, but his bosses have been applying pressure like you would not believe to try to recover that information. It's some pretty heavy shit on those missing files. Shit that has people worried about what could happen if it got in the wrong hands. A lot of folks—innocent people—could be killed."

The front door opened. They had been so engrossed in their conversation that neither sister had heard a key in the lock.

"Heyyyyy, bitches!" Tallhya barged in, loud and beaming with smiles. She walked into the sunken living room and stood in front of Simone, holding her hands out to the side. "Bammmmm, bitches! Boom-shaka-la!"

"Daaaaaamn!" Rydah was impressed

Simone gasped. "Oh my goodness!"

"You look amazing!" Rydah exclaimed. "Like a whole different person."

"And the swelling hasn't even gone done yet. My doctor said that there will be way more dramatic results in about two to three months."

"Girl, you look great. I'm so happy for you. I hope it truly makes you happy."

"She sure looks happy," said Rydah. "Happy, rested, and radiant. Shining and glowing and slim!" Rydah said.

"How does Dr. Fonz like it?" Simone asked with a raised eyebrow.

"He keeps telling me I didn't have to do it, but he comes over and checks on me."

"The doctor making house calls?" Rydah joked.

"Girl, yes! And you know Uncle Maestro all over him like the FBI, interrogating him."

"Oh, trust me I know. Better you than me. Girl, I'm glad you over there getting a taste of them," Rydah said.

"But you look great, girl, and so happy! That's why you smiling! You skinny and got a boyfriend."

"I don't have a boyfriend. But skinny? Yes, it's coming!" she said with smiles.

"We are happy for you. We truly are!" Rydah said.

The ruckus woke Wolfe from his sleep. He decided to get up and head into the living room to check out the results of Tallhya's surgery. But first he needed to brush his teeth, wash his face, and find some shorts to throw on.

"Well, thank you for having my back, but this meeting isn't about me. It's about you. You said you have something to tell us," Simone said.

Wolfe was about to slip on his shorts and wife beater but decided to ear-hustle a little longer before joining and kicking the bo-bo with the girls.

"I know," Simone said. "You sounded like it was so urgent on the phone, and since I've been here you've been kind of distant, not like your normal self."

Wolfe also wanted to know what was on his baby's mind. He wanted to be sure that her sudden funky mood didn't have anything to do with him. After all, he had just disposed of a few men and a no-good bitch. In his world, it was totally acceptable to eliminate one's enemies, but Rydah wasn't from that world. She was a lover of all things, seeing the best in everyone. One thing for sure, Wolfe thought, something very serious was going on with her, and she wasn't sharing it with him. So he'd have to find other methods to figure it out, even if it meant snooping.

"Come to think of it," Tallhya said, "you've been kind of off for a few days now. I thought I was misreading shit before."

"Are you okay?"

"Well, I want you to know that no matter what, I got you and I love you. You already know how I feel about you. So whatever it is, we can get through this shit no matter what."

Wolfe thought, *Enough of the fucking sentimental shit. Spit that shit out.* Curiosity was killing him.

Rydah looked at both her sisters. Simone took her hand, prompting Tallhya to put her hand around Rydah's waist.

"It's like . . ." Rydah couldn't quite get the words out.

Wolfe had never seen her speechless before.

"Are you pregnant?" Tallhya said, trying to guess what had Rydah so tongue-tied.

There was a brief silence.

Wolfe thought about what Tallhya had asked Rydah. How would he feel if the answer to the question was yes? He wasn't sure if he was ready for a family. It wasn't something that he'd put much thought into. For the first time in his life, he began to let his mind wander to places it had never been before. Maybe he needed to rethink the way he lived his life. Give up the streets. Focus on being a husband and the father he never had. The father that he wished he'd had. Hell, he had enough money for a few generations of his offspring to live lavish. Why not? If he was going to ever settle down and hang up boots, Rydah was the perfect woman for him. It felt weird

:o him, thinking of being all in with someone, but maybe the time was right.

"OMG! I'm going to be an auntie!" Simone got all excited, assuming that the answer was yes because Rydah hadn't said anything.

"I swear, I'm going to be a great role model. I'm not going to be with any crazy-ass shit. I swear, I'm going to love this child, and we are all going to give it everything we never had."

"We are. This child will have none of the dysfunctional bullshit we were subjected to growing up," Simone added. 'But I think this is the gift that this family needed to bring us all together."

Wolfe began to envision pushing a little girl on a bike or tossing a baseball to a son, and he couldn't help but to think of what a magical feeling that would be for him.

Until . . .

"I'm not pregnant. Not that I know of, anyway. But who knows? We do be getting it in every chance we get."

"Then what is it?" Simone asked.

"And bitch, you will fuck up a wet dream of a nigga behind bars. Damn!" Tallhya said, shaking her head.

"That would have been good for the family," Simone added.

"Well . . . I think what I have to say is good for our family. Well, at first I did, and then I thought about it long and hard, and perhaps maybe it's not."

Wolfe was still drifting off in his own fairy tale, one he never got to live as a kid. He was ready to get the sisters out of the house so they could begin practicing conceiving.

Tallhya clapped her hand one time. "Bitch, I'm going to fight you. You blowing my high off being fine with all these tight-lipped charades. Just spill it."

"I'm trying." Rydah took a deep breath. "I just don't know where to start."

"The beginning's always good," Simone suggested.

"All ears."

"So . . ." She looked at her sisters, and they looked at her in a way to egg her on to spit out whatever was on the tip of her tongue.

"I was curious to look at the files to see if anybody in Wolfe's camp was working with the police. Though I don't know many of his friends, I wanted to make sure none of his inner circle or security were snitches. Because Wolfe has always been nothing but loyal to my family and me, I wouldn't want any thing to happen to him. Especially by the law or the hands of a snitch." She shrugged her shoulders. "I don't know why. I just began to search a lot of stuff. I just felt like, why would God put this in my hands if it wasn't something I was supposed to see?"

Tallhya and Simone were both pin-drop silent, studying their sister's body language as she spoke.

"Then I became relentless, almost obsessed with trying to find something. Then I think, in a crazy way, my mind began to play tricks on me. I started to wonder about you, Simone."

"Me?" Simone questioned.

"I'm being real. Yes, you."

"Just hear her out," Tallhya said.

"I mean, I don't know much about you, and I'm still learning. Then, the fact that you are with Chase, and the events that happened in Virgina. . ." Rydah pointed out, "You can't blame me."

Simone was quiet for a split second, then reluctantly said, "No, I guess I can't."

"So I started to search Chase's case, looking for his case files of what happened in Virginia or anything on you. Just to see where he was and his thoughts on his reports as far as his job was concerned."

"And in regard to me, you came up with nothing! Right?"

"Nothing as far as you were concerned, Simone." Rydah looked at her. "Buuuut . . ."

"But what?" Tallhya defensively said. "I already know you ain't find shit on me."

"Let me finish," Rydah firmly said.

"Well, hurry the hell up, then. All that slow talking and knot-in-your-throat shit is blowing me." Tallhya looked in her sister's eyes.

"As I read all of Chase's stuff, I came across something both mind-boggling and interesting. I couldn't believe it until I got a trusted source to look further into it."

"What?" Simone said.

"And what trusted source?" Tallhya asked.

"Wolfe's investigator. He is loyal to a fault, and he finds and knows everything."

"God, Lord, you know I love my sister, and I'm grateful to her, but she is dragging this whole thing out, and I just pray, Lord, give me some patience." Tallhya looked up at the ceiling, saying a prayer.

"And it was true," Rydah said, as if she were talking in a riddle.

"Lord, just give me strength and patience. My sister is really losing her mind. Don't let this craziness be hereditary."

Simone looked at Rydah, "Okay, you are scaring me a little bit, and my mind is running crazy."

Rydah got up and poured herself a drink.

"This shit is heavy. She drinking," Tallhya said. "It's getting intense. She don't drink like that."

"Chase lied to you. He said he found Bunny dead, that she committed suicide."

"Right."

"It's true he found her in the bed at the hotel. However, she didn't blow her head off. She took some pills, but when he reached her, he saved her. He found her cell phone with her, and when he went through it, he saw that she had killed a guy in another room in the hotel. Once she came around, he convinced her to cut a deal with him to avoid murder charges."

"What?"

"Bunny is alive. He relocated her and offered her a better life. In return, she has to work as an undercover informant, to use her looks to lure some of the most dangerous criminals into dropping their guards."

"Bunny is alive?" Simone was confused.

"Yes." Rydah nodded. "The investigator got me these pictures." She went to the drawer and pulled out the photographs.

"Wait a minute. Bunny would never sign up to be a rat. She hated the police."

"I'm sorry," Rydah said, "but she did. I have concrete proof."

"Banks sisters don't do that shit."

"And Chase would never know that she was alive and not tell me," Simone added.

Rydah nodded. "I agree with you both, but I can't think of anything else that makes sense."

Simone stood up. She didn't know what to say, or what to think. "Bunny knows so much stuff that I can't say." Her mind drifted off, wondering what exactly Bunny had told Chase. Did Bunny tell Chase about her and Ginger killing Deidra and her boyfriend? And how Simone helped them cut up the body parts and get rid of it? About the banks they robbed? And the laundry list of other crimes they had committed together?

"This is just fucked up. Real fucked up. You have no idea," Simone snapped.

"I want her address. I think we should pay her a visit," Tallhya said. "And Chase? What about him? I thought you had him under the spell of your pussy. He's a threat. A threat that has to be dealt with."

"Shit is so real," Rydah said.

"You have no idea," Wolfe mumbled under his breath.

Wolfe had no idea that Rydah was in possession of the files. He wanted them all for himself, and nothing was going to stop him from obtaining them. His mind skated around the overflow of wealth and power he would have once he possessed the files.

Just that quick, Wolfe couldn't give one solitary fuck about any plastic surgery results of a fat bitch, or his dreams of having a family.

Instead, Wolfe got back in the bed, under the covers, and pretended he was asleep, as if he'd heard nothing at all. But under the high thread count sheets, all he could think about was how those classified files were going to be his in a matter of hours. He hoped that he wouldn't have to hurt anyone he cared about to get them—Rydah included. . . .